The Summer Series

C.J Duggan

The Boys of Summer
A Summer Series Novel, Book One
Published by C.J Duggan
Australia, NSW
www.cjdugganbooks.com

First edition, published December 2012

Edited by Sarah Billington|Billington Media
Copyedited by Anita Saunders
Proofreading by Sascha Craig & Heather Akins
Cover Art by Keary Taylor Indie Designs
Book formatted by White Hot Ebook Formatting
Author Photograph © 2012 C.J Duggan

The Boys of Summer is also available in digital at Amazon
Contact the author at cand.duu@gmail.com

PRAISE FOR

The Boys of Summer

Summer Lovin'

This book kept me up until the wee hours of the morning because I literally could not force myself to put it down – I just had to know what happened. Everything about The Boys of Summer absolutely blew me away.

Claire – Claire Reads

Best Contemporary Read of your Life

I cannot begin to describe the love I have for this book. The Boys of Summer is a story about self-discovery and first true love that will stay with you for a long time after you read it.

Hannah – A Girl in a Café

Fun, Flirty, Fantastic

All in all, if you're looking for a lovable and intense read, then this is for you. C.J Duggan has convinced me she belongs in the contemporary market and I cannot wait to read more from her.

Donna – Book Passion for Life

An Australian Gem

You won't regret buying this one; you'll totally fall in love with the story and all of the characters. C.J Duggan knows how to write a book you'll just be drawn into! I'm already waiting for the next one – impatiently, might I add! The Boys of Summer is an Australian gem!

Seirra – Dear, Restless Reader

Simply Perfect

Everything about The Boys of Summer was fantastic!!! C.J Duggan has written an amazing story and she was able to perfectly capture the Aussie summer, fun times with friends both new and old, and all the feelings of falling in love with the boy of your dreams. Bring on book two!!!

Tracey – YA Book Addict

Sweet, Intoxicating, Exciting

The Boys of Summer is a wonderful example of just how deliciously sexy, sweet and charming summer-fling books can be! A book that gives you goose bumps, makes you swoon over its incredibly handsome male cast, gets you hooked on the clever plot line and, ultimately, sends you out feeling all warm inside, satisfied and with a wide smile on your face.

Evie – Bookish

Also by C.J. Duggan

Stan (Summer Series Novella)
Max (Summer Series Novella)
Ringer (Summer Series Novella)
Forever Summer

Look out for
Paradise City
Paradise Road

www.cjduggannbooks.com

The Boys of Summer

It seemed only natural to nickname them the 'Onslow Boys'. Every time they swaggered in the front door of the Onslow Hotel after a hard week's work, their laughter was loud and genuine as they settled onto their bar stools. I peeked through the restaurant partition, a flimsy divider between my world and theirs. I couldn't help but smile whenever I saw them, saw him ... Toby Morrison.

Quiet seventeen-year-old Tess doesn't relish the thought of a summertime job. She wants nothing more than to forget the past haunts of high school and have fun with her best friends before the dreaded Year Twelve begins.

To Tess, summer is when everything happens: riding bikes down to the lake, watching the fireworks at the Onslow Show and water bomb fights at the sweltering Sunday markets.

How did she let her friends talk her into *working*?

After first-shift disasters, rude, wealthy tourists and a taunting ex-boyfriend, Tess is convinced nothing good can come of working her summer away. However, Tess finds unlikely allies in a group of locals dubbed 'The Onslow Boys', who are old enough to drive cars, drink beer and not worry about curfews. Tess's summer of working expands her world with a series of first times with new friends, forbidden love and heartbreaking chaos.

All with the one boy she has never been able to forget.
It will be a summer she will always remember.

Warning: sexual references, and occasional coarse language.

Dedication

Dedicated to my best friend, Sascha.
For the drama, humor, tears, support, loyalty and most of all love!
Bringing sanity to me each and every day.
I love you more than is measurable.

"Love is not necessary to life, but it is what makes life worth living."
— Anon

Chapter One

I shouldn't have opened it.

But I did. I mean, it's what you do when a wad of paper hits you in the back of the head, right? You unfold it in the hopes that maybe, just maybe, it might be a note confessing undying love from a green-eyed, dreamy, Italian exchange student. If there *was* such an exchange student at Onslow High. A girl could dream. There wasn't a boy in sight that you could even hope to admire, and there certainly wasn't anyone else you would even remotely want to attract.

My best friend, Ellie, plucked the scrunched-up wad of paper from where it had settled in my hoodie, which, to the boys behind me, served as a makeshift basketball ring. She was fast, real fast –even more so with her lightning-speed dagger eyes that she cast to those snickering in the back row.

"Just ignore them, Tess, they're not worth it."

I barely heard Ellie's words as I took in the crude drawing of me. I knew it was me, thanks mostly to the giant arrow that pointed to a box-shaped figure with the words 'TESS' highlighted. A stick figure would probably be flattering for most high school girls with image problems, but this wasn't stick form; it wasn't even a box. It was a drawing of an … ironing board? Was that what it was? A speech bubble protruded from the pencil-thin smile. To their credit, the smile was drawn in red pen. My guess, it was to offer the ironing board more feminine authenticity.

"Hi, I'm Tic-Tac-Tess," the speech bubble said. "I'm flatter than two Tic Tacs on an ironing bored." *Ironing board was spelled wrong, idiots!*

I stared at the image for the longest time, muffled laughter and the unmistakable sound of high-fives being slapped from behind me, but it was only the sound of an unexpected voice that finally broke my attention.

"Do you care to share, Miss McGee?"

Ellie's elbow in my rib cage snapped me out of my trance to find Mr Burke overshadowing our desk. His thick, bushy eyebrows drew together into an impressive, yet frightening, frown.

Frozen, I made no effort to hide the note that was all too quickly plucked from my hands. Mr Burke re-adjusted his glasses and cleared his throat as he slowly examined the crumpled paper that had held me so entranced.

I could feel it; all eyes were on me, and I tried not to cringe as heat rushed to my cheeks. My heart slammed against my rib cage; a new tension filled the air as the class fell silent. We waited, bracing ourselves for the outburst that Mr Burke was so famous for.

I flicked a miserable look to Ellie who offered her best 'don't worry' smile.

Along with the rest of the class, I held my breath and silently counted down. *In 5, 4, 3, 2, 1… cue the screaming.*

"WHAT IS THIS?" Mr Burke bellowed. His red face surpassed my flushed cheeks, a vein pulsing in his neck. Before I could form a sentence, he did the worst thing possible, the very thing I feared the most: he read out the note.

"TIC-TAC-TESS?" He held the drawing out to display to the class.

Oh God!

"Flatter than an ironing board, hmm?"

Oh no-no-no-no-no.

I slid down in my seat. *This couldn't be happening.*

I cursed the boys in the back row with their stupid red pencil, crappy illustration and subpar spelling. (It was Dusty Anderson. Had to be. Or Peter Bricknell – no one else in school spells as badly as him.) I fantasised about them being dragged out by their ears to the principal's office, systematically getting booted in the behind like in a bad slapstick movie. There was also lots of crying and apologising in my fantasy. I quite enjoyed watching Peter cry. Instead I was to be punished, as was the rest of the class. Punished by a whole lot of shouting, I mean. Mr Burke's irate, verbal onslaught ranted and raved about idiotic time wasting, short attention spans and even the evils of paper wastage. Never was bullying (or the fact they had spelled ironing board wrong) mentioned. I mean, seriously, how does anyone get to Year Ten and not know how to spell board?

No, the bad guys wouldn't be punished. Instead, what had begun as a private joke, generated from my evil ex-boyfriend and his lackeys, was now shared with the entire class. It would soon spread to the rest of Year Ten and then, inevitably, the entire school. Brilliant job, Mr Burke.

That was how it began. Pretty much one year ago today, I had become stupid Tic-Tac-Tess. Even when the more supportive teachers overheard the taunts and duly gave stern looks and warnings, it did little to appease the situation. Even though the hype had moved on to some other unfortunate soul, the latest being Matthew Caine's drunken, school social scandal that had him vomiting over Mr Hood's Italian leather loafers. The effects of that infamous day in Mr Burke's Biology class still haunted me.

There was no rhyme or reason to high school. What made you team captain one day could make you a social outcast the next. I was neither popular nor a freak-a-zoid; I was no one, a real Jane Doe, and that's the way I liked it. I avoided the spotlight, which ironically followed my best friend, Ellie, everywhere she went. Boys were like moths and Ellie was the flame, which in my eyes was not a great thing. I'm not a prude or anything, I've had boyfriends and done stuff with them, but she's my best friend and I'm just worried about her. And I had reason to worry: I had overheard canteen-line mutterings of Ellie being a 'slut', but I would never tell her that.

So I chose the comfort of remaining in my friend's shadow; beautiful, bubbly Ellie with her perky, honey-blonde ponytail, a light dusting of freckles on her perfect ski-jump-curved nose. Ellie always looked like she had stepped out of a 'Sportsgirl' catalogue. And there was Adam, our other bestie, who's full of charisma and charm, and he's really funny, too. Everyone loved Adam, particularly the teachers. He was late for everything, but when he *did* arrive, it was always with lesson-disrupting flair. With his bed-tousled hair and his beaming smile, he could charm the knickers off a nun. His words – not mine. Ew!

The three of us made unlikely allies, but we'd been friends all our lives. Sure, Adam would disappear at recess over the years for some male bonding, from the sandpit in primary school to the footy field at Onslow High. He would always return and plonk himself next to Ellie and me, leaning over to steal a chip from one of our packets, earning him a well-deserved punch in the arm that had him screaming in dramatic agony.

He was such a drama queen. Ellie and I always predicted he'd be an actor one day. "Destined to be a thespian," we told him.

Adam would do a double take, his eyebrows rising.

"A lesbian?"

Ellie and I would groan in unison. "No idiot, a thespian!"

"Oh, riiiiight." He would nod, a wry smile fighting to break out. He'd known exactly what we'd said. Yeah, that was Adam.

The two shining lights of my two best friends' personalities seemed to be a good buffer for me. Ellie said I was really intelligent and had the biggest brain out of anyone at school, but I didn't know about that. We all balanced each other out in some way and watched out for one another, and it was never more evident than in times of peril.

As Ellie and I turned into our Year Eleven locker room to gather our books for English, our smiles faded and I froze. Dread seeped into me just like it had in Biology twelve months earlier. Except this time, it was a thousand times worse.

I will not cry. I will not cry! I repeated to myself over and over again as my nails dug into my palms with such ferocity that they threatened to break the skin. Laughter, loud and low, surrounded me from all angles in the room. A mixture of faces represented shock, horror and disgust, but the general mood was hilarity. And relief that it was happening to someone else. My gaze shifted directly to where I assumed Scott would be, laughing the loudest, but he was noticeably absent. Only a few of his friends loitered, their beady eyes trying not to flick from me to each other. It wasn't working. They were obviously waiting for a reaction, one I would never give them. I never did.

I just stood silently looking at my locker. The door had been smeared with something brown and sticky. My breath hitched in a tight vice of absolute fear and loathing. I noticed what I suspected was a string of caramel drool that dribbled diagonally to a mashed, chewed, chocolatey nugget that appeared to have been regurgitated onto my lock. It was a bizarre moment of bittersweet relief. It was only chocolate … and spit. Yeah, my relief was short lived.

"Looks like someone had a nasty reaction to a Twirly Whirl."

Dusty Anderson deliberately bumped my shoulder as he walked by me. Laughter following him out.

"More like a Twirly Hurl," added Peter Bricknell. More laughter erupted, but strangely no high fives. I would have thought this was definitely a high-five occasion.

"Oh, fuck off!" Ellie yelled after them.

I think her outburst shocked me more than my defecated locker did. If steam could physically pour from someone's ears like in the cartoons, it would have been pouring out of Ellie right then. Instead, a death-like stare and flared nostrils had to do.

"Ellie, don't," I implored. "It'll just make it worse."

"Worse? Worse than this?" She pointed.

The few loiterers that had remained in the locker room slowly exited as Ellie continued her tirade.

"You know who's behind this, don't you? That low-life ex of yours, that's who."

I didn't need to agree; I knew it was Scott. It always was. Not to mention I was well aware of his particular fondness for Twirly Whirls. First there was the note in Biology that had sealed my fate as "that flat-chested girl" and the rumours he spread shortly after that claimed I was frigid.

But *this* was by far the worst thing he had ever done. Before this, it was the odd, empty Tic Tac packet in front of my locker. That hadn't happened in months, though. He had lulled me into a false sense of security. I was such an idiot.

I sighed and straightened myself to fake indifference.

"Well, I better get it off," I said as I walked over to the wheelie bin, dragging it over from the corner of the room to my locker and assessing the damage.

Ellie calmed down a bit as she came closer. I could feel her body tense, and she quickly looked away. "I'll, um, go and find something to wipe it off with." She started to back away.

"OK, but don't go and tell anyone – promise?"

Ellie sighed and looked at me, sympathy pouring past the anger. "I won't promise forever, Tess. If he pulls any more crap like this, not just this, but anything, I will not be silent." She left, to hopefully find some hospital-grade disinfectant and a blowtorch to open up my combination lock.

Ellie returned with some paper towels, and Spray and Wipe detergent she procured from the school cleaner under the strict promise it was not to be used as an ingredient for anything explosive and returned ASAP. I made some leeway by finding a stick and slowly peeled off the regurgitated, slimy mucus blob that sat directly on my combination lock. It was then I heard Ellie dry retching into her hand, turning away. Such help. I chucked the chocolatey stick in the bin and went to console Ellie, her colour drained from her face.

"You alright?" I couldn't help but laugh as I patted her on the back. She couldn't form words as the chunks threatened to rise.

Animated whistling closed in at a brisk pace (a sound I would recognise anywhere) and Adam waltzed in. His relaxed, calm demeanour didn't say, "I'm hightailing it to class because I am fifteen minutes late"; instead, his surprise registered as he rounded the corner of the locker room to see me and Ellie kneeling on the linoleum by my locker, Ellie's face hovering over the wheelie bin.

His eyes narrowed from Ellie's sweat-beaded face to mine. "What's wrong?"

Before I could answer, Adam's gaze moved beyond us and paused on the splatterfest that was my locker. The steely look of fury that had surfaced in Ellie earlier now travelled through Adam. He looked back at me and with a deep, calm breath he came to stand beside us to survey the damage.

"One guess," he bit out.

"Yep!" I turned to re-evaluate the situation. The sight hadn't improved much, even with the gooey blob on the lock gone.

Without another word, Adam dropped his backpack to the floor, wrenched the zip open and delved into the contents.

"You don't happen to have a pressure washer on you, by any chance?" I mused.

He ignored me; Adam was on a mission. I could tell by the crinkle in his brow that all too quickly vanished as he found what he was looking for.

He pulled out …

"A banana? Seriously?" He was an odd boy.

"Urgh. Adam, how can you eat at a time like this?" Ellie cringed.

Adam peeled back the yellow folds, biting a big chunk out, and chewed vigorously, raising his brows in a 'hubba-hubba' motion. He then walked over towards … oh no.

"Adam?"

He fell short just before Scott's locker and offered us his best winning smile as he swallowed his mouthful. He held the banana in the air like it was some talisman, some holy grail.

"Ladies, I give you the banana." With that, Adam smashed it against Scott's locker, smearing it in a vast sweeping motion. The mushy, granulated chunks were thoroughly mashed into the crevices of his combination lock. And Adam did this all while humming a joyous tune. He then hooked the banana peel through the lock loop; it dangled like a motley alien form.

Ellie laughed, sat back on her heels away from the bin and clapped her hands, colour finally returning to her face just as it drained from mine.

"Adam, what are you doing?" I was part horrified, and part in awe of his heroic gesture.

Adam stood back, hand on chin in deep thought as he admired his handiwork. "It will have to do! I'm really regretting not grabbing that chocolate Yo-Go this morning. That would have gone on real nice."

"Please, no more chocolate," Ellie begged.

Adam dusted off his hands, "Well, best get crack-a-lackin. Wouldn't want anyone to think this was some sort of act of revenge or anything."

"You know who they are going to blame, right?" I pointed to myself with double fingers. "Ah, hello."

"Don't worry about Snotty," Adam reassured.

"Besides, we can be your bodyguards," Ellie added.

"Well, either I'm going to need to sleep with one eye open, or you two will have to take shifts in watching over me so that I'm not murdered in my bed."

"Not a problem. I already climb into your room every night and watch you sleep, anyway," Adam winked.

"Pfft, dream on!"

Adam's wicked smile broadened. "Oh, but I do."

"Urrgh. If I wasn't going to spew before, I am now." Ellie rubbed her stomach.

I playfully sprayed Ellie with disinfectant, causing her to scream and leap to her feet, dodging behind Adam. She grabbed his shoulders and held him for ransom. He faked fear. "No, please, anything but that!"

I did a fake-out squeeze and they both winced, which had me giggling with evil pleasure. This went on for a few more minutes, dodging and screaming until Adam spotted the chocolate-covered stick protruding from the wheelie bin. I could see the cogs turning in his mind and they weren't just any cogs; they were evil cogs.

"Don't you dare!"

His smile was wicked; he deliberately watched my reaction as he picked it up.

"*Adam*!"

"Bwahahahaha!" He chased me around the locker room with the vile mucus-choco stick. It was a good thing that the locker room was set far away from the main school building; there was no fear our shouts would unveil our lateness to class. There was no controlling the fact that we were laughing so hard we could barely breathe.

Adam and I spent the next ten minutes spraying and scrubbing my locker while Ellie watched with a horrified expression from across the room. Adam worked on my lock as I wiped down my door.

"What's your combo, McGee?"

I raised my eyebrows. "As if I would tell you."

He sighed. "Relax, I'm not going to send you love poetry, I'm just going to see if it works."

I finished the last wipe and gave him a pointed look. "You are totally going to send me love poetry."

"Pfft, dream on!"

I slapped his shoulder and clenched my chest in mockery. "Oh, but I do."

Chapter Two

Third period and I was a prisoner in double English.

I prayed that Scott didn't need to go to his locker between classes. My heart pounded against my rib cage, and my hands were clammy as I watched the agonisingly slow tick of the clock above Mrs Romano's desk. Would Adam's actions start an all-out war? I already thanked the timetable Gods that Scott was not in my English class.

My plan was simple: hightail it to the locker room, grab my stuff and be gone before Scott even noticed his redecorated locker. Then I would just avoid him for the rest of the year. Which sounds totally hard, but wouldn't be considering there were only three days left of school. By then we would all be cheering 'School's out for Summer', Alice Cooper style.

Three days; three ... more ... days.

A wad of paper landed next to my hand, and I flinched, for more than one reason. Luckily, English was pretty safe, no horsemen of the apocalypse in this class, which made it a welcome refuge. I secretly unfolded the crinkled paper under my desk.

You smell like Spray and Wipe.

My mouth twitched as I glanced sideways to where Adam sat, two people across. I met his devilish eyes, and he grimaced dramatically.

I discreetly eyed Mrs Romano, sitting on her desk at the front of the class, eyes downcast, animatedly reading aloud from her text. I scribbled my reply and did the tap down the line to pass it along. Like a lady would. I focused intently on the book I was meant to be following along with, knowing that I wouldn't be able to contain myself as I envisioned the raise of Adam's brows as he read my reply.

What's that, banana man?

It went back and forth for the remainder of the class, which I was grateful for as it made the time fly. Once the bell rang, I was jolted into the cold, harsh reality that awaited me.

Lunchtime.

I didn't even think to wait for Adam or Ellie; I was too focused on running to the locker room and praying that the combination of detergent and boy cooties hadn't jammed up my lock. Adam had tested and opened it easily enough; surely it would be okay? I dodged and weaved through the thickening flow of bodies down the hall, cursing the distance between my locker and the English room as I got stuck behind a group of giggling Year Seven girls. I burst through the doors and quickstepped down the stairs. I heard the distant yell of "No running!" from Mr Hood, but I had to risk it. Detention would seem like a holiday camp compared to facing off with my ex.

After tripping over my foot and dropping a textbook, I inelegantly made an entrance into the locker room. There were not many people in there, but the few who were there were laughing, crowded around Scott's locker which had been marinating in banana for the past sixty minutes.

I ignored them and made a beeline for my locker with enough time to unload my books, grab my bag, and hide in a bush for the rest of the day. I froze, my sparkling padlock in my hand. What the hell was my combination? My mind had gone completely blank. Panic set in as more students flooded the room and saw Scott's locker. I bit my lip. No, no, no … I looked up, finding the eyes of Kim Munzel, the resident grunge girl of our year, on me. Her green, scary eyes were caked with heavy make-up that was partly covered by a gel-sleeked jagged fringe – the longest part of her crudely short haircut. She seldom spoke and when she did, it was with a bad attitude. So why was she smiling at me?

She grabbed her bag and walked up to me, her dog chain clinking on her low-rise baggy jeans. I turned my attention back to my lock, pretending that it was the most interesting thing in the world. At that point in time it really was.

What was the bloody number?

Out of the corner of my eye, I could see Kim had stopped next to me.

"Hey."

I glanced around. Was she talking to me? Oh God. Yes, she was looking right at me.

"Hey," I said in a small voice.

"Did you do that?" Her head nodded towards Scott's locker, which was now semi-circled by a crowd.

Before I could get my thoughts together enough to form a coherent sentence, her smile tilted to form an evil grin.

"Nice job." Her scary eyes looked me over as if giving me a seal of approval, and then she left. So. Weird. The crowd peeled back to allow her through. She had that kind of effect. The locker room was now full of students; a mad hub of activity for the lunchtime rush.

Oh God! I fumbled madly with my lock, guessing combinations in a frenzied effort. Scott would be here any moment. I turned the dial and tugged in desperation as if I was MacGyver and this was the last chance to crack the code before the bomb went off. Some people asked themselves: 'What would Jesus do?', but I always asked myself: 'What would MacGyver do?' MacGyver would probably be able to pick the lock with a crusty, chocolate-covered stick. I'm sure he could.

TUG! TUG! TUG!

I thudded my head against the locker; it smelt like disinfectant and was probably cleaner now than it had been in the past decade of use by past students.

I felt hot breath blow into my ear as a voice whispered, "4-3-2-5-9-6." I jumped, spinning around to see a laughing Adam.

"Geez, McGee, jumpy much?"

"432596! My combination! Oh, praise sweet baby Jesus." I turned the dial and heard the magical click of freedom; it was the most beautiful sound I had ever heard. Which was ironic considering it was counterbalanced with the most horrible sound I could have heard right then: Scott's angry voice. Oh crap!

"What the ...?" his voice trailed off as he closed the distance towards his locker. The crowd parted eagerly. They'd been waiting for this moment; their eyes darted from him to me and back again. Just as I feared, you wouldn't have to be a rocket scientist to figure out they would assume it was me. I swallowed hard, fighting the urge to throw up.

Adam stood stock-still beside me, silently taking in the scene. I felt the press of someone on my left. Ellie had appeared from thin air and was at my side. If it weren't for my bookend buddies, I feared my legs would give out. I slowly turned to my open locker; best not to stare. While I pretended indifference, I heard him yell out to me.

"Oh yeah. Nice one, Tess," he sneered.

I did my best 'I'm bored' look from my locker. Scott stood next to his. Wow, if looks could kill. He was flanked by nervous-looking buddies, who were slowly opening their own lockers. Some friends they were, none of them even offering to get him a paper towel.

Scott hurled the banana peel across the room and opened his locker as if it wasn't covered in mush. He threw in his books and slammed his door shut, casting me a filthy look before storming out. His entourage looked at each other and appeared to be as surprised as I was. Like the mindless zombies they were, they quickly scurried after Scott, throwing uncertain glares my way.

I was just about to let my shoulders sag in relief when I heard it, right next to my ear. The solitary sound of a slow clap.

Adam.

"Way to go, Tess, way to go!"

It was as if I had just been carried out of a factory by Richard Gere or something.

This was not how I expected the day to go. Although things had taken an unexpected turn that had me smiling into my opened locker, Scott's voice echoed in my mind.

"You may have won the battle, Tess, but you haven't won the war."

***

Lunch and the rest of the day passed with surprisingly little drama. Scott's banana-rised locker stayed like that for the rest of the day; I think he was trying to prove a point or something. The typical boy mentality of not caring, though the look he had thrown me had been chilling. If I knew Scott, it would be eating him alive.

Ellie and I walked in mirror image, our thumbs hooked into our backpack straps as we pushed our bodies forward to balance the weight of our textbooks on our backs. I had made sure I had packed up all my valuables from my locker in case there was a mysterious attack overnight.

Adam circled us on his bike.

"Sooo, have you thought about my business proposition?"

He wasn't addressing Ellie, he was addressing me. I knew he was, because I automatically cringed every time he asked the question, which had been every damn day for the past semester. I also knew it was directed at me because Ellie, from the very get-go, had squealed and said, "Count me in!" Traitor!

Adam must have read the look on my face.

"Aw come on, McGee! It's gonna be awesome!" His circling was making me dizzy.

"I just don't think I would be any good."

He rolled his eyes at Ellie. "I thought you promised to talk some sense in to her?"

"Hey! I've been on operation 'get a rocket under Tess' for weeks. I even got her parents involved."

"Yes, about that." I stopped walking abruptly to confront Ellie, nearly causing Adam to fall off his bike.

Ellie gave me her fluttery-eye blink of innocence, the very one that probably fooled all the boys. Well, it didn't fool me.

"Mum has been giving me hell, saying, 'It will be good for your confidence, Tess' and, 'It will give you some extra pocket money for the holidays' and 'You might meet some new people'." I repeated every Mum-saying with enough exaggerated whining to sound almost authentic. Even to my ears.

Ellie folded her arms. "And all that is so bad because?"

I paused. Because it was out of my comfort zone. I was not good in foreign environments. I wanted to spend the summer with Ellie and Adam riding down to the lake, watching the fireworks at the show and eating ice cream at the Sunday markets. I wanted to regain that same essence of past summers and how wonderfully lazy it had all been. Not slaving away at the Onslow Hotel.

"It's not rocket science, Tess," Adam said. "Come on, it'll be the three amigos. No parentals. We can play pool all summer long and get paid for it."

"It will be so fun," Ellie said, "serving drinks to hot guys." Boys were never far from her thoughts.

"Yeah – and cleaning up sticky messes and dirty dishes; sounds like a riot," I said. "Can't we just hang out at the lake?"

"We ALWAYS do that."

"Not last year."

"Correction – YOU didn't do it last year; you were attached to Snotty's face the whole holidays. WE went to the lake and the market and stuff, and this year we want to do something different, don't we, Adam?"

"Yes, yes we do, and we want to do it with YOU."

The Onslow Hotel was almost like a tiara of Onslow in that it was positioned at the very peak of a hill overlooking the entire town. Ellie and I painfully walked up there a few times, agreeing that 'Coronary Hill' was an appropriate name dubbed by the locals. We had learned our lesson and chose for future reference to trek the long way around the back roads on bike, swinging around the imposing hotel structure to the quick trail home. Our bikes had blazed a path downhill as we screamed, our feet on our handlebars. So Adam was predicting awesome times ahead at the Onslow Hotel? I seriously doubted anything with the word 'Onslow' in it could ever be connected to awesome.

It was obvious that the fore-founders of our grand community severely lacked in the imagination department. Onslow was a small town, population of less than three thousand, nestled in the valley of the Perry Ranges. It would be more in line with being a retirement village if the rolling hills weren't the backdrop to Lake Onslow, a sprawling mass of man-made lakes that swept as far as the eye could see. Local legend claimed that it was bottomless, and Lord knows we had tested the theory. So far, it checked out: we could never touch the bottom.

As students of Onslow High finished up from school, we would cut through Onslow Park, walk past Lake Onslow where the Onslow Hotel overlooked the town of … oh, what is it called? Oh yeah, *Onslow*!

They looked at me with their pathetic, pleading doe-like eyes.

Even after a full three weeks of having to endure 'that' look, I still felt my heart race in anxiety at the thought. I had never had a job before, even though my parents had nagged and nagged me to get one.

I knew all the answers to the questions I was about to ask, but I tentatively asked again, anyway.

"So how many hours?"

"Weekend lunch, twelve to two, and dinner, six to nine."

I didn't need to calculate, I had done it a thousand times. Adam was good, he didn't smile or even show an ounce of excitement. He was serious and business-like, knowing that if he was any other way it would scare me off.

"Ten dollars an hour?"

He nodded. "Cash in hand."

I definitely didn't need to calculate that either. I'd had all of my hypothetical money spent for the past three weeks.

Ellie wasn't as diplomatic as Adam, and started to bounce on the balls of her feet.

Adam inched closer, maneuvering his bike right up to me. "Come on, Tess. My uncle wants me to be dish pig for the holidays, doing it without you guys would make it what it is, a pretty shitty way to spend my weekends. But I don't know, I thought if you guys were with me it would be a blast. We always make our own fun, and just think of it. We can go and blow all our money together on Big Ms and dirty deep-fried chicken wings at the Caltex afterwards."

That had me frowning in disgust more than anything. He'd been doing so well until now, but suddenly it seemed like he'd totally forgotten who he was talking to. But I now saw something new in Adam's pleading eyes. He had made it sound like an awesome adventure because his uncle and dad had given him little choice for the weekends but to slug it out in dirty dishwater for a good chunk of his holidays. He had sold it to us on the angle of money, free soft drinks and an array of cute boys. Admittedly, it did definitely have its perks.

But the bigger reason my icy facade had started to thaw was because if I didn't do it, I would barely get to see my best friends on the weekends, and I wouldn't be able to join in on all the 'in-jokes' they would share from all that time together over the summer without me. Plus, Ellie would no doubt snag a cute, new, Onslow-Hotel-visiting boyfriend for the summer, and Adam would be buying everyone chicken wings at the Caltex and where would I be? At home, doing chores because my parents wanted to drill some sort of work ethic into me, in some other torturous way as a form of revenge for not getting a summer job with my work-savvy friends. There would be no ten dollars an hour for the displeasure either. I thought of one of my mental purchases, a cute little summer dress I had spotted in the window of Carters' clothes shop, and smiled.

I re-adjusted the weight of my backpack as I looked down at my foot, tracing a circle in the dirt. I squinted back up at Adam who was waiting intently.

"Does the restaurant have air conditioning?"

Adam broke into a broad smile, like a cat that got the mouse.

"Like a freakin' igloo."

Smug bastard, he didn't need to look so satisfied with himself. I fought not to smile and looked from him to Ellie, who was acting as if she had a brigade of ants in her pants.

I sighed in defeat. It wasn't the summer I wanted, but it was the summer I was stuck with. "Alright."

"Sorry?" Adam questioned.

"Alright, I'll do it."

"Sorry, I didn't hear you. Can you repeat that?"

"I'll do it!" All air was knocked from me when a squealing Ellie body slammed me into a bear hug.

Bloody hell.

"Okay. Well, hopefully Uncle Eric will think it's okay. He is pretty desperate, but I can't promise anything. If you're lucky, I guess ..." Ellie and I set in on him, giving him a dual beating in the rib cage, but he preempted the attack and sped off on his bike, our textbook-filled packs preventing us from giving chase.

Adam called back, flashing a winning smile.

"You won't regret it! We are going to have the *best* summer!"

Chapter Three

The arrangement had been to meet at the Onslow Hotel for orientation in our spare school period, so we could get the feel of our surroundings.

Little did we know it was actually an ambush and we were about to be thrown into the deep end. A billowing cloud of steam blew up into Uncle Eric's face, threatening to melt it off entirely. This was just as disturbing as the loud hissing sound he was creating in an attempt to froth up milk on the coffee machine. I looked on in horror; how was I expected to be able to master this beast of an apparatus? I had never made a cappuccino in my life! Ash teetered on the edge of Uncle Eric's cigarette as it wavered every time he spoke.

He was a big, bearded, gruff, biker-looking kind of fellow, who cared little for his health if the caffeine consumption and chain-smoking was anything to go by. As far as I knew, the reason Adam had roped us in to help out was largely due to Uncle Eric's wavering health. No doubt it was a bonus that we were still in school so he could pay us minimum wage off the books. Kind of like a sweatshop for child labour.

He gave us an assessing look.

"We could do with some fresh blood around here. Tess and Ellie will be front-of-house in the restaurant."

There was a not-too-subtle agenda: Uncle Eric tended to work in a way of capitalising on people's strong points so as to attract the right clientele. Little did he know that I was silently freaking out over a coffee machine, let alone what else this job might entail. *Just breathe*, I told myself.

Just. Breathe.

As if sensing my unease, Adam elbowed me and threw me a friendly, reassuring smile. Ellie, who was as giddy as a schoolgirl, flashed me her pearly whites as if what Uncle Eric was saying was truly magical. I felt nauseous with information overload. I had only been inside the Onslow a few times for the odd dinner gathering, but Mum and Dad were not regular pub goers. They were more accustomed to wine and home-based dinners with close friends than pub hopping.

Now the beast of a coffee machine lay silent, the noise replaced by yet another scary sound: Uncle Eric wheezed out an uncomfortable series of chest-rattling coughs. I folded my arms and fought not to wince as the sound and smoke blew my way.

"Thought you quit that nasty habit, Unc."

An older version of Adam appeared through the divider that sectioned the main bar from the restaurant – Chris. He brushed past us in the small space, ensuring he slammed Adam hard in the arm as he made his way towards a lower cupboard, crouching to search for something. They never used to look alike. Adam went through a phase where he thought he was adopted because Chris looked so much like his parents, but nowadays there was no mistaking the resemblance. Lean, with clear alabaster skin, big deep, dark eyes, and dark unruly hair. The main differences were that Chris kept his hair cropped shorter, he was taller, and he held himself differently. Adam was a lot more outgoing whereas Chris was the far more serious sibling; he tended to go about in life as if the weight of the whole world rested on his shoulders.

Chris found an exercise book and flicked through it, a crinkle forming between his brows as he concentrated.

"What habit? Coffee or smoking?" Eric mused.

"Both," Chris muttered. His brow furrowed further as he thumbed each page.

When we arrived to begin our trial at the hotel, Adam had looked forlorn. Not a good sign. Not much seemed to worry Adam, but when I saw Chris behind the bar taking stock of inventory, I automatically knew the reason behind Adam's sullen mood without even having to ask. Uncle Eric had chosen Chris to manage the bar.

Smart move, Uncle Eric.

Knowing what Chris was like, we knew he'd run a tight ship and not give us an inch, especially Adam. Suddenly goofing off and free pool seemed like an impossible dream. This was strike one against the 'dream job' I had envisioned. Strike two quickly followed.

Uncle Eric moved aside.

"Tess, why don't you make Chris a coffee? Show us what you got."

Oh God! Why didn't I pay attention to how he did it?

I moved closer to the machine, fearing it would come alive and burn me with its evil steam spout. I was just about to fake the 'I totally know what I'm doing' routine when – saved by the bell! The bell being the distant jingle of jewelry and a gay, breezy voice that could not be mistaken for anyone other than Claire Henderson. Eric's younger, oddly glam, attractive wife. Well, glam and attractive for Onslow standards, anyway. I had heard Mum and Dad say on more than one occasion that it was an 'odd' marriage, and not just for the obvious aesthetic reasons. Claire had a tall slender frame dripped in Gucci and smothered in French perfume. Her silky, ash blonde hair was never out of place. I know opposites attract, but seriously? Claire Henderson leant over the bar, reaching for the keys to her Audi convertible.

"Hello, poppets! What do we have here?"

"Orientation," Chris said. He flipped through the mysterious exercise book but with less interest now.

"Of course. Adam these are your friends, the ones you always talk about? You must be Tess and Ellie."

We offered pleasant smiles; wait a minute, I'm wrong. *I* offered that smile. Ellie was beaming in such a way I feared we all may have been blinded by it. She stepped forward with an animated hair flick.

"I'm Ellie Parker, Mrs Henderson." She took Claire's hand to shake. "I love your shawl. Wherever did you get it?"

Claire Henderson honed in on Ellie with interest.

"Why, thank you. It was a gift, to me from me." She winked, and she and Ellie beamed at each other, instant friends. It was so clear, Claire Henderson could see herself in young Ellie Parker. It was a like magnetic pull towards each other, like for like.

Ellie beamed, Claire beamed. They didn't just enter into a room, they filled it with their vibrant energy and just when I was about to ask my own question about the shawl, Claire's bright, friendly eyes cut from Ellie to me and dimmed. A crinkle pinched between her perfectly manicured eyebrows, a crinkle that looked as though it really shouldn't be there considering I'd heard she had her plastic surgeon on speed dial.

"Ah, Tess, sweetie. Tut tut tut." She waggled her finger. "Uncross your arms and stand straight. Body language is everything."

I quickly unfolded my arms and stood straight like a soldier. All of a sudden I was very aware of every body movement I was going to make. What else did I do unconsciously that might be offensive? I blushed and felt like a naughty five year old.

Without further thought, Claire jingled her keys.

"I'm off now, poppets, don't work too hard."

Oh, we weren't allowed to work too hard or have bad body language, I thought bitterly. And on the same breeze Claire Henderson blew in on, she blew away. Probably to her townhouse in the city that Uncle Eric purchased for her. Another conversation overheard from my mum to one of her friends.

"They don't even live together! He has his pub; she lives in the city all week. What kind of marriage is that?" my mum would ask in dismay.

One that obviously skipped the 'in sickness and in health' vows, I thought, as I studied Uncle Eric's grey complexion. No doubt made worse by years of working indoors in a dark bar surrounded by cigarette smoke and a lifetime of pub meals. Was this what he meant by fresh blood? My heart sank. I knew it was only weekend work, but it was a weekend with minimal sunlight, no fresh air and no lake.

This was going to hurt.

The remainder of the trial went on in a string of awkward chaos, even when Uncle Eric retired himself to his residence upstairs. Crusty old Melba, the kitchen hand, took over some of the orientation. She whipped us into polishing silverware and glasses, folding napkins and various other jobs that we all apparently did 'wrong'.

"Hearts like a split pea, this generation, honestly." Melba snatched a napkin out of Ellie's hand and showed her how to fold it the 'right' way. It was nice to see not everyone succumbed to Ellie's charms. Not even Adam's good nature could steer Melba in a less moody direction. And he had known her all his life.

"Did she really babysit you when you were young?" I whispered to Adam who was helping me frantically to polish cutlery.

"She sure did," he sighed.

"That is the scariest thing I have ever heard," I said. "I didn't know your parents hated you."

"I guess when you have three boys you need the Terminator for the job."

We snickered, and her beady eyes settled on us from across the dining room. We quickly looked back down and polished like we were demons possessed.

I went to get a cloth from behind the restaurant bar when I noticed that the book Chris had been so focused on earlier was, in fact, a reservations book. I skimmed a couple of pages, working out just how busy to expect my days to get. I found today's page and saw a reservation circled in pink fluro texta. It highlighted something sinister. A lunchtime group booking for fifteen … today!

My breath hitched. *They knew about it all along?* I wondered if Adam knew? Was this some kind of test? My heart pounded as the double doors swung open and a congregation of permed, blue-dyed hair poured slowly into the restaurant bringing with them a mass of high-pitched chatter.

Chris appeared beside me and reached for the book; he took in my ghost-white complexion with mock interest.

"I know, a pokies tour bus," Chris said as we watched elderly people flood into the restaurant. "It's as frightening as it looks."

What were they doing here? We didn't even have pokies, did we? Maybe they were just travelling through for lunch and then off to wreak five-cent havoc elsewhere. I swallowed my fear as a group assembled in front of me.

"Try not to stress, Tess. They can smell fear," Chris whispered into my ear. I barely registered his laughter as he returned to the main bar.

I would be fine, old people were nice. They would be easy, surely? Where on earth was Ellie? And Adam? They'd been at the table folding napkins a second ago, but the table stood abandoned now. All of a sudden the glint of spectacles shone my way in a domino effect. The old people shuffled towards me.

I fumbled for a notebook and pen, ready for action. Poised and standing straight behind the counter, I flashed what I hoped was a winning smile and not a scary one.

I can do this. No sweat, this I can do. Just take down the order and handball it to the kitchen. Piece of cake.

Just when I was about to write my very first order as a confident, gathered, working woman, the leader of the group merged forward. She smiled at me sweetly, putting me instantly at ease. Then she sucker punched me in the guts.

"We'll have twelve cappuccinos, please."

Shit.

***

After what could only be described as a hellish first shift, I sat in the main bar, deflated with an ice pack on my steam-burned arm. My eyes were watery from the pain of clumsily branding myself in my haste, but the watery eyes were mostly due to humiliation. To my utter relief, Melba had taken over the making of the cappuccinos. I worked the floor with Ellie to conquer the more straightforward aspect of taking lunch orders.

I mean, what could possibly go wrong? Apart from not knowing the lunch specials. Or whether we catered for the lactose intolerant. Or if our menu was diabetic friendly. Or if it was offensive to someone with coeliac disease. Was our menu *offensive*? Christ! Old people have a lot of problems. Of course, I knew none of the answers and my table of eight stared at me as if I was some idiot they wanted to squish with their walking sticks. I tried to take solace in the fact that Ellie knew equally as little as I did, but I heard a chorus of laughter at one point and saw Ellie charming her table and writing profusely. Her table was looking up at her with adoring smiles. I had looked back at my bored death stares.

It took all my strength not to get upset the fourth time I had to trail back to the kitchen to ask the short-tempered cook another question. I didn't know what I feared more – my table, who I had diagnosed with chronic evil, or the psychotic and feisty cook, who would throw pots and pans and swear profusely when things didn't go her way. There was not much of her, but geez she could swear like a sailor and throw a heavy-duty saucepan with force. The only thing that literally pushed me through the kitchen door and back into the restaurant was Adam and his infectious attitude, though a greater part of me wanted to punch him in the face when I thought back to the very reason I was there. I had been abused by Melba, a busload of geriatric gamblers and a psychotic red-headed cook.

And then a third-degree steam burn. Okay, probably not third degree, but it stung. I drowned my sorrows in a glass of Coke that Chris had placed in front of me without a word. The door burst open from the restaurant.

"THAT was the best shift ever!" Ellie beamed, followed in by Adam who still wore his dish apron.

"Seriously, how cool was that? It was so busy, but good. Made time go so fast, and I even got a tip." Ellie pulled out a five-dollar note with glee.

"Looks like you had a table of high rollers," I added glumly.

It was then that Ellie took it down a peg or two. "I saw you had to return a meal to the kitchen. What was with that?"

"Which time? When it was too hot? Or too cold? I actually contemplated blowing on her meal for her."

Adam winced; he didn't need to have the full account of my nightmare. He was painfully aware of every time I came through the kitchen door with a new complaint. Each time I did, a little piece of me died.

Adam slapped and rubbed his hands on his thighs.

"Well, the worst is over ladies, you survived your first shift initiation. It's all downhill from here."

Ellie clapped with joy.

"Yay." I glared at him.

Ellie smiled sadly at me. "How's the arm?"

I sighed. "I'm afraid I will never be an arm model."

"I'm so sorry, Tess. I know how much you were counting on that to get you through university," Adam said in mock sympathy.

"I was going to be a wrist-watch model. You know, travel the world, but, alas, it's not to be." I shook my head and tried not to smirk.

Ellie couldn't contain herself.

"You're such a dork, Tess."

"You are who you hang with," I threw back.

Adam squeezed in between us, threw his arms over our shoulders, and kissed us both on the head.

"Oh gross, boy cooties!" I squealed.

"Thank you for doing this. It'll get better, I promise. You, me, and McGee are going to have the best summer ever, you'll see."

Chapter Four

Last day of school was little more than a giant social event.

There were no classes of any substance; instead, students wandered aimlessly around the school grounds. We weren't privy to a 'muck up' day as we weren't Year Twelves and any mucking up from the senior students had been monitored so severely that we had half expected to see watchtowers constructed for teachers with binoculars and dart guns. Such limitations were largely due to an incident from two years ago that had Andy Maynard fused to a goal post with electrical duct tape by a group of hooded Year Twelve boys. The school frowned upon that and banned Muck-up Day all together. That didn't mean there wasn't any anarchy in the schoolyard.

Our theme for the year was Toga. All Year Elevens arrived draped in sheets that would have had all our mums going ballistic because we took them without asking. We all walked around, our shoulders exposed like we were in Roman bathhouses.

"It would be all so authentic if it wasn't for the gum leaf crowns everyone is wearing," Adam mused.

I re-adjusted my leafy headgear. "What choice was there? I think it looks good."

"Oh God, Tess, this is humiliating." Ellie's eyes darted around, hoping not to be recognised.

"Relax, Ellie, it's our last day of school, no one will even remember what we wore."

We weaved and maneuvered our awkward costumes through a group of Year Eight boys playing hacky sack.

"Yeah, well, if this makes it into the Yearbook, I will never forgive either of you," Ellie threatened.

"Oh, come on, Pretty Parker, just think of it as the multicultural aspect of the Miss Onslow Show Girl."

I cringed. There it was, the one thing that turned the usually beaming, bright, confident Ellie into a stone-faced Ice Queen.

Ellie had entered the Miss Onslow Show Girl Pageant in Year Nine (so she was old enough to know better), and it was something Adam had relentlessly mocked her about ever since. I recalled the glee in his mischievous eyes as we sat in the showground stands watching Ellie radiantly wave to the crowd. I thought Adam was going to pop a blood vessel as he fought not to lose himself to hysteria when the Mayor of Onslow, Hank

Whittaker, started singing Stevie Wonder's 'Isn't She Lovely?' After a full afternoon of sitting in the sun and being forced to witness every age bracket of the Miss Onslow Show Girl, I couldn't help but lose it, too. Maybe it was Adam's infectious laugh, or perhaps I suffered a touch of sunstroke? I don't know. More likely, it was witnessing Mayor Whittaker, a gangly, balding, fake-tanned man with unnaturally white protruding teeth and a torturous falsetto, mime as he captured a butterfly to his heart and then released it into the air, as if he was a Backstreet Boy. From that day on, any time Mayor Whittaker ran into Ellie, he would blind her with his bleached veneers and refer to her with his pet name for her. Hence, 'Pretty Parker' was born. It was no Tic Tac Tess, but still, Ellie came second and never entered again.

"There is no such thing as a multicultural section in the Miss Onslow Pageant, idiot."

Adam placed his hands up in mock surrender.

"Sorry, Ellie. I guess I need to brush up on my beauty pageant trivia."

I could see this getting ugly. "So, the break-up party tonight. What time do we rock up?"

Ellie's head snapped around. "What are you wearing? Do you want to come to my place first? We can pick something out."

"How come I never get invited to these pre-party fashion parades?" whined Adam.

We both ignored him.

"I haven't a clue, really," I said. "What time do you want to rendezvous?"

"Make it seven at my house. By the time we get ready, we will be fashionably late." Ellie flicked her hair over her exposed shoulder.

Adam rolled his eyes and mimicked Ellie behind her back. I threw him a discreet frown.

"Sounds like a plan," I said, as I lifted my awkward sheet to step over a wayward empty chip packet.

"So we're not wearing the Togas tonight, then?" Adam pressed.

"No," Ellie and I said in unison.

"Aww, come on."

"NO!"

Adam circled us, and chanted in his best imitation of a caveman voice while fist pumping the sky.

"Toga! Toga! Toga!"

We were about to pummel him in a joint beating when he tripped on the hem of his sheet and went flying in a very inelegant fashion that had him sprawled on the concrete, revealing his board shorts underneath.

I suppose we should have checked if he was okay, and not mortally wounded. We would have done so, too, if we weren't crippled by fits of laughter. Ellie even snorted. That made us laugh even harder, to the point that we all but forgot about Adam who lay there, possibly bleeding to death. But he wasn't. He leaned back, and squinted up at us with a wry smile spread across his face.

We bent down, offered him a hand to get up and helped him dust his once-white sheet off. His mum would not be happy.

"And that, my friend, is the perfect reason why we are not going in a Toga," I said.

***

According to Ellie, it was always important to make a grand entrance at a party, to have all eyes turned to us. In fact, she revelled in it. As soon as we arrived, Ellie was on the lookout for John Medding, who was hosting the break-up gala. He was your everyday sporty boy – popular, pretty cute. He would usually hook up with a girl when he had some Dutch courage from a few beers. He would then choose to never make eye contact or speak to her again. This was my forecast for tonight, given I had seen it a dozen times before, but Ellie didn't think that far ahead. For now her gaze circled the party.

I wanted to dance. I loved dancing. I wanted to move until my feet were blistered and every time a song I liked blared out of the speaker, my heart sank.

The makeshift dance floor was housed in an industrial-sized shed, filled with gritty machinery emitting the faint smell of oil. The large space was shrouded in flashing disco lights haphazardly hooked up to a twisted extension cord leading to God knows where. I had lost Ellie in the commute from the main house into the crowded shed. The party was massive! Obviously not an exclusive Year Eleven break-up party like originally planned, I couldn't even spot a familiar face. I busied myself with grabbing a Coke from one of the eskies when Ellie bounded excitedly up to me.

"I'm going for a walk with John," she whispered.

I didn't share her enthusiasm.

I watched Ellie walk hand in hand with John, until both were engulfed by the blackness of the night.

Instead of dancing like I wanted to, I found myself doing my usual best friend stakeout, perched on the bonnet of a car, legs crossed, staring anxiously towards the woods that surrounded the Medding property. Worse still, I was expected to be 'entertainment' for Zeke Walker, John's best mate. He caused the car to dip as he sat next to me on the bonnet.

Having realised that we were to be left alone together while Ellie and John went and 'admired nature', his presence caused me to slide to the furthest edge of the bonnet. I had played the friend part before, left with whatever prospective best friend belonged to the boy Ellie was crushing on. I had even kissed a couple to pass the time, but as Zeke skulled the remnants of his beer can, crushed it against his head and let out an almighty belch, I nearly fell off the bonnet in an effort to get away from him.

Ellie, you owe me big time!

Zeke, who was quite beefy and had a tendency to squeeze his pimples in class without apology, was one of those vile boys that had been put on this earth to make girls cringe.

"So, do you wanna fuck?"

This time I did fall off the bonnet, shocked at the out-of-nowhere question. He must have read the disgust in my look as he shrugged.

"You know that's what they're doing."

I ignored him. If I ignored him, maybe he would go away?

"That's what John said anyway, he said that …"

"I don't give a shit what John said," I snapped. Here was another one. John had clearly heard that rumour. He assumed Ellie was a sure thing. They both did. I was angry at Zeke and John for believing that. And I was angry at Ellie for not caring what they thought.

"Whoa, touchy!" Zeke said.

I wanted to stomp off, to leave Zeke, the belching idiot, to himself. But I felt uneasy and wanted to be there for Ellie when she came back, make sure she was okay. I wouldn't just leave her.

Silence fell over us again, except for the occasional belch or spit. Finally, it seemed that Zeke got bored with my enthralling company.

"Screw this. I have better things to do. I'll find out later how he went."

He walked back to the party; I glared at his back and fought to contain my anger.

"PIG!"

He flipped me the finger without a backward glance. I hated him, I hated him and I hated John Medding and all his stupid friends that waited in the wings for all the details. That was the only reason Zeke had stuck around, not out of concern for anyone's wellbeing, but to be the one to get the goss hot off the press.

Jerk!

I wanted to march into the woods, and yell for Ellie, when I heard the distant snap of twigs. My first thought was that maybe Ellie was headed back to the party. But my eyes soon adjusted to that of a darkened silhouette. The long confident stride of the stranger momentarily paused as if they had noticed me. My own form was clearly lit by the disco lights that flashed behind me. The stranger's walk slowed, appeared more guarded. They continued towards me, the lights that flickered from the party gradually lighting his face with an array of pulsing hues of colour. My tension should have ebbed at the sight of just another late gate-crasher to the party; instead, I sat transfixed. My heart stopped. I knew that face; it was a face I had always known. A face I hadn't seen in a really long time.

My head spun at the sight and the memory of Toby Morrison. A boy I had never spoken a word to, a boy I had always admired from afar. He closed the distance between us. He looked at me for what was probably the first time, though I had looked at him constantly. I held my breath as he stopped by the car, our eyes locked in a long moment, his lips parted with what would be our first exchange. I breathed in deeply and braced myself for the moment, the moment I had waited for as he finally spoke …

"Get off my car!"

I almost toppled over as I slid off the bonnet, mortified. He reached out to steady me as he laughed.

Was he laughing at me?

"Whoa! Easy there." He smiled wickedly. "Don't stress, I'm just messing with you. It's not really my car."

He steadied me with a gentle touch to my upper arm. A scorch mark burned into my flesh even after he removed his hand.

It was then that I realised I had a fist full of Toby Morrison's T-shirt gathered in my hand with a white-knuckled intensity. I must have grabbed a hold in an effort not to fall flat on my face and further disgrace myself.

Toby's eyes flicked down to his bunched T-shirt with an air of amusement. His brows lifted in a 'Do you mind?' gesture that caused me to let go as if I had been electrocuted. Being electrocuted surely couldn't have burnt more than my flushed cheeks at that moment. I prayed that the bad lighting masked them.

Toby half laughed as he plunged his hands back into his pockets and stepped to my side; he tilted a fraction closer as if he was about to reveal a secret.

"Relax … I would never own a Holden." He winked and then turned his confident stride towards the party.

I watched his figure as he retreated, and took a deep breath as if I had forgotten to breathe 'til now. My head whirled.

What had just happened? Toby Morrison had just talked to me. And had we just shared a joke?

Or rather he had made a joke, and I all but fell over and stared all googly eyed at him like an idiot and not said a word.

NOT. ONE. WORD.

I watched as his figure became smaller, but still clear enough to see that he was stopped every few feet with people and hand grasps and pats on the back. Everyone knew Toby Morrison, and I seriously wanted to, too.

When Toby Morrison disappeared into the thick of the party crowd, I took a moment to firstly move far away from the car, whose ever car it was. I needed to analyse what just happened, play by play, detail for detail. His smile, his look, his laugh, and his hand on my upper arm that I swear had burned into my skin.

My back rested against the chill of the cement water tank. I cupped my cheeks and felt the scorching burn of my skin.

A distant rustle interrupted my thoughts, and I noticed two figures had emerged from the woods. John was doing up his belt and Ellie was three paces behind readjusting her skirt, her hair all in disarray. John walked straight passed me and headed for the party. I guess the silent treatment began now and extended to Ellie's friends. I waited for Ellie, who seemed surprised to see me still waiting for her. I plucked a twig out of her hair.

"Why aren't you dancing?" Her voiced sounded sleepy.

"Oh you know, I don't have a dancing partner."

Now was not a good time to do the responsible, chastising, best friend speech. I could see that she looked past my shoulder, wondering where John had gone.

My anger had grown more like a swirling furnace in the pit of my stomach. Ellie faked indifference, something she always did when boys treated her that way.

"Have you seen Adam?" she asked.

I wanted to be snide and ask *how could I?* I had been busy hanging out with foul Zeke.

Except for my run in with Toby Morrison!

All of a sudden I didn't feel so angry anymore.

"You know Adam. If we were fashionably late, he'd be later."

We headed towards the thudding of the music, and weaved our way through the mass of bodies. I was acutely aware of the snickers behind their hands as they looked Ellie up and down. Guess news spread fast at the hands of John Medding. If Ellie noticed, she didn't let on. Instead, her head bobbed to the music as her eyes searched for Adam. I looked as well, but my gaze also searched for Toby, who wasn't anywhere. I wondered what he was doing at a Year Eleven break-up party, he had graduated from high school years ago. And more importantly, where had he gone?

We made our way past the shed and headed towards the house, opening the back door to be flooded by the pounding of a stereo. We slid past the crush of bodies wandering into what looked like a dimly lit, stuffy rumpus room filled with sporting memorabilia.

"Ellie! Tess!"

We turned and saw Adam in the distance, his body higher than everyone else's as he was dancing on a billiard table with a bunch of tarty-looking Year Ten girls. They appeared to be wearing more make-up than they were wearing clothes, and he wasn't so much dancing with them as wedged between them. They all jumped up and down which was a mean feat for that many people on such an apparatus.

Ellie and I shook our heads at the sight. Adam owned the platform with his bad rhythm and beer in hand, decked out in his mangy Toga. The only one still dressed like that at the party. Ellie and I recognised it as exactly what it had been meant: a sign of rebellion.

"Can you believe it?" Ellie shook her head.

I laughed at the sight. I *could* believe it, actually.

"Hey, look, I'll be back in a minute. I'm just going to see where John got to."

I cringed. Sometimes Ellie only saw what she wanted to. "Ellie ..." but she cut me off.

"Back soon!" She kissed me on the cheek and disappeared through the crowd.

I hated watching her go, watching her move towards her impending doom. As I worried, I felt the distinct caress of alcohol-infused, hot breath on the back of my neck. A clammy pair of hands blocked my vision.

"Suuurpriiiseee," a voice slurred in my ear. I broke free and spun around to see the bloodshot eyes of Scott Miller.

I screamed inside my head and frantically looked for an exit.

"Hey, Tessh. You're looking mighty fine tonight." His eyes moved over me with a slow caress in a way that made me feel dirty.

"Now, I have a bone to pick with you," he swayed slightly as he waggled his finger at me, a dopey look of mock anger on his face.

Why on Earth did I ever go out with him?

"Wow, with me? That's fresh." I crossed my arms. I was doing the thing my mum said over and over again: 'Never try and reason with a drunk person'. But a part of me wanted to know more about this bone. Another of mum's sayings was 'A drunk man speaks a sober man's mind'.

Scott pursed his lips together and screwed his face up in an over-the-top action that made him look ugly.

"I have a confesshion to make, Tesh."

"That you're an asshole?" I said.

He dramatically waved my sentence away and stumbled into me so he could whisper into my ear, which came out as more of a drool.

"I love you. I alwaysh have, alwaysh will. *Hic*!"

Oh, vomit!

Maybe that saying was wrong; maybe a drunk person just spoke bullshit. That's what I counted on, but then I saw the raw look in his eyes.

Oh God, was he welling up?

"Why did you break up with me? Do you think I want to be mean to you? You jusht give me no choish."

Before I could retort, I saw his lips pout and they came in for the kill.

Oh no no no ...

I tried to maneuver away, but he had me literally backed into a wall, and past Scott's face that loomed towards mine, out of the corner of my eye I saw that we had caught a group of people's attention. We had caught Toby's attention.

I wanted to die a small death.

Oh, urgh, Scott Miller's tongue was in my mouth. How did this happen? I pushed into his chest with all the force I could muster.

"Get off me, you creep!"

"Aw, come on, Tesh."

He reached for me again but stopped short. He spun around as an almighty crack sounded from behind him, followed by screams and chaos. The music stopped, panic set in as everyone looked around and wondered what had happened.

That's when I heard it, the sound that made my blood run cold, a sound so loud it could be heard above all others. Adam's agonised scream.

Chapter Five

"Pool tables are not meant to be danced on"

My dad's disapproving frown pierced us in his rearview mirror, where Ellie and I sat slumped in the back seat. They had been woken in the middle of the night with a reluctant phone call to pick us up from the hospital. After the initial panic, relief soon followed in the knowledge that we were unscathed. Well, mostly unscathed.

"Poor Adam," said Mum, more to herself than anyone else. "He looked as white as a sheet."

I fought not to burst out in hysterical laughter as I thought to myself, *yeah, whiter than his filthy Toga sheet*. Thankfully, I managed to control myself.

I was exhausted. We dropped Ellie off at home, and I nodded off by the time we made it to our house. I was jolted awake by the slamming of a car door, and managed to stumble my way inside and crash into bed.

The only thing that had me escaping my parents' fury was that I hadn't actually done anything wrong. I had scared them half to death by calling them from the hospital, sure, but I needed them to look at the bigger picture: I wasn't drinking or smoking or acting irresponsibly (aside from Scott's tongue in my mouth but that was *not* my fault).

I must have looked troubled at breakfast the next morning, because Mum gripped my shoulders and gave them a reassuring squeeze.

"Adam's going to be fine, honey."

Oh yeah, Adam.

Guilt seeped into me at the thought that Adam had not exactly been in the forefront of my mind. Poor Adam! He had been joyously rocking out when the pool table broke in half. He had done so well to balance and not fall over his Toga, which he'd ended up tucking into his shorts, offering partygoers a sight that could never be unseen. But no, it was not the Toga that had been responsible for breaking his arm in two places.

"I spoke to his mum this morning," Mum said as she topped up my juice glass.

I straightened in my seat for the update. "What did she say?"

"Adam was pretty drunk last night." Dad looked up from his newspaper, his eyes bored into me as if I was being interrogated.

"I hadn't seen Adam all night," I defended. "I was with Ellie."

A fact that would not comfort my parents. Over the past year, they had slowly started catching on that Ellie's taste wasn't for alcohol, her taste was for boys. Ellie wouldn't be the sweet, little, church-going, accountant's daughter forever. Even parents talked, and, all of a sudden, I felt uneasy.

Before the conversation could turn in a direction I didn't want it to, I excused myself from my parents' knowing gazes. "Speaking of Ellie, I might just give her a call," I said. "You know, to see if she's okay," and I scurried from the room.

One positive for Adam taking all the attention was that Ellie seemed unperturbed by the fact that John Medding was a giant douche bag.

Our telephone conversation was dominated by Adam and what had happened last night (minus my Toby encounter), but then it moved on to far less desirable topics.

"So what was with you and Scott? Seriously, Tess, what the fuck?" Ellie's angry voice pierced through the receiver.

"Ugh, I know!"

I threw myself back on my bed wanting to erase the entire memory of last night. Well, perhaps not the *entire* memory. I thought back to Toby appearing out of the dark – the blue, yellow and red flashing disco lights shining on his beautiful smile. Me stumbling rather inelegantly off the bonnet. I cringed. *So classy!* At least I hadn't burst into tears, that was something.

"Hey, did you notice some older people at the party?"

Ellie replied in a manner that had me imagining her shrug. "Older, younger, it wasn't just a Year Eleven break up, I think anyone was invited."

"But why would you want to go to a Year Eleven break up?"

"Tess, it's Onslow. People go to the opening of an envelope; seriously, what else is there to do in this town?"

"I suppose." I wrapped the cord around my fingers as I lay on the bed.

The thought had never even occurred to me that Adam wouldn't be okay to work the next night, which I guess it probably should have since he had a broken arm and everything. I called him after I spoke to Ellie; we chatted about how much trouble he was in and if he was in any pain. It all seemed so normal, so natural. So when "see you tomorrow night" was met with awkward silence from Adam, a newfound dread swept over me.

"You are going to work tomorrow night, right?"

More silence.

"Adam?"

"I'm sorry, Tess, I won't be able to."

I sat up straight on my bed, alarm settling in.

"Sunday?"

"Tess, how can I wash dishes with a plaster cast?"

"I don't know! Rubber gloves? Surely there must be something else you can do?"

Adam sighed. "It's not just that. Mum and Dad are pretty pissed at me. They think I broke my arm because I was drinking. They went on and on about it. Not to mention Mum's ruined sheets."

"Pfft, I told you," I groaned.

"Anyway, they don't have a great deal of trust in me; they say I have to earn it back. And they don't exactly want me surrounded by alcohol at the hotel."

My silence echoed down the phone. "So? When will you come back to work?"

"I'm not going to, Tess. I'm not allowed." I could hear the regret in his voice.

But that did little to appease me. "What?! What do you mean you're not working?"

"Mum and Dad are sending me to my nan's house in the city. They said that it will do me good to get out of Onslow, but I know that they just want me to be a slave to my nan."

"How long for?"

"Until my cast comes off – six weeks."

"Six weeks! Adam, that's the whole summer holidays!"

"I know, I know," he said, "believe me, I know."

I should have felt sorry for him, a whole hot summer imprisoned at his nan's house. Unable to go swimming in the lake, hanging out with friends, working at the Onslow Hotel that he had looked forward to all semester. All his summer plans gone, just like that. I *should* have felt sorry for him. But I didn't. I didn't feel any ounce of pity except for myself.

This was not what had been sold to me as a summer we would 'never forget'. "You, me and McGee," he had said. Now I was stuck in a job every weekend for the whole summer. Without Adam, it wouldn't be the same. Adam was like the buffer, always there to cling to when Ellie would wander off with some new boy. Adam was always there to make me laugh, or vandalise a locker for me in the name of revenge. He was my anchor, how could I do it without him?

Who would give me sympathetic looks every time I came into the kitchen with a complaint? Who would punch me in the arm after our shift and promise it would be better tomorrow, even if it was a total lie? I felt lost. My hands clenched the phone with a white-knuckled intensity. My heart sank with the thought of walking into the Onslow Hotel tomorrow without him.

And then the anger set in.

"Well, I am so glad I did you a favour. I really fancy whittling my summer weekends away in a pub infused with cigarette smoke and rude tourists."

"Tess, I'm sorry. This blows, I know. Believe me – I would give anything to be there. The thought of taking my nan grocery shopping while she counts out her change at the cash register in five-cent pieces does nothing for me."

Again, I had no pity. I would happily trade places, but my days of doing Adam Henderson any favours were over. Never again!

"Yeah, well, you have fun with that! I'll think of you with your sweet nan sipping cups of tea, while I get abused and have to dodge a frying pan from crazy Rosanna."

"Te…"

I slammed down the phone, cutting him off. "Not interested." I glared at the receiver.

***

"Poor Adam," Ellie puffed as we made our way slowly up Coronary Hill.

"Mmm," I replied.

"Come on, Tess, he didn't break his arm on purpose."

"Didn't he?" I gave her a pointed look. I knew I was sulking and being unreasonable, but Adam's words echoed in my memory: "The worst is over, it's all downhill from here".

How ironic, I thought, as I physically made my way *up* the hill to my impending doom.

My heart clenched as I looked over Lake Onslow. It was dotted with locals and tourists lapping up the remainder of the dimming sun. They would stay out for as long as the mozzie repellant lasted. It was a beautiful balmy evening, perfect for enjoying the breeze that flowed off the lake on a summer's night. Instead, I was about to enter the Onslow Hotel, which was like a giant tomb to me.

Ellie and I decided to mix it up. Instead of entering the restaurant via the beer garden out back we walked through the front bar entrance. It was five o'clock, so the place was deserted save for the odd widowed drunk that had been propped up at the bar surrounded by empty chip packets and pot glasses for what looked like a rather productive day. Chris gave us a curt nod as we made our way through the front bar to the restaurant.

"How's Adam?" Ellie asked.

"He'll live." Chris took the empty beer glass from his patron as a sign of being done – that, and the old fella had nodded off at the bar.

"Time for a taxi, Ned, before the riff raff get here," Chris yelled, jolting Ned from his slumber.

"Taxi!" the old guy shouted.

Ellie and I exchanged glances and couldn't help but giggle as we walked through to the restaurant.

Melba was wiping down tables. "You're late!"

I looked at the clock on the wall; it was two minutes past five.

"We were just ..."

"Loitering in the bar, I know what you young 'uns are like, but I have news for you – there'll be no jumping on the bar or table top dancing or breaking bones on my watch, ya hear?"

Oh goody! Another reason to hate us even more.

Melba gave us directions to prep the dining room before meals started at six. We busied ourselves to further avoid her wrath and gave each other the odd smirk as we settled into our work. It was then that Chris walked through the partition, weaving his way through tables and chairs towards us.

"Melba, is it possible that you are looking younger every time I see you?"

Melba scoffed, "Oh, you, quit it." She waved him away and quickly gathered up the extra tablecloths to carry back to the kitchen, a ruby red blush creeping up her neck and cheeks. My incredulous stare turned from Melba's retreating figure to Chris, who looked at me.

And there it was, that Henderson charm.

"What?"

I shook my head. "Nothing."

His face melted back to stone. "We have a promotion going on this weekend, for the Irish Festival."

"Ooh, to be sure, to be sure," crooned Ellie as she sidled up next to Chris, who all of a sudden looked uneasy. He took a subtle step back.

"You're to wear these as the uniform tonight."

"A uniform?" pouted Ellie.

"It's only for the weekend." Chris chucked us both unnervingly small black tops, which I held up against my torso with a gulp. Before I could question the size, Chris was gone.

"Come on, let's get changed before Mad Melba returns."

I had thought I looked summery with my leggings, ballerina flats and a long, flowy, dusty pink top.

That was before. I stood in front of the full-length mirror in the ladies' toilets, my mouth gaping open in horror. I had literally poured myself into what there was of the tight, black top with the Guinness logo on my chest.

"I can't go out there like this," I said. My voice shook.

Ellie stepped out from the cubicle tucking her top into her non-offensive skirt.

"What's the problem?" She froze when she caught sight of me.

"Wow!" Ellie's eyes widened.

I grimaced. "I look like I'm in a cat suit." Turning to the mirror, I tried to pull down the stretchy top but it infuriatingly drifted upwards.

"You look hot, Tess!"

I chewed on my lower lip, trying not to get upset.

"Can you please go ask Chris if there is another size? Something bigger?"

Ellie had to shake herself from her daze as her gaze looked over me. "Ah, Tess, I don't think–"

"Ellie, please!"

I paced the toilets, waiting for Ellie to return waving a XXXL top in her hand. Unfortunately, it was not to be.

"Tess, seriously, you look fine. In fact, you look smoking-hot fine!"

I didn't want to be 'smoking-hot fine'; I wanted to be blend-into-the-wall fine.

Ellie grabbed my hand. "Come on, we can't stay in here forever. Chris said we were going to be flat out tonight so we better get to it."

Perfect.

"Oh, wait." Ellie pulled me up, and all but yanked my arm out of my socket.

"What?"

Without a word Ellie yanked the elastic from my hair and ruffled it up.

"*Ellie*!"

"Just trust me," she said.

I took a deep breath and stood still. She ran her fingers through my hair and folded up the top half with the band, for a messy half-up half-down look, before fixing my fringe to frame my face.

"Much better!" She smiled.

We came out just in time for a staff meeting. Chris's words were cut off abruptly when he saw us join the group. His eyebrows raised in surprise as he took in my apparel. Not in disgust or mockery, but the way a guy checks out a girl. The way boys usually looked over Ellie. He coughed, cleared his throat and refocused on his clipboard. I felt the heat flood my cheeks as I quickly sat down in an attempt to hide myself behind a table. I sat next to Melba who didn't give me the same look of appreciation. She was looking at me in more of a '*You look like a whore*' way.

We were given our battle stations speech; what our roles were to be, and what was expected of us for the night. The Irish band would be setting up in the beer garden, and the restaurant was fully booked. My heart beat faster as I recounted my disastrous first shift. It hadn't exactly boosted my confidence (especially now that I looked like a ninja). Ellie was jigging her leg like she always did when she was excited.

For what time remained before the expected arrival of our first booking, I took it upon myself to memorise the dinner specials, taking note of any vegetarian selections. I tested my pen for ink, dated the order pad accordingly and, before I knew it, the six o'clock rush had begun.

I fumbled and stuttered at my first table, but luckily they were a family of locals. Ken and Wendy Martin and their three adorable kids. They were patient and kind, and helped ease my nerves. I took their order without drama and spiked it proudly on the kitchen spike.

"Order up!"

"Well, look at you," crooned the usually foul-tempered cook, Rosanna. She smiled at me, her demeanour disturbingly friendly. But I knew this was the calm before the storm.

"Twirl for me." She circled her finger in the air in a spinning motion, giving a wolf whistle of appreciation.

"You'll be breaking all the boys' hearts, Tess."

I cringed. "I don't know about that," I said, and quickly retreated from the kitchen, running straight into Ellie.

She pulled me into the alcove where the high chairs were kept.

"Oh my God, Tess! You should see who just came through the front door."

Before I could ask, she let out a squeal. "I'm going to take their order," she said, and disappeared.

Okey dokey, there was either a celebrity in the bar (in *Onslow*?), or a hot boy. My money was on the latter and my suspicions were confirmed by the distant hum of the jukebox, which meant that the poolroom was in use.

My friendly family table continued to be everything true and lovely, which almost made up for my next table … almost.

Chapter Six

My burden to bear for the night was to serve two posh tourists, who spoke in clipped sentences and looked at me as if they had stepped in something nasty.

The full-figured lady sported a grey bob that was immaculately kept in place. No, really, it didn't move; there must have been a full can of hairspray on there. She was clearly highly flammable. I clasped my notepad tightly, glancing around with unease; trust Claire Henderson to think candles would make for great ambience in the dining room. The place was a giant death trap for this woman.

She smiled at me but it didn't quite reach her eyes. Her husband complained about the lighting, the air conditioning, and the sound of the music filtering through the paper-thin walls of the poolroom. Their rudeness frazzled me, which was bad, as the last thing I needed was to make more mistakes as the night picked up in pace. More patrons poured through the restaurant's French doors, all sun-kissed and starving from their day in the sun. The restaurant was at full capacity, a buzzing cauldron of chaos, so when I brought out the wrong meal (because I had written down the table wrong), Rosanna started to lose it, and I quickly vacated the kitchen, slamming hard into Chris's chest.

"Whoa, Tess, slow down."

I bit my lower lip in an attempt to hide that I was upset.

"We're going to switch things up a bit, okay? Uncle Eric wants you to take over Adam's place in the kitchen for a bit. Thinks it might be for the best," he said.

Meaning I wasn't quite cutting it out front. A part of me was relieved, but another part of me was mortified that I had just been demoted, if only for the night. In other words, they thought I wasn't doing a good enough job. They would never have sent Ellie in to wash dishes, not in a million years.

"Ellie's going to take over your tables." Chris took the notepad and pen from me; another slap in the face. I nodded and solemnly turned back to the kitchen. My summer was now downgraded from hell to the pits of hell, with Melba and Rosanna.

Thanks, Adam!

I stood in front of the sink for what seemed like forever, overwhelmed by the huge pile of dirty pots and pans, and ever-increasing stack of plates. I didn't know where to begin. I tied the sodden dish apron around me, too afraid to ask if there were any rubber gloves. At least I wouldn't have to worry about being seen in my cat suit. As I waited for the sink to fill, I cast a look at my pride and joy, my meticulously French manicured nails. I had filed, shaped and coated them in preparation for my big working debut. I had always prided myself on having nice nails and thought I would put an extra-special effort into them, knowing I was to be serving customers. If I was to be incompetent, at least they could say, "Well, she had nice hands."

Nice hands that were now submerged in blisteringly hot, dirty, dishwater.

Ellie swung through the kitchen door, smiling like a Cheshire cat; she never said anything about my new position. She was too busy humming a joyful tune and spiking her docket.

"Order up!"

I unloaded a stack of dishes near the server, peeking at the docket and wondering if the little piece of paper had anything to do with her being in such fine form. A docket with several meals listed sported the heading *'The Onslow Boys' – (Poolroom)*. A little smiley face had been drawn into the O, and the penny dropped. Ha! Well, at least someone was having a good time.

There was much swearing and pot throwing at the peak of service. Through desperation, they had Melba take a few orders, and with Melba's people skills being what they were, it was a true sign that they were under the pump. At least I was friendly. For the most part, Melba was really a kitchenhand for Rosanna and they kind of complemented each other. What I mean by that is that Melba refused to take Rosanna's crap, so it worked.

I had created a clean space in my sodden little corner of the world; I even felt good about my achievement until I looked down at my destroyed nails, the once immaculate polish melted from the heat of the water. As I took a moment to survey the damage, the background was filled with more swearing and clattering, accompanied by the frantic dinging of the service bell, all of which I was sadly getting used to as the night wore on.

"Order up," Rosanna screamed.

Ellie was noticeably absent, which caused Rosanna to lose it big time. Before all hell broke loose, Chris burst through the kitchen door and spotted my nearly clear sink.

"You. Meals. Go. Now!" He held the door ajar, pointing to the restaurant.

"But Uncle Eric said I was to–"

"Uncle Eric is upstairs watching *Touched by an Angel*, so what I say goes; we need you to take the meals, now!"

I frantically untied my dish apron and smoothed down fly-away strands of hair that had curled from the steam. Before Rosanna hurled the meals across the kitchen, I grabbed them and headed through the door Chris still held open.

"Get them out of here! Get them out of here!" she screamed.

Happy to escape the mayhem and relieved I hadn't been knifed in the process, I looked at the docket that lay haphazardly on top of the chip pile on the dinner plate. It read the 'Onslow Boys'. With immense concentration, I walked two plates through the restaurant en route to the poolroom. The mystery of Ellie's disappearance was solved when I saw her taking orders for a table of twelve. She managed to glance at me as I walked by, and putting two and two together she pouted at the fact I was delivering 'her' meals.

I pressed my back against the swinging restaurant door and pushed my way through to the front bar. I had never been in the bar in peak hour on a Saturday night. Actually, I had never been in here *at all* until I worked here, so I wasn't entirely sure what would greet me as I walked steadily through my final barrier, a flimsy concertina partition, and into the bar. The smell of cigarette smoke and stale beer hit me first, followed by the loud music that flooded from the poolroom. The front bar was dominated mainly by an older clientele, enjoying the blessed happy hour. The bar aligned with an array of men in attire ranging from flannelette-covered work overalls, to stubby shorts and Blundstone boots. Foreigner's 'Urgent' blared from the speakers as I made my way gingerly through the mass of bodies. Men parted for me with lingering gazes. I smiled politely, excusing myself as I brushed by strangers, dodging and weaving with great care, holding onto the dinner with a white-knuckled intensity. I headed to the poolroom to deliver the Chicken Parma's to the smiley-faced Onslow Boys. I paused under the archway, taking in the packed, smoky poolroom. The music was twice as loud in here. Just as I summoned enough courage to yell out my order, I was drowned out by a blast of laughter and shouts as someone missed a shot on the pool table.

"That's two shots to us!" yelled a tall, muscular boy. Sean Murphy. I knew him mainly by his all-star status as the ruck-man for the Onslow Tigers. He was now looking at me with piercing baby blue eyes, a colour I had never seen before.

He flashed a smile that made my stomach flip, and as if sensing my predicament, he shouted out for me, "Grub's up! Tobias, it's your shot."

A lone figure leaning over the jukebox flipped through the song archives; he pushed his final selection before turning to grab the pool cue from Sean. I threatened to drop my plates when I noticed Tobias was Toby. *The* Toby! *My* Toby!

Our eyes locked, his brows raised in surprise, and then I realised he wasn't the only one looking at me. All of the Onslow Boys were looking at me like I was some kind of creature that had emerged from the lake. But when I caught their eyes roaming over me much like Chris's had, it made me suddenly super aware and self-conscious of my bodysuit attire.

I coughed and stammered, "Where do you want it?" As soon as the words left my mouth, I realised how suggestive it had sounded and mentally slapped myself.

There was a pause and a line of bemused smirks as I watched the same thought flick through their minds, before Toby broke off and headed to the pool table.

"Two shots, was it?" Toby asked.

Sean scratched his jawline and nodded. Trying not to smile.

"Just sit them down there, Tess,"

I flinched at the unexpected voice of Chris, from behind me where he stood manning the bar, his arms crossed. He was all business, no nonsense. I latched onto the clarity and put the meals quickly on the bar.

"Thanks, Tess." Sean smiled at me as he slid a meal down the bar.

I made my exit, stressed that I had at least two more meals to deliver to them without embarrassing myself. Again.

I took the shortcut through the opposite door to head towards the kitchen; I passed Ellie who was still busy with her mammoth table. When she saw me coming from the bar, she winked and gave me the thumbs up, and I couldn't help but smile and return the gesture.

I carried the meals back the same way and avoided the front bar all together. When I reached the Onslow Boys, I didn't need to ask whose meals I was holding. Toby and another boy, Stan, I think his name was, had pulled their bar stools next to Sean and a boy they'd nicknamed Ringer. I placed the meals carefully before Toby and Stan who both said, "Thanks." My heart did a little flip.

"Hey, Tess, is there any salt and pepper?" Sean asked.

"Oh … uh, I'll get some." I made a silent prayer that I wasn't blushing at such a simple question. I snuck back to the restaurant and grabbed a set. Quickstepping back into the poolroom, I passed them to Sean's outstretched hand upon my return.

He watched me intently. "What's your last name, Tess?"

Before I could answer, Toby spoke for me. "McGee," he said. He glanced up from his meal, confident about his answer and motioning for Sean to pass the salt.

He knew my name?

"Ahh, McGee, eh? Your parents own the Rose Café in Perry? That McGee?" Sean pressed.

"Ah, yeah, Jeff and Jenny McGee."

"Best pies in town," Ringer added with a mouth full of chips.

They all nodded.

"Thanks! I'll make sure I tell her the Onslow Boys approve."

Sean frowned as if what I just said confused him and Ringer, Toby and Stan looked equally confused as they eyed each other.

Sean swallowed. "The Onslow Boys?"

In that very moment I knew I had gone bright red; the Onslow Boys was Ellie's nickname for them. Not a common one everyone used.

"Oh, nothing," I stammered. "It was just something that was written on the docket, so I could find you."

Oh help!

Sean munched on a chip thoughtfully. "Let me see."

I cringed and reached for the crumpled order I had shoved in my apron from the plate. Sean took it from me.

His smile broadened. "The Onslow Boys."

"Don't forget the smiley face," added Stan, who peered over Sean's shoulder.

I felt like such a child. Sean handed the docket back to me.

"That's pretty cool. Boys, it would appear we have a new status; we now represent the entire town."

"That's a frightening thought," Chris added, as he appeared in the bar. He had a habit of appearing out of nowhere.

"Surely we could have been called the Onslow Men?" Ringer puffed his chest out.

"No, I think boys is appropriate for the likes of you lot," Chris said.

They all broke out with laughter. Stan threw a chip at Chris and the verbal onslaught continued. Chris gave me a 'back to work' look that made me scurry to action. I locked eyes briefly with Toby who seemed to be the only one not overly amused by the personal jokes being flung around.

I ducked into the alcove between the poolroom and dining room hall, stealing a moment to catch my breath. I had managed to see Toby twice in one week and he knew my name, not just my first name but my *whole* name.

He actually knew my name.

So? I thought to myself. It was a small town, everyone knew everyone's name, it was no big deal.

I couldn't help but press myself closer to the partition; I strained to overhear their voices that were mixed with laughter.

"So what do you think?" posed Ringer.

"What do I think?" said Sean.

"Yeah."

"I think she makes me want to drink Guinness," Sean said. That had them all laughing.

Guinness? I looked down in horror to see that exact word blatantly advertised across my chest.

"Easy, Tiger," Chris said.

"Whose shot is it?" added Toby, and the fray was broken with more trash talk about one another's pool skills. Mortified, I ran back to the kitchen with my head swimming in all that was the Onslow Boys and Toby Morrison, who knew my name.

By eleven o'clock, it was just Ellie and I left in the kitchen, washing all of Rosanna's pots and equipment.

"Chefs don't do dishes," Rosanna had said as she smugly made her way out of the kitchen.

We glared after her, the same thought no doubt crossing both our minds.

Chef? Pa-lease!

Rosanna had pretty much trashed the kitchen. Remnants of greasy food spattered on the work bench, spoons, pots, dishes, sodden tea towels and an overflowing rubbish bin. I could only imagine that this was a reflection of what inside her mind was like. Chaos. We were on the homeward stretch, wiping down the benches, both clearly exhausted by a long, hard night. When Chris walked in with a new set of dirty dishes he dumped in the sink, I dragged myself over to refill it with water.

"Leave it, Tess," Chris said, "you've done enough, come and have your knock-off drink."

We dragged ourselves into the main bar, pulling up the spare seats next to Rosanna who was devouring a smoke, and Melba who sipped on a vodka and tonic. Chris plonked two ice cold Cokes on the small table before us which we gratefully skulled in unison.

"Thirsty work, girls?" bellowed Sean, who appeared out of the poolroom making his way towards the gents.

I nearly choked on a bit of ice at the unexpected comment, which Melba and Rosanna thought was hilarious. They slapped their palms on the table with fits of cackling laughter.

"Don't worry love, Seany-boy has that effect on all the girls." Rosanna knocked my chair with her foot as she wriggled her pencil thin eyebrows in a 'hubba-hubba' motion.

"And he's really nice, too," added Ellie, dreamily.

"Ha! It's the nice ones you have to worry about," Melba said.

Our conversation was getting more and more bizarre in a really dysfunctional way; it was like a bonding session of sorts. And as Sean reappeared and walked back towards the poolroom, we all tipped our heads sideways, watching, in appreciation of such fineness.

Chris worked on drawing the blinds, switching off the main lights and deadbolting all the doors.

"Time for everyone to head home by the looks of it," I sighed.

"Oh, honey," Rosanna said, "they're just booting up, the night doesn't kick off till now." She butted out her cigarette.

"How so?" asked Ellie.

"They're doing a lock-in."

"What's that?"

"It's the lurks and perks of being mates with the nephew of the publican." Rosanna stood, hooking her handbag over her bony shoulder.

"Dropping me off, Melbs?"

Melba swallowed the last of her gin, slapping her hand on the table.

"Let's go. See you girls tomorrow at eleven. Don't be late."

Chris unbolted the back door and let them out. My shoulders drooped, my body unclenched. I saw Ellie do it, too. For the first time that whole night, Ellie and I collectively relaxed.

She leaned towards me. "So what do you think of Sean?"

What I wanted to say (but didn't dare – not here) was, '*what do you think of Toby?*'

"He seems nice, friendly enough." I shrugged. "I don't really know him."

"Hmm, I would like to, though," Ellie said. "I mean, seriously!" She had that glazed look in her eyes as she stared towards the poolroom.

Chris collected ashtrays and rolled up bar mats, hovering over us in a not-too-subtle gesture for us to get a move on. We skulled the last of our drinks and gathered our handbags. We were both exhausted and obviously not invited to the lock-in anyway. In order to get out the front we had to make our way directly past the poolroom, where a very merry Stan was shuffling to K.C and the Sunshine Band's 'Get Down Tonight'.

"Who put this on?" complained Ringer.

"Random," they all said at once. But the Boys sounded unconvinced, casting dubious glances at Stan who mysteriously knew all the words as he pointed to no one in particular.

Ellie and I couldn't help but laugh.

"Don't encourage him," said Chris, who couldn't contain his own smile.

"He's trying to psyche me out," Toby said as he concentrated on potting the black ball. He did, with ease.

He shook Sean's hand, who had now spotted us waiting for Chris to un-deadbolt the front door.

"So the 'Perry Girls' are off, then?"

"Perry Girls?" repeated Ellie.

He shrugged. "Seemed only fair to return the title."

She thought for a moment, and smiled. "'Perry Girls'. I like it."

Sean walked over and shook Ellie's hand, then mine.

"For services rendered in the line of duty." He smiled.

Next thing we knew, we were ushered over to Ringer who shook our hands and was fighting not to fall asleep at the bar.

"It couldn't have been an easy job, having that knucklehead order you around." He tilted his head towards Chris. "He's drunk with power, ya know?" Ringer winked.

"Watch it, Ringo, let's not forget who the gatekeeper is here," Chris said in mock seriousness.

Ringer shook his head. "See what I mean?"

And then there I was. Standing in front of Toby, who held his hand out to me. I placed my hand into his and memorised the pressure, the feel, the length of one-two-three shakes and then it was over all too soon. But he did look at my hand for a mere moment, his brow furrowed.

Oh God, was he looking at my nails? My mangy, chipped, dishpan hands?

Ellie didn't get past Stan who was still shaking her hand in a way that threatened to dislocate her shoulder.

"Come on, Chris, can we keep them?" whined Stan.

Ellie laughed and looked at Chris with the same forlorn plea in her eyes.

"I think the girls have better things to do than hang out with a bunch of derelicts like us."

The truth was, Ellie's dad would be waiting down the road to take us to our childhood bedrooms for us to curl up in our jammies in bed. It had been a long day, and I had felt exhausted, but I was suddenly wide awake, standing next to Toby.

Chris opened the front door, as if the matter was non-negotiable. This was obviously a boys-only gathering.

"Eleven am start, ladies."

With that, we were ushered outside and the door closed behind us. Standing in muted darkness, only small slithers of light streamed beyond the cracks of the window blind, the echoes of muffled laughter sounding from inside.

We started the trek down the hill towards the brake lights of Ellie's dad's car when Ellie asked, "So what do you think of Stan?"

I laughed. How things could change in an instant with Ellie.

I didn't answer. Instead, in the relative privacy of the nighttime track, I said, "That's funny, because I was just going to ask what *you* thought of Toby."

***

Ellie had threatened that she wanted to know all the details of this Toby crush the next day, as we couldn't exactly get into the details with Ellie's dad in the front seat. It was hysterical watching Ellie desperate to ask, but biting her lips together in front of her dad. Dads were a girl-talk-free zone.

After I had showered the sweat, grease and smoke away, I removed the remnants of my poor, melted French polish. I thought back to Toby's expression as he shook my hand. It was subtle, but obvious, that something had run through his mind.

It bothered me. I'm pretty sure my hand wasn't clammy or gross. The nails, it had to be my nails. I cringed, I didn't want to even think about it.

Before I slipped into a coma for the night, I dragged myself from my bed to my desk for my nightly ritual: to check my email.

To: tessmcgee

Toby Morrison eh?? You little Minx! Talk about must have made a good impression?

I want to know everything!!! I have a plan. Operation Toby?? (Don't stress just an idea)

ME first, which sounds better? Operation Sean? Or Operation Stan?

Decisions! Decisions!

Sender: ellieparker

To: ellieparker

Go to bed! Talk tomorrow. NO OPERATION TOBY! Do I make myself clear??

GOOD NIGHT!!

P.S Operation Stan!! I like his dance moves

Sender: tessmcgee

I was set for bed when I saw an email from Adam.

To: tessmcgee

Do you still love me???

How did you go tonight? I spoke to Chris, he said you smashed it! I take it he is not referring to a plate and assume you did well? Go you!! I knew you would do good. That is why I hand picked you, you know?

Seriously Tess, that's really great. I better go, Nan's telling me Matlock is on. Oh goody!

Sender: Adam I can jump puddles Henderson.

To: Adam I can jump puddles Henderson

How can I stay mad at you? I don't want to run the risk of your feelings being as delicate as your bones.

And I will have you know I did totally smash it!

In the kitchen!!!

I think it's just as well you hurt yourself, because I have found my calling in life. I am the Messiah of dish pigs!

Don't cry for me though. It kills me to admit this, but I didn't totally hate it. But if you repeat that I will just deny it.

Enjoy Matlock!!

Sender: tessmcgee

Chapter Seven

The Sunday lunchtime shift was dead. It was like a graveyard shift at best.

But why wouldn't it be? Everyone was lake bound and enjoying themselves. My heart ached as I looked out through the windowpane of the poolroom, which was, incidentally, my job for the afternoon: to clean off drunken blow fish marks from Saturday night.

"I don't remember reading this in the brochure," Ellie said glumly as she sprayed Windex and cleaned fingerprints off the jukebox. Her bracelets clinked with each vigorous rub.

"Melba said we had to 'earn our keep'," I air-quoted.

Chris was nowhere to be seen. He had his own room upstairs; more 'lurks and perks' of managing the bar, on top of lock-ins, was, obviously, free board. That left Uncle Eric in charge of the day shift, something he was much more accustomed to. The place was breezy; slower and less high maintenance during daylight hours with just a handful of church-skipping tradies having a quiet cold one as opposed to the rowdy twenty-something crowd of a Saturday night.

It would be our second day into the Irish Festival and I was prepped; I wore my infamous Guinness top with a black skirt so I didn't look like a body double for that 1960s chick from the Avengers. We had a few lunchtime walk-ins, mostly tourists all damp and sun-kissed from swimming or lying out by the lake. Seeing them put Ellie and I in a whimsical mood, so we made plans to break away to Mclean's Beach between shifts.

But until then, forced to endure everyone else enjoying their holidays, the afternoon dragged on. I couldn't stop myself from turning each time the front door opened, my heart skipping a beat in hope, but the Onslow Boys never appeared. I guessed that they had better things to do on a Sunday afternoon. I could only hope they'd venture out when the sun went down.

At shift's end, we bolted down the hill in a highly unlady-like fashion, bags bouncing on our shoulders, arms flailing, breaths laboured. Our minds focused solely on reaching McLean's Beach at the hottest part of the day. It would be crowded and overrun, no doubt, but not so much by tourists. The beauty of Maclean's Beach was that it was always crowded by locals rather than tourists, just the way we liked it. Although I would often complain about tourists, I did get it. How could I not? My parents constantly reminded me.

"No tourists, no livelihood, Tess."

Mum and Dad's cafe on the main strip of Perry – a direct line into Onslow – proved to be the perfect busy stopover. Mum was an excellent cook, taught from Gran and no doubt her Gran before her. She specialised in traditional family home-cooked recipes and Mum's homemade pies were a big hit. It had made my heart clench when the Onslow Boys gave them the tick of approval as the 'best pies in town'. I wondered if Mum would remember them coming in. I'd have to ask in a way that wouldn't make her suspicious or have me sound like a stalker.

As time ticked on towards the dinner shift, Ellie and I packed up our towels we had stretched out on for an afternoon sunbaking session and headed for the hotel. We walked past the mechanics, where I knew Toby worked. Naturally, it was closed on Sunday, but I did have the slightest hope that Toby might have been in there, anyway. He could be doing a bit of weekend catch-up. Being a sweltering summer afternoon and all, if he was in there, he'd most likely be shirtless. Hey, it was my fantasy.

My gaze skimmed the exterior of the closed building. Faded block lettering read 'Matthew & Son' on the tangerine and blue workshop. Toby's dad, Matthew Morrison, had been the local mechanic for as long as I could remember. It was where everyone went. Since he was the only mechanic in town he could have named his price, but he was a real decent bloke and always charged reasonably. Or so my dad said. I squinted at the sign; it should have really read 'Matthew & Sons' seeing as Toby and his older brother, Michael, both worked there. That in itself was a real testament to their dad. I mean, don't get me wrong, I love my parents, but I could *never* work for them. And believe me, they had tried. One of the upsides of working at the Onslow was my parents stopped pestering me. They seemed pleased enough that I had stepped out of my comfort zone and was trying, at least. One look at my lacklustre waitressing skills, and they would probably thank their lucky stars I'd never agreed to work for them.

"Well, look at you."

Ellie gave me a side-on look.

"What?"

"Checking out Toby Morrison's workshop. It's Sunday, Tess, he'll be long gone."

I should never have told her about liking Toby. She was like a dog with a bone. Even more frightening was the scheming matchmaking side to Ellie that I knew she'd lose control of sooner or later. Probably sooner. Ugh, why had I told her?

She frowned at me. "What's stopping you? Tell me one good reason why you won't go there, Tess."

We crossed the main street, leaving Matthew & Son behind.

I half laughed at her. "One? Ha! I'll give you five!"

"Go on, then!"

I held up my thumb to begin the count.

"One! Before two days ago, I am pretty sure he didn't even know that I existed."

Although he did know my last name.

"Two! And this is a pretty big one: he's what? Twenty-two? And I'm seventeen. You do the maths."

Ellie shrugged. "Maths isn't my strong point."

It was five years too many.

"Three! He is *Toby Morrison.* Popular, gorgeous, charming … and I am TIC TAC TESS."

Ellie sighed. "You're struggling."

"Four! He works, I'm still at school. I doubt he would be interested in coming to Deb practice."

Ellie rolled her eyes stubbornly. "I must say, I'm still unconvinced."

"And number five," I breathed out. I had a horrible suspicion. Although I hoped it might not have been true, I seriously doubted it. "Number five," I said again, "Toby has a girlfriend."

And her name was Angela Vickers.

You would have had to live on another planet to not know Angela Vickers. 5'10", blonde, hard to miss. She was School Captain when I was in Year Ten, and, oh, how all the boys mooned over her, with her perky blonde hair and perfect perky breasts. None of which would have mattered, only that even the likes of Toby Morrison was obviously not immune to her or her assets. It bewildered me that Toby was like all the other predictable males when he seemed so different from them. I had been in love with Toby ever since the first time I saw him.

At the end of Grade Six, all students from Perry Primary were taken for a one-day orientation at Onslow High School. We all gathered around like sheep staring in wonder at the 'big league' we were about to enter after our summer holidays. I was drawn to the burst of laughter that had me turning to see a boy, a boy with the most brilliant smile I had ever seen. I decided I simply had to know his name, and then, like a gift, one of the boys he was laughing with said it.

Toby Morrison.

I found out that his dad owned the mechanic shop in town, so any chance I had, I would deliberately walk past it hoping for just a glimpse or to cross paths with him. My heart was all aflutter with the sight of him, and merely the thought of him was what had me anxious to start high school, to the point I started marking down the days on my calendar.

Of course, I learned the hard way that he was in Year Twelve and had graduated by the time I started high school. So that was that. My crush on Toby faded away and life went on, even if I did always think of that smile every time I walked past his dad's shop.

For the next few years, I saw him only every now and then at the Sunday markets or more fleetingly down lakeside with his mates. It was by pure chance one time, when I was fourteen, that I walked past Matthew & Son and saw him out the front in grease-stained overalls, talking to a customer about their car. He looked older, his hair longer, hands covered in greasy remnants of a hard day's work.

He was working for his dad! And I nearly ran into a pole.

My heart had pounded just as it had that first time at orientation. My secret crush was just that, an utter secret. I told no one; I didn't even confide in Ellie or Adam. Especially not Ellie. I was always terrified about confiding in her over my secret crushes as I'd learned from experience that it usually resulted in her marching up to the boy I liked and blatantly grilling them with the most obvious question of all: "So what do you think of Tess McGee?"

So Toby had become a non-negotiable secret, for the years that followed I would obsess about him only to myself. Until one infamous day in Year Ten woodwork when the latest rumour had circulated to my table. The big news that Angela Vickers was going out with the mechanic's hot son. My heart withered at the thought, and, just for the record, bad news during woodwork is not ideal; I nearly lost a finger that day. I had to accept it: the Angela Vickers of this world would always get the boy, and I would always be Tic Tac Tess.

But then, at the Onslow Hotel I wasn't Tic Tac Tess anymore, I was just Tess or McGee. I was like anyone else. The horrors of high school would soon become nothing more than a distant memory, even if that was little comfort to me now.

"Toby has a girlfriend?" Ellie asked. "No, he doesn't. Who?"

I sighed. "Yeah, perfect Angela."

"Oh yeah, we hate her," Ellie said.

For the smallest of moments, I had forgotten. Like when he stepped out of the darkness at the party, or the way he looked at me when I brought the meals into the bar, or the feel of his hand touching mine. No doubt I had over-analysed his every movement, his every facial expression, but I'm allowed to. That's what girls do. For those fleeting moments, however, I had managed to forget all about Angela Vickers.

"So they're still together?" Ellie asked.

"I see her car parked at his place all the time," I said.

Ellie gasped. "What are you doing outside his house? You total stalker!"

"Shut up!" I said, blushing. I could feel the familiar burn in my legs as we started our climb up towards the Onslow. "It's not like that. His place just happens to be on the main road to Perry. It's kind of hard to miss."

You had to crane your neck and look really hard, of course, but I would leave that little fact out. I knew Toby had his own place, though I didn't know how I knew. It was like knowing Sean's name or Stan's name. You don't know how you know, you just know. It's what's part and parcel of living in a town with a population of less than 3000; you knew all kinds of irrelevant stuff about each and every one of them. Toby's place was a mission brown shack, set back off the main road with a long sweeping driveway hidden amongst immense bushland. Even though it was set back and private, you could always tell if he was home. His navy Ford ute parked in the drive or, worst case scenario, Angela's red Lancer parked behind it. He had lived there since he was in Year Twelve, and I thought it was so grown up that he moved out of home, unlike most eighteen-year-olds in town.

I tried to imagine what the inside of his house was like, or if he could cook and use the washing machine. I would imagine that he would be pretty good with his hands, seeing as he fixed cars for a living. All of the little quirks I had been obsessing about since I was thirteen were now back in the forefront of my mind. And admittedly, I had never felt so unhappy about it.

Chapter Eight

I walked towards the Onslow Hotel kitchen, ready to assume my station at the sink.

I thought I would save Chris the trouble of banishing me to the kitchen, and instead I used some initiative and went on my merry way. If you could call it that. But I was merry; I had taken off the remnants of last night's battered French nail polish, I was working my Guinness shirt with a non-offensive skirt instead of leggings, and I had even managed a bit of colour from the afternoon spent at McLean's Beach with Ellie. There was nothing like a healthy dose of vitamin D and the beginnings of a tan to boost your spirits. As I pushed through the swinging kitchen door, ready to greet cranky Melba and crazy Rosanna, I was met instead with a set of glaring blue eyes.

Eyes that were attached to Amy, Uncle Eric's fifteen-year-old only daughter. She was elbow deep in dishwater and stared me down with dagger eyes.

"Oh, hey," I said, "Amy, isn't it?" I smiled politely and wondered why she was there until Chris stuck his head into the kitchen.

"Tess, you're on the floor tonight."

Bewildered, I looked from Chris to Amy and back again, my surprise evident.

"Really?"

"Really," he said. "Unless you think you might suffer from separation anxiety from Melba and Rosanna?"

"NO!" I shouted, probably a bit too readily.

Chris smiled. "I didn't think so. Come on, Amy's gonna take your place."

I looked back at Amy, ready to offer her a smile, but her glare deepened and I side-stepped away. Wow. I was on the floor again. Guess I didn't do as badly last night as I thought. And this time I was determined not to stuff it up.

***

"What is this?" A long, immaculately manicured fingernail pointed to their plate.

I tilted my head and leaned down a little to have a closer inspection.

"Uh … a piece of capsicum?"

"And what was it that I specifically asked *not* to be served?" She gave me a hard stare, as I fumbled through the backlog of dockets in my booklet.

"Oh, uh ..." There it was, clear as day, scrawled in block letters.

NO CAPSICUM! I fought not to cringe.

"I'm sorry, did you want me to change it for you?"

The lady rolled her eyes at her friends.

"No, I think you have done quite enough." Her voice dripped with sarcasm. I skulked away. Wow, it was amazing how a rather upbeat day can be torn down within a blink of an eye.

Ellie met me at the cutlery drawer.

"Don't worry, Tess, I have something that will make you forget all about Cruella de Vil over there."

"Capsicum spray?" I asked in hope.

Ellie frowned, confused momentarily, but she shook out of it and plastered on a big grin as she handed me a docket.

"Take care of this, would ya, babe?"

She sauntered off to wait on the next table. In my hand sat a crinkled piece of paper. A dinner order for the Onslow Boys decorated with love hearts. It was then I realised the distant pulse of the jukebox through the wall; it was nothing compared to the beat of my heart.

There was a lull in dinner service, which had me anxiously awaiting the sound of the bell to tell me the order was up. I paced within earshot; twenty minutes went by before I heard that magical ding. I slid sideways as I overshot the kitchen door in my haste. Elegance and grace, as always.

I was there before Rosanna spiked the order as done. She wiped the perspiration from her brow and curved the other at me.

"I see the Onslow Boys have made quite an impression on you girls."

I tried not to smile; even Rosanna was calling them the Onslow Boys. I plastered on my best poker face, attempting to appear cool and casual even though I had never been so eager to deliver two Chicken Parmagianas in my life.

"Just be careful, hon," Rosanna said.

"Oh, are the plates hot?" I flinched back just before my hands made contact.

Rosanna laughed. "No, but hot boys can burn you just as easily."

Oh no! Love advice from Rosanna. Now was not the time for a deep and meaningful; in fact, with Rosanna, *never* would be the time. To avoid the next cliché, I quickly grabbed the plates and legged it. I was about two seconds into my commute when I realised maybe Rosanna's words did have a double meaning; the plates were bloody hot! I bit my lip as I quickstepped through the bar, scurrying as fast as I could to the poolroom. I breathed deeply and grimaced at the pain, and when I entered the poolroom, I managed to voice the fact.

"Ahh-eee-aaah," I said, "hot stuff coming through."

I dumped the plates on the bar, shaking and blowing on my now free hands.

Oh God, did I really just announce that to the room?

"McGEE!" Sean shouted as he looked up from his pool shot that he'd just pocketed with ease. He straightened and swaggered towards me, brushing passed me as he reached for his beer on the bar. He saluted 'cheers' towards me before taking a sip.

"Murphy!" I tipped my head.

"Ah, so you've done your research? You know my name."

"I think everyone knows your name."

"Really? Why?" he mused.

I gave him an incredulous look. "'Cos of footy, of course; star ruck-man, why else?"

Stan slapped Sean on the back as he took his seat to get stuck into his meal.

"It's that, or the fact that he's such a ladies' man," Stan teased.

Sean cast Stan a hard look as he watched his friend eat. "Don't choke on that, will you?"

My eyes locked with Toby's who was across the bar, about to swig on his own beer. He was smiling at his mates' banter, and his eyes never left me as he took a long, deep drink. My burning hands were long forgotten as I felt other areas of my flesh burn up, with those eyes on me. Toby swallowed his beer and opened his mouth to speak when he was cut off by two hands covering his eyes from behind.

"Guess who?"

He smiled broadly and grabbed at the hands.

"Vanessa?"

It was then that Angela Vickers swung around to his side, hitting him with her clutch purse.

"Real funny, and who is this Vanessa, huh?" She mocked anger, but it was quickly defused as she melted with Toby's blinding, beautiful smile. She closed the distance between them, claiming his lips passionately as if it were a long-lost reunion.

Ringer groaned. "Get a room you two!"

I quickly looked away. The thought of her running her hands through his hair, pressed up against him in an embrace was just too much to bear.

I made a quick exit back to the kitchen to grab the two remaining plates that had mercifully cooled to the touch by now. I had hoped to spot Ellie en route, in the hopes that maybe she'd switch with me, but she was nowhere to be seen. At the risk of the food getting cold, I had no choice but to grin and bear it.

"Tess, can you do a glass run while you deliver those?" called Chris from the restaurant side of the bar.

Oh great, what timing. A glass run when I couldn't get out of there fast enough. I set the meals down with no witty banter from Sean; he was too busy talking to Angela who had decided to perch herself on Toby's lap.

I slowly, methodically made my way around the edge of the poolroom, picking up empty beer glasses from the windowsills and barrels. I spotted an empty glass near Toby and Angela.

Oh great.

I shyly excused myself as I leant passed them to grab the glass. Angela, who seemed to not even be aware of my existence until then looked me over and gave me a cool, calculating assessment. She didn't like what she saw.

"Hey, bar-keep!" she shouted with a smirk.

"Her name's Tess, Ang," said Stan. For that I was totally in love with him and wanted to tell him thanks, but I didn't, as Angela had me in her sights. As she stared at me, all I could think of was *please don't call me Tic Tac, please don't call me that.*

I could see the nickname register in her cold eyes. She smiled slowly.

"Tess, would you be able to get me a glass of your house white?"

I was at first surprised by the simple question, and then I realised I would have to give her my standard answer.

"Oh … um, sorry, I'm not allowed to serve alcohol, I'm only seventeen." I blanched. Her brows rose in fake surprise. She damn well knew I couldn't serve her alcohol. She just laughed and waved me off as if to run along.

"Oh, never mind. Chriiiiissssss," she shouted down the bar.

Her attempt to make me feel two feet tall had worked. I became embarrassed and flustered. I went to add the last glass to my stack, but it slipped through my fingers and fell. Everything happened in slow motion until it hit the floor and shattered in a loud, almighty smash.

"Taxi!" several people called out and laughed. All eyes were on me.

The entire stack wobbled in my arms but Sean jumped up and steadied them for me.

"Whoa, careful!"

I pressed my free hand to my forehead as I surveyed the damage. After carefully placing the glasses back on the bar, I bent quickly to pick up the shards, averting my eyes from all their gazes. An extra pair of hands appeared in front of me and carefully picked up some of the larger pieces. Silently, Toby had crouched beside me and my heart swelled at his kindness. His hand then grabbed my wrist as I went to lift a smaller piece.

"Don't cut yourself."

I froze, suddenly aware of him touching me, and then all too quickly he removed his hand from my skin and I looked away.

"I'll get a dustpan," I said under my breath. I also wanted to get away from them, from Angela, who I could hear laughing behind me. I was so determined to get away from the shrill sound that I nearly collided straight into Chris, who was holding a broom and dustpan.

"Thanks." I reached to take it from him, but he moved them from my reach.

"No, it's okay, I'll take care of it."

"No, it's fine, I can–"

"Why don't you go and take over from Amy for a bit?"

I did a double take. In other words: *you have made enough of a mess, Tess, get back to the kitchen where you belong*. It felt like a physical blow.

I nodded and pushed passed him. Ellie gave me a smile and a little wave from across the restaurant but I just made my way to the kitchen.

When I informed Amy I was there to take over for her, she hooted joyously and ripped off her apron with lightning speed.

With a "See ya later, losers," she pushed open the door and was gone.

"What a little shit she is," Rosanna said.

I surveyed the sink area and my new work zone. It appeared that Amy had made more mess in her attempt to clean. There was water all over the floor, and the dishes still had remnants of half-chewed food and sauces on them. I had visions of her furiously dunking them in the putrid water, fantasising it was my head as she slammed them onto the dish rack in a rage. I couldn't blame her. I was about to do the same; instead, I would be imagining someone else. I would be dunking Angela.

Chapter Nine

I stole a moment in the ladies' room, perched on a closed toilet lid for a bit of chin-trembling.

Even Rosanna and Melba must have sensed the change as, for once, they weren't taking their anger out on me. Ellie definitely knew something was wrong when I declined the end-of-shift staff drink from Chris. The Onslow Boys and Angela were still in the poolroom, and I just wanted a discreet exit out the back way. Ellie also knew me well enough not to question me about it, at least not just yet. We made our way down the sloping stretch of road where we would wait for my mum to pick us up.

"Hey, do you wanna go for a ride tomorrow?" Ellie said. "We can pick up our pays and go and blow it all at Carter's. There's this cute little skirt that would look great on you."

This was Ellie trying to cheer me up.

"Sounds good!" I faked a smile.

After I completed my nightly routine, peeling off my half-drenched, smoke-infused clothes to have a long, hot shower, I fired up my computer and found an email from Adam.

To: tessmcgee

Bad news I'm afraid! There is a Magnum P.I marathon on and guess who is front and centre?

ME! Under sufferance of course.

Although don't jump to any conclusions if I return home with a handle bar moustache.

It doesn't mean a thing.

How's things in O town? Hope you're having fun without me.

Sender: Adam I can jump puddles Henderson.

I was so emotionally exhausted even Adam's email did little to perk me up. I couldn't help but think back to Angela's arms draped over Toby, her sardonic smile as she belittled me in front of everyone. The smashing of the glass replayed in slow motion, the brush of Toby's fingers as he helped me pick up the shards.

I felt like such an idiot. I should have insisted with Chris that I'd clean it up. I could only imagine Angela's snide remarks as Chris swept up the mess.

"Ha! I wish someone would clean up after me. That's what you get for hiring twelve-year-olds", she would have said. And then everyone would have laughed with her.

I groaned and cupped my head in my hands.

To: Adam I can jump puddles Henderson

Do it! Moustaches are hot!

O Town is just peachy!

Sender: tessmcgee

To: ellieparker

All good. I am looking forward to our bike ride tomorrow. X

Sender: tessmcgee

***

I pumped the pedals and pressed forward over the handlebars to surge myself over McLean's Bridge. On and on it went, a never-ending mass of concrete overshadowing Lake Onslow. Up the footpath then around the curb, I peddled like a mad thing. The hot summer wind threatened to burn my skin as I boldly sailed down Macquarie Avenue, riding with no hands.

This was the freedom I had yearned for and never in my life would I have believed I would have found it on a Monday. But it was the holidays now and things had been switched up. I would meet up with Ellie after lunch as planned. In an attempt to still my overactive mind and get the most I could from the day, I had grabbed my bike and headed around the back roads of Onslow. The Mitchum bike trail had some of the best bushland scenery around. Luckily, being Australia, I didn't have to worry about mountain lions, grizzly bears or wolves … just poisonous snakes, deadly spiders and the odd wayward wallaby that wandered down from the foothills of the Perry Ranges.

As I glided along the isolated road, I sought refuge amidst the trees that edged my way, blocking the searing sun in intervals of shade-light-shade. I had circled this area a hundred, maybe a thousand, times and each time there were new sounds, new scenes. It made me forget the mundane existence of all that troubled me. I stood straight up on the peddles, lifting my face to the sky and breathing deeply, feeling the flashes of the changing shades flicker spots under my closed eyelids. This was living. In a space that seemed like nowhere, there were no worries, nothing could touch me here. Nothing!

And that's when I heard a snap.

Remember the never-ending stretch of the McLean's Bridge? The one I just had to leave behind me? Well, that was nothing compared to the long, barren stretch of bitumen that faced me now. This seriously had no end, I was going to die here! Suddenly all the wonder and the beauty of my surroundings lost its lustre for me as I limped my bike back down the road. I stopped every few steps to survey the damage to my skinned knee that had already started scabbing over, thanks to the heat of the day.

As I stopped for the hundredth time, I was surprised and a little disappointed that there wasn't more blood flowing from my gaping wound. It stung like a bitch! I took my anger out on my bike by giving it a good kick.

"Stupid bloody chain."

It had snapped clean in half, causing it to make an infuriating clanking sound with every rotation of the wheels. I clenched my jaw and limped on.

Nature sucked. I hated nature; I hated the now seemingly blistering sun that threatened to burn my skin. I hated the trees, the lake views, the birdsong and, most of all, I hated my carelessness. No phone, no water, no sunscreen. From now on, I would pack a survival kit that would consist of my dad's Swiss Army Knife. For what? So I could clip my toenails and open a bottle of wine?

Real smart, Tess.

My God, the heat was frying my brain, maybe I was losing too much blood? I might need a transfusion by the time I made it around the sweep of the Horseshoe Bend, my next landmark that was still nowhere in sight. After that, there was a bit of a declining slope, nothing too major and then the caravan park, owned by the Remingtons – Stan's parents. Perhaps they would let me dial triple zero by the time I stumbled through their gates. Or my mum.

Failing that, the next stop was the Onslow Hotel, where I could seek shelter and water and be nursed back to health by Melba, Rosanna and Chris.

Yeah, I think I would pass on that one.

I had a better chance of backstroking across Lake Onslow. But even though it weighed me down and I was seriously pissed with it, I wouldn't leave my bike. She was last year's Christmas present, a deep midnight purple with a tan cane basket on the front, very Jessica Lansbury circa *Murder She Wrote*. In the beginning, Adam and Ellie ribbed me about it constantly, but guess who wanted their swimming gear carted when it was too awkward to hook onto their handlebars? Oh, how they loved the Grandma basket then. Not that it served me much good now, it housed nothing more than a beach bag with my purse which held a whole $15 and my student ID.

Each time the cool breeze flowed through the trees it whipped around me, fluttering my loose peach singlet and refreshing my skin that was slick with a light sheen of perspiration. I stopped in the shade of a towering gum tree. Letting the bike rest on my hip, I pulled my hair up off my neck and closed my eyes, allowing myself to cool and rest for five.

The serenity was disturbed by the distant sound of kookaburras mocking me with their laughter. I peeked one eye open and listened closer. A sound was slowly closing in with a murmur that became louder and louder. What was that … a car? Possible salvation? Oh, *please* don't be a serial killer. I was desperate, but not desperate enough to hitchhike with a scary local who liked to play the banjo. I grabbed my bike and continued to walk, cool, calm and collected, instead of sweaty, bloody damsel in distress. I would politely decline any invitation and rough it alone, surely it wasn't much further?

The thudding of a burly vehicle and sound of music closed in behind me. The engine slowed, causing the hairs on the back of my neck to raise. The music volume lowered.

Oh no, no, no. Please keep going.

I walked faster, looking straight ahead, my bike chain rattling more insistently.

Leave me alone, it's a nice summer's day, can't a girl take her bike for a walk?

The car crawled now, it could be a creepy white van with a hooded deviant behind the wheel, I just knew it. I had watched enough late-night horror movies with Adam and Ellie to know all about stranger danger. My heart was leaping out of my chest. I know I said I would never leave my bike, but, honestly, I was getting to the point of ditching the sucker and heading for the hills screaming MURDERER.

That's when I heard my name.

Chapter Ten

"Tess?"

I stopped abruptly, before I spun to see a navy Ford crawling along beside me. I tilted my head slightly and found a mystified expression peering out at me through the open window.

"What are you doing out here?" said Toby.

Toby? Toby was behind the wheel. It wasn't a serial killer, it was *Toby*.

I inhaled a deep breath of relief. "Oh, thank God it's you! I thought you were a murderer."

His brows raised in surprise.

"Are you alright?"

No, I wanted to pout, *I am suffering from sunstroke, dehydration, starvation.* And I was all of a sudden keenly aware of how sweaty and awful I must have looked. I discreetly pushed my fingers through my hair and smiled in good humour, my eyes flicking to my bike.

"I'm afraid she has given up the ghost."

Ugh! That would be something my dad would say.

Toby pulled over and got out of his vehicle in one fluid movement. He was in his work pants and work shirt that had Tobias embroidered in yellow on his pocket. The little detail made me smile. I had only ever heard Sean call him that, and I was pretty sure it was to deliberately hit a nerve.

He gave me a coy smile as he made a direct line to crouch and examine my bike. I was mesmerised by his swiftly moving hands; he had beautiful hands. I had often wondered how they always seemed so amazingly clean, considering his job was to be covered in grease and oil all day, every day. He must have some heavy duty industrial cleaner to wash his hands with every night. This thought led me to visions of him at home, showering, getting ready for a night out with the boys at the Onslow for dinner and pool. His hair was always slightly damp, with just the slightest touch of hair product. He wouldn't do much more than that, he didn't need to; he was naturally perfect. Whenever I brushed past him in the crowded poolroom, there was always a hint of a fresh, clean, crisp aftershave. It made me want to be close to him, to bask in all that was Toby.

I snapped myself out of my daydream when he looked back up at me.

"This chain's history. Where are you headed?"

I didn't want to confess I was just goofing around on my summer holidays, giving little thought to much else. That was the beauty of it. It was meant to be a voyage to forget all my troubles, all thoughts of him and Angela last night. And then here he was straightening up in front of me, looking down at me with those questioning brown eyes.

"Oh, I should be getting home, I hadn't planned on being out so long."

Ugh! God, that sounded like I had a curfew; that I would be in trouble if I didn't scurry home to Mum and Dad. Why didn't I just say I was headed to the Onslow to pick up my pay, because I was a responsible working woman? I could have even asked if he wanted to join me for a drink? Like grownups do. Have a friendly chat.

About what exactly? Cars? School? His girlfriend?

"If you want, I can give you a lift home," he said.

I tried not to look so overjoyed, but the thought of being rescued by Toby was an even better outcome than I could have ever hoped for.

"Yes, please! I don't want to die out here, not like this."

He smirked. "Murderers, death; you have a dark mind, Tess."

And before I could hide my smile, he grabbed my bike and lifted it onto the bed of his ute. The very same one I saw parked in his drive, or occasionally at the Onslow Hotel. Deep navy, big and bulky, this was a man's vehicle. A vehicle I was about to climb into.

I fought to overcome my nerves as I opened the passenger door. I hoisted myself up inside. Toby was busy securing my bike in the back. On the passenger floor was a lunch box and thermos. I slid my feet away from the items, which wasn't difficult considering the ample room inside. There weren't individual seats but a light cream bench seat, with nothing dividing me from Toby. I leaned my arm on the open windowsill and pondered. You could fit three bodies in for a ride with ease if someone was pressed up next to the driver. I wondered who had ridden in this car with him. Sean? Stan? Angela?

Okay, let's not think about that.

Toby pulled open the driver's door, and he filled the rest of the cab's interior. He fired up the beast of an engine and pulled into gear, gloriously tearing up the bitumen. I stole a quick glance in the side view mirror and grabbed my hair that was flailing around from the open window. I held it back at the base of my neck, and my wispy fringe momentarily blinded me. I stole a sideways glance at Toby. He met my eyes briefly and smiled. I looked quickly out the window. In my peripheral vision, I watched as Toby's suntanned arm rested on top of the wheel, his other arm leaning casually on the open window. He was relaxed and confident behind the wheel. It was of little wonder; if he got his learner's at sixteen he would have been driving for six years by now. I calculated it in my mind. I would have been 11 when he started driving. I tried not to think too much about that.

An awkward silence swept over us, only to be broken by Toby's cough before he spoke.

"So, where did you go last night?"

I tried not to shift in my seat at his question. I was hoping that my sudden disappearance after the glass-breaking episode would go unnoticed. I guess not.

"Oh, you know, kitchen duties beckoned."

"Oh?" He seemed surprised.

"Yeah, whenever a crisis breaks out they shine a giant K in the sky, and I hightail it."

"So you head to the phone booth and change into your apron and rubber gloves?" Toby's mouth turned up at the corners. Just a little.

"Isn't that Superman?"

"Oh right, sorry. My bad, giant K in the sky: you're rocking it Batman style."

"Exactly. Except if I was Batman, I wouldn't be needed in the kitchen full stop. Bruce Wayne doesn't do kitchens."

"You could serve customers like the speed of a bullet."

I laughed, shaking my head. "Again, Superman. Why don't you know this stuff? What did you do as a kid, spend it outdoors or something?"

"Misspent youth, clearly. I obviously don't know my superheroes at all." He frowned as if deeply distressed. "I must look into that."

"I would if I were you, that's kind of embarrassing."

He flashed a smile my way, before turning his gaze back to the road. There was more silence, but this time it wasn't uncomfortable. I turned to peer at my bike rattling away in the back.

"So, the old girl," I tilted my head backwards, "will she ride again?"

Toby glanced at me then back to the road; that elusive upward tilt of his lips reappeared as if he was fighting not to smile.

"Let me put it this way. I thought I'd have to surround it with some sheets and bring out the 22 to put it out of its misery."

My eyebrows rose. "You carry a 22?"

"You think carrying sheets isn't weird?"

"Yeah, but sheets aren't deadly."

"You haven't been to an all-boys boarding school."

"Ew! Okay, give me a gun."

There it was, that smile. He made no effort to hide it now. It shone brightly, lighting up his entire face.

"Are we talking about guns and dirty boys' sheets?" Toby frowned.

"You started it," I said. "Sheets aside, which I really don't want to know about, did you really go to boarding school?"

"Yep, my parents shipped me off in Year 7. The longest year of my life. I ended up just mucking up until they had no choice but to bring me home."

I stared at him for the longest time. Trying to imagine Toby ever being bad, I just couldn't picture it.

"So the sheets were that bad, huh?"

He burst out laughing; it was a wonderful sound, rich and warm. It made my skin tingle.

He shook his head as he refocused on the road.

"You have no idea!"

It was a bizarre conversation, our first formed sentences alone together. Well, there was the party but that doesn't count. How would I tell Ellie about my bonding session in Toby's ute?

She would squeal and insist that I tell her everything, and she'd ask the most obvious question. "So what did you talk about?"

Umm, guns and dirty sheets?

It would probably be better to go all cryptic and tell her: 'stuff'.

We pulled into my driveway; Toby killed the engine and jumped out, rounding the back of the ute to untie my bike. While I climbed slowly from the cab, I watched as he lifted my bike like it weighed nothing, his flexed, bronzed biceps the only proof of any strain.

"Where do you want it?"

In my bedroom.

I mentally slapped myself and fought not to blush.

He waited for me to answer.

"Umm, I just keep it in the garage."

He nodded and walked it over, leaning it against the far wall.

"Just there's fine," I said, "thanks, Toby." His name sounded so strange, so intimate on my tongue. I wanted to say it again.

He looked at the bike, in deep thought.

"You'll be out of action until you get a new chain."

"Yeah, I'll go and buy one tomorrow."

Because I was now a responsible working woman who could buy things like that. I would forgo the cute little skirt from Carters and buy a bike chain.

So depressing.

"Well, if you need someone to fit it …"

"Oh, that's okay, my dad will do it."

And as soon as the words came out, I wanted to kick myself, preferably with steel-capped boots. Had he just offered to fix my bike? And I had blurted out that no, my daddy would do it?

IDIOT!!

"Cool, well, they're not that dear so you should pick one up down at Mac's store."

I started to walk him to the car, but he paused, head tilted as he looked at my leg.

"You're bleeding."

"Oh, it's nothing, just had an up-close-and-personal encounter with the bitumen," I said. "It doesn't hurt."

Like hell it doesn't!

His brows creased with concern and he crouched to examine it closer. My breath hitched in my throat as he lightly touched the skin around my knee. I fought to keep my breathing steady with the intimacy of it. He straightened, his look still serious.

"I have a first aid kit in my glove box; come on, let's clean you up."

We had a first aid kit in the house, but I wasn't blowing it a second time. I followed him to his ute.

"Jump up on the tray," he called over his shoulder as he headed to flip open the glove box and retrieve a small, blue zip-up case. I had planned to follow his advice when I noticed, due to my five-foot-nothing stature and the height of the tray, there was no way I could master it gracefully. Before I could even voice the issue, Toby had read the troubled look on my face. Without a word, he was by my side. With a small smile, he placed the first aid kit and a bottle of water on the tray.

"Here." Before I had time to think, his hands were on my waist and, as if I weighed nothing more than a feather, he boosted me up to perch on the tray. I fought not to squeal in surprise and my hands grabbed onto his shoulders for leverage.

"You okay?" he asked, his hands still on my sides, as if securing me in place.

I nodded all too quickly. He smiled at the affirmation and let me go. I could still feel the pressure of his hands, the feel and flex of his muscles as I was suddenly airborne. I could tell I was blushing profusely and hoped it might pass as sunburn.

I straightened my leg for his attention, as he rummaged through the first aid kit.

I arched a brow. "Rescue many damsels in distress?"

A crooked grin formed on his lips, but he didn't meet my eyes. "Every day! It's a tireless job."

My skin tingled from his touch as his hand clasped under my knee to hold my leg steady.

"Looks like you're the Superman then? Coming to the rescue and all."

He grabbed a bottle of water, popping the top with his teeth.

"This might sting a bit, okay, Tess? But I need to clean it."

My heart fluttered every time he said my name, I liked the sound of him saying it. I had never, in all my life of pining over Toby Morrison, heard it from his mouth before today. It had stopped me in my tracks when I had heard it through the open window earlier; I had suspected, but couldn't quite believe it to be true.

"It's okay." I smiled down at him and then he tipped a slow stream of water on my grazed knee.

SON-OF-A-BITCH!!

My entire frame locked up with the flash of pain; Toby's eyes darted upwards to watch my face.

"Sorry." He grimaced.

I tried my hardest to maintain my dignity as I clenched my jaw and forced a smile.

"It's okay."

Toby worked methodically, gently dabbing at the cut with cotton wool and Bettadine. I came to believe this was how Toby approached all things in life. Not to say just because he was ludicrously handsome that he must be a perfectionist in everyday life. It doesn't work like that. But everything he did was carefully thought out. Planned. Whether it be choosing a song on the jukebox, taking a shot at pool, or cleaning a clumsy girl's scraped knee, everything he did, it seemed, everything he touched, he did with great care.

The sting ebbed as I concentrated on the pressure of his fingers placed intimately under my knee, his butterfly touches of dabbing on the ointment. Once satisfied, he tore the package for the plaster and with intense concentration slowly placed it on my knee. Oh, he was a perfectionist alright. And he was damn good with his hands.

"Done." He stood back to eye his handiwork.

"Thanks, Doc!" I said. "Will I dance again?"

"You will dance, ride and serve meals better than ever before."

I arched my brow and examined my knee.

"Bionic leg ointment?" I teased.

I loved to make his face change, his smile was so transforming, it was the thing I loved about him the most.

I held my breath when he reached to help me down from the bed of the ute. He placed me gently onto the ground.

"Thanks," I managed to breathe. We stood there a moment. I realised I was still gripping his upper arms and quickly let go, trying not to blush deeper in the process.

'You good?" he asked.

"Yeah, thanks!"

I pushed my hands into my back pockets. Toby lifted the back tray with a thud, locking it in place, and moved towards the driver's door.

Say something, Tess, say something funny, bring back that smile, give him something to take away and make him remember you.

Instead, I said, "Thanks again."

Brilliant.

He grinned, exposing all of those perfect teeth.

"You're welcome." He fired his ute to life, leaning his arm on the open window as he checked the view behind him. He looked at me.

"When are you working next?"

I was startled by the question. I must have sported an idiotic expression because he just stared with an amused look on his face.

"Oh! Uh ... Saturday! I work again on Saturday, 12 till 2 and then 6 till 9, depending on how busy we are, and then again on Sunday, same hours."

Was that too much information? It was. Shut up, Tess. It was a simple question, you babbling idiot.

He nodded thoughtfully as if trying to take it all in. I'd overloaded him, I knew it.

"Well, might see ya there?" He began to slowly edge back out of the drive.

"Unless there's a giant K shining in the sky," I threw back.

He let out that wonderful laugh again and looked at me, really looked at me, and smiled that smile.

"Well, then I'll know."

As I stood for what felt like the longest time, staring out into the distance where his car had disappeared, there were some things I knew for certain.

I really wanted to hear that laugh again, and I couldn't wait for Saturday.

Chapter Eleven

"SHUT UP!"

This was Ellie's usual reply to things that she was dumbfounded by, and my afternoon (okay, so it wasn't an entire afternoon) spent in Toby Morrison's ute was something to be dumbfounded about.

"You total slut!" Another term of endearment from Ellie.

I just smiled and stirred my iced chocolate.

"So what did you talk about?"

Milk spilt over the rim of the tall glass as I faltered at the inevitable question.

"Umm ..."

Superheroes, guns and dirty sheets! Superheroes, guns and dirty sheets, my head screamed.

I shrugged. "You know ... stuff."

Ellie slumped back in her seat and folded her arms. "You lucky biatch!"

Yes I was. I straightened, trying not to smile like the Cheshire Cat.

"And the girlfriend?"

And there went my smile.

I knew about the girlfriend alright, painstakingly so. Last night was my first actual exchange with her other than brushing by her in the halls of Onslow High.

I sighed. "Yeah, he's still with perfect Angela."

"We totally hate her, right?" Ellie said.

The worst thing was I didn't hate her so much as I envied her. The way she walked in and captivated a room, how she completely owned it. She ordered a glass of house wine with grace. Stood and chatted, even flirted with ease with Sean as her designer sunnies held back her sun-bleached fringe. In fitted jeans and killer heels she presented a cool, casual style all of her own. What little did it matter if she had snake eyes and a matching reptilian personality. Everybody loved her. Toby loved her.

Sensing the change in my mood, Ellie set down her own iced chocolate after a long draw.

"Spill. I want every single detail."

Ellie half choked on her drink when I mentioned the first aid incident. As I waited for her to catch her breath, she sipped more, with a frantic wave of her hand for me to continue, hanging on every word. I could see her mind ticking over frantically and knowing Ellie as well as I did, it was unnerving.

I tried not to even let myself feel giddy as I thought back on every look, every smile, every touch. He had a girlfriend. It had meant nothing more than Toby being a nice person. He'd only done what anyone else would have done, which kind of took the buzz out of the moment.

"This is huge!" Ellie said, nodding.

Oh no, no, no … just as I had come to the conclusion that it was nothing, she was going to read all sorts of stuff into it. I watched Ellie, her mind whirring as she plotted and schemed in front of me.

I needed an exit strategy. "So did you get a chance to speak to Stan on Sunday night?"

I relayed his effort of sticking up for me when Angela called me 'bar-keep'. Her scheming eyes clouded over with a dreamy, swoon-like quality as she melted in her chair before my eyes.

"He's so sweet."

Too easy.

"He is really nice, I think Operation Stan is a goer," I said, adding fuel to the fire. "So the fact that Stan is older doesn't bother you?"

Ellie straightened. "Pfft, no! Think of all the idiots I have dated that were the 'appropriate age'. They sucked."

She was right; Ellie didn't have any problems landing boys, but finding a nice, respectful one was a whole other story. Maybe she did need someone older; someone that would treat her with respect and tame her wild ways. Then I wouldn't have to worry about sitting on bonnets of cars with her latest conquest's grotesque best friend. It would be a win-win situation.

"Why? Does it worry you?" Ellie asked.

"Age difference?"

I thought of Scott, his clumsy fondling hand under my shirt, greedily grabbing at me. I never enjoyed any of his touches. I usually steered them away so as not to go too far. I wonder what he would have done if I had ever needed him, like today? I couldn't even imagine him being anything other than grouchy and put out, like he had been whenever I had my period and wouldn't let him put his hands down my pants. He was too dense to figure it out, but I had my period a *lot* when we were together.

I thought back to Toby; he was a boys' boy, sure, he could rough house and swear like the rest of them, but I could never imagine him being cruel. He never even seemed to get loud or obnoxious, not even with a few beers around his mates. Instead, he was always quiet and understated. And the guys seemed to respect him for that. But he was twenty-two. Five years my senior. That had worried me as recently as yesterday. But now … although he was older and his mere presence turned my mind to mush, I didn't feel anything other than really safe with him. How could that be bad?

"No," I decided, "no, it doesn't bother me."

The gurgling slurps of Ellie's iced chocolate were loud in the café (and embarrassing) as she finished.

"That's settled then. Operation Stan for me, and Operation …"

"*No*!" I cut her off.

"What?" she tilted her head innocently.

"Don't even think about it."

She blinked at me, like she didn't have a clue what I was talking about.

"What I was going to say, before I was so rudely interrupted, was Operation Summer Fun!"

I didn't believe a word of it. I folded my arms and curved my brow in disbelief.

"Fine! Have it your way … Operation Dull and Boring." She slumped back in her seat.

"Why do we need to be Operation anything?"

Ellie gasped in mock horror. "What are you saying? You mean just … go with the flow?"

I shrugged "Why not?"

She smiled sardonically. "Could be fun?"

"With you in tow, I have no doubt."

Operation "Go with Flow" had us pick up our pays from Uncle Eric at the hotel, followed by stalking the clothes racks at Carters. I held up a pale green summery halter that I had had my eye on for weeks. I pressed it against me, tilting my head in the mirror and admiring the sheer fabric. I shouldn't buy it. I needed the new bike chain. But it was so pretty … surely I could have both? I checked the price tag and gulped. No, no I couldn't have both. My heart plummeted as I placed the halter back onto its rack.

"What are you doing?" Ellie asked. "You have been mooning over that for weeks!" She passed me on her way to the changing room, her arms piled high with clothes.

"I don't have to have it. I can get more for my money with other things." Other less expensive things, less beautiful things.

We shopped in mind for the next weekend's shift, knowing that we didn't have to wear our Guinness tops anymore. Instead of the gorgeous halter, I bought a boat neck style top that was a bit clingy for my taste, but Ellie squealed and insisted that I *had* to wear it Saturday night. I also wanted to buy a new Lip Smacker lip balm, and some Impulse body spray. Our afternoon of blowing our wages actually perked me up for the weekend to come, and I was even surprised at the disappointment of realising it was only Monday.

I had ten bucks left over, allocated to Operation Bike Chain, though I didn't know if it was even nearly enough. What do I know about bike chains? And once my parents found out it had, in fact, taken me a mere three hours to blow my first pay, there would be no sympathy for my cause. My bike would be garage bound for another week until the next pay day. So I would be pounding the pavement as I didn't think it would be a good look to have Ellie dink me on her handlebars. We weren't thirteen anymore.

When I got home I lay all my purchases out on my bed, planning for a fashion parade. I had a thought that had me going into the lounge room and rummaging through dad's tape deck, all segmented in order. I shook my head at some of his rather disturbing choices in music but then I found what I was looking for. I padded barefoot back to my room, popping the cassette into my tape deck.

Don Henley started to blare out of the small speaker and I smiled to myself. I hung out in my room for the rest of the day, trying on different outfits, adjusting hairstyles, experimenting with make-up, all whilst dreaming the day away. I allowed myself this small luxury in the privacy of my own heart, because I knew that as soon as I stepped out into the real world, all my wants didn't count.

To: tessmcgee

Are you ready for your mind to be fully blown?

Something so big, so EPIC it will change your life forever?

Sender: Adam I can jump puddles Henderson

To: Adam I can jump puddles Henderson

You're coming Home???? :)

Sender: tessmcgee

To: tessmcgee

What if I am?

Have you fainted? Do you need to sit down??

I know how your life has been barren and lonely without me.

Sender: Adam I can jump puddles Henderson

To: Adam I can jump puddles Henderson

I cry myself to sleep every night.

WHEN?????????

Sender: tessmcgee

To: tessmcgee

Soon my pretty. Soon!

Don't know the full details yet, but I think they might be releasing me for a weekend for good behaviour. It's a small mercy. But I will take whatever I can get.

Excited much?

Sender: Adam I can jump puddles Henderson

To: Adam I can jump puddles Henderson

I wait with bated breath.

Let me know! xox

Sender: tessmcgee

***

A strip of light streaked through the darkness of my closed eyes. I would not let the pesky sun disturb my slumber, so I rolled over, away from the offending beam. I had managed to kick off my blanket during the night and the oscillation of the fan still didn't threaten to chill me. I remembered that the irritatingly bubbly weatherman had promised a scorcher, and I had fist pumped my way to the fridge to grab a Coke, thinking '*do your worst weather dude*'. But as the sun lifted and the breeze stilled, humidity was at its sticky worst and I changed my mind and cursed the summer and all who gloried in it.

A prod to my exposed foot caused me to drag it away from the edge. A tickle and I kicked out. Scratching my nose, I rolled over to push my face into the pillow with a sleepy groan.

"Wakey, wakey," an upbeat voice sing-songed. Mum.

"Noooo, go away."

"I have a surprise for you," she coaxed as I felt the mattress dip next to me.

She had my semi-attention now. I squinted at the clock.

"But it's so early."

The bright and breezy note in my mum's voice lowered in astonishment.

"It's 11.30!"

"Wake me in half an hour." I turned over, hugging my pillow.

"I guess you don't want this, then." I heard the rustling of a bag as she got up to leave.

I sat bolt upright, blinded by my wayward hair which swept across my face at haphazard angles.

"What is it?"

"Never mind, you're too tired," Mum teased.

"Oh, be the grown-up, Mum, what is it?"

Mum became all excited as she hid an object behind her back.

"Close your eyes."

I was fully awake now. I loved surprises. Had I told her about that top I had been eyeing off? She must have noticed I came home without it yesterday. I sat on my knees, pushing my bed-tousled hair back.

Holding out my hands, I closed my eyes. Mum placed something in them, and they dipped under the unexpected weight. Okay, definitely not a top. But it was solid and cool.

"Open your eyes," Mum said, barely able to contain her excitement.

I opened them with haste as Mum ripped the plastic from the top with as much flair as a magician pulling a rabbit from a hat.

"Ta-DA!"

"Oh ..." I said, "wow." That was about as much as I could muster as I took in the hot purple, marbled bike helmet in my hands with, oh Jesus, was that a lightning bolt on each side?

"Do you like it?"

"Wow. It's ... wow."

Mum nodded in appreciation.

"I saw you came home with another scrape on your knee, and thought you really need to have one of these. It's the new shape, like the racing people wear, very smart."

Smart was not the word I would have used. *Helmet hair* screamed inside me. I had never been so happy that my chain snapped, rendering my bike useless.

"I know you kids don't get around with helmets, but I think once one starts wearing them, it will catch on; the next thing you know, you'll all be wearing them."

I offered my best fake smile. "Thanks, Mum."

"Try it on!" She beamed.

I humoured her by placing the egg-like dome on my head. It slipped forward, into my face.

I gave her a double thumbs up. "Awesome."

She patted my cheek. "Looks great, you'll have to give it a test run."

I grimaced, trying not to overact my disappointment. I was a terrible actress.

"I can't until my bike's fixed; the chain, remember?"

"Oh that's right, well Dad can-"

"No rush, it's kind of nice walking – won't do me any harm."

In fact, I was pretty sure it may just save my reputation.

As Mum went to leave my room, she stopped and said, "I almost forgot." She fished out my mobile phone from her pocket that I had left charging in the kitchen.

"This thing keeps beeping at me." Mum wasn't very savvy with technology, and she handed it over as if it had a bad smell secreting from it.

I waited for her to leave before taking my helmet off with great gusto; I didn't want to hurt her feelings. I placed it on my chair giving it a horrified look.

Oh hell, no! Mum I love you, but this I cannot do.

A reminder beep went off, and I crawled back into bed to read 5 missed calls, 7 messages from Ellie. What the?

9.06 am

Oh me Gawd! Oh Me Gawd!

Ring me!!!

9.10 am

Why haven't you rung me??

9.38 am

OMG!! Check your emails woman!

And pick up your phone…I have to talk to you!!

9.44 am

OH MY GOOOOOOOD!!!! Tell your dad to switch your home phone over from the fax, I mean seriously!

9.46 am

Are you mad at me??

9.50 am

Because seriously now is not the time to be mad at me…TRUST ME!!!

10.00 am

I am coming over to kick your skinny butt!!!!!! Plus I want to see your face when I tell you!!!

I dove out of bed, tripping over my sheet that was tangled around my legs, while I attempted to dial Ellie's number and fire up the computer all at the same time.

I pressed the power button on the old computer and, as usual, it whirred, groaned and chugged to life. I swear, my parents had given me what must have been the oldest, slowest computer in the southern hemisphere. And if that didn't have my leg jiggling in impatience, I pressed the power on the modem and waited, waited and waited some more as the dialup beeped and buzzed, connecting to the internet. Thank God it was a separate line; between Dad's inability to switch the phone back over from the fax, or the fact that Mum and Dad were constantly using it for the business, I would never have got a look in. I convinced them on my sixteenth birthday that it was vital for my future study to get with the times. So they got me a secondhand computer and the internet with its own separate phone line. And I *did* use it to study. Right after I chatted to Ellie and Adam for a couple of hours each night on MSN Messenger.

Ellie wasn't answering; guess it was payback or she was riding over to kick my butt. What on earth had her knickers in such a twist? I was used to Ellie's dramatics, but this seemed different, far more intriguing, even more so than my hideous helmet.

Finally, my computer connected to the web, and I tapped into my email account. I expected to see one BILLION messages of harassment from Ellie, but there was only one from 8.04 am.

To: tessmcgee

Operation Go with Flow initiated!

Oh me Gawd! Oh me Gawd!

I hope you are sitting down, and I hope you have relieved yourself because otherwise you are seriously going to pee your pants!!!

I walked to the corner shop this morning to fetch the paper and who do I run into, in his work rig, fueling up?

That's right! Stan Remington, looking all windswept and interesting. Seriously he is so adorable!

Anyhow we got to talking and he invited us to go out on the boat with him and the boys…THIS AFTERNOON!!!!

Hold onto your helmet honey…(Oh yeah I know about that by the way. I mean I had to help your Mum pick it out and all. So cute don't you think??)

Anyway I will call you for rendezvous.

Meet the boys at the Onslow Hotel at 1pm.

Ellie X

P.S If you're wondering…Toby will be there.

PP.S And Angela has gone to visit her grandparents and won't be home for two weeks. (Just saying)

Sender: ellieparker

Boat.

Toby.

1pm.

Shit!

Chapter Twelve

I looked at the time in a panic as I tried to dial Ellie's number.

"Come on, come on, Ellie where are you? Pick up." My leg was jigging rapidly, what had she done?

By 12.00 pm I was showered, dressed and still unable to get onto Ellie. Now it was my turn to kick her skinny butt. You couldn't just drop a bombshell on someone and then not answer. Furthermore, you do not encourage and help your best friend's mum to pick out a hideous bike helmet and expect to get away with it. I would put that in the memory bank for later. For now there was nothing else to do but grab my bag and pocket my phone.

"Mum! I'm heading to Ellie's."

Luckily, Ellie lived only three blocks over (be it three large blocks). The weatherman's words echoed in my head. *It's going to be a scorcher!*

Lesson learned! I had water, sunscreen and coconut cream lip balm that I never left home without. I had opted for a light yellow summer dress. Cool and airy.

I found Ellie in her bedroom, looking radiant as ever in her cut-off denim shorts and halter top; she looked like a catalogue model, but that wasn't new.

"I trust you got my messages?" she asked as I entered. She was sitting at her dressing table, moisturising her long legs.

"Ah, yeah, are you serious?"

"I would never joke about such a thing."

I believed that. Boys were an extra-curricular activity Ellie took *very* seriously.

"Oh-my-God! Look at the time, we gotta go!" Ellie leapt to her feet and grabbed for her beach bag, eyes searching the floor for her thongs. "We have to meet at the hotel at one."

I had to force my heart to stop racing, everything was happening too fast.

"I have to swing by my house first and grab a towel and my bathers," I said.

"No time! I've packed you everything you need. Dad is going to drop us off. I told him we had a staff meeting and then we were going to McLean's for the afternoon. I suggest you tell your mum the same." Ellie shouldered her bag and squealed with excitement. "Let's go!"

I tapped my foot and bit my nail as I stood in the Onslow Hotel ladies' room,staring at two microscopic strips of bleached white material. Ellie had chosen a bathing suit for me. I use the term 'suit' loosely, as when one usually thinks of a suit, one would think of actual body coverage like the one-piece bathers I was more accustomed to.

I should have worked out something was a bit fishy when Ellie changed with lightning speed and left me alone in the change room, dumping the bag in front of me.

"There you go! Everything you need. I'll be out in the bar waiting for the boys."

I thought she was just overeager for them to arrive. I thought little of it until I took out the rolled-up towel and peered into an empty bag. My heart clenched with fear; in Ellie's haste she had totally forgotten a bathing suit for me! But as I unraveled the towel, a white square fell out, revealing two tiny pieces encased in a sheer, barely there sarong. My suspicion was right. She had forgotten a bathing suit, because this was barely anything.

I hated her, cursed her and stood there, staring for a full ten minutes. I couldn't go on the boat with them in this. And if I did, I just wouldn't swim. Simple. I could keep my dress on and have a bit of a tanning day. That'd be alright.

I gritted my teeth and tried the bikini on. I had never felt so utterly naked, not even when I *was* naked. I crept out to adjust the foreign pieces in the mirror and *Oh my God!* There was just so much skin … and was that a hint of cleavage? Not possible.

Ever since I had been branded Tic Tac Tess, I had taken to wearing loose, flowing tops that diverted all attention away from *that* area. It was not until I was forced to wear the Guinness top that I was forced to reveal any form of shape in that department, hence why I was so uncomfortable now. Not only were they out there for the world to see, but they were barely contained by tiny strings that felt like they could be blown undone by a breeze.

I was going to kill her! Before I could dive back in to the cubicle and change into my clothes again, Ellie burst through the door. My instant reaction was to cover myself with my arms as if I was standing naked, which wasn't too far from the truth.

Ellie's eyes bugged out; even *she* thought it was too revealing.

She looked me up and down. "Tess, you look amazing!" she gaped.

"Yeah, well take a good look because this is not going anywhere."

Ellie grabbed my arm, preventing me from walking back into the cubicle to change.

"They're here and waiting in the bar."

I frowned, pulling away from her. I didn't care; this was a bad idea. I should have known from the very beginning. I guess I did know, but I should have had a plan for when it happened, when the second I confided in Ellie she would be pushing me into things I didn't want to do. Now I was literally poured into a bikini that I would never have worn even in the privacy of my own bedroom, let alone in front of the Onslow Boys.

"Tess, trust me! You *want* to wear that. If you want to grab someone's attention, this is how I'd do it."

"I'm not you!" I snapped.

"No, you're not," Ellie said. "You're Tess and you're beautiful. And believe me, when people see the real you, Tic Tac Tess will be a thing of the past. Come on, Tess, just this once?"

It was like a physical blow, saying that name to me. Adam and Ellie never *ever* uttered those words, knowing how much the nickname hurt me.

There was a knock on the door.

"Come on, you lot, you ready?" called Sean. "You're taking so long the seasons are changing."

"Coming," yelled Ellie.

She gave me an imploring look, grabbing my shoulders and turning me towards the mirror.

"Learn to see what others see," she said as we both appraised my reflection, "because, believe me, that girl in high school, the supposedly flat-as-a-board nobody ... this is not her."

"Fine." I slipped on my dress over the bikini.

We weaved through the restaurant, sighting the Onslow Boys propped on stools in the main bar.

"Don't think I've forgotten about the helmet, either," I muttered like a bad ventriloquist, plastering a fake smile on my lips.

"Geez, did you wake up on the wrong side of the bed or what?"

I thought back to my lack of sleep, and Mum's annoying awakening.

"You could say that."

Sean and Toby led the way down to the jetty. Boats of all shapes and sizes dotted the harbour, a hub of distant splashes and screams echoed from the water as people lapped up what was the beginning of the hottest part of the day. We neared an impressive boat with navy inscription scrawled along the hull.

Southern Son.

"Whose boat is this?" I asked.

"Stan's, isn't he a nice boy?" Sean mocked.

Ellie just scoffed, tipping her sunnies on as she crossed her arms and looked out to the jet skiers, churning circles on the water.

Toby jumped into the boat followed by Sean as they went to work on their safety checks.

"You okay?" I asked Ellie. I hoped that she wasn't going to be in a mood for the rest of the day. Ellie didn't take too kindly to being stood up.

She flashed a winning smile. "Sure, this is going to be fun." She pushed past me, over the edge of the jetty and held out her hand. "Sean, could you help me?"

Sean dropped his rope and scooted over to help her into the boat. Ellie squealed and clung onto his arm as she landed awkwardly on the rocking deck.

"Careful," he said, steadying her.

I rolled my eyes.

Sean motioned me over and helped me into the boat. His hands circled my waist as he lifted me down. I had never had so many hands encircled around my waist in my life as I had in the last couple of days, and every time it made my cheeks flush from the intimacy of it. The ripped cords of muscles in his arms felt foreign under my touch. Scott had always been lean and gangly, like he still had growing to do, which he mostly did, he was a teenager after all, as opposed to the Onslow Boys.

I sat on the sideboard, watching Sean and Toby work with expert precision, finishing up the safety checks.

"Sweet! Full tank. Good on you, Stan, my son," Sean said.

"I think he had a big day planned," Toby said, more to himself than anyone. And my heart did ache a little for Stan, who was now stuck helping his dad on this hot, sweltering day, when he was supposed to have been firing up the engine, which Toby did instead.

As the engine churned dark water into white froth behind us, I thought about what we were about to do. I was about to embark on a day on the lake with *Toby Morrison*. If anyone had told me last week this was how I'd be spending my summer, I would have never believed them.

"Where to?" called Toby over the hum of the motor.

"McLean's?" posed Sean.

"Too busy," Ellie yelled.

"How about over Horseshoe Bend? Pretty secluded there," I suggested.

Sean smiled wickedly as he moved to sit beside Toby. "You want somewhere private, do you, Tess? What do YOU have planned for the day?"

I blushed, horrified at what he thought I was suggesting.

"I just meant …"

"You heard the lady, Tobias, drive her around the bend."

Chapter Thirteen

We powered along, giving a wide berth to all the other boats that were littered throughout the lake.

Once we were clear of them, Toby floored it, jerking us backward and causing Ellie and I to hang on for dear life. The thrill of the surge and the power of Stan's boat was exhilarating. It was fast; very fast. I looked at Ellie, who mirrored my own gleeful smile, as we set across the never-ending stretch of water, the wind spray of the water cooling my face.

"Faster!" Ellie yelled.

Toby leant sideways, struggling to hear. "Faster?"

"Yes, faster!" we screamed.

Toby accelerated before the words were fully out of our mouths, and we hung on with white-knuckled intensity. I dipped my head to prevent my eyes from watering. Sean and Toby were laughing as they looked back to check on us (probably to make sure we were still onboard).

All too soon, Toby lowered the throttle, slowing the boat down as we reached our destination. We were on the opposite side of town, and I could see just offshore the very place I had been limping along earlier in the week.

As if it triggered a memory in Toby, too, he turned to me. "How's the knee?"

It was now only an embarrassing pink mark and looked far less fatal. I tried to bend my knee away from his eyes.

"Oh, it's nothing."

"What's this?" Sean's ears pricked up.

"Nothing," Toby quickly changed the subject. "Help me with this, Sean." He concentrated on something complicated on the control panel.

I guessed that Toby didn't stop for an iced chocolate with Sean after dropping me home. Didn't tell him all about his afternoon and how he rescued me, fixed me up. Didn't exchange smiles and laugh at each other's jokes.

I guess that's not really a guy thing to do.

Sean obviously didn't know what Toby was referring to. It seemed his knight-in-shining-armour rescue apparently wasn't anything worth mentioning to his mates, unlike my analysed play-by-play and detailed breakdown of events with Ellie.

I knew boys were different, less analytical, less emotional than girls (I mean I had done the survey in *Cosmo*, so I was kind of an expert), but I wondered if Toby would look as disappointed as Stan did when he broke it to Ellie about not being able to make it today. And then I scoffed at the thought; why would he? He had a girlfriend, he was probably disappointed about *Angela* not being here. *Wake up, Tess!*

"Time to shine, Tess," Ellie whispered to me.

She scooted out of her denim cut-offs and peeled off her top, revealing a black bathing suit that exposed her flat stomach. Her suit was linked together by large rings along her sides, giving it the illusion of a one piece. Sean looked up from the logbook he and Toby were leaning over.

He smirked. "You girls must get the most unfortunate tan lines."

Ellie laughed as she adjusted the gold links. They really would leave unusual whites circles on her skin.

She looked at me expectantly.

"Where are the tunes you boys are so famous for?" Ellie asked. She stretched her long arms above her head, tying her hair up in a messy ponytail that always somehow managed to look good.

I took a deep breath. Here we go. I chucked my thongs off, trying not to think too much as I crossed my arms and peeled my dress upward, over my head. Thank God for all the times Ellie and I sunbaked in our backyards, turning every couple of minutes like rotisserie chickens, and the only time I ever exposed my midsection. One thing I wasn't bashful about was my ability to tan a sweet, golden brown colour. It was the best thing about summer: my hair lightened and my skin darkened. And at this very moment, my darkened skin was exposed to two new sets of eyes that trailed over my attire – or lack thereof. I quickly glanced away, embarrassed, as Toby and Sean's eyes lingered at my chest.

Oh my God, Toby was looking at my boobs.

Toby coughed and tried to find something on the boat to occupy his attention. Sean's brows raised, and he glanced at Toby with a not-too-subtle smile. Ellie looked triumphant, smiling, twirling her hair around her finger. I only prayed she wouldn't embarrass me further by giving me a thumbs up.

I pretended not to notice when Toby's eyes betrayed him, when his gaze strayed back towards me in a long, assessing look. He wasn't wearing sunnies either, so there was no hiding it. But he wasn't smiling like Sean had been; he seemed uncomfortable with it. With me.

I wasn't sure how I felt about that. Mission accomplished: I had gained his attention, yes, but I wasn't sure it was in a good way.

Ellie was working on sunscreening her nose and cheeks, slathering it over her neck and shoulders.

"Tess, can you do my back?"

I squirted the lotion onto my hands and rubbed it vigorously into her skin like I had done a million times before.

Ellie threw the sunscreen over to the boys, landing at Sean's feet. "That sun's got a bite in it."

They looked at the bottle, then uneasily at each other.

"Sorry, mate, but I am not lathering you up," Sean said to Toby.

"Likewise." Toby frowned.

Ellie rolled her eyes. "Honestly, what big babies! Here …" Ellie snatched the bottle off the deck and squirted some lotion on her hand as she approached Sean. Oh, she was good. "Turn around," she said, in a no-nonsense way.

Sean even looked taken aback. "Yes ma'am." He pulled off his shirt and tossed it on top of his bag.

Now it was our turn to try not to stare, and judging from the smile that crept onto his lips, he totally knew it. His broad muscular shoulders were something to behold on his six-foot-three-inch frame. A chiseled six-pack, I didn't even know guys in Onslow were built like that. He cast a wicked grin at us as he turned around to expose the taut curves of his smooth back. All of a sudden I was envious of the task Ellie had before her. Even Ellie, who was no stranger to the ways of skin on skin, seemed to pause and showed a moment of fluster. I tried not to smile. Was she blushing? She shook off her moment of weakness, placing it in that locked cage of hers, and rubbed the lotion onto his shoulders.

Sean stretched his neck and leaned forward a little.

"A bloke could get used to this. So what do they recommend? Application every hour?"

"Every four," Toby corrected, as he peeled his own shirt off and walked over to stand directly in front of me. I stood frozen with sunscreen-covered hands.

He gave me a small smile and said, "Be gentle with me," before turning his back to me.

I had so enjoyed Ellie's moment of unease. Not so much fun when it was me. The only difference was, unlike Ellie, as I studied the lean bronzed lines of his shoulder blades, I didn't have the skill to tamper down my awkwardness. Ellie threw over the sunscreen, which I dropped. Twice.

Toby flinched as I touched the middle of his back with my lotioned hand. I paused momentarily, and watched him relax before starting again. I started to rub it in until the whiteness disappeared, and it blended into his deep brown skin. His back was so smooth. Whenever I applied lotion onto Ellie, I did it with a slip, slop, slap and all done! She would always ask if it was rubbed in properly, and I usually lied and told her yes, even though it never was. I hated having sunscreen on my hands and just wanted to get it over and done with.

But in this instance I wanted it to last forever. I was slowly working in the lotion, sweeping circular motions, as I became more at ease with touching him. When I glanced at Toby's profile, I saw his eyes were shut, his expression serene. By this point, Sean was smearing his face with sunscreen and rubbing it over his chest, arms and legs as Ellie looked dreamily on. All too soon every last drop had been absorbed into Toby's skin and my job was done.

I coughed, and said, "Good to go."

I held up the tube to Ellie, miming for her to do mine, but she just shrugged and cringed, showing me her hands.

"Aw, Tess, I just wiped them clean."

I glared at her. "I'm sure that …"

"I'll do it," Sean and Toby said in unison.

Ellie smiled broadly. Her smug smile spoke for her. *'Aren't you glad you wore the bikini?'*

Sean and Toby looked at each other, surprised. Motioning to Toby, Sean swept his hand in my direction as if to say, *'After you'*, and now Toby was the one that looked out of sorts.

"You have to make sure she gets covered well, Toby; Tess burns easily," Ellie said.

It was an utter lie, which I made obvious when I glared at her. She dipped her sunnies down her nose to give me a wink before she pushed them back in place and leaned back on her towel in the sunbaking position.

With a subtle, deep breath, I turned around and Toby placed his hands gingerly on my back. I could feel his breath on my neck and my body swayed with each hypnotic caress. I fought not to let out a moan as he massaged the sunscreen into my muscles. It felt so intimate. I blinked with surprise as he dabbed sunscreen on the top of my ears.

"Oh, I forgot to do yours." I spun around.

His eyes went to my hands and a look flashed across his face, a look I had seen before, the night in the poolroom when he shook my hand.

"What?"

A crooked smile formed as he shook his head. "Nothing."

"What was that look for?" I pressed.

Toby grabbed my wrist and brought my hand up towards him, turning it from side to side in deep scrutiny.

"Your hands are tiny," he said.

"Shut up, no they're not. Thanks a bunch, I'll make sure to sign up for the freak show next time the circus is in town, shall I?"

A crease formed on his brow; he looked annoyed.

"I didn't say it was a bad thing." He grabbed my other wrist and turned my hands over so my palms faced the sky. He smiled slowly; my skin tingled under his fingertips.

"So dainty." He looked at me now.

"Dainty?" I repeated.

"Yep." He held his hand up in front of me and motioned for me to do the same. I placed my hand against his. The tips of my fingers only touched the top crease of his, he bent the tops of them as if to prove a point. I mock-glared at him.

"Don't be fooled," I said, "they pack a mean punch."

"I'm sure they could. At the right angle, they could slip between my ribs."

"They are not that small."

"What were you saying about the circus?" he teased.

I went to hit him with my freakishly tiny hands, but he grabbed my wrist, too quick.

"Oh, you're fast," he said, fingers locked around my wrist as I tried to pull it free. He grinned. "But I'm faster."

I struggled to break free from his vice-like grip.

"Tobias, didn't your mum teach you to play nicely?" Sean said dryly as he and Ellie watched on.

It was a Mexican standoff now; Toby didn't want to let me go in case I lashed out.

"Truce?" he offered, watching me suspiciously.

I smiled sweetly. "Truce."

He slowly let me go, and I calmly placed my hands by my sides. He seemed to relax, thinking it was over. I moved to brush past him and, with his back to me, slowly picked up the sunscreen. I silently pointed and squirted a stream right across his shoulders. He froze and slowly half turned towards me. I covered my mouth trying to contain my laughter.

He gaped at me, like he couldn't believe what I had done.

"Oops!" I said. "My dainty hands slipped."

He nodded as if all was fair in love and war. He went to reach for a towel but he faked out and instead lunged for *me*. I screamed, darting over the side benches and trying to escape him. I jumped behind Sean.

"Save me, Sean!"

Sean stood firm like a fortress protecting his people, until of course I realised his people was Toby. And I learned a very valuable lesson as Sean shrugged, as if to say *'What's a fella to do?'*

Toby stepped by him and grabbed me.

"How could you?" I cried at Sean in over-exaggerated horror.

Sean held up his hands. "Sorry, my sweet, brothers in arms."

Toby flipped me over his shoulder, my legs flailed and screams echoed across the ranges.

"Toby, put me down!"

"It's been nice knowing you, Tess." He walked me over to the edge of the boat.

I couldn't catch my breath for my own hysteria, it was like getting tickled to the point of madness; he eventually propped me down on the boat ledge. I was leaning precariously backwards, Toby the only thing keeping me from tumbling over the edge: his stomach pressed up against my legs, holding my upper arms.

"Don't you dare!"

His smile was wide and wicked, exposing all his bright white teeth.

He slowly pulled me towards him and leaned his head to the side. My ear tickled, his lips brushing against them as he whispered.

"Tess?" His voice was low and seductive. I was hypnotised by his proximity, his deep brown eyes. I couldn't form words, I just held my breath.

The corners of his lips lifted into a curve. "I'm sorry." And with that, he let go and I plunged backwards into the ice cold lake water.

Chapter Fourteen

I resurfaced, coughing and spluttering, completely sobered and most definitely no longer drunk on Toby.

Just as I gained my breath a huge explosion catapulted next to me, and I flinched against the force as rivulets of water and waves toppled over my head. All of a sudden, Toby appeared from the depths, flicking the excess water from his head in that famous head flick boys do when they swim. He beamed at me.

I retaliated with a splash of water to his face. "You're such a child." I glowered at him.

"Aw, don't be like that," he laughed.

Laughter rang from the boat as Ellie and Sean leaned over the rail, observing us.

"He had little choice, Tess, mutiny means walking the plank."

"Traitor!" I threw back at him.

Sean clenched his heart and looked hurt.

Toby caught my eye, and he didn't even need to say what he was thinking. We were on the same page. On the count of a silent three, we let Ellie and Sean have it. With a unified sweep of water, we saturated them with a giant splash.

Before we knew it, we were set upon by a six-foot-three-inch sized human bomb.

And it was ON!

I decided to escape the caveman display of who could outdrown the other and made a wide berth for the boat.

While Toby and Sean continued to wrestle like rolling crocodiles in the murky lake water, Ellie was waiting for me with a towel and a knowing smile as I hauled myself up the side of the boat.

Toby followed thereafter, causing the boat to dip slightly as he effortlessly hoisted himself in.

Glistening droplets fell off his shoulders and down his flat stomach. I eyed the beads with a slow, lingering look that made me want to reach out and touch them.

Sean was next. He scurried over to Ellie and captured her in a huge, soppy, saturated bear hug.

"Ugh, *don't*!" she grimaced.

"At least you didn't get thrown overboard," I said, as I threw an accusatory glare at

Toby. He shrugged as if he had no idea what I was referring to.

"It can be arranged," said Sean as he grabbed for his towel.

Boys.

"Don't even think about it," Ellie threatened.

I realised we could be hoisted overboard at any time if they suddenly felt like it. Although I had secretly loved every single minute of it, there was a part of me that wanted some form of revenge, for the sisterhood. Something to wipe those smug smiles right off their smoking-hot faces. And then I had a cunning plan, it was a risk, but I thought it was my best possible chance.

"You better watch your backs, boys, or you'll be the ones hoisted overboard next."

"That's some serious trash talk, McGee, you think you and your dainty self could take us?" Sean rubbed his head, eyeing me with interest.

I shrugged. "I think I could take Toby."

This scored me some laughing and incredulous looks from them both. Even Ellie lifted her glasses onto her head, her expression suggesting that I had lost my mind.

"Is that right?" Toby asked.

I tried to play it cool. "I'm just saying if push came to
shove ..."

I eyed Ellie, hoping to transport some sort of telepathic message to her, but she just stared back at me blankly.

"What do you think, Ellie?" I asked. "Do you think I could outdo Toby ... say to ..." I looked for a landmark and found one, "the pylon?"

The three of them followed my gaze to the concrete pylon that served as support at the base of the bridge; it looked like a little island. I had seen teenagers lounge and jump off it like a colony of seals, but today it was noticeably barren. Ellie's penny dropped; I knew it had because she gave me a winning smile, and if she was telepathically sending me a message, I could tell it was something like *'DO IT!'*

"Let me get this straight, are you challenging me?" Toby pointed to his chest, as if he could hardly believe it.

Cocky much?

I laughed. "Well, if you're too afraid ..."

"Whoa, whoa, whoa ... so what are you suggesting, McGee? That you could beat Toby to the pylon?" Sean said.

"Oh, I don't think, I know."

Trash talk was fun.

They both looked over my five-foot-nothing stance. I stood tall and proud, my hands on my hips. Who would have thought that a mere couple of hours before, I was hiding in the ladies' toilets at the hotel, threatening to go home? Now I stood, staring down two seriously hot boys, challenging them, in my soaking wet bikini. An element of self-consciousness came over me as I remembered just how much of my bare flesh was in front of them, a thought that ripped my focus back to the present.

A devilish smile formed on Toby's lips that silently said *'challenge accepted'*.

Ellie and I knew I wasn't outgoing or a go-getter. You wouldn't find me being the life of the party. I was more often than not a wallflower, praying not to be noticed. A creature of habit in all things school and home life, but when it came to the water, now that was where I shone. Naturally, like many a local, we were born on the doorstep of the Lake District. With a small population, there was little else to do for fun other than water activities. Whether it was swimming, water skiing, boogie boarding, fishing, canoeing, or something else – you name it. We were all water bound, one way or another.

My preference was (and always would be) swimming. No one had ever beaten me in sprints to landmarks. My mum's scrapbook was littered with first-place ribbons. I was small and 'dainty' but I was fast … *real* fast. I looked at Toby and knew I could take him.

Boys being boys, it was clear by the way they looked at me that they underestimated me. And Ellie knew it, too.

Ellie balanced on the edge of the boat, staring out to the pylon.

Toby and I looked each other in the eyes, like two opponents about to face off in the boxing ring.

"Okay! It's simple, when Tess beats you, she'll hand your arse back to you in a hand basket, does that sound fair?" Ellie said.

Only then did Toby's eyes frown from me to Ellie.

"Why don't we make this interesting?" added Sean. "Sort of 'winner takes all'."

"Oh, this sounds good," I agreed.

Toby laughed and shook his head. "You are something else."

My heart threatened to leap out of my chest, as I stared up into his eyes. His crooked smile formed on his lips.

"What do you suggest?"

I bit my lip. Exaggerating deep thought, I clicked my fingers in a Eureka moment.

"If I win, you fix my bike." I was quite pleased with this.

"And …" added Ellie, "until you do, you have to be her personal chauffeur and take her wherever she needs to go."

My head nearly spun off my shoulders as I threw a dirty look at Ellie, who seemed quite proud of herself.

Toby crossed his arms, uncertainty clouding his eyes.

"That's two things."

"What's wrong, Toby? You afraid?" Ellie teased.

He squared his shoulders. "Fine. Done. But if I win …" He thought for a moment, flicking a quick look to Sean. "If I win, you have to supply me and the boys with a stash of pies from your mum's shop. Freshly baked and delivered."

Like taking candy from a baby, I thought. And then my heart did a little flip at the realisation that he must have held my mum's pies in really high esteem.

"Shall I put my order in now?" Toby said. "The apple and rhubarb is a particular favourite of mine."

I held up my hand. "Best not to build up your hopes, save the disappointment."

Toby and Sean were enjoying this. In their minds, there was no contest. True, Toby could hurl me around like a ragdoll, but once he entered the water, I was lighter, faster and younger, something I would rub in after I won.

We stood on the edge of the boat, poised for the command. My heart raced as my adrenalin spiked. We gave each other a final long, lingering 'psyche out' look. When you chose to hang with the big boys, you had to prove your metal, earn your respect.

Sean shouted, "On your marks … get set … GO!"

I smashed into the concrete pillar with such force, waves of water carried me forward, and I had to place my hands up to stop myself from slamming into it. I knew I had won. It wasn't by much, but it was enough. Ellie screamed and jumped for joy, dancing around Sean on the boat, who stood with his hands on his head.

"Dude!" he yelled.

Toby and I clutched the concreted ledge, our breaths ragged and our senses blurry as everything slowly caught up to us. He was a mere inches away, looking at me. I managed to smile and once I gulped in enough air, I spoke.

"Hello, slave!"

The boys were surprisingly good losers, and Ellie and I weren't thrown overboard. Instead, after more cruising around the lake, we headed back inland and back to the Onslow Hotel for a drink.

I felt so giddy and fresh from the day in the sun with the boys. With Toby. And he hadn't laughed at me in my barely there bikini; instead, he had looked me over with a lingering male appreciation that I was happy to get used to.

I tied the sheer, matching sarong around my hips so that the split ran along my leg. We arrived as we had left, Ellie and I trailing the boys across the grassy embankment with Sean carrying our beach bag over his shoulder.

"Aren't you glad you wore the bikini?" Ellie whispered.

I just shrugged and played it down. I didn't want to have to admit I was wrong, *again*.

"Oh come on." She shouldered me. "Did you see the look on their faces when you took off your dress? *Priceless*!"

I wanted to press further; in fact, I wanted to stop her dead in her tracks and break out in song: "Tell me more, tell me more." But her thoughts had quickly moved on.

I was interrupted by her high-pitched, ear-tingling squeal. I followed her manic gaze just as she screamed.

"Adam!"

Chapter Fifteen

Adam stood at the top of the embankment under the sweeping verandas of the Onslow Hotel.

We charged forward, running as best we could in our flip flops and wet bathers as we passed Sean and Toby. Sprinting in a direct line, we smashed into Adam, giving him a dual, fierce, bear hug.

"So I guess you're pleased to see me, then," he laughed.

It seemed like an eternity since I had seen him, but really it had only been a few weeks. We were finally all together, where it all began. Even if the circumstances had changed, it mattered little; it was the perfect ending to a pretty freakin' perfect day.

The look Adam gave me as he stood back from our hug made me glance down to check I didn't have anything hanging out that shouldn't have been.

Nope, all in place.

Adam took a subtle step back and chose to strike up a conversation with Ellie. My excitement ebbed. Was that a look of disapproval? All of a sudden I wanted to run and grab my clothes. I felt naked, exposed; Adam had made me feel stupid just by one look. We sat down on one of the picnic tables. I was across from him and glad of the barrier it provided between us.

I had gone quiet, I couldn't help it. It wasn't like Adam to judge; it was the only way you could survive a friendship that involved Ellie. We had agreed the three of us would always be a judgment-free circle, and it had always been so … until now. He had put a damper on our reunion.

Toby and Sean brought out a tray of drinks and then remembered Adam's presence.

"Sorry, mate, did you want something?" Sean pointed to the bar.

"Ah, no thanks." Adam seemed edgy.

You know the old saying 'two's company, three's a crowd'? Well, the same applies for four's company, five is excruciatingly awkward.

If Adam hadn't turned up, the day would have probably ended with Ellie, Sean, Toby and I having drinks at the Onslow, reliving the day's events with further verbal sparring and razzing. I wouldn't feel ashamed by what I was wearing, and I most certainly wouldn't be sitting here in uncomfortable silence tracing the condensation on my pot glass, trying to stem the tide of anger at Adam that was building up inside me.

I had been so excited to see him. I had no idea he was going to be home this soon, perhaps he hadn't known either, or maybe he'd wanted it to be a surprise. Oh, it was a surprise alright, though it seemed more so for him.

I was itching to punch him in the ribs and ask, "*what was that look for?*", but while we sat with Toby and Sean, I kept quiet.

Sean glanced awkwardly between us and started up a conversation with Adam in an attempt to diffuse the tension. He asked him how things were in the big smoke and how his arm was healing. *Oh crap, his arm.* I snapped out of my daze.

"How is your arm?" I managed.

They both looked at me. Adam was about to reply when Ellie cocked her head.

"What's that scribed on your cast, some city chick's phone number?"

"Pfft, I wish." He twisted his cast so it was readable to us all. Scrawled on the inside arm of his cast in big, black, permanent texta was:

You're GROUNDED! Mum xox

"Kind of a buzz kill for the opposite sex, don't ya think?" He smiled.

I smiled to myself. Typical Adam.

Ellie shrugged. "I think casts are cute."

"Hey, there's Stan," Sean said. We all swiveled around and sure enough, there was Stan through the window at the bar, talking to Chris. Ellie sat up straight; her expression may have been one of disinterest, but her body language gave her away entirely.

"So it is," Ellie said. She pretended not to care but, oh, she cared alright.

"It was nice of him to lend us his boat for the day." I subtly kicked Ellie under the table.

Adam picked at the frayed edge of a beer coaster.

"Now there's a man who burns easily." Sean took a swig of his beer and looked pointedly at Ellie. I didn't get it. Was he saying Stan got sunburnt easily or … I don't know. Was he being metaphorical and saying Stan was a sensitive soul who got burned in love easily? Either way it was directed at Ellie, and by the look on her face, she couldn't decipher what he meant either.

Matching my silence, (in fact trumping it), Toby sat next to Adam, playing with his mobile, intently scowling at the screen.

"What's up, Tobias?" Sean said. "Trouble in paradise?"

"Hmm? Oh … yeah, something like that," Toby said, climbing to his feet. "I'll be back in a sec." He walked off without even looking up, only noticing Stan coming out with Chris as he dodged them.

"What's up with him?" Stan said with a frown.

"Woman trouble."

Stan and Chris groaned as they made themselves at home on the picnic table bench.

A spike of jealousy ran through me as I pictured Toby speaking to Angela on the phone at that exact moment. She would ask him what he had been up to, and he would shrug and say nothing, and that every waking moment without her was torture and please come home soon. Okay, so maybe it wouldn't be *exactly* like that, but my imagination was my nemesis so I zoned out in a cloud of misery.

I caught Adam staring at me, that quizzical frown back in place as he studied me. Seriously, what was his problem today?

"So!" Stan began. "Seeing as though I busted my rump today helping my old man, he agreed that we could have the shed tonight for some extra-curricular festivities." Stan addressed us all, but his lasting gaze was on Ellie, checking her reaction.

"Are you actually going to show up at this event?" she said icily.

He tipped his drink to her. "Yes, ma'am. Gonna crank up some tunes and dust off the old pool table."

"Shweeeeet!" Sean sing-songed.

"Ladies?" Stan asked.

Ellie replied enthusiastically on our behalf, but my inner conscience was thinking about what my mum and dad would think about going to a twenty-two-year-old's party until all hours. I had been out all day and the details of my whereabouts had already been sketchy at best. I hadn't mentioned the Onslow Boys to my parents; I didn't think they'd understand. To them, boys (aside from Adam) were all after one thing: to deflower daughters, get us pregnant and ruin our lives. My parents had nothing to worry about in that area. Seeing as though I was still most likely the last living virgin in Onslow and surrounding regions, I was pretty safe.

But I really wanted to go to this party.

After a while, my heart sank as I realised Toby wasn't returning to the table. I didn't want it to end on such an anti-climactic note. It had been the perfect day. I thought dreamily about the way his hands had glided over my skin, how he held my wrists with such gentle strength, or of when he placed his hand against mine, smiling at the difference. He had been so animated, so lively, more so than I had ever seen him. Maybe that was the way he was with his mates? I rarely saw him uninhibited. I doubt it was due to anything I did; sure, he gave me a look over when he saw me in my bikini, but so had Sean. They were guys and that's what they do; it didn't mean anything.

But Toby wasn't like the other boys; he seemed reserved, quiet and respectful – aside from throwing me overboard, but I liked that side of him, his playful side. And then I envisioned him throwing Angela overboard, and all of a sudden I didn't like that side to him nearly as much.

The Onslow Boys said their goodbyes and said they would see us tonight.

"Hey, Ellie," Stan said as the boys headed towards the door, "can I talk to you for a sec?"

She sighed deeply, but I knew she was secretly delighted.

This left me and Adam, who sat directly opposite me, giving me a strained smile. Oh, no you don't, I thought; there was something underneath that facade that bothered me, and I had to clear the air.

"Why do you keep looking at me like that?"

"Like what?" His eyebrows shot up, like he was genuinely surprised.

"As if there's food on my face and it turns your stomach."

"Wouldn't it be easier to say a look of disgust?"

"Is that what it is? I disgust you?" My voice rose.

"Oh God, Tess, no … Jesus, keep your voice down," he said, glancing around. "No, that's not it at all." He looked forlorn.

"Then what is it?" I demanded.

"It's nothing, you're just paranoid."

"Don't give me that, I know you well enough to know every single one of your looks, and I have never seen that one before, so spill."

By now the coaster in Adam's hands was shredded into a million tiny pieces, and he was staring at his little pile of cardboard when he offered a low, casual, one-shouldered shrug.

"You look different, you seem different."

I was taken aback, was he serious? I straightened.

"I'm not!"

"Yeah, you're right, okay, good, I'm getting a drink."

"Whoa, whoa, whoa," I said, "back it up, buddy, don't think you can bail on this. What do you mean I've changed? We've barely spoken to each other, how can you gather that?" Had the city pollution warped his brain?

He brushed bits of coaster off his hands.

"Don't mind me, I'm just tired. I only got back this morning and I'm beat."

"So, guess you won't be going to the party, then?"

He scoffed. "Party? You're a real party goer now," he said sarcastically.

He was really starting to tick me off.

"Well, how's about you go and take a nap and wake up on the right side of the bed before you come and see me again." I got up to leave, but he followed me.

"Tess, come back, don't be mad."

I swung around to face him "Don't! God, Adam, this the first time I've seen you in ages and this is how you act?"

He stared me down. Yeah, this wasn't going anywhere.

"You know, I was actually looking forward to you coming home, but I didn't think you would make me feel …" I broke off looking out at the lake.

"Feel what?"

God, wouldn't he take the hint and leave me alone? I cut him a dark look.

"Make me feel bad about myself."

His brows rose as if I had dished out a physical blow. *Good.*

I turned, chin held high, and strode away.

Chapter Sixteen

After the long, agonising walk home, I shuffled my flip flops across my front lawn and thought to myself how heat stroke can make you delirious.

I stood in the open doorway of the fridge, basking in the coolness that poured over my overheated, sweat-sheened skin. I greedily downed a bottle of water. It was a good thing that Mum and Dad were out as I made my way to peel off my bikini, ever grateful to be rid of it as I headed for the shower.

I let the lukewarm cascade of delicious clean water wash all the sand, sunscreen and sweat from my body. What a disappointing, frustrating end to what had been such an amazing day. Adam's distance, Toby disappearing without so much as a "catch ya later". No, he had to leap to Angela's beck and call. I was grumpy and tired; maybe there was something to Adam's claim of fatigue making him act strange towards me.

But I wasn't in the mood to make excuses for him. I was now too busy trying to think of my own excuses, if I was going to get to Stan's party tonight. I sat on the edge of my bed, the towel wrapped around me. I had darkened at least two shades today, with a slight tinge of red that I hoped was my temperature and anger and *not* sunburn. It was nearing on 6 o'clock, and Mum and Dad would be home any minute. I was pretty beat. Did I even feel like going to the party? Did I just want to crash and wallow? You bet I did. I had dressed myself in my cut-offs and spaghetti strap navy singlet when the phone rang.

"Where are you?" Ellie all but shouted down the phone like a pissed-off parent.

I yawned. "Home."

"I'm coming over." The line went dead.

I groaned and flung myself back on the bed. And so would begin an array of predictable events.

It would start with "What are you wearing? We have to get our stories straight, what's wrong with you? What do you mean you're not going? Of course you're bloody well going!" and so on until I gave in and just went to the party.

My head pounded already.

There was little time to corroborate stories before my parents got home. I felt bad about the half-truths I was feeding them of late but I needed to have some sort of fun over the holidays, it just happened to involve a twenty-something-year-old's party. A twenty-something-year-old *boy*. This wasn't going to be easy.

Mum and Dad had just pulled into the drive when Ellie rocked up in her Sunday best. She radiantly beamed a smile at my parents and chit-chatted pleasantly with them. If only they knew what happened as soon as my bedroom door was closed, and she flipped her backpack off, the contents vomiting onto my bedspread. She all but cried a war chant as she stared me down and started whispering about tonight's plan of attack.

My parents seemed happy enough that Adam was back in town and that we had plans to meet up with him. Those usual occurrences meant late nights watching DVDs at one of our houses. We didn't give the specifics, but I told them I would have my mobile on me. They just told us to have a good time. With an "I'm not sure what time the movies will finish" I was curfew free. Mum and Dad were usually in the deep stage of sleeping by the time I crept through the door. Not that I had made a habit of it. And this was the first time I felt the pang of guilt, because usually what I had just said was the truth.

I folded my make-up bag and choice of clothing in Ellie's pack; we would go via her place for the change so as not to raise any questions. Ellie's mum was a nurse and on night shift, so we could be in and out undiscovered. Ellie's dad would barely glance up at us, especially if the cricket was on. I had always thought her incredibly lucky to be given such a free rein, but now, the lack of attention they paid her made me kind of sad.

"So has Adam been filled in on our plan of deceit?" I asked rather unenthusiastically.

"He has and he is going to meet us there." Ellie looked at me side on as we walked along the street.

But I didn't offer any reaction. I half expected her to ask what was going on between us but either she didn't want to pry or she was way too distracted by Stan and his impending party to worry herself with the drama. I was betting on the latter. She talked animatedly about Stan, and how he had apologised again for not coming. Said he'd make it up to her. I'd tuned out by the time we crossed McLean's Bridge.

The plan was to rendezvous at the Onslow Hotel, before wandering off to Stan's later on. It felt surreal and a bit intimidating walking up the grassy embankment, even though we had been there only a mere hours beforehand. This time the sun had dimmed and the fairy lights lit the eaves above the picnic tables that were now occupied by a mass of people, enjoying the music from within. We had never been here when we weren't working. Never been ordinary patrons. I felt as if I didn't know what to do with my hands, as if I should be reaching and collecting empty glasses on the way in. We were stared down by a group of older girls, and were cast a wink and a smile by a guy we brushed passed; some older gents nodded "Ladies" as we weaved our way to the bar.

Chris was flat out taking money and filling pots; he looked up to see us standing before him as he pulled on the beer tap. His serious gaze didn't change.

"Two Lemon Ruskis, please, Chris," Ellie said sweetly.

"Everyone's in there, don't draw attention to yourselves." He set two glasses of coke on the bar for us, and walked away to serve the next customer. I guessed that was a no to the Ruskis, then.

Ellie slumped in bitter disappointment. "Could we look any more like teenagers?"

"We are teenagers," I said.

"Yeah, but I don't have to be reminded." She took a long draw from her straw. "I suppose people might think it's Bourbon and Coke?" she said hopefully.

"Well, don't complain too much, they were free. I doubt Chris's generous mood will last."

The poolroom was packed, a trail of gold coins lined up along the pool table's ledge indicating there was a fair wait for the next game. The forty-four-gallon barrels dotted around the room were stained by circles of drinks and ashtrays, as people sat around them on bar stools. The couch in the far corner was overcrowded to the point people were forced to sit on the coffee table or perch on the arms of the chair. The French doors were wide open letting a breeze roll off the lake and filter through the bar, which helped a little with the smoke and strong cologne all the boys caked on for the night's festivities. I was only interested in one kind of cologne and I looked around, wondering who Chris had been referring to when he directed us to the poolroom.

Then I saw him.

Toby was leaning in the alcove of the French doors, talking to someone I didn't know, a shorter guy with a buzz cut and a sock tan that clashed against his boat shoes. He leaned closer to him struggling to hear over the loud music. 'Hurts So Good' blared from the flashing jukebox. A couple of girls flipped eagerly to find some Shania Twain. Ellie spotted Stan leaning over the bar for a straw; she made her way over, sneaking up behind him, and whispered in his ear.

"Hands behind the bar, please," she said. He spun around, grinning from ear to ear.

"You're not going to tell the big guy upstairs, are you?" he teased.

"Maybe, can't make any promises."

I wanted to roll my eyes at the goofy looks they were giving each other, but an inner pang of jealousy overcame me. I envied how they could be openly flirtatious with one another. They were sending out signals to each other, and they both knew they were reciprocated. I was used to unrequited love and just as I was about to cast my usual doe-eyed longing glance across the room to the boy I knew I couldn't have, I froze to see his eyes were on me. I smiled, and he mirrored me. I made my way over, and he watched my every step as he took a deep drink from his beer then placed it on the window ledge and leaned back on the doorframe.

I looked at his beer with an arched brow.

"Can't even hold your own beer," I said. "Are your arms that sore from all the swimming today?"

"Almost as sore as my ego, but I'll live." He looked at my drink with a frown. I didn't want to have to confirm I was only drinking Coke. I wanted to pretend as Ellie had done that I was not seventeen, and that I was just hanging with a boy in a bar on a summer's night.

"I'll have the contract drawn up by my solicitor and have it to you as a matter of urgency." I felt nervous, half thinking that he would laugh at me and say, *"You didn't expect me to follow through with the bet, did you? I was only joking, kiddo."* But instead he grinned; it was the teeth-exposing kind, the true grin, the unhinged Toby that made my tummy flutter.

"I suppose two out of three would be out of the question?" he mused.

"Not on your life, I couldn't handle the humiliation," I said.

"Yours or mine?" he laughed.

"Wow, were you seriously not there today when I shamed you? You were literally choking on the lake water I was kicking up in your face."

He crossed his arms, laughing. I sipped on my drink, innocently looking at him, loving every minute of our exchange, the exchange I was hoping to have this afternoon that never happened.

Toby was wearing jeans and a navy polo shirt. He smelled amazing, his cologne was fresh and sharp. I wanted to step closer to bask in it all.

Instead, I played it cool, waiting for his retort.

"Tess, if it wasn't for your manicured nails, I would have beaten you today, that's how close it was, photo finish."

"You mean I have my dainty nails, on my dainty hands, to thank?"

He picked up his beer, and then nudged me playfully with his foot.

"You know I didn't mean anything by it, right? When I said your hands were dainty. I meant it as a good thing."

"Oh yeah, sure." *Act cool, Tess.*

I knew it wasn't meant in a spiteful way. Had I gone home and looked up the meaning of dainty in my pocket Macquarie dictionary? Maybe. Did the meaning state:

Dainty: Delicately pleasing in appearance of movement?

It sure did.

And perhaps he didn't know the meaning of the word so thoroughly as I did now, but it definitely wasn't meant as a bad thing.

As we gave each other a sly smile, each almost lost in our own world, a figure walked in the open French doors and wrapped herself around Toby like an octopus.

"There you are! I wondered where you got to." Angela smiled.

And the moment was gone.

Angela completely ignored my presence, turning her back to me as she pawed at Toby who stiffened in the surprise of her appearance.

So much for being away for two weeks.

"You sure you won't come?" She pouted.

"No, you go with the girls. Have a good time." He held her upper arms, which were linked around his neck. I tried to sidestep away. I wanted to dissolve into the crowd, retreat into wallflower Tess again. I was about to back out of the French doors when I heard it, that all-too-familiar voice shout out from behind me.

"TIC TAC?"

Chapter Seventeen

There are many levels of mortification.

I turned slowly around and there he was. Scott, frozen on the footpath outside the French doors, looking at me as if he couldn't quite believe his eyes. Oh no. No. Shattering a glass had been embarrassing. Wearing the teeny tiny bikini had been humiliating. But nothing – nothing compared to the flush of mortification, the rush of horrible high school memories. I felt it in Mr Burke's Biology class when he read out that stupid note and coloured the rest of my high school experience with that stupid name. But nothing compared to the shame I felt now, in front of the Onslow Boys – in front of Toby.

Angela, Toby, the girls at the jukebox, Sean from outside and even Chris, flat out in the bar, still managed to hear over the deafening music and collective chatter. He may as well have shouted through a megaphone, it was *that* loud.

"I thought it was you, we were just on our way to Stevie's when Dusty said, 'Hey isn't that Tic Tac?'" Scott said. "I thought 'no way is it Tic Tac; Tic Tac Tess would never be hanging in a bar'."

Oh God, could he say that name any more times?

It was like someone punching me, again and again, punching a hole in my chest. And the worst thing was, he wasn't even trying to be malicious. To him, it was just my name.

But to me, it really wasn't. I couldn't breathe. I had to get out of there. I had to. Scott was polluting the air with his mouth, and I could feel Angela and Toby's eyes burning into the back of my head. I just gave a small smile and excused myself, darting through the crowd, straight to the refuge of the Ladies' toilets.

Again!

I slammed through the door and clutched the basin with a white-knuckled intensity, thankful that I was alone. I flipped on the faucet and concentrated on the water, its circular motion around the sink and down the drain as it made its way out into the great beyond. Oh, how I wished I could go where it was going. I didn't dare look at my reflection; I didn't want to see my scarlet flushed cheeks, or the tears that welled in my eyes. Why here? Why now? I had been doing so well. I had finally started to become something more than high school, more than that name. But then Scott thrust me straight back there. No, he had done worse than that, he had brought it into my new world, where

I was not Tic Tac, I was simply Tess McGee.

I had become a girl that could hold her own, could verbally spar and even flirt with the best of them. But now it was all tarnished. As soon as I gathered myself, I would walk out of here and just go home. It was a good plan. Ellie wouldn't mind, she had Stan to hang with, and I would be home by a decent hour, and keep my parents happy. Win-win.

The door opened, and I knew it would be Ellie checking on me. But it wasn't. Angela sauntered in and propped her designer bag on the basin as she smoothed out a perfectly manicured eyebrow with the tip of her equally perfectly manicured fingernail.

I busied myself with washing my hands, a task I pretended to be so fascinated by, that I couldn't even tear my eyes from them. She was still; I could feel her watching me in the reflection of the mirror. I pretended not to notice. She tilted her head a little in my direction.

"It's Tess, isn't it?" she asked in a gentle voice.

"Yes," I managed to say.

She ran her fingers through her hair, fixing her already perfect reflection.

I could see her eyes dart to my chest, and I felt myself flush even further, if that was possible.

"You're not small, you know?"

Oh my God, this was not happening?

She turned fully to me, facing me directly. There was no denying it: yeah, this was really happening.

"He's probably never even touched a booby in his life." She shrugged and turned back to the mirror to reapply her lip gloss. "I would seriously doubt he is an expert on the subject." She pouted at herself in the mirror and scrunched her hair.

Was Angela Vickers going all deep and meaningful on me? And did she seriously just say booby? Who *says* that?

She cast me a fleeting smile and without a word, picked her bag up off the counter and sashayed out of the bathroom.

I stood stunned from what I could have sworn was a small act of kindness from Angela Vickers. I didn't know exactly how I felt about it.

I could do one of two things. Get Chris to sweep up my shattered ego off the poolroom floor, while I ran out the back door. Or two, I could play the 'ignorance is bliss' hand and go out and pretend that it didn't even happen, all while completely avoiding Toby for the rest of the night. I was so humiliated I couldn't even bring myself to look at him. Maybe Adam was right. I had changed, and Scott had wrenched me jarringly back down to reality. Reminded me who I was. I pulled my mobile out and began to text.

To: Adam

Fashionably late as usual? Where R U at bozo?

We're at the O Hotel.

A second later the screen lit up.

Adam

Bozo?? I'm out the front.

And with that, I gathered myself together (making sure I didn't look too pitiful) and left my refuge to hang with Adam. Instead of going with the flow, I was going to go with what I know. And I knew Adam.

We made peace. Things seemed back to normal between us as we both obviously didn't want to bring up the conversation from earlier. Turned out Adam was only home for the weekend, so I was glad that I had this time with him. We sat on the outside picnic table, sharing a packet of crisps, when we saw Angela and four of her friends pile into a car. They were way too overdressed for Onslow. They must have been heading to Redding, the next biggest city half an hour away; it was the place to go once you turned eighteen.

Adam snared the last chip.

"So you going to Stan's later?" he asked.

"I don't know, not fussed either way."

"Who's going to look after Ellie?"

"I think she will be right. Stan's a good guy."

"Yeah. I don't think she'd know if we were there or not, the way they're making doe eyes at each other." He shuddered.

"Well, well, well, what do we have here?" My seat dipped as Sean sat down next to me. Toby was right behind him, standing at the head of the table. His cool, reserved manner was back and I mentally slapped myself for the flips my traitorous stomach made at the sight of him.

Get a grip, Tess.

"We're heading off soon, there is far too much Shania Twain pouring out of the jukebox."

"The netball girls are on a bit of a rampage tonight," added Toby.

Sean stood. "You coming?"

I made a point not to look at Toby even though I could feel his eyes on me, waiting for my reply. Instead, I looked at Adam and posed the question to my best friend.

"What do you wanna do? It's your weekend."

"Hmm. Shania Twain or a party at Stan's?" He drummed his chin thoughtfully with his finger.

"I don't know how much better it will be," Sean said. "I'm pretty sure you'll be reduced to witnessing Ellie and Stan suck face all night if their actions in the bar are anything to go by."

I cringed. I'd left her alone for five minutes, and she had already publicly disgraced herself.

"One thing I *can* be sure of, though, there will be no chick power ballads," Sean added.

I pouted. "What? No 'I am woman, hear me roar'?"

"Definitely not!"

Either we were to stay at the Onslow with the netballers and be subjected to tabletop dancing or head to Stan's for a game of pool and semi-decent music. Deep down, okay, not even too deep down, I knew what my choice was. I knew it the second I looked up at Toby.

We walked through the night, making our way to the caravan park nearby. We gave up worrying about waiting for Stan and Ellie who were stopping every five minutes for a quick pash against a tree. I wanted to get as far away from them as possible. The rest of us walked in uncomfortable silence, and Ellie giggled and squealed followed by sucking noises behind us. Over and over again.

I felt the butterflies in the pit of my stomach. I didn't miss Scott, that was for certain, but I did miss the weight of a boy on top of me, making out for hours, and chaste stolen kisses on the walk home at night. I missed the heart palpitations and the strange stirrings I was only just beginning to understand. I missed being the object of someone's affection.

As we walked, Adam and Sean played footy with a crushed beer can, even going so far as to run some commentary for themselves. According to the commentators (Adam and Sean), Sean was the number one Champion in the World and Adam was the undefeated five-time Premiership Captain.

They were somewhat ambitious. I laughed at their deluded fantasies as they darted further in front of Toby and me.

And then I was painfully aware that I was walking in the dark with a boy. Not *a* boy, *the* boy. But I couldn't have him. I couldn't steal kisses from him. I shouldn't even look at him the way I do, the way I always have. Still, it didn't stop me from wanting to walk closer to him, just so I could listen to his breathing or his low laugh as Sean tripped over his own foot.

"And the World Champion goes down!" he mused.

"Oh no! The impact of his ego hitting the ground could tilt the world off its axis," I added.

"Tsunamis and earthquakes will ripple through the world."

"A crater will form and create a new lake system."

"Where are you heading? Oh, we're just going to Lake Sean."

We both lost it in dual fits of laughter at our own commentary.

"What's so funny?" Sean asked, but we were far too amused to answer.

We stopped at the gate to Remington's Caravan Park, thinking it only appropriate to wait for the host of the party to lead the way. Toby climbed onto the gate and sat, while I fidgeted with impatience and shuffled from one leg to the other. Finally, a figure appeared from the darkness. Ellie was walking, her eyes cast down, arms crossed against her chest as if stemming off a wayward chill that didn't exist.

"Where's Stan?" Sean asked.

She walked straight past us through the gate. "Who cares?" she said coldly.

Adam and I looked at each other with grim expressions.

Uh-oh.

"Is she alright?" Toby jumped down from the gate.

"Yeah, it's probably nothing," I said. Knowing Ellie, it was definitely something, so friend duty beckoned, and I followed her into the park.

I sat opposite Ellie on one of the logs that had been cut purposefully and arranged in a circle. So campers could sing 'Kumbaya', probably. It took everything in me not to so much as crack a smile as I stared blankly at Ellie, registering what she just told me. She was pretty upset so I had naturally thought the worst: that nice guy Stan wasn't actually a nice guy after all and tried to force Ellie into something back in the bushes. But as unlikely as it seemed, I was truly taken back when I found out why Ellie was *actually* so distraught.

"You know how I have put on a bit of weight since school stopped …"

I didn't know or notice. Still I humoured her with patient silence, urging her to continue.

"Well, we were kissing and his hands were wandering around my back. Which distracted me and I just said to him as a joke, 'Don't touch my flabby bits' and then he said 'But I like every part of you, even your flabby bits'. Can you believe he said that?"

I cringed inwardly, not because he said what he said, but because my heart went out to the guy. What had been meant as a really nice compliment along the lines of 'I like you just the way you are' had received punishment. He had suffered one hell of a case of foot in mouth that would take Ellie some getting over.

"He said I was fat!"

I grabbed her hand and gave it a reassuring squeeze. "Oh Ellie, that's not what he meant."

"Well, that's what he said." She sniffed.

Oh God, how did I even begin to save this train wreck? I knew she wouldn't see reason. So I did what best friends do. I deflected.

"Scott called me Tic Tac in front of the entire bar, in front of Angela and Sean, Chris and Toby."

Ellie's eyes narrowed with sympathy. Yep, it was working.

"Don't worry, Tess, they don't know what it stands for."

I gave a half smile. "Angela knows what it means, so they'll know."

"Oh, fuck Angela," she snapped.

My eyes widened.

"Who cares, anyway, stuff them all, let's go find Adam and have a good time. We can make our own fun. You, me and Adam and my back fat."

I burst out laughing, and even Ellie joined me. We had managed to drag each other out of the depths of despair once again. We heard a snap of a branch to see Adam appear with a guarded look on his face.

"Everything okay?" His eyes flicked from my face to Ellie's.

We could only manage to nod.

"Do you need me to call Stan out? Kick his arse?"

This only made us laugh even harder.

"I'm serious," he straightened. "I could take him."

Ellie snorted which made Adam break into a smile and join us in our laughter. The kind where the outside world would look in on us and think we were mad. Though it had been a bit rocky this afternoon, we were back. We understood each other perfectly and no matter what, we would always be there for one another.

"Oh, my God! I gotta go pee, wait for me?" Ellie wandered off to find the toilet block. I wiped away tears that had emerged after laughing so hard. Adam straddled the log to sit next to me.

"Seeing as this seems to be some kind of circle of truth," he said, "I have a confession to make."

All of a sudden, I was very sober and my laughter died down as I looked into Adam's serious, earnest eyes.

"I did give you a funny look today." He started to pick at the bark on the log, a sign that he was uneasy.

"I just didn't recognise you; when I was standing on the porch at the hotel I saw Ellie walking up with some girl, and I was watching this girl, in this hot, white bikini, and I thought I have to know this girl, and then you came closer and I saw it was you, but it couldn't be you. This girl was so carefree, confident. I thought it was the sexiest thing I had ever seen. Then you looked up and saw me, and the look on your face was the Tess I knew. The goofy Tess McGee. I was a bit taken back. I saw the way Toby and Sean were looking at you, and I kind of went all Alpha male on you."

He smiled sadly.

I didn't dare breathe or think about asking what he meant by the way Sean or Toby looked at me. I just remained quiet.

"I was just being a jackass. I had only been away for a few weeks and I felt, I don't know, replaced. Pretty stupid, huh?"

"Yes," I said, "idiotic! As if I could replace you!" I kicked him. So he wasn't judging me – well, not in the way that I had thought.

"Adam, you're my best friend and that's not going to change, I can tell you that, so stop going all Alpha on me, okay? Unless you want to avenge my honour with a banana because you can totally do that anytime you want."

He kicked me back, and we were us again.

"So … you thought I was sexy, huh?"

He threw his head back and groaned.

"You thought I was sexy." I grinned.

Adam rolled his eyes.

"You totally love me, you want to write me poetry, and …"

Adam covered my mouth with his hand, which only made me laugh. "What is revealed in the circle of truth remains in the circle of truth."

"Nuh-uh, only if the circle of truth has a cone of silence and as you can see …" I lifted my hands up to the sky. "Nothing."

He gave me a bored look.

It was then a delayed thought registered. "So what you're saying is the goofy Tess you know is *not* sexy?"

"Ugh, Tess, quit it already!"

"No, no, I want to know," I said. I pointed to myself. "You wouldn't want to tap this?"

"Right now I want to choke you."

He slid over to me and grabbed me closer to him. My smile fell from my face with the unexpectedness of it. His hands cupped my face, his lips hovering above mine.

"You seriously want to know, Tess?"

He closed the space and claimed my mouth with an urgent, hot, delving kiss.

He smiled. "You are sexy, in your own goofball way, you're sweet and beautiful and smart and funny and, although you kiss to the point where I feel like I want to go back for seconds, you're my best friend, and that's why I don't want to tap that."

I was breathing heavily, he had wiped my brain blank, all thoughts, all smart-arse retaliation, everything evaporated from my mind. He thought all those things of me, but, above all, he valued our friendship. It was something I would cherish for the rest of my life.

There was a coughing sound, and I broke away from Adam with such speed I nearly toppled off the log. The Onslow Boys stood before us. Sean gave a wry smile. Toby was deadly serious, and poor Stan's worried eyes weren't focused on us; he had his own troubles. My eyes darted back to Toby, who unflinchingly stared back at me with a deep, burning gaze.

"Don't mind us." Sean propped himself on the opposite log. As usual, Toby chose to stand.

"Do you know where Ellie went?" Stan asked. "Is she still pissed?"

Adam answered for me. "A word of advice, Stan, let that one cool down for a bit."

***

It was Ellie's laughter that sent me in the opposite direction of the toilet blocks. I found her near the swimming pool talking to a couple of tall boys with towels draped around their necks, smiling down at Ellie.

"Tess! Come and meet Wes and Mark."

I didn't want to meet Wes and Mark. I just wanted to get to the shed, and I wanted Ellie in tow.

I offered a pleasant enough smile as I turned to Ellie. "They're waiting for us."

"Oh, right!" Ellie agreed (thank God!).

"Do you guys wanna come to a party?"

"Uh, Ellie, I don't think we're in a position to invite people," I whispered.

"Oh, it'll be fine." She waved me away, which really got my back up.

"Half of Onslow will be there, and the boys are staying at the caravan park anyway, right?"

I knew exactly what she was up to, and I did not like 'Operation Make Stan Jealous' one bit.

"Whatever! Do what you want, I know you will anyway," I snapped and walked off without so much as a backwards glance.

I loved Ellie, but she sure could infuriate me sometimes.

Chapter Eighteen

I followed the thunderous rock music that filtered through the night.

It led me towards a giant shed that housed an array of mis-matched sofas, a pool table, a folded down table tennis; aside from the high tech stereo and a giant television, the rest looked like stuff that had been salvaged from hard rubbish day. It was a man's paradise!

Sure the style was stuck in the 70s, but the shed was packed with people, most I had never seen before. Seriously, *did I know anyone here?*

'Heartache Tonight' thumped out of the mounted sound system, and I tried not to scoff at how appropriate the song choice was. I spotted Toby reading the back of a CD cover near the stereo, when he looked up at me.

I wandered over. "Your choice, no doubt?"

"What makes you say that?" He looked back down at the cover.

"Oh, I don't know, seems like your kind of music. Plus you were playing The Eagles in your car."

He didn't say anything.

I picked up the cover to the album, looking over the track list. It was the same as my dad's tape I had been listening to in my room.

"I like number nine," I announced.

Toby didn't respond; instead, as the song faded out he took the CD from my hands and put it into the player, flicking it to song nine. Then he turned and sat on the couch.

Huh. Maybe he'd had a fight with Angela? I silently hoped so. I sat next to him as Timothy Schmit's voice filled the room, with 'I Can't Tell You Why'. I tilted my head down, getting in his eye line to coax him to look at me.

"Please don't make me have to use a really hideous cliché," I whined.

That had him looking at me, frowning as if he didn't speak English.

I rolled my eyes. "Fine. You asked for it: penny for your thoughts."

"Oh." That made him smile. "Yeah, that's pretty hideous."

At a loss as to what to say, I thought I would give not being a smart arse a go and see how that worked.

"Look, you don't have to fix my bike. I was just razzing you about it."

His gaze flicked up. "No, no, a deal's a deal … I don't mind."

"Just saying."

"Do you need a lift home later?" he blurted out.

I stammered at the question.

"That was a part of the second condition, wasn't it?"

"Ah, yeah, it was." I felt all uncertain and coy.

"Just checking." He leaned back on the couch, his eyes lighting with that familiar spark.

"I haven't read the contract yet, so I'm a bit fuzzy on the details."

I smiled and shook my head. "My secretary is so fired."

Toby seemed to relax. "Give her a go, she's probably out on the town with the netball girls."

"Ha! Even more reason to sack her."

"I wonder if there is any Shania Twain in here somewhere." He jumped up to paw through the CD collection again.

"Don't you dare." I grabbed his arm, pulling him backwards. His eyes darted to where my hand rested on him. I didn't move my hand, I couldn't physically bring myself to break the contact; all of a sudden there were no smiles, no jokes, just him and me and our space on the couch. I could only hear the music and be aware of the heat of his skin and the rapid rise and fall of my chest in this moment.

The only thing that snapped me out of my daze was Toby's words which seemed low and raspy.

"Is Adam your boyfriend?" His gaze flicked over my face as he waited for my answer. My mouth gaped open; I couldn't hide the fact I was dumbfounded by the question.

I blinked quickly and took my hand from his arm. I struggled to construct a legible sentence.

"Oh – um, no, we're just friends, it's not like that."

His stony expression didn't falter, didn't reveal any kind of emotion. He was so hard to read, and I wanted to read him so badly. He gave a small nod and handed me the CD cover.

"Better go and make sure these guys aren't cheating." And without another word, he got up and headed towards the pool table.

I tried to gather my thoughts. He had been intense and distant, and then we were joking and then BAM, an out-of-the-blue question, and then he was gone.

I didn't want to sit there with a perplexed look on my face all night, so I headed for the fridge for a drink, only to spot Ellie walking into the shed with the taller tourist, Wes. Oh yes, she did!

Adam wandered over and took the open can from my hand.

"She works fast."

Everyone's eyes went to Stan who was standing by the pool table, glaring at the happy new arrivals. Toby patted him on the back and handed him the pool cue, flicking Sean his own unamused look.

"What must people think of us?" I said.

"Ellie's her own person. It's got nothing to do with us."

"Yeah, but guilt by association and all that."

"I don't think you could ever be compared to Ellie, Tess, you two are chalk and cheese."

Ellie laughed obnoxiously loud at whatever Wes had said. My heart sank. Ellie's stupid games really bugged me. I just never understood the logic; you like someone, they like you, isn't it a no-brainer? My gaze rested on Toby who was lining up for his shot.

What would I know? When I wasn't making out with my best friend, I was mooning and flirting with a very-much-taken twenty-two year old. Yep! I was all about the moral high ground.

"When did things become so complicated?" I sighed.

"No idea. I must say, I'll be glad to head back to the city and watch re-runs of M*A*S*H; you girls are far too exciting for me these days."

"Oh? Must be the new Tess, that's far too cool for school. Got to make sure I don't lose myself by the time you get back next."

I elbowed Adam playfully.

"You better not."

I frowned. "I won't, dummy."

"Just saying." We turned to watch the pool game.

"Do you want some words of advice, Tess?"

I glanced at Adam's profile as he sipped.

"Don't give your heart away too easily." He turned to me. "Make him earn it."

And with that, cheers echoed throughout the shed. Toby potted the black.

I'd had enough of cryptic messages, and didn't get a chance to ask Adam who exactly he was referring to. Who had to earn my heart? And why didn't I get the chance to press him further? He was suddenly too busy glaring across the room. I followed his gaze and my eyes froze on the only thing that could possibly have evoked such a reaction in Adam, because it evoked the same in me.

Scott, Steve and Dusty walked into the shed like a bitter wind. So much for avoiding the horrors of high school.

Sean sauntered over to get another beer from the fridge beside us.

"What is he doing here?" Adam spoke, low and bitter.

I just shook my head in amazement. "It's Onslow. You can't swing a dead cat without hitting someone you know."

I wondered how Ellie could stand it? Hooking up with all these different boys and constantly running into them. But then again, nothing much really got to Ellie, I mused, as she flirted with Wes right in front of Stan.

Sean followed Adam and my seething glares.

"What's the deal?"

"Tess's ex." Adam glowered.

Sean laughed with surprise. "Geez, Tess, how much more of a trail of broken hearts can you leave? You're a lucky man, Adam, best defend your honour."

"We're just friends!"

Adam frowned. Maybe that had come out a bit loud.

"You don't have to sound like the idea repulses you so much."

"That's my cue," Sean said, retreating back to the pool table.

Scott made his way over to us.

"Don't you move," I warned Adam.

"Hadn't planned on it."

"Tess, Hendo, what's happening?" Scott spoke like we were long-lost buddies.

"Thought you were going to Stevie's?" Go on, run away, I thought.

"Apparently this is where all the action is." He looked over at Ellie and Wes who were getting closer and closer, leaning in to each other to speak over the music, which wasn't that loud anymore.

Scott's gaze focused on me, giving me a long, lingering once over, with a smile I just wanted to wipe clean off his face.

"Looking good tonight, Tess."

"Well commit it to memory, because we're out of here." Adam grabbed my hand to leave, but Scott stepped in front of him.

"Whoa, whoa, whoa, Hendo, I was just talking to the lady."

"Lady, is it, tonight?" I said. "Not frigid, or Tic Tac or some other degrading nickname?" I spoke slowly, quietly, but I couldn't wholly contain my venom.

"Oh, come on, Tess, you know I'm just razzing."

"Step aside, Millo," Adam said sarcastically.

Scott's smile turned snide. "Wait a minute, Tess, you're not fucking Hendo, are you?" He started to laugh like the snivelling germ he really was.

"No, she's fucking me."

A deep voice floated over from behind Scott, who instantly sobered, his eyes widening as he turned to face a wall of Sean's muscular chest. Sean looked down on him with a cold, hard stare. The entire shed went deathly quiet as they watched the showdown. I squeezed Adam's hand, threatening to break his skin.

"What of it?" Sean's voice was low and filled with malice.

I heard Scott gulp as he assessed the danger he was in. His eyes darted from Sean to me as if hardly believing that such a pairing could be possible. I just smiled sweetly at Scott, quirking my brow, silently daring him.

Go on, just try it!

"Your shot, babe." Sean passed me the pool cue. Because? … Oh yeah. I was like, totally playing pool with my fictional boyfriend.

I took the cue from Sean who stepped aside, touching me lovingly on the lower back to usher me past.

Oh, he was good.

He continued to stare down Scott who couldn't hold eye contact.

"You come near Tess again, and you and your friends will be fish bait. My old mate Tobias over there …"

Toby gave him a two-fingered salute from his brow.

"… Well, his family is connected to the Mafia, and they don't look too kindly on little boys walking in uninvited and harassing our friends."

Toby flicked me a perplexed look, like he had no idea what Sean was talking about, and Stan's smile reappeared to the point he had to turn his back on the scene so as not to give the game away.

Steve and Dusty looked like a pair of rabbits in the headlights.

Steve croaked, "We were just leaving, weren't we, Scott?"

Scott nodded quickly and backed away, his face ashen.

None of them dared to even look my way as they quickly made their exit. As soon as they were gone, well, that's when laughter erupted.

Sean came up to me. "Sorry, Tess, no doubt we're going to be the next hot gossip in Onslow."

"I dare say all of Onslow and Perry will know by now," added Adam.

"The Mafia? Really?' Toby shook his head.

"How come you didn't give my family underworld status?" Stan asked, his expression surprisingly earnest.

"Come on, Stan. Look at Toby, all dark and broody, he could easily be linked to the mob, now if you were connected to the Irish mob, you would have been perfect."

"Maybe next time." I said. Stan seemed to have momentarily forgotten about Ellie and Wes, until she spoke.

"That was the funniest thing I have ever seen, can we hire you for all occasions?"

"Weddings and Bar Mitzvahs." Sean nodded.

Ellie came over and hugged me. "We're heading off now," she whispered in my ear. I shot her a look that begged her not to, but she just winked at me, her mind made up.

"Might see you guys later." She deliberately directed her speech away from Stan who had immediately soured again. Poor Stan.

This was one night I would not be waiting for Ellie. She made her own decisions so she could deal with the fallout. Wes took her hand and guided her out of the shed. The party atmosphere fizzled out as we all watched them leave.

Adam whispered in my ear. "So that's okay with you, is it? Making everyone believe Sean and you are together?"

"Ellie is about to wander off into the dark with a stranger and you're asking me about a mythical relationship? If it means Scott leaves me alone for the rest of my life, then Onslow is welcome to think I'm Sean's girlfriend.'

I turned from Adam to walk over to Sean. I stood on my very tippy toes and, placing my hands on his shoulders, I kissed him on the cheek.

"Over the top, but thank you."

Sean beamed a winning smile at me. "People talking about me and you? I don't mind the thought of that one bit."

The moment for appreciation was interrupted by a thunderous crack of the billiard balls as Toby broke with a shattering force.

"Sean, you're up!"

Chapter Nineteen

Great. Both Adam and Toby seemed in a mood.

Tonight was not turning out to be ideal. The rest of the night went by with a certain lack of drama. I just sat and watched the boys play pool, drank too much soft drink and tried to forget about Ellie.

They tried to coax me into playing pool, but my heart wasn't in it. Adam snapped out of his bad mood after a little while, never one to hold a grudge, but Toby seemed a little off, just like he had been when I first walked in. Maybe he was thinking about what Angela was getting up to. Maybe he was annoyed by all the teenage gatecrashing and resented Adam and I even being there. I managed to convince myself that it had something to do with me, to the point I felt utterly miserable and decided to bow out early, say my goodbyes and go home.

Adam agreed to walk with me, and then the Onslow Boys had had enough too and decided to walk with us back to the Onslow.

Stan walked us out to the gates, he had his hands in his pockets, shoulders slumped, forehead furrowed; he looked like he had seen better days. I wanted to tell him to forget Ellie, to say something that would make him feel better, but I had nothing to add. Probably just as well because now, surrounded by his mates, was not the time or place.

We navigated our way through the darkened streets, the four of us walked the long stretch back to the Onslow Hotel. I only hoped that we wouldn't bump into Ellie on the way.

Sean talked a lot, mostly just to drown out our gloomy silence.

Adam and even Toby added additional remarks on the fishing at the weir, but I zoned out midway, setting a fast pace, eager to end the night. If they thought I was quiet, no one said anything. They might have thought I was upset over the Scott incident or Ellie. I doubted they would ever suspect in a million years that it was actually because I feared that any ground I'd made today with Toby was lost. I would go home and he would go home and Angela would probably get dropped off at his place tonight. I felt sick to my stomach. And angry. How could I have been so stupid? I knew he had a girlfriend. There was no way me and Toby could end well.

It had been great of Sean to defend my honour, but in all honesty I was a little put out that it hadn't been Toby. Of course, it wouldn't have worked because everyone knew he was with Angela. Still, I wondered if he was annoyed at Sean, dragging him into it. Who knew? All I knew was every time I tried to catch his eye he would make an effort to avoid mine. He walked on the opposite side of our group, Adam and Sean between us. I didn't know what his problem was but all of a sudden I didn't care as I could see the glowing window lights of the Onslow Hotel. It wasn't quite twelve yet, so there was still time for a lock-in. It occurred to me this was probably their plan: play more pool, reclaim the jukebox and say goodbye to us pesky teenagers.

Adam was crashing the night at the Onslow. He had his pick of the rooms upstairs as most tourists stayed in the holiday parks rather than stay at a pub with its overpriced, un-refurbished rooms. So vacancies were pretty high at the Onslow, they made more money out of meals and the bar than having to worry too greatly about accommodation. Uncle Eric didn't have much flair for such things and Claire Henderson was never around. I gathered she must have been present at some stage as there were touches of her taste dotted all around the restaurant. John Waterhouse paintings lined the walls, a shiny black grand piano, plush mahogany and cream rugs with black fringed borders, antique-style furnishings and subtle lighting added for ambience. The woman was highly strung, but I couldn't fault her taste.

Sean and Toby walked in the open door heading straight for the main bar. I paused outside and Adam hovered, waiting for me as I dialed my mobile.

Ellie's phone went straight to voice message, and I sighed in irritation as I waited for the beep.

"If you received this message I can only assume you haven't been murdered and buried in a shallow grave somewhere. It's 11.40 and I'm heading home."

"How you getting home?" Adam asked.

"It's a nice night." I shrugged. "I'll walk."

"And you're worried about *Ellie* being murdered."

"I'll be fine, I've done it a million times from yours and Ellie's houses before."

"That wasn't quite so far."

"Stop being an old woman."

"I can't help it, I've been hanging with one for too long."

"Well, you are who you hang with."

"Well, in that case don't go turning into an Onslow Boy, you're too pretty for that."

"I don't need to turn into one, I'm dating one, apparently."

Adam grimaced. "Yeah, well, that's going to be around like wild fire by tomorrow. Hope no one congratulates your parents for gaining a new twenty-two-year-old son-in-law."

My smile dropped from my face. "Oh God. I didn't think of that."

Adam nodded. "Oh, I did."

I bit my lip. "Man, if Mum and Dad hear that, I'll have my arm in a plaster cast like yours with 'grounded for all eternity' marked on it."

"And Sean will be fish food."

"Or pie filling." I cringed.

"I'll walk you home."

"No, no, no ... You're on a good behaviour bond, remember. Just stay here, I'll be fine. Most of the moon is up. It's light and a nice night. I'll be okay."

"I'll get Chris to run you home."

"Will you stop? Chris is busy. I. Will. Be. Fine." I kissed him on the cheek. "Goodnight."

"What, no tongue?" He smiled wickedly.

"Shut up! Or I'll get my big twenty-two-year-old footy-playing boyfriend to beat the crap out of you."

Adam imitated Scott to a T, fidgeting and gulping in a convulsive way that had me laughing until it hurt.

"Night, Bozo." I backed away, knowing that if I didn't he would talk me into letting him walk me home. He looked at me with an uncertain frown on his face.

"Text me a progress report on the way home, I want landmarks and updates until your foot is in your front door, you hear me?"

"Yeah, yeah."

Once again, I made my way down Coronary Hill, leaving the distant weekend noises of the hotel behind me. I managed one look back when I reached the bottom; Adam was a speck on the verandah silhouetted by golden light. I knew he would stay there until I was out of sight. As soon as I made my way around the bend and hit Main Street, I texted him.

To: Adam

Turned a corner happy now?

He texted back.

To: Tess

Yes! Now go on, git!

I strolled leisurely along Main Street. Onslow was relatively well lit in this part of town, but the moon hung like a beacon lighting the way in darker spots, and I never once felt afraid. I knew this town like the back of my hand, it was as much a part of me as was the smaller territory of Perry which housed nothing more than a milk bar, a post office, and Mum and Dad's cafe on the edge.

I texted Adam again as promised.

To: Adam

Brimstone Street. Still alive.

There were still a couple of cars around, mostly young joy riders, but they paid me little attention, their music up full, probably headed for McLean's Beach or up to the Point to go parking.

It took me no time to make it to the fluro lights of the 24-hour Caltex. I texted Adam the breakthrough.

To: Adam

Pit stop at the Caltex. Yay!!

I perused the shelves, but didn't find anything of interest. I went to the ladies' room where the fluro lights continued, highlighting the dark circles under my eyes from smudged eyeliner and my hair all curled with the humidity of the night. I saw very little point in making any touch-ups aside from my lip smacker. As I went to dry my hands with the towel dispenser I glanced to my right and froze midstep. There, mounted on the wall, was the condom vending machine. It brought back a memory of when Ellie and I had come in here one afternoon after being at the lake all day. We were in Year Seven and we saw this very same machine. We dared each other to put in some coinage and get one out each. We giggled while we did the unthinkable. We held the silver foiled wrappers in our hands like it was this wondrous, mysterious thing, which it was. Then Ellie said we should have a competition, see who would be the first one with a chance to use it. She was all wide eyed in excitement.

"Okay," I agreed, feeling like a daredevil, even though we both knew Ellie would win. I hadn't even kissed a boy, whereas Ellie definitely had. We giggled as we got one for Adam as a joke. We put them in our Hang Ten wallets, bought ice creams and went on our merry way. That night at dinner I couldn't take my mind off the 'thing' in my wallet. It felt like it was burning through my pocket. The very sin of it. I was so sure Mum and Dad knew what I was up to. I didn't eat much, for the fear of looking them in the eye. After tea, I went straight to my room and took the foil square out of my wallet and hid it in the shoebox with all of my other keepsakes that I hid in the back of my wardrobe. I breathed a sigh of relief, but jumped out of my skin when Mum knocked on the door.

"Tess hon, *Monkey Magic* is on." If I didn't go and watch my favourite show like I did every other night, they would definitely know something was up.

For weeks, every night before I went to bed, I peeped into my shoebox, secretly smiling at the thrill of rebellion I felt by possessing something so forbidden. I didn't know how Ellie felt, although I knew for a fact she carried it with her because she was bragging to the girls in the school toilets and showing them.

Adam, on the other hand, thought it hilarious and broke straight into it as we sat on the banks of Lake Onslow in our secret place we used to go swimming and fishing. He thought it brilliant to put over his head and blow it up so it expanded into a big white dome.

"You really are a dickhead, Adam," Ellie had laughed, which caused him to laugh and the condom went flying off his head. I picked it up with a stick, Ellie and I both looking at it with wide, horrified eyes at the sheer size of it. I gulped and we both tilted our heads in wonder.

"Surely it's stretched." Ellie looked on in distaste.

Adam was lying on his back, squinting at the wrapper.

"It says extra extra large," he sighed. "Gee, I hope it fits."

He threw a cheeky smile our way.

"It does not say that," I snatched it off him.

He just shrugged, put his hands behind his head and closed his eyes, lying in the sun. It was then that my breath hitched as I read the packet.

"What does it say?" Ellie whispered, moving closer, balancing the parachute on her stick. I swallowed hard and looked at Ellie in dismay.

"It says regular," I whispered, and we both turned to look at the limp white rubber thing on the end of the stick.

"Jesus!"

I smiled at the memory of how excited we had been over such a thing. Ellie now popped coins in it like it was a gumball machine. I even noticed Adam's flash of the infamous square foil in his wallet when he paid for things.

I knew Adam had done it when he went out with Nicky Briggs last year for eight months. They were all over each other, and he was forever catching the bus to her house after school. I was secretly jealous of Nicky taking up so much of Adam's time and when I overheard Nicky and Adam had done it, I unexpectedly felt a deep misery. I felt like I was the last standing virgin alive. Which was actually most likely true.

I put a coin in the slot and pulled the lever, then grabbed the foil packet that fell out. A different kind of thrill surged through me as I held it now. When I was in Year Seven, I often wondered who my first would be, but never really into the scary technicalities like I did now. Ellie often told me details of her being with boys, and although it embarrassed me, I was also fascinated at the same time.

"Does it hurt?"

"At first," she had said, "but then it's better and better." She smiled dreamily. "Honestly, Tess, you don't know what you're missing out on."

I placed the condom in the inner pocket of my handbag where I kept my compact. I didn't exactly want anyone to recognise that unmistakable flash of silver that I had seen in boys' wallets all over Onslow. And then I thought, what difference did it make? According to the population, as of tomorrow, I had been sleeping with Sean Murphy. My stomach did a little flip at the thought of being so intimate with the likes of Sean. I shook my head; hanging around condom vending machines was sending me crazy. That or the fluro lighting.

As the automatic doors opened, and I stepped out of the Caltex, I froze stock still. A familiar navy Ford ute was parked in front of the shop. It was unmistakable, as its owner was leaning casually against the car door, his arms folded with almost an air or amusement, as if to say, "Fancy meeting you here."

"Adam said you were walking home, nice night for a murder."

I rolled my eyes. Traitor.

"What is with you guys and murder?"

"I watch *Crime Stoppers*."

"Yeah, well, so do I and apparently Mafia-affiliated men driving navy pickup utes are to be avoided at all costs."

"Is that so?" he smirked. He was back.

"Afraid so." I tried not to give up my smile so easily, but it was difficult when his was so damn contagious.

He raised his brows, sighed and straightened from his casual lean to shoving his hands in his pockets, glancing back at his ute.

"Well, this is awkward."

He walked to the passenger door and opened it, waving his hand in the direction of the interior.

"Deal's a deal!"

I looked down at my feet. "Um …"

"If you're wondering about my drinking, I was drinking Coke for the last four hours. I'm good to go."

Had he really? I frowned, trying to remember the pool game at Stan's, but other things must have distracted me. Every time I looked at Toby, it wasn't to check out what he was drinking.

"You didn't not drink because of me, did you?"

That caught him off guard. He glanced at the Caltex roof, his shoes, then back at me.

"Well, a deal's a deal."

My shoulders slumped, mortified. He had sacrificed a night out with his mates to play chauffeur to me because of our stupid bet. I bit my lip; the look of dismay must have been all over my face.

"Hey, Tess, I don't mind, it's no big deal."

"I didn't want to ruin your night."

"You didn't," he said earnestly.

"I feel awful, I don't mean for you to think that –"

"Tess!"

He cut off my rambling and pointed.

"Get in the bloody car."

Chapter Twenty

I was in Toby's car. Again!

We drove around the streets of Onslow with the windows wound down, the summer breeze blowing my hair.

José Feliciano was on the radio crooning out his version of 'California Dreaming' and I thought I would die from happiness. I looked at Toby's profile as we pulled up to the only set of lights in the whole town, and he tapped his fingers on the steering wheel.

He caught me watching him. "What?" he smirked.

The breeze had been cool on my skin but now we had stopped, the warmth in the air came back to me.

I looked at him, really looked at him. The glow of the streetlights behind him … I didn't know what to say. My gaze flicked to the bow of his lips, and I quickly glanced away.

I looked at my hands that fidgeted in my lap. "So you're not mad at me anymore?"

Before he could respond a sounding horn blasted from behind us. The lights had changed, rocking Toby into motion. As we moved our way forward and back into the present, my phone rang and Adam flashed up on the screen.

"Hello?"

"Are you a ghost speaking from the afterlife?"

Toby threw me a questioning look. I mouthed 'Adam', then realised maybe he was still trying to decipher what I had just said to him. Something I regretted as soon as the words left my mouth, that's what. I was after affirmation, the kind only insecure teenage girls would ask for, and that was the last thing I wanted to come across as.

I rolled my eyes. "That's right! And I am going to haunt you for the rest of your days."

"You hadn't checked in so I thought I would … what's that noise?"

"I'm hitchhiking."

There was a moment's silence on the phone, and then he twigged.

"Toby found you!"

"Yes, you dibber dobber."

"Hey, don't blame me, when I said you had walked home he basically accosted me and then high-tailed it after you. I said if I knew you, you would stop at the Caltex for junk food."

"Oh, you think you know me, huh? Well, it so happens I didn't buy a thing."

Condom! Condom! Condom!

"Nothing from a certain vending machine?" His voice was teasing. I nearly dropped my mobile switching to the other ear away from Toby. Damn him! We had been friends for too long.

"No!" I said a little too high-pitched.

Adam chuckled on the end of the phone. "You so did! And you can't even blame it on Ellie this time."

"I'm hanging up now."

"Oh, hang on a minute." There were muffled voices followed by scratching and static.

"Tess?" Sean's voice came on the line. "Can you please put Toby on?"

"Oh, um, he's driving. Hang on a sec, I'll put you on loud speaker."

"Tooooobyyyyyyyyy, Toooooooobyyyyyyy," sing-songed through the phone like a nightmare.

"Can you come and pick me up? Old buddy, old mate, old pal … what do you say?"

Toby sighed and gave me a bored look.

"Do you mind?" he asked.

A destination to delay me from getting out of this car, hell no.

"Fine by me."

"Be back there in five." Toby worked to turn the car.

I was just about to hang up when Adam's voice echoed through the loud speaker.

"Tess? Okay, so where were we before we were so rudely interrupted? Oh that's right, you went and got yourself a co…" I hung up the phone with lightning speed and threw it on the dashboard.

Toby did a double take. "Everything okay?"

You mean apart from forgetting to turn off the loud speaker and nearly having my best friend reveal that I was packing heat? Apart from that, fine!

I texted Adam a very brief 'SHUT UP!' message and then placed my phone on silent. If Toby wondered what Adam was talking about, he didn't let on. Maybe I bought myself a *Cosmo* mag or something. That could work.

We pulled into the Onslow car park, which was nothing more than a big circular space of gravel out the front of the hotel. There were people everywhere, loitering, most intoxicated after a big session. We couldn't see Sean, and neither of us really wanted to get out of the car.

Near the front entrance a fight broke out; there was a lot of pushing and shoving before their mates held back the two obviously hammered guys.

We wound up the windows at this point and waited for our package to be delivered.

We both jumped as a sound thudded against Toby's window.

"Toby!" A muffled sound with a smattering of condensation as Angela pressed herself drunkenly against the glass that she then proceeded to kiss.

This could not be happening.

"I missed yoooouuu…" she crooned. Toby unwound the window, and Angela's eyes lit up now that there was nothing stopping her from getting her claws on her man.

She paused as she caught sight of me, tilting her head in wonder. I gave a small smile.

"Tic Tac?" she said. I flinched. So much for our bathroom bonding, at least her predictable behavior made it easy for me to hate her. "What are you doing in here?"

Toby saved me from answering. "I'm just dropping Tess and Sean home."

"Sean?" Angela's eyes squinted into the interior thinking she might have overlooked him the first time. How anyone could overlook Sean's six-foot-three stature, I couldn't be sure.

"He's inside, do you want to grab him for me? I don't want to leave the car."

Her smile didn't quite reach her eyes. "Sure thing, babe, I know the law doesn't look too kindly on people leaving kids in cars." She looked pointedly at me and laughed at her own joke.

Before she went, she pulled Toby into a full-on kiss, her eyes on me, laying claim on her man. Finally she pushed him away and zig-zagged through the crowd.

Well, that was awkward.

At least she didn't call me out and try to claw my face off, but the night was still young. We just sat in silence. I could tell Toby was embarrassed by public displays of affection. It was always Angela pawing at him, and although he looked at her affectionately and smiled, you would never see Toby getting all gooey. I was thankful for small mercies because I didn't think I could stomach that. Sean stepped through the front door, sauntering his way across the gravel with a pot glass of beer in hand.

He came around to my passenger side to get in.

"You can't take that with you," I said.

"It's for my collection, don't tell Chris." He put a finger to his lips and climbed in, his giant frame filling the inner cabin. I scooted over to the middle, and he leaned on me, spilling a bit of beer on himself. It was at this point I realised I was pushed right up against Toby, his bare arm burning against mine. I gave him an apologetic smile, even though I was not in the least bit sorry.

Toby whispered to me, "I think we better get him home first, if he passes out we'll have no hope."

"Agreed." I muttered and tried to push Sean away from crushing me.

"Hey lookie, it's my girlfriend." Sean put his arm around me. "What's for tea, honey? Are all the house chores done?"

"One: in your dreams, and two: it's the 1990's, not the1950's, you sexist pig."

I felt the vibration of Toby's laughter through his arm as we both watched Sean's brows rise in surprise.

"Tess, will you marry me?" Toby laughed.

I blushed, not knowing what to say, when a familiar cackle sounded from across the drive. Angela had stumbled over in the garden. Her equally drunk friend tried to help her up, but she was too busy laughing.

"Wow, someone's drunker then me. Impressive." Sean threw back another mouthful of what looked like flat, warm beer.

Angela hauled herself up and spotted us again.

"Heeeeyyyyy, where are you going?"

"I'm just going to drop –"

"You can't go." Angela pouted, glanced around her and then cupped her hands around her mouth. "Chris is going to do a lock-in." She whispered in a loud, obnoxious way, as if she was privy to this amazing secret. As I looked over her dishevelled state, I knew Chris wouldn't let her stay; she was a loud, messy drunk and Chris wouldn't have that time bomb in his pub. Lock-ins were risky enough. All hush-hush as the beer continued to flow past their 12 o'clock licence. It could mean big trouble for Chris and his uncle if they were found out.

I prayed that my little cozy refuge, pressed up against Toby, wouldn't be spoiled if Angela convinced him to stay with her. But he didn't budge.

"Stay here, Ang. I'll come and get you after I drop them home."

Her eyes cut daggers at Sean and me, like he had chosen us over her. Which he kind of had.

She shrugged. "If I'm here, I'm here."

"Don't be like that, I won't be long."

She flicked her hair and walked off in a huff. What a child. I could stress and blush, and ask all the stupid naive questions in the world, and I still would look more mature than Angela Vickers every time. Toby stared after Angela with a deep scowl; he resonated such anger, I was sure he wouldn't go after her. His jaw pulsed as he tightly clenched the steering wheel.

"She'll be alright, she's got her friends. She'll be here when you get back." I tried to pacify him like the idiot I was.

She's a freakin' idiot!

"Yeah," Toby said as he started up the engine. He slung his arm over the seatback to check his back view. "I'm not coming back."

Chapter Twenty-One

Life could be worse than being wedged between the Onslow Boys in Toby's ute.

Sean suggested we go for a drive, and from the moment we had left Angela back at the Onslow, a new-found awkwardness had settled over the three of us. Toby's solemn silence was thick and heavy; I couldn't see his face, but I could feel the tension in his body where it was pressed against mine. I stole a quick sideways glance at Sean who could only respond with a helpless shrug.

Regardless of the change in mood, I was glad we were churning into the darkness; the last thing I wanted was for Toby to have a sudden hit of remorse and head back to the Onslow to pick Angela up for a make-up session … yeah, I didn't want to think of that.

The possibility of turning around became bleaker as we drove further and further away from the hotel, veering onto McLean's Bridge en route to Perry. My heart spiked with panic; maybe Toby took going for a drive as a male bonding thing? I didn't want to go home yet! Sure I had desperately wanted to earlier, but now? Pressed next to Toby, feeling the warmth of his skin against mine; I never wanted to go home.

I listened to the rhythmic hum of wheels along the stretch of the never-ending concrete bridge that connected me to my impending doom. Home.

Be cool, Tess, be cool!

Then Toby sped past the turnoff to my street and kept driving up the winding road into the dense bushland. I tried not to smile too wide as relief flooded through me. He continued passed the Rose Café, leading deeper and deeper into the Perry Ranges, veering down the Point turnoff.

We were heading to the Point?

We climbed higher and higher. Toby laughed for the first time when he noticed that I was making a funny jaw movement to force my ears to pop.

"There's chewy in the glove box." He motioned with a head tilt.

I leaned across Sean who was like a brick wall; he lifted his arms to maneuver out of my way a bit, allowing me access to the glove box. The inside of the ute cabin was claustrophobic, pressed in between Sean and Toby – but don't get me wrong, I wasn't complaining! The glove box light momentarily highlighted a bemused smirk on Sean's face, as if he was loving every minute of me lying awkwardly across his lap. Was the chewy worth that smug look? Yeah, I decided, it kind of was, as I accidentally on purpose elbowed him in the side as I straightened back into my seat.

"Ugh! Christ, Tess." Sean clasped his side.

"Oops, sorry!" I offered sweetly, unwrapping and popping a piece of gum in my mouth. Toby took a piece from the pack.

The close proximity of the cabin wasn't the only thing that caused a swirling giddiness in my stomach. I had never been to the Point at night. Come to think of it, I had only been there a handful of times during the day.

Once was with my Uncle Bernie who loved to go bird watching (yeah, that had been a riveting afternoon), so much so that my mum promised she would never subject me to it again. The other time was for a Grade Six field trip to replant trees after a bush fire swept through the ranges.

The Point was a popular haunt for young rebellious delinquents who were looking to hang out. I knew this because I had witnessed plenty a young couples stopping off at the cafe in the early hours of the morning. Their kiss-swollen lips, dishevelled hair and creased clothing. Oh, how I secretly envied them.

Unofficially, the Point was the designated playground for the eighteen-plus crowd, mainly because, thanks to the steep incline, you could only access it via car. Adam, Ellie and I had attempted it once by bike, but the winding ranges were far too steep for our little peddling legs; it didn't take long for us to breathlessly voice, *"You know what? We can totally wait 'til we're older".*

The shadows of bushland passed by in a blur; I tried not to imagine what my parents would think. Me, travelling to the Point with two twenty-two year olds; I quickly shook the thought from my mind. No time for guilt tonight. It took us about ten minutes to make it to the final turnoff, abandoning the bitumen and winding up the rough dirt track that seemed much steeper at night. Up and up we crawled, not seeing more than a metre or so in front of us. The canopy of trees cast an eerie blackness, and as I looked out at the dense scrubland, I thought it would be the perfect place to bury a body. Had Toby and Sean not been debating the hard-hitting topics like chickens being the greatest of all of God's creatures, I might have been a little bit nervous.

"Chickens?" Sean said in disbelief. "What about echidnas? They're so tough you could run over one in your car, and it would still be alright."

Toby chewed thoughtfully on his gum for a long moment. "Yeah, echidnas are pretty cool." He nodded.

Yep, pretty thought-provoking stuff. I stifled my smirk, and my thoughts switched momentarily to Ellie. I wondered where she was right now. A part of me knew I should have stayed with her, but if I had, I certainly wouldn't be pressed up against Toby, mere metres from the Point. Instead, I would be playing lookout for Ellie and her new fling; God only knows what kind of company I would be keeping.

The track evened out at the very top of the climb. It was so dark it felt like we could have easily driven off the edge of the earth for all we knew, but like everything with Toby, he maneuvered his way up the track with great care.

The Point was a mass clearing on top of one of the highest parts in the Perry Ranges. Sheer rock boulders sloped downwards into the abyss of darkness that ended with the distant twinkle of the town lights of Onslow. A derelict, boxy, wooden shack sat to the right of the clearing that had once been the fire observation tower. Over on the left of the clearing stood two ugly pylon towers, servicing as some beacon of technology. They were fenced off but it still didn't prevent adrenalin junkies scaling them and climbing the pylons on drunken dares. Miraculously no one had plummeted to their death, yet. At least, not that I'd heard of.

And sure enough, tonight we were not the first car to crunch up the gravel track to the Point. Three other vehicles were parked in a circle and a crowd of people perched on bonnets. As we edged closer, Toby sounded the horn and wound his window down. He pulled over to where Ringer stood, cigarette in one hand, can of Jim Beam in the other.

"Well, if it isn't the Onslow Boys. What brings you to this neck of the woods?" Ringer took a long draw of his ciggie, past his smirking lips.

"We're out of options, we have partied it and pubbed it," Sean said.

"And now your here parkin' it?" Ringer laughed.

"Not with you bunch of pervs." Toby smiled.

Ringer looked at me as if seeing me for the first time.

"McGee!! What you doing stowing away with these bums?"

"Oh, you know, enjoying the view." I looked out towards the dark smudge that would be Lake Onslow, speckled with dotted lights from the town.

Toby steered us slowly closer towards the edge where the lookout was more prominent.

"Whoa, hang on a sec," Sean said, "you two kids take a look at the pretty lights, I gotta go whizz."

Sean climbed out and stumbled into the night.

Toby smiled and placed Sean's empty pot glass in the cup holder. "Although I don't doubt his authenticity, something tells me he won't be heading back in a hurry."

I cast Toby a questioning look.

He drove forward bringing his ute closer still to the edge. He pushed it into park and killed the engine, flashing me a devilish grin.

"He's afraid of heights."

We were silent for a while as we stared at the beauty of our little town. Growing up in Onslow seemed mundane, even claustrophobic at times, but sitting above it, as we did now, it looked well … kind of beautiful. Toby shifted and relaxed in his seat. I became all too well aware that I was still pressed right up against him, I hadn't even bothered to move across when Sean had gotten out. I was torn between scooting across, because that seemed like the appropriate thing to do, or not saying a word; act like I didn't even notice and stay right where I was.

I chose to be ignorant a little bit longer.

Toby gripped the steering wheel with one hand.

"What made you think I was angry at you?"

Damn! Memory like a freakin' elephant.

Just because I desperately wanted to forget the things that came out of my mouth didn't guarantee others would.

"Oh no … I just thought you seemed a bit quiet tonight, that's all. I didn't think it was solely directed at me."

Yes I did.

He nodded, seemingly satisfied with my answer.

He laughed a breath through his nose.

"I think you would be the last person I could be angry with."

My head swung around to look at him but his eyes were diverted as his fingers played with a thread on his shirt.

"I'm sorry about how Ang treated you tonight," he said.

My mouth gaped. "It's not your fault," I said.

Angela had pronounced Tic Tac in front of Toby as a means to deliberately humiliate me. Fresh anger boiled to the surface. Actually, yeah, maybe he should apologise for her. It was because of boys like him thinking she was a goddess that gave her grounds to be so cocky. My silence must have made Toby uncomfortable because he pressed further.

"You know, I had a nickname in high school." My head snapped up, that had my attention.

Oh God, he knew, he heard. Of course he did.

"Oh?"

He gripped both hands on the steering wheel sighing deeply as if psyching himself up to tell me. I tucked my foot under my leg, settling in, waiting for Toby to continue.

"They used to call me Toby–Wan."

Okaaaay? I frowned, unsure as to how it compared.

He looked at me expectantly. "Toby-Wan-Kenobi," he repeated slowly, as if my first language wasn't English.

My hand flew up to my mouth to mask the smile that automatically formed on my lips.

Oh please, don't laugh.

He smirked. "You think that's funny?"

I shook my head violently, biting my lips, trying not to lose it.

"On the contrary, Star War's references are hot. Gives you street cred."

"Yeah, not quite."

"I thought you were going to say Tobias."

"That, and they used to call me Toblerone."

"Hey, I wouldn't object to being named after that."

Toby shook his head in disbelief. "Chicks. Always with the chocolate."

"Always!"

We stared at each other in silence, neither one of us looking away.

"Thanks for telling me your nickname." I smiled. "It's not quite the same, but I can appreciate it."

Toby's gaze never wavered from mine. "People will always make fun of what's different, Tess."

An uncomfortable shiver ran down my spine. Even Toby knew I was different. That I was awkward, clumsy and clueless.

I broke eye contact, untucked my leg and sat up straight. "Yeah, I'll definitely look out for that circus when it comes to town next," I said, focusing intently on the twinkling stream of car lights below.

That was Toby's cue to insist that he didn't mean it that way. I was not a freak, and he was welcome to gush about how wonderful I am.

Instead he laughed, which had me frowning his way again.

"What?"

"Well, if they set you in the kissing booth, let me know, I am always willing to donate for a worthy cause."

Was he flirting or being friendly?

Toby collected himself and shifted in his seat, his arm brushing against mine, causing my skin to prickle with the sensation of his skin on mine. "Sorry I dragged you up here, I sort of didn't even ask if you wanted to?"

"No! No, I wanted to. I mean you really didn't have to give me a lift home, I didn't expect you to."

Moon rays filtered through the windshield, giving the cabin an otherworldly glow.

Toby's perfect teeth were illuminated when he smiled. "You know, you are the worst winner!" He shook his head. "Ever since you won the bet, you've been apologising. Just go with it, enjoy it, because I assure you, next time ..." - he leaned closer - "... you will not be the winner." He pulled back, smug.

I curved a brow. "Next time?"

He nodded. "I fully intend to redeem myself."

"Want a chance to rebuild your shattered ego, do you? I bet you're itching to fix my bike so you can be rid of me once and for all." I shouldered him gently, teasing him as I would Adam. And then I realised what I had done; I had treated him like my friends. He looked down at his shoulder, then up at me. His eyes shadowed with untold meanings that I couldn't read.

"What if I didn't want to fix your bike?" he said in all seriousness.

"Why, is my company so stimulating that you can't bear the thought of being without me?" I teased nervously.

I was aiming for light and airy, but something must have gone wrong with my delivery because Toby's face went blank. He looked out into the lights of Onslow, ran his tongue over his bottom lip and sighed.

"Bring the bike in on Monday, and I'll have a look at it."

"Oh, okay, sure." My heart sank. That was rather anticlimactic.

He tapped his fingers on the steering wheel. A silent awkwardness had swept over us.

"We better get you home. The last thing you need is for rumours to circulate tomorrow that you went parking up the Point with Toby Morrison."

A thrill shot through me at the thought of such a thing. A girl could get used to that idea.

"I can see it now, love triangle splashed across the local news," I said, again attempting with the lame nervous humour.

Toby frowned as he started up the car. "Yeah, Ang would love that."

And there it was, how to kill a conversation. All good humour died a sudden death. We picked up Sean who was socialising with the masses and edged our way down the winding ghostly roads of the ranges. I was now definitely ready to go home.

Chapter Twenty-Two

It was 2 am when I tiptoed into my house.

I was unaccustomed to such big days and heavy nights that had me traipsing across the countryside and emotionally dragging myself backwards through a hedge. I was exhausted and managed to crash fully clothed into bed. Judging by my numb arm the next morning, I'm pretty certain I never moved, not once.

When you lie to your olds there comes a certain responsibility to follow through the next day. A shadow of paranoia followed my every move. I had some scrambled eggs and a side of guilt for breakfast, trying not to make eye contact with my chatty mum. They grilled me with a myriad of questions, like, "What did you have for tea?", "What movies did you watch?" and "What time did you get home?" I had to think on my feet with my best 'I'm not guilty' responses. My inner monologue was screaming *liar!* I tried not to choke on my breakfast juice as my conscience laid into me with steel-capped boots. My next point of call was to word up Ellie, and fast. That's if she wasn't too sleep-deprived from last night's escapades.

Ellie's phone rang out, and I was quietly pleased. I wasn't in the mood to chase her down and listen as she retold what an amazing night she'd had. I placed the receiver back on the hook and sighed with relief. Oh well, I'd see her at work. *Work, ugh.* Still suffering from my own sleep deprivation, I had to really psyche myself up for my afternoon shift. The only thing that kept pushing me through was that Sean and Toby said they would come in and annoy us for some lunch. Every time the front door of the main bar screeched open with its hundred-year-old unoiled hinges, my heart rate spiked with anticipation. Mostly it then plunged just as quickly as my searching eyes saw crusty locals, or nameless tourists, pour through the door.

I had suspected an unbearable afternoon with Ellie's voice ringing in my ears as it usually did the day after her conquests, so when I was met by her with silence that stretched on for an uncharacteristic age, well, I admit, it got the better of me.

"So how was your night last night?" I asked as she fumbled in the linen cupboard with some tablecloths.

Ellie shrugged and offered a weak smile. "It was alright."

"Just alright?" I tipped my head, trying to see her eyes.

She nodded lightly but I saw her chin quiver, and with that, friend mode kicked into gear. Lunch had not officially begun yet, so I ushered Ellie into the ladies' room. I guided her into a cane chair that was wedged in the corner next to the sink and hand dryer. This place was so handy for meltdowns and emergencies.

I sat her down, making sure she didn't bump her head on the hand dryer. "Ellie, what's the matter? Did someone hurt you?" I crouched in front of her.

Her eyes widened. "No, nothing like that, it's just …" Her voice broke away.

I grabbed her hand to urge her to talk. "Well, what then?"

Her big, blue eyes welled with tears as she looked down at me.

"Why am I always so stupid? It's like I'm floating above my body, and I can see the things I'm doing and hear what I'm saying and I go to scream but nothing comes out."

Had Ellie had a breakthrough during the night? Guilt usually didn't follow Ellie's escapades. "What brought this on?"

The tears began to flow now, and my heart broke for her. Ellie was the rock in our relationship, so seeing her crumble … well, it really rocked me, no pun intended.

Struggling as to what to do, I grabbed her some toilet paper.

"I saw Stan on the way to work." She took it from me and blew her nose.

I cringed at the thought; this town was far too small. Maybe Ellie wasn't as immune to his presence as she pretended.

"Was he mean to you?"

I imagined Stan giving her the cold shoulder, a death stare, even maybe calling her on a few home truths. After last night, any of those reactions would have been warranted. I felt awful for thinking it.

"That's the thing," she sobbed, "he was really nice to me, lovely in fact. The same Stan, he treated me like nothing had happened. If anything, he stumbled over his words and apologised to me and said that he didn't mean what he said."

Well, yeah, I could have told her that. Oh Stan! Will you ever find out that your maturity in the matter had made such a breakthrough? I wondered.

"So, this Wes guy?" I pressed.

"I don't want to talk about him, I don't even want to think about him, I just want to pretend none of it even happened. Then I don't have to think about what a horrible person I am."

"You're not horrible; you're hard work, I'll admit, but you are the sweetest person I know." I shrugged. "I love you."

"You're the only one." She blew her nose again.

I knew this was coming from deeper wounds, from a family in which she felt like a third wheel to her parents' independent lifestyle.

"And Adam, and we're awesome."

She laughed through her tears. "Yeah, I guess you are pretty awesome."

"Are you sure that Wes guy didn't do anything?"

"No, he was fine. I've had worse. And after seeing Stan this morning, it just made it hit home all the more."

It was right there and then that I, Tess McGee, decided to step up to a challenge, for once. A cunning plan stirred within my brain. It was called Operation Mend Stan. I wouldn't voice my genius; Ellie was still pretty raw and needed some time. I had also seen the hurt and anger in Stan's eyes last night; he could poker face his feelings all he liked, but I knew he would still be angry inside. I would have to proceed with caution, but I knew it was the way to go.

After pacifying Ellie and managing to sneak back into the restaurant away from Melba's scrutiny, I grabbed a heap of serviettes to take into the main bar. What met me there had me grinning from ear to ear. Sean, Ringer, Stan and Toby were all lined up along the bar, throwing beer nuts into each other's mouths.

"You do realise that unwashed, dirty old man hands have been in those nut bowls," I said.

Just as Stan caught the last flying nut he broke out into a coughing fit, spluttering as my words resonated. All eyes swung around to me. But it was Toby's broad boyish smile that really caught my attention. It soon fell into a cringe as the four of them picked up their drinks and washed the beer nuts down, with repulsed shudders. Sean pushed his beer nut bowl away with distaste.

I giggled and plonked down beside them for a spell.

"Heard any good gossip lately?"

Sean straightened. "Apparently some hot footy player is dating some pretty little waitress from the Onslow Hotel. It's quite the scandal." He winked.

My eyes widened, my blood running cold. "Really?"

Sean laughed. "Actually, I have no idea. I've been working all morning." He shrugged. "I didn't get sledged for anything."

"Give it time," Ringer said. "Good gossip needs time to grow and mature, like a fine wine."

"Or a jumper that warms with age," added Toby dryly.

I heard the cool room door fly open, and I quickly hopped off my stool and got back to something that resembled work.

I headed back to the restaurant and brushed past Chris who was carrying a slab in from out back. I paused, then slipped through the partition and turned to the boys, offering some last-minute, friendly advice.

"Remember, boys, hands off your nuts."

Chris almost lost his grip on his cargo. As I slid through and stood behind the partition I could hear the uproarious laughter; Stan had nearly choked on his beer, and I could hear someone pummeling him on the back as he coughed and fought for air. I peeked through the partition, seeing Toby's shoulders vibrating from laughter.

Shaking his head, he turned to Stan. "She is something else."

***

Chris pushed through the swinging kitchen door, spiking a lunch order docket for the Onslow Boys, something I silently resented; it was, after all, my job. Maybe he didn't like the nut comment?

Geez, what a square.

Even though it killed me, I decided to let Ellie take the meals out to them, so she could reacquaint herself with Stan. After how she behaved last night, I didn't know how the others would respond to her. They seemed pretty loyal guys. I could only hope that if Stan was alright with her, then they'd respect his wishes and take their cue from him.

And that's exactly what they did. Ellie picked up and was back to her normal self by the end of the shift. I bet guys our age wouldn't have been as mature about it.

We were on the homeward stretch when we heard the creaking of the staircase that led down to the main reception area of the restaurant. A rather seedy, sorry-looking Adam shuffled down the stairs, hair all messy, sleep still in his eyes.

"Where am I?" he croaked.

"You're not in Kansas anymore, Toto, that's for sure." Ellie looked him over with a bemused frown.

He clasped his head in his hands. "Why are you shouting?"

"What on earth did you do last night after I left?" I asked.

"Lock-in," Adam groaned.

Ellie and I looked at each other in surprise. "You mean Chris let you stay?"

"Don't sound so surprised," he snapped at me.

But I *was* surprised. Chris wouldn't let me and Ellie in a lock-in and Adam was Chris's younger, grounded, naughtier brother. He was always extra hard on him. The whole thing made no sense.

"He got me to take over the bar for a bit." Adam gingerly pulled out a chair and pressed his forehead to the tabletop.

Now this made even less sense.

"He left you in charge?" I asked, my disbelief pouring off me.

"Yes! God, is there an echo in here, or something?"

"Why would he do that?" Ellie asked.

He looked up at us as if we were deluded, and then it was like a light bulb went off in his mind – a low, painful, groggy light bulb.

"Oh, that's right, you weren't there." He buried his face in his hands and attempted to wipe the sleep from his eyes.

"Weren't there for what?" I pressed.

He lifted his head out of his hands and a huge, cheeky smile broadened across his face.

"When Angela Vickers puked all over the bar."

Whaaaaaaat?

Gold! The stuff to tell your grandchildren. Adam relayed how Angela Vickers had been dancing drunk on top of the bar. Chris had been yelling at her to get down but she just ignored him, so when he yanked her down to kick her out, she spewed all over the bar, the floor and herself.

Awesome!

Chris ended up taking her home because everyone else had been drinking. And that's when Adam stepped up to the plate. A win-win situation for all, apart from Angela. So sad!

The boys finished their counter meals and waited around until Ellie and I knocked off. Even though I was surviving on little-to-no sleep, I had never felt so alive. I washed dishes with great enthusiasm, polished silverware like a thing possessed. I noticed the same eagerness in Ellie. We both had a core focus: get the work done and start living again (between the hours of two and six).

The only person who didn't seem to be so in love with the world was Adam. He glared at us from across the room every time we made so much as a clinking noise with the cutlery.

Every time the kitchen door was pushed open, and we brought food out, he turned a deeper shade of green until he couldn't take it anymore and quickly disappeared, clawing his way pitifully back up the stairs. We didn't see him for the rest of the shift. Some catch up.

At shift's end, Ellie and I darted behind the door where we kept our bags in the restaurant section of the bar. We didn't need to talk; there was a humming undercurrent of excitement running through each of us at hearing the jukebox in the poolroom and that familiar laughter. We took turns in fixing our hair in front of the small mirror, crudely nailed to the wall. We sprayed some Illusion Impulse body spray to mask the eau de Windex and sweaty kitchen hands that we currently smelled like. We topped up our lips with strawberry Lip Smacker. I could tell Ellie was a bit apprehensive. Stan and the boys were being pleasant enough to her, which helped, but she was still embarrassed. This made me strangely happy. It was like this new Ellie, with a conscience. I liked it. Maybe Stan was rubbing off on her.

"Okay, I'm going in." Ellie breathed deeply. "Wish me luck."

"You don't need any luck." My words came out funny through my stretched lips as I applied the sweet lip balm.

I spun around but she was gone.

I had a sudden thought and delved my hands frantically into the pocket of my soiled apron, which I had hung behind the door. I sighed with relief as some small objects made chinking sounds as my fingers brushed them. My rings. I had almost forgotten to put them back on after dish duty. As I placed the gold circles back onto my fingers I heard the unmistakable blast and hiss of the steam from the coffee machine, followed by a crude coughing fit. I peeked around the door to see Uncle Eric brewing probably his ninth cup of coffee for the day.

"Ah, young Tess, just the person I was looking for!" He poured the frothy milk into his mug. "Would you like one?"

Had he just coughed all over the mugs and coffee machine? I decided to pass, and made a mental note to Spray and Wipe the coffee machine tonight.

"No thanks," I said.

"Well, come join me in the beer garden for a bit, I want to have a quick chat."

Uh oh.

Chapter Twenty-Three

My mind was reeling as I tried to think of all the possible reasons I needed to be pulled aside.

Was he unhappy with my work? Was it about hanging out in the bar after hours? Was I fired? I felt sick.

The beer garden was a grapevine-infested Amazonian jungle, dotted with tiki torches and picnic tables. A rather exotic refuge if I didn't readily associate it with Uncle Eric's passive chain smoking. It was his own kind of sanctuary; where he sat with his coffee, paper and cigarettes when the day allowed him to get away from the bar. A place where he and his poker buddies sat in the evening, gambling and smoking cigars.

A brick BBQ and vine-covered gazebo sat in the corner and was a nice space, even though the area needed a desperate blower-vac. Today was slow and calm with Chris covering in the bar, while Uncle Eric led me out to his refuge at an umbrella-decked table with his coffee in hand.

The day was warming up, but I wasn't sure if it was truly hot or if it was my nerves that made me flush as I took a chair opposite Uncle Eric.

"You enjoy working here, Tess?" He tapped a cigarette from his pack.

I gave it a brief thought; I guess I did, now that I thought of it. I was both pleased and surprised by this revelation. I seemed to have found my feet now, even knew what I was doing … kind of.

But why was he asking? I squirmed in my seat. Maybe I wasn't doing as well as I thought; maybe Chris had reported back one of my earlier calamities.

"Relax, Tess," Uncle Eric chuckled. "Don't look so worried. I hope you enjoy working here, you've been a real asset to our staff."

My shoulders slumped with relief.

"Thanks, I really do like working here. It was a bit hard in the beginning when I was trying to get my head around things, but I like to think I'm not making too many mistakes."

"You can't learn if you don't make mistakes." He flicked his ash in the ashtray. "You seem to fit in very well."

I smiled. It was nice to hear these things.

"You seem to get along well with Chris's friends."

My smile slipped a little. "Yeah, they've been really nice to me."

He took a deep drag of his cigarette. "They're good boys."

His gaze then flicked to mine. "Sean Murphy is a particular fan of yours, I hear."

My smile was all but gone, and I could feel the colour drain from my face.

Flicking another ash, he sighed. "There's not much that gets past me, Tess, there isn't much a publican isn't privy to. Though I don't tend to listen to much idle gossip, when something concerns me, I listen. I'm not going to give you a fatherly lecture, or pull the boss card on you, Tess. I just want you to be careful. I know that this is your first job and it's all new and exciting. But these boys, these young men," he corrected, "however nice they may be, well, they'll have different expectations compared to the high school boys you're accustomed to. They won't settle for hand holding for long, and I don't want you to feel pressured into anything you may regret. Not on my watch."

"You don't have to worry, Uncle Eric, we're just friends. It's not like that."

"I see the way you and Ellie look at the boys. I don't expect you all to be saints, I just don't want to see anyone hurt, or do something they'll regret. You're a good girl, Tess. I wouldn't want anyone to take advantage of that."

I'm sure in years to come I would look back at this and be grateful for his concern, but right at that very instant I was looking for the closest way to escape. He must have sensed my unease because he allowed me a reprieve.

"So I'll see you back here at six, then?"

I nodded with my best 'nothing weird just happened' smile.

"Thanks, Uncle Eric, see you later."

I shot to my feet and as I was nearly home free, he said, "Tess?"

I paused, cautiously turning at my name.

"If you need to speak about anything, me or Claire are always happy to listen."

I wanted to die.

There was a certain amount of discomfort from having your boss assume you were having sex when you weren't *actually* having sex. Now every time Uncle Eric looked at me, I knew that was somewhere in his head, and that idea freaked me out. The only thing that would get me through the evening shift was the fact that Uncle Eric retired early, otherwise it would have been Mission Avoid Uncle Eric's Knowing Eyes.

I entered the poolroom like a zombie, perching on a bar stool next to Ellie.

"What's wrong?" she asked.

"Oh, nothing. I'm just tired. I might head home, catch up on some sleep before tonight."

After all the buildup and enthusiasm for knocking off to hang with the Onslow Boys, all of a sudden I didn't want to be anywhere near them. If that was what Uncle Eric was thinking, what would others be? When Sean had defended me against Scott, I thought it was heroic, awe inspiring; to be honest, a bit of a joke. But now the news had travelled and to, of all people, my boss, it somehow didn't seem so funny anymore. I felt ill.

As a group of tourists flooded the poolroom, I took the opportunity to sneak away. I didn't even speak to Toby or the boys. Ellie said she wanted to stay a bit longer, her nervous gaze constantly flitting to Stan. I nodded, distracted, as Uncle Eric's mortifying words repeated through my mind.

***

Walking through the front bar as I started the evening shift, my gaze instinctively turned towards the poolroom. Surprisingly, I spotted Sean, alone at the bar. He wasn't often on his own so I jumped at the opportunity to give him the heads up on what was going around.

I hadn't anticipated how hilarious he'd find it. Sean's entire body convulsed in spasmodic fits of thigh-slapping laughter.

I glared at him.

He wiped away tears and fought to catch his breath. Chris walked through from the main bar, casting a curious gaze from Sean to me.

"What's so funny?"

"I think I'm to expect a heart to heart with your uncle soon, Chris." Sean saluted him with his beer. "I can't wait."

I rolled my eyes. "You're seriously demented, you know that, right?"

"Maybe we should get Unc to chaperone us like in the olden days, he could walk ten paces behind us while we take a turn in the garden."

He was loving every minute of this.

"Or better yet …" I leaned closer. "My dad can escort you to a shallow grave in the Perry Ranges, because if he finds out, that is going to be a far more probable outcome."

"If who finds out what?" Stan said, as he and Toby walked through the poolroom door.

My heart leapt at the sight of them. I hadn't even heard the door open. Stan was in his usual good humour, but Toby looked between Sean and me in guarded silence.

It made me uneasy; aside from the small exchange this afternoon over the beer nuts, we hadn't spoken at all since the ranges. Now there was not so much as a hello; he didn't say it, so I didn't say it.

Since Sean had been alone in the bar, I'd figured Toby must have had better things to do tonight. But here he was, flicking his wallet out of his back pocket and ordering a beer, looking better than ever. Tonight he'd opted for jeans and a Pink Floyd T-shirt under an open black and white checked shirt; his hair was still damp from the shower and glistening from a little carefree product application. It probably took him only seconds to arrange it into its gorgeously disheveled state. It was sexy. He walked behind me to settle on a stool, and the fragrance of his aftershave made me want to press closer, but I had to control myself. Even if I did want to squeal and jump up and down clapping like a wind-up monkey with brass symbols for hands.

"Oh nothing, just some trouble in paradise." Sean winked and gave me a wicked smile.

It was nice that he found it all so amusing, but I'd been serious about my dad not being happy. I didn't even dare let on that I was spending most of my days with a group of men (though young ones). There was no way he or Mum would approve.

I shrugged and gathered the last of the empty pots and pints on my way to the kitchen.

"It's your funeral."

I gave Toby a wide berth as I headed back to the kitchen. Though I was over the moon to see him, I didn't want him to think that he was in any way obligated to take me home after work. This spur-of-the-moment bet was starting to seriously backfire, and I wished that I'd never made it, or at best that I'd let him win. I would have made him his damn pies and that would have been the end of it. Maybe now he'd be greeting me with a smile instead of this weird silence. I may not have acknowledged him, but it's not like he acknowledged me. Ha!

Geez. And I was critical of Ellie's mind games. Could it be that I was playing my own? Either way, I'd told myself on the way back up Coronary Hill this afternoon that the next time I saw Toby Morrison I would play it cool, and that was exactly what I'd done. I just didn't expect him to do it, too, and so well.

Chapter Twenty-Four

Tonight Onslow hosted its famous annual Summer Show.

There were food stalls that sold hotdogs, fairy floss, kebabs and Danish pancakes; there were craft stalls with handmade jewelry, tie-dye clothing and knitted blankets and toys that smelt like lavender and old ladies. Come midnight, fireworks filled the night sky, casting a glorious reflection over Lake Onslow.

Everyone in Onslow and the surrounding regions flocked to these events. It broke the monotony of daily life in these sleepy towns, and got everyone together. For me, it had mostly been worth going because every year I had been guaranteed to spot Toby.

This year, I'd hoped it would be different, that I wouldn't be mooning over Toby from a distance.

Ellie and I didn't even manage to break out a sweat in the evening shift, only a handful of meals for the regulars and a few touristy blow-ins for drinks. Yet with so little to do, I hadn't even noticed the bar empty out. Without even a goodbye, the Onslow Boys were gone. So much for me not caring. Chris didn't seem to care about missing out on the show. I suppose he wasn't exactly a show bag kind of guy. Still, I would have thought he would at least want to hang out with his friends.

I did my best not to openly whine about my reluctance to be at work. I didn't want to be that girl, but being next to Ellie's increasingly enthusiastic nature (it seemed things were back on track and she'd made amends when I slipped out between shifts) tended to drag me down further. I delivered a meal to a couple enjoying the sunset on an outside table. My heart ached as I could hear the distant beat of music, laughter and screams from the show. It taunted me. I had never missed a Summer Show. Ever. Sadly, there was a first time for everything.

I had just hoped it wouldn't have been this summer. So far, my holidays had wildly exceeded all my low, low expectations, not to mention confused me more than ever. And now I was angry, angry at being stuck here, angry at Ellie's happiness, at Toby for the effect he had on me.

I would be stuck working until midnight, probably witnessing the fireworks on the front porch of the Onslow (if I was lucky), in my smoke-infused work clothes. Ellie was miffed about it, too, but was pacified by checking her mobile every possible chance behind the staff room door. She would smile and giggle and sigh with every incoming message. Stan.

Ellie would no doubt meet up with him after work, he would come and pick her up, and hopefully offer to take me home so I could go to bed and dream about the things that were a joke to think I could have.

By eleven I was wiping down the last of the kitchen benches; I wasn't able to hear the distant screams from the show, which I was happy about. I was about to throw myself in the fires of hell when I took it upon myself to grab a bucket and dust pan and clean out the open fireplace in the front bar. I moved the fireguard and was about to get on all fours when a voice startled me.

"We have a cleaner that does that."

Chris leaned against the bar, his arms crossed, gaze transfixed on the mute TV. Was he watching *Grease*?

"Well I wish you had've told me that when I was scrubbing the kitchen floor."

Chris shrugged. "She's no spring chicken, you did her a favour."

"Yeah, well, I don't think this fireplace has been cleaned out since 1974."

"You can do it if you want, I just thought you'd have preferred to head down to the show."

I froze mid-sweep, studying his emotionless face as he watched Olivia Newton John sing 'Hopelessly devoted to you'.

"Oh, um, does that mean that ..."

He sighed. "Knock off, Tess, it's dead tonight. Go and enjoy yourself."

"Ellie, too?" I all but squealed.

"Do you honestly think I could stop her? Go!"

I returned the fireguard quick smart, doubling back to the kitchen to dump the cleaning supplies. Ellie was sitting on the kitchen bench with her mobile when I burst through the door.

"Think you can get us a lift?"

My mood had lifted (as any person's would for early release on their sentence for good behaviour).

The show turnout was huge, bigger than last year. I had felt the giddiness of what it was like to go to the show, but this year it wasn't for show bags, water fights, or rides. This year I just wanted to hang out with fun people. The very people we now pulled up next to. Stan parked next to a huge convoy of utes and cars lined up along the edge of trees opposite the main strip. It looked like a Show and Shine inspection except the cars weren't anything special and just had a bunch of people hanging out, like they did every year. I remembered always looking over at the older crowd that lurked along this strip and thinking, wow! They were out of school, had jobs, drove cars and were *so cool*. Now here I was, climbing out of Stan's Hilux, about to infiltrate the gang.

"Well, look who finally made it." Sean was perched on the edge of a ute; everyone turned to witness our arrival. A sea of inquisitive eyes rested on us, but there were two sets in particular that made me wish I had been dropped off at home instead.

Toby's unreadable gaze and Angela's murderous one.

Angela was wrapped around Toby like one of those anacondas you see on the Discovery Channel. Seriously, she was going to give him a neck injury. I had to pretend like they weren't there, that I had no interest in their presence. Yeah, that would be best.

I, the third wheel, broke away from Ellie and Stan who had managed to not unlink their hands since exiting the car. I made my way over to prop myself next to Sean on the ute tray, the only friendly face I knew.

"How was work?" He nudged me with his shoulder.

"Dull and long."

"You missed me that much?" Sean grinned.

Rolling my eyes, I said, "So what have all the cool kids been up to?"

"Oh, you know, leaning on cars trying to look cool. It's exhausting."

"I think the problem is that you're just not doing the lean right?"

He curved his brow at me. "Is that so?"

"Yeah, you have to give it more elbow action, perhaps the odd bobbing of the head to an imaginary beat."

"Like this?" He propped his elbow on the edge of the ute for the cool casual lean and then bobbed his head in an over-the-top fashion that made me giggle.

I grimaced. "You look like you have a nervous tic."

"Ha! A *cool* nervous tic." Our laughter broke off at the slamming of a car door. Toby's car door.

"Are we going to the Point?" Toby seemed impatient when he spoke. Snappy. Sean jumped off the tray and stretched, revealing a flash of muscled stomach in the dark.

"Okey dokey." Sean groaned mid-stretch.

"Did you just say okey dokey? Is that the lingo for yesterday's generation?" I teased.

"Yesterday's? Youch! So what should I be saying? 'Like, whatever dude!'" He drew it out like an American surfer boy.

"Now you just sound like a Teenage Mutant Ninja Turtle." I shook my head, my legs swinging from the tray. The engine to Toby's ute roared to life as he revved the accelerator an impatient two, three times.

"Any day now, Murph." Toby adjusted his mirror in agitation. Angela was busying herself by looking in the reflection of her side mirror, pouting and fixing her lip balm.

Sean turned to me, offering me a hand off the edge of the tray. "We're all heading up to the Point to watch the fireworks, you wanna come?"

Stan broke away from nuzzling Ellie's neck. "Best seats in the house."

"Okay, cool."

We all piled into Stan's car, Sean in the front passenger seat, Ellie and I in the back. Half a dozen other cars followed as we left the Show behind and made our way out of Onslow, over McLean's Bridge and up into the Perry Ranges. Toby's car was directly behind ours and the last in the long line weaving up the hills. Our windows wound down, the hot summer night whipped through our hair. Stan navigated the turns like a rally driver, and I tried not to think of the increasing drop on my left as we climbed higher and higher. Instead, I kept turning to see if Toby's headlights were visible; his car was close enough behind us for me to see their silhouettes but not close enough to make out faces. No doubt Angela was burning a hole in the back of my head.

It was then I saw the flicker of Toby's indicator. He turned into a side track, marked by a sign I couldn't make out.

"Oooh, looks like someone has their own fireworks in mind," laughed Sean, looking in his side mirror.

"Where are they going? Should we wait?"

Stan peered into the review mirror. "They're heading to the Falls."

My stomach plummeted. Everyone knew about the Falls. There was only one reason anyone went to the Falls of a night time, and it wasn't to see the impressive waterfall that flowed into a series of natural pools. It was a parking hot spot. If you wanted to socialise, make out, watch fireworks, you went to the Point. If you wanted privacy, you went to the Falls.

"I doubt they will be gracing us with their presence this evening," Sean half laughed.

"No wonder Toby seemed so toey," added Stan.

I stopped looking back; instead, I focused on the back of Sean's seat.

That was that, then. I convinced myself that it should be a relief. I didn't have to waste my time with romantic fantasies, by analysing every look Toby gave me, every touch. That was that. The last nail in the coffin. Absolute closure.

Ellie reached for my hand in the darkness and gave it a squeeze of silent support. It was then I felt the ache in my heart, the churning of my stomach. I breathed deeply to control the emotion that threatened to well. If this was a good thing, then why did it hurt so bad?

Chapter Twenty-Five

The fireworks were spectacular, something to truly behold and remember for all of our lives.

Or that's what I guessed, since I hadn't paid any attention or cared in the slightest. The rest of the evening went by in a blur of self-pity. I should have gotten Stan to take me home straight after work, but no, that would have delayed the inevitable, no matter how much it hurt. I guess I needed to see it. See Toby's indicator flash through the darkness and his ute peel away.

After the fireworks display, and what felt like an agonisingly long time of forced socialising, me, Ellie and Stan mercifully wound back down the hill again. Sean decided to stay on at the Point because apparently the night was young. He had tried to convince me to stay but all I wanted to do was take my sorry self home and fall into a coma for the rest of the summer. Stan's phone had beeped with a message while he drove but he couldn't look because it was in his back pocket. We pulled up at my house, and I said my goodbyes and dragged myself up the garden path. I was at the front door when Stan yelled out to me.

"Tess, wait!" He was frowning at his mobile screen. I was about to shush him when he held his phone out to me and said, "This is for you, it's from Toby."

I dropped my bag and practically tripped over my own feet as I quickstepped back to the car, suddenly not giving a damn if Stan woke the entire neighborhood. I grasped the car windowsill and tried not to look desperate, but I wasn't pulling it off too well.

"What does it say?" I asked, trying to keep my breathing even.

Stan passed the message to Ellie; he squinted, struggling to read it. Ellie held it up to the overhead light. She winced and her sad eyes turned up to me, her smile pained.

"He wants you to bring your bike into the shop tomorrow, so he can fix it."

I snatched the phone from her hand. It did say that, but Ellie had left out the last detail.

So I can get it out of the way.

You know how I said that the turnoff to the Falls was a last nail in the coffin? I was wrong. Fixing my bike was it. He would fulfill his end of the bargain and get me and my bike out of his way. I had been half tempted to get Stan to text back, 'whatever, never mind', but then I thought, No! I would take the moral high ground.

To prove even further that I had no-hard-feelings-let's-be-friends, I chucked in my own deal. I spent the portion of the next morning at the Rose Café making pies. Much to my mum and dad's surprise, I negotiated some hours helping them out at the shop if I could make up some pies. Mum and Dad kept casting me wary looks as if there was some alien creature in their kitchen. I suppose there was.

"So what are you going to do with the pies?" Mum asked.

"My bike is getting fixed today; it's a kind of payment, a little thank you."

"How very Dr Quinn Medicine Woman of you; sure they don't want to trade for eggs and chickens?" Dad laughed.

I just glared at him as I rolled the pastry with my pin.

"And they're okay with that?" Mum frowned.

"Yes, it's all sorted. Apparently your pies are quite the hit among many."

Mum straightened with pride.

'Well, I have a new recipe. We should try it."

I held up my hand. "No, Mum, it has to be made by me, and I'm doing the Summer Berry pie deal."

I had watched my mum make these pies a hundred, maybe a thousand times, so I was confident in being able to replicate the same crisp, sweet, sugary flavour. I made four large ones in total.

Three were Summer Berry marked with a pastry 'O' for Onslow Boys, and one was baked with a 'T' for Apple and Rhubarb pie. Toby's favourite. I didn't want to take so much pleasure in making something for Toby. I wanted to slap myself for lovingly painting the egg wash on the T with a smile. Until reality flashed back in the form of that flicking indicator that changed everything.

Dad had offered to give me and the bike a lift into town, but it was not an overly hot day. The walk was so calm and peaceful until I made it to the main strip and that peace turned into sweaty-palmed anxiety as I approached Matthew & Son. Hopefully Toby was out and I could just handball my bike to his dad and then hightail it out of there.

No such luck. The radio was blaring with the Eagles and the shop was empty aside from a pair of unmistakable legs that lay under an old, metallic blue Kingswood, one foot tapping to the beat. A muffled voice sang and whistled from under the car. I coughed and rang my bike bell and the voice froze. In one fluid motion Toby wheeled himself out from under the car, casting a winning smile that flashed brilliantly white against his grease stained face. It was the smile that caught me off guard, the one I certainly didn't expect to see greeting me. Talk about four seasons in one day; one minute he would be all smiles and joking, the next I couldn't even get a hello.

I tilted my head to the music. "What, no Glen Campbell?"

It was a universally known fact that if you passed by Matthew & Son, you would always hear Glen Campbell from the stereo.

His smile broadened. "Not on my watch." He maneuvered his way to his feet and wiped the excess grease off his hands onto a cloth.

"Well, you knew I was coming, so I guess I'll never truly know."

He crooked his finger and motioned me to follow him. I leaned my bike on the steel pole in the middle of the room and went with Toby into the office. It was a small, paper-infested space with a map-filled cork board and empty boxes piled in the corner from incoming parts orders.

Bills were spiked and clipboards with scrawled details were racked. Toby opened a filing cabinet stacked with cassettes. He grabbed one and held it out to me. I smiled. Glen Campbell's *Greatest Hits*.

"I knew it."

"Right." He took it from me and placed it back in its slot, and picking up its case, he showed me the inscription on the side. 'Matthew Morrison' was written in thick black texta.

"Dad's stash." He placed it down, picking up the next box. "Mike's God-awful stash." Sure enough, 'Michael Morrison' was inscribed on the side. He then picked up the last box, raising his brows. "My stash."

I eyed him warily as I checked out the spines of the tapes. The Beatles, The Eagles, Credence; sure enough, no Campbell.

"Still quite the mature-aged selection," I mused.

"I like to think of myself as an old soul."

I picked up a cassette I wasn't familiar with. "Sam Cooke?"

Toby's face lit up as he took it from me. "Ah, now he is an absolute favourite, you've probably heard this in my car." He looked at me expectantly.

I bit my lip in deep thought.

Toby shook his head. "You don't know who Sam Cooke is?"

I grimaced. "Maybe if I heard him …"

Toby ejected the Eagles cassette, popped in Sam Cooke and pressed play. A melodious tune oozed out of the speakers and I instantly recognised it as the song that had played when Toby had driven me home from Horseshoe Bend.

The wind flapping around the cabin, Toby's bicep flexed with tension at the wheel. The awkward side-smiles at one another in our first real encounter together. The first time we were alone.

Sam Cooke was singing through the stereo about a cupid casting its bow, and I was lost with the wonder of his beautiful voice.

Our trance was broken by an incoming whistle to the tune, and Toby's dad entered the office, pausing in surprise at the sight of me.

"Oh, hello."

"Ah, Dad, this is Tess."

"Hi, Tess." He shook my hand with vigour; I could feel the roughened calluses from years of labour.

"So what are you kids up to?"

Toby squirmed uncomfortably, it seemed no matter how old you got, there was a universal trend: parents were put on this earth to embarrass. But I didn't think Toby's dad was embarrassing, he was friendly, and charming. He had laugh lines in all the right places with dark blond hair and tanned skin. You wouldn't have automatically thought them father and son but then Matthew Morrison smiled and suddenly there was no mistaking the link.

"We were just discussing Toby's love for Glen Campbell." I smiled sweetly. Toby laser beamed his gaze into mine, silently imploring me to be quiet.

Matthew's brows raised in surprise. "Really?"

"Mm hmm." I nodded.

"He is the best!" Matthew added excitedly. "Guess all those years with Glen Campbell playing at home finally paid off. I knew you'd come around, son." He patted Toby on the shoulder. Toby looked pained.

"Why, on his sixth birthday we bought him a cowboy suit and he used to ride around the yard on his stick pony."

"Right." Toby snatched the cassette cover out of my hand. "Time to go." He ushered me towards the office door.

I had to laugh. "Nice to meet you, Mr Morrison."

"Please call me Matthew." He tilted his head and smiled.

I grabbed the edge of the door, buying some time as Toby pushed me forward.

"Well, Matthew, I would really love to learn the rest of that story someday."

Matthew rubbed his lightly whiskered chin. "I dare say I can even drag out some old photos." He winked.

"Oh, now that I would love to see."

"Out!" Toby grabbed my hand from the doorframe.

Back in the garage, I grabbed my bike and brought it forward for inspection, but I was more keen to unveil my prized pies.

I wheeled the bike over. "I brought you a present."

Toby looked over the bike, looking not in the least bit excited.

I rolled my eyes. "In the basket."

This only resulted in a curved brow of skeptical interest as he lifted up the blanket over the basket as if he were expecting a striking cobra to rear up.

"No you didn't ..." He ripped the white and red check cloth from the top.

"Freshly made this morning by yours truly." I beamed.

He cocked his head as he noticed the pastry initials.

"Oh, um, these are the Summer Berries. 'O' is for Onslow Boys." I blushed. "And 'T' is for ... well, it's your favourite Rhubarb and Apple."

He looked into the basket with a deep affection as if it housed a litter of fluffy kittens. He looked up at me.

"You didn't have to do that, you know."

I shrugged. "I know."

We looked at one another for a long moment, and then all of a sudden the speaker dipped and stopped and Sam Cooke was playing again, crooning out 'You send me'. Toby's gaze quickly darted down, with what I thought was a blush.

I mentally slapped myself for getting carried away. I was here so he could fix my bike, and the deal would be finished and there would be no more obligations to one another; he now had pie so all was fair. It was then I noticed Toby had looked back at me.

"What?"

He frowned, making me feel uneasy. He stepped closer looking at the side of my face.

"Keep still."

I froze "What?!"

"Don't panic, you just have a little something." He reached out and wiped his finger down my cheek.

"There."

The penny dropped as I saw his face break into a cheesy grin. I walked to peer into the side mirror of the nearest car to find a long, black streak down my cheek and Toby trying not to drop my bike as he laughed, waving his dirty hand at me.

"Oldest trick in the book."

I rubbed my cheek. "Almost as old as your taste in music."

"Right, that's it." Toby leaned the bike next to the car and held out his greasy hands to grab me.

I ran, squealing. "Toby, don't!"

I reached the safety of the street outside and Toby paused in the archway.

I wiped my cheek vigorously. "Is it gone?"

Toby shrugged with a devious smirk on his face. "Guess you'll never know, just like the Onslow Boys are never going to know about those pies."

I gasped. "I am so going to tell them."

He shook his head. "I have your bike for ransom now."

"You're a cold-hearted man, Toby Morrison."

Toby leaned against the doorframe, arms crossed as he looked me squarely in the eye. It was unnerving, as if he was peering all the way deep inside me, into my soul. All of a sudden he wasn't smiling anymore; his whole demeanour had sobered.

"So I have been told," he said in all seriousness, and with that he straightened, uncrossed his arms and turned and walked back inside, leaving me in the street, breathless and confused.

Chapter Twenty-Six

To keep my mind busy, and to the utter shock of my parents, I offered my services to the Rose Café' from Mondays to Thursdays.

I know, right? I just couldn't take lying on my bed being in my head all day. Or worse, hanging with the Onslow Boys. With Toby and Angela.

Once over their own shock, Mum and Dad had agreed wholeheartedly and even insisted I was paid properly and everything. Looks like that top I had been eyeing off wasn't so far away, after all. It was good to be there, we all liked it. Over summer, the peak tourist season, I usually rarely got to see my parents at all.

And it's not like I had anything better to do. Ellie started spending her every waking moment with Stan. Adam had headed back to his nan's in the City.

It wasn't until Thursday afternoon at the café that I saw a familiar six-foot-three figure at the counter, peering into the glass cabinet. He was wearing his navy work shirt and pants and an impressively fluorescent orange safety vest, with reflective trimming.

I walked up slowly. "I'm sorry, sir, but I'm afraid your attire is in a serious colour clash with our décor."

He turned abruptly with a surprised smile. "McGee!"

"Murphy!"

"What are you doing here?"

"I work here Monday to Thursdays."

"Two jobs? You put us all to shame."

"No I think that fluro vest ensemble puts you to shame."

I walked around the counter to grab an order docket. "So I have to ask. Did you happen to receive a pie this week?"

Sean looked at me blankly.

"A Summer Berry pie?"

Still nothing. I shook my head. "Unbelievable, you wait 'til I see that Toby Morrison."

A spark of recognition flickered in his grey-blue eyes.

"If you are referring to a parcel I received at work containing a crust of a pie with a note saying, 'Tess made us pie. It was delicious', then, yes, I received a secondhand portion of pie."

My jaw fell open. “That is so mean. The pies were meant to be for all of you.”

“Pies? Plural?”

I told him about the pies I had lovingly made from scratch and instead of being mad, Sean laughed, scratching his chin.

“Right! Well, I guess this means war.”

“Uh oh!”

“It’s been a long-standing Murphy-Morrison tradition, war has,” he said. “It was his turn for payback. Now it’s my turn. I’m going to have to have a think about the next one. However long it takes.”

“Riiight, okay,” I said, “well, I’m not getting involved. I don’t want my bike mailed back to me in pieces.”

“Fair enough.” Sean went back to studying the contents of the glass cabinet. I watched him as he chose. His cheek dimpled for a second and was gone again. It was an unexpected delight each time he smiled, but he wasn’t really a smiler, more like a wicked grinner. He looked older than twenty-two, but maybe that was because he was so filled out, so muscular, that it made it hard not to ogle him. His short-cropped hair made it hard to decipher what colour it was, probably brown. He wasn’t beautiful like Toby, but he was handsome.

“Why don’t you have a girlfriend, Sean?”

Had I said that out loud?

He leaned on the counter studying me like a bug under a microscope.

I blushed, flustered. “Sorry, that’s rude, it’s just I don’t understand why you wouldn’t.”

He nodded. “Because of my dynamic personality and my freakishly handsome good looks?”

“Never a serious answer with you, is there?”

His mouth curved at the corners, and he adjusted the serviette dispenser on the counter. “I don’t know, why don’t you have a boyfriend?”

It was my turn to fidget under scrutiny. “Guess I just haven’t found the right one yet.”

A moment passed between us of mutual understanding. It was nice. It felt like I was connecting with Sean for the first –

Mum sidled up alongside me and pretended to look at something on the cash register. Typical Mum move. She stared at the register with a look of fierce concentration, a scowl that didn’t lift when she rose her gaze to Sean and held it there. Oh my God … what had she heard?

Then I remembered that I wasn’t at the Onslow. Any fun, harmless bantering (if not borderline flirting) with an older boy wouldn’t be looked on kindly by my bosses here.

How much had she seen?

“Tess, honey, why don’t you jump on the coffee machine and fix table five some cappuccinos for me, please. I’ll serve this young man.”

Mum handed me a docket from her apron pocket. In other words, get away from my daughter. Yeah she’d been listening alright.

Sean’s Adam’s apple bobbed as he swallowed.

I would prepare myself for twenty questions later.

I made my way towards the opposite counter and started work on table five's cappucinos. Funny, considering my early fear of this apparatus, I now fancied myself quite the barista extraordinaire. I even went so far as to make quaint little shapes with a shake of the cocoa powder dust. No wonder my parents looked at me suspiciously. What had I become?

After serving Sean, Mum came over all smiles, an enigma of easy going. I knew she wasn't feeling easy going, and I knew what was coming next.

"So who was that?" This was just the beginning of my interrogation. I supplied the details she could handle, but failed to mention that Sean and his friends were a big part of my extra-curricular activities. I also failed to mention that Ellie was dating Stan Remington, or that Toby Morrison himself was fixing my bike. I knew if I gave my mother too much information she would piece it all together and draw her own conclusion.

Men-drinking-taking-advantage-teenage-pregnancy-*game-over*! My parents were prone to jumping to this conclusion. I think they were overrating my effect on the opposite sex.

So I played it down and soon she was partially satisfied, got bored and gave up, leaving me with a sceptical, wary 'I'm-not-thoroughly-convinced' look on her face as she put table seven's croissant in the toaster.

As November merged into December, Christmas-party season was well underway and the Rose Café had been booked for the local doctor's surgery shindig on Friday. Mum and Dad had pleaded for me to help and said they would make it financially worth my while so I couldn't exactly say no. Besides, I knew how busy it was and rushed off their feet they were. It's not like I wasn't going to get anything out of it: it was money and, not to mention, sure to score me some brownie points with the olds.

And it was just one night; what's one night in the grand scheme of things? I mentally chided myself any time my heart ached about not seeing Toby. I had to stop myself from thinking that way. He didn't belong to me; he was well and truly Angela's.

Although I could have sworn there were times when something passed between us – looks, touches, even the gaps in conversation.

When we sat in his car at the Point that night, I thought that maybe, just maybe, for the smallest of moments that he felt what I felt.

Argh! I was thinking about Toby again! Maybe a night away from the Onslow social scene would do me some good. Let them converge on the hotel without me.

I knew Ellie would be there because when she called me she whinged and whined incessantly about the fact I had to work.

"But it's Friday." The horrified words travelled through the phone receiver.

"I know, but I promised."

I then used my skills of deflection and switched the subject to Stan. Worked like a charm. Apparently, they were going to the hotel to hang out, and then the group would head up to the Point. Relief washed over me, because witnessing Angela and Toby together was definitely not my idea of a good time.

"Come on, Tess, at least come to the Point with us after, you'll be finished by then, surely."

No. *No*. I would take a stand. One night off. Surely I could manage that.

Chapter Twenty-Seven

Ellie wouldn't exactly miss me in the company of Stan; no one else really existed in their sickeningly loved-up little world.

I was tired of seeing their constant displays of public affection, the kissing and cuddling and hand holding. Tired and envious of it. There were no emails from Ellie with updates of Friday night shenanigans when I checked on Saturday morning; no text messages, either. Yep, Ellie was off the radar alright. She had a boyfriend. It wasn't official as such, yet, but I knew the pattern: when Ellie was unreachable, she was happily lost in Boyfriend Land. Someone who I knew was definitely not in Girlfriend Land (more so Nana Land), was Adam. He was proving to be an excellent pen pal.

To: tessmcgee

Kill me now! Seriously!

I am set to go on a shopping expedition to Central Plaza tomorrow with Nan and Aunty Claire. You know what that means? Hours spent at Millers, Lincraft, Spotlight, oohing and aahing over the feel of fabric. And gossiping over gluten free cake, over how Mum should be more independent and how she's getting too skinny on her latest Weight Watchers obsession. And then I'll be forced to have a haircut that I don't need at one of those 'Just Cuts' sweat shops. I am predicting at least 8 hours of hell. But I don't need to complain. How is working for the parentals? I must say I'm not sure how I feel about all this work caper.

OMG Tess. Are you changing?? Remember you have to let me know.

Sender: Adam I can jump puddles Henderson

To: Adam I can jump puddles Henderson

I have changed! I am rolling in the $$ now, so I can go to large shopping complexes and ooh and ahh over the feel of fabrics.

Do you want to come? Ohh that's right…you're 'busy'.

Shame you can't come home this weekend. There is a Cricket Club disco in the beer garden tonight. (So I have been told via a blunt voice message from your brother) Which means Chris and Uncle Eric will be running around stressed and snappy as they try and set things up. Oh yay!

I saw your mum the other day, she hasn't lost too much weight she looks fantastic! Do I sense a bit of the green eyed monster in Aunty Claire? (Don't repeat that)

Sender: tessmcgee

To: tessmcgee

I am so going to repeat that.

Sender: Adam I can jump puddles Henderson

I smiled to myself, shook my head and logged off. I was not relishing the thought of this afternoon's shift back at the Onslow. I predicted chaos. Chris would be in a foul mood, snapping at everyone, and I'd be exposed to plumber's crack from Uncle Eric as, ciggie hanging from his mouth, he tried to connect extension cords. Melba would be muttering under her breath and Rosanna wigging out over bookings. It would be like Irish weekend, but worse.

On the plus side, I had never felt so rich. Mum and Dad had given me a rather healthy pay packet which I'd sat on my bed and counted over and over again. After finding out about the disco, I thought, what better way to treat the hard-working woman in me than with a shopping spree.

I hitched a ride into town with Mum, and I couldn't help but stare at Matthew & Son as we drove by. The lights were off and the garage doors were pulled down. I didn't have much time before I had to get ready for work, but managed to stock up on moisturiser, lip balm, some make-up and Impulse spray. I made a quick dash to Carter's to finally buy that top I'd been mooning over all summer. The top I had tried on a hundred times. The top I loved, the top that was GONE.

I frantically flicked through the racks; maybe someone moved it? No-no-no. I asked the peroxided, bubblegum-chewing shop assistant if there was another one in stock. She shrugged. "Sorry hon. What's there is there, must have sold it."

I trudged slowly out of the shop. *I would not cry over a top.*

I would, however, be severely depressed and moody for the rest of the day. My heart wasn't into shopping anymore and I slumped myself back to the car for Mum to take me home. Ellie had texted me to say that she was going to be late and not to wait for her. She was no doubt just crawling out of bed after a late night rendezvous with Stan.

Whatever.

When Mum dropped me at work, it was exactly as I'd expected: chaos. But it was good chaos. I walked through the beer garden entrance expecting to find nothing good. Instead, I was amazed. The dance floor was prepped, the DJ station in place and a man was working on the lighting. There was no shouting, or bum crack, it all looked rather under control.

I swooped down on some dirty dishes (probably from Uncle Eric's breakfast) and made my way to the kitchen.

Amy was sitting on the bench swinging her legs, seemingly in a good mood. Until she saw me. Her smile vanished, and she glared at me in her usual death stare I'd grown accustomed to. Talk about holding a grudge. Beside her, Melba peeled carrots and Chris leaned casually against the bench, his hip cocked and arms crossed. Rosanna was flailing around the kitchen in her usual flurry of insanity.

"I mean it, Chris, this kitchen is getting shut down at nine pm sharp! My kid's sitter charges like an asshole a minute after that, and I will not be taking a single order after nine."

I wasn't completely sure what an asshole charged, but it made me smile. I did find

Rosannaisms quite funny when they weren't directed at me.

I took the initiative of filling the sink up and making a start on the mess from breakfast. Plus, I didn't mind making Amy look bad; that was a small part of it.

"Don't stress, Rosanna, I've got it. Nine sharp," Chris repeated.

"Anyway, I think it's only fair, we want to go to the disco, too, you know," Amy piped up.

Chris raised his eyebrows and turned to Melba. "Is that right, Melba? You hanging to bust a move on the dance floor tonight, too?"

Melba just scoffed and brushed away his words. "Oh, you."

"How about this? Kitchen shutdown at nine sharp and as long as things are shipshape here, the rest of you can knock off at ten."

I spun around. "Serious? Ten?"

Chris turned as if noticing me for the first time. "Just this once."

"Hells, yeah!" Amy screamed and swung her legs more rapidly.

"But this kitchen has to be spotless," Chris added before leaving.

"Looks like you will be busting a move after all tonight, Melbs," Rosanna teased. "Where's my drink, chook? I'm thirsty like a son of a bitch."

Amy passed Rosanna a pot of soda water which she drained in three giant gulps.

"Now, spill! Right from the start, this is some good shit." Rosanna leaned forward, her full attention directed at Amy, kitchen work forgotten now that she had negotiated her nine pm knock off. She seemed more relaxed, for now. Was that just soda water?

"What have I told you two about gossiping?" Melba said with exasperation.

Rosannna waved her off. "Oh, shush. You love it, go on, chook."

Chook's (or rather, Amy's) beady eyes swept around the kitchen, as if she was some kind of P.I, before settling into the gossip she was about to unload. Such an attention seeker, I thought, as I dipped the wok into the sink to soak.

"Okay, so I wasn't allowed to stay out to watch the fireworks (which was so unfair) and my friends were having a party at McLean's Beach, and I couldn't go because my dad's a dick and he thinks I'm, like, going to get pregnant and drink and shit."

I raised my brows as I set into scrubbing a pot. It sounded familiar, but, wow, she had a mouth on her. Either this was how fifteen-year-olds talked now, or Amy had been hanging out with Rosanna for too long.

"Anyway, I had to wait for Dad to go to sleep which took *forever*, because he never really settles until he knows everything is locked down. So, no worries, I knew the party wouldn't be cranking up 'til later, anyway. So it was real late when I climbed out onto the fire escape for my grand exit."

"I don't know if I should be hearing this." Melba frowned.

"Anyway ... that's when I heard the voices under the stairs. I was like, shit!, and ducked like a ninja. And that's when I saw movement. Two shadows talking under the stairs. I thought, ooh, gross, slobbery drunks pashing in the beer garden. So I had to get a better look, right?"

"Of course." Rosanna nodded vigorously, hanging on every word. And then I noticed – so was I. I had been working on the same plate for the last five minutes.

"But they weren't pashing, they were sitting on the bottom steps, and one of them – the girl – was crying ... like *really* crying, while the boy rubbed her back and then she looked up at him and was like, why? Why would he do that? And I was like, holy shit, I know who that is."

"Who?" Rosanna, Melba and I all asked at once.

And before Amy could deliver her climactic line, Ellie burst into the kitchen.

"Toby broke up with Angela!"

The plate slipped out of my hands and smashed into a million pieces. Ellie had solely addressed this to me with an elated spark in her eyes.

Everyone looked at me. At the china shards at my feet. At Ellie, then back to me, as if the information should have meant something to me.

Which it did.

Oh my God, it did.

Amy gave Ellie a pissy look. "You ruined my story."

"Sorry."

"So it was Angela?" Rosanna asked. "Under the stairs?"

"Yeah, and Chris," Amy continued. Apparently, the reason why Toby was moody and fidgety on the night of the Summer Show was not because he was taking Angela up to the Falls for some canoodling. He was taking her to the Falls to break up with her.

Angela had then relayed it all to Chris in between sobs in the wee hours of the morning. She had begged Chris, asking if he had known about it and why Toby would have wanted to break up with her.

"What did Chris say?" Melba was hooked like the rest of us.

Amy shrugged. "Some big speech about people growing apart and things happening for a reason. Deep shit. He was real careful not to be specific and break the bro code."

"The bro code?" I asked.

"Yeah. He would have totally known why Toby dumped Angela. Guys *do* talk. At least those ones do. Not to mention Chris is like David Bowie in that Labyrinth movie. That guy is all seeing, all knowing. Has a crystal ball or something. What he doesn't know doesn't exist. Lurks and perks of the profession I guess."

"Well, no wonder he was Angela's first point of call then," Rosanna mused.

"Your turn. What do you know?" Amy snapped at Ellie.

"Stan told me. It was an accident. I asked him who was coming to the disco tonight, and when I name dropped Toby and Angela, he had this funny look on his face; it was enough to tell me something was up. So I made him spill."

Amy gasped. "You broke the bro code?"

Ellie straightened with pride. "Guess I did."

With each placing of individual cutlery on the table, it triggered the same thing over and over in my mind.

Toby broke up with Angela – Toby broke up with Angela.

Those headlights I had watched with great interest through the back window of Stan's car, the indication to the Falls that all but broke my heart and changed everything. The text message to Stan about bringing in my bike the next day. God, he sent that after he'd broken up with Angela.

My head spun. Toby had been single when I went to the shop, when we teased each other about song choices, when he wiped grease on my cheek. He did seem more relaxed than the night before. But I would never have guessed why.

Ellie found out from Stan that the Onslow Boys, including Toby, would be in attendance tonight, but Angela had gone away for a girls'/healing weekend.

Ellie clicked her fingers in front of my face, snapping me out of my own frazzled thoughts.

She giggled. "I know what you're thinking about," she sing-songed.

I was speechless, absolutely at a loss, as I fumbled my way through the silverware.

"You know, breaking the bro code is really quite simple." She leaned forward and whispered, "You just threaten to hold off on the goods!"

"Ew! Ellie, too much information, thanks."

"I'm telling you, works like a charm." She winked. "I'll get some dirt before tonight, just giving you the heads up."

Ellie was loving this, but I was uneasy.

Obviously, the entire saga was intended to be hush-hush. And I didn't want Ellie to be too inquisitive in case Stan became suspicious.

So, Toby was a free man; that didn't change things. Maybe he wanted to be single? To be free of women, to hang with the boys.

No, it didn't change anything. I would still just be Tess. The same dorky girl getting her bike fixed.

Then why was it that during the break before the dinner shift I checked my messages every two seconds in case Ellie had an update? And I got ready three hours before my shift began, paying particular attention to every detail, ensuring everything was perfect.

I was in the shower, exfoliating, shaving, conditioning up a storm when I heard my bedroom door open.

"I'm just going to the cafe, hon; have fun at work and don't break a leg on the dance floor," my mum yelled out.

My mouth was full of toothpaste as I paused brushing.

"Bwye Murm." I heard my bedroom door close.

In a burst of steam, like a magician entering the stage, I exited the bathroom. Hair in a turbanesque twist on my head, towel wrapped around me, I froze in the doorway thinking perhaps I was seeing a mirage, that my mind was heat affected from the shower, because hooked on my mirror was the light mint top I had dreamed about for all eternity, the one that had been sold. I walked over to it, touching the soft, silky fabric to ensure it wasn't a dream. A note was clipped to the hanger.

To our hard-working daughter.

We are so proud of you.

Thanks for all your wonderful help and for being an utter joy.

Lots of Love Mum and Dad. x

P.S. Ellie helped us pick this out.

My chin trembled as I picked up the top, the top I would definitely be wearing tonight.

Hours later there was a knock at the front door. I knew it would be Ellie trying to catch me out undressed, unprepared. She loved fussing over me before any big event, to do my hair and dress me up like a life-sized Barbie doll. No luck this time. I was ready, dressed and primed to go when I opened the door.

"Tess!"

"I know, amazing, right? I'm actually ready." I circled with pride.

She beamed at me. "You look beautiful."

I grabbed her in a bear hug. "Thanks to you I do."

Ellie laughed. "You could wear a hessian bag and you would still be gorgeous."

"Well, you're my best friend, you're supposed to say things like that."

Ellie walked in, a smile stretched across her face.

"Firstly – no, I don't have to say things like that, and secondly – I'm not the only one who thinks you're beautiful." She wiggled her brows at me.

"W…what?"

Her smile broadened, barely containing her excitement. "I know something you don't know," she sing-songed tauntingly.

"Tell me."

"Sorry, I have to honour the girlfriend code."

"The girlfriend code?"

"Let's just say, Stan confided in me something that I vowed I would never repeat."

"That's really touching." I moved from the front door into the cool of the lounge, trying my best to disguise my rapid breathing as my heart hammered against my chest in anticipation.

If I didn't take the bait Ellie would get bored.

She followed me into the lounge. "Yep, something *very* interesting."

"You're right, don't tell me. You don't want to break that girlfriend code, now." I straightened the pillows on the couch. My heart pounded like crazy.

I could see Ellie's excitement dipping. "It's something about you." She stood with her hands on her hips.

I cast a fake grin. "That's nice."

Oh God! Tess, just breathe, don't freak out.

Ellie's mood darkened. "It's about someone thinking you're pretty. Goddamnit, Tess, don't you want to know what it is?"

"But the code."

"Oh, screw the code, come on, sit here." She slapped the couch cushion next to her, and I obeyed.

I squeezed my hands together in my lap, in an attempt to disguise the slight tremor of anticipation. "Ellie," I paused, "I know this might sound strange, but do you mind if you don't tell me? I kind of just want to go along with things and just enjoy the summer. Go with the flow, remember?"

What the … what was I doing? What had I just done? I could hear the words coming out of my mouth, but I seemed powerless to stop the utter stupidity I was speaking.

Ellie looked at me as if I was some wacko. "Are you serious right now?"

Was I? What was wrong with me? Any normal, red-blooded teenage girl would have thrown themselves at Ellie's feet and begged for details, had her repeat them several times, asked for the tone of voice it was said in, facial expressions, time and setting of conversation. All the usual over-the-top analytical questions. What was I afraid of? That something that I'd wanted for so long might be possible? That what I'd felt with Toby wasn't imagined? After so long of having an unrequited crush … I didn't know how to digest the possibility.

I nodded adamantly, the tension ebbing from my veins. "I am. I don't want to know."

Ellie watched me for a long time as if half expecting me to change my mind. I met her look unwaveringly.

The corner of her mouth tilted. "You are unbelievable."

"Why, thank you."

"Okay, so I won't break the code, but all that aside, can I give you some friendly advice?"

"Okay …"

"When you knock off work tonight, go looking for Toby, because, trust me, he will be looking for you."

Chapter Twenty-Eight

I was stalling; I knew I was. Delaying leaving the sanctuary of the toilets.

The door burst open with the sound of laughter and I snapped out of my daze. A couple of girls stumbled in, swaying their way into a line in front of the mirror, though one headed straight to the empty cubicle. I dodged the incoming traffic with a polite smile.

"Pass me a tampon, ho face," the girl from the cubicle yelled out.

Charming. I left them to their affectionate name calling.

The evening's older clientele huddled around the main bar inside. Not really into the disco scene, their entertainment for the evening was Uncle Eric behind the bar. Chris was, no doubt, manning the beer garden bar, cutting off (and trying really hard not to strangle) the drunken just-turned-eighteen crowd.

I weaved my way around tables through the closed, dark restaurant to the sliding door out to the beer garden.

Looking through the thick glass, it was actually quite pretty now the sun had gone down. The entire garden was enclosed by overgrown ivy, which Eric or somebody had woven with fairy lights. It made the space feel intimate and cast a romantic glow throughout. Huge glass vases filled with lit candles dotted each picnic table and speakers were strategically placed around the perimeter for everyone to enjoy.

Shame about the choice of music, though. I could hear 'Kung Fu Fighting' muffled through the glass door, no doubt ten times louder out in the garden.

I took a deep breath and opened the sliding door. It opened directly onto the dance floor, where a sea of drunk girls flailed their arms around in what I could only assume was their attempt at dancing. It was what I imagined walking into a snake pit would be like.

The poor choice in music only seemed to encourage the drunken horde of screaming, laughing girls. There was a mixture of muffin tops protruding from tight-fitting jeans, short skirts and boob tubes. Bare arms struck *Karate Kid* poses, karate chopping each other to the song.

As I stepped out into the garden, sliding the door closed again behind me, I was blinded by the flashing, spinning globe above the dance floor that was the disco ball, before I took a deep breath and zig-zagged through the mass of writhing bodies, intent on avoiding the smoke machine as it belched out wads of nastiness that would no doubt induce asthma attacks and coughing fits in the boozed-up girls on the dance floor.

I actually would have quite liked to see that.

Stan was perched on a picnic table, Ellie in front of him, his legs straddling her hips and her arms snaked around his neck. Ringer sat at the same table with his girlfriend, Amanda, whispering sweet nothings into her ear. I looked around the shadowy garden and the dance floor and all of a sudden felt very alone; no Toby, no Sean in sight. Looked like my only option was to sit with the happy couples and become the dreaded fifth wheel.

I plonked myself on the bench seat with a sigh, only to notice I didn't have a drink. Damn.

I had nothing to occupy my hands with. It wasn't because I was thirsty; I looked around the packed beer garden and seriously doubted all these people were all so parched at this one particular moment. It wasn't about thirst, it was about keeping your hands busy. It was a social thing. If you didn't have a drink you could smoke, or text someone. I had nothing to occupy my hands with so I awkwardly folded them in my lap. I tried to be cool, tried not to look around too much in search of Toby. I tried not to interrupt the canoodling couples.

I gave off an air of nonchalance, when really I wanted to stand on a picnic table with binoculars and search for him. I felt a dip in the seat and then the press of heat next to me as Sean sat and slid along the wooden plank to bump into me.

I quirked a brow at him.

"You're going to get a splinter in a very unfortunate place if you keep sliding along like that."

Sean held a jug of beer and with a steady hand he topped up his pot glass, a smile on his face.

He nodded in the direction of Ellie and Stan. "I think the only ones in danger of getting a splinter in unfortunate places are those two."

They sat in front of me, kissing and pawing at one another, completely oblivious to everyone around them. Honestly, couldn't they get a room or something?

"You want to give it a go?"

My head snapped around towards Sean.

He tipped his head back and gave a deep belly laugh.

"The look on your face is classic. You don't have to look so frightened, Tess, I was referring to a beer."

He held out a freshly poured pot towards me with a knowing twinkle in his eye. He wasn't just referring to the drink. We both knew it.

I straightened my back and lifted my chin. I didn't want the drink, but I took it, had a sip and nursed it like an old familiar friend. Sean watched me with an amused smirk. Damn him.

"Of course," he said, "if you had something else in mind, I would be open to suggestions." He took a deep swig of his glass.

"What? Dry humping on picnic tables?" I posed innocently.

Sean coughed, spluttered, and beer shot out his nose. He thumped himself on the chest, his eyes watering.

Ha! One-all! I proudly took a sip of my beer.

Urgh, it was awful.

I gagged and squinted, after far too big a mouthful.

"How do you drink this stuff?"

Sean fought to speak past his spluttering. "Even worse, try swallowing it down the wrong way." We must have looked a funny pair, coughing, wincing and spluttering.

I was hyper-aware of every movement as I scanned the beer garden. My heart fluttered, pulse thumping in my ears. Beads of sweat dribbled down my back and I started to feel nauseated. Maybe it was the heat? I took another swig of my pot in the hope it would cool me down. Urgh! Maybe it was the beer? My stomach churned, and I fought not to cringe afterwards, because that's not what cool people did.

I caught Ringer giving me a long, side-on look.

"What?"

"Better not let Chris catch you with that."

Oh, right. I'd forgotten that I was downing alcohol in a public place. So weird, society's rules. Sure, people could dry hump and make out, that was acceptable, but underage drinking was seriously frowned upon.

I wanted the ground to open up and swallow me whole from the embarrassment. I hated being reminded of how young I was. I pushed the beer away and wiped the cold condensation from the pot glass on my thighs. I straightened defiantly before getting up, walking a direct line to the bar where Chris was pouring a line of shots.

I needed something to wash down the aftertaste. Something legal.

Chris glanced up at me as he reached the last shot glass. "The usual?"

I nodded. "Straight up on the rocks."

"Coming up!" He smiled, flipping a glass into his hand and scooting ice into it with smooth precision.

Chris handed me my Coke, and then looked directly at me. "Hey, Tess?"

"Yeah?"

Oh God, did he see me with the beer?

He leaned forward so we could hear one another.

"Do you think you could go and request some decent music? I don't think I can handle more crap like this."

My shoulders sagged with relief. That I could do.

As I carried my drink carefully over to the DJ, I dodged a few flailing limbs as they struck their best Saturday Night Fever poses.

Dear God.

The DJ was housed in a little protective alcove with black velvet drop sheets behind him, which advertised in tacky, glittered block letters 'DJ Rosso'. Doesn't everyone secretly dream that their name would be up on velvet someday?

The disco ball glinted off the thick gold chain around Rosso's neck and he kept re-tucking the cigarette behind his ear so the ladies got a good look of his arms in his muscle top. He probably didn't even smoke, just thought it made him look cool.

My eyes watered as I leant towards DJ Rosso; his cologne took my breath away, and not in a good way. I asked if it was possible to play something a bit more modern; he shrugged and pointed me to behind the velvet curtain where I found a thick, yellowing, well-used book full of songs. Thumbing through the selections, I took my time in the privacy of the little alcove. I took my job seriously; I had to save the party from cheesy hits of the '80s.

I leaned against the table, sliding the book towards the disco lights that didn't quite reach behind the curtain, only in dim flashes from the disco ball. A trail of fairy lights twinkled above me, but they weren't exactly bright enough to read by.

The song ended and another started up. I noticed the difference straight away as 'Funky Town' died out and a slow melodic guitar swept into the space. A pleased patron let out a 'woop' somewhere on the other side of the curtain as Live's 'Lightning Crashes' filled the speakers. A smile curved my lips. I loved this song.

I held the book closer to my face, squinting at the song list.

"You'll hurt your eyes doing that."

I squealed and spun around, knocking my knee on the table. The book fell out of my hands but Toby caught it in a juggling motion as he tried not to spill his Corona.

Toby.

"Sorry, I didn't mean to scare you," he said, grinning that gorgeous grin. My heart hammered against my ribs like an excited butterfly. I fought to catch my breath.

"You chose this song?"

"Guilty." Toby took a long swig of his beer, but his eyes never left me. He leaned forward, placing the book back on the table next to me.

"You don't need that, haven't I taught you enough about good music?"

I tilted my head to look up at him, he seemed different, more relaxed than I had ever seen him. I wondered what number Corona that was in his hand.

"I like this song." I smiled, my gaze darting downward. If this was a staring contest, he would outdo me every time.

I didn't know if it was the Corona, or the song, or the secluded atmosphere. This new, electric swirl of tension between us drew my gaze back to his, into those eyes. His tall silhouette glowed with the backdrop of fairy lights, his beautiful face lit by the blue, green, red strobes through the fabric.

"So, what's it gonna be, McGee?"

He shifted his weight from foot to foot and inched closer to me. He was so incredibly close I could feel the heat of his skin, feel his breath. I struggled to answer; it felt like my brain had completely shut down.

His gaze flicked to the song book with an amused smile. "What song have you chosen?"

"Oh," I said, blinking, "right … um …" I burned red, thankful for the dim light. I turned but his hand stilled me; he clasped my elbow and drew me around to face him.

I was drowning. I was drowning in him. My heart raced, and I couldn't think of a thing to say, all song choices, all reason, all ability to construct coherent sentences was lost. So I just said the first thing that came into my head.

"Is your name really Tobias?"

What …? Why had I …? Why was I such a freak?

Amazingly, he didn't seem taken aback by my random question. Instead, the edge of his mouth curved up, and he handed me his beer as he reached into his back pocket and flicked out his wallet. He frowned, holding it high to find some good lighting. He caught the edge of a wayward fairy light and dragged it down towards us.

I had to step closer to him in order to see the licence. As he held it over us, the fairy light lit my face; it wouldn't hide any blushes. On the plastic card, I saw the line of a serious face, a frowning younger image of Toby, which made me smile. I then saw, right there in block letters, sure enough it read: Tobias E Morrison.

"Satisfied?" he asked.

I curved a brow. "What's the 'E' stand for?"

Toby laughed and tucked his wallet back into his pocket.

"Not a chance." He took the beer from my hand, his fingers brushing mine. Goosebumps prickled on my heated skin.

I crossed my arms. "Come on, *Tobias*, don't be shy."

He finished off the last of his drink and placed it on the table beside him. Without a word he grabbed my hand and elevated my arm, leading me into a twirl as Live's lead singer (and a whole bunch of party goers) hummed on the other side of the curtain. I went with the twirl, and he pulled me back towards him, closer still.

He was trying to distract me. He was pretty good at it.

I tried to remember to breathe as he held me close.

"Nice distraction technique," I said.

He snickered, pleased. "Pretty good, isn't it?"

"I didn't think you were a dancer."

His hand squeezed mine and a flicker of some new emotion spread across his face. He leaned so close to me I could feel the press of his lips against my ear.

"Who said anything about dancing?"

He pulled back slowly keeping his face near mine. I was dumbstruck, the way his heated gaze rested on me with a knowing smile, his words … was this really happening? He stilled, watching me. I swallowed hard. Toby Morrison slowly closed the distance between us, his eyes closing. This was really happening. This was really –

The alcove was flooded with light.

"Where's the song book? I don't see it?" A beehived, sequined girl flung the curtain out of the way and stumbled into the alcove. "Roooоosssoooooo, I can't see it," she whined, hands on her hips, ignoring us completely.

Toby let go of me, grabbing the book to hand over to her. She accepted it with a hiccup instead of a thank you and stamped her way back to the DJ. The curtain snagged on the edge of the DJ booth, leaving us exposed.

Toby picked up his empty beer and waved it with a shy smile. The moment was gone.

"Better fill 'er up." He went to step through the curtain and then paused and turned back.

My eyes lit up hopefully.

"Did you want a drink?"

Oh. I glanced at my Coke on the table, now watered down from the melted ice.

I offered him a weak smile. "No thanks."

He turned to go, and my shoulders drooped. I looked at my feet with a sigh. When the curtain didn't lower again as Toby left, I looked back up. He was still there. And he was staring at me. I couldn't read his face; I didn't know what he was thinking. What was he doing?

Just when I thought he would turn to leave, he stepped forward, back into the alcove, placed his empty bottle on the table and in one fluid moment, without taking his eyes from me, Toby yanked the fabric back into place, enveloping us in darkness. My heartbeat spiked at the unexpectedness of it. Toby strode towards me, his hands cupped my face and his lips claimed mine. My surprise soon melted into his touch, my hands entwined around his neck as I kissed him back. Toby's hands were in my hair, his soft lips brushed against mine, gentle at first and then more intently as the pressure of his kisses coaxed me to open my mouth, his tongue delving gently to taste my own. I followed his rhythm and pushed more eagerly against him, my hands moved to divide the thick, silken folds of his hair. I had dreamed of those lips, but never had I imagined they would be so soft, so utterly mind shattering. A small noise escaped me in pleasure; I could feel Toby smile against my mouth as he slowly edged me back against the table, the weight of his body pressed against mine; it felt like a dream, like I should wake at any moment, but no, this was real, this was definitely real!

My hand slid up under the back of his shirt to feel the long, lean flex of his muscles. Toby shuddered as my finger lightly traced his spine downwards, he kissed me so passionately as his hand slid towards my hip, down along my thigh, bending my leg to curve around his waist. I thought I might die of happiness then and there at such an intimate gesture. The edge of the table dug into me through the thin fabric of my skirt, but I didn't care. All I knew was Toby, the feel of him moving against me, the sensation of his tongue in my mouth, of his hands circling gently on my skin. As if breaking the trance, he let my leg slowly fall to the ground and eased his body off me a little, but his lips still hovered over mine. Our breath laboured, he reached out and tucked a wayward strand of hair gently behind my ear and his thumb slowly ran down my cheek. His eyes flicking momentarily to the motion of my tongue sweeping along my bottom lip, Toby pulled away slowly, a knowing tilt to his luscious mouth. He backed away and with one last lingering look he grabbed his empty bottle, peeled back the curtain and was gone.

Chapter Twenty-Nine

I wasn't overly surprised that as I lay in bed after the disco, sleep eluded me that night. I stared up at my bedroom ceiling replaying the evening's events over and over in my mind.

I had kissed Toby Morrison. I had fucking kissed Toby Morrison!

Or more to the point, *he* had kissed *me*, and I had most certainly kissed him back, oh yes I had.

When Toby kissed me it was like I burned from the inside; I had never felt more alive, more wanted. The edges of any doubts I'd had, had melted into him. It had been fast, hot and completely unexpected, and then like that he was gone, leaving me in the darkened alcove, my hands shaking as I had touched my kiss-swollen lips.

When I had finally ventured out from behind the curtain, I had watched Toby's every move. He had mingled at the disco, his eyes darting towards me every now and then with an amused glint. And what did I do? I sat at the picnic table in a catatonic state of shock. As midnight struck, I lost Toby in the crowd as everyone poured out of the beer garden and lingered on the footpath under the bug-infested lights. I wandered around, trying to seek him out, but his truck was gone. It was a bittersweet feeling; he was gone but the memory of his kiss replayed in my mind.

The sun eventually crept into my room, and if I dozed at all, it had been briefly and with a wicked smile on my face.

It wasn't a dream.

As I skipped into the kitchen, already showered and ready for work, Mum and Dad both did a double take. Dad peered at the time on the microwave and cast a confused look back at Mum.

"Good morning!" I said, giving him a kiss on the top of his head.

"Who are you and what have you done with our daughter?"

I rolled my eyes and opened the fridge. I was absolutely ravenous.

"Going somewhere?" Mum looked alarmed; my early rising had deeply unsettled their routine.

I shrugged grabbing the milk. "Work."

"Honey, it's 7am, you don't have work for another five hours."

Yes, five long, hideous hours. I couldn't wait to see Ellie to tell her what had happened last night. I had thought of messaging or emailing her, but I wanted to see her reaction in person.

Five long hours away also meant hours without seeing Toby.

"What's wrong with being organised?" I threw back.

"Nothing, it's just …" She floundered to think of something. Poor souls, I thought, first a summertime job, then helping them at the shop and now rising with the sun; it was all too much.

"What time did you get home?" Dad asked over his paper.

Uh-oh. If I told them, it wouldn't take them long to calculate just how little sleep I'd had and then they'd get all kinds of suspicions as to what had made their daughter so chipper this morning.

"Oh, not too late, you know how I love my beauty sleep."

He nodded and turned back to his paper, accepting it.

Boom! That's how it's done. Bullet dodged … for now.

***

Ellie sat opposite me in the restaurant, before we officially started our shift. She had just listened intently to my play by play of the night's events: from the encounter behind the DJ station, to *the kiss*, to Toby's disappearance. I retold it beautifully, played it out to full dramatic effect.

Not once did she interrupt me or look shocked or even happy for me. Instead, she listened with a pained expression on her face and an uncharacteristic silence.

Quite frankly, it wasn't the reaction I had expected.

I fidgeted in my seat. "What? What is it?"

"Nothing." She couldn't even bring herself to look at me as she smoothed out invisible creases in her black apron.

I frowned. I didn't get it. Last night, she had been my own personal cheer squad, told me to seek out Toby because she had inside information that went in my favour. What had changed?

"Nothing?" I repeated. "Well, THAT'S crap!"

Ellie sighed and finally spoke. "I just don't …" She broke off as if picking her words carefully.

"You just don't what?" My patience was wearing thin. "Out with it."

She gave me a sad smile. "I just don't … I don't want you to do what I do."

I crossed my arms defensively. "And what's that exactly?"

Ellie shifted in her chair. "I don't want you to jump in the deep end with him. Hold back a little."

"That's not what you were chanting last night."

"I know, but take it from someone who knows."

"Knows what?" I said. "Has Stan said something?"

"No! No I don't even think he knows anything. We haven't even talked about last night."

Didn't surprise me, I seriously doubted they could speak much with their tongues in each other's mouths all the time.

Ellie grabbed for my hand and gave it a squeeze. "Just don't let yourself be the rebound girl."

"The rebound girl?"

"Tess," she continued carefully, "he only just broke up with Angela after dating for *over a year*."

I took a deep, calming breath. I didn't want to hear this.

"Just don't expect too much, okay? Just take a step back."

I pulled my hand away and pushed my seat back. It gave an ear-piercing scrape against the polished floorboards.

"Noted," I said, "thanks for the pep talk." I got up to walk towards the kitchen. If I didn't move now, I would say something I would regret.

"Tess, wait." Ellie caught my arm, jolting me to a stop. "I'm sorry, that's great, I mean really great. I'm excited for you. I just don't want you to get hurt, that's all."

"You mean you just don't want me to have a life," I bit out.

Hurt flashed across Ellie's face. "That's not true."

"Isn't it? Well, maybe if you'd thought outside your little world for one moment, you could have saved me from making such a huge mistake."

I spun back around towards the kitchen, tears threatening to overflow from my eyes. She wasn't allowed to see them, she wasn't. This time she let me go; she didn't call out. This time she didn't say a word.

I had wanted Ellie to squeal and hug me and help me with my next outfit to dazzle Toby in, to keep me filled in on the Onslow Boys' next social event. But as we worked together in silence for the whole shift, I knew it wouldn't happen. As much as I fought against it, Ellie's words rang in my ears and fed into my paranoia. Why did he kiss me and then just leave? Maybe he wasn't into it. No, no he was definitely into it. A myriad of thoughts crowded my overworked mind; it was a full-time job pushing my doubts aside. As if that wasn't bad enough, my heart all but stopped when I heard the front door screech open and familiar laughter filled the front bar. I found an excuse to go to my bag behind the door so I could peer inside at the boys as they pulled up their bar stools.

Sean, Stan and Ringer looked over the menu.

No Toby.

I loitered a little longer and eavesdropped on their conversation.

"Where's young Tobias?" Chris asked, handing over their drinks.

I pressed myself against the wall, hanging onto every word, and peeked through the crack in the restaurant divider.

"I dare say he is probably facedown in a world of pain right about now," Sean said with an evil smile.

"He was pretty wasted," Chris laughed.

"'Coronas are the devil's brew', I believe he said?" added Ringer.

They all shuddered and laughed. "I doubt we'll even see him today. Serves him right."

Their conversation shifted to lunch, and I made my way back to the restaurant before Chris saw me. He hadn't seemed that drunk to me, but what did I know? 'Devil's brew' and 'wasted' ran through my head as I pictured Toby at home, feeling sick and sorry for himself and the stupid things he'd done the night before. Like kissing the rebound girl.

I felt sick. I told Ellie as I passed her that the boys were in the bar and made my way, once again, to the refuge of the ladies' toilets.

***

I managed to hold it together. I tried not to think too deeply about all my fears about kissing Toby and the way he'd up and left like that, with no warning. I felt exhausted. I just wanted to go home and crash into oblivion before the stress and agony of the dinner shift. I wanted to avoid Ellie's eyes that would no doubt reflect a silent 'I told you so'.

When I finally made it home between shifts, scuffing my feet as I trudged towards the driveway, I froze. My bike was propped up under the carport, sparkling, shiny and fixed. I wondered if my lack of sleep was making me hallucinate.

My heart threatened to beat out of my chest; I ran up the drive and clasped the handles. Yep, it was real. I dashed inside but the house was empty.

"Damn it!"

I frantically dialed the shop number and heard my mum's usual spiel after the second ring.

"Good afternoon, Rose Café, Jenny speaking."

"Mum!"

"Oh, hi honey, how was work?"

"Just awesome, hey listen, my bike?"

"Oh yes, sorry, I meant to put it in the garage but I was running late."

"When did it get dropped off?"

"Not long after you left for work, just five minutes later, and you could have ridden it there. You could have finally used your new helmet."

I cringed away from the receiver.

"Who dropped it off?" My voice seemed smaller now.

"Matthew Morrison, himself, did. I was late for work because of it, got caught up chatting to him. He's such a lovely man, isn't he? And a real fan of my pies, so he's definitely in the will."

A coldness settled over me. Toby's dad dropped it off? Toby had gotten his dad to return my bike instead of him. That clinched it. He was avoiding me. The bike was fixed, so that was that. He didn't need to see me anymore. Hot tears welled in my eyes. I was so *stupid*.

I tried not to sound too different on the phone; Mum could sniff out unhappiness like a bloodhound.

"Cool, thanks, Mum. I better go."

"You can ride your bike to work tonight," Mum said, sounding excited.

"Yeah." I tried to match her enthusiasm. "Yay!"

The phone clicked as she hung up, and I listened to the silence of the empty house. The realisation swept over me.

I was the rebound girl.

Chapter Thirty

I was so tempted to call in sick, to avoid the rest of the weekend and everyone in it altogether.

But Chris could have eyed the beer in my hand last night, combined it with my silence during lunch service, and it wouldn't take him long to conclude that I wasn't sick, I was hungover. He'd give me the sack for that, I just knew it. It was a tempting thought, to be honest. Maybe if I broke my arm, I would be sent away to my nan's house in the city for the rest of the summer. Not that I had a nan in the city, but still. I needed Adam. He could have cheered me up, especially in lieu of Ellie's and my heated debate at lunch.

After a catnap, I showered and had a quick bite to eat. Although I felt human again, I didn't feel much better until I started getting ready for work. In the process, my self-pity morphed into determined resilience as I stared hard into the mirror.

I opted for a cute little top and skirt. If I was going to face an audience, I was at least going to do so looking hot.

As I walked into the bar that afternoon, I had on my best happy-go-lucky face and flashed the customers a winning smile and false confidence that had everyone fooled. Mostly everyone knew me by now, and I was always greeted with either a 'Tess!' or 'McGee!'.

Days of Tic Tac Tess were light years away. I couldn't believe that used to be my biggest problem: a stupid nickname by an immature boy.

I hung my bag up behind the door. Ellie's bag was already there. I was still mad at her, but it would take far more energy to keep up the silent treatment than to be civil. She couldn't rain on my parade anymore, because I simply wouldn't confide in her about my love life. I knew that would hurt far more than the silent treatment, even though, in its own way, it was kind of the same thing.

Ellie was still on edge around me as if she wasn't wholly buying the act, and I knew that if anyone could see through it, it would be her.

Rosanna, Amy and Melba seemed to suspect something was amiss though I chatted animatedly to them about all sorts of things. Maybe too animatedly. I was over-the-top bubbly with the customers, and I even caught Chris giving me a confused frown. After a few hours, my face ached from all the smiling, and I was exhausted. How could Ellie stand this all the time? Being a wallflower conserved so much more energy. I let my smile slip for a breather as I gathered some cutlery for a table. Beside me, Ellie reached for some silverware for her table.

"Toby's here," she whispered.

And when I met her eyes, she smiled a small smile and then whisked herself away.

Oh shit.

I had no intentions of running to the poolroom, or even crossing his path at all if I could help it. Even though I had completely resented Ellie's advice, I knew there was something to it. I already felt like a big enough idiot.

When Chris asked me to deliver a meal into the poolroom, I paused so long he thought I hadn't heard. I had heard alright. Even though the order of a single bowl of chips didn't have 'Onslow Boys' written on it, it didn't have to; to me, the poolroom was a no-go zone. Enemy territory. I had to woman up. The last thing I would do was get Ellie to run the meal for me, so instead I ran fingers through my hair, straightened my clothes, took a deep breath and grabbed the meal.

It felt like every step I took was in slow motion. The achy melody of Portishead echoed from the poolroom as I dodged traffic in the front bar on my way. All of a sudden, I wasn't paranoid about dropping the plate or spilling the contents, I was just hoping that Toby might have been in the men's room when I delivered the meal.

No such luck; I spotted him through the alcove, laughing at some bad shot that passed from his opposition. He leaned casually against the windowsill, pool cue in one hand, beer in the other. He didn't look hungover to me, I thought. As I paused, watching on just beyond the doorway, his eyes flicked up and met mine just as he was about to take a shot.

My breath hitched at the acknowledgement; the first time since last night. The contact was broken when Sean heckled him to hurry up and take his shot. He did, making the white ball rebound on the cushion and pot the wrong ball.

"Oooooh, two shots, son!"

The poolroom filled with cheers and exclamations of shock at the rare occasion Toby made a mistake on the pool table. The boys pounded him with back slaps and ruffled his hair. He shook them off with a smile. My face felt on fire; he'd lost concentration because of me.

I hurried into the poolroom, trying not to draw attention to myself while they were all preoccupied.

It was then that I looked at the order. 'Bowl of chips' with an angry face next to it, in Ellie's handwriting. Then I realised why, as a group of Angela Vickers' friends sat around a barrel on stools, pursing their lips in disdain as they sat in the corner feeling superior.

Awesome, I thought. Icing on the cake of a brilliant day.

"Bowl of chips," I said in the friendliest way I could.

Three sets of cold, angry eyes met me, all casting me a death stare.

They begrudgingly moved their drinks aside for me to place the bowl down. I offered them another friendly smile and escaped while the going was good.

Only to be stopped by a shrill voice.

"Hey, bar-keep!"

I turned, dread swept over me; the snarky comment had drawn the whole room's attention.

My brow quirked in question as I met her gaze. Just try it, I thought. I was in no mood for her.

The girl's manicured claw pointed to the chips.

"We said chips and gravy."

The docket didn't read with gravy, but the customer was always right, no matter how evil they were.

"I'll grab you some," I replied sweetly.

The blonde with her eyes a little too close together feasted distastefully on a chip.

"And we said chicken salt, not ordinary salt."

"God, who would have thought you would actually need a brain to waitress," Pencil Eyebrows scoffed.

I bit the side of my jaw, ready to grab the bowl from the barrel and pelt them with chips when I heard a voice next to me.

"Lay off, Jules." Toby lingered near the French door, chalking his pool cue.

Pencil Eyebrows had a name, and now her death stare was focused on Toby.

"Oh, I forgot that jail bait here was you guys' little pet. I guess you can't handle a real woman with a brain."

"Which instantly rules any of you out," Toby added coolly as he blew the excess chalk off his cue and gave them a knowing smirk. Laughter and catcalls sounded in stereo as the Onslow Boys overheard the exchange.

"Go fuck yourself, Toby."

Jules stood up, chucking a handful of chips at him and stormed out, earning me three bumps in the shoulder. But that did little to upset me when I met Toby's gaze, and he gave me a wink.

Sean slung an arm around my shoulder. "Never mind them, Jail Bait, they can't help it. They were born with chronic evil."

I smiled at Toby. "You okay? You're lucky a wayward chip didn't take out an eye."

He laughed then, the warm familiar one I loved to hear.

"Could have been worse, there could have been gravy."

I sighed, my attention moving towards the mess that had been dumped on the floor.

I retreated for a dustpan and headed back in, ice broken by, of all things, a bowl of chips.

Chapter Thirty-One

"Seriously, what is the point of going to the Point?" Stan whinged.

"Well, do you have a better idea, lover boy?" Sean smashed the billiard balls with a satisfying crack.

Stan shrugged. "I don't know, just thought we could try something different, that's all."

"McLean's Beach?" someone chucked in.

Sean faked snoring.

"How about the Falls?" added Toby, as he flicked through the jukebox's song selection.

"What? Hang out with all the deviants?" Stan scoffed.

"I don't know, Stan, sounds like your kind of scene."

He flipped Toby the finger.

Toby grinned wickedly before turning back to his task with a shrug. "There's good swimming there, that's all, it's hot enough, it's just an idea."

"Swimming at the Falls, eh?" Sean rubbed his soft stubble in deep thought. "Why not?"

"Whatever, can we wait for Ellie to knock off work first?"

"Aw, don't worry Romeo, we won't leave without Juliet." Sean grabbed Stan and made kissy noises. Stan pushed him over.

I couldn't help but smile at their banter as I gathered the last of the chips from the floor; my smile slowly faded when I caught Toby staring at me.

He was leaning back against the glass display of the jukebox, his arms folded. "So, you in?"

Play it cool, play it cool.

I shrugged. "I guess."

***

Whoops and cheers echoed down the dirt path as the boys raced each other towards the secluded swimming hole down the bottom of a rocky incline. I could hear the distant thundering of the waterfall clearly, even though it was still a fair distance off.

Ellie and I lagged behind as we climbed out of Ringer's car, shaking our heads as we secretly wondered who were the teenagers among us.

"Are we okay?" Ellie asked as we shut the boot and carried our borrowed towels.

I bumped her shoulder. "Of course."

I could make out her brilliant white smile in the moonlight.

As we neared the path, our attention turned toward the slamming of a car door, where Toby stood leaning against his ute.

"You not swimming?" Ellie asked.

"Nah, I'm just the ideas man."

"Cool, well, I better go make sure these fools don't kill themselves." Ellie flashed me another smile and ran after the boys.

Toby pushed off from the door, hitched himself up onto the back of his tray and made a place on one of the rugs. He casually patted the space next to him, and I attempted not to smile too broadly at the relief of such a small gesture.

"Unless you wanted to swim?"

Before he could even finish his sentence, I chucked the towel into the tray and climbed up and over to sit next to him.

"I guess that's a no then?"

"It was a terrible idea, I can't believe they're all down there." I laughed.

Toby lay back, linking his hands behind his head and closed his eyes.

"A terrible idea, or a brilliant idea?" He peeked an eye open before closing it again with a smile.

I was suddenly very aware of how alone we were. The distant yells and cascading water were a million miles away, or so it felt.

I picked at the frayed edge of the rug. "Thanks for fixing my bike."

"Oh," he smirked, "that."

"Yeah. I'm back on the road again."

"Yeah, I was kind of pissed at my dad," he said, his eyes still closed.

"Why?"

"He didn't ask me. He just thought he'd do me a favour and deliver it for me."

"Well, that was nice of him."

"I guess. It's just … I wanted to deliver it myself."

Relief flooded me. In a moment of panic, I had feared the worst, that he was avoiding me. But he wasn't.

"Well, it was a good effort to fix it while you were hungover."

Toby's eyes opened as he frowned at my words; he straightened.

"The boys said you were hungover today."

He still looked confused. "Oh! I didn't fix the bike today."

Now it was me who looked confused.

Toby fiddled with the frayed edge of the rug, his hand close to mine as he spoke, not looking at me. "I fixed the bike the day you gave it to me, Tess."

My frowned deepened. "Why didn't you tell me? You know … give it back?"

He looked at me now. "Remember I said, 'what if I didn't want to fix your bike?'"

I remembered. "Yes …"

"I didn't want to fix it, because I liked driving you places."

I stared at him, unable to believe it was true.

"Not that I was the most reliable taxi service." He rested his elbows on his bent knees.

"Oh, I don't know," I said, "you were there when it counted. Saved me from perishing on the Horseshoe Bend. Took me on my first drive to the Point to watch the fireworks, it was only last night …"

His eyes flicked up to mine as I broke off at the last two words. Last night.

"Yeah, last night," he repeated.

"Guess you won't be drinking Coronas again anytime soon."

The corner of his mouth curved up. "Not if I can help it, no."

He regretted drinking the Coronas; I wondered if he regretted anything else as well.

I shifted to sit next to him and leaned against the cabin rear window.

Don't jump in the deep end, Tess, play it cool.

Pulling back and taking it slow was good advice. That's what I decided to do.

"Am I just the rebound girl?" I asked. That didn't last long.

Toby stiffened, his scowl deep and so penetrating I had to look away from it.

"What makes you say that?"

Now I was uneasy. Me and my big mouth.

"Because we are sitting in probably the same place you sat a week ago when you broke up with your girlfriend."

I regretted it as soon as the words left my mouth. I could feel Toby's anger pouring off him in waves. Suddenly going for a swim seemed like a great idea.

"I see," was his cold response.

I cleared my throat, finding myself utterly fascinated with the edge of the rug I fiddled with. I couldn't take my eyes off it, couldn't look at him.

"I'm just saying that you don't have to worry about me expecting anything more. I know last night was just a bit of fun, and that if you had any regrets today, to not worry about it. It is what it is, and I'm cool about it."

Stupid words. Stupid words coming out of my stupid mouth.

I expected his shoulders to slump in relief or his icy exterior to thaw, but it didn't. He seemed more agitated as he ran a hand aggressively through his hair.

"Is that what you think?" he said. "That I regretted last night?"

I looked at him then, trying to hide the hurt in my expression.

"Don't you?"

He sat up straight and grabbed my hand to stop it from fraying the edge of the rug.

"I may have been buzzed last night, but I remember everything. I can't promise you that I won't want to drive you home, or kiss you like crazy again. Because I will. I do." His eyes shifted towards my mouth and then back to meet my eyes.

"I like you, Tess."

I was supposed to act cool and indifferent and hold back from falling in too deep right now.

Take it slow, Tess. It's good advice – take it slow!

I kissed Toby for the second time. I pushed him to sit back against the window as I straddled his lap, feeding the hunger, living for the moment. We weren't coy and polite this time; Toby's hand slipped under my shirt, his fingers skimming my bare belly, his mouth catching my exhales as I cupped his face and tilted his head to the side for better access to his lush mouth.

Toby nipped playfully along my neck, which made me giggle. He grasped the curve of my knees and drew me closer. I felt the unmistakable evidence of his desire pressed between my legs as his hands slid up my bare ribs and pushed under my bra to touch my breasts. I rocked slowly on his lap pressing into his touch, never feeling more alive than with the new sensations that tingled in foreign places. Never before had I wanted Scott or any other boy to touch me as I wanted Toby touching me now. I relished in the brush of his work-roughened fingers gliding over my skin and the way he moved under me. His hands suddenly bunched my skirt up in his fists as his tongue filled my mouth to duel my own.

I braced myself for the hand that was sliding along my thigh, daring to delve between my legs to explore me like no other had. But just as his finger pulled the elastic of material he froze and panic shot through me at the thought that all of a sudden he had come to his senses, that he thought it – us – was a bad idea. I breathed hard, tried to catch my breath as his head tilted to the side, listening for something. That's when we heard it, the incoming laughter and voices of an approaching stampede of swimmers.

I slid off Toby's lap and worked at adjusting my skirt and fixing my hair. Toby had a far worse problem as he pulled on his shirt to hang over the large tent in his shorts. We sat apart and cast knowing smiles to one another as we both tried to gather our breaths and look casual, like we were just hanging out, not dry humping in the back of his ute.

Toby looked around and feigned surprise at the disheveled, soaking figures that approached.

"Back already?"

"Tobias! That was the *worst* idea you have *ever* had." Sean shivered.

"I take it you didn't have fun, then?"

"Ffffucking ffffreezing," he stuttered.

Toby flashed a grin towards me. "I guess we had a better time?"

I blushed and glanced away.

A better time? Oh yeah we did.

Chapter Thirty-Two

Mum and Dad gave me Monday and Tuesday off to make up for my work-filled weekend.

They said I couldn't work seven days a week, even though they did and they still wanted me to have *some* fun this summer because I was working so hard. It made me feel a bit guilty considering I was telling them so many white lies lately about where I was and who I was with. The last thing I wanted was to smash the illusion of being the perfect daughter, especially given my extracurricular activities with a certain gorgeous twenty-two year old who could kiss like no one else.

Ellie's ongoing advice played on my mind even though I was convinced that I wasn't Toby's rebound girl seeing as he obviously had some feelings for me.

He said he liked me, and he had fixed my bike ages ago and that was when he was still with Angela. Ellie thought that was a major development.

I thought the mere fact I had kissed Toby twice was an *epic* development.

But Ellie still wanted me to take a step back, which meant no accidentally going past his work and 'bumping' into him and no joint daytime trips mid-week with the Onslow Boys, (which I thought ludicrous and unfair).

"Trust me, Tess! Haven't you heard the old saying treat 'em mean to keep 'em keen? The more unavailable you seem, the more he'll want you."

"That sounds like playing games to me."

"You'll thank me when he's pawing over you at the weekend, begging for your time."

Talk about confusing advice. If not a tad hypocritical.

Apparently the boys had gone water skiing mid-week and McLean's Beach Friday night, and with the view of 'playing it cool', I didn't go to either and now Saturday lunch and well into Saturday night, Toby was a no show. Great plan, Ellie.

I gave her my best 'not happy' look.

"Don't worry, they'll be here," Ellie reassured me.

And the Onslow Boys did rock up. At least Stan and Sean did. No Toby, though. Ellie gave me a worried look, and I went back to the kitchen. Obviously, 'absence makes the heart grow fonder' was more like, 'out of sight, out of mind'. As I dumped dirty dishes in the sink, I vowed never to take Ellie's advice again.

"What's your problem?" Amy glared as dirty dishwater splashed her in my dumping fury. I stormed out the back to kick a milk crate across the cement and slumped on to the back step to take a few breaths. I was angry at the world, at Toby, but mostly at myself.

Maybe I *was* the rebound girl.

At Sunday dinner service, when Toby was a no show again, doubt rose in me. Apparently the Onslow Boys had gone fishing, which was just Jim-dandy, but a whole week had gone by and the buzz from last weekend was quickly wearing off.

"You stress too much, I haven't exactly seen a heap of Stan this weekend either," Ellie said.

"You mean aside from your mid-week catch ups and yesterday and today? That's not classified as 'a heap'?"

"Not for our standards."

I really didn't give a crap about what their standards were, I was too busy feeling sorry for myself as I sipped on my Sunday night after-work staff drink. I hit the heavy stuff tonight. Double shot raspberry lemonade; yeah, I was depressed.

"You may not think it now, but in time you'll thank me for this."

I just grunted into my syrupy lemonade. The weekend was over. I felt like a little lap dog waiting for the door to open, waiting for the boys to come waltzing in. Ellie had tried to find out more info from Stan about their whereabouts and if they were coming in, but they must have been out of range. We couldn't even grill Chris, who was absent from his usual weekend shift. He wasn't out bonding with the boys; instead, he had taken a break to go to the city and stay with his nan and Adam.

Adam. I wished Adam were here. Ellie was sapping my energy with an entire summer devoted to her. I needed a buffer.

I nearly knocked my drink over at the sound of the door; I whipped my head around so fast it threatened to snap off my neck. A lone figure walked through. Stan. My shoulders slumped as Ellie brightened.

"Hey, you!" She beamed, swiveling in his direction.

His smile was warm and authentic, his eyes lit up when he saw her and there was no doubt how he felt about Ellie. There was no guarded, unreadable, broody expression on Stan's face. He was an open book; they both were.

Ellie flung her arms around his neck and kissed him. He held her, causing Ellie's feet to hover off the ground.

Stan winced. "Ah, Ellie watch my sunburn."

He was noticeably flushed, and Ellie pulled back his collar with a gasp.

"Stanley Remington, you deserve a right arse kicking."

I shook my head. "Boys and their inability to rub sun screen on each other."

"Believe me, it's not worth the hassle." He cringed as he sat down.

"I can see that." I eyed him skeptically.

"So where is everyone?" Ellie asked innocently.

"Home, I guess, big day."

Stan looked beat. A combination of drinking and sunstroke was nasty indeed. I wondered if Toby had suffered the same fate? He wouldn't burn like Stan because of his beautiful olive complexion, but I was appeased by the fact that they had had a big day and that was the reason they didn't come in tonight. But still. Stan had; he would have walked on fire to get to Ellie. My heart spiked with jealousy at how their relationship had developed.

Stan and Ellie dropped me off at home, early even for a Sunday night, on what had to have been the most anti-climactic weekend of the summer. With no Onslow Boys and no Chris to hold a lock-in, the bar had closed an hour early and so there I was, sitting in my room all before midnight. My dad had even stirred to get a drink and seemed utterly amazed I was home already. At least that would make me look good, I thought.

I checked my emails knowing there would be nothing from Ellie. Her emails became less and less frequent these days. Plus, she was no doubt in Stan's bungalow right now sponging him down with aloe vera cream.

Old faithful Adam, however, sat in my inbox, which made me smile no matter what my mood.

To: tessmcgee

Guess who can finger knit? Jealous much? Yeah you should be!

Hey I will finger knit you a scarf, I think if I start now it should be ready for winter in about 4 years' time.... Watch this space!

So what's happening McGee?? Chris is here but he won't dish the dirt, he is such a killjoy. I wonder when Mum and Dad are going to tell him he's adopted?

Maybe this Christmas?? Hand over his Bruce Springsteen's Greatest hits CD with a P.S...You're adopted!

Live to hope.

Sender: Adam I can jump puddles Henderson

To: Adam I can jump puddles Henderson

Sorry dude! There is no mistaking your family resemblance. Brothers to the bone! If anything, I suspect you were cloned from the same petri dish, aside from the whole serious broody thing (Don't tell him I said that).

If you can't manage the adopted angle how about dropped on his head as a baby? That might explain a few things. But then again you might have been dropped on your head as a baby too? Which in any case would also explain a few things.

Like ah Finger knitting??? What the?

Sender: tessmcgee

To: tessmcgee

People are afraid of what they don't understand Tess. Finger knitters everywhere have been suffering from the prejudice for centuries. I have to say I am a little disappointed in you.

Considering I fell off a billiard table recently I think I will avoid the whole dropped on head topic, it might back fire.

What are you doing home from work?

Sender: Adam I can jump puddles Henderson

I hit reply. I wanted to tell him about my horrid weekend, about Ellie's boy theory which I was seriously starting to doubt. I wanted to tell him each scenario and every painstaking analysis I had all week. But in order to do that, first I would have to tell him about the boy. Something I had been avoiding and something I couldn't do via email.

Screw it, I thought, and picked up the phone.

My fingers threaded nervously through the curve of the phone cord as it rang. Then he answered. Much like Ellie, there was surprised silence after I told him a (sugarcoated) version of events. He didn't need to know about the dry humping. But if he was about to echo the same spiel as Ellie, for one, I didn't think I could stand it and two, maybe they couldn't be all wrong?

Adam blew out a breath. "You've been busy."

"Oh, you know, just the typical summer drama." I winced.

"Tess. I have been finger knitting. A typical summer is not in my existence."

"I guess you'll have to live vicariously through us, then."

"I'll say. Toby Morrison, huh?" He sounded as if he needed it to sink in, as the phone line fell into more silence.

"So do you think I'm the rebound girl?" I asked, afraid of the answer.

"Possibly. But aren't we all on the rebound from someone? I mean, no matter how much time goes by, the next person will always be the rebound person. Was Stan the rebound guy for the tourist sleaze bag? Or was the tourist sleaze the rebound from Stan?"

I sat up straighter now. "I guess."

"Do you want some advice?"

I nodded, which in hindsight was pretty dumb on the phone but he continued anyway.

"Don't over-think it. Trust me, blokes aren't complicated creatures."

"So do you think I should hold back?"

"What for? If you like him – I can't believe I am having such a chick conversation with you – but if you like him, let him know. Not in a stalkerish 'I want to have your babies' way, but if you wanna hang with him, do it. If he's keen, he'll appreciate your honesty more than playing stupid games with him. Good God, woman, you're taking boy advice from Ellie? Seriously?"

"You weren't around, Adam! Besides, it's not exactly like I talk to you about this stuff."

"Yeah, well, this is the one and only time I like not having a vagina."

"Gross."

"Like I said," Adam continued, "the male species isn't as complicated as you think, so just go with it and do your own thing."

I felt a wave of relief pass over me at Adam's no-nonsense, honest words. Maybe it was because it was what I wanted to hear, but it was also good to get a guy's point of view. Adam was my last point of call before I picked up my mum's copy of *Men are from Mars, Woman are from Venus.*

"Thanks, Adam."

"No sweat. I better go, this scarf won't knit itself, you know."

"You sure you don't have a vagina?"

"Whatever, Toby lover!"

"Don't say anything to Chris, okay? It's not exactly common knowledge."

"Ha! That's what you think."

I froze. "What's that supposed to mean?

"Here's another helpful insight into guys, Tess: opposed to what girls think, mates talk. We are mostly apes with our brains in our pants, but don't underestimate the power of the bro code."

"The bloody bro code."

"It is a strong, unbreakable bond."

"Ellie broke it," I laughed.

"I bet she freakin' did." He laughed, too.

"Any last words of advice, oh wise master?"

"If you take up finger knitting, make sure you use talcum powder so the wool doesn't rub on your fingers."

"Got it. Anything else?"

"Stop playing games and go get him."

As I hung up the phone, that was exactly what I decided to do.

Chapter Thirty-Three

I had looked down this drive maybe a thousand times before, but none of those numerous times held as much weight as it did now.

I lowered my foot to balance my bike as I came to a stop. A singular porch light shone like a beacon down the long curving driveway, casting a shadow across Toby's car.

Light on. Car in drive.

He was home. I supposed anyone would be at 2am on a Monday morning. I was in two minds, I was ready to turn around and head for home; I paused, a murmur of music inside had my heart thumping in a matching rhythm. He was definitely home, he was awake and before nerves demanded I leave, I walked my bike down the drive, towards the light, towards the music.

I propped it near the wall of the cabin, moving through the darkness of the carport, skimming myself sideways so as not to scratch Toby's car. I placed a hand against the bonnet. Cold, Toby must have been home all night. I realised how creepy that was so quickly pulled my hand away.

Stop being such a stalker, Tess!

Before I could put too much thought into where I was and what I was doing, I followed the ever-increasing thud of music that led me around the back. Then I had a thought. *What if he wasn't alone?* I faltered for a second, then pushed forward. If I chickened out now I would never get any peace. I wanted – needed – to do this so before any more self-doubt forced itself into my mind, I turned the corner.

A dim single bulb lit the back deck that housed a couch … in which Toby sat. And he was alone! Surprise lit his face as he saw me. He paused mid-sip of his beer, and went to speak then thought better of it.

As he sat there, all relaxed, nursing his stubby, my heart leapt into my throat. He was so incredibly sexy in low-rise jeans and a black Bonds singlet, he was barefoot with bed-tousled hair and he was here, at his home, sitting and staring at me.

All of a sudden I felt weird and out of place.

An amused crease tilted his brow. "What are you doing here?"

What was I doing here?

When I didn't answer, Toby melted further into his couch, swigging on his beer, only momentarily taking his eyes from me.

"You want one?" He held up the stubby.

"Sure."

He stood, towering over me. Skimming past as he walked towards a bar fridge on the back deck, I quickly concentrated on trees that lay beyond Toby's backyard, silhouetted in the moonlight. Crossing my arms and staring into the nothing, it took every ounce of my strength not to watch Toby bend to the bar fridge, clinking the bottles as he rearranged the shelves. I didn't really want a beer, but I thought it would make me seem less awkward, have more of a purpose, because that's what friends do, right? They hang out on back decks listening to music and downing a few beers.

As I tried to justify my presence, something blisteringly cold pressed against the back of my neck. I gasped and stepped away, spinning around. Toby grinned wickedly as he held out a beer.

"Cold enough?"

I rubbed the back of my neck and threw him my best death stare. That only seemed to amuse him more. His gaze dipped to my shoulders, then back up to my face again. He stepped forward, all amusement suddenly sobering into that serious gaze I'd seen so often.

"You caught a bit of sun today." He ran the back of his knuckles gently along my upper arm. His hands were both full of our beers but that didn't stop him from touching me. I didn't know if it was the shock of the ice-cold beer on my neck or Toby's touch that caused gooseflesh to form on such a warm night.

The song ended, and Toby's attention was drawn away from me, snapping me out of my own daze as he placed my beer into my hand.

He disappeared through the sliding glass door; I could barely make him out in the dim interior. He restarted his tape, the same melodious symphony I'd heard from the driveway.

I took a swig of beer and fought not to choke on the vile taste of it. Seriously, how did people drink this stuff?

Toby increased the music's volume this time, and I was plunged into blackness as the back porch light switched off. Toby skimmed through the sliding glass door and moved towards the couch again.

I had an idea of what the darkness meant; it was a 'do not disturb' sign. I swallowed deeply. I could just make out Toby as a light from the kitchen window shrouded the couch in a light orange glow through the mottled glass.

"Do you like this song?" I asked.

It's his tape, he put it on, of COURSE he likes this song.

"It's my absolute favourite," he said in a low, dreamy voice. He sat back down on the couch and slowly patted the space next to him.

Why is it that people take a long swig of alcohol before they do something they need courage for? One sip could hardly give me enough to conquer my nerves and fears, so I took two big ones and sat next to Toby.

"What's it called?" I asked, trying not to cringe at the disgusting taste, to keep the conversation flowing casually.

Toby's arm lay carelessly across the back of the couch, my neck pressed against it. The couch seemed a lot smaller than it looked. It was cosy; I relaxed into the dip in the middle so that I leaned in to Toby. He ran his fingers through my hair in a slow, comforting motion. I closed my eyes and rested my head on his shoulder.

"It's called, 'A Change is Gonna Come'," he whispered into my temple.

Toby leaned forward and rested his beer on the floor with a delicate thud; my eyes opened, breaking my dream-like state as he took the beer out of my hand and placed it on the floor next to his. All of a sudden finding a place for my hands didn't matter as Toby closed the distance between us. My tummy tingled with the gentle, lingering touch of his lips to mine. I reached up, my fingers entangled through his thick, dark hair as our bodies pressed closer, melting into each other as the music played and the darkness hid our roaming hands. Toby broke away first, leaving me breathless and fearful that he had decided to stop, but his eyes met mine in a silent question, and I gripped his singlet and pressed my forehead to his.

Toby's breath drew in a long shudder. "Are you sure?"

I answered only in trailing light kisses along his jaw leading to his mouth. I could feel Toby's Adam's apple swallow hard, his breath laboured as I playfully hovered over his lips, deliberately looking into his eyes as if memorising the moment. I captured his beautiful mouth with a sweet, teasing caress, and that was all the invitation he needed.

The couch creaked with each movement as the weight of Toby's body pressed down on me, and we desperately maneuvered into place. I could taste the remnants of beer on Toby's tongue, but it was strangely intoxicating on him: I liked it, as opposed to when drinking it myself. His hands moved, skimming up my thighs, bunching my skirt to my waist. Each movement was slow and deliberate at first, as if with each bold unraveling he expected me to stop, push him away, but every touch only caused my stomach to twist in excitement. A heated look of understanding flashed in Toby's eyes as he knelt back and looked down at me. I sat up, peeling my top over my head, and we lay down again. The heat of our bodies melted together, his strong assured hands grabbed at the elastic of my knickers and dumped me out of them. Panic jolted through me in the swift movement as Toby's dark form hovered over me, blocking out the moon. It was then I heard the confident fumble and flick of his jean button and then the zip.

This is really happening, this is really happening.

Toby lowered my bra strap, then paused. "You're shaking."

Was I?

I fought to keep my breath steady. "I don't mean to, I just …"

Toby's voice was low, soft near my cheek.

"We don't have to …"

"I want to!"

If he stopped looking down at me and just kissed me that was all I would need. Instead, he kept his concerned gaze focused on me, his beautiful face highlighted by the tinted, mottled glass from the kitchen. It shone a warm glow across us.

Toby's lips tilted, forming a coy, lopsided smile. His fingers traced lazy, comforting circles against my skin.

"It's only me, Tess," he whispered.

It was all I needed to hear. I pushed myself up to sit before him and gathered the fabric of Toby's singlet, slowly peeling it over his head.

I knew this face.

I knew this boy.

My fingers traced a line over his smooth, bronzed skin, from his shoulder, across his collarbone; they trailed a long, teasing line down to his jeans. His breath hitched as my fingers rested on the parted buttons of his Levis, and I couldn't help but smile.

Did I know what I was doing? Did I have any idea of what I was getting myself into?

He snaked his arm behind my back and lowered me onto the couch again. In that very moment, there was only one thing I knew for certain: I wanted Toby to block out the moon.

Chapter Thirty-Four

We lay on the couch in silence for the longest time.

The music had long since stopped and a warm, gentle breeze swept over the deck, cool against my dampened skin as I lay in Toby's arms.

A deep chuckle vibrated against my cheek.

I tilted my head up. "What?"

"Nothing. I just thought I was in for a quiet night, and then you showed up at my door."

I leaned on my side and looked down at his flushed face. "Do you wish I hadn't?"

He ran his fingers through my hair. "No, I'm glad you did." He smiled. "You lunatic."

I frowned and went to hit him but he caught my wrist, dragged me down into a heated kiss, and I crumbled into him. Toby pulled down the rug draped over the back of the couch and arranged it over us. We lay in a twisted cocoon until the first rays of light pierced the sky. I managed to doze in short bursts, but even though I was sore and exhausted I couldn't still my mind.

Wow. So that was sex.

I lay on my side and watched Toby's peaceful, sleeping profile; the rise and fall of his chest; his arm curved over his forehead, and his perfect bow shaped lips slightly swollen from our kisses. He looked so young, and I smiled as I pushed a wayward strand of hair off his brow. He rolled toward me, blindly moved my wrist away from his face, snaking an arm around me.

"Get some sleep, McGee," he mumbled.

I giggled. "I can't."

He peeked one eye open. "You're going to kill me, go to sleep."

"Oh that's right. I'm much younger than you, I keep forgetting," I teased.

He poked me in the ribs, and I squirmed with laughter. His eyes were still closed but a broad smile spread across his face.

"Get some sleep, Tess."

I nestled into Toby's warmth and closed my eyes, but sleep did not follow easily.

Hours must have passed as the sounds of bird calls in the surrounding bushland greeted the morning. Toby stirred next to me, and I knew what he wanted. I wanted it, too. This time it was easier. His movements were slower, his mouth captured my gasps and moans. He pushed me to new points of madness, a blinding intense place, a place I never knew I could belong, but Toby took me there.

I was still sore, but I was able to immerse myself in his warmth. There was nothing else in that moment except Toby and me as he gathered me against his chest, both breathless; his thumb stroked my bottom lip as he tilted my head up, to look into my eyes.

"You're shaking," I whispered.

He kissed the top of my hair, and I listened to the frantic beat of his heart; I smiled, revelling in the fact that I was the one responsible for it.

Sleep must have found me eventually, as I jolted awake when the blanket shifted. Toby sat up stretching, his bones clicking and popping as he stifled a yawn. I smiled, shifting towards him, squinting; I shielded my eyes against the morning sun's rays. As Toby shuffled his jeans on, I watched the muscles contort in his back. He glanced back down at me with a coy smirk.

He leaned back on his elbow, his eyes studying mine and we watched each other openly, comfortably. Toby's hand rested on my stomach and as he began to sit up he froze as his gaze dropped towards my crumpled skirt pushed high above my waist.

He sat upright, swearing under his breath.

"Jesus, Tess!" Frantic, apologetic eyes met mine.

I sat up to see dried blood smeared against my thighs.

"Shit, I'm sorry. I didn't know, I just thought that … oh, Christ, did I hurt you?"

I shifted the skirt downwards as I sat up and gave him a reassuring smile.

"Only a little." I grabbed his hand, but he flinched away which hurt more than anything that happened last night.

"I'm so sorry, Tess. I thought, if I had known …"

Suddenly all the wonder and beauty of the languid, lazy affection we had shared moments before was gone, overcome by shame and guilt. As I searched for my shirt and undies, wanting to quickly cover myself, I hardly noticed that Toby had moved away from me. The sliding door was shoved open, and Toby appeared with a washcloth. He knelt down and wiped at my legs, his gaze intense, focused, as if erasing the blood would erase what happened last night.

I stilled his hand and took the cloth from him.

"Thanks."

Comprehension dawned on his face, and he left to let me clean myself up. I stood up and wiped my legs clean, then redressed. I found the empty condom wrapper at my feet, which I discreetly tucked into my shoe. I flamed crimson, in the heat of the moment I hadn't even thought about it, hadn't even realised Toby had used a condom. I was silently thankful that he had.

Toby came back outside, this time in a clean T-shirt and holding a glass of juice.

I held the cloth awkwardly, my cheeks burning with embarrassment. He handed me the juice and took the cloth from me.

"It's okay," he said, "I'll sort it." He ducked back inside and quickly disposed of it before returning with his own glass of juice. I wanted to die.

I gulped on my pineapple juice in an effort to distract myself from the awkward silence that loomed over us.

After a moment, Toby took my glass and set it aside. He lifted my chin to meet his eyes.

"You okay?"

I tried to smile and nodded, but it wasn't very convincing.

"You're a bloody lunatic, you know that?" he said, lips tilting into a lopsided smile as he shook his head.

I relaxed slightly as his fingers brushed against my cheek to tuck a sleep-tousled strand of hair behind my ear.

"So I've been told."

He bent down and kissed my forehead, and then my lips, but they didn't linger.

"I better get home," I said, "I don't want anyone to file a missing person's report."

He walked me round the front, his hands plunged into his pockets, neither one of us looking at each other.

I grabbed my bike and we stopped at the end of the drive, in silence.

What do you say in times like this? "Thanks for last night"? "You were great"? "We should really do this again sometime"? "Thanks for taking my virginity"?

Not that one.

Instead, I settled for, "Okay, well … see ya."

I didn't look back as I started wheeling my bike down the street, knowing I couldn't hide my cringing face, knowing the dull ache between my thighs.

"Tess?"

I paused, my heart stopping at the sound of my name. He watched me thoughtfully, blinked, and it was once again broken by a smile.

"See you on the weekend?"

I wanted to cry with relief at such a minor semblance of normality. I smiled back.

"Sure," I nodded.

Once I walked around the corner, I straddled my bike with a deep breath against the pain and rode home with the sun in my eyes, a thousand memories swimming through my mind and a dumb, dreamy smile on my face.

Chapter Thirty-Five

I did it ... twice! No, I had done it *twice* with Toby Morrison.

I stood in front of my bedroom mirror with a towel wrapped around me, wondering if anything had changed; if I were to walk down the street, would people look at me differently? Could they tell? I towel dried my hair in the same daze I had been walking around in all morning.

I crept into the laundry to put my stained and rumpled clothes in the wash myself. Mum and Dad didn't need to see this. I checked my pockets as my mum always did, in case of coinage and wayward chapsticks. I had lost far too many to the washing machine; it wasn't funny. And when my Cherry Bliss chapstick had worked its way through Dad's work whites, well the parentals were not happy.

I praised small mercies as I reached into my skirt pocket and fumbled against not a lip smacker, but the crinkling of a foil packet. I quickly pulled it out and revealed the torn, empty condom wrapper. In my haste this morning, as I had kicked off my shoes, the foil packet had stuck to my foot. I'd scooped it up and shoved it in my pocket in a desperate attempt to hide all evidence.

Now, I held it, in my home. Thank God I'd decided to wash my *own* clothes. I had a horrific flash of my mum emptying my pockets and finding it.

I dumped my clothes in the washer, piled in ample detergent and high-tailed it to my room, only to be stopped by Mum in the hall.

"Are you doing your washing?" She looked at me with surprise.

"You don't have to look so horrified." I clenched my fist tighter, holding onto its contents. Panic prickled down my spine.

Mum shook her head. "You never cease to amaze me, Tess."

I was certain of it. I was sure Mum would have been amazed that I'd snuck out last night and back in this morning undetected, and she'd sure be amazed at what I held in my sweaty palm right in front of her. Here she was thinking I was her little angel, when I had never felt more like the devil as her loving eyes looked over me.

She pecked me on the cheek. "You've been such a help this summer, thanks sweetie." I breathed a sigh of relief as I quickstepped to my room, the foil wrapper burning a hole in my hand.

"Tess?"

"Yes?" I flinched, all too guilty as I turned back around.

"Why don't you ask Ellie over tonight? You haven't had anyone over these holidays. You can have a girls' night. Your dad and I won't be home 'til late."

"Okay, thanks Mum."

As I closed my door, I pressed my back against it and exhaled in relief. Losing my V plates last night with the boy of my dreams, and tonight a slumber party with my BFF. How unpredictable was my life? I dragged the shoe box from my wardrobe and placed the empty wrapper beside the expired foil packet from when I was thirteen. I couldn't help but shut the lid with a goofy smile.

That night, Ellie sat at the breakfast bar, watching me suspiciously as I covered a pizza base with cheese, humming joyously over such a mundane task.

"What's with the Mary Poppins thing?" Ellie asked. "Why are you so happy?"

"What? God, just because I do my laundry and make dinner without a scowl, what's weird about that?"

"You did your own laundry?"

"Uh, yeah, my arms aren't painted on, you know."

Such a dad saying, I thought.

"You're working two jobs and doing your own laundry? Please tell me it is under sufferance from your parents. Like you're being punished or something."

"Nope!"

"Tess, you had to be begged to get *one* part-time job these holidays, what's happened to you?"

Toby, I thought. He made me want to be a better person, a more mature person, responsible as he was and had been even when he was my age. It would sound dumb if I said it, though.

Toby and I parted on such good terms that I had been humming and smiling all day, but as the light dimmed and the sun set, so did my doubt. I thought back to the look on his face when he realised I had been a virgin, the way he had stammered 'had I known'. Had I known, what? Would he have not touched me? Would he have backed off completely? I tried to block out the negatives, my embarrassment, his anger at himself, his regret. Instead, I wanted to think about the moments of pleasure, the feeling of his breath on my neck, his mouth on me, how he held me after and folded his fingers through my hair the way he seemed to like to do.

I sighed, wiped my hands on the tea towel and glanced at Ellie. I had debated if I should tell her, and how to do it. I knew I would regret it, knowing she wouldn't approve.

But of course I was going to tell her. How could I not? Before she had arrived, I'd prepped the cassette player in the kitchen. As she watched me suspiciously, I walked over and pressed play. I looked Ellie dead in the eye, watching her expression as Madonna's 'Like a virgin' blared out of the speakers.

"I made it through the wilderness," Madonna sang and Ellie frowned with confusion as it slowly registered. Her gaze flicked to the stereo, then to me and widened in shock.

"No way!"

"Way." I waited and watched as an array of emotions played on her face.

Confusion, doubt, disbelief, horror and then a grin.

"Toby?"

I lashed out with a flick of my tea towel. "Of COURSE, Toby. Who else? Jeez, Ellie."

"Oh my God, Tess." She rounded the counter and gave me a huge hug, leaning back to slap me across the arm.

"Hey!"

"What did I tell you about playing it cool?"

"That hurt." I rubbed my arm in a scowl.

"I bet that's not all that hurts." She curved her brow, giggled and slapped me on the behind, sauntering back to sit at the breakfast bar.

"I must say, that was rather dramatic. I've never had news broken to me via song before, thanks, Tess."

I placed the pizza in the oven.

"So? When did this happen?"

"Last night," I said, "at his place."

Ellie drew in a breath. "Tell me more, tell me more." She leaned forward.

"What else is there to tell?"

"Ooooh, no you don't! Tessa Ellen McGee, I have told you every dirty little detail over the years, you're not getting out of this."

Yeah, every dirty detail, except for important things like blood and awkwardness afterwards. I knew I shouldn't have told her, now she wants to know EVERYTHING.

"It's private," I said. "I'm not you, okay?"

"Come on, tell me."

"I don't want to, Ellie."

"But I tell you everything."

"No."

"Please? Come on, so how big –"

"I said NO, Ellie!"

Ellie closed her mouth, shocked. A newfound silence set over us; she looked hurt but quickly swiped it away.

"Whatever. I better get going." She slapped her palms on the counter for leverage as she got up to leave.

"What?" I said, confused. "I thought we were going to watch a movie, have a slumber party. Pizza won't be long."

"Yeah, well, I forgot I have my own slumber party to attend to with Stan." Ellie sidestepped to the door.

"On a Monday night?" I crossed my arms sceptically.

"Not so different from your escapades last night, now is it?" And she was gone.

Ellie left without a smile or a backward glance. I had offended her. My worries had been founded. With or without Madonna's aid, telling Ellie had been a mistake.

I didn't know exactly what to expect from Ellie when next I saw her; I knew she was mad and just like every other time she was mad, the silent treatment ensued until she got over it.

But as for Toby, as each day passed at the Rose Café, I half expected him to wander through the door with a smile. Not that he had ever done so before, but now I hoped, I don't know, that something had changed. He had made no promises, no declarations of love but as each day went by that I didn't hear from him I felt more miserable than ever. Come Saturday night, when Toby was a no show at the hotel, I'd had enough of lying in my bed, night after night, every detail of *that* night on repeat in my mind.

I didn't know for sure, but it was in the air. It felt like everyone knew. Any time Toby's name was mentioned, Ringer smiled at me and Chris frowned in disapproval … but maybe I was just paranoid.

"You're being paranoid!" Ellie said (yeah, she was talking to me again).

"So you haven't said anything to Stan?"

Ellie rolled her eyes. "Not everything's about you, Tess.'

For the first time in … well, forever, Chris let Ellie and I stay for a lock-in. The outside lights were switched off and the hotel was cast into darkness. The blinds were drawn and the inner lights dimmed. All but the selected few patrons were booted out and with the doors locked, Chris jumped the bar to join in with his mates.

From what I had gathered in bits of conversation and from Ellie, Toby had gone to the city to pick up a car with his dad and wouldn't be back 'til late. Then he and the boys had an early fishing adventure on the lake.

All was of little comfort to me. By midnight I'd had enough; without Toby, the lock-in was kind of boring as Ellie and Stan canoodled by the jukebox, Ringer nodded off to sleep in the corner and Sean and Chris argued over pool table rules.

So they wouldn't make a big deal of it, I snuck out the back and into the night. The gravel crunched under my feet, and they pounded a steady pace towards a destination I wasn't so sure I should be going.

If he had wanted to see me he would have been there, no matter what kind of day he'd had. I felt sick with the thought that everything that went on between us would change. In a bad way. That he thought it such a huge mistake he would avoid me for the rest of the summer. I wanted to know, I *needed* to know that we were okay. I needed to tell him that that night had been great and not to regret it because I certainly didn't. Above all, I wanted to tell him I was glad he was my first and that I wouldn't change a thing. And if I was brave enough, I would tell him I would really like to do it again.

My mind flashed to the new foil package that was in my back pocket, from my own packet from the Caltex. I thought it rather presumptuous of myself but better to be prepared.

Little did I know that protection would be the least of my problems.

As I rounded onto the main road, closing onto Toby's street, I had already rehearsed what I would say a thousand times. I was in danger of seeming like a stalker, winding up at his place uninvited *again.* But I needed to put my mind at ease, get all of these emotions off my chest. By the time I turned into Toby's driveway, I had worked myself into such a determined state that I had no time for fear or doubt, I just had to march on in there and face Toby. As I marched up Toby's driveway, I spotted something and stopped. I froze, stock still, all my bravado, all my hope plummeted with a heartbreaking thud. Toby's back light was in 'do not disturb' mode and Angela Vickers' car was in the drive.

Chapter Thirty-Six

I didn't go in. I couldn't. Instead, I walked around Onslow through the night with no purpose, no clear direction.

Toby and Angela Vickers. I was numb. The numbness was so debilitating, all I could sense were my rapid, shallow breaths. Had I been walking for minutes, hours? I couldn't be sure. All I knew was I had backed out of Toby's drive and walked and walked, as far away as I could. I didn't allow myself to think, to feel anything. I put up a wall to everything except my breathing, the rhythmic sound that drove me away, as far as I could go.

Random strobes of lights pierced the darkness as Saturday-night joy riders passed me on the main strip. It was only when a flick of a high beam from behind and a frantic sounding of a car horn caused me to pause and shield my eyes.

A window rolled down, and it took a moment for my eyes to adjust, for my mind to clear as I peered into the car to see Ringer's girlfriend, Amanda, behind the wheel, Sean beside her. He leaned across her, peering out at me.

"There you are. You went AWOL. What are you doing roaming around on your own?"

"N-nothing," I croaked out.

"We're heading to the Point, wanna come?" Amanda asked.

Before I could decline, I heard the click of a car door.

Sean was out of the car, holding the front passenger door open for me. "Hop in the front, Tess, I won't subject you to the torture of sitting with these goons."

His gaze dipped to the back seat. Amanda's brother, Ben, and Ringer sat there, exchanging insulted glances. I hadn't even noticed they were there.

"I would hop in if I were you, it's not every day Sean gives up a front seat for someone."

Before I could object, Ben passed a West Coast Cooler through the window.

"Here, hope you like wine."

I eyed the bottle, grateful it wasn't beer. "What's with you and the girly drinks?"

He shrugged. "They're Amanda's."

"Oh, whatever, Ben. Don't hide your love for chick drinks behind me." Amanda cast a dark look in the rearview mirror.

I unscrewed the top and skulled half the bottle in one go. I wanted to feel a different kind of numb. When I finally dipped my bottle, four sets of eyes rested on me with a mixture of surprise and respect.

Sean frowned at me. "You alright, Tess?"

I took another swig and snapped my lips in a gasp of appreciation.

"Yep! Let's go!"

By the time we reached the Point, I had downed two West Coast Coolers and was handed my third with a lecture to slow down from Sean. He half laughed about it, but I could tell he was serious.

But I didn't care. I just needed to forget. Forget Angela's car in the driveway and most certainly forget Monday night ever happened.

I felt sick.

The Point had filled out to a respectably sized gathering. Someone pushed an old metal drum out the back of their ute and they filled it with twigs, newspaper and a dash of lighter fluid, and it wasn't long before a circle of people stood and sat around it.

"A bonfire in this heat?" I mused.

Sean shrugged. "Feels pretty stupid standing around in a circle without one."

"What, like fire creates ambiance?" I scoffed.

"Amongst other things. You don't think it does?"

By now I was a little buzzed, the alcohol chilling me out somewhat. This was what I was after, but it wasn't enough, so I followed Ben and Ringer as they towed the esky toward the fireside. A chilly breeze blew in over the tops of trees and penetrated the Point, dropping the temperature within minutes. I guess the drum wasn't as ridiculous as I first thought. I went to crack the lid of the esky when it slammed back into place. Sean sat his arse down on the cooler.

"Do you mind?" I said.

"Oh sorry, did you want a drink?" He batted his eyes at me innocently. Like hell.

"Yes, Grandpa," I said, "move."

Sean nodded gracefully and lifted so he could delve his hand into the icy recess, only to pull out a can of Coke, which he slapped into my palm. I snatched it out of his hand and threw it over the cliff towards the flickering lights of Onslow. I stared at Sean in my best death stare.

"Geez," he said, "I hope that doesn't break a window." Sean curved his brow.

I held out my hand again with a 'don't mess with me' look on my face. Sean handed me a Cooler, his face unreadable.

Sure, he probably thought I was crazy, but what did I care? Judge away. The opinion of the Onslow Boys meant bugger all to me at this point, and all I cared about was working on my alcoholically fuelled buzz.

I squeezed onto the esky next to Sean. As I took a deep swig, I could feel his eyes burning into the side of me.

"*What*?" I snapped, glaring at him, challenging him. The light of the fire accentuated the twinkle in his eye as he fought not to smile.

"Your lips are swallon," he said. "Looks like pash rash."

There was no danger of that, I thought. Lips hadn't touched mine in six whole days, and those particular lips never would again. I thought about Toby's lips on Angela's and wanted to throw my drink. I wanted to start walking again, away from here, away from these people, away from everything. I was so angry I couldn't bear it. The wine fueled my fire instead of numbing it.

Not-too-distant laughter broke me out of my thoughts. I noticed two snickering idiots, Carla and Peter, two of Scott's friends from school. How did they get up here? Was no place sacred? They had always taken great delight in making me miserable. They walked by, and Carla elbowed Peter and laughed behind her hand at me.

"Friends of yours?" Sean asked.

I looked down at my drink and started picking the label off. "Doesn't matter where you go in this town, you always run into someone you don't want to."

My voice was lower, calmer. I was weary. It seemed like I'd rolled through anger; I could only guess I was spiraling into self-pity as I let the judgmental snickers affect me.

Sean leaned in and spoke quietly into my ear.

"Do you want to go for a walk?" His brows were furrowed in concern. I looked around the people at the Point, including Carla and Peter, and I decided that it was exactly what I wanted to do.

"Grab me another drink, okay?"

Sean sighed. "Yes, ma'am."

We trudged through the darkness and navigated the rocky terrain far enough away that the sounds of laughter and music from a car stereo grew faint. A cylinder of light and sparks shone into the sky from the fire. We walked in the opposite direction at the base of sloping rocks behind the shack of the fire lookout. The moon was full and high enough in the sky for me to make out Sean's broad back as I carefully followed him.

Sean effortlessly wove down the path in a fast stride, my drink dangling from his fingers. I stopped and leaned against a boulder to catch my breath.

"Wait," I huffed, "slow down."

Sean paused, turning back.

"One of your steps is equal to, like, six of mine." I could make out the brilliant white of his teeth. He tilted and looked at my legs.

"Sorry, I forgot."

I reached out for my drink. He held it towards me but just as I was about to take it he lifted it out of my reach.

"Don't be a dick." I jumped but he held it up and away.

With hands on my hips, I glared at him and hoped there was enough moonlight to show my murderous look. Sean lowered the bottle and just as I reached for it, he lifted it again with a laugh.

"You're such a fucking child!"

"Am not times infinity, no returns."

I tried not to laugh but couldn't help it and leaned against the rock, arms crossed, refusing to play the game. Sean handed me my drink and joined me against the rock as I twisted the top off. The metallic snap and hiss of bubbles from his can as he opened it pierced the silence.

We both took a swig.

"Can I ask you a personal question?" Sean flicked the ring of his can away into the darkness.

I followed suit and threw my bottle top. "I guess." I suddenly felt uneasy.

"What's going on with you and Toby?"

Any momentary light mood Sean had put me in was overshadowed by a searing pain as my mind flashed back to Angela's red Lancer behind Toby's ute. I turned away, hoping he hadn't noticed my reaction.

"Nothing, why?"

"Just wondered."

I looked back at him. "Yeah, well, there's absolutely *nothing* going on."

Sean's eyes narrowed in thought, looking at me as if he was weighing something up in his mind, his expression unreadable as he took in my answer.

"Fair enough." We were quiet for a moment. "Can I ask another personal question?"

I sighed and tilted my head at him in annoyance. It made him smile.

"Can I kiss you?"

Wait … what? All thoughts, good and bad, evaporated from my mind. Sean gazed up at the stars, as if he hadn't said a word, hadn't asked me that bonkers question. An outrageous question, a question that had me thinking, and then moving and him looking down at me. And then the next thing I knew I was kissing Sean Murphy.

Chapter Thirty-Seven

Maybe it was the buzz of the alcohol?

Or the secluded darkness and the attraction I had always had for Sean, but as he lifted me and pressed me against the rock I knew that it was all in an effort to forget. I kissed Sean so fiercely it had taken him back initially, his brows raising in surprise as my hands wrapped around his neck, my tongue slipping inside his mouth. Sean broke away breathless, holding my wrists and looking down at me like I was a stranger. Then, as if reading my pleading gaze, silently telling him that this was what I wanted, what I needed, he pinned me against the rock and met my urgent, forceful kisses. As our mouths feasted on one another, I knew it was exactly what I needed. My mind was clearing, erasing every touch, every memory, every moment with Toby Morrison. And as Sean lifted my leg to bend around his waist, I wanted to hurt Toby, hurt him like he hurt me. A new excitement ran through me, a new urge as I moved and moaned against Sean's muscular frame, his arms pinning me in like a cage, lifting me as if I weighed nothing. I wrapped my other leg around his waist and gasped at the new pleasure I felt as he pressed in between the junction of my thighs. Now all thoughts of anyone else were gone as I was blinded by the thrill that threatened to surge as Sean's hips rocked into me. We were fully clothed but with heated, passionate kisses and touches I was on the edge, and as his hand slipped from my breast to between my legs and his friction intensified, the pleasure so intense, so unexpected, I screamed into his shoulder and went limp in his arms. Sean's groans ebbed as my own died and he slumped, his weight on me pinned me to the cold slab that stung through my shirt and, what I suspected, grazed my back now I could feel the sting.

Hot breaths heated my neck, and then Sean's gravelly voice half laughed in my ear.

"Christ! I haven't come that hard since high school." He chuckled and kissed my neck.

I let the aftershock of my climax ride over me; I felt the wet patch and the bulge pressing against me from Sean's jeans. I pressed my face into the alcove of Sean's neck, and sobbed. I sobbed so hard and so violently my body shook. All my hurt, anger, confusion and shame flooded through me.

"Hey, hey, hey ... what's wrong?" He cupped my face, forcing me to look into his worried eyes.

"What's wrong, did I hurt you?"

I laughed through the tears. "Hurt me? No." God, if only he knew what he just did to me. "I'm sorry." I broke away, straightened my clothes and fixed my hair. I tried to wipe my face.

"This was a mistake. I shouldn't have come here with you."

Sean rubbed my arm. "Do you want to go home?"

I hiccupped and nodded. "I'm sorry," I whispered.

He smiled. "Hey, don't be, come on."

We walked back to the group, moving slower this time and together. Sean kept glancing at me as he stepped over rocks and steadied me as I went along. As we walked back into the clearing of the Point, Sean pulled his shirt over his crotch and I straightened my skirt and top. We rounded the corner of the old fire shack and walked right into the path of Carla and Peter. Their stunned gazes roamed over our dishevelled states, my bloodshot eyes, our kiss-swollen lips. They exchanged knowing smirks and walked off without a word, whispering and snickering to each other.

I couldn't take any more. I had never felt so ashamed; I had used Sean and behaved in a way … who was that girl out in the bush with him? She didn't seem like Tess, that's for sure.

***

I squinted one sleepy eye open as my phone chimed. A text message.

Breakfast at the Diner you dirty stop out. From: Ellie.

I had disappeared on her last night without a word, something we promised not to do to one another, so I figured I owed her. Plus, I had to tell her that my Toby phase was well and truly over and that I didn't want to talk about him, ever again. My summer was to enter a new phase and this one didn't involve the Onslow Boys – any of them. It was the only way I could see surviving with my reputation intact, not to mention my sanity.

I was exhausted, my hair still damp from my hot shower – a useless attempt to get rid of my hangover. Stupid West Coast Coolers. It really was the devil's brew.

A block away from the Caltex diner my phone chimed a message from Ellie:

Toby's here :)

A cold shiver ran down my spine. She thought she was passing on good news. I paused and contemplated going home again, but then squared my shoulders, held my head up high and kept walking.

Sure enough, a long line of cars parked out the front, and right in the middle of the car park was Toby's navy Ford ute. I recalled the vague mutterings of the Onslow Boys' fishing trip. Was that today? All of a sudden, I felt grateful for stopping by his house; it would prevent me from mooning over him and making an even bigger fool of myself than I had already. Even though my head tried to convince myself, my heart wasn't buying it for a second.

I pushed through the door. The Caltex booths that lined the front windows were packed and, as usual, the place was a hub of activity. Sunday mornings were always chaotic at the Caltex, a regular meeting point before people set out on their lake-bound adventures. More importantly, you could fuel up on greasy eggs and bacon after a boozy Saturday night. My stomach churned; I couldn't think of anything worse. A sea of inquisitive eyes rested on me, including Toby's. A boyish smile lit his face when he looked up from his menu; I never hated him more because my traitorous heart still skipped a beat at the very sight of him. I exchanged niceties and said hello to everyone and no one in particular, making a point of not looking at him. The Onslow Boys and company occupied two booths; there was only one space left and mercifully it wasn't in Toby's booth.

Everyone slid sideways and bunched up a little closer to allow me space; Sean moved his things and shifted without a beat even though he was in deep debate with Stan who sat opposite with Ellie. I didn't even mind the fact I was wedged in next to Sean. When he dropped me home last night, we had agreed our tryst in the bush would be our secret. Even now, the fact he didn't offer me a reassuring smile made me grateful and relax a little. Unfortunately, the line of our U shaped booth had me sitting directly back to back with Toby. He was so agonisingly close, I could feel the seat dip and shift every time he moved.

Ellie beamed at me and raised her brows as if I was sitting in the best seat in the house. It seemed to take all her effort not to give me a double thumbs up, and I was definitely grateful that she didn't. Sean slid me a menu.

"Something to reline the stomach?"

"Coffee to reignite my shattered soul."

He laughed. "With a dash of fruit-flavored wine?"

"Sean, I swear if you don't stop talking, I will claw your face off."

Sean cat-called and laughed a deep, happy laugh in typical Sean fashion. I smiled back. Even though we had overstepped a massive line last night, nothing had changed. That was something, at least. I tried to swallow the nauseous feeling that swelled in the pit of my stomach; being so close to Toby was killing me. When it came to him, no matter what beautiful, friendly and totally oblivious smile he threw my direction, I knew nothing would be okay with us. I tried not to let my heart spike each time I heard his voice from behind me, I felt the clamminess of my hands trying to keep my breaths even. Being so close to him, to Sean, I couldn't take it. I had to get out of there.

"Where did you get to last night, anyhow?" Ellie tried for mad, but she was more curious then anything.

Sean didn't flinch, but I must have shifted uneasily, and the booth behind me shifted with movement, and I watched Toby pass and walk towards the counter. He was back with Angela. I meant nothing to him. My misery spiral was interrupted by the sound of skin sliding against vinyl.

"Hey, did any of you hear about last night?" Amanda's elbows appeared over from the other booth and rested on the back of our seat between Sean's head and mine.

I gripped the salt shaker.

"No doubt we're about to," mused Stan.

Amanda looked around like she was some A-grade spy before she continued.

"Guess who's back in town?" Her eyes lit with excitement.

She had all our attentions now.

"Angela Vickers," she whispered, perhaps a bit too loudly, as she flicked a glance towards the counter.

The salt shaker flew out of my hand and rolled across the table. Sean grabbed it and gave me a weird look as he placed it back in the holder.

"So?" Sean snapped as he moved his head away to avoid Amanda's elbow.

"*So*, apparently she went round to Toby's last night."

Ellie's eyes widened, her gaze darted to me, and I was all but ready to get up and leave. The last thing I needed was details.

"Apparently, she rocked up at some ungodly hour, drunk off her head and started roof rocking his house."

A snort escaped Stan and Sean broke out in laughter.

"It's not funny," Amanda continued.

"He had to call her parents to come get her. She was smashing the place apart, broke all his lights with rocks, broke a window ..."

My eyes darted towards Toby who was in a conversation with a local by the counter. Oh no.

"Then what happened?" Ellie pressed.

"Her mum and dad came and got her and, boy, were they pissed. Her mum went right off at Toby, saying he broke their precious daughter's heart, she even slapped him across the face."

"How do you know all this?" I said.

Amanda smiled. "I know everything." With a wink, she looked pointedly from me to Sean and flopped back down in her seat again as Toby returned.

What had I done?

Ellie missed nothing. She looked from Sean to me with a troubled expression.

My throat closed up, my heart beating rapidly. The diner started feeling too small; way too small. I needed air. I needed to get out.

"I have to go." I jumped out of my seat.

He wasn't with her, he wasn't with her.

As I strode across the car park, the door slid open again behind me.

"Tess, wait up." Ellie followed me. "What's going on?"

"Nothing, I'm just hungover."

"Bullshit. What's wrong with you?"

How could I summarise the week's events in a Caltex parking lot, within a stone's throw of the Onslow Boys?

"What's up with you and Sean?"

"Nothing," I said too quickly

She rolled her eyes at me, her jaw set. "I saw the look you two gave each other after Amanda said that stuff, why don't you tell me anything anymore? I thought we were best friends."

"We are."

"No, best friends tell each other things. They're not all secretive and leave in the middle of a lock-in without telling me. It's like ... who are you, Tess? I don't even know you these days."

My stomach soured. "Sorry to be so inconvenient, Ellie. For once, I have a life and you can't stand it. What do you want me to do, wait on the bonnet of cars for you for the rest of our lives?"

"What are you talking about?"

"You know what I'm talking about. If you think I've changed, then you're right. Maybe I have. It's called not living in your shadow anymore, so get used to it."

Ellie watched me for a moment then stepped closer, her look grave. "Tess, I just don't want you to whore around."

"What, like you?" I regretted it the moment it left my mouth, I regretted the look of hurt it caused to flash across her face and I regretted hearing her response.

"Go to hell, Tess."

Ellie walked off just as Stan approached, hearing the final outburst. In a way I wished she had just hit me; I deserved it.

The door slid open again and Stan and Ellie passed Sean, Ringer and Toby on their way back. Oh God. I would have completely crumbled, except Sean handed me a coffee in a polystyrene cup.

"You forgot this."

"Thanks."

Sean and Ringer walked on towards the car, readying themselves for the epic fishing adventure, leaving Toby who stood next to me, the two of us alone for the first time since … well … just since.

If he asked me if I was okay, I might have screamed, but in typical Toby fashion, he didn't pry.

"I didn't know you liked coffee." He slid a pair of Ray Bans on, shielding him from the bright morning glare.

I tried to smile but I knew I didn't pull it off. I blinked away the tears that threatened to come and wished I had my own pair of Ray Bans to hide my eyes.

How was all this possible? How had I managed to do so many stupid things in such a short span of time?

Toby sensed my mood and struggled to find words of ease.

"Well, if I don't get sunstroke, I'll see you tonight?"

"Sure."

Sean and Ringer cat-called for Toby to hurry up, and he gave me a shy smile as he walked away.

"Toby!" I called after him.

He turned, peeling off his shades so his eyes met mine. It was like a silent exchange before he broke into a brilliant smile, and I knew instantly he wasn't trying to avoid me. If anything, my guilt over last night's train wreck had me wanting to avoid him and his beaming smile. A smile that still showed even after last night and his showdown with Angela, he was still here smiling at *me*. He winked at me, a secret between just the two of us, replaced his shades and jogged towards the ute and his boys, without a care in the world.

What had I done?

Chapter Thirty-Eight

I know I said Ellie usually got over things, but this time was different.

The afternoon shift was tense and awkward as my attempts at small talk with her, let alone apologise, were met with stony silence. Any time our paths crossed in the restaurant, Ellie made a not-too-subtle attempt to avoid me all together. In the evening, when I made my way into the kitchen, I felt sick at the thought of enduring more of the same cold treatment.

I deserved it, I knew that, but it didn't mean I had to like it.

Laughter echoed out from the kitchen as I pushed my way through the swinging kitchen door. Ellie, Rosanna and Amy stood around the prep area. I was met with a casual 'hello' from Rosanna and Amy. Ellie's laughter dried up and her smile dropped at the sight of me. She pushed her shoulders back and with a casual flick of her pony tail, gathered her apron and left the kitchen without a word.

"What's going on between you two?" Amy frowned.

"Long story." I sighed. It wasn't really that long; I just didn't want to talk about it with the likes of Amy and Rosanna. Amy shrugged and continued her conversation with Rosanna. I pulled my rings off and dropped them into my apron pockets, glancing wearily at the kitchen clock – 5:55pm; it was going to be a long, long shift.

At least my fallout with Ellie took my mind off other things, the things that really troubled me. It was the only positive point I could take from the drama. I looked blankly at the docket whose table number I had forgotten to write down; Christ, I couldn't even remember who I'd served. This mistake wasn't an isolated incident tonight. As soon as I thought I was getting my shit together at work, I was back to making stupid mistakes, like the good old days. I walked from the restaurant into the bar trying to jog my memory. Was the salmon for that old guy with the comb over? How about this Lamb Rogan Josh; had that lady in the leopard print ordered it? Had I served her? I had no idea. Shit! I didn't fancy being yelled at by Rosanna, not tonight. I moved towards the poolroom and frowned at the docket, hoping if I stared at it hard enough, it would jolt my memory.

But it didn't. Instead, my body was jolted as I slammed into what felt like a brick wall. Knocking me off balance, I juggled the plates precariously.

Oh no, oh no, don't drop them, oh no …

A pair of hands reached out to steady me.

"Whoa, look out!" Toby held me still for a moment until I seemed to have my balance again.

I didn't drop them, thank God I didn't drop them.

He grinned down at me. "You okay?"

I had been so distracted I hadn't even heard the front bar door open, or seen the Onslow Boys walk in, until I had collided with one. Sean and Stan were behind Toby, trying not to laugh. My face flushed.

"Sorry, I was in the zone." I stepped from his grasp, the small space in front of the door seemed claustrophobic all of a sudden; Toby's hands dropped but his touch had burned into my skin.

"Stop manhandling the staff, Tobias," Sean muttered into Toby's ear as he pushed passed Toby who still blocked the front door. Stan followed but didn't contribute. I guess Ellie must have told him what we were fighting about. What I'd said.

"Rough night?" Toby asked.

"Yeah, I just wish it would be over already."

"So I guess the last thing you want to do is go for a drive after work?"

"What?" I said, in perhaps a too high-pitched voice.

"Did you want to go for drive," he repeated, "with me?"

I tried not to smile too widely. "Um, yeah sure."

He nodded, a lopsided tilt to his mouth. "Well, you know where to find me."

He weaved his way through the poolroom, his skin darkened by his day fishing in the sun. He must have gone home and changed – now he wore a navy T with khaki cargos and boat shoes. He didn't smell like fish, but the Cool Water aftershave I had eyed in his console, it was my favourite smell in the whole world now, much more appealing than cooking oil and garlic bread which infused into my clothes each night. Seeing Toby (or rather, *colliding* with Toby) had lifted my spirits, and the thought of leaving here with him after work made my stomach flip in excitement. It was an unexpected delight in what I had thought would be a night from hell. Now the night couldn't end early enough, but for a whole other reason. And just as I pushed my way back into the kitchen it came to me!

"Table number 29!"

As Ellie and I filled out our time cards in silence, Chris poked his head into the restaurant bar, twirling the hotel keys around his finger. "You girls staying for lock-in?"

Ellie waited for me to answer first.

"No, I'm going to head out."

Ellie said, "Then I'll stay." Another not-too-subtle jab; Chris shrugged and headed out back.

I went to get my things.

"What, you're not going to stay to cross Chris off your list?" Ellie said. They were the first words she'd uttered to me all night.

"Ellie, look, I ..."

"Or is it Ringer's turn tonight?"

"Ellie, I'm sorry I said that."

"Yeah, well in future, it's best not to say anything at all. Shouldn't be too hard, you seem really good at it now."

Ellie filled out the last of her hours and spiked them near the till, without so much as a backwards glance. I sighed and leaned on the restaurant bar, cupping my forehead in my hands. A dull ache had slowly formed in my head over the last few hours, and I wished it would just stop so I could think straight. As soon as I got home to lie in the darkness, staring at the shadows on my ceiling, I knew I would think of a million clever things to say, an amazing, award winner of a speech that would have won Ellie over and made us best friends again. But right now, I had nothing.

"Are you meditating?"

I jumped and spotted Toby standing over my shoulder. Chris must have flicked the main switch off because the restaurant was dark. With my eyes closed, I hadn't even noticed, which added to my shock when I opened my eyes to see the shady figure next to me.

I clutched at my heart. "You're like creeping Jesus."

He laughed. "Sorry."

I spiked my time card with a sigh. "Can we get out of here?"

"Your chariot awaits."

"In the form of a blue Ford ute?" I curved my brow.

"But of course," he said in an over-the-top French accent.

"Sacre blur, bad accent alert!"

"Wow," he said, "Le rude?"

"Le sorry?"

"Le hurt." Toby clutched his heart.

"What can I do to soothe your shattered ego?"

Toby drummed his chin thoughtfully, pacing around me. He stopped just near enough to whisper in my ear.

"Le kiss?" He circled his arms around my waist, and I couldn't help but giggle. The feeling of being hidden in the dark with Toby, as if nothing had changed, made my heart swell with joy, until a flash of last night with Sean came to mind and I felt the waves of guilt wipe the smile from my face.

"How's about le hurry up, so I can le lock up, Peppi Le Piu."

We both flinched at the sound of Chris's voice right by us.

He flicked on the light with a sigh. "I trust you two love birds will be making a back exit?"

Toby scratched the back of his neck and smirked; Chris attempted a serious expression, but he couldn't pull it off. He unlocked the beer garden door, and we made a quick escape.

"Speaking French, Tobias?" Chris said. "Must be love?" He groaned out the last word as Toby sucker punched him playfully in the ribs as he passed, the way it seemed even grown boys do.

As Toby and I weaved our way carefully around the tables and patio heaters in the unlit beer garden, he clasped my hand from behind and tugged me into him. I giggled giddily as he pulled me into an even darker, secluded alcove. I was so close against him, I could feel the warmth of his breath on my face.

"What do you know? This is where it all began," he said.

"Began?"

"This is exactly where I was when I wanted to kiss you," he whispered, his lips brushing along my neck causing me to melt under his touch. "So bad."

I breathed deeply trying to blink my way out of my daze when I realised we were standing where the DJ, fairy lights and black velvet curtain had been the night of the disco.

"Except this time there's no drunk netballer squawking at us," I teased.

"I wouldn't care if the seven horseman of the Apocalypse charged through the garden right now, nothing's gonna stop me from doing this." He leaned down and captured my lips with tenderness, a completely perfect kiss, like it always was. I lifted myself on the tips of my toes to meet him. His hands fisted into my hair, making no apologies as his kisses intensified, became more forceful. He wasn't back with Angela. I'd been so wrong. He still wanted me. It wasn't a mistake; he didn't regret *that* night at all. Toby Morrison wanted me.

Chapter Thirty-Nine

We drove to McLean's Beach and parked off in a leafy, secluded section just off the sand.

It wasn't the prettiest part of the beach, nor the biggest. It couldn't cater for more than a few at a time, which was what made it so perfect. The ute's headlights lit up abandoned sticks fishermen had wedged into the muddy embankment to stand their rods in. Apart from that, the beach was untouched. There were no other signs of civilisation. We were well and truly alone. As soon as Toby had put his car into park, I was already straddling his lap, kissing him deeply. It mattered little that the steering wheel jutted uncomfortably into my back; being in Toby's arms was all that I cared about.

I suppose we should have had the 'talk'; gone over where we were both at and where things stood between us. Even though all we did was make out and roam each other's bodies with our hands, neither of us wanted to break the moment. Not until there was a distant boom and burst of colour in the sky.

"Look at that." Toby nodded over my shoulder.

Fireworks lit the sky in a cascade of sparks and colour, it felt like they were swirling and exploding just for us. This part of the world at McLean's Beach was not only a secluded haven, but it was also the best position from which to watch fireworks I had ever been to, even better than the Point. They were far, yet seemed so close, like our own personal show. I rolled off him and sank onto the bench beside Toby, and we watched the sky in wonder. Toby wrapped his arm around me as I lay my head against his shoulder. When I wasn't transfixed with the beauty of the fireworks, I splayed my hand against his, linking our fingers together. Toby's other fingers folded through my hair in lazy strokes that made me smile with happiness.

"Don't fall in love with me, Tess."

I blinked rapidly, shocked back into the moment. It was like a record being scratched, or the slamming of a finger in a car door. I looked at him quickly, but his eyes were fixed on the fireworks.

Where had that come from?

Suddenly all the beauty, the intimacy of our entwined fingers, our closeness, felt cold.

"Don't flatter yourself," I said and sat up straight, breaking the connection.

Toby sighed. "I just don't think I'm the right guy for you."

Here we go, I thought. I wanted to physically brace my hand against the dash. Seemed he wanted the 'talk' after all.

"Let me save you some time," I said. "I'm seventeen, you're twenty-two, 'you're a nice kid and all, but let's face it' and blah, blah blah. Spare me the speech, okay?"

Toby grasped the steering wheel, I could see his jaw clench. "That's one way of looking at it," he said, "but I was thinking it's more to do with, 'what does someone like you see in someone like me?'"

My mouth fell open, and I quickly closed it. Was he serious? He couldn't be …

Toby rolled his eyes in frustration as if I was an idiot for not getting it.

"Tess, you're smart, beautiful … you're young! You have your whole life in front of you. I don't want to be a complication in that."

I could hardly believe what he was saying. I wanted to laugh, I wanted to cry, I wanted to beat the crap out of him for being so ridiculous.

I took a deep breath, then another one, thinking about what I wanted to say. "You know, before I started my job at the Onslow I guess my life was pretty uncomplicated. You know why? Because I was nothing. I just had Ellie and Adam. I couldn't talk to anyone else, really. Hell, I couldn't even make a bloody cappuccino without blushing. I was scared of everything; I wanted to just stay under my rock. Do you know how debilitating it is to live like that? Being terrified of everything, everyone? Being afraid of saying the wrong thing, wearing the wrong clothes, putting the wrong song on the jukebox? I have to think and analyse *every* step of my existence with this terror that I am going to fuck it up."

Toby listened, watching me; he didn't break contact, didn't even blink, as if he was peering deep into my soul. I guess after saying that, he pretty much was.

I broke from his gaze and looked down at my hands in my lap. "Then I met you and the Onslow Boys and everything changed. I can't even try and put into words how liberating it is. For the first time in my life I feel free. You did that. So if I was to choose? Then I choose complicated," I said, with a nod of finality. I met his eyes again in a silent challenge. "I choose you."

Toby looked at me for the longest time. It was hard not to break eye contact, but I simply refused to. Soon, a small smile tugged at the corner of his mouth. I swear, I didn't even realise I'd been holding my breath 'til that moment.

Toby shifted his gaze out the windscreen, into the darkness over the water. The fireworks were over; I hadn't even noticed.

"Remember the first night we spoke?" he asked after a while.

"You mean when you told me to get off your car?"

Toby threw his head back and laughed in a way I had rarely seen.

"You should have seen your face."

"You nearly made me cry, you know," I said with a wry smile.

Toby fought to contain his laughter. "You know most girls would have told me where to go, or flipped me off." He shook his head. "But not you."

"Yeah, I know, rabbit in the headlights, such a good look."

"That's the thing. I've never met anyone like you, Tess. You think you're a no one?

You're so wrong. *So* wrong. You stand in a room with all the Angelas, even the Ellies. None of them can compare to you. I remember when you started working at the Onslow, I couldn't keep my eyes off you. You were so terrified. You weren't full of yourself like other girls. Every time you walked into the bar, you were like a breath of fresh air. Even when Angela was a bitch to you, you rose above it. You made me see the difference in people. You're not a nobody, Tess, you're a somebody."

I let his words run over me as I tried to fight the tears that prickled at my eyes. I didn't need to ask about last night with Angela – I should never have doubted him. I was a somebody. My chest swelled with such intense emotion I didn't think I could bear it.

"Tess, the other night when we …"

I closed my eyes, a single tear rolling down my check.

"Don't. Please, Toby. Don't spoil it."

Toby took my hand into his.

"Why didn't you tell me?"

I buried my face in my hands, afraid to meet his eyes, embarrassed about my coming confession.

"I'd liked you for so long, I was afraid that if I told you, you might have not wanted to … continue."

Toby laughed.

"Tess, there isn't a drunken, screaming netballer in the world that would have made me not want to … continue. I just may have gone about it a little differently."

He squeezed my hand gently, and I leaned into him once more, resting my head on his shoulder.

"So, you liked me for a long time, huh?"

"The longest."

"How long?" I could tell he was smiling.

I cringed. "For a stalkerishly long time."

"And how long is that exactly?"

"I saw you from across a crowded school yard."

"What? School?"

"I was doing my Year Seven orientation, and you were in Year Twelve standing with a bunch of boys."

"Wow," Toby said, "you little perv."

I giggled and the tension ebbed away. We fell into a comfortable silence for a while, but Toby broke it with a sigh.

"What are we doing?"

I moved then, climbing into his lap. I linked my arms around his neck. That was enough deep conversation. I pressed light kisses against his mouth, gently biting his bottom lip, and he dug his fingers into my back with approval.

"Well, whatever we're doing, can it be done at your place?" I whispered against his mouth.

He tilted his head back and cocked an eyebrow.

"Are you trying to seduce me, Miss McGee?"

"Is it working?"

Before I could kiss him again, in one fluid motion he slid me off his lap and turned the key in the ignition. I giggled at the unexpectedness of it and straightened beside him as he pulled into gear.

"You betcha."

Chapter Forty

I sent Ellie what seemed like my hundredth email, begging for forgiveness.

The long, drawn-out silence of our fallout had reached a new level, a level we had never been to and I was scared our friendship might not recover from.

I was startled out of my gloomy thoughts when Mum tapped lightly on my door.

"Tess, hon, Ellie's here to see you."

I all but knocked over my desk chair when I stood up. I was afraid to hope that she'd come on good terms.

Relief flooded through me the moment she coyly stepped passed Mum, into my room, and offered me a friendly smile. Everything was going to be alright.

As soon as Mum closed the door, I body-slammed her with a bear hug.

"Jesus, Tess, it's not like I just returned from war or anything."

Tears squirted out of my eyes and there was nothing I could do to stop them. I was just so relieved. I could hardly stop myself as I sniffled and sobbed and headed into blubbering-mess territory.

Ellie rubbed at my shoulders, "Don't cry, please don't cry, Tess, its okay."

She sat me down on the bed, squeezed my hand and waited out my mini breakdown.

"I'm so sorry, Ellie, I'm so sorry for what I said and for what I didn't say," I blubbered. "You're right, best friends should tell each other everything. You're always so open with me and I should be with you, because you really are my best friend in the whole wide world." I knew I was babbling, but everything spilled out in such a rush Ellie had to clench my arm and tell me it was enough.

She grabbed me a tissue and waited for me to catch my breath.

"It's me who should be sorry, Tess." Her eyes began to well, too.

"You have nothing to be sorry about." I sniffed.

Ellie's chin trembled. "I always just expected you to be there, waiting around for me. You were right, I didn't want you to have a life. I was a selfish idiot."

"Well, we're even then. We can call it a draw in the 'being idiots' category." I squeezed her hand reassuringly.

Ellie just shook her head. "It's not even."

I looked into Ellie's red-rimmed eyes and a coldness swept over me as I tried to read the level of dread in Ellie's expression. I let go of her hand.

"What did you do, Ellie?"

"That's just it, I haven't done anything. Me and Stan, we haven't you know ... done it."

I paused, surprised. "Really?"

"Yeah."

I slumped on my bed in relief. "Ellie, that's a good thing," I assured her. "It just means that you really like him, that when it comes time it'll be really special because you care about each other." I swelled all over with such affection for Ellie, my best friend, so proud of the new leaf she had turned over this summer.

My words, however, did not seem to console her. Ellie couldn't even look at me; instead, she shredded a tissue in her shaky hands.

I scooted closer. "Ellie?"

"I'm so scared, Tess. I'm so frightened of doing it with Stan."

This vulnerability in her was new, and I was so happy to see it.

I smiled. "Because you like him so much?"

It was then that Ellie's tear-brimmed eyes met mine.

"Because I'm a virgin."

***

I stood at the kitchen sink, slowly downing a glass of water with a shaky hand. I was grateful I was home alone, as any attempt at coherent conversation would have been lost on me. My mind was mush and had been ever since Ellie left.

Ellie was a virgin.

Could I believe anything anymore? Once I had picked myself up off the floor where I'd fallen off the bed and got over the sting of the carpet burn on my elbow, what followed was an epic confession from a blubbering Ellie that left me shocked, stunned and shocked all over again.

Ellie confessed that the reason why the boys were so mean to her was because she refused to put out, but she agreed to let people believe she had. Little did she know that those lies would end up being the only reason boys wanted to be with her.

I couldn't believe it. What about her confidence? Her knowledge? Her sage advice?

Probably stupid *Cosmo* magazine.

Ellie said she had adopted the certain image, the reputation she had so fully, that she didn't know who the real Ellie was anymore.

And then she met Stan.

He didn't want her for sex; he was with her because he liked her: the real Ellie.

The clincher in the surrealness of her confession was when Ellie turned to me and asked:

"So, what's it like? You know ... sex."

I had blinked frantically, and my mind had gone blank. I just couldn't process that question, not from *Ellie*.

I had been with Toby a mere hours before, and I still struggled to form an answer to that question.

I had given as much detail as I was comfortable with. But as I stood at the kitchen window in the comfort of my own company, I remembered every detail from last night. It had been amazing, but my body had tensed momentarily as it remembered what it had done with Sean only a night ago.

Chapter Forty-One

To: tessmcgee

Cc: ellieparker

Lock up your daughters, Onslow!

I'm coming home!

Sender: Adam I can jump puddles Henderson

Adam's grand homecoming coincided with another disco in the beer garden. Okay, so maybe Ellie and I had begged and pleaded with Uncle Eric and Chris to hold one that weekend. Hell, we wanted to celebrate.

The best thing about having inside connections was that we managed to get the disco organised for the Friday night, a non-work night! I even suggested to Chris he could promote Amy from dish pig to fill-in waitress. He begrudgingly agreed to give her a go and that resulted in Amy becoming President, Vice President and Secretary of the Tess McGee Fan Club. No more dirty looks for me!

Amy skidded through the back sliding door to the beer garden where I sat with Ellie in a shady spot where only a small slither of sunlight reached.

"Tess, I heard your phone go off." Amy handed over my bag.

"Ta."

She smiled brightly and ran back to the restaurant to get stuck into her waitressing chores.

"She is the most enthusiastic waitress I've ever seen," Ellie said with a laugh.

My screen was lit up with the words '1 new message'.

Toby.

A smile broke out across my face.

"One guess." Ellie playfully kicked at my chair.

Life was easier now, better. I didn't have to snoop around corners for secondhand information or rely on Ellie to give me the update on when the Onslow Boys would be coming in. Instead, Toby and I texted. We had each other's numbers now. It was officially on, but we were still keeping quiet about it, keeping it on the down low for a while. We hadn't seen each other since that night at McLean's Beach and then his house; he was either at the garage or I was at the café.

So I couldn't help but beam when I read the message.

See you at 8

Toby.

"Is he sending you love poetry or something?" Ellie peeked over her shades, shades she didn't really need now that the sun had shifted.

I sighed. "Not exactly, but it's good enough for me."

I went home to change, the thought of arriving at the disco all fresh and clean, instead of stinking of kitchen fumes, my hair shiny instead of limp from steam over the stove and sink was a nice change. A brilliant change. I glammed up some fitted jeans with some fancy heels and a baby blue halter that contrasted nicely against the tan of my skin.

Ellie had arrived early to meet Stan for dinner so I knew I would be making a solo entrance. I made a point of arriving later than eight. I aimed for cool and casual, which I probably wasn't pulling off very well as I weaved through the crowd, ducking and stretching to see a familiar face.

So much for a grand entrance – I didn't know any of these people. Had I gatecrashed a private function? It was then that a pair of hands covered my eyes, and I heard the unmistakable taunt of a familiar voice.

"Look out, lady! I have use of both my arms now."

I spun around and flung myself into the two fully functioning arms of Adam.

"Hey, you!"

Adam crushed me in his grip, but I gave as good as I got.

"I missed you," I said.

Adam smiled. "Tess, stop flirting with me, please. Speaking of, where's Pretty Parker?"

I whacked him in the upper arm. "Don't start."

Adam screamed so loud, people stopped mid dance to glare at us with disapproving stares.

"*Stop* it, Tess! I have delicate bones."

I went to retort but Adam was body slammed as a squealing Ellie appeared from nowhere and threw herself onto him in a hug.

"Why aren't I a chick magnet like this with all the girls?" His voice was muffled as he tried to blow Ellie's hair from his mouth.

"Because you belong to us!" Ellie declared.

Adam threw a look behind him to Stan, who watched on in amusement.

Adam shook his head. "Chicks! They're just so needy. On the email, the phone constantly. It's exhausting."

"This coming from someone who fingerknitted us friendship bracelets and mailed them to us?" I added.

"Oh wow! Would you look at that?" Adam pretended he saw someone in the distance and waved to a girl. She looked confused and glanced behind her to see who Adam was waving to.

"I'll be right back, better circulate. People get really funny if you don't say hi." He was quickly swallowed up by the crowd.

There was a downshift in lighting and the music slowed as The Cranberries song, 'Linger', filled the night for the lovers in the garden. Ellie and Stan took to the dance floor, to not do the Robot or the Sprinkler but just to hold each other and sway. I smiled,

Ellie finally got her Prince Charming.

As my gaze drifted, I saw Toby at the entrance, eyes locked on me. He broke into a broad smile as he weaved his way through the crowd, not taking his gaze from me. Not once.

I folded my arms. "You're late."

"You're beautiful." He smiled wickedly. "Especially when you're mad."

Ringer squeezed past, guiding Amanda through.

"Why don't you ever speak to me like that?"

Toby punched Ringer in the arm.

Ringer turned shrugging his shoulders.

"Incidentally," Sean's voice jolted me. I had forgotten that we stood in a very public beer garden. "Ringer does speak to Amanda like that, when he's drunk. It's not pretty." In true Sean fashion, he was happy and carefree.

Luckily, though, we hadn't talked any more about it or anything. It seemed we were cool. Nothing had changed between us since that night at the Point. Ringer flipped Sean the bird and took Amanda to the dance floor. Toby, Sean and I stood on the edge, watching the couples hold each other close and sway. Guilt spiked through me any time I was with them together. I forced it down, fearful it would seep into my time with Toby. I had to tell him about Sean. I knew I did. But not now. Toby gently rubbed a lazy circle with his thumb on my palm.

A collective scream whooped out of the dance floor and the unmistakable guitar strums flowed through the speakers, as 'Wonderwall' sounded. This song was everywhere and everyone – even, tragically, my dad – seemed to know all the words. Ellie and Stan stumbled over, pulling the three of us onto the dance floor where there was an explosion of smashed bodies pushed together in the cramped space. Nobody cared, as the DJ lights flashed to the beat and everyone swayed and belted out the chorus. Toby held my hands, anchoring me to him in a rare, unnoticed moment in which everyone was lost in the music. We broke eye contact as Adam appeared and slung his arms around our shoulders, forcing us into some bad side-shuffling dance moves. Ringer and Amanda slow danced to our left, Ellie and Stan sang joyfully into their mimed microphones, jokingly serenading each other while Sean played air guitar like no one else. We drowned out the music as the whole disco sang at the top of their lungs. We linked into a chain of slung arms and twisted limbs. A group of friends enjoying a moment.

'Wonderwall' faded out and was replaced by 'Bow River', a real Aussie anthem by Cold Chisel. Non-dancer Toby quickly took his exit from the dance floor and mimed to Sean asking if he wanted a drink. Toby leaned into me, he was warm and smelled incredible.

"You want a drink?"

I shook my head, and he winked and squeezed my hand as he vacated the dance floor, sidestepping a flailing girl. Sean took my hand and started to Rock 'n' Roll dance with me in very uncoordinated moves that eventually just led him into flinging me around the dance floor like a rag doll. He flung me towards him too fast, and so quick that I slammed into him and stopped hard, my nose smashed against his chest. I probably would have been in pain if I hadn't been so winded.

“Sorry ’bout that.” He tried to not laugh through his breaths, but it was evident we were both beyond it.

I rubbed my forehead. “That’s going to hurt tomorrow.” Sean had stopped laughing, instead he seemed distracted by something near the bar. I tried to follow his gaze but my view was blocked by the crisscross of the dancing crowd.

“What’s wrong?”

I wasn’t sure he had heard me until he flicked an agitated look my way.

“Nothing, just wait here, okay?”

Okay, Mr Cryptic.

Whatever. I continued to dance by myself, lost in the feel of the music. Suddenly Adam and Ellie flanked me, and my stomach fizzed with excitement. I thought we were about to tear up the dance floor school-social style. Ellie dug her fingers painfully into my arm; I went to shake her off until I followed her horrified gaze and then the music died.

Chapter Forty-Two

Everyone stood frozen on the dance floor.

At first we were confused, but it didn't take long to work out what was happening. My heart clenched.

Toby and Sean were facing off by the bar, and before I could even wonder what had happened, they had each other by the scruff of their necks, hands fisted in each other's shirts. Glasses shattered as Toby threw Sean against the bar.

"FIGHT!"

"Tess, don't!" Ellie tried to hold me back, but I broke away and pushed through the stunned crowd towards them.

"Toby, Sean, stop it!" I screamed, trying to get their attention. I slapped at their arms, trying to break their hold on each other, but it was of no use. Their eyes were locked on each other, murderous.

An arm snaked around my waist and pulled me back.

"Adam, let me go!"

Chris grabbed Toby, and Stan and Ringer worked to edge Sean away. They grunted and swore as Toby and Sean struggled away from them and towards each other.

"Stop it!" I screamed, tears threatening to spill over.

"Get him out of here," Chris yelled at Stan and Ringer, but Toby broke free and in a silent rage was the first to leave.

Adam let go of me. My heels clicked frantically on the concrete as I chased after Toby. Sean's hand reached out and grabbed my upper arm, preventing me.

"Tess, don't." His tone was fierce, his expression grave.

"What is wrong with you? Let go of me!"

"He knows! Alright, Tess? He knows."

My head swam. How? How did this happen? It all became perfectly clear when I saw, further down the bar, Carla sipping on her drink, all innocence and sweetness. I caught a sideways glance at a smug-looking Peter.

She turned to face me. "Oops." She shrugged. "I guess he didn't know."

I broke away from Sean. He didn't try to stop me.

I ran as far as I could before ditching my heels, and then pounded the pavement with such force it wasn't long before I could faintly see the long stride of Toby's silhouette up ahead.

"Toby, wait!"

He stopped, as if flinching at the sound of my voice. I ran up short, trying to catch my breath.

It was then I cringed against a new sound, a series of running steps behind me. Ellie, Adam, and the Onslow Boys coming up short, their breaths laboured.

I made sure I got in first.

But before I could speak, Toby spun around, his gaze searing into me as he walked towards me.

"Deny it," he said, "tell me nothing happened."

My mouth gaped open, and I stumbled to form words, which just made him angrier.

"It's not what you think." My voice quivered.

"Did he touch you?"

Oh God, please don't do this.

"It happened the night Angela was at your house. I saw her car in the driveway, what was I supposed to think?"

Hurt and disbelief flashed across Toby's face.

"You think that little of me?"

"It's not what you think, Toby." Sean's voice came in from behind me. "We're just friends."

I stepped closer, reaching out, but he flinched away.

"*Don't.*"

I could feel myself falling apart in a blind panic. "Toby, please don't do this."

He refused to look at me. A long moment stretched between us, his jaw clenched in anger. Just as I was certain he was going to walk away, and I'd never see him again, Sean stepped forward.

"If you're going to take the high moral ground, Toby, then why don't you start by being honest with Tess?"

Honest? What?

Toby glared at Sean, a silent warning that made goosebumps form on my flesh.

"I swear to God, Sean," Toby bit out.

I looked from Toby to Sean and back again. "What's he talking about?"

"Go on, Toby, tell her. Tell her of the job offer you accepted in the West."

Sean turned to me. "Toby's moving. He's leaving Onslow." He turned back to Toby. "I bet you didn't tell her that."

"Toby?" I said. "*Toby.*"

A raw emotion flickered briefly in Toby's eyes, but he shut it down. He looked at me, unflinching. "Yeah, well, there's nothing keeping me here now."

And just like that, he walked away.

Chapter Forty-Three

If there is one thing worse than self-pity, it was other people's pity.

They all looked at me with solemn, knowing gazes and sad smiles, and worst of all, they kept asking, "Are you okay?"

No, I was not okay.

It was as if someone had punched a hole in my chest and every rational slice of my brain refused to function. Ten days had passed since the disco without a word, not even a glimpse of him. I stopped checking my phone every few minutes after the seventh day. He hadn't come to the hotel all week.

I sat in a booth at the Caltex with Sean on a Tuesday afternoon, the one person who didn't offer sad smiles or patronising words of comfort. He was just as lost as I was.

"Have you seen him?" I asked.

"Yeah," Sean said, "and he's pretending nothing happened. Every time I go to talk to him about it, he refuses to."

Like I never existed.

"God knows what Carla said to him." I sighed.

Sean scoffed. "I knew as soon as I saw him over at the bar. Carla was whispering in his ear. Then he turned around and looked at me dancing with you, and I knew. In one look, I knew." His eyes focused on his fingers as he rubbed condensation off his glass.

I felt for him; he was at as big a loss as what I was.

"At least he'll talk to you."

Sean shrugged. "To be honest, I don't know what would be better. He's not the same with me, things probably won't ever be the same again. You don't betray a mate like that. You just don't."

He'd lost his best friend, and it was all because of me.

"How were you supposed to know? We hadn't told anyone. And now you guys are fighting … Sean, I'm so sorry."

Sean grabbed my hand. "Hey! Don't you dare say you're sorry, it wasn't your fault."

"But it was," I said.

"You'd have to be blind not to know Toby liked you. It was me, I shouldn't have crossed the line."

I sighed. "Well, it hardly matters what his feelings *were*, anymore. It's pretty clear what they are now."

"He'll come around," Sean said, but he didn't sound convinced.

"Before or after he moves away?"

"In his defense, he took the job way before you came around."

"Is that why he broke up with Angela? Because he was moving away?"

Sean watched me for a long time, as if gauging whether or not I was serious.

I was deadly serious.

He stood, tossing a couple of ten dollar notes by our bill.

Was he going to answer?

After a second, Sean sighed. "It was you, Tess. He broke up with Ang because he was falling for you." He patted my head and walked out the door.

Toby had broken up with Angela to be with me. I felt worse than ever.

Two weeks. Nothing.

It was over. It was really over. I had surpassed the tears, the anxiety attacks and churned it into resignation. Though it had felt like so much more at the time, I had had my first summer fling. Toby would go to his new job, I would go back to school and normal life would start all over again.

I searched desperately for a silver lining; if Toby moved away I wouldn't be forced to see him with someone else, and if he wasn't around, I would find it easier to get over him.

Ellie even offered her own words of wisdom: "I think the fact that he took it so badly is a real testament to how much he liked you."

I curved a sceptical brow. "Grasping at straws much?"

I dragged my raggedy soul through Christmas, offering forced, half-hearted smiles and false cheer over the festive season. Work at the café and hotel was extra difficult. I was forced to be pleasant as I served the never-ending mass of customers. I'd sucked it up as much as I could, though, because I could sense Mum and Dad catching on to my despair.

I'd almost convinced myself that I would be okay as long as I could fake it. But then Ellie and Adam's parents came over for a BBQ; the forceful smiles and laughter was exhausting.

Adam perched himself on the island bench while I washed dishes in the kitchen.

There was a sense of great unease between us. It was all me. I couldn't let my guard down; I was afraid of letting down that barrier, of exposing my soft underbelly I fought so hard to keep hidden. I was tired, so tired of the way my insides ached.

I felt Ellie press beside me as she took the plate and washcloth from me.

"I don't think you can get that any cleaner, you know. You've been washing it for the past ten minutes." She smiled at me with that sad, sympathetic smile.

I flicked a bashful gaze at Adam who was looking at me as if waiting for me to crumble at any moment.

Ellie took over the dishes. She seemed nervous. Maybe it was me; things were strained between the three of us lately, and I knew it was my fault.

Adam sighed. "Just tell her, Ellie."

My head shot around to face her, suddenly alert.

"What? Tell me what?" I said, my eyes darting from Adam to Ellie and back again. "What are you talking about?"

Ellie placed the dish in the drainer and faced me as she dried her hands.

"They're having a farewell party for Toby tomorrow night."

She swallowed deeply, her eyes flicked nervously to Adam. "It's at Stan's shed, so you don't have to worry about running into him at the hotel …" She broke off.

"But we're not going, right, Ellie?" Adam added.

Ellie shook her head violently. "Of course not."

My sweet, foolish friends. I smiled sadly out through the kitchen window. It was blindingly bright outside, a beautiful, sunny day. The blue sky blurred in my vision. I shifted and anchored myself to clasp the sink and avoid my friends' pity. My tear-filled gaze rested on the towering Ghost gum near our driveway, where it cast a shadow over our sunburnt lawn.

I remembered the day we stood on the front lawn, the same kind of sunny afternoon when Toby gave me a lift home from Horseshoe Bend. So many times I wanted to step over that line, not thinking how it could change everything, alter our newly formed friendship; if only I hadn't made that stupid bet, what would have happened then? Toby and I would be speaking, Sean and Toby would still be best mates. I would probably be going to Stan's tomorrow night to say goodbye to him, to wish him a happy life. Knowing what I did now, would I have changed a thing? Would I have taken back the feel of his hands on my skin? The linger of his soft lips on mine, the way he could bring me undone in ways I had never known I could feel?

No. I wouldn't change a thing. I couldn't regret what we had, our days in the sun, our nights in each other's arms, I could never regret or give those memories up. And that was what they were now – just memories.

It was truly the end. As if the knowledge slammed into me, my guard shattered and I cupped my face into my hands, sobbing with such force my entire body shook. I felt the circling of a pair of arms and then another, stroking my hair, my back. Adam and Ellie were there when I fell, like always. Ellie rubbed my back and cried with me, Adam pressed his lips to my temple and hushed me with words of comfort.

It was over; with a bone-jarring certainty, I finally accepted it was over.

***

The next day was a Friday night, the night of the party for Toby, and Adam and Ellie took me out for dinner. Though they didn't say as much, I knew it was to cheer me up. I could, of course, think of other places to eat than the Onslow, but Adam was keen to play pool and listen to some tunes, so who was I to rain on his parade? After my breakdown yesterday, I wanted to redeem myself by ending the awkwardness that existed between me, Ellie and Adam. The summer hadn't exactly gone as planned, so tonight was more about recapturing the essence of our friendships, and less about my misery.

Just make it through one more night of faking it, I told myself. It would get easier, surely?

I asked Mum to drop me off right out the front of the Onslow.

What did I care if my parents gave me a lift? My days of making grand entrances and tracking up that bloody hill were over. A lot of things were over.

Adam was sitting at the picnic table out the front when we pulled up, watching Ellie pace back and forth in front of him. As I neared, my movement caught their attention. I flashed them my best smile. I could do this. It would be fine. My smile slowly evaporated as I took in their anxious eyes that darted to each other, then both at me.

"Ah, Tess," Ellie said, "you're here." She stopped pacing, but still wrung her hands anxiously. "How about we go get some Chinese at the Golden Dragon?" She walked briskly towards me. Adam stood, nodding his head as if it was the greatest idea in the world.

"Chinese? But what about playing pool?" I turned to Adam.

"Yeah, well, you know, with my history I should probably steer clear of pool tables." Adam linked his arm with mine and led me towards Coronary Hill, Ellie scurrying along behind. Was I being frog marched down the hill?

"What's wrong with …" I stopped dead in my tracks, and Ellie slammed into me from my sudden stop.

Toby's ute was in the car park, along with Ringer's, Amanda's … everyone was here. How had I not seen them?

"I thought you said Toby's farewell party was at Stan's tonight."

"Yes, well, it seems tradition dictates that they have a few here, before heading to the party." Ellie grimaced.

Of course it did.

"I'm sorry, Tess, we honestly didn't think they'd be here." Adam touched my shoulder. "Come on, let's go."

"No!" I said. "I'm not leaving. I came here to have dinner and play pool, why should I leave just because of him?"

From the looks on their faces, Ellie and Adam thought I was out of my mind; they probably thought I was on the brink of another hysterical breakdown like last night. I cringed at the memory.

"Tess, do you really think that's such a good idea?" Ellie asked.

I rolled my eyes. "They don't own the place. Besides, we're all mature adults. We can be in the same building."

"But the same room?" Ellie said, biting her bottom lip.

"You sure?" Adam asked, like he wasn't buying my bravado for one second.

"I'm sure!" I spun around and stomped back towards the Onslow. As I closed the distance, as coming face to face with Toby again became an impending reality, I lost all my nerve. I was so completely and utterly unsure. My heart raced so fast I could feel the deepening thrums pulsing in my ears. What the hell was I doing? Was I crazy?

I took a deep, shaky breath as my hand splayed against the front door, ready to press it open with that familiar screech. I paused outside, staring at the timber, the only thing that separated me from the inside – from Toby.

"Tess?" Adam's voice pressed against my right ear, I could feel his hand on my shoulder. "We don't have to …" And before Adam finished his sentence, I pushed the door open, flooding the main bar with sunlight.

Chapter Forty-Four

Distant laughter filtered through the thin walls of the poolroom into the restaurant. The bass beat of the jukebox thumped loudly, disturbing the calming musical stylings of Enya that played from the speakers where we sat in the dining room.

Adam quirked a brow over his menu. "Enya? Seriously? Oh, Uncle Eric, I'm appalled."

I shrugged. "Blame your Aunty Claire."

Adam raised a sceptical brow. "Aunty Claire is never here."

All our gazes turned from our menus towards the bar where Uncle Eric stood whistling animatedly while he brewed a coffee. Adam shook his head. "And here I thought Uncle Eric was more of an AC/DC fan, but Enya?"

We cast knowing smiles at one another as our eyes flicked back to our menus. An old familiarity settled over us. The same effortless, friendly banter flowed like it did before the summer had begun, before Adam was sent away, before everything turned to shit. Well, mostly everything.

"So are you going to see Stan tonight?" I asked Ellie as I poured a glass of water from the carafe.

The simple enough question seemed to unease Ellie. "Ah, no, not tonight. Tonight is *our* night."

It was meant to be a touching sentiment, but I could tell there was no conviction behind the statement. Though she tried to disguise it, she was disappointed she wouldn't be seeing Stan, which was stupid because he was only a room away in the poolroom. All through dinner, I tried not to think about the fact that Toby was in there, so agonisingly close. When we'd walked through the front door, none of us glanced over there. I didn't even know if Toby knew I was in the building. We had simply veered sharply right and headed for the restaurant.

I looked at my two best friends: Ellie desperate to see Stan and Adam pining every time he heard the crack of the cue against the billiard balls. Instead of me faking it tonight, they were faking it, as well. They were putting on brave faces to cheer me up, to make it all about me, courtesy of my Toby-fuelled mini breakdown. They were such good friends. The best.

Enough was enough. I was a good friend, too. If I couldn't suck it up for one night, perhaps the last night I would ever be in the same room with Toby again, then I was just a coward and a shitty friend, too.

I pushed my chair back and stood up. "Let's go."

Adam frowned. "Where to?"

"I'm going to kick your arse on the pool table."

A wicked grin formed across Adam's face as he turned to eye Ellie. She straightened in her seat.

Adam nodded his approval. "That a girl."

We left our table and rounded the corner to the poolroom. *Okay, no biggie, I could do this. They didn't own the place and besides, they were probably gone, on their way to the party at Stan's by now and the poolroom would be ours for the taking.*

Oh fuck.

The Onslow Boys were very much in the poolroom, ever present. Sean, Stan and Ringer stood around the pool table, cues in their hands. Toby stood alone, flipping through the song selections at the jukebox.

He looked good.

It had been two whole weeks, yet my traitorous heart still skipped a beat. The very sight of him turned my thoughts into mush, and my body into a heightened state of long-suffering desire. I tried to remind myself that what I now suffered was what I had always known – unrequited love from afar. But it was just that much harder, having had it and lost.

When Toby saw me, there was no surprise, no emotion at all. It was as if he saw straight through me.

This was a bad idea.

The other Onslow Boys were their usual jovial, easygoing selves. Stan's eyes lit up as soon as he spotted Ellie; ditching his pool cue, he made his way over, pulling her into a big bear hug. Ringer shook Adam's hand, and they started up their own conversation. But I was distracted as one song ended and a new one began: Marvin Gaye's, 'Heard it Through the Grapevine'.

Smart arse.

I watched as Toby turned back around to the jukebox and flicked through to select another song.

The atmosphere in the room was tense. Usually Sean would make fun of someone, we'd all have a laugh and it would be over. But not tonight. Sean raised his eyebrows in my direction when the song started up, but aside from that tiny gesture, he focused on his conversation with Ringer and Adam on pool tactics. Sean restricted himself to banter with his mates rather than be too openly friendly to me like he would have in the past. Much like the summer holidays, everything I had known with the Onslow Boys was drawing to an end; in a few weeks, I would be back at school and my part-time work at the Onslow would be over.

The sudden realisation hit me; this was it. This would be the last time I saw Toby, this would be the last time we'd all be together like this at the Onslow.

And we were going to let it end like this?

The tension between Sean and Toby, too, was obvious as they cast each other wary glances. I wanted more than anything for things to be the way they were again. I was just a girl. I seriously wasn't worth ending their friendship; they had to know that, right?

All I knew was I had nothing to lose, because I had already lost him.

I strode across the poolroom, past the boys, straight to Toby. Beyond my better judgment and all the courage I had mustered up, I stood before him and stared him straight in the eye. There was a flicker of surprise and a new tension swept over us.

"So this is how it's going to be?" he asked. "A showdown, here in front of everyone?"

My shoulders involuntarily slumped at his question. "Is that what you think I'd do? Humiliate you, like some screaming banshee?"

He looked at me pointedly, and then I remembered Angela Vickers, the worst screaming banshee of them all.

To be honest, that kind of pissed me off. Not the screaming banshee type of pissed, but to lump me in with Angela? I was the pretty fucking *insulted* type of pissed.

I sighed heavily. "I just wanted to say goodbye, that's all.

And …" *oh God, this was so hard,* "and good luck!"

The tension in Toby's shoulders melted, his eyes darting across my face suspiciously, warily, like he was waiting for the vindictive punchline. I met his gaze full on, and a familiar song filled the speakers. Live's 'Lightning Crashes'. It was the very same song that played the night of the first disco behind the velvet curtain. What was he playing at?

I swallowed hard. "I haven't had the chance to talk to you …"

Okay, Tess, keep it together.

"… And I just wanted to say thank you."

His frown deepened. "Thank you?"

Oh God, I was lame …

I glanced around, embarrassed, I edged to the corner of the room for some semblance of privacy; Toby moved with me.

It took all my strength to meet his eyes. "For a brief moment, you made me believe that I was a somebody, that, above all, I wasn't like the other girls. And I'm not." I stepped forward, so he could hear me over the music. "I know it really doesn't seem that way. And it kills me that I let you down, that I did something so stupid because I jumped to the wrong conclusion. I don't want you thinking I am anything other than who I am, who you got to know this summer."

Toby was so still, so unmoving, if it wasn't for the flex of his jaw muscles I would swear he had turned to stone.

"But you have to know, I'm really sorry. I'm sorry that I didn't tell you about Sean, but there would be days of not even seeing you, of not knowing if what was happening with us was serious. I had no idea of knowing. When I saw her car in your driveway, I thought that you and her …" I bit my lip, the memory of that horrible, regret-filled night flooded back to me. "If you don't understand how sorry I am that I hurt you, that I never would have done it intentionally, if you don't get that, then you don't get me."

I couldn't look at him anymore; I knew my eyes were a window straight into my heartbroken soul. But he was so silent, I thought maybe he hadn't heard what I'd said at all. I couldn't say it again. I couldn't …

And then he spoke. His voice was low and raspy. "I get you."

I looked up at him in surprise.

"The thing is, Tess, if you think I would be with you one night, and then go back to Angela …" He shook his head. "Then *you* don't get *me*."

We stared at one another for the longest time. I guess we didn't really know each other. I finally broke away, knowing it would be the last time I would see Toby. My heart threatened to break at the thought.

"Well, it doesn't matter anymore, does it?"

"I guess not." Toby said coldly. It was as if a knife was twisting in the pit of my stomach.

"Bye, Toby." Before I realised it, I'd held out my hand. I cursed myself as it hung between us. I had never felt like such a loser than in that moment.

A handshake, Tess? Seriously? Just walk away, you idiot! Walk away!

Before I could inwardly scream at myself any more, Toby took my hand, squeezing it in a firm but gentle shake. His eyes rested on my hand. It was reminiscent of the first time we shook hands in this very room; aside from the party, it was our first real interaction, our first real hello, and now it was our very real end.

"Bye, Tess."

I slid my hand from his lingering clasp and, without meeting his gaze, walked through the crowd to Ellie.

I swallowed down the tears enough to hold it together. "Can we go now?" I said in a quiet, trembling voice.

"Of course, let's go."

Chapter Forty-Five

I rounded the corner of the locker room, trying to get my head around the new Year Twelve layout and fall back into the routine of school.

On the first day back, I knew I was out of sorts because, of all things, I was happy to be back at school. So wrong, I know.

With a sigh, I opened my new locker and gathered my bag. Irritating laughter bounced off the metal lockers and echoed around the room. A few lockers up from me, Carla unlocked her locker and cast me a smug smile.

"How was your summer, Tess?"

I narrowed my eyes. Before I could reply, another voice interrupted me.

"Shut up, Carla!" Scott opened his locker on the other side of her.

Carla's gaze flew to him in utter surprise.

He stared her down. "Leave Tess alone."

At a loss for anything intelligent to say or do, Carla just scoffed. "Whatever." She slammed her door with a bang and made sure she cast me a murderous look on the way out.

Scott gave me an awkward smile as he gathered his books and walked away.

Had he actually called me Tess?

Adam and Ellie walked around the corner and spotted me.

"There you are? You ready?" Ellie smiled.

We made our way out through the gates and under the 'Onslow High' arch. The grounds were swarming with everyone's excitement of surviving their first day back.

"Chris is picking me up, you ladies need a lift?" asked Adam.

"No, I'm right," Ellie said. "Stan should be here somewhere." She eagerly looked out over the road at the long line of parked cars, biting her lip in anticipation. Her eyes searched down the road when she suddenly froze.

"Tess."

Adam and I were equally confused until we followed her gaze, and that's when I saw him.

Toby leaned against the driver's door of his ute, arms crossed, his gaze unreadable, and fixed on me.

"Tess, are you okay? Do want us to wait?"

Ellie and Adam were just as rigid with shock as I was. It took me a moment to offer any kind of acknowledgment.

"It's okay." I took a deep breath. "I'm sure this won't take long."

Adam grabbed my bag. "We'll wait."

"Okay," I said, but I doubt it was even audible. I willed my legs to move, and after a moment, they carried me across the road, my hands fisted at my sides to disguise the tremor.

Just breathe, Tess. Just. Breathe.

As I stopped in front of him, he straightened, pushing his hands deep into his jean pockets.

What was I supposed to say? Hey? How's it going? Instead, we just stood there. God, this was horrible. What did he want me to say? Oh God, what if he wasn't here for me? What if –

"You didn't come to my farewell party at Stan's?"

Was he for real? I had said my goodbyes.

Toby shifted, but his seriousness remained. "Shame. It was a good party."

He was bummed I'd missed a good party a couple of weeks ago? I didn't understand. Everything about our exchange was so wooden, so unnatural. It hurt.

I hadn't seen him in weeks, and yet as I spotted him across the school, my heart spiked its betrayal like it always did. I would never get over this boy; saying goodbye was the hardest thing I had done. I'd known he was still in town until today and, for some reason, knowing he was still in Onslow had appeased me, because he was still near. But now with his departure looming over me, over us, of him really leaving, of him standing in front of me, he was killing me all over again.

His head tilted slightly, his lips twitched. "Don't make me say it."

I paused. "Say what?"

"Penny for your thoughts."

"Oh." I smiled weakly.

Awkward silence wedged its ugly way between us.

"So, you're leaving?"

His fleeting moment of humour sobered as he nodded.

I was drowning inside. I dug my nails into my palms. I had faked being okay for so long, that now I needed to be stronger than ever, and I could feel my façade crumbling.

I was about to say, "Good luck" and scurry away when he stepped forward. "I head off in about twelve months' time."

"*What*?"

What did he just say?

A smile broke out on his lips.

"I *am* going, Tess, just not today."

Was he taunting me? Was he trying to punish me by giving me false hope, only to rip it from underneath me? He could have been, but I didn't believe it, because I *did* know him, and he wouldn't do that.

"I don't care about what happened with Sean …" He took in a deep breath. "Okay, I do care. But not enough. Not enough to walk away."

"But your job …"

"It can wait."

I could feel myself falling, the walls were crumbling with a fear to hope, to believe.

"So you're not leaving?" I whispered.

Toby reached for me, took my hands, squeezing them. "How can I? Ya see, there's this girl, and I'm kind of crazy about her."

My heart pounded against my chest.

"I've done a lot of thinking; all I know is I should have told you that ages ago." He pushed a wayward strand of hair from my brow.

I glanced around. "Did you want to talk about this somewhere else?" I asked.

"Oh, I think right here is perfect for what I need to do."

Toby smiled his perfect, wicked smile, the very one that melted me. I thought my heart might stop as he edged closer, tilting my chin up with his hand.

"What do you need to do?" I whispered.

"This." He captured my lips in a long, lingering kiss. My walls came crumbling down as I melted against him, his arms encircled me, and I was lost to the feel, the memory, of all that was Toby.

Lost in the happiness as I folded my arms around Toby's neck, we both flinched at the blast of a horn as a car pulled up beside us. Chris, Sean and Adam looked on from their seats with big, goofy grins.

Chris shook his head. "Settle down you two, there are children present."

Adam held up his hands. "Seriously, why look at me when you say that?"

Sean ignored the brotherly sparring as he grinned at us, bobbing his head in approval. "'Bout bloody time."

A second horn sounded from behind; Stan waved his arm out the window. "Come on, people, move along, nothing to see here."

Ellie sucker punched him from her passenger seat.

"Where we headed?" asked Toby, taking my hand in his.

"Well, nowhere too extravagant, it is a school night," Sean teased.

Toby flipped him the finger and everyone laughed.

"Follow us," Chris said.

Toby and I slipped into the ute, and he started the engine.

I slid over to the middle to belt in and lean against his side.

"We're going to do this? For real?"

Toby frowned. "What, follow Chris? Well …"

"No, I mean us, you and me?"

A smile lit up his face. "Yes, ma'am!"

My heart swelled at the way his warm eyes rested on me for the longest moment before he turned the wheel to fall in line behind Stan.

"Then there's one thing I need to know," I said, in all seriousness. And there was. One thing I had wondered about above all others.

Toby frowned with uncertainty, his eyes flicking to me and back to the road.

"What's that?"

I leaned into him, smiling through my words as I whispered, "What does the 'E' stand for?"

Toby broke out in a fit of deep, rich laughter. Shaking his head, he said, “Ernest … My middle name is Ernest.”

Ernest. It made me love him all the more.

Epilogue

6 months later

The place was deserted.

And why wouldn't it be? Toby and I sat in the main bar of the Onslow Hotel on a Tuesday night.

Toby grimaced. "I'm sorry this isn't much of a way to spend your birthday."

I clasped my necklace for probably the hundredth time, admiring the beautiful chain and gold disc pendant that had an italic 'T' engraved on it.

A 'T' for Tess, a 'T' for Toby.

"It's perfect!" I leaned over to show him how perfect.

"Keep it PG guys, I'm still here." Chris looked on in distaste, as he had a tendency to do whenever we were around.

"What are you doing hanging in a bar midweek, anyway?" Chris posed.

I straightened on my stool. "Hey, I'm eighteen now! I'm completely legal, so rack 'em up, bar-keep." I slammed my hand on the bar way too hard.

Chris looked on with a 'kill me now' expression; he poured a glass of the house white and placed it in front of me.

"On the house, Birthday Girl."

"Thanks." I smiled.

Even though I was secretly miffed that I had to remind Chris that it was my birthday (I mean, I had reminded everyone I had ever met for the past month that I was turning eighteen), it wasn't just Chris that disappointed me. My own parents, my flesh and blood, had sung me a rather quick, halfhearted version of 'Happy Birthday' before they ducked to work, with promises that come the weekend they would make it up to me. I had received a rather animated text from Ellie saying 'Happy Birthday' and 'call you later'. At least Adam had come over, even if he hadn't stayed long.

I had been on the verge of cracking open a tub of ice cream out of depression until Toby picked me up. I had been spilling out all my troubles when he asked me to pass him something from his glove box. I was so engulfed in self-pity I passed the white box with the pretty red bow to him without even taking a breath. I only paused when he pulled over and looked at me with an incredulous smile.

I touched my necklace again at the memory. Every time I did, Toby broke into a smile, pleased.

He picked up his beer, and held it up towards me.

"A toast to the Birthday Girl."

I grabbed my ever so grown-up house white and clinked our glasses together.

I was finally an adult!

I took a deep, confident gulp, only to gag when it went down the wrong way. My eyes watered as I tried to draw breath. Toby thumped me on my back as I coughed and spluttered all over the bar.

Yep! I may be eighteen, but the stuff was still vile.

Toby tried to salvage my dignity. "Chris, can you grab us a glass of water and some menus, mate?"

Chris managed the water. "Sorry to be a killjoy guys, but I'll have to call last drinks. I'm shutting up soon."

Toby did a double take. "What, no dinner?"

Chris shrugged. "Sorry mate, it's what happens mid-week."

I looked at the wall clock, it was only 8.30pm, and I was starving. I saw the disappointment in Toby's face so I didn't press the issue. Yeah, this was turning into some birthday.

I didn't even manage to finish my glass of water as Chris stalked up and down the bar, collecting beer mats, and wiping down.

Okay, okay, we're going, geez ...

I grabbed my bag and went to walk out the front when Toby grabbed my hand.

"This way." He pulled me in the opposite direction with a devilish smile.

"But the car's out front."

He dragged me along until we were engulfed by the darkness of the restaurant, where he paused and kissed me into silence.

"I thought you might want to do some reminiscing in the beer garden." He nuzzled into my neck. I giggled as his breath tickled me.

My eyes darted. "What about Chris?"

Toby kissed me again, and all of a sudden I didn't care anymore. This was the best birthday ever.

Just as I was relaxing, getting lost in his kisses, he broke away.

"Come on." He tugged me into action; my mind was still drunk from his kisses.

I followed his long, confident stride through the dark restaurant, and he guided me to the sliding door that led out to the beer garden.

Now was as good a time as any, I thought.

I stopped him, just as he was about to open the door.

"Toby, there's something. Well, there's something I've been wanting to say."

And just as I was about to form my next sentence, the sliding door flew open and lights flooded the garden.

"SURPRISE!!" roared the crowd, followed by a rather hideous and ill-matched version of 'Happy Birthday'.

I shielded my eyes as they adjusted to the brightness, my other hand clutching at my racing heart.

They were all here. Mum, Dad, Adam, Ellie. To my right, Uncle Eric, Claire, Amy. Melba and Rosanna clapping in front. And a line of beaming Onslow Boys.

My eyes welled.

They hadn't forgotten.

After the initial shock I turned to Toby. "You!" I went to whack his arm but he caught my wrist and pulled me into a hug. "Happy Birthday, Tess," he whispered into my temple.

"Alright, alright, that's enough of that, you two." My dad broke in and took my hand. He flicked Toby his regular '*the jury is still out on you*' glance. It always mortified me. It had been six months, and Dad still hadn't fully accepted Toby. Toby still suffered through uncomfortable family dinners/interrogations. Mum, on the other hand, loved Toby and came over to link her arm through his with an apologetic smile.

Dad walked me over to a huge table fully set with gold embossed china and sparkling crystal wine glasses, and draped in crisp white linen. Tea candles and vases of white Iceberg flowers ran down the centre. My chin trembled; it was so beautiful, and it was all for me.

"Melba and I set it out this afternoon," Amy blurted out.

"It's beautiful." I touched one of the intricately folded napkins.

I sat at the head of the table, Toby to my left and Mum and Dad to my right. My eyes trailed down to the long line of friends before me.

Ellie was explaining to Adam the order of cutlery to eat with, Sean debating Aussie rules with Stan, Claire Henderson fussing over Uncle Eric's tie.

Whoa. Uncle Eric was wearing a tie?

My heart swelled with a deep, immense love for them all. Even for Melba and Rosanna who ushered behind Amy with platters of food. Food that Rosanna constantly reminded me that she had spent *all* day in the kitchen cooking.

Toby leaned into me. "What was it you had to tell me?"

I blushed at the memory. "Oh, I'll tell you later."

Toby's frown was broken by the clinking of a fork on a wine glass.

Ellie stood up, her eyes already shiny with emotion.

"Adam and I flipped a coin over who would do the best friend speech. Even though Adam lost, he said he would be pacified with the knowledge that Tess secretly held a flame for him."

Laughter was amplified by Chris punching Adam in the arm.

"What? It's true; sorry, Toby."

"Anyway, I'll make this quick. To Tess …" She held up her glass. "… the most amazing person I know. My life will always be brighter because you're the one that shines next to me."

"To Tess!" Glasses clinked all down the table, and Ellie wiped her eyes.

I fanned my face to stop the tears from overflowing. Toby winked at me and squeezed my knee.

A long line of embarrassing speeches followed. About my hopeless bar skills from Chris, my cappuccino fear from Melba, the girl in the white bikini from Sean that made me blush crimson.

"What bikini?" my dad asked, before the subject was swiftly changed. The only person that didn't speak was Toby, who sat silently by my side.

After the cake and embarrassing childhood stories and what seemed like hours and hours of laughter, the party wound down and guests left. It was time to clear the table and blow out the tea lights. I instinctively went to grab the empty glasses.

"Leave it, honey, it will all be there tomorrow." Claire Henderson smiled as she and Uncle Eric retired for the night.

They were the last to leave; now only Toby and I remained.

"They better hope it's all there in the morning. What's the going rate for fine china on the black market these days?" Toby said, as he looked over the messy table.

I sidled up to him, wrapping my arms around his neck. His attention quickly snapped from the table to me.

"I have a bone to pick with you, Toby Morrison."

"I have been keeping this party a secret for three weeks! My life would not have been worth living if I slipped up."

I laughed. "Not that! I do believe you promised me some beer garden reminiscing?"

A wicked smile broke out on his lips. "That's right, before we were so rudely interrupted."

A stillness swept over Toby. His smile changed into a serious intensity as he swallowed hard. "I love you, Tess McGee. I don't do big funny or heartfelt speeches in front of people at birthday parties, but I'm excellent in private alcoves in beer gardens." He paused. "Okay, that sounded really bad, what I mean is …"

I kissed him into silence. I pressed my forehead against his with a sigh. "I love you, too, Toby. In fact, that's what I was going to tell you before we walked into the beer garden. Right before the really bad singing started."

Toby chuckled. He let out a sigh of relief. "Ready to reminisce?"

I whispered my final word before he closed the distance.

"*Always*."

An Endless Summer
A Summer Series Novel, Book Two
Published by C.J Duggan
Australia, NSW
www.cjdugganbooks.com

First edition, published July 2013

Edited by Sarah Billington|Billington Media
Copyedited by Anita Saunders
Proofreading by Sascha Craig, Lori Heaford & Marley Gibson
Cover Art by Keary Taylor Indie Designs
Book formatted by White Hot Ebook Formatting
Author Photograph © 2013 C.J Duggan

An Endless Summer is also available as a paperback at Amazon
Contact the author at cand.duu@gmail.com

An Endless Summer

Sean looked out over the lake, squinting against the sunlight. He turned to me, his expression sobering as his eyes flicked over my face in silent study.

"Come on, Amy, I saved you once, I'll save you again."

I met his stare unflinchingly. "I don't need saving."

A wicked grin formed slowly on his face. "Don't you?"

After a rebellious summer night that almost claimed her life, Amy Henderson – the Onslow publican's only daughter – is sent away to suffer a fate far worse than any other punishment:

Boarding School.

Three years on, a now nineteen-year-old Amy returns to Onslow for the summer. What once was a cauldron of activity with live bands, hot meals and cold beers, the Onslow Hotel now lies dark, deserted and depressing. All fond childhood memories of loitering on the hotel stairs and eavesdropping on customers' colourful conversations are in the distant past.

How had her dad let it come to this?

With the new threat of putting the Onslow up for sale, Amy reluctantly turns to a local tradesman for help: Sean Murphy, the very same Onslow boy who saved her life all those years ago. With his help and that of some old friends, the task is clear: spend the summer building the hotel back up to its former glory or lose it for good.

In an endless summer, Amy soon realises that sometimes in order to save your future, you have to face your past, even if it's in the form of a smug, gorgeous Onslow boy.

Dedication

Dedicated to Lesley.
It started with a random act of kindness, and even after all this time you are always going above and beyond.
Thank you a million times over for being a part of this incredible journey with me.

"If you want to know where your heart is, look at where your mind goes when it wanders."

- Anon

Chapter One

Summer of '96, Onslow.

"There he is!"

My best friend, Tammy Maskala, was deeply, madly in love with Sean Murphy. Like, truly stalkerish type love.

Tammy and I had been friends forever. We turned sixteen on the same date, snuck out, hung out, and did everything together, but what Tammy wanted to do more than anything, or *anyone,* was Sean Murphy. We had spent an entire footy season freezing our butts off sitting in the football stands every home game to watch Sean ruck for the Onslow Tigers. I had personally been more enthralled with my bucket of chips than Aussie Rules, but every time Sean even so much as touched the ball, Tammy would elbow me, squealing in delight. I just got annoyed if it knocked a chip out of my hand.

Of course, Tammy was absolutely terrified of talking to Sean or engaging in any activity with him other than deep, longing sighs from a distance. That summer, Tammy said things were going to change and that was it. The only thing Tammy needed was a little helping hand from – yep, you guessed it – me.

"You know him," Tammy pleaded with me.

"I don't know him."

"You see him *all* the time."

"He's best friends with my cousin Chris."

"Exactly!" Tammy sighed in dismay. "You are *so* lucky!"

Many of my friends thought that growing up in a pub was the coolest thing ever. However, it wasn't as glamorous as it seemed. More often than not, I was something that was underfoot, shooed out of the way from oncoming traffic, a.k.a. patrons. I was ushered from forbidden places, lectured for loitering on the stairs, or chastised for eavesdropping on "adult" conversations. I always felt in the way and come summertime, when the season picked up and the tourists flowed in, I was *always* in the way.

By a young age I had learnt to entertain myself and tried to stay out of everyone's way. I remember on my thirteenth birthday, I had been given my first set of rollerblades, a brilliant ploy to keep me outdoors. I would race around and around the cemented verandah of the Onslow Hotel; it was like my very own roller rink. My rollerblades were presented to me with strict instructions, though: No rollerblading down Coronary Hill. I knew that. I mean, come on, did they think I had a death wish?

On the very day I got my rollerblades I had been gingerly rolling back and forth on the verandah, gaining my confidence, when Sean and his mates Toby, Ringer and Stan, rocked up for their usual Friday night drinking session. Every Friday night, without fail, they came in after work for a parma, some pool and so much beer they usually ended the night with an air guitar competition. I could always hear them from up in my room at three in the morning, arguing over the winner. I was *not* eavesdropping. Okay, so maybe a little. Anyway, they arrived all freshly showered and changed from their day's work and I watched them swagger across the car park in a chorus of animated conversation and laughter. I skidded to a halt on my blades and grabbed onto a beam for balance, peering out from behind a verandah pole as they approached.

They skipped every second step up to the verandah before Ringer noticed me standing awkwardly, knock-kneed in my netball skirt and with knee and elbow pads on, clasping the pole.

"Look out, what do we have here?" Ringer announced, playfully pulling on one of my plaits as he passed.

"Looks like we have ourselves a roller-girl. Come on, show us what you got," Sean teased.

"I'm not showing you," I said with a sneer. Truth be told, I was terrified of falling flat on my face. I couldn't go more than five metres without wobbling, flailing and crashing into a wall.

"Hey, Chook, is Chris behind the bar?" Toby asked.

I nodded. I was always nice to Toby. He was my favourite of all Chris's friends.

"Sure you won't show us a trick before we go in?" asked Stan as he turned towards the door.

"Well …" I lifted my chin. "I can do this …" I pushed myself off the pole and gathered enough momentum to work myself into a full three-sixty spin. It was going so well and was pretty impressive until my blade clipped a rough bit of concrete and I swayed sideways.

The boys' reflex reaction was to flinch; they all raised their hands at me in an 'easy' motion. But it was fine. I caught myself. Their bodies all visibly sagged with relief when I didn't face plant into the concrete. After successfully completing my Evel Knievel stunt, I smiled sweetly with my best 'Oh yeah! Look what I just did!' expression.

They all seemed rather impressed, except for Sean who stood leaning in the doorway with his arms crossed, his lips twitching as if fighting a smirk. I glowered at him.

"Bloody hell, you gotta do it faster than that, Chook."

Sean reached out, took me by the hands and pulled me along the concrete.

"Sean, don't!" I screamed.

He abruptly stopped me before breaking into a wicked smile. Then, he dragged me along some more in the opposite direction, his height and strength the only things preventing me from falling as he flung me around on my blades.

I screamed in terror, begging for him to stop as I barely missed knocking my shin against a giant terracotta pot plant. I just knew I was going to break a leg if he didn't let go. All the boys watched on, laughing, as Sean finally slowed to a stop, grabbing my shoulders to steady me. I grabbed onto a verandah pole, my voice hoarse from screaming, my heart pounding out of my chest.

"Now that's how you do it!" Sean laughed before following the others in the front door.

"You're such a bloody child!" I yelled after him. He winked and disappeared through the bar door. It was a place I wasn't allowed to go, so I glared at their backs furiously as their laughter was engulfed by the closing door swinging shut behind them.

I had never really had much to do with Chris's friends when I was younger, except when they used to come and taunt me at the pub. When I started waitressing at sixteen, however, I saw them a bunch more.

I tried to convince Tammy to waitress as well, as it would be her best chance to talk to Sean, but she was way too shy. So instead, Tammy lived vicariously through me, asking after every single shift if I had run into him, or seen him at the hotel. She begged me to tell her everything. Waitressing also gave me privy information as to where 'the Onslow Boys' would be. I wasn't sure why they were nicknamed that (I mean, there were other boys in Onslow), but it was something most girls called them so I figured I may as well, too.

"They're heading to MacLean's Beach after lock-in tonight," I said with a sigh into the phone. It seemed like all Tammy and I ever talked about was where Sean was and what he was doing. Just for once, I wanted to have a conversation about something else.

"Oh. My. God!" Tammy said, squealing. "Amy, we have to go."

I rolled my eyes. I was no stranger to sneaking out. I'd done so only last week to go down to a party by the lake when Dad said I couldn't go, but the last thing I felt like doing was stalking the Onslow Boys. It sounded boring.

"I don't know; they usually don't finish up from the lock-in until after one in the morning."

"Oh, please, Amy, you have to come with me. I'm going to talk to him tonight. I'll do it. I swear I will."

I wanted to bang my head against the receiver and come down with some mysterious twenty-four-hour bug that rendered me housebound. But, like I did every other time, I caved.

"Okay, but you better do it!" I told her.

I would sneak out, sure, but if there was one boundary I would never dare cross, it was stealing booze from my dad's pub. I knew Chris kept an up-to-date inventory down to the very last drop and messing with the stash wouldn't be worth my life.

So that was Tammy's area: I would agree to come and she would supply the booze. She'd raid her mum and dad's stockpile from their garage, like she always did. Apparently, they never suspected a thing.

Come one-thirty a.m., after changing and waiting impatiently for the sound of the front bar room door to slam, I legged it for the back staircase. Tiptoeing carefully downwards, I winced at the sound of a creaking step underfoot. I froze, hoping not to be heard. But it was okay – Dad was long asleep; if George Michael wailing from the jukebox failed to stir his slumber, then nothing would. As meticulously planned via in-depth phone conversations, I met up with Tammy a little way off from MacLean's. Giggling, we propped ourselves on top of a sand dune overlooking the sparkly, dark stretch of Lake Onslow.

"Wait here," Tammy whispered. I'm not sure why she was speaking so quietly since we were on our own.

Tammy disappeared behind a bush and I heard the rustling of a plastic bag. Under the white glow of the full moon, she returned with something in her hand.

"Ta da!" Tammy produced a cask of peach wine and two plastic cups.

"Classy!" I mused.

"I call it Dutch courage," Tammy said.

She squeezed on the tab, trickling a clear, fruity wine into her cup, then mine. We pressed them together in a mock clink, giggling "Cheers!"

"Here's to me talking to Sean Murphy tonight," Tammy said. She took a deep breath and skulled her wine.

I just shook my head and followed suit.

***

After a cask of wine and a shared six-pack of smuggled VB cans from her dad's stash, we were feeling good and zigzagging our way towards MacLean's Beach. Falling in the soft sand, we laughed hysterically over how uncoordinated we were. How we stumbled to the actual clearing of MacLean's, I will never know, but we did. Then, we attempted to be suave and sophisticated and walk as straight as possible through the crowd, give or take losing it in hysterics every now and then. I made a mental note to avoid my cousin Chris, but luckily through my blurry vision I couldn't spot him.

"I don't see Sean anywhere," whined Tammy. She collapsed into the sand, her face crumpling with sorrow.

"Shhhh," I said, as I waved her words away. "Be cool!"

"I am never going to get to talk to him, am I?" she asked, looking as if tears would start dribbling down her cheeks at any moment. "Never, never, never."

I blocked out her incessant complaining and kicked into friend mode: I needed to find Sean. I squinted my eyes at the sea of bodies dotted around the beach.

I spotted Alex Keegan; he was friends with the Onslow Boys, surely he would know.

"Hey, Alex!" I called out, stumbling a path to him. He turned, surprise dawning on his face as he saw me.

"Past your curfew, isn't it, Amy?" he asked as he looked me over.

Rather rich, I thought, coming from Alex who was only a year above me.

In a cocky move, I swiped his beer from his hand and took a long swig. I smacked my lips in appreciation.

"I won't tell if you won't."

Alex shifted uncomfortably, like so many of the boys did. Dad had threatened half of Onslow with very bad things if they so much as looked at me.

It was absolutely mortifying.

"Where's Sean?" I asked with my best smile and then lifted the can to my lips again.

Alex frowned and snatched the beer back from me. "Who wants to know?"

I rolled my eyes, snapping quickly out of the sweet-girl act. "Just tell me!"

He eyed me sceptically, weighing up whether to tell me or not. After a long pause, Alex tilted his head to his left. I followed his gaze out onto the lake.

"He's on Stan's boat with a few others."

In the darkness, I could make out a distant light on the water.

Okay, that was *not* part of the plan. I didn't want to be the one to break it to Tammy, but she was right. It seemed she wasn't finally talking to Sean tonight. Ugh!

I coaxed Alex into giving me a few beers and he begrudgingly obliged. As we drank together, he noticeably relaxed, which was made obvious when his hand snaked out and settled around my waist.

My eyes flicked out towards Stan's boat, much to the annoyance of my new BFF, Alex.

"Hey, what's he got that I don't got?" Alex pulled me into him; I could smell the alcohol and cigarette smoke on his breath against my neck.

Gross.

I pulled away and smiled at him sweetly before leaning in to whisper in his ear.

"A boat."

I walked backwards, away from Alex, beers in hand, and made my way back to Tammy who had passed out on the sand.

I knew what would wake her up: It was time to put this Sean matter to bed once and for all.

Dumping the beer stash next to Tammy's corpse, I walked towards the edge of the water, peeling my top over my head and tossing it onto the shoreline. Cat calls sounded from behind me.

"Yeah, baby! Take it off!"

I flipped my middle finger at no one in particular as I flicked off my shoes and struggled to unbutton my denim cut-offs, shimmying out of them while trying not to fall over.

The warm water lapped at my toes and a thrill shot through me as the sensation tingled around my ankles, my calves, and then my thighs as I walked into the lake in just my bra and knickers. My feet sunk into the muddy bank, slowing me down as I made for the light of the boat and the distant laughter offshore. I was going to swim out to them and give them a piece of my mind – those anti-social pricks!

"Oops," I giggled, losing my footing.

A breeze blew and gooseflesh rippled along my skin; all of a sudden the water didn't feel so warm anymore. But I had to do it. Tammy needed to talk to Sean and she needed to do it tonight.

I heard distant calls from the shore as I dived into the lake. I resurfaced, gasping at the unexpected chill of the water. I pushed forward, breast-stroking towards the light. I couldn't tell if the noise of people talking and yelling was from behind or in front of me, but it wasn't like it mattered; they weren't talking to me. I could only kick into the oblivion. It wouldn't take long to get to the boat. I was a good swimmer and Chris would soon be dragging me onboard giving me a lecture. Then I'd tell them all off for ditching the party and Sean would come to shore and meet Tammy, whom I was certain he didn't even know existed. He would see how amazing she was and they'd fall in love and Tammy would finally leave me in peace. I would never have to hear the name Sean Murphy again.

My breath laboured. I blinked against the water that splashed in my face with each stroke. I couldn't see the light anymore; my arms were cold now, heavy, and refused to work. I wanted to stand up and head back to shore, but there was no bottom.

A surge of water crashed over my face and filled my throat. I choked on the unexpectedness of it. It lapped again and my head bobbed under the surface. I bobbed up again, a panic spiking through me. This was *not* fun. This wasn't what was supposed to happen. I wanted to get out now, but there was water everywhere. I was being swallowed up by the night; there was just black sky above and black water all around.

All I could hear were my gasped breaths and the beating of my heart echoing in my ears as I sank and surfaced, sank and surfaced again, somehow unable to float anymore. I clawed at the water. I wanted to scream, but my mouth filled again and again with water and I went down deeper. Even as I tried to kick my way free, I was consumed by the darkness of the never-ending stretch of nothing.

My insides burned as I thrashed in a panic against the engulfing blackness. This was it, this was the end, I thought. I realised I was dying and there was nothing I could do about it. It was an unnerving experience, accepting your fate like that – letting go of the fight, sinking farther into the abyss to meet the end. The fear dissipated. I wasn't scared anymore. My death was so peaceful, so quiet, so very beautiful.

Maybe it was a dream – this wasn't happening – maybe that surge of water and whoosh of bubbles that filtered next to me was my mind playing tricks. The iron grip that swooped around me and grasped me tightly, the one that pulled me upward with such almighty strength. I must be asleep, I thought. It was a nice dream … until I resurfaced.

"Amy! Amy! Look at me, look at me!"

I double-blinked my eyes to clear my blurry vision. I struggled to fix on the person yelling at me, a voice coming from a face -hovering above. Beautiful blue eyes narrowed in panic and a strong, vice-like grip on my shoulders, jolting me to focus.

"Get back, give her room!" he shouted.

Droplets of water dripped onto my face as hands moved and cupped my cheeks.

"Amy, you're going to be all right," he spoke softly, gently. "Everything's going to be all right."

***

I was drunk and passed out in my knickers, according to Tammy's retelling of the events the next day. She told me Sean had dived into the water and duck-dived several times before he found me and dragged me to the surface. She said he screamed for someone to call an ambulance as he carried my lifeless body out of the lake. He gave me mouth-to-mouth and worked on pumping my chest until I vomited up half of Lake

Onslow into the sand. When she mentioned the mouth-to-mouth detail, I could tell she was secretly pissed that I'd had Sean's mouth on mine, but it wasn't like she was going to admit to it.

As for me, I had lain in a ball in my room for three days after, silently wishing I had drowned that night, rather than face the embarrassment of it. My chest was still bruised from where Sean had pushed so hard that he'd nearly cracked a rib. It sure felt like he had.

My parents were furious. I had to be ambulanced to the hospital and, after the initial fear passed, they moved on to rage at me for having snuck out, and then hushed angry whispers outside my room.

I half expected I would be grounded for life, but instead it seemed as though I was to suffer a fate far, far worse.

I was being sent to an all-girls' boarding school in the city.

I wiped away the tears, my throat scratchy from hours of silent sobbing in my room, mixed with swallowing half of Lake Onslow.

As my tears dried, my throat was parched. I listened to the silence downstairs and cautiously crept out of my room, hoping not to bump into anyone. Especially not my traitorous parents. I would just slip downstairs to the kitchen and grab a Coke, and then sneak back upstairs again, no one the wiser.

As I crossed the landing, I stilled at the sound of distant voices that filtered through from the main bar downstairs.

Before I'd even thought about it, I crept down the stairs towards the voices, cutting through the restaurant and pushing myself against the partition. I squinted through the gap in the dividers.

Sean stood in the bar facing a grim-looking Dad.

"Well, I just wanted to make sure she was okay."

"We appreciate it, Sean. We can't thank you enough." My dad shook his hand.

Sean tapped him on the upper arm and offered a reassuring nod.

"No need to thank me, Eric, I'm just relieved Amy's all right."

My dad pulled Sean into a hug.

"Thanks, mate!" He tapped Sean hard on the back and pulled back, sniffing. I watched as they both stood there awkwardly for a long moment.

Sean scratched the back of his head.

"No worries." He offered a small smile.

"How about a beer, son? My shout." Dad moved behind the bar; the awkwardness gone.

"Yeah, great." Sean moved to follow Dad but stilled, his eyes flicking towards the partition. I held my breath; I dared not move. Could he see me?

Sean broke into a broad smile and winked. I expelled a shocked breath and ducked from the opening, my heart racing a million miles an hour.

Oh God! Oh God! Don't tell on me! *Please*. I waited, half expecting the partition to be wrenched open and I would be plucked from my hiding place in my PJs, caught spying yet again. But when nothing happened and the conversation continued, I slowly moved to peek through the opening again.

Sean had moved and was sitting at the bar now, talking to my dad about footy. I backed away and ran towards the stairs, up and into my room, the first smile in a long time lining my face.

Chapter Two

Summer of '99, The City.

There was a creature in my house.

Dragging its feet along the kitchen lino, it expelled a yawned, bad-odoured breath, all the while scratching its butt crack and raiding the cupboard.

Yep, Dad's home.

I had never lived with both of my parents for a long period of time; it just never happened, not in my world. Mum lived in the city; Dad lived in the country at the pub. They weren't separated or divorced or anything, they were very much together. They spoke every day, they liked each other; heck, they even loved each other. It was just the way it was. When I was younger, I thought everyone's parents lived like this. It wasn't until I was older that I started to realise my little family was seriously screwed up. Seeing how I was the only child, guess who inherited all the crazy? Yep! Lucky me!

I peered over the back of the couch and caught my sneering reflection in the lounge room sliding-glass door. My headphones sat crookedly on my head, a deep frown etched across my brow. I slipped down and resumed my position: my long legs stretched out across the couch, my fluffy, purple dressing gown twisted around my PJs. I reaffixed my headphones and cranked up the volume on my Discman as an attempt to block out the rustling sounds from the kitchen. Noises I had been trying to ignore for months. The sounds, I guessed, that would transform into animated chatter as I sensed my mother, Claire Henderson, click-clacking down the hall.

She swung into the kitchen with her breezy, sing-songy voice. I peered over the couch again and, sure enough, there she was in her long, flowing, silk nightgown, her ash blonde hair gathered into a French twist. She was bright-eyed and glowing, always looking like a million bucks even first thing in the morning. Freaky ageless genetics? Perhaps. Wasn't sure if I'd inherited them, though. A close personal relationship with Dr Baritone and his Botox needles was more likely. My mum leaned into my dad and gave him a passionate kiss on the lips. *Gross!*

Unfortunately, it was not uncommon behaviour for my mum. My dad, Eric, on the other hand, who stood there canoodling with her in the kitchen, this was not how I remembered my dad. He was big, burly, bearded Eric Henderson, a generational publican in Onslow, a country town a mere two hours away. He was funny, great with people, knew the business, and ran it well. But this man spooning out a grapefruit for breakfast was not my dad.

One night, I overheard Mum crying on the phone, offering my dad an ultimatum, and the next thing I knew, Dad was on our doorstep, moving in. My dad had decided to go on this dramatic health kick: he quit smoking, cut down his drinking, and joined Jenny Craig. He'd lost a stack of weight and even shaved off his beard. And, the incredible shrinking man was now dressing younger, too, and, God help me, had even started strutting around like a rooster in a hen house. And the worst thing? My mum *loved* it.

My mum's attention turned from her loving husband and landed on me as I stared on in distaste. "Morning, honey!"

I sank back into the couch and thought if I didn't move, maybe I'd be left alone.

No such luck. My headphones were peeled off from behind me.

Okay. Now I was pissed.

"What's on for today, then?" Mum asked, innocently enough as she smiled down at me. There was a none-too-subtle probe to her question – with this question there always was. It was the question I was asked *every* day, and it was a trap.

"How about we get dressed today?" My dad leaned against the archway to the lounge room, taking an irritating sip of his soy, low fat/no fat, sugar-reduced, low GI drink.

I liked how he said 'we', as if his jab wasn't solely directed at me. It wasn't as if anything had changed, I did what I always did at home with Mum. The only difference was that Dad was here to point out the things he didn't approve of.

When it came to me, it seemed like he approved of nothing. Especially since my decision to defer from uni for twelve months, the biggest mistake I could possibly have made, or so I was reminded *every* day. A familiar anger bubbled under my skin.

I pulled myself up into a sitting position. "And what is it you two lovebirds have on for today?" My voice dripped with sarcasm.

Mum straightened with interest. "Your father's taking me on a date."

Ugh. Another one? Seriously?

They gave me an over-enthusiastic rundown of how, after yet another day of living out their second honeymoon, they planned to come home and watch a double episode of *Ally McBeal* on Prime Time. I had to get out of here!

Later that night, my parents relaxed in front of the TV. Dad slinked his arm around Mum and stole a wayward chip from the bowl. Mum playfully slapped his hand away. Rolling my eyes, I crept out and shut the door on their uproarious laughter as cutesy, crazy Ally McBeal fell over her own feet, *again*.

I switched the phone to my other ear where my friend Mary waited.

"What did you say?" I asked, lowering my voice.

"Where are you going to go?"

More laughter erupted from the lounge. My glare towards the offending sound was my usual expression these days, and with all that frowning and scowling I, too, was going to need Dr. Baritone's Botox before too long.

I shuddered.

"I don't know," I sighed. "Anywhere but here."

I guess I should have been happy for my parents. Most normal offspring would have been relieved that they were working things out, reigniting the flame so to speak, and I thought I would adjust to the change of Dad being a full-time presence in my life. But, to be honest, it was rocking my world. In a bad way. It was rocking a world that, since I finished school, Mum and I had lived in exclusively the majority of the time. Just us. Dad didn't belong here, he was a country boy; his role in my life was to provide me with an escape, a place I could go for school holidays and weekends. A place to get spoilt with an endless array of raspberry post mix and limitless packets of salt and vinegar chips.

My dad was the coolest. Or he had been. To all my friends in the city, I was this rich kid with a country mansion and my own multi-roomed hotel on the lake. When I was younger, I would literally bounce on the balls of my feet at the thought of going to Onslow; I longed for school holidays where I would pack up my swimmers and thongs, don the floppy hat and war paint my face with fluoro zinc cream before heading to the lake with all my country friends. Onslow was the ultimate escape; it allowed me absolute freedom and some of the happiest times of my life.

I froze, zoning out from Mary's chatter on the other end of the line as my eyes fixed onto a photo on the fridge door. It was a picture of me from years ago sitting outside the Onslow Hotel on a picnic table, my gangly legs hanging over the edge, and a goofy, forced smile on my face. At a guess, I must have been fourteen. I could usually tell my age in a photo. Closed-mouth smile: braces. Bright, beaming smile: post braces. By the awkwardness of this photo, I was definitely sporting a mouth full of metal, but, more disturbing than that, was I wearing a …

"Skort?" I grimaced.

"Amy? Amy? Did you hear me?"

"Oh, sorry, what did you say?"

"Seriously, you're not thinking of leaving the city for the summer, are you? Like, where would you even go?"

My eyes never broke from the goofy, suntanned, happy fourteen-year-old me, perched alone in front of the sweeping verandah of the Onslow with its heritage green roof and cream brickwork.

I broke into a toothy grin at the thought of being alone, just like that girl in the photo. I plucked it off from under the magnet.

"Mary, did I ever tell you about my mansion in the country?"

Chapter Three

"You have got to be fracking kidding me!"

Yes, I said fracking. It's what a life of growing up with my mother had reduced me to – compromised swear words. Even though she tried her hardest to stamp dirty words out of me with the best private, all-girl education money could buy, my sailor-mouth habit was never completely cured. It was Dad's fault, really. All the foul language I learned was a direct result of my time spent hanging with him at the Onslow. Even though I refrained from saying the *real* 'F' word, Mum still loathed my rendition and eventually just gave up trying to stop me altogether.

Speaking of giving up, I stood outside the Onslow Hotel and stared up at the building in mystified horror. I would have thought maybe I was tired and grumpy due to the bus trip from hell, or that maybe I was at the wrong place and didn't even realise it.

Or maybe I was hallucinating this monstrosity.

But no. I wasn't.

I had not expected this.

My heart sank at the sight of it: the overgrown lawn, the dirty ring-stained picnic tables, cigarettes, and broken glass near the front door, a couple of empty bottles on the windowsill. The windows were smudged and grotty – even the overhanging Carlton Draft sign dangled from a snapped chain, squeaking in the faint, hot breeze that blew. I half expected a tumbleweed to roll past me and a lonely wolf cry to echo through the hills. If we had wolves in Australia. Okay, a dingo, then. The atmosphere was that of a horror movie, an eerie, deserted scene.

I shielded my eyes from the beaming sunrays and hoped against hope that what I saw before me was a mirage, a nightmarish illusion.

But no. It wasn't.

The Onslow Hotel had been downgraded to the Norman Bates Motel. How long had Dad been in the city? A couple of months? Not even. He hadn't just upped and left, he'd put the Onslow staff in charge and he'd done the odd check-in and business call on the phone when he wasn't wining and dining Mum.

What the hell had happened? How long had the Onslow been like this? This was not what I expected to arrive to. Not. At. All.

***

My hand traced along the peeling, blistered paint of an outside picnic table, the very same one I'd been sitting on in the photo when I was fourteen. I had thought that merely being here would transport me back to that time, a happier time.

But I was so wrong.

My zombie-like, depression-filled trance was broken by the sound of an approaching car. The screaming of the fan belt was only out-blasted by the deafening sound of heavy metal music from the stereo. A weather-beaten, white Mazda hatchback scaled up Coronary Hill and sped into a long, winding circle. It flicked up gravel as it turned and halted with a violent jolt in the Onslow car park. I sidestepped away from the picnic table and into the shadows to get a better view of the new arrival and to avoid being seen.

Blissful silence followed as the engine of the Mazda was shut off and the car door flung open with a pained screech. I ducked behind an overgrown bush and took in the lean figure of a guy, somewhere in his mid-twenties, in fitted black jeans, boots and a crumpled white shirt. Dark, greasy hair fell to his collar. He readjusted his shades and stretched his limbs to the sky with an almighty groan before reaching into his top pocket for a ciggie. My first thought was that he might be a weary traveller making a pit stop; he looked like a wiry musician, maybe? Or a grubby stand-up comedian looking for a gig at the local. He bent into his car and reached for something in the back seat. Just when I was sure he would bring out a guitar, he pulled out a leather jacket and haphazardly slung it over his shoulder before slamming the car door.

His boots crunched over the gravel as he made his way towards the hotel. Reaching into his pocket, he foraged around to expel a long chain with an array of keys – keys I would recognise anywhere. They were Dad's.

With his brief distraction, tall, dark, and greasy kicked a wayward can as he stepped up to the porch.

"Piss and shit," he mumbled.

Charming fellow.

He unlocked the door with expert ease; he was obviously well used to the old door, the special twist and jiggle the lock needed before it would open – something only a few select people would know about. Once he unlocked the main door, he moved on to the side poolroom French doors and it suddenly dawned on me: After Chris left, Dad had put on a new barman – this must be him. Matt, was it? What the hell was he doing – or, rather, *not* doing – and more to the point, what the frack was he doing opening the hotel at two p.m. mid-week, or any day of the week, for that matter? For as long as I could remember, the Onslow Hotel was a seven-days-a-week trade, three hundred and sixty-five days of the year. Not even Christmas was sacred (something I'd been painfully aware of when I was a kid). At the latest, the pub would open its doors at ten a.m. Monday to Saturday and eleven a.m. on a Sunday, and as far as shutting up at midday went, it just didn't happen. The restaurant may have been closed, but there was always someone to mind the bar. Always.

My troubled thoughts were jolted by a mobile phone ringing. My heart leapt at the unexpectedness of the sound blaring from Matt's phone.

He fetched the mobile out of his shirt pocket. "Yello? Maaaaaaaaate," he drawled as he disappeared inside the hotel.

I stepped out from my hiding place in the bushes, feeling suddenly stupid for spying on him, a stranger. Surely there must be a misunderstanding, maybe a family medical emergency, or maybe Dad had negotiated some hour change or something. Not likely, but it's not like it was something he would have necessarily told me.

As a thousand thoughts ran through my mind, my gaze lowered onto a smouldering ciggie on the ground near the garden bed. Matt must have flicked it before he answered the phone. The smoking cylinder was in good company with what seemed like a hundred other half-smoked ones. Not a single one of them had actually hit the designated smoke trays provided for smokers. I stomped on the lit smoke and anger pulsed through my veins.

Oh, hell no!

I twisted my foot into the earth, trying to contain my fury. Once the ciggie was well and truly obliterated I decided that the time for lurking in the shadows was over and headed towards the open bar door, towards home.

I was well accustomed to the smell of faint cigarette smoke and stale beer. After all, I had spent the majority of my childhood living here, but the interior was dank, dark and smelly for other reasons. The small amount of sunlight that filtered through a broken Venetian blind highlighted a stream of unsettled dust particles. They danced before my eyes that strained to adjust to my grim surroundings. I heard a one-sided, muffled conversation from the restaurant bar out back. Matt was rummaging around, still on his phone.

"Yeah, mate, nah, nah, nah, I told you! It's sweet."

I worked on twisting the lever of the Venetian to let in some sunlight.

"Can I help you?"

I turned to smile sweetly and met the wary face of Matt, who pocketed his phone. His beady eyes swept briefly over my face and then slowly lingered on my body with sleazy approval.

Ew.

I wanted to wipe that smirk off his face. Instead, I forced my smile even broader.

He relaxed his stance, leaned his hip against the bar, and crossed his arms.

"Well, I must say, this is an unexpected start to the day."

"A rather late start to the day, isn't it?" I quipped.

He looked like he had slept in his clothes, so it probably was his start.

"Well, whatever it is, it's a welcome start to the day." He smiled.

Ugh! Gross.

"The name's Matt." He held out his hand. "Matt King, but the locals call me Kingy." He added a wink.

It took every ounce of my strength to reach out and take his hand. I grasped it as firmly as I could, just like my dad had taught me. Dad always said you could tell a person's worth by their handshake, and, sure enough, Matt's shake was clammy and limp. Seemed about right.

"Amy. Amy *Henderson*."

I watched with great delight as the colour drained from Matt's face. His smile fell as his handshake turned to dead weight.

That's right, dip shit, that *Henderson.*

I sighed and looked around with my hands on my hips. "Well, I can't say I like what you've done with the place, but I guess it can be expected to be a bit stuffy. It's not like it's used to being closed up for such long hours," I said, giving Matt an extremely pointed look. "And opened so late in the day. Nothing that can't be fixed with a bit of TLC, isn't that right, Kingy?"

Matt's mouth gaped, seemingly struggling to string together a coherent sentence.

I shouldered my bag. "I'm beat. I best drag myself upstairs and unpack." I flashed another winning smile.

Matt just nodded, it was like he had seen a ghost, and I guess he kind of had – a ghost of Henderson's past.

I made a point of pulling open each blind I passed in one violent yank that in return made Matt wince from the bright sunlight. Each tug was like marking my territory; stamping a claim on what was mine. Dusty, dirty, dank and depressing as it was, there was no taking the Onslow away from me. I headed towards the partition to peel myself through the restaurant to the back staircase.

"Oh, Matt?" I stilled and turned towards him.

His troubled, dazed eyes met mine.

I held my hand out … "Keys?"

Chapter Four

Unlocking the door, I kicked it open and dropped my bag inside.

Urgh. What was that smell? I winced and covered my nose, my eyes threatening to water with the pong that emanated from Dad's two-bedroom apartment above the pub. The place looked eerie and deserted, as if Dad had literally upped and left for the day and simply not come back. His reading glasses were lying on an open book and the cushions were all skew-whiff on his favourite chair. It had his unmistakable butt indentation in the brushed suede fabric, created from many years of sitting there, kicking back. A stack of newspapers made for a stained side table; cigarette burn marks had singed the carpet; an overflowing ashtray sat at the foot of Dad's chair; and there was a stack of pizza boxes on the coffee table that could barely be seen under all the paperwork and junk. It was the epitome of a bachelor pad set in the pits of hell; it was as disgusting as a teenage boy's bedroom … I imagined.

It would have deeply saddened me that my father had been living like this, if I had allowed the emotion to override my anger. Which I didn't.

I kicked an empty, crushed soda can across the room and stormed towards the window to open it. I needed fresh air; bile threatened to burn the back of my throat if I took in one more putrid breath. I unclipped the latch on the window and groaned in frustration as the old-style latch window wouldn't budge.

"Come on!" I bent my knees and pushed upwards with all my might, but it was no use. I felt all hot and flustered and I had to get out of this space. I stepped to my left and flung aside the heavy red velvet curtains that smelled of cigarettes and second-hand smoke. As I pushed aside the drapes, I revealed a set of grotty French doors that led onto the balcony.

Oh, please open.

I turned the lock on the handle and twisted with a silent prayer. A magical click of freedom and the door opened, rewarding me with a burst of fresh, crisp air that rolled in directly off the lake.

I stepped out and embraced the sun on my face and inhaled a much-needed breath. The balcony creaked and groaned under my feet and I smiled at the familiarity; it was as if the old girl was speaking to me. I clasped the railing and looked out over the lake and the town of Onslow that nestled directly at the bottom of the hill. The hotel was perfectly positioned up here, overlooking Lake Onslow. I was so immersed in nostalgia looking out at the sweeping views that I had almost forgotten the ashtrays, empty beer bottles, and pizza boxes, the smell! Oh, the smell …

Yeah. I had *almost* forgotten.

I was snapped out of my trance by the slamming of a car door and the annoyance of someone whistling. The tune floated up to the balcony, crystal clear and pitch perfect.

I leaned over the railing and tried to make out who was approaching the hotel from the car park, but I was too late as the footsteps made their way underneath the balcony.

Curiosity got the better of me. I pushed off the railing to head downstairs to catch a glimpse of who exactly was coming in, but I'd only made it halfway across the landing when I froze. That quaint, familiar creak of the balcony now roared with an unnerving groan, and there was a violent tremor underfoot. My eyes widened and fear spiked through me as I felt the wood underneath give way.

It all happened so fast: One minute I was up on the balcony admiring the breathtaking views of Onslow; the next thing the floor gave way and, with an almighty scream, I grabbed at everything – anything – and was hanging on for dear life. My fingers hooked with white-knuckled intensity onto the base lip of the French doors, the only thing that kept me from completely falling through the cave opening below me that half my body had already fallen through.

I didn't want to die. I screamed again in shock, legs flailing, clawing at the lip to keep myself from falling farther.

"Matt!" I screamed, "Maaaatttt!"

But it wasn't Matt's voice that answered.

"JESUS CHRIST! KEEP STILL!"

I couldn't look down, I couldn't bring myself to. I could only guess that the mysterious whistler received a nasty surprise when he'd walked under the balcony. He was probably getting an even bigger surprise, considering my T-shirt was caught on a piece of debris and bunched up to my armpits.

I couldn't have cared less if I was dangling butt naked at that moment. All I was aware of was the heaviness of my body, the ache in my arms and the black hole below me that the hotel balcony had crumbled into.

But what I feared the most was the clamminess of my hands as they slowly slipped from the ledge.

"I'M SLIPPING!" I cried out.

"HOLD ON! I'M COMING UP!"

However irrational and ridiculous I could be sometimes, even though I was most likely about to fall to my death, a new panic flashed in my mind. I didn't want anyone to see the state of my dad's putrid apartment.

"NO! NO! DON'T COME UP!"

I finally made out Matt's panicked voice. "Aw, man, I am so getting fired for this."

Yeah, don't worry about me, arsehole!

"Probably, mate, but I think that is the least of our problems," the whistler's voice snapped.

"YOU'RE GOING TO BE ALL RIGHT! I'VE GOT YOU, LET GO!"

"WHAT?!" Was he for real?

"LET GO! I'VE GOT YOU!"

"... NO!"

"TRUST ME, LET GO!"

I wanted to debate this all day; where the hell was he? He clearly didn't have me, I wanted to defy the voice that tried to encourage me that I would be okay, but the choice was taken out of my hands as I felt my fingers lose their grip on the French door in a final slip.

I fell. I screamed; my arms grazed along the broken opening, my stomach plummeted; this was it. I would be pulverised by the cement landing; I would break my bones and crack my skull. But as I screamed in absolute terror at my impending fate, my fall was broken by strong, steely arms. I collided with a torso. I fell into him so fast, so violently, I literally heard the air being knocked out of his lungs as we both flew backwards, hitting the ground in a unified "Oomph!"

I clenched my eyes firmly shut, afraid to move as my heart threatened to pound out of my chest. My throat felt raw from screaming, but I didn't seem to be dead.

I felt a light tap on my shoulder blade and I opened my eyes.

"Are you all right?"

My head was resting on a muscled chest – I could feel the thunderous frantic beat within him that matched my own. I was clenched in a vice-like embrace in the stranger's arms, who cradled me still, and more alarmingly I was spread-eagled, lying on top of him. I lifted my head and pushed upwards. My panicked eyes met with vivid, baby blue ones that stared at me, narrowed in concern.

They widened in sudden realisation.

"Amy?"

I paused mid-movement, my hands splayed across his chest as I stared down at his face. Once the world had stopped spinning, recognition must have dawned on my own face, too.

"Sean Murphy?" I said, mainly to myself.

I felt his laughter vibrate against my palms splayed out on his chest.

His once rigid body collapsed on the ground. He cupped his face in an exhausted groan. "You just took ten years off my life!"

I glared down at him. "Trust me, it didn't do much for me either."

He moved his hands away from his face to reveal a boyish grin.

He shook his head. "One minute I'm walking along, minding my own business, and the next thing I know the bloody pub falls down and I'm nearly pancaked by a screaming girl; I thought all my Christmases had come at once." He continued to laugh. "Not the pub falling down part, but the damsel-in-distress thing wasn't bad."

I sat straight up and crossed my arms in distaste. "I see *you* haven't changed."

He lifted himself onto his elbows. "Honestly, Amy, you say that like it's a bad thing."

Matt's cough interrupted my seething reply. Once I'd looked up at Matt, then back at Sean, I realised in a stroke of horror that not only was I still on top of Sean but I was straddling him rather inappropriately. I locked eyes with Sean, his brows raised in amusement. I stumbled to my feet like I had been struck by lightning and accidentally stepped on him.

"Ah, Jesus, Amy!"

My cheeks were on fire as I manoeuvred myself to my feet. Matt offered Sean a helping hand off the ground and, as he dusted himself off, both sets of eyes froze on me. My eyes narrowed in confusion and I followed their gazes. I looked down to see my shirt had been torn clean in two. My black lace bra was exposed to the world, totally and utterly out there saying *hello boys!*

I gasped and clenched the fabric together, mortified. Could this day get any worse?

Before I disgraced myself any further, I gingerly excused myself and turned towards the hotel door. I paused mid-step and spun around to face Sean.

"Is there something you wanted?"

Matt brushed past me, not even managing to look me in the eye.

Sean stepped forward, plunged his hands into his pockets, and shrugged. "I was just stopping by for a cold one. Say g'day to your dad."

"Well, he's not here," I said, perhaps a bit too quickly.

Sean nodded. A wry smile formed on his lips. "Well, a cold one then?"

"Sorry, we're closed." And before he could ask another question, I stepped into the hotel, kicked the door closed, and leaned against it with a deep sigh.

Mortified!

I shifted to my left a little, leaning slowly to peer out through the dirty windowpane. Sean stood staring at the closed door, perplexed. He rubbed his stubbled chin and looked upwards to the newly formed skylight in the balcony. He smirked.

"Just go, *just go*," I whispered under my breath.

"Are we really closed?"

I flinched at the unexpected voice right next to my ear, as Matt's narrowed eyes followed what I was looking at outside.

We were closed all right; I just hoped we weren't condemned.

Chapter Five

I studied my reflection in the bathroom mirror and surveyed the damage.

One grazed elbow, a few scratches, a torn shirt, amazingly no bloodshed, but just like my top, my dignity had been well and truly trashed. Groaning, I cupped my face and leaned against the sink; at least I hadn't been in a skirt, wearing a G-banger …

Small miracles, I guess.

My fringe parted as I blew out a laboured breath, my hands falling at my sides, exhausted. I straightened, a new thought running through my mind.

"I could have died," I said aloud to myself. "I could have totally died."

I reached into my pocket for my phone, punching in the numbers with fierce intent.

The phone rang, one, two, three times … "Hello?" my mum's upbeat voice answered.

"Mum!"

"Oh hi, honey, did you make it all right?"

"Yeah, well …"

"Oh, that's wonderful. Guess where your dad's taking me?"

The last of Mum's voice was drowned out by the loud ear-bleeding burst of an engine; I winced away from the phone.

"What is that?"

Vroom… Vroom…

"Oh, that's your dad's new bike." Mum's voice held an excited thrill.

"Whaaaaat?" I said. "You have *got* to be kidding me, a motorbike?"

"A trike."

Oh, this was getting worse.

Mum could barely contain her excitement. "He's taking me for a ride!"

"Dear God …" The midlife crisis had reached a new level and now he was dragging Mum into it, down the Western Ring Road like a bat out of hell, no doubt. God they were so *embarrassing.*

"Mum, I don't think …"

"Honey, I better go! Your dad's got the motor running. Ooh, wish me luck!"

Before I could so much as think, the line went dead.

I looked at the phone, confused. There had been a pretty important point to my phone call, but I had been completely sidetracked by Mum's erratic excitement. I envisioned them screaming up the highway, two middle-aged misfits getting their kicks, pulling over for a pit stop somewhere, pulling off their helmets and pashing madly …

Shudder.

What had happened to Claire Henderson? The Claire Henderson I knew would never get on a motorbike, purely because it meant she'd get helmet hair and that just wouldn't do.

I wandered dazed into the apartment and banged my knee on the coffee table.

"Ahhhh, sonofa … Ahhhh!"

How much more could my body take? I plonked onto the coffee table that was covered in papers and remotes. It could have been my near-death experience, fatigue from travel, or the overwhelming mess that lay before me that made my shoulders sag. What had seemed like a brilliant idea, to escape to the country for the summer, was literally falling apart. While Mum and Dad lived up the summer in the city, I was trapped in this smelly, grotty tomb. I wanted to run screaming, and maybe if I rang up now I could book a ticket on the first bus for tomorrow morning. I didn't want to stay in the Onslow; not like this.

I shifted awkwardly on my lumpy, makeshift seat and grabbed the one thing that jabbed into me: a dog-eared copy of *House and Garden* magazine? Ha! Surely it was Mum's, but as I eyed the date, September 1999, I knew it couldn't be. It was only a few months old; Mum hadn't been here for months and months. What had Dad been doing with *House and Garden*, of all things?

I flicked open the cover, half expecting it to reveal a fishing magazine inside. Instead, it fell open to a folded down page. There was writing scrawled in the corner: Dad's writing. Clearing any doubts I had, I cocked my head and read, 'Claire's dream kitchen,' with an arrow pointing to the image on the page. The photo was of a sleek, white kitchen with modern stainless steel appliances.

As I flicked further through the magazine, a smile curled my lips up. It was marked with several dog-eared pages of interest: a cosy lounge, a circled wall colour Dad would like for the living room, page after page of little comments on what he liked. My smile faded as I flicked through to another page.

A picture of a beautiful bedroom. A paper chain lantern was draped over the headboard of a gorgeous wooden bed with matching desk and a plush wingback chair. The bedspread was a lighter shade of a divine purple that offset the deep colour of the walls. It was such an intense colour, but the room could take it because the trimmings were a crisp white with polished floors and a gorgeous feature rug. It was so beautiful my fingers trailed over the glossed image to trace along the arrow to the scrawled handwriting that read, 'Amy's room'.

I blinked rapidly to clear my blurring vision as I focused on Dad's handwriting. He knew what I liked. He must have sat here in this room, looking at beautiful pictures, daydreaming about the things he wished he had, the things he would like to have been able to give us.

It spoke to me, such a subtle gesture, because it was so unexpected and completely something I would do. People always said I was my father's daughter; I had always scoffed at the comparison. Dad was a big, gruff, bearded bloke I didn't like much being compared to, but maybe sometimes I was like my dad in other ways?

I lifted my gaze from the show-home display of dreamy, unlived-in images of perfection, to my bleak, littered surrounds. My heart sank.

Oh, hell no! This shit would not fly with me.

I squared my shoulders and chucked the magazine on the couch. Standing up, I circled the room with my hands on my hips.

"Nope, this won't do at all," I said aloud to the room.

The cogs in my mind started whirring and thoughts of a bus ticket home were long gone.

I walked over to the window I couldn't open before and wiped a clean spot in the grimy glass. The sun twinkled on the lake's surface – so beautiful, so familiar. I slowly tore my eyes from the view and looked back into the apartment and then back to the scene outside.

I smiled, slow and wicked. "It's time to take out the trash!"

Chapter Six

The seventh black garbage bag flew down the chute.

The chute being my earlier, self-made, human-shaped skylight through the balcony floor. I dusted my hands off on my jeans with immense satisfaction as the last garbage bag made a clinking crash on top of the rubbish mound. It was so damn therapeutic; I had gone from tired, bruised, and down-and-out to having a new lease on life.

I had peeled off the threadbare throw covers from the couch, and cleared all the empty food containers, boxes, papers, bottles, and ashtrays. Instantly it had created clean spots throughout the apartment.

Well, sort of.

I lifted up an old beer bottle and it left a clean, circular marking in the thick layer of dust; this was the pattern all over the apartment. I worked on stripping cushion covers, bed sheets, doonas, and took down curtains, making a pile in the middle of the living room. They were ready to be washed for the first time in, well … I didn't know how long. The last curtain crumpled in a heap on the floor and a cloud of dust shot into the air. I coughed up a storm, wiped my brow and re-evaluated the scene: Was I actually getting anywhere?

Yep! Time for a break, though! I headed downstairs, swung around the end bannister and dragged my feet across the restaurant towards the front bar. Grabbing a bottle of Coke from the lower fridge, I selected a pot glass and went to shovel some ice from the bucket. But all there was in there was water.

"Damn it."

I rolled my eyes, cursing Matt, and looked around. Melted ice was the least of my problems; the bar was filthy, unstocked and disorganised. And deserted. It was also the first time I realised that I was utterly alone here. Never in my life had I seen the bar unmanaged, or the place entirely empty. Even on its quieter days, there had always been a wayward drunk propped up in the corner, or a few locals in for a cold one and a quiet game of pool. I had sent Matt home with little thought that it was something my dad would never have done in a million years, no matter how bad things got.

The thought unsettled me some; what if Dad found out I had closed the pub? He would be furious and I would be whipped home so fast my head would spin.

Ha, I thought. I looked around at the cracked lino behind the bar, the shrivelled, two-day-old lemon wedges near the cash register, the smell of rotten, unwashed beer mats that festered on the bar. It was his fault! He had abandoned this place and left some useless bartender in charge. And where was the rest of the staff? The cleaner, the cook, the waitress, the dish pig … where were the *customers*?! There was no life here. The Onslow Hotel was dead.

I made my way around from behind the bar, careful not to spill my warming Coke, and headed into the poolroom. As I walked through the entry, it was sticky underfoot. Gross. I noted the stained outline of a spilled drink from God knows when. I slammed my Coke down and leaned over the bar in search of something to clean with. It took some finding. After I had wiped up the sticky residue, then I would rest, I promised myself.

On my hands and knees, I worked on edging through the sticky, dirty mark that had splashed against the skirting; it smelled like something fruity and stale. My intense concentration was disturbed by the screeching of the front door on its hinges. I was flooded with sunlight. I cursed under my breath; obviously Matt hadn't locked the door on his way out. I sat back on my heels and held my arm to my face, shielding my eyes from the light.

"I'm sorry, we're clo—"

I eyed a tall figure leaning against the doorframe, sporting a smug smile.

Sean.

I was suddenly aware of how disgustingly dishevelled I must look, kneeling amidst a sticky, soap-sudded mess, water staining my T-shirt, wisps of hair escaping my ponytail. I wiped my brow and pushed away the strands of hair that blocked my vision. I warily dropped the scrubbing brush back into the bucket. Sean leaned carefree in the doorway, the backdrop of sunlight glowing around his six-foot-three stance. Down on my knees before him, I suddenly felt so incredibly small. My eyes trailed over him; his Blundstone work boots, navy blue work pants and matching navy singlet. His folded arms accentuating the broadness of his chest. My eyes met briefly with the amused glint in his. His brows rose as his teeth flashed under a cheeky grin.

"You've missed a spot."

My cheeks flushed as I thought he was referring to my eyes that had unashamedly roamed over him, but as he glanced to the floor, I snapped out of my daze and looked down to a grubby spot I had indeed missed.

Nothing infuriated me more than that old, smart-arse, 'missed a spot' joke. It was something I had always heard from my older cousins, Chris and Adam, who had loved to taunt me every summer when they'd helped out at the pub. Sweeping in the beer garden, you missed a spot. Varnishing the silver, you missed a spot. Washing a dish, you missed a spot. My scowl deepened at the memory as I stood and dusted the grime from my knees, dampened from kneeling in dirty, soapy water.

I grabbed the bucket and made my way to walk around behind the bar.

"We're closed," I threw over my shoulder.

Walking in the little alcove that housed the sink and dishwasher, I tipped the dirty water from the bucket down the sink and winced at the putrid blackness of the once fresh liquid. Rinsing the bucket out and putting it back where I had found it, I vigorously washed my hands before paper towelling them dry. I made my way back behind the main bar, where Sean had already pulled up and relaxed onto a stool, propping his elbows on the bar.

"Bad day?" he asked with an amused lift of his brow.

"You mean apart from nearly falling to my death? No, other than that, I'm just peachy."

Sean's smile broadened as he tapped his hand on the bar. "That's the spirit!"

I didn't share his enthusiasm. I knew I was being unreasonably snappy; it wasn't Sean's fault that my dad had turned out to be a chain-smoking hoarder who had left the family business to a lazy douche like Matt to run into the ground.

I sighed, my shoulders sagging as I lowered my guard, just a little.

"Do you want a drink?"

If Sean was surprised by the offer he didn't show it; instead, he nodded his agreement. "Please."

I mirrored his nod and grabbed a glass from the stack. I straightened as I motioned to pull the lever of the VB tap forward, all of a sudden self-conscious as I felt Sean's eyes on me in my peripheral vision. I angled the glass and an amber stream flowed into it, before I quickly straightened the glass to ensure it formed the perfect froth to finish, like my dad had taught me. I was hit with a wave of nostalgia, a tiny smile threatening to curve the corners of my mouth at such a small pleasure, until what had begun as a steady stream of beer started to cough and sputter violent spurts of foam into the glass. I instantly pulled the lever back to stop the assault.

"Oh, for frack's sake! The barrel's empty. This is … " I threw my hands up in dismay; I didn't know whether to laugh or cry hysterically. Oh the irony … a pub with no beer. "This is just great."

Sean leaned over the bar and grabbed his beer, studying the half-filled morsel that resembled more of a soft serve ice cream than a drink. He placed it back down, trying his utmost not to smirk as he looked at me. I wanted to wipe that smug look off his face. I knew what he was thinking.

How does a publican's daughter not know how to pour a beer?

I was about to defend my honour, insisting it was the end of the barrel, but he spoke before I had a chance to form the words.

"Did you just say frack?"

My mouth gaped; I could feel my cheeks burn at the question.

"Pfft … no!" I lied.

Sean broke into a broad smile. "Yeah, you did," he teased.

"I don't know what you're talking about." I cleared the beer away, avoiding Sean's knowing eyes.

"Well …" Sean stood and stretched his arms over his head. "Today has certainly been a day of firsts."

"Did you want a stubby or a can or something?"

"Nah, that's okay. So where's your dad? Will he be back soon?" He walked over to peer outside through the grotty window.

I must have looked dumbfounded because I kind of was. Dad losing weight, quitting smoking, and heading to the city to woo his wife was common and mortifying knowledge. It was one of my huge reservations about coming back to Onslow for the holidays. I would be escaping Mum and Dad, but I wouldn't be escaping their figurative ghosts, even after Dad's three-month stint at home full-time. All any local would have to do was look up the hill to see the Onslow abandoned and overgrown. Like a giant rotting hotel that the crazy publican had chucked in for love.

"Where have you been living? Under a rock? Dad hasn't been here for months."

Sean lazily shrugged one shoulder, as he tore his eyes from outside to me.

"I wouldn't know, I just got back."

"Back from where?" The words fell from my mouth before I could stop them.

"I just finished a contract up north, building a school there in Warrentye."

I looked blankly at him – I had no idea where that was. It sounded far away.

"It's where I've been living the last two years."

Okay, that made sense, I thought as I nodded my head. "Yeah, I just got back too," I confessed.

I had probably been away longer; my memory searched for the last time I was home at the Onslow. I froze, my eyes darting back to Sean. He must have read something in my expression as he straightened.

"You all right?" he asked.

I was instantly transported back to my last time in Onslow; my cheeks burned, mortified at the memory of the last summer I had seen Sean Murphy three years ago.

The summer he saved my life.

Chapter Seven

"You look like you've seen a ghost," Sean said.

Maybe I had; the ghost of summers past. The last thing I wanted to do was go down memory lane. Seriously. Some things just needed to remain in the past. Maybe Sean had forgotten that night.

I really hoped he had.

"Oh, I've just had a really long day."

Sean studied my face for a long moment, silently gauging if I was telling him the truth. Finally he nodded, as if accepting my excuse.

"Well, want some advice?"

I raised my brows in interest.

He pushed off from the wall and leaned in towards me, whispering into my ear.

"Lock the door."

I followed him outside, stepping over the pile of garbage bags from upstairs, which Sean eyed with interest. He stepped wide along the verandah that was filled with debris. Looking above, his brow creased in deep thought.

"Have a look." He pointed. I followed his line of vision.

"The beam's rotten. No wonder it caved."

I squinted up to the broken, damp-stained beam. "I dare say you have a downpipe overflowing somewhere it shouldn't be." Sean walked along the verandah. He touched the posts, and strained his neck to inspect every single inch.

"I'll have a look around, but hopefully by the look of things it's just an isolated section." Sean scratched the stubble on his chin in deep thought, lost in the throes of his profession. He had been a builder for as long as I could remember, but had gone on his own a few years ago and made a name for himself; apart from being a womanising footy player, he was also a skilled tradesman. At least that was what I had heard before I'd left Onslow; no doubt the footy playing and womanising were also still favourite extracurricular activities.

I leaned against the door and inspected a chipped nail I had earned from a day devoted to cleaning.

"Well, that's a relief," I said unenthusiastically.

Sean flipped out his mobile. "What's your dad's number? I'll give him a quote if he wants."

My head snapped up. "No!" I yelled, reaching out to grab his wrist. Sean froze, an amused quirk to his lips as he looked down at my hand. I pulled it away.

"Um, I just mean that … he's probably busy and …"

Sean broke into a broad grin as he pocketed his phone. "You haven't told him."

I straightened. "I tried, but, like I said, he's busy."

"O-oh! You broke the hotel!"

"Pfft," I said darkly. "I think it was pretty broken before I got here." My eyes rested on the pile of rubbish that blocked the path to the main door.

"Yeah, what's with that?" Sean took in the overgrown surroundings, his smile sobering into a grim line.

I didn't want to get into that; I didn't even want Sean looking around like he did, judging, just like the rest of the town probably was.

"Hey, um, sorry about slamming the door in your face before," I said.

Sean turned with interest, his brows raised.

I felt like I wanted to squirm under his smug scrutiny, but I held my ground. Sort of. "I just, um, forgot to, um …"

"Construct coherent sentences?"

I glowered. "Shut up!" I moved to snatch up a garbage bag for the skip around the back.

Always the smart-arse.

"What I meant to say is thanks. Thanks for helping me today."

"Why, Amy Henderson, you're making me feel all warm and fuzzy inside." Sean grabbed one of the other garbage bags and slung it over his shoulder, following me.

"Yeah, we'll call it a momentary lapse of sanity."

We carried our clinking bags of rubbish off the verandah down the uneven, cracked path that ran around towards the back entrance where the large skip was kept. Slinging my cargo into the grubby recess, I dusted my hands off and went to thank Sean for his help, but thought better of it as we turned to head back around the front.

"You know, I was serious, I can give you a quote if you want."

I had only been at the Onslow for one day and already I had seriously damaged the property, alienated the only staff member and shut down the pub for the first time in its history. A big part of the reason I had vehemently objected was if Dad had found out I had shut down the pub a mere hours after my arrival, nineteen or not, I would be banished from the Onslow quick smart. Regardless of the damage Dad's neglect had caused, I was not mistaken to believe I would be in serious trouble.

"I can't pay you to fix it."

Sean looked troubled. "Why would you pay? I'd be quoting for your dad."

I stopped dead in my tracks. "Dad can't know. If he finds out what happened today I would be …" I was blabbering, and the last thing I needed was to reveal too much about how, even at nineteen, I really didn't want to get in trouble with Mum and Dad. Especially now that they were a combined force and on the 'same page' when it came to me.

I had heard it all; they were worried about me, what was I going to do with my life? When was I going back to uni? In a nutshell, my life was going nowhere fast and after nineteen years of not worrying too much, now that Dad was home and he had undergone such a life-changing journey, all of a sudden he was determined that I make something of my life and Mum was his biggest fan. What a joke!

"You're serious?" he asked.

"Yes."

We stepped up onto the verandah again, closing the distance towards the garbage bags.

"Well, call it a momentary lapse of sanity but …" He looked up. "There is a gaping hole in your balcony. He's going to find out."

"I know, but …" I sighed. "I'll figure something out."

I went to take the bag from Sean's grasp but he refused to let it go, so we stood there joined by our mutual grasps of the black garbage bag.

The last thing I needed was to get a lecture from him about how stupid that sounded. I was just about to shut this whole conversation down before he started laughing at me … but then he didn't. He just stood there, staring, no smile, no expression at all other than a questioning frown and a firm, unrelenting grasp on his side of the bag. He didn't have to voice the words that he no doubt thought – that I was out of my mind and pathetic for keeping secrets from my parents like a kid scared of getting caught after breaking a window with a cricket ball.

"Well, good luck with that," Sean said. He let go of the bag. "See you around, Amy Henderson."

That infamous crooked quirk to his lips was back before he tore his eyes away, hopped off the verandah and headed towards his white twin cab Toyota. My heart sank a little; was I actually disappointed that he hadn't challenged me, questioned me, or insisted he help offload the rubbish for me?

I watched as he climbed into his work rig that sported his name and mobile number on the side in blue print, advertising his business: 'Sean Murphy This N That Building'.

He put on some sunnies, fired up his ute and worked to turn the steering wheel in a cool, confident, one-handed turn. He backed it up, pulled into gear, flashed a winning smile and sounded the horn in a series of honks before he blazed a circled cloud of dust and flew down Coronary Hill.

As the dust cloud settled, I suddenly felt exhausted and alone, just me and the dilapidated Onslow. I accidently stepped on a garbage bag.

"Crap!" Correction. Just me and a pile of garbage. Oh joy.

Chapter Eight

By ten o'clock at night I was showered again and in my PJs.

Dad's apartment still smelled like the remnants of cigarette smoke, after thirty-plus years of chain smoking. The walls were even stained, that passive yellowing smoke colour. I had scrubbed and rubbed, washed and polished, and yet the apartment still didn't feel right. I had attacked the kitchenette with some hospital grade disinfectant, but I had yet to clean out the fridge.

I had only opened it for a nanosecond and closed it so quickly I could barely believe that such a short glimpse could have evoked such terror in me. The amount of rotting food and sludge that had pooled at the bottom of the fridge was truly repulsive and, after the day I'd had, I wasn't ready to tackle that just yet.

I unclipped the sheets and doona cover I'd hung out earlier from the line at the back of the beer garden and basked in the sweet lavender fragrance that emitted from them. Finally, something clean and fresh. I couldn't wait to collapse in a heap into them. I had downed a packet of nuts and another Coke that had seen me over the line, but I was so busy that I didn't overly notice my exhaustion until I hit the wall. I didn't think my brain could function much longer without food; I would get some supplies tomorrow.

I shuffled my bunny slippers up the stairs, my arms full of linen, when I paused on the landing. I stared wearily towards the apartment door, then turned to the opposite hallway. I flicked on the hall light, lighting the long narrow hall, and made my way to the fourth door on the right. Inside, I switched the light on and found a double bed with a navy, plaid bedspread and a poster of Jimi Hendrix on the wall. I smiled. The fourth room on the right had always been my cousin Chris's room when he came to help out in the holidays. He was the oldest of all my cousins, seven years older than me and best mates with Sean. The room hadn't changed a lot; aside from being bare. It just lacked his clothes and crap strung all over the place. I flicked the light off, shifting the pile as my tired arms began to feel weighed down with the load. At the end of the hall, last door on the right, I opened the door and revealed a room with a desk, another double bed stripped of blankets, and a washstand jammed in the corner. The room was more barren and unlived in than Chris's, but it would always be Adam's room, Chris's younger brother. I'd loved having them around for the summer, although I would never admit that, but come summer again I looked forward to my cousins being back to stay and help out at the Onslow. Each summer, I had been instantly transformed from being an only child to having two older brothers. As I looked at the abandoned room, my heart swelled at all the memories of growing up here. The times we would play murder in the dark and go hide in one of the many guest rooms, or how they'd take me out on the lake waterskiing, something I had always been happy to do until that night before I was sent away. I swallowed down the memory as I clicked off the light.

I hadn't been back in the lake since that night. I hadn't exactly had the chance to, either, seeing as though I had been frog-marched off to the city after the whole sneaking-out, binge-drinking, almost-drowning debacle.

Yeah, that would do it every time. Even looking out onto Lake Onslow from a distance, a certain chill and apprehension swept over me that I hadn't been able to shake in all this time.

It had been three years.

I made my way straight across the hall, readjusting my bundle of washing on my hip so that I could open the door. As I flipped the light on, I was instantly calmed.

My room.

One thing had to be said about Dad's lack of decorating skills – my room had pretty much been left as it was. It was like a giant time capsule of my childhood, and, better yet, it didn't smell like smoke. A Party of Five poster on the wall, a white dressing table with my rainbow-coloured nail polishes and feather boa draped over the mirror. Purple was my favourite colour and a common theme throughout my room. It was only highlighted by the stark white of my wrought iron bed. My room lay directly across from Adam's and I remembered how in the middle of the night we had often snuck out of our rooms and lain in the hall, framing our faces with torches and trying to outdo each other with ghost stories. It had been so creepy, but so fun. I stepped inside and dumped my linens onto the bed. This was where I would sleep; this to me was home!

***

I peeled one eye open as I was awakened from a deep sleep.

What the hell was that noise?

The sound of distant yells and clanking drove me from my bed. Stumbling for the curtain, I pulled it to one side and was instantly blinded by sunlight.

Ugh, what time was it? I cringed away from the offending beams and let the fabric fall back into place.

I pressed the light on my Baby-G watch: six-forty-five a.m., holding it up to my face as I struggled to wake up.

Oh, hell no!

I grabbed for my bunny slippers and flung the door open. As I stomped down the hall, the noise became louder and my fury spiked.

"Some people are fracking unbelievable!"

Winding my way downstairs into the foyer of the restaurant, I was now wide awake and mad as hell. Who the hell was here at six-forty-five a.m.? Was this Matt's idea of a joke? Or inconsiderate neighbours? Okay, so I was in a lone hotel on a hill with my closest neighbours being a five-kilometre trek away, but still. It could have been.

I shrugged off the thought; regardless, there was a hell of a racket coming from my doorstep and I was pissed. After yesterday's nightmarish introduction to the Onslow of today, I had been exhausted and planned to sleep the summer away. Well, if not that, I certainly hadn't planned on being woken up at six-forty-five a.m. But it seemed someone had other ideas.

I unbolted the front door in the main bar and threw it open. I charged out to give whoever it was a piece of my mind, when I nearly collided with a pole.

A pole?

"Watch it! We haven't taped it off yet!"

A hand grabbed my elbow, yanking me aside and out of the path of another pole. I stumbled, but the vice-like grip held me upwards and refused to let go.

"Nice slippers!"

It was Sean. He was holding my arm, smiling down at my fire-engine red, fluffy bunny slippers, complete with floppy ears and googly eyes.

I wrenched my arm from his grip.

"What are you doing here?" I snapped.

I needn't have asked the question; after I had gotten over my confusion I knew exactly what I had run into.

"I'm baking a cake, what does it look like?"

My eyes narrowed. "Scaffolding?" I spun around. "Who said you could put scaffolding up?" My heart spiked in a sudden panic that maybe Sean had rung Dad last night after all.

"Hey, Amy!" Stan skipped up the steps towards Sean. "Was this what you were looking for?"

"Yeah, thanks mate." Sean took the brackety-looking thing from Stan's gloved hand and studied it.

Stan stood beside me, folded his arms and admired their handiwork.

"Don't worry, Amy, this will be fixed in no time. We'll tape it off and put up hazard signs." Stan flashed a boyish grin. "Good as new."

Stan had always been the most jovial of the Onslow Boys, and the one I had seen the most of over the years. He and Chris would often come and stay at our town house on a weekend for the odd footy match or concert. With his floppy, auburn-brown hair, his bright blue eyes and fair skin, he exuded a shy, friendly quality that was always sweet and appealing. The total opposite to Sean Murphy.

"Sean, can I talk to you for a minute?"

I offered Stan a small, apologetic smile as I headed inside. As I dodged the pole they'd erected and opened the door, I didn't miss the deep sigh from behind me. I could only imagine the eye roll Sean had no doubt thrown Stan as he reluctantly followed me. I waited in the alcove that led into the poolroom. Arms folded, I tried to look lethal; I caught my reflection in a glass pane and gasped. It seemed I'd bypassed lethal and had landed on ridiculous. My bedhead, bird's-nest hair stood up in a frizzy crest, my deep purple singlet top, and matching purple and mint green striped PJ bottoms accentuating the bunny slippers. I tried to frantically run my fingers through my hair and had to stop as I heard Sean's heavy work boots thumping towards me. I pushed aside my fringe, and crossed my arms back into place.

Pfft, what did I care what I looked like? It was only Sean.

Sean, who was now leaning into the alcove, his body mirroring mine. He wore a navy blue Bonds singlet that exposed the taut curves of his tanned biceps, and navy shorts with boots and socks that my eyes flicked to with a bemused smile.

"I bet you get a nasty sock tan."

Sean looked down at his boots and then back up at me. He then leaned over and pulled down his sock and revealed, sure enough, a paler strip of skin.

"Holy crap!" I said and shielded my eyes. "I've been blinded."

"They're not *that* white, smart-arse," Sean said defensively. He looked down with a frown and studied his ankles.

"Hey, it's okay, I understand. Occupational hazard."

Sean's eyes narrowed. "Is this why you had to pull me aside? To check out my tan lines?"

My smile slipped away from my face as I remembered why I had called him in.

"No!"

"Are you sure? Because I can show you some other tan lines if you want …" Sean moved to slowly peel his singlet up over his chiselled stomach.

This time, I was momentarily blinded, but in an 'Oh my God!' kind of way.

After I had stared open-mouthed and let my eyes trail over the wall of flesh, my mind worked to form a coherent sentence before he completely took his top off.

"No! No, it's all right, I don't need to see."

Didn't I?

Sean shrugged and let his top fall back into place with a smug smile. Oh, he thought he was so clever making all the girls speechless just by the flex of a muscle.

Well, not *this* girl.

I had been momentarily intrigued, but that was it.

I plastered my best 'I'm so bored right now' expression on my face as we stared one another down. Sean's eyes were lit with a silent knowing that made me want to lash out and take that smug look off his face.

"I can't pay you for this," I said, in all seriousness.

"That's all right, that preview was a freebie." He winked.

My arms flew by my sides and I exhaled in anger as I stomped my foot.

"God damn it, Sean, can't you be serious for one fra—"

Don't say fracking, don't say fracking. "For just one minute?"

Sean's brow curved. "Did you just stomp your foot?"

I fought the urge to do it again; it was a knee-jerk reaction after every frustrating, smart-arse retaliation.

It took every ounce of my strength to control the anger that threatened to consume me. I closed my eyes and breathed deeply.

"What I meant was, I can't pay for you to fix the balcony, Sean," I said. "Not right now; I have to get my head around so many things and at the moment I don't want Dad knowing about it. I was going to tape it off and put signs up. No one walks up there anyway and you said the rest was secure, it was just that one beam, so I think it can wait a bit … right?"

"What are you trying to get your head around?"

"What?"

Was he actually asking a serious question? Sean looked stern; his smile had gone.

"What's there to get your head around?" he asked again.

I scoffed. "Look at this place! It's disgusting; do you honestly think that a gaping hole in the verandah roof is going to drive people away? No! They're *already* away. One look at this place from a distance does that, let alone stepping inside." I stopped talking, knowing I had already said too much. It was one thing to voice what I knew to be true; I didn't want to talk about the embarrassing state of the Onslow with anyone else, though.

I wanted to sweep it under the carpet, stop everyone talking about 'the Hendersons'.

You know the mother ran away from Onslow and the father went mad and chased her. Now the spoilt, nasty daughter is back for the summer.

Oh, I could just imagine what they were all saying, and it bothered me – *really* bothered me. I wanted to show them, show them all. But I had to do it my way, and that meant on a tight budget and didn't involve a builder and scaffolding.

Sean didn't say anything for the longest time. I thought maybe for once I had rendered him speechless but then, just as I thought I would glory in the possibility, he broke the silence.

"Who said I was charging?"

I stilled. "What do you mean?"

He rolled his eyes. "I'm not charging you for repairing the balcony."

I must have looked dumbfounded and I could see he was now pleased with himself for rendering *me* speechless.

Once what he had said had registered in my brain, I wasn't thankful. I was angry. "Thanks, but I don't want your charity."

Sean's eyes narrowed in anger. "Charity?"

"Look," I said. "I appreciate it, but I am not having a pity party."

"Is that what you think this is?" Sean said incredulously.

"Isn't it? Look, Sean, I don't–"

"Just hang on a second …" he interrupted.

"End of discussion," I said. "Sean, I'm not—"

"LET ME FINISH!" He raised his voice.

"NO!"

"AMY …"

"FOR FUCK'S SAKE, SEAN, STOP TRYING TO RESCUE ME." I screamed.

Chapter Nine

This time, I *did* render him speechless.

I could feel the anger as it pulsed through him, and radiated outward from his eyes as they burned into mine. All of a sudden I felt really small, so I broke from his gaze.

"Amy?" His voice was lower, gentle.

"Please, Sean, I don't need your help."

"I'm not trying to be the knight in shining armour, here."

I scoffed, still refusing to look at him.

"I'm not asking for repayment, Amy, because your dad has been good to me over the years. Hell, I practically spent my early twenties in this place. I'll fix it, it will be done and no one has to know."

"I'll know."

Sean sighed heavily. "Bloody proud, pig-headed Henderson, just like your old man."

"Well, I would sooner be that than a self-centred egomaniac who thinks he's God's gift to women."

Sean laughed. "I saved you from breaking your neck yesterday, I'm offering to fix your balcony today for free and *I'm* self-centred?"

"Well, chuck in MacLean's Beach and you have your heroic trifecta." The words tumbled out of my mouth before I could stop them. The last thing I wanted to ever remember was that night. The one where Sean had pulled me limp and lifeless out of the water. It had been a constant source of embarrassment for me. Everyone knew about it and, what was worse, it was exactly the reason I had been sent away. It wasn't that I was angry at Sean; it wasn't his fault. I mean, he saved my life, but I didn't want him to be my constant saviour. I needed to save myself sometimes.

If anything, Dad owed Sean big time, he had said so himself, and apart from the odd free beer, I'm pretty sure Dad had never been in any position to pay him back. So the last thing I needed was for a debt of gratitude to pile up against Sean any more than it already had; it wasn't fair and I wouldn't do it. He had done enough.

Sean had stilled, the memory of MacLean's Beach that night dawning on him.

"Christ! That was the last time I saw you? All those years ago?"

I had done it now, me and my big mouth.

"Yeah, well, that was ages ago." I could feel my cheeks burning.

Sean shook his head at the memory. "You scared the hell out of me that night."

This was exactly what I didn't want – a trip down memory lane.

"That's settled then, so you will just take it down, right? The scaffolding?"

Sean snapped out of his thoughts, his confused eyes staring my way, a small, wicked smile forming on his face.

"I don't know, I guess I'm speaking to the wrong person. I mean, it's your dad who owns the place. I guess I should really be asking him." He reached into his pocket for his mobile.

Son of a bitch!

"So this is how it's going to be?" I bit out.

"Lose some of that pride, Amy." Sean's thumb hovered over the call button. "Accept a helping hand once in a while."

My frown deepened.

Sean sighed. "It's not charity. If you want, I can offer you mate's rates and you can have your precious little bill. You can pay it back whenever you want and your dad doesn't have to know. How's that sound? Deal?"

I thought about it for a moment. I had no idea how I planned to pay it back, but I would. I *so* would. I squared my shoulders.

"Deal!"

Sean pocketed his mobile with a smile. "Right! Best get back to it then."

Before I could offer up a forked-tongued retaliation, Sean peeled himself from the alcove and walked out of the door.

***

Being up at this hour when I didn't have to be was unthinkable, but then again so was pulling out a long line of mouldy hair from the shower drainpipe. I gagged as I placed the vile tendril in the bin and washed my hands with blistering hot water. I cleared the condensation from the mirror and stared at my reflection. My hair was now dampened from the shower, my face was fresh and make-up free. I stuck out my tongue to judge its colour, not that I exactly knew what I was looking for even if I was sick. And I was ill. I was completely revolted by this place, at least.

By nine a.m. I was showered and dressed, but for what exactly I wasn't sure. Each time I heard a chorus of laughter or a raised voice or power tool from outside it grated me.

My stomach rumbled in protest and I remembered how the hotel wasn't even stocked with things like food! I grabbed my bag from my room and made my way downstairs; I wanted to distance myself from what had now turned into a construction site. A few hours out would do the trick.

I stepped out onto the verandah, super aware of what would greet me now: a jungle of steel poles stood as support under the gaping hole in the balcony floor, with a board placed under the hole as something to walk on until they fixed it. Stan was up on the boarded platform, whistling along to the radio. Yeah – a radio! They had certainly settled in for the day.

Stan looked down at me with a smile.

"You off, then?"

"Yeah. Just have to get a few things from town. Looks like he has you doing all the work."

Stan laughed. "He wishes." He plonked down into a sitting position, his legs dangling over the edge.

I wondered why Stan was here helping Sean, anyway. Last I knew, Stan had been working elsewhere in town, but that was a while ago.

"So what have you been up to, Stan?"

"Oh, you know, work and more work."

"So you're just helping out Sean?"

Stan looked at me, confused. "We work together."

"Oh?"

"Yeah, Sean came and saw me when he got back, made me a deal and here I am."

I nodded. At a loss as to what else to say, I was about to ask how his girlfriend, Ellie, was going. Then, I quickly stopped myself as I remembered they had broken up a few years ago. Before I put my foot in anything else, I decided I'd better get going. I wasn't exactly up with the latest in Onslow happenings.

"Well," I said, "don't work too hard."

I turned to walk down the steps before it registered. "Stan, did you want anything from down the street?"

Stan's smile was more striking than the sun. "No thanks, Amy, Sean's popped down for some smoko, best not spoil my appetite," he said with a wink.

"Okay, no worries, see ya later."

I headed towards the downward slope of Coronary Hill; I would no doubt be puffing and panting up it on my return, arms loaded with bags. I wasn't exactly fit. For now, though, the downward walk was awkward, but manageable.

I had made my way down the last of the hill, walking out on the flattened edge of the bitumen into town, when I saw a white twin cab Hilux in the distance, making its way towards me.

"Oh, great!" I said, tipping my head back and groaning.

It slowed, as I knew it would, and had a suntanned arm leaning out of the opened window as it pulled to a stop. A smile beamed at me from the driver's seat as the driver pulled back his sunnies to rest on his head.

Sean.

"I would offer you a lift, but I'm afraid that might be considered charitable. I wouldn't want to give you that dastardly impression."

I tilted my head and smiled sarcastically.

"Hey, I brought some smoko." Sean leaned over to the passenger side. He held out a Chico Roll and a strawberry Big M to me.

I cringed at the thought of devouring that for breakfast.

"No thanks, I'm just heading into town to get some supplies."

"You sure? This will give you all your daily calcium needs and …" he said. "What exactly *is* in a Chico Roll?"

It was a good question. "I hate to think."

Sean studied the giant Aussie version of a spring roll before he shrugged and bit into it.

"Mmm, it's good. Sure you don't want some?" he spoke with his mouth full.

I screwed up my nose as I watched him. "As tempting as it looks, I think I'll pass."

Sean swallowed and winced. "I think it's got cabbage in it."

"I'll definitely pass."

I started to walk again but instead of leaving him behind like I intended, Sean put the ute in reverse and drove backwards alongside me.

"It won't take us long to finish what we're doing," he said.

"Great!"

"We'll be all clear and out of the way by the weekend."

"Sounds good."

"You are opening for the weekend, right?"

I stopped.

What day was it?

"Today's Thursday," Sean said, as if having read my mind.

Open for the weekend? Was I going to open today? Was Matt even coming in? I hadn't even thought about it. Crap!

I half laughed to myself. "Would anyone even notice if we didn't?" I asked.

Sean looked at me side on for a long moment. "Wow! Is that the sound of defeat, Henderson?"

Ha! Wouldn't you love that? I thought.

I straightened, squared my shoulders, and quickened my pace. "Best get back to work, Sean, I'm not paying you to eat Chico Rolls. We'll be open!"

I heard his laughter over the engine … "Yes ma'am!"

Against my better judgment, as he put the car back into drive and roared away, even though I was terrified, I smiled.

The weekend loomed and I had no idea what I was doing.

Chapter Ten

After downning a civilised sandwich from Betty's Bakehouse …

I scanned the aisles of the local IGA supermarket, filling my trolley with cleaning products and food, and counting my blessings that Jan and Roy, the owners, made home deliveries. I dreaded walking back up Coronary Hill enough already without having to lug a week's worth of shopping too. I studied the product information and weighed up which bleach would be the most effective when I heard voices from the next aisle over.

"He's back in town, I see," a hushed voice said.

"Yes, he's been here a few weeks now," a second voice joined in speculatively.

I smiled and shook my head, just envisioning the two local ladies clutching at their pearls as they gossiped in the supermarket aisle. Not much had changed in Onslow.

"Apparently he secured this massive building project. Built a multi-million dollar school."

I stilled. *Pardon?*

"Yeah, I heard that he cashed in big time."

"Well, no doubt; he has just put in an offer on the old Ellermans' lake house … in cash."

I leaned closer to the disinfectant products, trying to peek between the bottles to the next aisle.

"I always knew he was destined for something big," the first one said. "My heart just broke when he injured his knee."

The second voice sighed. "Football was everything to him, wasn't it? Such a shame."

"The Onslow Tigers lost out big time that day."

Silence followed and I envisioned their grave heads nodding as they reminisced.

"Well, things happen for a reason. I am a big believer in that."

"Oh yes, absolutely; I mean look at him now. Back, and bigger and better than ever."

"Bigger and better? Are you not telling me something, Loz?"

A chorus of giggles sounded and I slowly manoeuvred my trolley to get a better look through the shelves. I spied Loz, a blushing thirty-something blonde, holding a basket. She was a lot younger than I'd imagined.

Loz elbowed her friend. "Carly! I'm a married woman."

"Oh, yeah, and you don't fantasise about Sean Murphy? I can only hope that one day something needs fixing at my place so I can give him a call."

I rolled my eyes as more giggles sounded.

"Well, let's just say …" Loz looked around, "he could leave his drill piece under my pillow any day of the week."

And in that very moment of me not paying attention to where I was going, my trolley ran straight into a display of stacked baked beans. A hundred cans tumbled to the floor, clinking and clanking and rolling, making an almighty crash. The wayward tins rolled in all directions. My cheeks flamed with embarrassment as I went to ground, trying to stop the avalanche of falling cans from rolling out of control, but with little success. Not only had I interrupted the gossip session, I had caused calamity through the whole supermarket. Roy came sweeping along in his white apron; Jan hurried over from the deli, gasping in horror. Not at the wrecked display, as I thought for a second, but at me.

"Oh, my poor dear, are you all right?" They both helped me to my feet, their sweet faces furrowed in concern. Although I didn't doubt their sincerity – from living at the Onslow all my childhood I'd seen that expression on Dad before – that look also meant, 'Please don't sue us.'

"I'm so sorry; I wasn't looking where I was going." I went to pick up the cans, but Roy and Jan ushered me away.

"No, no, we'll take care of that, young Amy, don't you worry yourself, it happens all the time," Roy assured me. Which wasn't very assuring, actually.

I moved aside, my cheeks burning in mortification as Loz and Carly, the horny housewives, looked me over in a cool, calculating assessment.

I turned from them and said in my loudest voice, "Hey, Roy, Sean Murphy is doing some renovations at the Onslow; you wouldn't happen to have any drill pieces, would you?"

Roy thought for a moment. "Yes, I'm sure I do. Come with me, we'll check out the back."

I followed Roy, making sure to smile sweetly as I passed the now gaping, horrified housewives. I'd never seen cheeks go so red.

Strangely, I didn't feel so embarrassed over a few cans of baked beans anymore.

***

I carried the essentials, such as food and hygiene products, up the hill back to the Onslow and, even toting so few items, the trip up the steep incline just about killed me. My home delivery would be coming later in the day; it would give me enough time to think about what the hell I was doing before I set myself to do more cleaning. This was not the summer I had planned for, that was for sure.

My arm muscles burned by the time I lugged myself across the drive. I spotted Sean and Stan sitting on the steps of the Onslow, talking animatedly and nursing bottles of Gatorade.

Stan saw me first, and it wasn't until I had closed the distance that Sean's gaze followed Stan's. Stan jumped up and grabbed my bags and I tried not to sigh in relief.

"I bet a lift never looked so good." Sean saluted me with his drink.

"That's not all that looks good around here, apparently," I said.

"Oh?" Sean quirked his brow before taking a drink from his bottle.

"Mmm, I overheard some horny housewives in the supermarket, and apparently you, Mr Murphy, can leave your drill piece under their pillow any day of the week."

Sean spat out a stream of blue Gatorade that led him into a coughing fit. Stan burst into hysterics and barely contained himself as Sean fought to catch his breath, his eyes watering.

I smiled and stretched my arms above my head. "Looks like it's going to be a beautiful day."

I grabbed the bags from Stan and, without a backwards glance, made my way inside.

***

After psyching myself up for the next challenge, I cleaned out Dad's fridge. It wasn't pretty. At first I doubted if it would ever be the same; the smell of the rot and wet goo at the bottom of the veggie drawer was enough to make me dry retch. I had scrubbed and rubbed it within an inch of its life. Now it was ready for some non-expired food.

I placed the shopping in the bar cool room until I'd faced off with the fridge. Just as I was about to yank the heavy cool room door open, the hotel phone rang. I flinched at the high-pitched sound; that phone never rang – well, not while I was ever here, anyway. Surely Mum and Dad would ring my mobile?

I eyed the phone like it was some cornered, deadly creature. I picked it up.

"H-Hello?"

A loud chorus of coughing made me flinch away from the receiver.

"Amy?"

"Yes."

"Oh, hey, it's Matt," a raspy voice spoke softly into the receiver.

"What's up, Matt?" Although, I could probably guess.

"Yeah, listen, I won't be able to make it into work today." Cough-cough-cough. "I've been up all night, crook as a dog."

"Oh, no. That's awful," I said, without any enthusiasm.

"Yeah, I'm just going to sleep all day. Hopefully it's just a twenty-four-hour thing."

"Here's hoping!"

I slammed down the phone, thus ending the coughing attack.

"Wanker!"

"Nice to know it's not just me who cops it."

I flinched to see Sean standing at the bar.

"Jesus, Sean, don't you knock?"

He shrugged. "It's a public place."

A closed public place.

I couldn't be bothered arguing.

"What do you want?"

"I need to access upstairs."

I did a mental check of upstairs; it was less smoke-infused than it had been yesterday, and at least it was now dust and grime free: passable for public inspection.

"Okay."

I felt Sean's eyes burning into the back of me as his heavy footsteps followed me up the staircase.

"So you're going to be a home owner, I hear," I said over my shoulder.

"Indeed."

"The Ellermans' lake house?"

We reached the apartment door. I could hear Sean chuckling so I turned to see him shaking his head.

"What?"

"You went into town for a few hours and now you know all the goss."

"Well, not all of it."

Sean stood so close to me on the landing. It was a hot summer day and the upstairs was always warm if the doors weren't open for the air flow to filter through the building. I felt claustrophobic as I reached my sweaty palm out to the handle of the apartment door. I could open it, walk in, create more space between us, but Sean's eyes pinned me there; they questioned me with a mocking glint and a crooked curve to the corner of his mouth.

"Tell me, Amy, it wasn't you asking the locals about me, was it?"

I blanched, horrified by the question. "No!"

"You sure? You weren't looking for a character reference?"

I cocked my head and smiled. "Now why would I need one of those? I know exactly what kind of character you are, Sean Murphy."

"Is that right?" He stepped closer, forcing me to lift my head to meet his eyes. He was so close we were almost touching, but I refused to be distracted. Not by the heat that emanated off his body, or the smell of his sharp, musty aftershave, or the feel of his breath. I refused to be sidetracked by the vivid blue of his eyes.

By anything.

Two could play at this game. I stepped closer as I looked him straight in the eyes.

"That's right."

"And what kind of character am I, then, Amy Henderson?" His voice was lower, hypnotic, and I fought not to be lost in it.

I smiled sweetly. "I think I've already told you."

His eyes flicked over my face. He studied me with intense scrutiny and his gaze rested on my mouth for a split second and then back to the staring competition. Was he the one getting distracted now?

I bit my lower lip and his gaze followed the brief action; yep, he was distracted, all right.

His Adam's apple bobbed as he swallowed. "Tell me again."

"You mean the part where I called you a self-centred, womanising egomaniac? Or do you want me to elaborate on that?"

He quirked his brow. "I thought you'd have had a better imagination than that."

My eyes narrowed as he leaned towards me. I froze as he closed the distance. My heart pounded in my chest and it was as if all the oxygen was sucked from the space between us. I bit my lip again, trying to control the shallow rise and fall of my chest as Sean leaned in and grabbed … my hand? He placed his over mine that held the doorknob to the apartment. He twisted the handle until it clicked and pushed lightly, trapping my hand under his. He didn't let go, his cheek was near mine and it puffed out in a wicked grin.

"After you," he whispered. His breath tickled against my cheek.

I wrenched my hand from under his, pushed the door wide open and strode in, grateful for the space as I walked to the farthest corner of the room. The French door was open, just how I had left it, in the hope that a constant flow of air would filter through the apartment. It was working. I had never been so grateful for the luxury of fresh air as I breathed it deep into my lungs, fighting to control the beating of my heart. I could only hope that I wasn't scarlet red as I suspected my cheeks were. Oh, wouldn't he just love that?

I avoided eye contact and looking at Sean in general. "Balcony's that way." I pointed at the open French door and then mentally slapped myself.

Where else would the balcony be, Captain Obvious?

If Sean had thought my stating the obvious was as dippy as I'd thought it was, he didn't say anything.

He walked towards the open doors and stopped short of the hole in the floor.

I watched him hesitate. "I thought you said it was safe to walk on?" I asked, moving to stand beside Sean and peering out onto the balcony.

"It is," he said.

"Then it's okay to walk out there, right?" I asked.

When he didn't answer, I took that as a yes, and stepped out onto the balcony, ensuring I gave that entire missing section a wide berth. I cocked my hip against the railing and looked out, down the hill at Lake Onslow, grateful that I could enjoy the view again.

I released a contented sigh. "Is there any place as pretty?" I turned, expecting to see Sean by my side, but he hadn't moved from the apartment – not one step.

"I'll take your word for it," he said.

I frowned and hoisted myself up to sit on the ledge. Sean's brow furrowed and it was almost as if the colour visibly drained from his face.

I hooked my arm around the beam for support. "What's wrong?"

"Do you really have to sit up there?"

My eyes widened. "Why? Is it not safe?" I looked around.

"I don't think sitting on the edge of a two-storey building is *ever* safe, no." His expression was serious, all humour long gone. This was a side of Sean I didn't expect.

Interesting.

"So, doing this would be a really bad idea then?" I pulled myself up to stand on the ledge, holding onto the pole, like I had done a thousand times before when Mum and Dad weren't around.

Sean's eyes widened in horror.

"Amy, get down," he bit out. He tentatively stepped forward onto the balcony, before stopping on the threshold.

I half expected Sean to march over, rip me from the ledge, and carry me downstairs over his shoulder while spouting out a giant lecture. My stomach flipped at the very thought. But instead, Sean's jaw clenched and he gritted his teeth. He wasn't looking at me; his focus was on the hole in the balcony. His hand grasped the doorframe with a white-knuckled intensity.

It was then that it dawned on me. "Sean, are you afraid of heights?"

"Can you just get down from there?" he snapped.

"How can a builder be afraid of heights? It's like a doctor being afraid of blood."

"Amy," his voice warned.

I should have enjoyed watching him suffer, but somehow, seeing Sean paralysed with fear like that was not in the least bit satisfying.

"All right, all right." I jumped down from the ledge. "You okay?"

"You know those things that seem like a good idea at the time?"

"Yeah."

He swallowed. "Well, this was one of them."

Chapter Eleven

"Hi, love, how's everything going?"

I cringed at the sound of my dad's voice on the phone. I had been distracted mid-mop of the bar room floor when I answered my mobile without even looking at the screen.

"Oh, hey, Dad. Yeah, everything's good."

Aside from the hypochondriac bartender and the builder with vertigo, everything was just Jim-dandy.

"And how's Matt going? He's a top young bloke. If you need anything you just let him know and he'll take care of it."

I frowned at my phone. Was he talking about the same Matt?

"Uh, yeah, he's good." I tried to put the mop silently back into the bucket.

"Has it been busy?"

Oh God! Talk about asking tough questions.

"Oh, you know, it's pretty steady, but I don't think the summer crowd has kicked in yet."

Lies, lies, lies.

"Well, when things pick up like it always does over summer, Matt says he has a few mates that can help out."

Matt's mates? I could just imagine.

"We'll see how we go."

"That a girl! I bet you're too busy working on your tan anyway. You just leave the business side to Matt and enjoy yourself."

I tried my best not to openly scoff.

"How's Mum?"

"Well, that's why I called."

My heart clenched. "Is everything okay?"

"Oh yeah – of course – sorry to scare you. I just called to let you know that I'm surprising your mother with a trip away."

My heart started hammering against my ribs again and I let out a breath I hadn't even known I was holding. "Oh? What did you have in mind?"

"A trip down the coast, you know, like she often talks about?"

Actually, Mum mooned over Europe mostly, but I guess this was Dad's compromise.

"Do you think she'll like it?" His voice had a childlike hopefulness to it. Knowing how materialistic and superficial Mum was, I was in no doubt that she would love it.

"As long as it's luxurious and not camping, I'm sure it'll be right up her alley."

"That's what I thought." He could barely contain his excitement. "I'm taking her out for dinner tonight, going to spring it on her with a gift voucher to a spa ... on the coast." He chuckled to himself, humoured by his genius plan.

It was hard to hold a grudge against him, hearing him so upbeat and excited. It was a side of Dad I had not grown up with, so this new midlife-crisis persona was really unusual.

"Well, good luck!" I said. "No doubt I'll get an enthusiastic phone call from Mum later."

"Here's hoping, hey?"

An awkward silence settled over us, as the conversation dried up.

"Well, better let you go, you're probably itching to get down lakeside with your friends."

I looked at the mop bucket. "Yeah, sure am."

"Before you go, love, your mother and I talked about it and thought, seeing as you're going to be in Onslow for the summer, we'd pop some money into your account. You know, for incidentals and stuff for the hotel. I know you have your own money but just in case you need anything."

My heart spiked in approval. "Uh, yeah, that would be great. Thanks, Dad."

"No worries. If you need any more just let us know."

"I'm sure it will be fine."

***

Holy *frack*!

I stared wide-eyed at my ATM receipt. There were way more zeros than I had expected. 'Incidentals' I gathered, were for cleaning products and basically everything Matt didn't seem to think it necessary to stock up on, like soap or toilet paper. At nineteen, I felt kind of guilty receiving any kind of allowance; it was kind of princessy, but it was also how our family worked. I had always been in a comfortably wealthy family and Dad provided for me and Mum and we didn't question it. But now, I was questioning.

Where was it coming from? How was Dad affording to dish out money like it was growing off a tree when the Onslow was literally falling down around me? Obviously he had invested way too much trust in Matt the Rat, and Matt was no doubt feeding him utter falsehoods over how the business was running. Had to be, or else Dad would have done something.

I pocketed the receipt with the ludicrous figure on it and made the decision to leave it as emergency stash only. Even though the Onslow was one giant freakin' emergency, I needed to think about what I was going to do. I couldn't have the hotel closed forever and the balcony repair job was almost complete, which was great. It just left the rest of the hotel that needed drastic attention.

Matt graced me with his presence again on Friday, after having made what seemed like a miraculous recovery from his deathbed. He busied himself around, opening and closing the fridge doors in the takeaway section of the bar.

I sat propped on the bar, flicking channels on the TV. "I stocked it yesterday," I said, rather unenthusiastically.

"Ha! So I see. Seems like I'm out of a job."

I should be so lucky.

I flicked off the TV. "Hey, Matt, can I ask a stupid question?"

Matt stilled from looking inside the fridge and appraised me with guarded uncertainty.

"Where are all the staff?"

"The staff?"

"Yeah, we're just about in the peak season. Where are they? Surely there can't just be you?"

Matt straightened and puffed out his chest. "Why not?"

"Have you worked here at the Onslow at summertime?"

"No."

"Well, it gets busy – *real* busy. There are two bars and a restaurant. Although it seems patronage has dropped off a bit, I think we can get them back. We need more than just you."

Matt looked unenthused.

"We have regular tourists that come back every year, Matt, and they will be coming again whether you're prepared for them or not. Regardless of what has happened, I think we can get this place up and running, back to its full potential."

"So does this mean the bar's open?" Matt asked.

I took a deep breath and tried not to slap him upside the head. "It has to be. It may not be up to scratch yet, but we can't make improvements if we don't have money coming through the door."

"So ... what do you want from me?" Matt looked disgusted, as if everything I had said was a major buzzkill.

I sighed. "I want you to do your job!"

Heaven forbid he do anything more than that. I leapt off the bar.

"I think I will hire someone to come and mow the lawns and do some weeding," I said.

Matt's interest peaked. "Oh, yeah? Well if you need any extra sets of hands, I have a few mates."

"No, it's okay," I said. "I've got it sorted." At least, I thought I had, because what I was about to do was an absolute last resort and it scared me to death.

***

I sat in a sunlit parlour. Floral-covered La-Z-Boys flanked a 1960s-style gas heater topped with an array of shiny porcelain cats. The living room was filled with doilies and knick-knacks, but not a speck of dust on any of it.

I expected no less from Melba Stewart. Melba, a robust, portly woman with a matron-style bun and a no-nonsense attitude waddled into the room with a tray of tea and biscuits. She had worked at the Onslow since I was born and had pretty much raised me when my parents were too busy.

Melba handed me a china teacup. "You don't still have three sugars, do you?" she asked, a look of disapproval marking her face.

"Afraid so," I said. "But, hey, it's my one vice in life."

She pursed her lips together, not buying my line for one second.

I smiled. "I've missed you, Melbs."

Melba scoffed, brushing my words away, a clear sign that she was trying to fob me off before she became emotional.

I didn't know where to begin. Did I strike now that her soft underbelly was exposed, or did I wait until a few more words were exchanged? I decided to go in for the kill.

"Been to the Onslow lately?" I asked, innocently, as I sipped on my tea.

"Ha! What on earth would possess me to do that?"

This wasn't going to be easy.

"But you have at least seen it, haven't you? You know, from a distance?"

"Just spit it out, Amy. What do you want?"

Oh, she knew me too well.

"I need your help, Melba."

Her icy facade refused to thaw; her eyes were so dark, I was almost intimidated myself … almost. I'd seen that look a million times.

"Dad has put this bloke Matt in charge."

"Oh, don't even mention that buffoon's name; what an utter idiot he is," Melba cut me off.

I smiled. "Well, Melbs, it seems we're in complete agreement there. I didn't know where else to go. I got such a shock when I came home; it's taken me days to get over the amount of work that's in front of me just to get the place presentable again. It's just all such a mess and I don't even know where to start." I poured it all out. The days of pent-up anger and sadness, everything I hadn't dared admit or even acknowledge, just flowed from me.

Melba sat across from me, motionless, still like a statue, and studied me intently. I was about to ask if she had heard anything I had just said when she breathed in deeply.

"And what makes any of these things your problem?"

I paused.

"Because it's my home. And I can't for the life of me believe that it has just been let go."

"Well, ya father doesn't seem to care all that much." Melba pronounced 'ya father' with such venom I knew I had hit a nerve in coming here.

It had been late last year when I'd overheard Dad say that Melba had left the Onslow. I had been in such shock I had wanted to go straight back to Onslow and beg her to come back. Melba was such an integral part of the Onslow. Sure, she was mean and bitter and pedantic, but she ran the restaurant and the kitchen like a well-oiled machine. Dad basically had nothing to worry about when it came to that part of the business because Melba ran the show, and ran it well. But now, without her …

The fact that she had left made no sense at all, and any time I asked about it Dad always brushed it off or shut down. But as I sat across from Melba now, I knew she still cared about the Onslow; I read it in her deep, troubled sigh as I told her how bad things really were. If Melba had been around, there was no way the Onslow would be in this state. Any time Dad had left whatever bartender in charge in the past, Melba was always the go-to person. She secretly ran the show.

"Yeah, well, Dad's on a bit of a 'journey of self-discovery' at the moment." I tried not to cringe.

"Ha! Just like a man, they can never multi-task."

"Yeah, well, he's lost all this weight, and just upped and came to woo Mum back. And it worked. It's embarrassing. They're like a couple of teenagers." I shook my head, half expecting Melba to mirror my horror. So the fact that she was smiling made no sense at all.

"What?"

"So he does listen after all, the old fool."

Melba must have read my confused frown and silence.

"Oh, I suppose he wouldn't have told you, would he?"

"Told me what?"

"Twelve months ago, your father was a different man. I'm not talking about the man you see today or the man you knew before. He was someone else, unhealthy, and miserable, in an absolute rut of self-pity, and I was sick to death of watching him slowly kill himself. He would stay in bed for days at a time; he stopped sponsoring the cricket club and hosting functions. He wasn't doing anything except dwelling in his own misery. He hired that Matt, thinking he would be the saviour, but all he did was add to his troubles."

It was hard to hear what Melba was saying, to envision Dad living that way. Mum and I had been living it up in the city. I hadn't given too much thought to what Dad was up to. I had just naturally assumed he was living the dream; I mean, what grown man wouldn't want to own a pub, and drink, smoke and socialise all day long? But in reality, it seemed, it hadn't been working at all. It had all been a lie. How had I not seen it?

"So what changed?" I asked.

"I left. I wasn't there to see how it changed. After your mother gave him an ultimatum, something I'm sure he was just going to let go, I gave him my own ultimatum."

My eyes widened. "And that's why you left?"

"Ha! Not before having a humdinger of a fight with that stubborn mule."

I winced.

"I called him every name under the sun, and you know how I feel about such language, but I was furious."

"And then you left."

"No, Chook, that's when he asked me to leave … and never come back."

Chapter Twelve

That was not exactly how I expected the story to go.

"Well, regardless of what was said, he obviously listened to you, Melba. By the sounds of it, your tough love saved Dad's life."

Melba didn't seem appeased by this; she just sat back in her La-Z-Boy and rocked gently.

"He saved one area of his life but let another go," said Melba.

"But that's it, he can't let it go, and he can't do it all by himself. Melba, there are NO staff. No one. Just me and Matt the Rat and that's not enough. I need help. I need *you*."

Melba's shoulders sagged sadly; her icy exterior was thawing.

My heart clenched in hope.

"I'm sorry, Chook. But when your father told me to leave and never come back, I said on my oath that I would *never* come back. And unless Eric invites me himself, I cannot in good faith walk back in that door."

Melba and her bloody moral high ground. I wanted to scream, to kick, to cry, but my heart sank far too low to fight for it.

I nodded. "That's a shame, because regardless of what's gone on between you and Dad I'm the one that needs your help, *I'm* the one that's drowning."

"It's not your fight, Chook."

"Isn't it? If you think about it, the ultimatum you gave Dad wasn't your fight, either."

Melba stopped rocking; her eyes cut into me and I knew I'd gone too far and it was time to leave. I stood and hooked my bag over my shoulder.

"Thanks for the tea; no one makes it better than you."

And before she could reply, I made my own way out the door.

***

By the time I got back to the Onslow, I was so immersed in self-pity that I almost didn't notice that the scaffolding had been taken down. It was only a voice from nowhere that abruptly stopped me from pushing my way through the door.

"See? Told you it would be finished."

Sean was perched on a picnic table, sipping a cold beer. He pointed above my head with a broad smile. I followed his eyes to see that the hole was completely patched and a new support beam in place. I smiled.

"Looks great."

"Wow! High praise indeed."

Sean reached down into an esky by his feet, his hand delving into the icy recess, and produced a cold stubby and held it out to me. Condensation dribbled down the sides.

"Want one?"

I eyed it sceptically.

Sean rolled his eyes. "Relax, I bought it from you. Put money on top of the till and everything. Bought ice from the servo; I'm a paying customer, I promise."

"Our *only* customer," I said. I closed the distance and took the cold stubby from his grasp. My fingers brushed his and I was unnerved by how that made me not want to meet his gaze.

"Thanks."

I stepped up and sat on the opposite side of the table, not too close.

"The lawns look good." Sean took a sip of his beer.

I turned to see the freshly cut grass and whipper-snipped edges.

"I hadn't even noticed."

"No, you were too busy sad sacking it up the drive."

"I was thinking," I said defensively.

Sean shook his head. "You think too much."

"Yeah, well some of us have to do the thinking for everyone." I spotted Matt through the hotel window, doing nothing more than slouching against the bar and laughing at the TV. My brows narrowed as I took a long sip of beer.

Sean followed my line of vision. "What's the go with him?"

"My dad, in all his wisdom, put him in charge."

"I see."

"I suppose you're going to tell me what a great bloke he is and that Dad was right to trust him with the Onslow?"

"Not at all. I wouldn't put him in charge of a lucky dip."

I couldn't help but burst out laughing.

"Well, there's a sound I haven't heard in a long time."

"Yeah, well, there isn't a whole lot to laugh about these days," I said. I picked at the label on my stubby, keeping my fingers busy.

Sean finished off the last of his beer in a long skull before getting up and chucking it in the nearby bin.

"How old are you now, Amy?" he asked. "Eighteen?"

I straightened. "Nineteen."

He nodded, in deep thought. "So you're nineteen, it's Friday – soon to be Friday night – and you're basically the gatekeeper of the local pub and yet there's nothing to laugh about?"

"It's a burden," I said, "not a never-ending party."

Sean sealed the lid on his esky and tapped it into place.

"Well, that's because you're not doing it right."

"So what? What would your advice be, hmm? Invite some friends over, get hammered, have a lock-in and pash someone in a dark alcove somewhere?"

Sean smiled and exposed a brilliant line of straight, white teeth. "Exactly." He gathered his esky and started to walk towards his car.

"See you tonight, Henderson. I'll be the one loitering in a dark alcove somewhere," he teased.

"Very funny."

Sean reversed his ute and flipped his sunnies into place before flashing one last smile at me and pulling out onto the road. He sounded the horn in two quick toots.

See you tonight?

Shit! Tonight? Friday night.

Much to my horror and regardless of whether the hole was now fixed, the weekend had arrived and there was nothing I could do to stop it.

***

We had no cook, no wait staff, one half-hearted bartender, and me. I prayed for a quiet night in the bar, but it was not to be. Somehow the mid-week scaffolding, the doors being closed, lawns mowed and the mumblings of a DIY project had piqued the locals' interest. Seemed they'd got to thinking the Onslow was undergoing renovations. I guess it kind of was, seeing as though you could now walk around the bar room without your feet sticking to the floor. You could even lean against the bar without wetting your arm on putrid, soggy, stale beer mats. You could see through the jukebox glass to select songs now that I'd wiped the weeks, possibly months, of grubby fingerprints away. If anyone asked for a beer now, chances were it was actually stocked and cold. I had made a mad dash to the supermarket to grab some boxes of salted nuts and potato chips. I figured maybe it would hold off endless questions about non-existent dinners.

I found the chalk on a shelf behind the bar and wrote on the restaurant blackboard and bar menu: *New and improved menu coming soon.* It was an utter lie, I had only just gotten past stocking the cool room and making sure things were clean in the bar. I wasn't ready to tackle the kitchen and restaurant yet. I hadn't even dared to wander out and check the state of the beer garden. I made sure the doors were locked; for now, it was all off limits. It had to be.

My stomach fluttered with nerves as a large group of young locals poured through the door and made a beeline for the bar. Matt struggled to keep up with their orders. I jumped the bar and chipped in with pouring drinks. I made sure not one glass remained empty, something Dad had instilled in me. Never leave a glass empty. I worked fast and hard, which seemed to rub off on Matt, much to my surprise.

After an empty week, the Onslow filled up at the end of the work day. We literally ran from one end of the bar to the other, criss-crossing from the main bar up to serve drinks in the poolroom. I scooted along, holding three beers in my hands and propping them on the bar top.

I tapped into the cash register. "That will be seven dollars fifty."

A twenty-dollar bill hung in my peripheral vision and I grabbed it, ready to make the quick exchange, but as I pulled it, it refused to give and my eyes darted up to meet Sean's. He grinned down at me. He held the twenty dollars in a vice-like grip and I tugged harder, smirking.

He let go of the bill. "Smile, Amy." He gathered the beers with ease in his large hands. "The Onslow is back in business."

I worked quickly to deposit the twenty dollars. "Hey, don't forget your change."

"Keep it," he said. "Consider it a tip for a job well done." He winked before turning towards the pool table.

There was no time to debate the point. A sea of arms waving money meant thirsty patrons. Maybe we'd be all right after all.

Adrenalin carried me through. Sean was right, we were busy and the money flowed in. Matt and I struggled to keep up, but we did. We even exchanged a few smiles, exhilarated by the buzz of the room, the music on the jukebox. The Onslow was alive again, and my hopes soared. Maybe I had been overwhelmed at first because I hadn't been back to Onslow for years. I had been living in our beige, modern town house in the city, so of course it was a shock to come back. Now, Matt was finally pulling his weight, picking up the challenge when I needed him most – perhaps I had been too quick to judge and all I needed was to give him a chance.

I was about to turn the corner into the main bar to tell Matt that he was doing a great job and to take a ten-minute break, when I saw him working the cash register with expert fingers. I smiled and went to call out to him over the music, when I saw him, with just as much expertise and quick fingers, slip a twenty-dollar bill from the till into his back pocket. It was so fast I almost missed it. I would have thought I had imagined it if it wasn't for the way he looked behind him and started to whistle nervously.

My heart sank: any hopes that had been lifted tonight crashed down with an almighty thud. Matt walked towards me as if only just noticing me.

"Bloody hell, I don't know about you but I'm knackered."

"Yeah, me too," I said with a half-smile. "Hey, listen, do you mind if I take a break? I just need some fresh air."

"Sure, I've got it."

I bet you do, you sly thief!

Without a word, I walked from behind the bar like a zombie. I zigzagged my way through the crush, and pushed my way through the door out into the summer night, fighting the tears that wanted to fall.

Chapter Thirteen

I was well aware of the irony.

I left Matt alone in the bar while I sat on the picnic table outside in the garden, while he no doubt robbed us blind.

I just had to get out of there, though. The disappointment that rolled off me was palpable, each drawn-in breath became tighter and my hopelessness threatened to drown me.

I couldn't do this.; I would have to ring Dad first thing and tell him what was going on, that this just wasn't working. And then, I remembered the excitement in his voice about surprising Mum with a holiday. Hell, he had probably already done so by now. I checked my Baby-G watch: eleven p.m. Yep, they would be celebrating and making plans by now.

I rested my elbows on my knee and cupped my hands in my face.

How was I going to tell him?

How was I going to break it to him that the one person he had trusted to run the Onslow in his absence had, instead, run it further into the ground and was stealing from him.

The picnic table was off to the side and mostly hidden by bushes, so I had hoped for a moment's privacy to collect my thoughts away from the drunken revellers. But when I heard the high-pitched giggle and voices approach, it was clear someone else had had the same idea.

"Oh my gosh! Did you really fix this?" a high-pitched chipmunk voice cooed.

"Yes, ma'am. Some fine craftsmanship indeed."

Oh, hell no!

I peeked through the bush as dread seeped into every fibre of my body. I knew that voice. And, sure enough, there he stood, all six foot three of him, beer in one hand, arm slung around some blonde bimbo.

This was not happening.

I shrank back and scooted as far back on the table as I could manage, hoping not to be seen.

A tremor of anger ran through me. I was annoyed at my parents, at Matt and at Melba, but mostly I was furious at myself. How had I thought I could save this sinking ship all by myself? And, more importantly, why did I even want to? There was nothing here for me now. Any friends, any fond memories I'd had, had drowned that night in Lake Onslow. I wiped at a tear that dribbled down my cheeks, a tear that made me angrier at how stupid I was for letting everything get to me, and the angrier I got, the more emotional I became.

"I bet you're really good with your hands," the blonde bimbo crooned.

I felt sick.

Blondie pulled Sean off the verandah and led him along the drive. Their feet crunched underfoot as they came into view, clearly lit by the lights that flooded out through the windows of the hotel.

Sean's arm was slung over her petite frame again. I didn't want to watch this. I slid my hand sideways to give myself leverage off the table, when a rough splinter jammed into my finger.

"Shit!" I cried out in pain. The sharp stab was all I needed for the tears to flow. As if that wasn't bad enough, Sean and Blondie stopped still, turned back, and peered into the darkness. Sean stepped forward, his arm still around the girl's shoulders. He frowned ... "Amy?"

Oh, fuck! Go away.

"Are you all right?"

"Yep!"

No.

"Fine, thanks." I tried to keep my voice even, but it was so not working.

Sean's arm fell away from the girl and he left her in the drive and closed the distance towards me.

"Hey!" she pouted, hands on her hips in annoyance.

"Hang on a sec," Sean said, without looking back.

I squeezed my finger, trying to prevent the throbbing sting. I turned my body away from him, hoping that he would just leave.

"Amy?"

"Go away."

"What's going on?" His voice was low, gentle.

"Nothing, please just leave me alone."

I felt the table dip next to me.

Yeah, that really worked.

His hand grabbed my chin and forced me to look at him, revealing my shiny, bloodshot eyes to the light.

I swallowed hard. "I'm fine."

"I can see that." His eyebrows were furrowed. "You going to tell me what this is all about?"

My chin trembled and I held up my hand. "I have a splinter."

God, I was pathetic.

Sean's eyes bored into me as if he was waging on whether I was seriously crying over a splinter or not.

"Seeeeaaaaaaaaaan!" a long whiny cry came from Blondie. "Are we going yet?"

"In a minute," Sean said, turning back to face her. "Hey, how about you go grab us some takeaways?" He reached into his back pocket.

This seemed to work as she strode over, snatched the money from Sean, shot me a parting death stare, and hobbled on her high heels back inside.

With her gone, Sean focused his attention back on me. "Let me see." He grabbed my hand and pulled me closer, turning it towards the light. "I think you'll live, it's not that deep." He half smiled at me. He held my gaze as he pulled my hand to his mouth. "Hold still."

The words whispered onto my flesh and my eyes widened as his lips covered my finger, his teeth gently nipping at my flesh and, with the slightest of pressure, he sucked the splinter shard out of my finger. I watched on in frozen awe as he lowered my finger, now free from the shard. It was so insanely intimate, all tears and self-pity had been wiped from my mind, until he broke the silence.

"So, are you going to tell me what's really wrong?"

I tore myself away from his gaze and looked out into the dark. He tilted his head, getting into my line of vision to try to coerce me to look at him.

"Come on, I just saved you from losing a finger, the least you could do is tell me what's got you so worked up. I thought you'd be happy; the place is jumping like the days of old."

I shook my head, emotions threatening to spill over the edge. I hated being so vulnerable, especially in front of Sean.

"I can't do it. It's too massive. It's too big; I was kidding myself to think I could fix this place by myself."

I could feel Sean's eyes burning into my profile. I thought he would never speak; his silence obviously meant I was right. This wasn't for me – what did I know about renovations and running a pub? The sooner I just let it go and went back to the city, the better.

"It is massive," Sean agreed. "Undeniably it's tough and unrelenting and monotonous and endless." Each word was like a nail in the coffin, cementing my decision.

Sean grabbed my elbow and forced me to look into his serious eyes.

"And if it was anyone else they wouldn't stand a chance, but it's not anyone else; it's you."

I shook my head, the only thing I could do to show him how wrong he was.

"It's you, Amy. You know this place, you *are* this place. The Onslow stands because the Hendersons built it, made it. And although it seems like it's going to be a miserable, endless summer …"

He stood up. "Just hold on, okay? You can do this, Amy."

Our eyes locked and something passed between us, as a long, lingering silence washed over us. The intense silence was quickly shattered by a high-pitched voice.

"Woooo, I got stollies, babe."

Sean turned and caught the stumbling blonde girl.

Any moment shared and all meaningful words spoken now seemed null and void, as Sean looked at me, embarrassed.

"You going to be all right?"

"Yeah, I think so." I tried my best to smile. "Thanks, Sean."

He opened his mouth to reply, but the blonde pulled him away.

They peeled away into the darkness, their silhouettes swallowed up by the night. Just when I thought Sean's kind words had soothed me into rising above my situation, somehow, as I stared off after them, I had never felt more miserable.

Chapter Fourteen

I couldn't bear to look at him.

I was lucky if I mumbled two words to Matt for the rest of the night. Come time to close up, I gave him the task of ushering people out and was fast to close the door behind him.

He stared at me from the other side of the glass and looked at me like I was an alien.

"Don't you want help cleaning up?"

"No. I'll do it."

"So, no staff drinks then?"

"No." And with that, I deadbolted the door and pressed my back against it with a relieved sigh. I should have really made him stay, made him earn his keep, but I just couldn't stand being in the same room as him.

I pushed myself wearily off the door and trudged around the bar, lowering all the blinds and collecting empty pints, shots, cocktail, and pot glasses along the way. Dumping my stack on the bar, I worked on rolling up the damp beer mats and emptying ashtrays into the bottom foot tray near the stools.

A loud series of knocks pounded on the front door and my mood darkened. It was either some drunk begging for a last-minute takeaway slab of VB or, worse, Matt had come back. I was betting on the latter. They pounded on the door again, this time harder. I was not in the mood for this. I stomped to the front door, unbolted the deadbolts in a rage and whipped open the door.

"I said *no* …"

My words cut off; I stared like a stunned mullet as my eyes flicked from a wall of chest up to meet the bemused smirk of Sean.

"What's that you were saying?"

"What are you doing here?"

I looked around him, waiting for the shrill voice of his earlier companion, but she was nowhere in sight.

He was alone. Maybe he'd forgot something. My weary eyes looked back up at him.

"Can I come in?"

I stepped aside, allowing him to brush past me. I deadbolted the door after him and turned off the main outside light.

I tried to keep my voice even and matter-of-fact as I returned to cleaning up. "Where's your date?"

Sean pulled up a stool and watched me with interest. "Date?"

I rolled my eyes as I unloaded a new stack of glasses onto the bar next to him. "The pouty blonde who was admiring your handiwork, amongst other things I'm sure," I mumbled under my breath.

I couldn't stop the snarky words that tended to fall out of my mouth around him. I shouldn't have even acknowledged anything; I mean, what did I care who he was with? I started loading the dirty pots onto the dishwashing rack.

"Oh, Lisa." He smiled. "Yeah, she's a handful all right."

I fought not to slam down each glass on the tray.

I forced a smile. "She sounds like a riot."

I could feel Sean's eyes on me, judging my expression, waiting for me to elaborate. Why should I? I didn't care who he was with or what he did with his free time. Or who. I loaded the tray into the washer, slammed the door, and pushed the power on. I straightened up and met his eyes.

"So where's Lisa now? Waiting for you to grab more booze? Is that why you're here? You know we're closed, right?"

Sean's eyes narrowed. "If you must know, I kissed her goodnight and sent her on her merry way home."

My stomach twisted in a pang of jealousy as I imagined her snake-like arms wrapped around his neck, her hands in his hair, his hands on her tiny frame, holding her to him. My miserable and unreasonable thoughts were broken as he stood from his stool.

"I'm not here for more grog because unless it's free flowing from the person running the show, which I'm pretty sure is you, I would never beg or expect it after hours."

Sean pushed in his bar stool. "I was just doing a welfare check, but I see the tears are gone and you're back to your old self. I'll be off then." He headed towards the door.

I just stammered, watching him go, trying to find the words to make him stay, to tell him I was an idiot, just being a jealous fool. *No*, I wouldn't say that, I wasn't jealous, why would I be? My head was all over the place tonight, why would I admit to a moment of insanity? I was tired and stressed; that was probably why I was being so snappy and unreasonable – had to be.

Sean unbolted the door and opened it to walk away and disappear out into the night.

"I have to fire Matt," I blurted out, causing Sean to stop mid- step. He turned back, a silent question in his eyes.

I walked around the bar, my hands wringing a damp dishcloth.

"He's stealing from the till."

Sean closed the door and walked towards me with a guarded, unreadable expression on his face.

"Are you sure?"

I nodded. "I saw him slip a twenty in his pocket from the register."

"Have you checked to see if the till balances?"

I blanched, unable to look at him. "I have been so flat out I didn't even think to check what the float was before; I wouldn't even be able to guess what it was, and I don't want to ask Dad, he'll just get suspicious. It's something I shouldn't really care about since I'm, you know, not 'working here' or anything."

I was pretty certain the till had never added up, not even when Dad was running the place personally. Dad was always ripping out the odd note for ciggies, and shouting drinks to mates; on that alone I was pretty sure it had never balanced in its life.

Sean rubbed at the whiskers on his chin, something he tended to do when he was deep in thought.

How did I know that?

"The only staff member I have and he turns out to be a thief," I added glumly. "Now do you still think I can do it?"

"Eternally pessimistic, aren't you?" He smirked.

"Do you blame me?" I asked, lifting the stools up on top of the bar.

Sean started gathering glasses from the other end of the bar. "No business is smooth sailing; you just have to ride it out. Look at the bright side. You had a full bar tonight; people are looking for somewhere to go and this is the place."

"Yeah, money's flowing in and a chunk of it is probably going into Matt's pockets."

"Let him go and don't pay him what's owed; hopefully you will be able to make up some ground that way."

"I guess."

The phone rang behind the bar; we looked at each other, confused. Who was ringing at twelve-fifteen a.m.?

Sean's brow arched. "Expecting someone?"

"Nobody rings that phone, except Matt." I would never give him my own number.

"Where is he, anyway?"

"Sent him home. I kind of locked him out."

"Maybe he's about to do you a favour and quit?"

I quickly walked around the bar to the cream landline phone mounted to the wall. "Believe me, after the way I treated him tonight I wouldn't be surprised. Hello?"

"Amy?" My mum's voice sobbed through the receiver.

My smile instantly fell as my eyes fixed with Sean's. "Mum?"

"Amy, it's Dad … He's had a heart attack."

Chapter Fifteen

"He'll be all right."

Sean's words were barely audible as I zoned in and out, listening to the whirrs of his Toyota Hilux's engine. The vibration of the passenger glass window massaged my temple as I stared out at the dark. Our headlights illuminated the white stripes of the highway as we distanced ourselves from the winding Perry Ranges and headed towards the city. Two long hours away, the longest of my life.

As I had crumpled to the floor and dropped the receiver, Sean had rounded the bar in one fluid motion, breaking my fall. He'd held me in his arms as he picked up the phone to find out for himself what had made the colour drain from my face.

Sean had to convince me that my dad had not died, that he'd suffered a heart attack, and was being looked after in the hospital. I hadn't even asked if Sean could take me to the city. He had just told me to grab my things while he scrawled a note and taped it on the front door.

Sean just did. Without question, without hesitation.

"Thank you," I whispered, the tears flooding my eyes.

"Did you say something?"

I closed my eyes and turned my face into the window, praying that if I slept the tears wouldn't come. I felt Sean place his hand on my shoulder and he rubbed it gently.

"Get some sleep; I'll wake you when we get there."

***

I woke up stiff from sleeping so awkwardly upright in the car. Dust particles danced on the stream of light that filtered through the windshield. Sean's car seat was tilted back and his arms were crossed; he leaned his head against the seatbelt strap and was fast asleep.

I rubbed my eyes and looked out through the windshield to discover we were in a car park. I twisted around to look out of the back window. We were at the hospital.

What time was it? And why didn't he wake me?

The dashboard read six a.m. I tapped Sean on the arm.

"Wake up!"

Sean stirred, unwrapping his arms and slowly stretching them above his head with a moan.

"Why didn't you wake me?" I frantically searched for my other shoe.

Sean yawned, rubbing the sleep from his eyes. "We arrived at three in the morning."

"Mum's probably wondering where I am." I opened the door.

"She doesn't even know we were coming straight away, she probably went home."

"Did you even check?" I snapped, slamming the car door. I bolted towards the administration entrance.

The automatic doors hissed open and the receptionist told me to follow the long, navy line along the wall. It led me through a maze of twists and turns, through double doors to where I needed to be. As I pushed through to a vast, white, U-shaped waiting room, I saw Mum walking down the hall, dunking her teabag like a zombie. Her hair was dishevelled and I could tell she had been crying. The sight of her scared me; it was an unkempt Claire Henderson, and that was something you would never normally see.

"Mum!" I ran to her and hugged her so fiercely she nearly spilled her tea out of her polystyrene cup.

"Amy, sweetheart! What are you doing here?"

I looked at her incredulously. "Of course I'm here. Dad had a heart attack – I had to come."

Mum cupped my cheek with a sad smile, her weary eyes trailing over me, but then something caught her attention over my shoulder.

"Is that Sean?"

"Mrs Henderson." Sean nodded.

Mum sighed. "One of these days you boys are going to have to start calling me Claire – you make me feel old." Mum ran her fingers through her hair and straightened her shawl, no doubt mortified that she was so unkempt in front of him.

"What are you doing here?" She looked from him to me.

"Sean gave me a lift," I said.

"Oh, that's right; he was with you when I called." Her eyes flicked from me to him and back, the speculative cogs turning in her head.

"Sorry, Sean, it's been a long night," she said.

"No worries, Mrs. He— I mean Claire."

"How's Dad?"

Mum smiled and hooked her arm in mine. "Come and see."

***

Dad was sat up in bed, smiling broadly. I would have been relieved if it wasn't for the intravenous drip and oxygen tube in his nose.

"Chook! What are you doing here?" His bright eyes narrowed towards Mum. "Claire, I told you not to say anything."

"She's your daughter! She has a right to know."

"That's right! I'm glad Mum told me, I would have been seriously pissed if she hadn't."

"Amy, language." Mum frowned.

I rolled my eyes and sat in the seat next to Dad's bed. "Are you going to be okay?"

Dad laughed. "I'll be fine, just had a little turn."

I knew he was sugarcoating it.

"You know, that's the last time I try to surprise your mother," Dad said. "I thought she would be the one clutching her heart in amazement, but it turned out it was me."

"That's not funny, Eric," Mum chastised.

"No, you're right, love, sorry."

"So what has the doctor said?"

"I'm to take it easy – no coastal trips, skydiving, or clay pot making." He winked at Mum. Okay, I seriously didn't want to know what that was about.

"And *no* stress," Mum added.

"Yeah, that's a big one." He smiled at me.

"Maybe your body's in shock after the health kick," I said in all seriousness.

"I'm sure it's a combination of a lot of things, Chook."

"Your father and I are going to work on some things, to make life a bit easier."

I nodded. "Sounds like a plan."

Thank God I hadn't unloaded all the issues of the Onslow onto Dad; I would have blamed myself for this. That was it, then: the Onslow was my problem. No more complaining or blaming, I would just get on with it. For Dad.

Dad smiled. "I know I may be hooked up like Frankenstein's monster in a hospital bed, but I can't help feeling like the luckiest man alive right now."

I gave Mum a dubious look. "Have they put Dad on drugs?"

He chuckled at me. "What I mean is, I have my two beautiful girls by my side and that makes me the luckiest man alive."

***

I spotted Sean out in the waiting room, sitting next to the vending machine. He had his elbows on his knees and was intently reading the label of his energy drink. I paused a moment and smiled at his intense, crinkled brow, his stubbled cheeks and dishevelled hair. I noticed the receptionist staring at him as well, chewing on her pen with a glazed look in her eyes. And why wouldn't she? Even in his sleep-deprived, dishevelled state, there was no denying his presence. His square shoulders filled out his shirt, betraying the long, curved muscles that were snug against the material. He was sex on legs.

I snapped myself out of the moment, pushing those kinds of words out of my head as I approached him. He lifted his eyes and instantly sagged in relief as he saw my smile. I plonked down next to him, playfully nudging him with my shoulder.

"Everything okay?" Sean asked.

I sighed. "Yeah, I think it will be. Just a real fright for everyone."

I unashamedly looked into Sean's eyes and he gazed back, unflinchingly, into mine. I held him there, taking in the vivid blue irises and the way a darker ring of blue circled it. It was as if no one else was around, or mattered, and I was glad because I wanted him to believe me when I told him what I had to say.

"Thank you, Sean. Truly. I know I can be a snarky, impossible princess sometimes."

His brows rose.

"Okay, most of the time. You say you're not a knight in shining armour, but I don't wholly believe that."

"I thought you didn't want to be rescued?" He reached out to me, delicately moving a strand of hair out of my eyes.

"I don't, but I do need a friend to tell me to wake up to myself every now and then."

"Oh yeah? And how do you think that will work?"

I shrugged. "I'll probably still tell you where to go," I said, "but I'll be thankful to hear it."

He threw his head back and laughed, crossing his arms and shifting in his seat. I punched him in the leg.

"Shhh …"

He sobered and looked back at me with a wicked grin. "Don't you go changing, Amy, not one single thing."

I could feel myself blush as his eyes burned into me. I bit my lip and peered down, suddenly unable to look into those eyes.

Someone coughed and Sean sat up straight and there was Mum, her gaze working between the two of us. Sean stood and scratched his head tiredly.

"Ah, I might go get something from the vending machine." He pushed his hands into his back pockets.

"There's one behind you," I laughed.

"Oh, right. Um, yeah, no, I think I'll get some fresh air and bin this." Sean held up his empty bottle and excused himself quickly.

I couldn't help but laugh again. It was always semi-amusing to see my mum's look of stone turn grown men into babbling fools.

My laughter died when I looked back towards Mum, her same stony expression focused on me.

So maybe it wasn't just grown men she could reduce to unease. Mum adjusted her shawl and sat next to me. I smiled uncertainly again when she clasped my hand in both of hers.

"This. Has. To. Stop. Now," she said to me, enunciating each word with an underlying sternness.

I frowned. "What are you talking about?"

Mum's eyes flicked towards the direction Sean had just left in. "Whatever is going on between the two of you has to stop."

I could feel the hairs on the back of my neck rise. I slipped my hand out of Mum's grasp, straightening. "There's nothing going on."

"Amy, you know I don't suffer fools."

"There's nothing happening between me and Sean Murphy." I tried to keep my voice down.

"You were together late last night."

"He was helping me clean up the bar."

Mum's eyes narrowed. "Where was Matt?"

Oh crap!

The rat was out of the bag.

"He wasn't feeling too well so I shut up for him."

Mum inhaled dramatically and rubbed her temples. Jeez, if she reacted like this to something so trivial, I hated to see what she would do over the truth.

"I curse that bloody pub," Mum said. Those were harsh words coming from her, so I knew she was upset. "It's not enough that it's taken ten to twenty years off your father's life, but now it's eating into yours as well."

"It's not," I said. "I'm fine. It didn't worry me, Mum, I wanted to go back, and if I can help out while I'm there …" *Like single-handedly rebuild the rotting hotel from the ground up and re-launch it to the masses again* ... "Well, so be it."

"You're meant to be having a summer holiday."

"A holiday from what? Shopping and sleeping my life away in the city? Bumming around aimlessly in my gap year? Don't even get me started on that. Accepted into a Bachelor of Arts, I don't even know what that means. A major in history … What am I supposed to do with that? I will most likely end up a teacher … When did my future spiral out of control?"

"If having an education and future prospects is 'spiralling out of control' then I'm not one bit sorry for that."

Mum was getting defensive.

"Mum, I'm not ungrateful, but seriously, I don't mind being at the Onslow, and if it means I have to use some elbow grease then big deal, I can handle it. I don't mind."

Mum sighed. "It's no use arguing over this, it's neither here nor there. Your father and I have spoken about it and after yesterday it's only cemented our decision. We're going to put the Onslow on the market."

Chapter Sixteen

"*What?*" I cried out. The woman at the nurse's station shushed me and shot me a disapproving look.

"Amy, please don't be difficult about this," Mum said. "Not now."

"Difficult? What's there to be difficult about? The fact that you weren't even going to tell me?"

Mum picked an invisible thread from her shawl. "I don't know why you're so upset. You haven't even been to the Onslow in years."

"THAT WASN'T BY CHOICE!" I couldn't contain my anger.

"Amy, stop it! People are staring."

"Oh, I'm sorry, I'm a little upset. You have just ripped the carpet out from under me, that's all."

"Don't be so dramatic."

My blood boiled as my anger escalated. "What does Dad say about this?"

"Your father needs to alleviate the stress in his life and that pub is the biggest burden on all of us."

"Ha! It's kept you in designer clothes all these years." The words came out before I had a chance to reel them back in. Mum cut me an acidic look that could have melted glaciers. I squared my shoulders and fought not to shrink away, to hold my ground.

"I suggest you go back to Onslow and enjoy what's left of the summer; your father and I will sort things out when he is well enough. I'm sorry you've taken this so badly, but it's the only way," Mum said. "I'm not losing any more years to that pub."

I stood up. "I want to speak to Dad."

Mum lowered her voice. "You are not bothering your father about this, do you hear me? He doesn't need you carrying on about it and that's final!"

I turned, hoping she wouldn't see the tears that burned in my eyes.

"I mean it about Sean," she said. "Don't play with fire."

"I told you, we're just friends."

Mum's dark blue eyes flicked over my face. "He doesn't look at you like a friend."

This time I did walk away, and I made sure I didn't look back.

***

I all but ran through the automatic hospital doors, breathing in a lungful of fresh air, trying to still the beating of my heart as anger continued to swirl inside me in disbelief. I wiped my eyes. She would not make me cry, *she would not make me cry*!

I had shed far too many tears these past twenty-four hours.

Enough was enough.

"Amy?"

I swung around, never so happy to see Sean's friendly face.

"Everything okay?"

"You know, you ask me that a lot."

"What does that tell you?"

"That it's time to 'suck it up, Princess.'"

He shook his head. "I'm not saying a word."

"Can you take me home?"

"To your mum's house?"

I turned and strode towards the car. "To Onslow!"

***

Seeing the rolling hills of Perry was a welcome sight. An immense joy swelled inside me as I wound the window down and stuck my head out, closing my eyes and lifting my face up to the sun. I hadn't told Sean about my mum's plans to sell. I just wanted to sit with my thoughts, with my own plans. A part of me worried that if I voiced it out loud it would make it all a reality and I couldn't deal with that, not right now.

Sean tore his eyes briefly from the road to look at me. "Anyone would think you were happy to be home."

"I am!"

"I bet you're tired."

"You would think so, but I actually feel … I don't know. Strangely upbeat."

"Give it time, you'll hit a wall mid-afternoon."

"Great! Just what I need for Saturday night."

Sean frowned. "So you're actually going to open tonight?"

"Why wouldn't I?"

"I just thought after everything you might want to take it easy."

I couldn't afford to lounge around, now more than ever. If the Onslow ran at a loss and turned into the burden Mum believed it was, then there would be no negotiation. Even though I was pretty certain there wouldn't be much room for negotiation anyway, I had to try.

We pulled into the Onslow in a long semi-circle up the drive. Matt's car was parked out the front and it looked like the note had been removed from the front door.

"Bloody hell, don't tell me he's used some initiative and opened up …" I shook my head.

Sean clenched the steering wheel. "What are you going to do about him?"

I banged my head against the car seat. "He's gotta go."

"Do you want me to come in?"

"No, I'll be all right."

"What are you going to do tonight? You can't run the bar on your own."

I shrugged. "What choice do I have?"

Sean broke into a slow smile.

"What?"

"To think you were perched on that picnic table last night ready to chuck in the towel, and look at you now. Your dad must have said something to you; something's lit a fire inside you."

Sean was impressed about my turnaround, as if I had been on some kind of journey of self-discovery and now I was going to take on the world. I had to face reality, and if that meant telling Sean the truth then I knew I could trust him.

I gazed out over the freshly mown, sloping grass embankment that led up to the beautiful, big Onslow Hotel. It was the place of my childhood and my heart ached with the possibility of not wandering through its rooms, perching myself on a stool, or looking out over the lake from the best view in all of Onslow ever again. I smiled sadly at Sean.

"They're going to sell the Onslow."

Sean stilled, looking at me with a grave uncertainty as he waited for me to continue.

"Mum thinks it's a burden, that this place is to blame for Dad's health. She says they've talked it over and reckon it's for the best to sell."

"And how do you feel about that?"

I thought about the question. "It makes me want to prove them wrong, show them that it may not have been in the past, but this place could be the best thing that ever happened to us."

Sean looked past me, his eyes sweeping over the Onslow with the same familiarity mine did. It was then that I noticed that same spark lit his eyes as he looked at me.

"Then let's see you do it."

A mutual understanding formed silently between us.

I shifted my focus to Matt's beat-up Mazda.

"First things first."

Chapter Seventeen

"I don't know what you're talking about."

Matt sneered at me, his arms crossed in a defensive challenge.

"It's quite simple: you can either give back the money you stole and *then* I fire you, or you can just go and I keep what is owed to you. Either way, you're fired."

I heard the distant crack of billiards. I had tried to convince Sean that I didn't need him on standby but he had negotiated himself as merely an early paying customer, playing pool … by himself.

Nothing strange about that …

Matt was not taking my ultimatum well, so the fact that Sean was close by gave me a boost of courage to play hardball. From the moment I walked through the door, Matt had been all sickeningly concerned and fraught with worry over Dad, asking if there was anything he could do. As soon as I mentioned we needed to have a 'chat' he snapped into the sneering, glaring douche I had always pegged him for.

"You can't fire me. You've got no proof, sweetheart. Just because you're the publican's daughter doesn't make you Mother-fucking-Superior."

Okay, that didn't even make any sense.

I sighed, bored more than threatened.

"This is useless. I'll just cut my losses and opt for the latter. Forgive me if I don't offer you a reference." I hopped down from my stool and made my way around behind the bar.

I could see he was stunned that I had meant what I said. A blackness swept over him and even though Sean was just in the next room, I still felt uneasy.

"Keys?" I held my hand out.

Matt glared daggers at me but I didn't budge. I looked him directly in the eyes, challenging him.

He delved into his pocket, yanked out his set, and threw them on the bar.

"Here you go, you little bitch, you're welcome to this fucking cesspool."

He snatched up his jacket and stormed out of the bar, slamming the front door behind him.

Sean slouched in the alcove of the poolroom, cue in one hand, beer in the other.

"So that went well, then?"

I shook my head. "He didn't punch me in the face, so yeah. Excellent."

Sean placed his pool cue aside and flipped out his mobile.

"What are you doing?"

"Calling a locksmith. I wouldn't take any chances."

I shivered, looking out of the front window. The dust still hadn't settled from where Matt had driven off, chucking an almighty burnout in the drive.

"Do you think someone could come out today?"

Sean smiled at his phone. "I think I know just the bloke who can hook us up."

He lifted his phone and waited. "Ringer! What are you up to?"

***

Ringer downed his beer with impressive speed, smacking his lips together in appreciation. "Thirsty work, that is."

"So I see." I arched my brow at Sean who just smiled and winked as he drank from his own glass.

"So just send the bill directly here and I'll take care of it," I said.

"Uh …" Ringer paused mid-sip, looking from me to Sean with unease.

"What?" I looked at Sean who was staring at the ceiling in despair.

Oh, I see. "Sean, you are not paying for this."

"It's not like that. Ringer owes me a favour, don't you, Ringer?"

Ringer put his beer on the bar with deep confusion. "Do I?"

"Jesus H. Christ!" Sean rolled his eyes at the ceiling.

Ringer slowly caught on and finally played his part. "Oh, yeah, yeah, that's right, from that one time. Yeah, yeah ... I totally owe you *big* time." Ringer nodded.

Sean shook his head. "Remind me never to do a bank job with you."

"What?" Ringer asked incredulously.

"So, gentlemen, if you don't mind; Ringer, can you please send the bill to me?"

Sean scratched his stubbly jaw and eyed Ringer, who turned to him, holding his hands up in a question.

"You know, I can't remember you writing anything down," Sean said, "when you were doing the locks, Ringer."

Ringer shook his head in fierce agreement. "True, I really have to start getting better at that."

"Terribly neglectful, our Ringer."

"It's true, I am." Ringer saluted me with his beer.

"This is pathetic," I said, trying not to smile.

"So I'm guessing," Sean continued, as if I hadn't even spoken, "there's no paper trail then."

"And without a paper trail…" Ringer added.

"There's no bill." Sean looked bitterly disappointed.

I folded my arms. "It doesn't matter what I do or say, you two are going to conspire against me."

"Why, whatever do you mean?" Sean asked innocently.

I just shook my head. I was ready to try somehow to convince Ringer to give me the bill, when a figure appeared in the doorway.

"Look out! Here's trouble," said an old familiar voice.

Toby Morrison stood in the doorway, taking off his shades and smiling at his two mates. Sean and Ringer spun around, astonished, as if what they saw before them was a mirage.

"Tobias Morrison! How the bloody hell are ya?" Sean leapt off his stool and shook Toby's hand before pulling him into a bear hug. Ringer flanked his other side and ruffled his hair up.

"When did you get back, you old dog?"

Toby pulled his head away, laughing. "Just now. I saw your cars parked out the front and thought, nothing much changes in Onslow."

"Yeah, you're right about that." Sean slapped him on the back, grinning.

I stood behind the bar, looking on with a broad, goofy smile. It was the first time I'd seen the Onslow Boys together in years – it seemed maybe it had been years since they *had* been together.

I let them have their boyish reunion and was happy to do so until Toby's coffee brown eyes passed Sean and rested on me.

"Well, not everything stays the same … little Amy Henderson?" Toby approached the bar with uncertainty.

I blushed. "Not so little anymore."

Toby looked amazed. "I'll say."

Toby opened his mouth to talk but Sean interrupted him. "So where's Tess at?"

"I dropped her off at her mum and dad's house so she could freshen up first."

My ears pricked up. Of course, if Toby was back it meant Tess was, too. I wanted to dance on the balls of my feet with excitement. I hadn't seen Toby's girlfriend for years, but we often emailed each other. It was hard to believe that once upon a time I used to be horrible to Tess. She'd been a waitress here – I was fifteen and she was a few years older and helping out my dad for the summer. I cringed at the memories of how I'd behaved. She was the sweetest, kindest person I knew; there was good reason why everyone loved her. When she finished Year Twelve, Toby and Tess moved to Western Australia where he got a great job as a diesel mechanic and Tess went to university. Tess had talked about how they wanted to drive across the Nullarbor and back home one summer, but they never got the chance because they were always working. Well, I guess this summer it finally happened and I was thrilled about it.

"Is Tess coming by later?" I asked hopefully.

"For sure. Actually we kind of hoped we could have dinner here?" Toby looked for a bar menu.

"Oh." I cringed. "We don't have meals on at the moment, sorry."

Toby smiled. "No worries; just means I can flog these blokes on the pool table instead."

Sean and Ringer cat-called in outrage. "Challenge accepted," Sean said.

I shook my head, laughing at the familiarity.

"Toby, did you want a drink? On the house."

"No thanks, Amy, I better get back and see what Tess is up to."

"Come back around seven, give yourself a chance to warm up before you disgrace yourself on the pool table," said Sean.

Toby grinned before putting his sunnies back on and heading for the door. "Yep! Nothing changes in Onslow."

Chapter Eighteen

It was hard to believe that in the last twenty-four hours, I had been to the city and back, fired my sole staff member, and now was looking at opening and operating the bar all on my own.

It was a little overwhelming.

Ringer and Sean left not long after Toby, each having some things to catch up on and no doubt needing to freshen up before they met up with Toby tonight. I wanted to pull Sean aside and talk to him about the whole locksmith bill, but he didn't give me a chance.

I scrawled 'Open at six p.m.' on a piece of paper and stuck it to the door. Figured I'd give myself a chance to freshen up, have a shower, and get ready for the full-on night that was to come. Much to my astonishment, Matt had started restocking the cooler room that morning, so that was one less thing I had to worry about.

My mobile rang when I was in the shower, but a herd of wild horses could not have driven me away from the delicious cascade of water that re-energised me. Covering myself in a towel and my hair up in a turbanesque wrap, I picked up my phone and found one missed call, one voice message. Mum.

"Hi, honey, it's just me," she said. "Hope you got back safely. They're releasing Dad in the morning, so don't stress. He's well and will be home soon. Love you and talk to you soon."

Aside from our rather heated discussion this morning, it was classic Claire Henderson to just forget about what had happened, as if the conversation had never taken place, and we would just go on our merry little way. Until she had some real estate agent goose-stepping through the property with a clipboard, no doubt. I wondered what would happen if Dad demanded she give up her swish town house in the city because it wasn't 'financially viable'. What then? I knew she would have a pink fit, that's what. I couldn't wait to get Dad on his own – it was my hope that Mum hadn't managed to brainwash him into believing that selling the Onslow was a good idea. The Dad of old would not have agreed in a million years to sell the pub, but the Dad of new? The hip, gel-in-hair, clean-shaven, metrosexual, post-heart-attack version of Dad? Well, I didn't entirely know. If there was one thing I agreed with Mum on, though, I wasn't going to stress him out with my vehement disapproval of selling. Instead, I would let my actions speak louder than words: I would bring the Onslow back to life, prove that it *can* be financially viable and show them exactly why they shouldn't sell.

It was four-fifty p.m. and I suddenly felt ill. In a bit over an hour, I was going to open the pub for the first time, and run the bar on my own. On a *Saturday night*. I couldn't bear to think about it.

I blow-dried my long, brown hair into sleek, straight strips where it fell midway down my back. Lately I had been sleeves up, scrubbing floors, cleaning windows and drains, scrubbing fridges, and doing little else, but no doubt generally looking like a sweaty feral. But tonight was different. I was going to be the face of the Onslow, the acting manager, so to speak. I wanted to make an effort, to look nice. Decent. Dare I say … sexy? *Cringe.* I thought of all the reasoning behind my sudden effort in my appearance. But against my better judgment, every now and then Sean's voice kept popping into my head, or a memory of his wicked smile. As I put my mascara on, my mum's words echoed in my head.

"He doesn't look at you like a friend..."

I had desperately wanted to ask her to explain herself but it had been more important for me to make my point and walk out. There were moments when something exchanged between Sean and me, I couldn't deny that, but it was probably just a mutual understanding. He wanted the Onslow to succeed just as much as I did. He had just come back to town and the hotel held a lot of memories for the Onslow Boys. That's why he was so passionate about helping it thrive; it was for the Onslow. It wasn't about me.

Ditching the denim shorts and T-shirts that I had been knocking around in lately, I opted for one of the two dressy outfits I had managed to pack: a red halter top and black fitted pants. I adjusted my top in the mirror, hoping it wasn't *too* sexy for Onslow standards. Oh God! I had no idea. I needed girl advice, but all I had was a load of boys.

I looked at my phone, chewing on my lower lip. Could I call Tess? I shook the idea away. No, she was probably exhausted and catching up with family; the last thing she would want to do was come here and give me fashion advice. Even if she was coming out later, anyway.

I paced back and forth behind the bar, watching the clock tick down until my palms became sweaty and nervous pains twisted my insides. Ah, screw it! If I didn't have someone here to distract me I feared I might vomit. I picked up the phone and called the McGee house.

***

Not only was Tess eager to see me, she wholeheartedly agreed to come over and arrived in record time.

"Look at you!" She quick-stepped to me across the car park, her arms wide open. She pulled me into a huge hug. "You're so tall!"

She looked me over and hugged me again. "You are so beautiful, Amy. Gosh, I've missed you!"

Tess hadn't changed a bit. Her golden hair twisted in natural waves to her shoulders, her eyes were a beautiful greeny-blue. Her petite stature made me feel like a giant Amazon woman next to her.

"Thanks for coming," I said lamely.

"I was so happy you called. Where is everybody?" She looked around the pub, studying her surroundings.

"There have been a few changes," I said with a wince.

"Okay, is this a one-drink story or a two-drink story?"

"Tess, there aren't enough drinks in this entire bar that would cover it."

"I think I'll take a seat, then."

I blabbered everything out to Tess, starting from Dad's journey of self-discovery, to me rocking up and falling through the balcony (which Tess tried her hardest not to laugh about).

"It's not funny!" I said, fighting not to laugh myself.

I recapped the horror of the thieving barman, the fallout with Melba, my dad's health scare and the big plan to put the Onslow on the market.

Tess listened intently, never tearing her eyes from me. "So you're here doing all of this by yourself?"

I shrugged. "As of today, yeah."

"You're going to be running the bar on your own? On a Saturday night?" she asked disbelievingly.

I shifted nervously in my seat. "I have no choice, Tess."

"Isn't there anyone that can help out? That wants some part-time work?"

"I haven't even had a chance to think about it. I fired my barman a mere hours ago. I got back from the city this morning; I haven't exactly had a chance to recruit."

Tess frowned in deep thought. After a moment she offered me a small smile and reached for my hand. "It's going to be all right. We just have to get through tonight and then tomorrow – sleepy Sunday shift, right? We can sit down and work out a plan. I'm home for most of the summer. Come Christmas it will run like a dream."

"That's if it's not sold out from under me before then."

There was sadness in Tess's eyes; she would be a terrible poker player. "Let's take one day at a time. We can only do our best."

"We?"

"You didn't honestly think you'd steal all the glory, did you? You know, I was kind of worried I might get bored after a while being back in Onslow, but now I see there is little chance of that. Project!"

I smiled wryly. "Be careful what you wish for."

Tess laughed and lifted her Lemon, Lime and Bitters. "Here's to Operation Save the Onslow." She clinked my Coke-filled glass.

"That sounds suspiciously like something Ellie Parker would say." I curved my brow.

Tess choked on her drink. "Oh, I totally forgot. Ellie's coming home for the holidays too! She gets back tomorrow morning."

"Awesome, it's like the gang is back together."

"Almost." Tess's excitement ebbed and I knew she was talking about my cousin, Adam. Adam, Ellie and Tess had been best friends since kindergarten and continued to be all through school, but as everyone moved from Onslow and discovered new interests and lived their own lives, it seemed sometimes people just grew apart. It's natural, I guess, but it didn't mean you didn't still think or care about them.

"Have you heard from him?" Tess asked.

"Only through Chris or Aunty Lynda and Uncle Ray. He moves around a lot. I think he's pretty high up in the rankings. Apparently he is a real fitness freak now, too. Who'd have thought, Adam in the army, being all disciplined and stuff?"

Tess laughed. "Well, he always had so much energy to burn off; it sounds perfect for him."

"Yeah, I guess." I looked around the empty bar – it was hard to imagine that it used to house all of us three years ago. Adam, Chris, Stan, Ringer, Toby, Tess, Ellie, and Sean. And me, I guess.

"Amy." Lost in thought, my head snapped up to look at Tess, who smiled her sweet, warm smile. "You're going to be just fine."

Chapter Nineteen

"How do I look?" I asked, hoping for some last-minute advice before I officially unlocked the door.

Tess looked me over. "Stunning."

It was almost as if I expected a sea of people to emerge from the outside as I unlocked the door, as if the Onslow was in such hot demand that I would have to unlock the door and just stand back. But it was all rather anticlimactic – there wasn't a huge onslaught of locals and tourists that stampeded me; in fact, for the first hour there was no one. I needn't have worried about being prepared for the worst because the worst didn't happen. Well, not until nine p.m., because that's when the night officially turned to shit.

The Onslow Boys were noticeably absent, but Tess had received a text from Toby saying they were all out having a look at Sean's lake house. I couldn't help but visibly sag in disappointment when Tess read out the message.

"They'll be here, Amy. Just later on," she assured me.

"Yeah, no worries." I half laughed it off, as if it really didn't matter one way or another. But it did matter, more than I would ever want to admit. There was a steady influx of people now, old faces and new, but somehow it lacked that certain something. Or someone. It was a good night, but it wasn't magical. I mentally slapped the thought aside and just kept busy, filling glasses and retrieving them off tables to be cleaned, then filling them some more. Tess offered to help, although I wasn't exactly flat out so it wasn't necessary. She sat at the bar chatting with me instead. It looked like I wasn't in any need of backup, after all, I could handle it, until the bar room door opened in a long, aching screech. I turned expectantly, thinking maybe the boys were here at last.

Instead, I saw a figure appear in the entrance with a few friends in tow … Matt.

Oh, perfect.

His beady eyes rounded the bar and like a lion stalking a gazelle they landed on their intended target: me. He saluted me with a cocky smirk and then said something to his sidekicks that I couldn't quite make out over the noise of the jukebox. His friends looked me over with a long, cool, assessing gaze before the three of them slinked their way into the poolroom.

"Friends of yours?" Tess asked with interest, having watched the whole show.

"Remember the thieving barman?"

Tess's eyes widened. "You mean the one you fired *today*?"

"The one and only." My lips pursed into a grim line. "I wonder what he's doing here."

"I don't know, but I bet it's trouble," Tess said.

"He's got some nerve, that's for sure."

"I don't like the looks of this. I'll call Toby and see where they're at."

I grabbed Tess's hand before she could reach for her phone. "No! No, look, it's all right, they're not doing anything. I can handle it."

For now, I wanted to hold my own. I didn't want the Onslow Boys to run to my rescue; I didn't want *anyone* to. The last thing I wanted was to portray a damsel in distress. I was a Henderson, for God's sake. Matt was on my turf and I doubted he was stupid enough to try anything. Was he?

As if on cue, smashing glass sounded from the poolroom, followed by the scraping of bar stools along the floorboards. Yelling travelled up to the main bar. Tess and I looked at one another before I dashed up to the other end.

People stood around, giving the huge puddle of shattered glass a wide berth.

"What happened?" I questioned.

Matt's mates snickered as he held up his hands in mock innocence. "They just fell off the table." He smugly perched himself on the arm of the sofa near the jukebox. My eyes trailed around to take note of anyone else's rendition of events, but the ones who hadn't already turned away and started up conversations again just glared over at the mess, as if it was nothing more than an annoyance – an inconvenience for them. It was obvious no one was going to give them up.

I made my way back into the main bar. I wanted to avoid Matt, even though I was absolutely infuriated to see him. I didn't want him to think that he was getting to me. I couldn't help but remember the look he gave me when I accused him of taking the money. This day was starting to seriously suck and I wished the Onslow Boys were here already. But they weren't. I had to play it cool, had to appear in control, and that was exactly what I did.

I begrudgingly swept up the shards of glass with Matt, the smug bastard, looking over my shoulder with glee. A surge of tourists and locals flooded the pub and all of a sudden I didn't have time to worry about Matt and his snivelling sidekicks. With the shattered shards of broken bottles carefully discarded, I was run off my feet, focusing solely on filling up glasses, and keeping my head above water. I stole a moment to do a quick glass run when I was abruptly halted by a hand gently but firmly grabbing my elbow. I spun around in surprise, my eyes widening when I looked up into the eyes of Sean, a grimness to his face that made me worried. Before I could ask what was wrong, he guided me into the alcove that linked the bar and the empty restaurant. A thirsty patron called out in dismay as he waved money at the bar.

"Pipe down, she'll be a sec," Sean yelled angrily.

We were pressed into the tiny space, hidden, not to be seen by anyone. My heart thudded, his grasp still on my arm, his breath flowing down on me. I was all of a sudden very aware that I hadn't checked my appearance for a while. I must have been a mess. I licked my bottom lip, a testament to my un-glossed, neglected lips, and I suddenly would have given anything for my coconut cream lip balm.

He squeezed my arm as if to bring me back from the brink of my daydream.

"Amy."

Oh yeah, right … the present.

"What? What is it?" I gave him my full attention.

"Amy, there's something written on the men's room wall." Sean's voice was low and soft, his look grim as his brows creased down.

My stomach plummeted. "How bad?"

"It's bad. Do you know who would have done it?"

I didn't have to think too hard to come up with one, and one only, suspect. I glared towards the laughter that echoed out from the poolroom. I spotted Matt gyrating astride a pool cue as if it was a pony, his friends bending over in fits of laughter … idiots!

"One guess," I said.

Sean's jaw visibly clenched, his anger evident as he followed my gaze.

Toby sidled up next to us, his stern look matching Sean's. "Hey, Amy," he said. "Do you want us to get rid of them?"

"It's okay, I'll deal with it," I said.

Sean didn't let go of my arm. "Bad idea."

My eyes rested on his hand on my arm, unable to hide my annoyance.

"What choice do I have? He's done enough damage to this place. Enough is enough." I pulled my arm away from Sean.

I weaved my way through the bar and ran straight into Tess.

"Queue's building up. Hey, is everything all right?"

I sighed and looked over at a trail of empty glasses aligning the bar top and tables, evidence of an escalation of rowdy pub-goers.

"What are you like at pouring beer?"

Tess's eyes widened. "It's been a while …" She sounded unconvinced, but offered a final nod. "But it's fine, I can do it."

"Thanks, you're a life saver."

Tess put her game face on and took over the bar to deal with the ever-increasing crowd of thirsty patrons. I made my way towards the poolroom where Matt was now dangerously spinning the pool cue in an arc in front of him, making hooting noises like he was Bruce Lee or something.

It was an unsettling sight, but it was nothing compared to what was about to unfold. A new song started on the jukebox and Matt discarded the pool cue and pumped his fists in the air.

"I freakin' *love* this song!"

Everyone in the room exchanged disturbed glances as Matt hoisted himself on top of the pool table, scattering the balls. The two locals in the middle of a game swore at him, but he didn't care. In a high-pitched whine, Matt started to sing the Bee Gees' 'More Than a Woman.' Everyone looked on in confused horror before breaking out in laughter.

He flailed his arms around in the air and knocked his head on the overhead lampshade. It swung, light jumping about and casting shadows over the room like the disco ball from hell.

I didn't know about anyone else, but I'd had enough. I pushed my way over to the jukebox, squeezed my arm around the back and got it! Mercifully, I pulled the plug.

A chorus of outrage filled the room, but no one protested louder than Matt.

"What the fuck?" He stood on the pool table glaring daggers at me; I guess messing with a hardcore Bee Gees fan was dangerous territory.

He jumped off the table and stalked towards me with a hard stare. He moved up close, right into my face, trying to intimidate me. I pushed past him. I had always struggled to comprehend what makes people do what they do. What makes bad people be bad?

Tonight, I had no answers.

Once I had put some space between us I spun around to glare at his back.

"Hey!"

He turned around to me, his brows rising in surprise as a sleazy grin formed on his face.

"I think it's time for you to leave." My voice shook in anger; I hoped it didn't come across as fear.

He laughed and cast a cocky glance at his mates and leisurely leaned back on the bar. He crossed his arms in defiance.

"Oh, yeah? On what grounds, babe?"

I smiled back sweetly and casually closed the distance between us. I stepped right up close; I was the one now getting into his face.

I could see him visibly relax as I leaned in to whisper, "On the grounds of this."

And quicker than anyone could catch on, I picked up his pot of beer from the bar and threw it on his crotch. He jerked away from me in shock and his friends scurried out of the way.

"Go home, Matt. You're drunk. We don't take too kindly to blow-ins pissing themselves on our turf."

He pulled at his pants as the look of disbelief on his face contorted to that of seething rage.

"You little bitch," he spat out.

He stepped forward towards me. Before I could flinch away from him he was suddenly jerked to a stop by a vice-like grip that had grabbed at the material at the scruff of his neck, and pushed him violently against the wall.

"Looks like you lost the pissing contest, old mate," Sean growled into his face.

Matt tried to push off the wall away from Sean, but Sean leaned more heavily against him and it was no use. Matt's mates belatedly rushed in to throw their weight around in his defence but hands gripped the backs of their T-shirts too and they found themselves slammed against the wall by Toby and Stan. A series of pushes threatened to spill over into a bar room brawl. What was I supposed to do? I tried to fight past Sean's back but he infuriatingly blocked my way.

"You need to keep your bitch on a leash," Matt said. I think he realised what a huge mistake it was to call me that the instant Sean's sweeping elbow connected with his jaw.

One of Matt's mates tried to intervene. "We were just going, weren't we, Matt?"

Sean and Matt were locked in death stares as Sean held him against the wall, the tips of his toes barely touching the ground. It was a standoff, but Matt was the first to look away. His face flushed scarlet, no doubt due to oxygen deprivation from Sean's bear-like grip around his throat.

"Yeah, we were just going," Matt croaked.

Sean held onto him for a moment longer, waiting for Matt to break his resistance, which he did. Matt put his hands up as if to show peace. At that sign, Toby and Stan let go of Matt's mates, and they all pushed off each other with dirty looks and silent threats.

Matt straightened and looked at his mates and adjusted his crumpled shirt.

I stood off to the side and glared at him, but he didn't meet my eyes as he followed his mates past me and out of the door.

He walked deliberately close by me on his way out, stopping only briefly to have his final say under his breath.

"With a daughter like you and a shithole like this, no wonder the old man had a heart attack." He smirked, triumphant that he had had the final say.

My fury spiked into a blistering rage as soon as Matt turned to finally walk away, to leave the Onslow. Nothing could stop me. I charged; I jumped on Matt's back and laid my fists into him. He toppled forward, which gave me a better vantage point so as to pull his hair and pound into him some more.

Matt cried out, "Get this crazy bitch off me!"

I laid into him with a guided commentary:

"THAT'S for letting the grass get too long."

WHACK.

"THAT'S for opening late every day."

WHACK.

"THAT's for stealing from my family."

WHACK-WHACK-WHACK ...

The only thing that prevented me from pummelling him into a pulp was the unexpected grip around my waist that scooped my flailing, kicking frame off him.

"Put me down!"

Another arm pinned my arms down, and carried me out of the bar like a pole – a pole with kicking legs.

"Come on, badass, time to go," Sean half laughed in my ear as he strained to carry me away. He carried me through the front bar, the crowd of drinkers parting like the sea, and all the way out through the front door of the hotel. The cool breeze skimmed my heated cheeks. He placed me down and I continued to squirm to get out of his grip. *Why did he have to be so strong*?

"Do you promise to be good?"

I stopped shifting and squirming and attempted to catch my breath. I could feel Sean's laboured breaths on the back of my neck. I couldn't promise anything, my temper was still boiling over.

"Let. Me. Go," I bit out.

A chuckle, rich and deep, vibrated through his chest against me.

"I don't think so, little wild cat."

I arched my head to the side so I could see him, his breaths still as laboured as mine. But his breaths weren't through exertion; these breaths were strained for a whole other reason as I felt the heat of his skin on mine. I strained my neck around and looked into his eyes, eyes that were studying me. He was contemplating whether to release me, with all the seriousness as if he was contemplating releasing a caged animal. The sternness in his expression fell away as he caught my eyes.

A little smirk tilted the corner of his mouth.

"You're a feisty one, aren't you, Amy? I don't mind admitting, you scare the hell out of me."

"If you don't let me go, I am going to open up a can of whoop ass on you."

This had him throwing his head back with laughter, which just made me even angrier and I jerked and kicked about some more.

"What a terrifying thought!" he said. His grip tightened to still my movements.

"What ya got there, Seany boy?"

A deep, burly voice emanated from the darkness. Big Sam, who worked at the local council, appeared from the drive, making his way up onto the verandah. He had a curious, bemused look on his face as he studied the situation. I tried to struggle free again, thinking surely this would embarrass Sean into letting me go. But his embrace was tighter than ever, as I was pressed against his ribcage.

"Look out, Sam, she's a real live wire."

Sam paused, about to open the pub door.

"Well, careful you don't get electrocuted, young fella."

"It's all good, Sam."

His grip loosened a little and I stopped fighting. I suddenly felt a little mortified by my actions. I would have tried to run a hand through my hair, if they weren't pinned to my sides. Oh God! I had started a bar room brawl. I had been *in* a bar room brawl. In *my* bar room!

"Enter with caution, Sam."

"Trouble?"

"Oh, I think Toby and Stan have everything under control; just some trouble with a few blow-ins."

Sam shook his head. "Bloody tourists. Be good, kids."

Having left us alone, I was now super aware of Sean's arm around my ribcage, pressing under my bra line, intimately close to the swell of my breasts. His other arm was swooped around my lower stomach. The heat seeping from skin to skin was so intense I thought I would be burned by his touch. A touch I found myself leaning back into. His chest was like a living, breathing wall – so sturdy, so strong. His thumb stroked my upper arm in a soothing, circular motion. I could sense his lips near my ear as his breaths swept across my cheek. I slowly lifted my eyes to him. Gone was any sign of amusement or even concern. Instead, there was something I hadn't seen before, and didn't know how to name it. His eyes flicked across my face in a deep study. His gaze flicked from my eyes to my mouth and quickly back again. It was so fast I thought I had imagined it. Was there a silent question behind that foreign look? It seemed like hours had passed since I had pleaded with him to let me go. Now, having seen that raw look in his eyes, it had me wanting the opposite. Before I could open my mouth to voice just that …

"Amy?"

The trance was broken. Our heads snapped around to see my cousin Chris standing at our side with his duffel bag slumped over his shoulder and murder in his eyes.

"What the fuck is going on?"

Chapter Twenty

Sean's arms fell away almost as quickly as I leapt forward.

Chris dropped his bag to the ground. His eyes narrowed and flicked from Sean to me and then back, his penetrating glare resting on Sean, who scratched the back of his neck and attempted not to smile.

Oh God, please don't smile …

I could see a familiar tension pulsing through Chris's veins as he fixed his lethal stare on Sean.

"Chris, what are you doing here?" I asked, trying to deflect his attention and rage – a rage I was all too familiar with; it was the same fury that arose any time his kid brother, Adam, pushed him to the edge. It usually resulted in a joint beating of one another. My eyes widened at the memories and I moved to quickly stand between him and Sean.

"Hey, quit it!" I pulled at Chris's top, causing his eyes to narrow down towards me.

"I said, what are you doing here?"

His serious gaze burned into me and I suddenly regretted redirecting his attention.

"What's going on?" Chris bit out.

"N-nothing," I said, lifting my chin up defiantly.

I felt Sean shift behind me as if he was going to support my claim, but the tension was interrupted by the screeching of the bar door followed by the blast of music from within.

Tess popped her head out before locking onto us with a big smile.

"They're gone. Toby and Stan had the pleasure of escorting them out back with a bit of friendly persuasion."

"Escorting who?" Chris called from behind me.

Tess squinted beyond us. "Chris? What are you doing here?" Tess beamed.

I spun around, annoyed enough from his macho BS and the habit of him cutting me off and ignoring my questions. Same old Chris.

"Yes, Chris, what are you doing here?" I said.

This time it was Sean's turn to interrupt. "I called him."

"What?" I said. "Why?"

He shrugged in that casual, careless way of his. "I thought you might have needed an extra set of hands."

Oh, did you now?

"Don't give me that look," Sean said.

"What look?"

"The look that tells me I am in serious trouble when you get me alone."

Tess snickered and I could feel myself turning a deeper shade of red. Chris coughed and I broke contact from Sean's knowing eyes.

"So does anyone want to tell me what's going on?" Chris asked, clearly annoyed.

I sighed. "You better come in and pull up a stool."

***

At midnight. it was time for the lights to go out and the doors to be deadbolted. I pressed my back against the last of the locked doors and blew out a deep breath. I heard the muffled chatter and the jukebox with the volume down low from the poolroom where only the select few still sat around the couches – not select in the fact that I had invited them, but that they'd invited themselves. Still, it was only Toby, Tess, Stan, Sean and Chris so I didn't entirely mind. After all, they had prevented me from scratching out Matt's eyes; that would have been really bad for business. In the last hour before lock-up I had managed to enlighten Chris on what I had discovered upon my return to Onslow, including Matt the Rat and the fact that Dad seemed completely oblivious to it all.

Chris was living in the city and apparently had gone straight to the hospital to see Dad, but there had been no mention of my being at the Onslow until Sean had called him. When Chris mentioned that last part I couldn't help but glare towards Sean who was playing pool with Stan, just like old times.

"Looks like I got here just in time." Chris looked at me while taking a long drink of his beer.

"Why?"

He cocked his head. "You mean apart from attacking the patrons or finding you with Sean Murphy?"

My eyes flicked to him, alarm undoubtedly obvious through my suddenly tensed body.

"I assure you, there is nothing you should read into either of those situations."

Chris placed his beer on the bar and crossed his arms as if he didn't believe a word I had just said. Suddenly I wasn't so eager to remain in the poolroom anymore to be judged by my cousin's suspicious brown eyes; instead, I had to face an entirely different situation.

I tossed the cloth into my bucket of soapy, hot water and grabbed an extra bottle of Spray 'n' Wipe and a Brillo pad. My semi-punishment for bar room brawling was to clean the profanity off the walls in the men's room. Even if Chris hadn't told me to, I would have done it anyway. I couldn't bear to have it there another second.

"I'm going in," I called to the poolroom. Juggling my stash of cleaning supplies, I pushed my back against the men's room door. The stench hit me first, an indescribable odour that was powerful enough to make my eyes water. Boys were so gross. As I propped the door open with a chair from outside, hoping to let some air in and dilute the stench somewhat, I thought, here I am on a Saturday night about to scrub the men's room. Wonder what others are doing on their summer holidays?

The thought was wiped from my mind as soon as I looked at the wall over the urinals. Rage filled my insides at seeing the disgusting caricature of me in a lewd act with a boy, scrawled onto the wall in black texta. If I had had an inkling of just how degrading the image was going to be, I would have done more than throw a drink on the creep. Now the stench wasn't the foulest part of this room, and I didn't want that drawing on the wall another minute. I sprayed the wall and scrubbed it within an inch of its life. I paused only every now and then to wipe a wayward tear that fell down my cheek. I heard footsteps approach the men's room.

"I'm in here …" I yelled out, mainly to prevent any embarrassment and possible exposure of boy parts, when I broke off mid-sentence. Sean stood in the doorway.

"Hey," he said.

"Hey," I croaked back.

"They said you were in here."

"Do you need me to leave for a minute?"

"Oh, no, no, I came to see you. You calmed down now?"

I wanted to say I had, but the emotions running through me now made me anything but calm. And now that Sean was here my heart threatened to jump out of my chest.

"I'm fine," I lied.

Sean closed the distance between us, and my heart pounded faster as he reached out and took the cloth from my hand.

"Come on, two of us will get this done quicker."

We set on scrubbing away the graffiti, which was now just a large, black, indistinguishable smudge. Relief filled me with every scrub as I dipped the cloth into the now lukewarm water.

I couldn't help but break the silence with what was at the forefront of my mind.

"Are you in trouble?"

Sean paused mid-scrub and cast me a questioning look. I rolled my eyes.

"With Chris."

"Oh."

"I thought you might have been forbidden to come in here or something."

A smile spread across his face that I didn't expect.

He coughed. "I don't think I have been 'forbidden' to do something since I was five years old."

That wasn't an answer so I just stared at him.

"Chris is cool. All is well."

Oh goody!

I really needed to curb my inner sarcastic voice.

With both of us working on it, the wall was as good as new in no time, the horrible drawing just a memory.

We stood back and admired our handiwork.

"We've created a clean spot," I said.

"I don't think these walls have been disinfected for … well … ever." Sean glanced around with a look of distaste and he tossed the cloth into the bucket I held, filled with mucky water.

"Thanks," I said. "You always seem to be helping me clean up a mess."

"You've certainly livened things up around here." He took the bucket from me and we both gladly exited the men's room.

After scrubbing my hands elbow deep in boiling hot water, I dragged my feet into the poolroom where I slumped onto the couch, zoning out of the conversation. I was exhausted, physically from pub room brawling and emotionally from Chris's drama and disapproval. And Sean – what was with that tonight? Not to mention that I smelt like a urinal.

"Earth to Amy."

I lifted my head from my hands. "Huh?"

Tess sat on the arm of the couch, touching the top of my hair. Chris stood beside her.

"Poor thing," Tess said. "You must be exhausted."

"Yeah, bar-room brawling will do that to you," Sean said over the crack of the pool cue against the billiard balls. I just ignored him.

"Did you hear anything we just said?" Chris asked, annoyed.

"Sorry, what?"

Toby laughed and plonked himself on the couch opposite us. He crossed his legs on top of the coffee table and folded his arms behind his head. "Looks like someone is going to have to be carried up the stairs tonight."

I yawned my words out. "I'm alriigggghhht."

"Pfft, totally," Stan laughed, turning from the jukebox.

Tess cut them down with a stern look. "What we were saying is we should have a fundraiser for the pub."

My interest was piqued and I sat up straight. "What kind of fundraiser?"

"Save the Onslow," Chris said.

"No." Tess shook her head. "It should be something to do with your dad, get all the locals together as a kind of community spirit thing to help out in his time of need. We could hold a sausage sizzle and promote a working bee or something."

My shoulders slumped. "What if nobody comes?"

"That's a hell of a thing to say," Sean snapped, mid-stride as he lined up to take a shot.

My eyes raised in surprise. "Is it?"

"Yeah, it is." He challenged me. An awkward silence broke out over the group as Sean and I faced off.

I gave him a bored look. "Well, guess you would know; you seem to know everything."

"You shouldn't be so hard on your old man. Believe it or not he is well respected in Onslow and there are a lot of people out there that will help." He leaned over to take his shot as if automatically ending the conversation, dismissing the idea that I would have anything to add. My blood began to boil.

"Is that right, is it? Well answer me this then: Where are they now? Because I don't exactly see anyone breaking down the door with casseroles and get-well cards to see if

Dad is okay. Actually, I haven't seen a goddamned soul around here, except for sleazy, troublemaking blow-ins who only want to rip the place off."

"Amy, come on." Chris sighed.

I cut him a dark look. "Don't you start. Did you pay for that beer?" My eyes flicked towards his empty glass on the bar. Chris's eyes darkened as if what I had said had cut him to the bone. I regretted the words as soon as they'd flown venomously from my mouth. Without breaking his eyes from mine, Chris stood, dug into his back pocket and flipped out a twenty, slamming it on the bar.

"Keep the change, I'm hitting the sack. Gotta get up and earn my keep." He started for the door.

"Chris, you don't have to do a day shift," I called after him.

He turned to me, my blood running cold at his stare. "What alternative is there, Amy? Families stick together, don't they?" he said icily before leaving the room.

Chapter Twenty-One

After slipping Chris's twenty-dollar bill into an envelope and writing 'Don't be a dick' on it, I tiptoed up the hall and slid it under his door.

After our rather heated exchange I had time to think it over and let it seep in just how relieved I was that Chris was here. I knew he wouldn't have hesitated the moment Sean called him; he had always been loyal like that. Sure, he had the tendency to be hard on people, but it was only because he expected the best. Chris always put in a hundred and ten percent so I couldn't fault him for expecting a lot from others, too. It would be a massive contrast between Chris being here to help compared to the likes of Matt the Rat.

I cursed as a floorboard creaked underfoot as I made my escape down the darkened hallway. The hall was suddenly illuminated with light as a door opened behind me. Chris stood there, shirtless, with his electric toothbrush in hand, frowning at my 'deer in the headlights' stance.

He held up his hand as if telling me to wait a sec, disappeared from the doorway and I heard a gargle and spit, and he then reappeared, wiping the excess toothpaste off his lips with the back of his hand.

"You going to bed?" he asked.

Way to go, Captain Obvious.

I chose against the sarcastic response and just nodded.

Chris leaned against the door frame. "So, do you think they'll really sell?" His eyes were serious, but they had softened. Maybe he was tired, like me.

"I honestly don't know."

Chris didn't reply. Instead, he looked off into the swirl of the '70s carpet, thoughtfully, as if he wasn't entirely present in the here and now.

After a while he broke the silence. "Do you want them to?"

"No." My response was immediate, certain.

Chris broke into a slow smile, for the first time all night. "Okay. Then let's do this."

I didn't know entirely what 'this' meant, but by the wicked glimmer in his eyes it seemed it meant he and I were in this together, and for the first time in a long time I felt part of the family again.

"Okay," I agreed, smiling back. It was almost like a mutual truce and, as I noticed the glint of humour in Chris's eyes, I relaxed. But then that same smile slid away as he stepped back into his room, the sound of paper crinkling under his bare foot.

Uh-oh!

Chris frowned, lifted up his foot and tilted his head sideways. "Don't. Be. A. Dick?" he read aloud.

"GOODNIGHT!" I quickly backed away, quickstepping my way to my room, and slammed the door.

***

I sat bolt upright in bed as incessant pounding on my door threatened to break it from its hinges.

"Wakey-wakey!" Chris yelled.

Did he seriously just say wakey-wakey? Dork!

"Come on, get up, Amy! You didn't think you could sleep in just because I was here, did you?" he called, his footsteps receding down the hallway and away from my door.

I rubbed at my eyes. What time was it? Heaven forbid I sleep in on a Sunday during my holidays. Oh, the horror! But he had a point, I guess: just because he was here to help out didn't mean that I would … Holy hell, it was six a.m.! Was he freaking insane?

I threw myself back onto the bed and tucked myself into the doona like a cocoon. *Chris, I love you, but seriously ... No way!*

I stirred again later at a softer knock and as I peeked one eye reluctantly open I saw piercing sunlight pushing its way through the cracks of my curtain. I would have mistaken it as a rather unlike-Chris awakening but then his voice called through the door.

"Amy, you better get up, there is someone here to see you." For a moment I thought perhaps it was a dream, but then of course I knew it wasn't as the door opened and Chris turfed my hairbrush at me from my dressing table.

"Up!"

Luckily for him the brush missed, but it didn't stop my dramatics.

"Doooooooon't," I whined.

"Move it!"

"Ugh, all right!" I snapped. "Who's here?" I stretched.

"Come and see." He smiled and left, leaving the door wide open.

Jerk!

I didn't want to jump to his beck and call – I didn't want to start a pattern of being his little soldier taking orders – so I took my time having a shower and getting ready for the day. I figured it was most likely Sean who had dropped in like he seemed to have developed a habit of doing lately. Most likely he was here to taunt me.

When I rounded the corner into the bar, I froze. My heart stopped for a moment and I'm sure a look of astonishment aligned my face. Was this a dream?

"Melba?"

Sure enough, there she sat, her portly frame perched on a stool at the bar, her legs barely able to rest on the rail at the bottom of the bar stool. She clasped her hands in her lap, her posture super straight, as always. She gave me a thin-lipped smile, as if she wasn't entirely happy to see me.

"What are you doing here?" I approached her cautiously as if any quicker and I might spook her.

"I heard about ya father." The icy facade had still not thawed. She said 'ya father' with the same level of disdain as last time. But this time her eyes weren't as harsh as she looked at me. She must have stopped in to see if I was all right (which was a huge concession considering she had vowed never to step back into this place). I was touched. Knowing Melba and her vows, just being here must have been huge for her.

"Yeah, Mum called before; he went home this morning. He is doing okay. He just has to take it easy."

Melba scoffed in reply.

I perched on the stool next to her, giving Chris an uncertain look.

"Thanks for stopping by, Melbs, I really appreciate it."

Melba's leg jiggled up and down with nervous energy; there was something obviously eating away at her as she became more agitated.

"I've been thinking," she bit out.

"Oh?"

"Well, I've heard things. And it's just absolutely ridiculous having a pub with no food; it's just not right."

It took all of my strength to keep a blank face, to not show so much as a smirk, and I definitely avoided Chris's eyes. I wanted to believe I knew where this conversation was headed, but I was afraid to hope, to believe in the possibility. And just as I tried to convince myself otherwise, Melba confirmed my hopeful thoughts.

"If we're going to open for lunch and dinner, we're going to have to pull the kitchen apart and scrub it within an inch of its life."

I couldn't fight it now, my lips tilted upward. "We?"

Melba's brows fell forward. "Don't be smug, Miss Amy Henderson, it doesn't become you."

I hopped off my stool, throwing my arms around her in a big bear hug. "Oh, Melba, I'm not smug, I'm grateful … I'm *so* grateful!"

Melba fidgeted under my embrace; she never did do warm and fuzzy well and had always tended to avoid such things like 'emotions'.

"Yes, well." She straightened on her stool. "There is one stipulation."

"Name it." I nodded, a little bit of fear fraying the edge of my mind.

Melba gave me a long, cool stare. "I don't want your father to know I'm here."

My shoulders slumped in relief and I couldn't help but get the giggles.

"I mean it, Amy, or I won't do it … As far as your father is concerned I have nothing to do with the place."

I shook my head, more laughter pouring out from me.

"What's so funny?" Melba crossed her chubby arms.

"Melba, as far as keeping secrets from Dad goes, get in line."

Chapter Twenty-Two

After letting the whole Onslow saga pour out to Melba for what felt like the millionth time, I finally had a chance to get excited about what was unravelling.

Sure, I had to spend the morning listening to Melba moan and scoff with every drawer, door and food container that had expired before I was born.

I lifted myself to sit on the hotel kitchen's island bench and cast Chris a grim look as he leaned through the doorway.

"What an absolute disgrace; I have a good mind to ring your father and give him what for," Melba said, wrinkling her nose in disgust at the grime she was scrubbing loose.

"Uh-uh, Melbs," said Chris. "You're not here, remember?"

"And don't you forget it." Melba stabbed her finger in the air at us, before disappearing into the cool room. A muffled gasp of horror sounded from inside. I looked at Chris, cringing at the thought of what Melba had discovered now.

He held up his hands in defeat and backed away, sporting a huge grin as he did so. "I'll leave you two to it, shall I?"

"Chris," I whispered. "Come back here!" My eyes darted to the cooler and then glowered back at him as he saluted and walked through the swinging kitchen door.

I moved to follow him when I was jolted by the unexpected sound of Melba's raised voice.

"Would you look at that?" She held out a mouldy pot with what looked like something that had once been a piece of … broccoli?

I grimaced. "Gross. I bet if you poked that with a fork it would say 'ouch'."

"Absolutely … dis-gus-ting!" Melba enunciated the words like a hoity school ma'am, and even though I loved her more than anyone in the world right now for coming to help me out, it didn't mean it was going to be a barrel of laughs.

***

A yawn escaped from me and I could feel my bones click as I stretched, walking through to the main bar. After spending the day cleaning the kitchen with Melba, I was exhausted. Even so, I still managed to throw Chris a good scowl as I walked past him.

"Finished?" He raised his brows in amusement.

I would have given him a forked-tongued retort, but I instantly saw that he hadn't exactly been slacking these past four hours. The mahogany bar shone and I could smell the furniture polish as soon as I walked through the doors. The tray that edged around the bar's base designed for wayward cigarettes and rubbish had also been emptied and polished. The floorboards still had that streak of freshly washed dampness to them.

It seemed a shame to lean on the newly polished bar, but I was so tired. I pinched the bridge of my nose and closed my eyes.

"We're finished for today."

"How long before we're up and running in the kitchen?" Chris asked.

I sighed. "We'll hit it hard tomorrow and then go and look at getting some food, work out a basic menu to begin with and trial it on a lunch shift."

I half expected Chris to comment on what a great plan that was, but he didn't reply.

I lifted my head up and looked at him expectantly. His eyebrows were furrowed as he gave me a long, side-on look.

"What?" I straightened. "What's wrong?"

"You look so pale."

"Gee, thanks." I self-consciously ran my fingers through my hair.

"I'm just saying you look washed out. When's the last time you left this place? Took some time off?"

"I went down the street the other day," I quipped.

"Running hotel errands doesn't count."

"I went to the hospital to see Dad."

"That *definitely* doesn't count."

I shrugged. "Well I just have to get on with it."

"How about you take a break, get some fresh air?"

"What about you?"

"I'm fresh blood, remember? I only blew in last night."

A break from the Onslow did sound rather amazing – to be able to sit elsewhere in the peace and quiet, the sun on my face, the reflection off the water. What bliss.

"You should go for a swim or something, perk yourself right up."

Chris's words were the equivalent of a record being scratched; they wrenched me from my daydream. A coldness swept through my body as my heart spiked in a panic at the very thought of going into that lake. It was something I hadn't done since *that* night, something I had no intention of revisiting ever.

"Wow. By that reaction I'm guessing that's a no."

"I think I'll just go for a walk," I said. "Get some vitamin D."

"Sounds like a good idea," Chris said as he poked the recess of the ice bucket with a spoon.

"You sure you don't mind?"

"Go, before I change my mind."

He didn't need to voice it again. I dodged around the bar stool and, with a new-found energy, grabbed the front door and it let out that old, familiar screech as I threw it open. A warm, summer breeze hit my face and all of a sudden I didn't feel the least bit tired; I had never felt more alive.

***

Okay, so it wasn't far. I didn't go on some grand adventure, but still the view was amazing. I had bolted across the grassy embankments that headed down to flatter ground and down towards the jetty. A long line of boats dotted the water along the way, the distant echoes from thrill-seekers ringing out along the long mass of sweeping water that stretched as far as the eye could see. I hunched over, catching my breath.

Christ, I was unfit. Still, why wouldn't I be? I couldn't exactly go frolicking among the suburban streets of the city, Julie Andrews-style. The city had always lacked such conveniences; it had been perfect for Mum and her high-spending lifestyle but when she'd upped and moved while I was at boarding school, no one had bothered to ask me what I wanted. I guess I lost that right: sneaking out, binge drinking and nearly drowning; the parental trifecta of horror.

As usual, and for the lack of anything else to do, I was drawn towards a vacant picnic table on the edge of the grassy embankment that overlooked all the water action. Stepping up, I moved to dodge the dried bird poo and sat in a relatively clean spot on the top, stretching out my long legs to rest on the seat. I placed my hands back on the table ledge and closed my eyes against the blinding sunrays. I enjoyed the warmth of the hot summer wind as it rolled in from the lake. I smiled against the humming of the boats and jet skis, the laughing of terrified children as they were flung along the water's surface in their giant, inflatable tubes. The callings and joy the summer brought out in people, the long-lost sounds of my childhood – all the things I had missed these past summers living in the city. I would never get tired of hearing it, and just when I thought I could finally relax away from my usual surroundings, my eyes snapped open to the sound of a voice I would recognise anywhere.

Chapter Twenty-Three

"You'll get burnt!"

Ugh!

I straightened from my reclined position to see Sean standing before me in knee-length boardies, and … *Good God, he's not wearing a shirt.* I quickly averted my eyes as I wiped my hands on my shorts from touching the grimy tabletop.

I could only imagine his smug smile broadening at my lame attempts not to eye his six-pack; he was such a smart-arse. I sighed and stared intently at my fingernails.

"I think there's more chance of you getting burnt than me," I said, coolly looking up to meet his eyes.

Look at his face, look at his face; don't look down, don't look down.

"So the princess has escaped from her tower," he said with a devilish grin.

"Does that make you the Court Jester, then?" I mused.

Sean swept his hand to the sky and bowed low. "Yes, m'lady."

I framed my face with my hand, shielding my eyes from the blinding sun. "You're an idiot!"

"I would prefer to think of myself as a lovable rogue."

I shook my head and a sudden silence swept over us. I looked past Sean to see jet skis churning circles in the water.

Sean followed my line of vision. "You gonna go in?"

My attention snapped back to him. "No!" I blurted out a bit too fast.

Sean's smile evaporated. He stared at me as if gauging if I was serious or not.

"Well, you can't sit here all day staring off into the distance." He leaned closer and lowered his voice. "It's kinda creepy."

"Is that right?" I said, squinting back up at him.

Sean nodded. "Creepy."

I rubbed my palms along my thighs, wary of getting too much sun. I caught Sean staring at my motion before he quickly looked away.

He cleared his throat. "I'm just finished here; how about we go on a land expedition, then?"

"Land expedition?"

"Yeah, I've got to pick up some supplies from down the street."

"Wow, sounds like a riot," I mused.

"So eager to get back to your tower, Princess?"

I paused before I let out a sarcastic comeback (my natural defence), and thought about what exactly waited for me back at the Onslow. Chris shouting orders and a semi-trashed kitchen. Yeah, I think I could live without that for a bit longer.

"All right, Captain Excitement, take me on this life-changing land expedition then." I climbed off the tabletop and brushed peeled paint flakes from my shorts and hands.

"Life-changing? I'm afraid I've oversold it to you. The last thing I want is for you to be disappointed."

I smiled sweetly as I sidestepped towards the car park. "I bet that's what you say to all the girls."

Sean paused. His brows creased in a mixture of horror and confusion, the corner of his mouth curving incredulously as he began to follow after me.

"What did you just say?"

I just giggled and sped up, my head darting backwards to see where he was. As soon as the words had tumbled out I knew it meant trouble; I had read it all over his face. When I ignored the question it just dug me into a deeper hole.

"Right! That's it!" he said, and ran after me.

I screamed. Bolting across the car park, finding it hard to run in my thongs, it wouldn't take much for Sean to reach me; three of my steps were equal to one of his and with him giving chase I was doomed from the start.

"Sean, don't!" I screamed breathlessly as I struggled to scramble up the grassy knoll towards the car park. Finally I lost my thong and faltered.

That was all he needed to seal my fate. I felt the whoosh from behind and my world spun as I was rolled onto my back, the spiky blades of grass digging into my shoulders as he pinned my arms to the ground with his iron grip.

"Sean, get off me, you dickhead!" I squirmed under him but it was of no use. He had me pinned. His thighs trapped my hips into place as his laboured breaths blew down on me. I stopped myself from fidgeting as I became very aware of how intimately we were pressed up against one another.

Sean grinned down at me. "Dickhead?"

"Get off," I bit out.

"Say you're sorry."

My mouth gaped open. *Never!* I told him just as much with my silence and a mega-death stare.

Sean leaned closer. "Amy. Say. You're. Sorry!"

I yanked my head to the side, refusing to look at him, breaking away from his face that hovered above mine.

"Fine! You asked for it."

Sean mercifully lifted his weight off me, but it was a short-lived relief as he yanked me to my feet by my wrists.

Grabbing onto my upper arm, he marched me back down the embankment, my feet skidding in resistance. My other thong slipped off my foot and lay abandoned behind us. Before I could let out another protest …

"Leave it!" Sean said. "You won't need them where you're headed." He dragged me along in a fast stride, my feet barely keeping up as I padded along the grass barefoot.

"Where are you taking me?" I demanded.

But before he could answer, I became all too aware of where we were headed.

"Sean, no!" I pulled away, using all my strength and putting all my weight on the heels of my feet, digging into the sand. My heart raced as I breathed heavily, my breath laboured in fear. An all-consuming terror overcame me as he pulled me closer to the water.

"Sean, please stop!" I begged.

A group of teenage boys sat on the edge of a fence, laughing at the hilarious act of revenge. Sean marched towards the jetty. I was screaming now, pleading in mumbled forgiveness.

"I'm sorry, okay? I said I was sorry!"

"I'm afraid it's too late for that," he said as he pulled me along, my feed padding along the wooden boards of the jetty.

Sean whipped me around, smirking down at me as if this would be my very last time on dry ground before I went over the edge.

"Any last requests?"

By now I was shaking like a leaf, my eyes wide and watery with fear. It was no use voicing anything; I couldn't have if I'd tried. My throat stung from screaming. I was that girl on roller blades being flung about all over again, except this time my fear was absolute. I shifted miserably from one foot to the next, the hot ground stinging my feet. My eyes bore into his good-humoured ones.

"Ready?" he said.

Before I could burst into tears, Sean threw me up over his shoulder and I closed my eyes. But as Sean started to walk my eyes flew open again. The world was awkwardly upside down but he wasn't walking towards the jetty or the water. He was carrying me away from it, back towards the car park. Perhaps it was the blood rushing to my head or the new confusion of our direction and …

Did he just slap my butt?

I didn't allow myself to breathe a sigh of relief – first off, because I didn't trust a thing Sean Murphy did and secondly, because my stomach was constricted by being carried over Sean's shoulder. Carried like I weighed nothing more than a feather. I heard the distant cat-calls and wolf whistles from the teenage boys as Sean carried me like a caveman.

We finally came to a stop by his car and Sean set me back on the ground. I pushed away from him and leaned against the passenger door, fighting to reel my emotions in.

I was seething, breathing heavily, my hair in disarray as I fought to stop the tears from spilling over.

He raised his eyebrows at me in surprise. "At the risk of being barred for life from the Onslow, I would never have gone through with it."

"Yeah, well, you're a real fucking gentleman." I pushed him out of my way to walk past him. I didn't make it two steps before he had snaked his hand around my arm and pulled me back.

"Yeah, well, you're no lady with a mouth like that."

My eyes flicked down to where his hand held my arm. "Let. Me. Go." I was getting really tired of Sean flinging me around like a rag doll.

"No, not until I say I'm sorry."

I started to demand again that he let go when … *Wait, what?*

"Unlike you, Amy Henderson, I'm not too pig-headed or proud to say I'm sorry."

"Is that your version of an apology, is it?"

He studied the lines of my face, lines that were no doubt still etched with dread; I couldn't help it. The thought of being plunged into the water was so debilitating I could feel my hands trembling in a mixture of anger and fear.

Sean gently released my arm and leaned one arm on the passenger car door beside me. It was almost as though I could hear the cogs of speculation turning in his head.

"Amy, you can't live in Onslow and not swim." He paused. "Can you swim?"

"Of course I can swim!" I snapped. "I just don't swim … here."

A sudden realisation lit Sean's face as if he had read the uneasiness in me.

I brushed my hair back into place, feeling a nauseated twist in the pit of my stomach. "I haven't been swimming since *that* night," I said lowly, looking down at my bare feet. More silence – I knew what was to come. He would offer me words of comfort, as the realisation slowly dawned on Sean why I had been so terrified of the water. He would comfort me, tell me how he had been frightened that night, too. I could see it in his eyes as he towered over me. The fear in his vivid, blue eyes was the first thing I'd seen; it was the one thing I remembered clearly from that night.

I fidgeted under his silent scrutiny, the anger slowly lifting in me, as he was no doubt thinking of something to say, pitying me.

"You were thrashing around like a piranha from memory," he said, breaking the silence.

I glared up from my feet. "You paint such a vivid picture."

Sean moved forward, causing me to shift back against the car.

His boyish grin sobered as he looked at me side on. "Come out with me, on the boat."

"I've swum," I said defensively, "in pools and stuff. Just not … *here*."

"What about the Falls? I could take you there. I think there's this log lying across a ravine; I could dance across it for you, Swayze-style!" Sean started jiggling side to side, singing, "Hey, Baby, I want to know-o-o, will you be my girl …?"

A wry smile broke across my face.

"Now that I would like to see."

I envisioned Sean plummeting into the ravine and I giggled at the thought.

"Or we could go swimming here and I could lift you over my head."

"At the risk of me kneeing you in the face and drowning you, I think not."

"Just saying. Nobody puts my piranha in the corner."

Pushing myself off from the car, I said, "One: I am not your anything, and two: seriously, what's with the *Dirty Dancing* references?"

Sean looked out over the lake, squinting against the sunlight. He turned to me, his expression sobering as his eyes flicked over my face in silent study.

"Come on, Amy, I saved you once, I'll save you again."

I met his stare unflinchingly. "I don't need saving."

A wicked grin formed slowly on his face. "Don't you?

***

I decided against the land expedition with Sean and thought I would just trek home instead. I went to retrieve my thongs but they were gone, along with the fence-sitting delinquents …

"Great! Just great!" I said, throwing up my hands.

I limped my way across the spiky grass – my baby-smooth city feet were not exactly accustomed to traipsing around the outdoors. Sean leaned against the car, his arms folded, attempting not to smile.

"It's not funny," I yelled out to him.

His lips twitched. "I never said a word."

I made a final sweep of the area before hobbling my way back onto the pavement. Sean fired up his ute and reversed, pulling up beside me. Without a word he leaned over and pushed the door open in a non-negotiable 'get in' way. I might have argued the point if my feet weren't on fire, but instead I quickly hopped in, lifting my legs onto the dashboard and sighing in relief. Sean eyed my legs and I could see the look of unease as I rested my feet on his polished black dash. I took a chance to peer around the interior, which was so clean you could eat off the floor. If you really, really wanted to.

I was used to the empty food containers, crumbs, and drink bottles of Dad's car or even Chris's. A smile tugged at my mouth. It brought a new meaning to Sean's apparent unease at getting footprints on his dash.

Well, too bad.

I planted the soles of my feet firmly on the dash. I adjusted my seat back and settled myself in. He would soon wish he'd helped me find my thongs. Sean's jaw clenched with tension in his attempt to not be agitated by my feet. He pulled into gear and headed for the car park exit and onto the main road. I flipped the sun visor down, flinching as a catalogue landed in my lap.

A paint catalogue?

I tilted my head to study the writing. Dulux interior.

"Brainstorming, are we?" I asked. I picked up the brochure and flipped through the tiny little squares of colour.

"I'm trying to pick something to bring the lake house back from circa 1977."

"Let me guess – mission brown and avocado?" I teased.

"What's wrong with my mission brown trimmings?" Sean asked.

"Nothing, I think brown is seriously underrated."

Sean's eyes flashed from the road to the brochure momentarily. "So what would you choose then?"

My eyes landed on a colour before Sean had even finished the question.

"Portland Stone." I pointed. "It's warm and light and exactly the same colour I want to paint the dining room at the Onslow. It could work for modern or traditional interiors."

Sean eyed the sample sceptically. "Portland Stone," he repeated.

I chucked the book aside with a sigh. We came to an intersection; Sean flicked his indicator to turn right towards the main street of town.

"Ready for your life-altering adventure?"

I gave him a bored look. "I can hardly contain my excitement," I said in an unenthusiastic, monotone drawl. All I wanted was to go back home, but Sean obviously had his own agenda.

Typical.

He flashed a winning grin. "Good. Let's go!"

Chapter Twenty-Four

I was thankful for small mercies.

Sean's little adventure involved nothing more than stopping off at the local hardware store to pick up a tube of Space Filler.

Utterly thrilling.

He took the scenic route from town to the hotel. I insisted he drop me at the bottom of Coronary Hill. Barefoot or not, I could hobble along as best I could. I would just have to suck it up.

Sean pulled over at the bottom of the incline. "Ashamed to be seen with me, huh?" he asked, curving his brow.

"It's called preserving your life; you want to grow old, don't you? Because, trust me, the last thing I want is to be lectured to death by Chris about you. Seriously, between him and Mum I don't think I could …"

"Whoa, hang on. What has your mum said?" he asked, confusion lining his face.

Fuck!

"What? Oh, no – nothing."

"Amy, you couldn't lie straight in bed."

"I told you, it's nothing."

"Amy?"

"Just drop it, okay?" I snapped.

"Right, fair enough." In one fluid motion, Sean leaned over and pushed the passenger door open and unclicked my seatbelt. It happened so fast I was looking at the open door and back at him, mouth agape, as I struggled to think what to say.

"Sean …"

"You better get going before someone sees you." He wasn't being nasty, he just said it in a matter-of-fact way. I knew enough to know that all of Sean's good humour had slipped away.

It made me feel stupid and embarrassed. I didn't want to argue the point because if he asked again what Mum had said …

He doesn't look at you like a friend.

Well, I could never voice that; it was just too mortifying to repeat.

So I opted for some humility instead.

"Thanks for not throwing me in. The lake, I mean."

Sean nodded in acknowledgement, but he didn't look at me. Why was his coldness annoying me so much? Usually I would give anything to have a moment's silence around him. No smug, smart-arse innuendoes, no cheesy punchlines, no smile; basically, no Sean.

Far out, why is this getting to me?

"You better go," he said, starting the car back up, still not looking at me.

Well, screw you, buddy. I was the queen of the tantrums and no one was going to take my title. I slammed the door shut, which finally made his eyes snap towards me. I still sat beside him.

He curved his brow in silent question.

"Just drive me up the bloody hill."

Big baby!

Sean took immense joy in speeding up the hill, making a long, grand, unnecessary sweep around the drive at a hundred miles an hour, before coming to a violent jolt directly outside the Onslow's entrance and sounding the horn several times with a winning smile.

"See ya, honey!" he shouted.

I glared at him. Suddenly, the silent, broody Sean of before seemed oh, so appealing. I opened the door and paused mid-climb as my eyes fixed on an audience watching my arrival. There they were, sitting at the picnic table: Toby, Tess, and Stan all staring on with guarded amusement. It was Chris's open scowl that caused me to look away and shoot dagger eyes back towards Sean before slamming the car door again.

"Aw, is this our first fight?" he asked, clutching his heart.

I gripped the edge of the window glass and leaned my head in, plastering on a sinister smile. "Oh, you don't want to fight with me."

"Sure I do." He puffed out his chest.

"Really?"

"Haven't you heard? Making up is half the fun," he said, grinning from ear to ear.

"Hey, Sean, you stopping in for a cold one?" called Stan.

"Nah, mate, I'll catch ya later. I've got a few things to do," he yelled before he set his eyes back on me. Lowering his voice, he said, "I'll leave you to deal with Chris's lecture, shall I?"

I stepped back from the car, glowering. "Coward!"

Sean laughed. "Say 'hi' to your mum for me." And with that, he tore off out of the drive, churning up stones and leaving a trail of dust to settle behind.

"No wonder our fucking driveway needs re-stoning," Chris bit out. He was obviously already pissed and I so wasn't in the mood for a lecture, especially with an audience. I knew as soon as I turned around it would begin.

"When I said have a break, I didn't mean an all-day expedition with— Where're your shoes?" His eyes fell to my dirty, bare feet, confusion spreading across his brow.

"Chris, not now!" I said, cutting him off and padding inside. I felt like a defiant teenager acting out against my parents. It was not too far from the truth, seeing that Chris always treated me like a child.

I swung open the un-oiled hinges of the front bar door and stomped into the main bar. I managed to stub my toe on a bar stool that hadn't been pushed in by some lazy customer.

"Son of a—!" I shouted, shoving the bar stool in as best I could, hopping on one foot. "Bloody, lazy, stupid—" I was cut off mid-rant by a voice from behind me.

"You better not let Melba hear that come out of your mouth; she'll take to you with a bar of soap."

I spun around to see a grinning Ellie Parker lingering in the doorway of the ladies' room.

"Oh my God! Ellie?" I limped towards her wrapping my arms around her.

"Hey, Chook." Ellie squeezed me hard before letting go and standing back to look at me. "Look at you! Bloody hell, what did they feed you at boarding school?"

I laughed, the full weight of Ellie's words resonating as I realised I had actually grown taller than her.

The last time I had seen Ellie was, at a guess, two years ago. I ran into her and her mum shopping at Northland Plaza in the city. At the time it had taken me completely by surprise to see someone from Onslow – it had filled me with a familiar nostalgia for a place I had been banished from.

Ellie was as I remembered her: bright, perky and confident. Her straight, honey blonde hair fell over her shoulders, her skin was tanned a golden brown; she always looked like she belonged in a *Sportsgirl* catalogue. She was effortlessly beautiful.

My attention was momentarily swayed from her to the loud banging on the window. I turned to see Chris holding up two fingers in a peace sign. At first, I thought he was apologising until he yelled, "Two more beers."

I sneered, almost tempted to hold up *my* version of two more beers but thought better of it.

"Didn't he give you the afternoon off?" Ellie piped up. "That's what I heard …"

I limped around behind the bar, grabbing two fresh pot glasses on my way. "Guess I will never live it down."

Before Ellie could start a girl-power, feminism-infused rant, Tess pushed through the front bar door, dismissing the dilemma. "Oh, don't worry about him; we have much more important things to discuss." Tess delved into her bag, barely able to contain her excitement. Ellie looked on with less enthusiasm, like a child half expecting a B-grade magician to pull a stuffed bunny out of their hat.

Tess located a notepad and pen, placing them on the bar so she could delve back into the recess to grab her berry bliss lip smacker.

"Let's talk working bee," Tess beamed.

***

In typical Tess fashion we spent several hours discussing tactics for the fundraiser, and the best way to organise a working bee. Our in-depth conversations seemed to appease Chris. When he, Toby and Stan came in from outside due to the fading light, he dragged up a stool next to Ellie. He glanced over at Tess's serial-killer-like handwriting and said, "Looks good."

Coming from Chris, this was high praise indeed.

As the sun went down, the bar didn't see much more action which was usual for a

Sunday shift. Just a few drop-ins for takeaway slabs and a handful of disappointed tourists who had wandered in from the caravan park looking for a feed. It really bothered me that the restaurant was not operational at such a vital time. Luckily, Tess was full of ideas.

"Your parents would honestly do that?" My heart swelled.

"Not only would they, but they would be happy to help."

"What have I missed?" Stan's voice called as he entered the bar from the men's room.

"Only the fact that Tess's *amazing* parents are coming tomorrow to help work out a menu for the restaurant."

Stan leaned against the bar, reaching for his beer. "Sa-weet! Go Mr and Mrs McGee – you should construct a giant golden M on a pole out front in their honour."

"Hmm, a giant golden M. I'm not a hundred percent certain but I have a feeling that might be trademarked, somehow," I mused.

"Oh, right. Bugger." Stan shook his head.

"Such an ideas man," quipped Toby, giving his mate a pat on the back. "Not just a pretty face."

Stan worked in an impromptu series of muscle flexes.

Tess rolled her eyes as she closed her notepad, and turned to Ellie.

"You used to date him." Tess laughed.

Ellie smiled as she chewed on her straw. "Hey, Stan, you never flexed your muscles for me, though," she teased.

Toby reached out to grip Stan's biceps. "What muscles?"

"Right! That's it." Stan grabbed Toby in a headlock, their stools screeching against the floorboards as they roughhoused.

Tess blew out a deep breath as she turned away from the wrestling match. "So, Ellie, you can organise the flyers for the working bee and barbecue; Chris, are you going to call up Eric's mates and get them on board?"

Chris nodded. "I'll also handle the stock, make sure we have plenty of stuff ready for the day and set up a few eskies in the beer garden."

"Dad's got an industrial pressure washer I'm going to grab tomorrow and start working on the front," Toby added, hunched over, catching his breath from his battle with Stan.

"And Ringer's going to be here with his ute – said he'd do a dump run for us," Chris chucked in.

"Where is Ringer, anyway?" Ellie frowned.

"Right where we should be." Toby eyed his watch. "We better go," Toby announced before spinning Tess around on her swivel stool and placing his hands on the bar, caging her in. She squealed at the unexpectedness of it and playfully slapped at him, but her surprise was gone in an instant when he kissed her goodbye.

Chris looked on in distaste. "Ugh, nice to see you guys are as stomach churning as ever."

"Shut up! I think they're adorable," I said.

Toby wrapped Tess in a bear hug and grinned at Chris and Stan. "See? She thinks we're adorable."

"I had forgotten you were headed to Sean's tonight." Tess did her best not to sound disappointed, but wasn't quite pulling it off.

"You sure you don't want to come?" Toby rubbed her upper arms.

"No, you go and have your male bonding thing. Thank him for the invite, though."

"And from me," Ellie added. "Tell him we'll come out soon."

I glared into the ice bucket as they talked – my effort not to react at the mention of Sean's name and the fact that he was having some sort of gathering and had failed to mention it to me.

Not that I cared; it would be a nice change not to have him darken my doorstep. The sheer amount of useful discussion we had got through tonight had been massively productive without his sarcastic quips and smart-arse innuendoes. In fact, it was bloody blissful. I smashed the ice with my spoon.

I stopped to see Stan eyeing me, a speculative look on his face.

"All right," he said, slowly turning his attention from me. "Better get this show on the road."

I gathered up their empty pot glasses, then waited as Chris skulled the last of his and passed it to me.

"You right to lock up?"

"Of course."

"I don't know how late we'll be," he added.

"That's all right, I'm not your keeper." I couldn't help but throw in that little jab.

He frowned. "I'm not yours, either."

"Really?"

"I'm just looking out for you."

"Chris, I swear, if you start giving me a talk about 'the birds and the bees,' I may be forced to stab you with this spoon."

Chris's mouth gaped. *Is he blushing?* I tried to stop my lips from pursing at the utter amusement of rendering Chris speechless.

"Don't be stupid. Jesus, Amy." He looked around him, making sure the others hadn't overheard.

I loved embarrassing him. "Chris?"

"What?" he bit out.

"Just go!"

Chapter Twenty-Five

It became disturbingly apparent that I didn't have one lethal weapon in my bedroom. Not one.

I knew this was a fact when I was woken at four a.m. by the slamming of the back hall door and the sound of footsteps. The sound of footsteps alone wouldn't normally have evoked fear in me, but no one used that door – no one! Chris hadn't returned from Sean's because he had already drunk-dialled me at two a.m. saying he was crashing on Sean's couch for the night.

I scrambled out of bed, my heart thumping, my pulse racing, as I searched for a weapon by the light of my mobile phone. If this was Chris's idea of a joke I would kill him. I couldn't imagine anyone even thinking of coming up the hotel's back staircase. You had to access it from the beer garden and we'd roped that off – no one ever used it. Before I could wrench the door open to potentially yell at Chris, a coldness swept over me. I wondered if maybe Matt had used the back door?

I heard a crash and the sound of muffled swearing out in the hall and I flinched away from my bedroom door handle.

Oh, my God, someone is really in the hotel.

Did I check the back door when locking up? Why didn't I check the back door?

I scurried over to my bookcase, wishing that I had a letter opener or a javelin or *something*; damn my lack of interest in pen pals and school sports. My heart lurched in my chest as the light in the hall flicked on, the luminous rays flooding under the crack of my door. I let out a series of shallow breaths as a new fear swept over me. I blindly grabbed at the first solid thing – a heavy, hardback book – and I carried it as a shield towards the door. I lifted the book above my head, but it wasn't very threatening as my arms violently shook. I heard the footsteps coming up the hall towards my door. I was trapped. I had to think fast – once that door opened I had to do something. I grabbed for my pillow, a moment of new-found power surging through me. I worked quickly to pull the cover off, discarding the pillow and replacing it with my … I tilted my head as the faint strip of light highlighted the title: *Macquarie's Dictionary*.

Yeah, I could spare it. I slipped it into the pillowcase, scrunching together the opening and swinging it over my shoulder like Santa would if he were Rambo. I took my place behind the door, slightly comforted by the weight I had at my back.

I wasn't religious, but in that moment, as the shadow of two strips stood in front of my door and my handle slowly started to turn, I closed my eyes briefly and prayed for help, for some almighty saviour that I would confess all of my sins to if he had my back just this one time. That was right before I unleashed hell.

I grabbed the pillow case and swung with an almighty crack across the back of the dark figure's skull. He clutched his head and fell over with a pained cry, before I swung again and whacked him directly in the shoulder. He crumpled to the floor with an "Oomph" as I danced around him like Muhammad Ali ready to take another jab. The stranger rolled onto his back and held up his arms protectively.

"Amy, stop! It's me!"

I froze mid-swing, my eyes adjusting to the flood of light that filtered in from the hall now that my bedroom door was fully open. I could now make out the crumpled figure lying on his back, clutching the back of his skull, his face twisted in pain.

"Ahhh, Amy, what the fuck!" he cried.

I dropped my pillowcase in a thud, my hands covering my mouth in horror.

"Oh, my God," I knelt down. "I am so, so sorry." I tentatively reached out, but he flinched away.

"Not as sorry as I am! Jesus!" He let out a series of coughs. "Some bloody welcome party."

My guilt soon channelled into annoyance as I stood, my hands on my hips. With a deep sigh, I stepped over the fallen body and flicked on my bedroom light.

"Honestly." I turned to look at the sorry sight. "Adam Henderson, what the hell did you expect sneaking in the back door at four a.m.?"

Adam edged himself towards the wall to lean against the door jamb. "I didn't want to wake anyone." He cringed with every movement.

I crossed my arms. "Well, I heard you coming a mile away. You suck at being quiet."

Adam wiped at his mouth and peered at his hand as if he expected to see blood.

Now he was just being overly dramatic.

"You're just lucky I don't own a javelin," I said.

"I'll let you know how lucky I feel in the morning." He pressed his back against the door and closed his eyes as if he was trying to channel the pain.

"Well, in case you hadn't noticed, it is the morning – just really, really fracking early."

Adam broke into a smile and momentarily peeked one eye open. "Still replacing your swear words, I see."

"Shut up!"

"Just say it, Amy, say the word."

"No."

"Go on," he teased.

"No."

"You know you want to." He smirked.

Yep, Adam was back. My annoying, unco, over-dramatic cousin was home and who even knew he was coming? I sure as hell didn't.

He opened his eyes, squinting up at me. "Say it."

"Adam?"

He looked at me pointedly now. "Yes, Amy?"

"Get the fuck out of my room!"

***

Come morning (the real morning where the sun is up in the sky kind of morning), I walked into the main bar and saw Adam perched there flicking through the pages of … *Oh God.*

"You know, it's amazing," he said.

I cringed at every page he turned of the *Macquarie's Dictionary* that lay before him on the counter.

"What's that?"

"I was hit in the head with a dictionary and all of a sudden I have all these words in my head. Like concussion, hallucination, malnutrition …" He slammed the dictionary shut. "Like, seriously, is there any food here? I'm *starving*."

I flicked him with a tea towel. "Mind your manners, mister. We're fixing that today, actually. The McGees are coming over to help us out with the menu."

"McGees?" Adam straightened and rubbed his stomach.

"*The* McGees." I said with a smile.

Adam's brow furrowed as he looked over the dictionary again. "I haven't seen them in ages."

"Yeah, well, maybe you would have if you weren't such a snob."

Adam's eyes snapped up, his face darkening. "Snob?"

"You're the one who ran off and doesn't keep in touch with anyone."

"It's called the army," he said in his defence.

"So what? No phones or computers in the army?"

"You're sounding more and more like Aunty Claire every time I see you."

My grin fell. Adam's words were like a slap in the face – I knew I hadn't exactly been thrilled about being compared to my father but when it came to being compared to my mother (and not in a complimentary way), it didn't sit well at all. Adam must have read it all over my face.

"Dis-tract: Verb. To draw away or divert the mind." Adam nodded as if what he was reading was truly fascinating.

I gave him a bored look before I grabbed for the book and spun it around towards me. I read with intense concentration.

"Hmm." I tapped my chin, and then honed in on one particular word and smiled.

"Uh-oh." Adam said with a smirk.

I cleared my throat. "Dis-turb: Verb. To interrupt the quiet, rest or peace, to throw in commotion or agitate; disorder; unsettle: to disturb the working of a program or disturb someone's sleep."

"Does it say, 'resulting in being clobbered to death by a dictionary'?" Adam asked.

"That's exactly what it says."

"Forgive me if I am rather dubious; you can look that up if you want. Du-bee-us."

Adam stood and pushed in his stool. "I'm heading down the street for something to eat. Do you want anything?"

"No thanks."

He went to open the door, but moved aside as it swung open, nearly hitting him in the face as a rather dishevelled Chris slumped in the doorway. His clothes from yesterday were creased and he wore dark sunnies inside. He looked ten kinds of hungover and I couldn't help but smile.

"Worst. Night's. Sleep. Ever," he said, groaning.

"With a side of hangover?" Adam looked over his older brother, revelling in his discomfort.

Chris flipped his sunnies onto his forehead and squinted his bloodshot eyes as if he had only just noticed Adam standing next to him.

"So, the prodigal son returns." Chris half laughed before putting his sunnies back into place.

"In good time, I see."

Chris scoffed and pushed Adam out of the way as he skulked his way inside.

"I wish my head hurt for the same reason yours does," said Adam.

I threw him a dark look – the last thing I wanted to go through with Chris was another one of my recent bursts of violence. I seemed to be demonstrating them a lot lately.

Adam winked before opening the door. "Just going down the street, do you want anything, Chris? Cow tongue wrapped in tripe and dipped in beer batter?"

Chris, who by now was slumped with his forehead to the bar, managed to exert enough energy to flip Adam the finger.

Adam caught it and clutched it to his heart as if he had been blown a kiss. "God, I've missed this place." And with the screech of the door and the sound of Adam's animated whistling flowing into the distance, he was gone.

"Sean has an uncomfortable couch, then?" I asked.

Chris lifted his head with a groan. "What bloody couch?"

I giggled, reached for a pint glass and filled it with water. "How did you get home?"

With a shaky hand, Chris carefully concentrated as he gulped down a mouthful, before gasping his answer. "Sean dropped me off."

I paused.

He didn't come in?

My first reaction was disappointment, although I couldn't think of it that way. It was just a response because I had wanted to talk to him about the working bee. That's what it was. Tess hadn't mentioned what part Sean had said he would play, even though he had done more than his fair share in helping and no doubt had other things to do – like actual *paid* work.

I then replayed yesterday in my head. Maybe I had offended him in some way? The invitation to hang at his house last night hadn't been extended to me. The other girls had been invited so it obviously wasn't a boys' night, but not me. I tried to tell myself that I was grateful for the peace away from his smart-arse contributions, but maybe he felt the same way? Maybe he was glad to be away from the cranky, high-maintenance publican's daughter? Maybe he had just wanted to give the working bee and me a wide berth? I was lost in my thoughts and none of them made me feel anything other than disappointed. I needed to get a grip – far too much energy was being spent thinking about Sean Murphy.

I shook the rambling thoughts from my mind and eyed Chris's practically green complexion. I didn't feel in the least bit sorry for him.

Chapter Twenty-Six

Another full day spent in the kitchen at the Onslow didn't seem so bad.

Melba, Ellie, Tess and I were all scrubbing every nook and cranny of the kitchen, rewashing pots, pans, plates and cutlery. Bagging up linen for the dry cleaners and working together like a well-oiled machine. Our cleaning frenzy soon spilled over into the restaurant, where we opened the sliding door out into the beer garden to get some fresh air filtering through.

"Whoa! You're going to need a machete to get through that." Ellie grimaced at what had once been a beautiful, shady, well-kept beer garden, dotted with picnic tables and fairy lights, the perfect escape on a summer's evening. It now stood overgrown with ivy, tables all dismantled and set against the wall, the paved courtyard littered with leaves and debris from the overgrown surroundings.

It was overwhelming.

Dad had *really* let this place go.

"It beats me how Adam managed to find his way to the stairs without injuring himself," I said, shaking my head.

Ellie's head snapped around to face me.

"What?"

"Adam actually navigated his way through this mess in the dark." I said with a half laugh.

It wasn't until I noticed Ellie's big, blue eyes shift from me to Tess, who also stood frozen mid-wipe of her table, that the penny finally dropped.

"Oh, uh, yeah, Adam's home."

Ellie looked at Tess and then back at me.

"When?"

"Only last … Well, this morning actually. Scared the crap out of me too. Talk about a grand entrance."

Tess laughed. "That's Adam."

"No, seriously, I thought it was someone breaking in. I attacked him with a hardback dictionary."

Ellie finally broke into a smile. "Did you hit him really hard?"

"So hard."

She nodded. "Good."

"So where is he now?" Tess beamed.

"Good question. He went out this morning but he hasn't come back yet – he's probably avoiding Chris. He's not in the greatest of moods."

"Pfft, what else is new?" said Ellie.

I had never fully realised what Adam's absence had meant to the likes of Tess and Ellie – he was always just my pesky cousin I would see in the holidays. For the last couple of family gatherings, Adam had been noticeably absent. He'd been off travelling and busy being an international man of mystery. I had emailed him a few times, telling him about what was going on, but his responses were always few and far between and pretty generic. I used to shrug and think *whatever*, but I couldn't imagine how it would have felt being on the receiving end of his silence as a close friend. I knew how close Tess, Ellie and Adam were. I could hear it even now as the three of us retold famous Adam stories, and there were plenty to choose from.

In the hours of dusting, polishing, vacuuming and airing out the restaurant, we had pretty much recounted all of their high school years to the present in the Adam files. As I wiped the blackboard clean, I retold the story of last night's events with great animated detail to Tess and Ellie. They listened intently and bent over in hysterics. I re-enacted Adam's cries and head holding, trying not to lose it myself as I thought back to last night. I was about to finish in a grand finale when I was interrupted by an unexpected voice.

"That's not very nice, Amy."

I whipped around to see Adam leaning casually in the door frame of the restaurant.

Oops!

"I'm going to put a bell around your neck," I said, placing my hands on my hips.

Adam walked past me, ruffling up my hair as he made his way over to Tess who was frozen as if she had seen a ghost. Without a word Adam smiled and pulled her into a bear hug and within seconds she melted into his arms.

I stood awkwardly to the side – it seemed strange witnessing this reunion. It felt like it should be private, that I should discreetly step away and give them some space. I probably would have if I hadn't looked at Ellie, and found, surprisingly, that she stood off to the side, glaring daggers into Adam's back.

Adam's arms fell away from Tess as she wiped away tears from her cheeks and laughed gently.

He playfully knocked her on the chin before turning to Ellie who still looked like she had laser beams shooting out of her eyes.

In true Adam style he ignored her rather obvious body language and broke into a broad smile.

"Hey, Pretty Parker."

Tess and I cringed in unison at the nickname Ellie had always despised above all others; a nickname she was stuck with since her second placing at the Miss Onslow Showgirl in Year Nine. It was a sore point and Adam knew it.

Adam reached out for Ellie, but with lightning speed she uncrossed her arms and slapped his arm away.

"I'm still mad at you, Adam Henderson!" she bit out.

Adam's brows rose in surprise, then relaxed in amusement as he noticed Ellie wringing her hand. Cursing under her breath because she had hurt it.

"Jesus, when did you get so buff?" she winced.

Adam laughed, looking at his arms, which had obviously beefed up – it was the first thing I had noticed. Adam had changed from a floppy-haired, wiry boy to … well, a bit of well-formed beefcake. If he wasn't my cousin, of course, I'd guess he was hot. I cringed at even having *thought* that.

Adam opened his mouth to speak but Ellie soon cut him off.

"Two words – *two words* – you sent me."

"Ellie, I—"

"You could have picked up a phone, written letters, sent smoke signals, anything!"

"Ellie …"

"I don't want to hear it, Adam, I don't want to hear it! You up and ditched me. There is *no* excuse."

"You're right," Adam said.

"You … w-what?" Ellie stuttered.

"I'm a grade-A dickhead, who needs to be flogged with a dictionary."

I let out an exacerbated sigh. "Oh, my God! I am never going to hear the end of that, am I?"

Adam stepped slowly closer to Ellie, carefully, as if he might spook her.

"There is no excuse." He reached out and gently cupped her face. "I'm so sorry."

Against her better judgment I could see Ellie leaning into his hand. Oh, he was good. I wasn't sure what he was doing in the army besides lifting weights, but he had become such a smooth talker that I think Adam seriously needed to reconsider his position in life and be a hostage negotiator or something.

It took a mere moment for Ellie to throw her arms around Adam in a fierce hug before drawing back and hitting him really hard again.

"Don't call me Pretty Parker."

***

I had started the late shift with a spring in my step and a song in my heart. Okay, maybe that was overstating it, but still, the day had been massively productive. The kitchen and restaurant were gleaming and after the interesting Tess–Adam–Ellie reunion, Tess's mum and dad rocked up to help out with menu ideas and cook up a few samples. They brought tubs of ingredients and easy-to-follow recipes: simple, hearty food, which was what they were famous for.

Tess's parents owned the Rose Cafe in Perry, a small border town separated only by the Onslow Bridge. They had won numerous awards over the years, including being the back-to-back title holders for 'Best Pie.' They even had a house specialty pastry dubbed the Onslow Boy – hilarious.

Tess's parents were wonderful; they were light, bubbly and so generous with their time. I hugged the bejesus out of them before they left, fearing it would never be enough to show how grateful I was for their invaluable help. The McGees even offered to help out with catering for the working bee, and doing a few lunch shifts until we got on our feet.

The last cook we had that I could remember was a dishevelled, grotty man by the name of Dezi. I had wondered where Rosanna, our bad-tempered, pint-sized cook before him, had gotten to. According to Melba she had met and fallen in love with some guy over the Internet and he had relocated her and the kids up along the coast somewhere. Not that I was considering rehiring crazy Rosanna … Although she was very entertaining. I had often wondered what she was doing now. I hoped she was happy.

I looked over the handwritten menus we had worked on that afternoon and smiled, filing them in the bookings folder near the till. My eyes trailed down the line of the bar, pleased by the customers that were dotted throughout the hotel. The jukebox blared from the poolroom as did animated laughter and chatter; it felt so good.

Tomorrow the working bee would officially commence. Chris and I were even going to interview a couple of potential people to take on for staff, as Tess, in all her wisdom, had put up some flyers: 'Help Wanted'. Things were looking up!

And then the phone rang.

Chapter Twenty-Seven

Honey, we're coming up!" My mum's voice beamed down the phone.

"Wait, what?" My heart threatened to beat out of my chest.

"It won't be this weekend, but probably next weekend, providing your dad's up to it."

My shoulders slumped in relief.

"Everything all right, hon?" Mum's voice kicked into concerned-parent mode, so I amped up the 'everything's awesome' cheerful vibe and told her I couldn't wait to see them.

Once I had said my goodbyes and hung up the phone, any positive walking on sunshine feeling I'd had before was swallowed up by a dark cloud. Now I had a deadline. I had to pull out all the stops, had to show Mum and Dad what this place could really be and convince them not to sell.

I sighed and pinched the bridge of my nose, feeling the familiar pulse of a headache coming on.

"What's up, lamb chop?" a voice asked – an unmistakable voice.

I looked up to see Sean with his infamous high-wattage smile.

"Lamb chop? You are such a poet."

"It's certainly no *Romeo and Juliet* but with our history with balconies I think we best avoid Shakespeare."

Sean's fingers tapped the bar. I hadn't even noticed he had come in. He must have slipped through the door and into the mass of bodies in the poolroom.

"So you had a bit of an all-nighter last night?" I tried to sound breezy as I grabbed for a fresh pot glass.

"Just downed a few beers on the deck – made for a rather colourful evening. Shame you couldn't make it."

I nearly overflowed the glass with beer, quickly having to twist the tap off in my moment of distraction.

"Well, I wasn't invited, was I?"

"What?" Sean said. "Chris said you were manning the pub so you couldn't make it."

I must have looked dumbfounded, because I truly was. I guess in a sense it *had* been my turn to man the bar, but they had left after lock-up so I could have gone, and I certainly didn't need Chris answering for me.

"You didn't know?" Sean eyed me with interest.

I looked down, not wanting to show him how furious I was with Chris.

"Sean, buddy, we're up!" Ringer yelled from the poolroom. I listen as he racked up the billiard balls.

I worked on fixing up the froth-to-beer ratio in Sean's pot so that it looked less like a glass of ice cream.

"You better go. If you have any chance of winning you'll have to break."

Sean smiled, knowing exactly what I was talking about. Ringer was a terrible breaker and a less-than-perfect doubles partner.

"Can you bring that up for me?" His eyes flicked to his beer as he walked towards the poolroom.

"Coming right up!"

I wiped my alcohol-soaked hands, grabbed Sean's beer, and walked up to the other end of the bar where all the action was. 'When The River Runs Dry' was playing from the jukebox, but it was the unmistakable thunderous crack of the billiard balls that grabbed my attention as Sean instantly pocketed a ball with his impressive break. He was wearing a basic white T-shirt but when he leaned over the table and positioned himself for the shot, cords of muscle drew tight and accentuated every curve.

"You might want to close your mouth."

I was jolted back to reality to see Ellie standing at the bar with Tess just behind, exchanging smiles.

"Oh, um …" I stammered, my cheeks burning scarlet. Damn him.

Ellie and Tess cast each other knowing looks and pulled up a seat at the bar, hooking their handbags on the backs of their stools.

"We're just teasing," Ellie said. "I think we can all appreciate that the Onslow Boys offer a nice view."

I worked to busy myself, placing Sean's beer on the side of the pool table and wiping the bar down. I disposed of an empty glass, placing it in the dirty dish rack, and erasing the damp circle, wiping it away as if it would deflect Sean's existence. It probably would have worked if he hadn't been standing in front of me, flipping out his wallet.

"Ladies." He nodded at Tess and Ellie.

They nodded back in unison. "Sean."

"Double trouble." He flicked out a twenty, drawing my eyes to his wallet where I saw the unmistakable gleam of a silver, square condom packet in one of the slots. My stomach flipped and I didn't know where to look. Mercifully, Sean snapped his wallet shut and replaced it in his back pocket as he put the twenty on the bar.

I quickly moved to the till to get his change.

"So what?" Ellie perked up. "Tess and I are trouble and Amy isn't?"

Oh God, leave me out of this.

I had intended to leave his change on the bar but Sean held out his hand.

I placed the note and coinage into his palm, his fingers brushing mine. A small thrill shot through me at the tiny gesture. I'm sure he meant it to.

Damn him.

"Oh, she's trouble all right." His eyes bored into mine as a devilish smile curved his lips. "Trouble of the worst kind."

I folded my arms.

"Well, best stay out of trouble's way then," Ellie said, shooing him away.

He pocketed his change and grabbed his beer, heading back to the pool table. "Nah, trouble never looked so good," he said with a wink.

If I wasn't blushing before, I was definitely flaming now, and the fact that I could feel Ellie's and Tess's eyes on me didn't help.

Ellie shook her head, looking from me to him and back.

"He is unbelievable."

"Still the same old Sean." Tess said with a laugh.

"I actually think he's gotten worse," Ellie agreed.

"He has always been a shameless flirt," said Tess.

I sighed, folding up the dishcloth. "He drives me mental."

"I think Sean was put on this earth to drive women mental," Ellie said, "and it appears to be working." She saluted me with her drink.

An uproarious yell sounded from the pool table as the boys bellowed, "Two shots!" I took the chance to steal a look at Sean who had Ringer in a headlock, ruffling up his hair.

"Sometimes he is so thoughtful and nice," I said, "and then there's the times (and that's the majority of the time) when he's cocky and smug, and suggestive and immature and I just want to strangle him!"

Tess smiled, raising her glass. "Yep! That's him, all right."

"Sometimes ..." I leaned forward, lowering my voice, "I fantasise about tripping him over."

Ellie clapped her hand to her face, trying to stop the contents of her drink from snorting out of her nose as she coughed, while Tess patted her on the back.

I couldn't help but join in. Once Ellie had regained her breath from the choking and laughter, she grabbed for my cloth to wipe away the mess she'd made on the countertop.

"You know, there is an easy way to render Sean speechless," said Ellie.

I stilled, *incredibly* interested in what she had to say.

I held up my hand. "Hang on a sec! I want to give you my complete and undivided attention." I threw the cloth into the sink and walked into the main bar.

"Chris, I'm taking my break now!"

***

Ellie, Tess, and I collectively sighed as we settled into the puffy couch in the main bar. We were tucked away from the rest of the mayhem near the unlit open fireplace – it was far enough away from the calamity of the poolroom, but still in direct line of sight to spy on those making all the noise.

Exhibit A: Sean Murphy. *Naturally.*

"It's really quite simple," Ellie said.

I sipped on my Coke. "Well, please explain. I would give anything to wipe that smug smile off his face *just once*." I had a fifteen-minute break to find out how to take down the giant and see if it was as easy as Ellie believed.

"Sean is a grade-A flirt and in particular loves nothing more than to see women blush."

"I'm not a blusher," I said, not at all convincingly.

Tess winced.

I slumped. Oh, how I wished I wasn't like all those girls, all those bashful, giggly girls and housewives who batted their eyelashes and treated Sean like some Greek god carved out of marble.

I peered towards the poolroom and watched Sean and Ringer pretending their pool cues were light sabers as they duelled, *Star Wars* style, with Stan offering helpful commentary.

"Use the force, Sean, use the force."

I shook my head.

I turned to Ellie and Tess. "What do you suggest?"

Ellie grinned at Tess. "There is only one way to solve a problem like Sean Murphy."

I edged closer on my seat as if Ellie was about to reveal the secret of life.

"With Sean, you have to give as good as you get."

My shoulders slumped.

Well, that was anticlimactic.

"But I do! I answer him back all the time and it does nothing."

Ellie rolled her eyes. "Not that!"

"Then what?"

"The next time he flirts, or is suggestive, you do it back."

What?

"Flirt with Sean?" I asked, curling up my lip with distaste.

"Think about it; it's genius. He won't be expecting it and the shock value alone will shut him up. Even if it's just for a moment, think about how blissful that moment of silence will be."

"She has a point, Amy," Tess said.

I was more sceptical. "You really think it would work?"

Ellie shrugged. "What have you got to lose?"

My dignity.

"I'm telling you!" Ellie said, slapping my knee. "He won't see it coming, especially from you."

My brows lowered. "Why especially from me?"

"Well, because it's you. You're little Amy, the publican's daughter. You're like everyone's kid sister."

My eyes widened. I could feel the hairs on the back of my neck rise. I tried not to openly scowl at the words and look insulted, even though I was. 'Little Amy, the publican's daughter' – it was what I'd got my whole life …

Well, not anymore.

I stood and forced a smile. "Oh, right. Of course. Well, I better get back to it."

Tess looked warily up at me. "You okay, Amy?"

"Yep! I am now. Thanks for the heads up, ladies, I can't wait to put it into practice."
Ellie's brows rose. "So you're actually going to give it a go?"
I shrugged. "If the opportunity arises."
Ellie broke into a wicked grin. "Oh, it will."

Chapter Twenty-Eight

Before I returned to the bar I ducked out the back way towards the ladies' room to freshen up.

I peeled through the partition into the dark restaurant and was weaving my way through the tables when a voice sounded from behind me.

"You know, I don't think I like the sound of that plan."

I jumped, clutching my heart as I turned to see a shadowy figure leaning on the bar near the partition.

"I swear to *God*, Adam, if you creep up on me one more time …"

"I wasn't creeping – *you* were creeping. I was just standing here minding my own business."

I looked around in the dark room, confused. "What are you doing in here? Hanging out in the dark? It's weird."

"I was about to walk through the bar, but I didn't want to disturb your little slumber party chat."

Oh God, he heard everything.

Anger seethed through me. "So what, you just thought you'd lurk in the shadows and eavesdrop? Nope, nothing creepy about that."

"I was not eavesdropping," Adam said defensively.

"Good!" I turned to continue towards the ladies' toilets.

"But about that plan …" he called after me.

I paused, sighing deeply as I turned.

"Plan?" I opted to play dumb.

"About getting even with Sean."

"From the *private* conversation you weren't listening to, you mean?"

Adam leaned over the bar to turn on a lamp near the coffee machine. "Yeah, that one."

"Let me guess … You don't approve."

Adam blinked, adjusting to the lamplight. "I don't, but not for the reasons you think."

I stared blankly at him. Adam rolled his eyes.

"Sounds an awful lot like game playing to me."

"So?"

"*So*, game playing sucks. And there is this raging testosterone inside of me that makes me feel like I should defend my brother-in-arms from your wicked ways."

The penny dropped. "Don't you dare!"

"What? Tell Sean? Hmm, I wish I could promise that but after my head injury my mind has been terribly forgetful lately."

"What do you want?" I asked through gritted teeth.

"It's not blackmail."

"Isn't it?"

"What if your devious little plan backfires?"

"It won't!"

I was getting testy. To be honest, I'd had no intention of putting Ellie's plan into practice. I was really disappointed with her advice. I'd instantly disregarded it, in fact, but now that Adam was putting in his advice on behalf of the brotherhood ... Well, it pissed me off.

"So it's all right for you boys to be giant smart-arses and womanisers but heaven forbid if we give it back?"

Adam opened his mouth to speak but closed it again, thinking better of it.

"What?" I said.

"No, nothing."

"What were you going to say?"

Adam rubbed his hand through his hair and looked around, possibly for an exit strategy. What had started out as a possible innocent taunt from him had turned into something messier.

"It's you, Amy. I just don't want you to embarrass yourself."

My mouth gaped open as if the wind was knocked out of me. What was with people thinking I was still this little publican's daughter crap? That I was still the same unco kid with braces loitering on the steps of the Onslow? Maybe that was the way they remembered me, but I wasn't that girl anymore. I was nineteen, for God's sake! I'd had boyfriends, a bunch of them. I could hold my own and I could give just as good as I got.

I was the one who had wandered into this disaster of a hotel and made the decision to turn it around; to fight for it. The little publican's, cute-as-a-button, innocent daughter? *I don't think so.*

Adam must have read the rage all over my face. "So ... no game playing, right?" he asked gently.

I just scoffed. "I don't have time for games." I didn't even wait for his response; I just turned and walked away.

***

I couldn't shift my mind from *the game*. I was constantly on edge any time Sean came near me, or if I looked and caught Adam's knowing eyes, or caught Tess's and Ellie's raised brows of encouragement, and, oh God, did Ellie just give me a thumbs up? Subtle as a sledgehammer.

Chris's voice jolted me from my thoughts. "You right to lock up tonight?"

He was another one to add to the mix. I still hadn't forgotten how angry I was at him for not telling me about my invite to Sean's. What else had he been deciding on my behalf?

"Where are you going?" I asked.

"A group of us are headed up to the Point, for old times' sake."

"Yeah, well, I guess I have no prior invitations so it looks like I can close." I watched for a reaction, but he didn't even flinch.

"Thanks, Amy, I owe you one." He ruffled my hair in that annoying way boys do. I sneered as he went back into the main bar. I would still have words with him, but just not right now. I turned to see Sean standing before me, placing his empty glass on the bar.

"Nice hair."

I must have visibly flamed, as I cut him a searing look that only seemed to amuse him more.

I changed the subject, running my fingers through my hair. "So, didn't get a lecture from Chris last night?"

Sean crossed his arms and leaned on the bar. "What about? Keeping you all to myself yesterday?"

It would have been a perfect opportunity to flirt back; it was an open invitation waiting for me to wipe that devilish grin off his face. Instead, I fought the flame of crimson and settled for my usual snarky comeback.

"Not brave enough to say that in front of Chris, though, are you?"

"Ha! Chris doesn't scare me. It wouldn't be the first time we've come to blows."

"Really?" I asked, surprised.

Sean looked on reflectively. "Year Ten, we had a duel in the school ground over Sharnie Maynard."

"Over a chick?" I asked. "Now why doesn't that surprise me? Who won?"

"Neither. It turns out she had the hots for Toby all along."

"Oh dear!"

He shook his head. "Broke my heart."

"Well, if it's any consolation, my best friend had the massive hots for you."

Sean stilled, his brows furrowing. "Who?"

I sighed. "Tammy Maskala."

The blankness never left his face, just like I suspected all those years ago: he didn't even know she existed.

I rolled my eyes. "About so high, mousey brown hair, big blue eyes, lurking in the shadows every place you went."

"Don't know her."

"Well, trust me, she loved you!"

"Is that so? So what's Tammy up to these days?"

Something unexpected jolted in the pit of my stomach, a sudden urge to shut up about Tammy.

I shrugged. "I think she's married."

Liar!

"Probably got a couple of kids."

Liar!

"Probably doesn't even live here anymore."

Liar! Liar! Liar!

As far as I knew, Tammy had never moved away and I had never heard of her mythical marriage or children, but for some utterly disturbing reason I didn't want Sean asking questions about her. I knew it was insane; it wasn't like she was his type anyway and she was probably long over him by now …

Oh, my God, I was going straight to hell.

Sean studied me for a long moment as I tried to act nonchalant by picking an invisible thread off my top.

"Fair enough," he said. "You seem to have your finger on the pulse there."

I smiled weakly. "Yeah, we kept in touch."

Liar!

"Sean, mate, we're up!" Stan called out as he racked up the billiards.

"Thanks, mate! I was starting to get a bit weary of Amy's incessant flirting." Sean rolled his eyes at Stan.

My draw dropped and I gaped incredulously.

Stan laughed. "Yeah. Jeez, sounds rough."

***

The more attuned I was to Sean, where he was and what he was doing, the more it made everything about me wooden and unnatural.

I cursed Ellie and her idiotic advice – it was a stupid idea; I was *not* going to flirt with Sean Murphy.

"Because it's you ... you're like everyone's kid sister."

I glowered to where Ellie and Tess sat on the couch, taking my fury out on the ice bucket, stabbing it violently with the spoon.

"Whoa, easy! What did that ice do to you?" Chris squeezed past me, grabbing a couple of pot glasses to fill at the tap.

"I just called last drinks; do you want to sweep around and do a glass run for me?" Chris asked.

Thank God, a means to an end!

I was mentally exhausted by what had been a massive day and a never-ending night. I swept around the bar, collecting empty glasses and the odd empty chip packet. I weaved my way through the poolroom and all the people holding onto the dying minutes of the night. One last drink, one last pool game, one last smoke before the strike of the clock, one last song on the jukebox. I headed towards it to collect the empty glasses on top of the flashing fluoro pink dome. I stilled, seeing the familiar broad back of Sean, one arm leaning against the machine while the other flicked through the song choices.

I walked up to stand beside him.

"Play Kenny Rogers?" I asked innocently.

He broke into a brilliant smile, not once taking his gaze from the folders that flipped before his eyes. "Not a chance."

"Don't be like that – 'Ruby' is a classic." I reached for the glasses on top of the jukebox and accidentally brushed against him.

"Off to the Point then?" I asked.

"Well, there isn't anything else going on." He pushed his song selection in before looking down at me.

Curving my brow, I teased, "What, no damsels in a short dress to escort home tonight?"

I was beginning to loosen up and feel like my normal self for what felt like the first time tonight.

Bob Seger's 'Night Moves' flooded the speakers as Sean cocked his hip against the machine and folded his arms. He looked at me for a long moment. "That's the unfortunate thing."

"What's that?" I asked with a frown.

"I can't exactly walk the publican's daughter home," he said with a glint of amusement in his eye.

Maybe it was the knowing look, or the fact that last drinks had been called and the night was over, or maybe it was the term 'publican's daughter' that had me thinking about what Ellie and Adam had implied. That I was just the same little Amy as when I was fourteen.

A surge of defiance surfaced in me and, as Sean's last words hung in the air between us, I took the chance, the one moment I might never have the courage to act on ever again. I did my best seductive look – I bit my lip and slowly moved forward. I reached for the empty pot glass Sean held, deliberately sliding my fingers over his, slowly, softly, as I pulled the glass from his hand. I quirked my mouth and looked into his eyes. I leaned closer still, speaking so no one else could overhear, and shrugged one shoulder.

"You can always walk me to my bedroom."

Chapter Twenty-Nine

I had aimed for a moment of blissful silence, so when his response was that of catatonic shock I began to worry.

All amusement fell from Sean's face as his eyes flicked rapidly over mine, as if he was looking at a stranger.

Yes! Victory! I had rendered him speechless.

When he swallowed deeply and seemed incapable of responding, I smiled my best sultry vixen smirk and walked away, with my head held high. Okay, I might have put a little bit more thought into swaying my hips than usual.

As I rounded the corner out of sight, I broke into a winning grin. I wanted to fist pump the sky and do a little dance at the satisfaction of wiping that smug look from Sean's face.

Chris jumped the bar. "So you sure you're right to lock up?"

"Yep!" I saluted, still running high as I kept picturing the priceless look on Sean's face.

Chris cast me a doubtful look. "You all right?"

"Yeah, why wouldn't I be?" I scoffed at him.

"Because you look different. I don't know, you look … happy?" Chris had said every word as if he was deeply troubled by the possibility of me being in a good mood. I didn't know how I felt about that – surely I wasn't such a grouch, was I?

Toby walked into the front bar, guiding Tess by the hand. He looked at Chris. "Ready?"

"Yep! What are the others doing?" Chris asked.

"They said they'll follow us up there."

Chris nodded and turned back to me. "I'll move them out. You lock up behind?"

"What, you're not coming, Amy?" asked Tess.

I smiled. "Not tonight, I'm pretty beat." I followed them to the door as Chris worked on rounding up the poolroom patrons, making sure all the pool cues, billiard balls, and glasses were accounted for before everyone left. Drunks had a habit of pinching anything that wasn't nailed down.

Ellie shouldered her bag and made for the door. I wanted to catch her eye on her way out to give her a cheeky thumbs up, knowing she would know exactly what it meant.

I didn't need to as she made a beeline for me, grabbing my arm, and pulling me aside, her serious eyes zeroing in on me.

My smile vanished. "Ellie, what's wrong?"

Ellie seemed really highly strung. "Whatever you do, don't go flirting with Sean, all right?"

My stomach plummeted and my mouth ran dry. "W-why?"

"Adam must have overheard us talking about him."

I relaxed a little. "Yeah, bloody big ears. It's all right, I already know."

However, Ellie didn't look any less worried as she shook her head.

"He let it slip, Amy."

"What?"

"After you left Sean at the jukebox, Adam, who I might add has had waaaay too much to drink …"

I looked over Ellie's shoulder to see Adam and Stan shadow boxing each other on the way out of the door.

I'm going to kill him.

"What did he say?"

"I'm not sure exactly, but he must have lectured him or something. Sean's definitely onto us, because Adam came up to me and said he was a dead man."

"Who, Sean?" I asked.

"No, Adam. He thinks you're going to kill him."

Oh, I was going to murder him, all right. I felt instantly sick. Sean now knew that I was deliberately bunging on the seductress act. I would never forgive Adam and his big ears or his fracking big mouth.

"Don't worry, Amy, you can just deny it. Say Adam's just talking drunk talk and he is an idiot. No damage done, right?"

I bit my lip and didn't answer. "Oh shit," Ellie said. "What have you done?"

I grimaced. Ellie pushed me farther to the side and lowered her voice. "Right, here is what you have to do. Act as if nothing has happened. If he doesn't mention Adam, you don't mention it. If he tries anything, play dumb and just go with it. Knowing Sean, he will be out to press your buttons, so don't let him win, okay?"

I rubbed my temple – this had gotten way out of control way too quickly. Adam had asked me, what if it backfires? Well, now, thanks to the drunken little shit, it had.

Big time.

I nodded, taking a deep breath. "It's all right. You're all heading to the Point, so I'll just avoid him till he leaves and lock up." Then, I'll hide under my bed and never come out again.

"Good plan." Ellie nodded.

"Come on, Parker, you're holding the line up." Chris held the door open for the stragglers.

Ellie hugged me goodnight. "See you tomorrow, Chook."

"Ellie!" Chris warned.

"I'm coming!"

I followed Ellie over to the exit and took the door from Chris, who walked out after Ellie. "Make sure all the main lights are off."

"Yes, Dad. Night, kids," I yelled.

I shut the door, deadbolted it and twisted the locks into place. With a sigh, I ran my fingers through my hair and walked into the poolroom to hang up the cues that had no doubt been left on the table, like always. I stopped in the archway that led into the poolroom. Sean sat casually on the edge of the table, his elbows on his knees, rolling a well-worn cue in his hands. He straightened as soon as he saw me, the same wicked grin slowly spreading on his lips.

"Ready to be walked to your bedroom?"

Fuck!

Ellie's words echoed in my mind: *"He will be out to push your buttons, so don't let him win."*

My gut reaction was to say something snide and tell him in his dreams, but the simple fact was that I actually did have the upper hand. I knew he knew, but he didn't know I knew he knew. Oh yeah, this was so simple.

"How did you manage to escape Chris's security checks?"

Sean hopped off the pool table and walked over to the mounted rack on the wall. He slotted his cue back into place and shrugged one shoulder in that cool, casual way he always did. "I hid under the pool table."

"What?" I laughed.

Sean worked on grabbing the other cues off the pool table and securing them back into place. "Yeah, it wasn't my proudest moment."

My smile slowly fell as I realised that he had deliberately hidden out so he could 'walk me to my bedroom'. I was suddenly well aware of how alone we now were, just Sean and me. I was snapped from my anxious thoughts by the sound of stool legs being scraped along the floorboards. Sean tipped the stools upside down to rest on the bar: the night-time ritual.

"Do you want a job here? We're hiring, you know …" I mused.

He lifted the last of the stools next to where I stood, before smiling down at me wickedly. "You just can't handle being without me, can you?" His knowing eyes waited for the reaction he was no doubt expecting.

It took every ounce of my being to fight against what would have been my natural, snarky reaction. I met his gaze unflinchingly, giving him nothing. I pushed off the wall I was casually leaning against – I could almost feel the heat radiate off Sean we stood so close, but not touching.

"Kill the lights. I have to empty the beer trays and give the bar a wipe down," I said matter-of-factly, before skimming past him to head to the main bar.

"Yes, ma'am! The sooner we get this shut down the sooner we can get out of here," he called after me.

I couldn't see his face as I walked away, but I could tell by his cocky words that he was no doubt grinning from ear to ear, the smug bastard. At least turning away from him I was able to sneer slightly, letting out some of my pent-up frustration.

Adam Henderson, you are a dead man.

I emptied and washed the beer trays, rolled up the beer mats, and wiped down the bar. I turned around and slammed straight into Sean.

"Watch it!" I snapped, rubbing my shoulder.

"Sorry, I just came to empty the ice bucket." His eyes darted to the container that now lay filled with ice cold water and only a few dismal floating chunks of ice.

"Oh, okay, thanks," I said, inspecting my shoulder for instant bruising.

Sean had plunged the poolroom and the outside into darkness. Now, only the main light in the bar remained on. I knew once that went out, there was no going back. I should just admit defeat and say, "All right, the jig's up, you win. Now get out," but a part of me hated the fact that he was enjoying trying to make me squirm. He was intently watching my reactions, every smile, and every quip. He was expecting me to fail or to concede defeat, which only infuriated me more. It was like a game of chicken or who would fold first.

As I went to the final light switch, my heart leapt in my chest as fear set in. I didn't know what kind of game I was playing or how completely out of my depth I was getting, but as my hand hovered over the switch I took a deep breath. Sean leaned on the bar looking expectantly at me. His twinkling eyes and confident, relaxed manner made me want to punch him in the face. It was also all I needed to make my decision.

Challenge accepted, Sean Murphy.

I smiled slowly, making sure that I held his gaze long enough before making my next move.

"Ready when you are," I said as I flicked the switch and plunged the bar into complete darkness.

May God help me!

Chapter Thirty

What was I doing? WHAT was I doing?

My head screamed with every step I took up the staircase. My stomach twisted with every light switch I flicked off as I passed, leaving pitch blackness behind me.

On most nights, I yawned and stretched and casually made my way up the staircase, but tonight each step was a step deeper into trouble, as I was acutely aware of the presence of Sean right behind me. Even in the dark it felt like his eyes were burning into me. I faltered on one of the steps, stopping to gain my balance when Sean walked straight into me.

"Owww!" I said, a bit dramatically.

"Shit, sorry," he whispered.

I pushed him in the chest. "Why are you whispering?"

There was no one else here. I swallowed deeply. Just me and Sean Murphy walking up to my bedroom.

We continued up the stairs, guided by the light that glowed down from the landing. We made our way to the top, Sean peeling off to the left, me to the right. We both turned, looking at each other, confused.

"Where are you going?" I asked.

Sean frowned. "Where are *you* going?" He looked towards the door of my Dad's apartment.

"My room's this way." I tilted my head towards the hall.

Sean raised his brows in surprise. "Well, I was going to have a coffee first and unwind but I see you don't want to muck around." He smiled a devilish flash of white teeth.

"Oh, umm, did you want some ...?" I was mortified by the insinuation that I was eager for him to be in my bedroom.

"It's all right, I can take a hint." As he passed me, he deliberately brushed against me as he made his way up the hall.

I glared at his back. *He is loving every minute of this*, I thought bitterly. I had to break from my scowl as he turned with a questioning look and pointed to a door.

"Keep going, last door on the left," I said, trying to keep my voice even.

The walk down the narrow hall was the longest of my life. I tried not to meet Sean's watchful eyes as he stood, waiting by my door, without a care in the world. Was I really so proud as not to admit defeat? To own up to the fact that I was trying to beat him at his own game simply to teach him a lesson? That I knew what he was up to and, nice try, buddy, but I'm calling you out on it? All these thoughts ran rapidly through my mind as I closed the distance between me and Sean and my room. And then another thought entered my mind.

Shit, did I make my bed this morning? Do I have any dirty underwear slung on the back of the chair?

I couldn't remember. *Oh shit, oh shit!*

I hoped the bad lighting in the hall would mask the anxiety on my face, the look I knew I was barely concealing.

Sean casually stretched his arms above his head as if he didn't have a care in the world, before he waved an arm towards my door, beaming. "After you."

I could hardly believe that a messy room was actually even a concern considering I was about to let Sean Murphy into my bedroom. I calmly twisted the handle and pushed the door open as I would have any other night. If I was to survive this I would just have to play it cool. Any reaction would tip him off. This was a battle of wills. Who would fold first? Who could push the other to their breaking point? And then a thought slammed into me.

What if he doesn't fold?

I was jolted from the fear of such a thought as Sean took a running dive onto my bed, bouncing once, twice, three times, like a giant kid. The springs of the mattress groaned under the pressure as he adjusted the pillows and cushions so he could casually lean back and watch me in the doorway. He entwined his hands behind his head and threw me his best cheesy smile as he sighed in delight.

I cocked my brow. "Make yourself at home."

He rolled over onto his stomach, leaning over to look under my mattress. "Nice bed!"

His voice was muffled as he spoke directly into the darkness under my bed. God, I hoped he couldn't make out all the junk under there, plus a decade's worth of dust, no doubt. I quickly turned off the main light, which drew his attention instantly.

I then realised how suggestive that might have come across so I scurried over to the lamp and fumbled for the switch on my desk. In a blind panic I struggled, and swore under my breath before mercifully finding it. With a click, my bedroom lit with a warm, subtle glow from my leadlight lamp.

Yep! Real smooth, Amy.

Sean still lay on his stomach, except his fascination had moved from under my bed to me as he hitched himself onto his elbows. The real me wanted to tell him to take a picture as it would last longer, or to not even think about getting any ideas – the lamplight was not to build ambience, it was to stop you seeing surface dust. Yeah, it didn't sound all that convincing even to my own ears.

Then I noticed his eyes moved from me to behind me. I turned to follow his gaze. Before I could raise a question, he hitched himself up and off the bed and was over to me in three quick strides.

"What do we have here?" Sean leaned past me and plucked something off my shelf with lightning speed, holding it up to the lamplight.

"A Rubik's Cube?" I asked, stating the obvious.

He bounced the perfectly aligned cube in his hand, studying it. "I haven't seen one of these in years."

I straightened. "Well, I'll have you know," I said, plucking it from his hands, "that I am the Messiah of the Rubik's Cube."

Sean looked over at me. "Is that right?"

"*The* Messiah," I accentuated the words with confidence.

"Oh, really?" He copied my actions from a second earlier and plucked it from my hand. "Well, let's see you undo THIS."

Sean turned his back to me, twisting the cube every which way in a conspiratorial fashion. He glanced over his shoulder at me every now and then to ensure I wasn't peeking. It was the first time I allowed myself to openly roll my eyes at him as he spent what seemed like an eternity unravelling the colours of the Rubik's Cube.

"Ah-ha!" He spun around and presented the cube to me, all twisted, the colours speckled throughout it. "Let's see you get out of this one." He smirked.

I sighed and grabbed it from him, as if bored by the challenge. Unlike Captain Mysterious, I chose not to turn my back. If anything, I wanted him to see exactly what I was about to do.

I blew on my knuckles for dramatic effect. "Watch and learn. Watch. And. Learn."

Sean scoffed and folded his arms as if waiting for my failure.

I honed in on the green centre piece and worked on unscrambling the rainbow of twisted pieces. I had no time to watch for Sean's reactions as I concentrated and counted my move notations.

Right inverted, right and down, I twisted with lightning speed, working through the algorithms in my mind.

Front inverted, up, left inverted, up inverted. I twisted on, speaking in my own language that I knew few could follow. Even fewer had a clue what an algorithm was all about. At first it didn't look like much, as if I wasn't getting anywhere, but I kept twisting, and twisted a series of carefully planned out sequences, my eyes darting over my quick-moving hands.

Right inverted, down inverted, right, down.

The corner of my mouth pinched into a smile when a wall of green formed in all its glory. I was on the downhill stretch now.

I stole a look at Sean who was watching my hands, captivated by every twist. I dug in, twisting in a blinding fury until I triumphantly held the perfectly formed cube up to Sean resting on my palm. My mouth twitched with a silent 'shove that in your pipe and smoke it.'

Sean stood, stunned, staring at the perfectly aligned cube in my palm. He disguised his smile by rubbing his hand over his jaw and lips. I squared my shoulders, waiting for an apology.

He nodded. "Wow," he said, plucking the cube from my hand and examining it thoroughly.

His eyes flicked up from the cube to me. "You really are a dork!"

My mouth gaped open. “Shut up!” I lashed out to hit him, but he was too quick and caught my wrist with his free hand, holding me in a firm grip.

“You’re so violent, Amy,” Sean mused.

I twisted, trying to free myself from his grasp. “Gee, I wonder why?” This time I glowered at him unapologetically.

Sean chucked the Rubik’s Cube aside, before he reached for my other wrist and pulled me closer to him.

My breath laboured, not in fear but at the unexpected thrill that surged through me as my body pressed against his. Sean’s grip was still firm, but it was the working of a slow, hypnotic circle he traced in the palm of my hand that had me melting slightly into his hold.

“Is that why you brought me here, Amy? To play games?”

I could feel the warmth of Sean’s breath near my cheek as he leaned in to speak into my ear.

I swallowed hard, moving my head to the side. What could I possibly say? “Unlike you, I don’t play games”? But that was exactly what I was doing and I was playing against a professional player. Women were his hobby. I had seen it time and time again over the years downstairs in the Onslow; Sean being pawed over by all the beauties in town, admired like some god with their googly eyes and irritating giggles. Women threw themselves at him. And what was I? Some boarding-school city novice, who had spent her entire teenage years fabricating sex stories in the toilets of a private all-girls school. The only real sexual experiences in my whole life had been stolen moments in the spare room of my boyfriend’s house when no one was home. Simon had been a nice enough boyfriend, but the earth hadn’t moved; not once. My heart had never threatened to pound out of my chest with him, not like it was doing right now just from being so close to Sean.

The smell of his rich cologne, the feel of his work-roughened hands on my skin. What girl in Onslow hadn’t fantasised about having Sean Murphy in their bedroom come night-time, all alone in the dark? I fought to not make eye contact, afraid of what I might feel if I looked into his blue eyes; eyes that I could lose myself in, even from across a room.

Damn him!

I yanked at my wrists, but it was of no use; Sean just pulled me around like I was a rag doll and propped me on my desk to sit. Letting go of my wrists, he stood so close I felt like I was pinned, anyway. I rubbed at my wrists, casting him daggers. He smiled his crooked smile.

He placed his hands on either side of me. He leaned into me, his legs pressing my legs apart. I could feel his lips press against my ear. “How far are you willing to go, Amy?”

Chapter Thirty-One

How had this happened? When had I completely lost all control?

I had gone from supposedly having the upper hand, to everything turning upside down.

Sean was pushing my buttons again. He had a masterful way of making me come undone simply by a look, or his incredible smell, or the heat and feel of his hard body pressed against mine. Everything about the position, pressed between my desk and his body, should have made me feel trapped. I should have wanted to slip a dictionary inside my pillow case and whack him over the head with it.

But part of me didn't want to do that at all, and that scared me. A piece of me enjoyed his touch and wanted to meet his challenge and that's what all this was about, wasn't it? Not letting him win – hadn't that been what had got me here in the first place?

I didn't know anymore. My head was fuzzy from his close proximity; I could barely think of what my next move should be. Then, like a hammer, it hit me: it was my turn to throw out a question, put the ball back into his court.

I let my defences down; I melted my rigid posture and slid forward, forcing him to move back a little to let my feet fall to the ground. He straightened, watching me with uncertainty.

I couldn't help but smirk. Was that an air of unease surrounding him? From the way I'd moved forward, not taking my eyes from his, not once, I felt a surge of power. I had been so overcome with the what-ifs that I had completely lost focus.

It was about pushing him, making him feel uncomfortable. I had to spin this whole thing around. I edged forward, placing my hand on his chest until the backs of his legs hit the edge of my bed. Sean glanced back, then quirked a brow at me. I pushed him as hard as I could, forcing him into a sitting position. His cocky smile had vanished; instead, he looked up at me with a guarded, serious expression.

It was a standoff all right, move for move. He knew I was bluffing; he had said as much with his mocking words. *"How far are you willing to go, Amy?"*

He expected me to fold and then he would laugh with victory and get up and walk out of my room. Head out to the Point so as not to waste the night.

I was just Amy Henderson. The publican's spoilt daughter, everyone's kind of friend. For a moment I felt a cloud sweep over me – a dark cloud of resentment.

Things had changed. I was Amy and I wanted people to see that. But above all, and as much as it disturbed me, I wanted Sean to see it. See that I had grown up and that there was more to me than my snarky comebacks and moody aggression.

With all these thoughts running through my mind, suddenly it wasn't about winning a game or having the upper hand. It was about proving to myself that I wasn't a spoilt child wanting to get her own way, to always be the winner.

Before I could voice my defeat, before I could say, "Congratulations, you've won," Sean stood up.

The planes of his face softened, lit with the warm glow of the lamp. "Amy, I—"

Before he had a chance to finish his sentence we both were jolted by a loud, fisted knock on my door.

"Ammmmyyyyyyy," Adam's inebriated voice sing-songed through the door.

My eyes widened as they darted to Sean. "Hide," I mouthed.

"Where?" he whispered.

Oh shit, oh shit ... Where do you hide a six-foot-three wall of muscle in a bedroom?

I mimed for him to help me slide my sideboard in front of the door, to stop Adam from flinging it open. Sean silently edged it into place before diving behind the door.

"Ammmyyyyyy," Adam continued, talking into the door. It was like a horror movie.

I thought maybe if I didn't answer he might think I was asleep.

"Amy, I'm sorryyyyyy, please open the door." The handle twisted and the door creaked. Sean moved behind me, pushing his back against the door to reinforce the barrier. Adam didn't stand a chance with Sean on my side.

I pressed my finger to his lips urging him to remain silent.

"Amy, come on. I'm really sorry, okay? I didn't mean to tell Sean; it just slipped out."

Sean's eyes snapped to mine: the jig was up.

"All right, I may have let it slip and I may have or may not have given him a lecture about not going near you."

Ha!

I stole a look towards Sean. Yeah, that worked.

He didn't appear to find this situation in the least bit amusing. His head was turned in to the door panel, but I could see the clench of his jaw line as if what Adam was saying was not going down too well with him, either.

Adam just needs to shut up.

"All right, all right. Fair enough," Adam said with a hiccup. "But just so you know, you don't have to worry about Sean. He assured me you're not his type."

I stilled, frozen, as Adam's words cut me to the core. I didn't know why, but it was as if a knife had been plunged into my stomach and twisted. I tilted my head away from Sean, not even wanting to look at him or for him to read the unmistakable change in my eyes, the hurt written across my face.

"Night, Amy. You have permission to pummel me tomorrow, because I know you will anyway."

Oh yes, I will.

Adam's drunken footsteps made their crooked way across the hall and into his room.

"Amy …" Sean whispered.

I held up my hand to cut him off. "He hasn't closed his door," I snapped at him.

We waited on a sound that never came, fearing what I suspected. I started to move the sideboard back into place, with Sean quickly helping me. I still couldn't bear to look at him so I busied myself instead on opening my bedroom door a crack, pressing my eye against the opening.

"Oh, great!" I whispered.

"What?" Sean tried to lean forward to look but I elbowed him away.

Just like I had suspected. Adam's door was wide open and, right before me in plain view, he sat lounging in a fluoro orange bean bag, his game console in his hand, playing 007.

I closed the door with a quiet groan.

"What?" Sean kept his voice low.

"He's playing the PlayStation."

"So?"

"*So*? He's doing it with his door open," I snapped.

Sean still looked at me as if he really couldn't understand what the issue was.

"Knowing Adam, he'll be playing it for hours and hours. You're stuck here, Sean."

Under normal circumstances, Sean would have made some lame joke about being stranded alone in the dark with a girl for hours. Instead, he just looked troubled.

"Yeah, don't worry," I snarked. "I'm none too thrilled about it, either. We can only hope he might pass out or something, but knowing Adam, the night owl, he'll probably be awake all night." I grimaced.

I had lost count of the endless nights of my youth in which I had stumbled across the hall, half asleep, at some ungodly hour. I would throw Adam a sleepy, dirty look and pull his door shut to muffle the sounds of the game music blaring from his TV.

There was no chance of doing that tonight without him cornering me for a deep and meaningful, and the last thing I wanted was for Adam to get deep about anything while Sean was within earshot.

I glared at the door with my hands on my hips, searching for a solution and, more importantly, to avoid Sean's gaze. Adam's words still circled around in my mind.

He assured me you're not his type.

What type – easy and stupid? I then thought about one of the big-breasted, petite blondes he usually walked home. I seriously doubted they would have wooed him with their Rubik's Cube skills.

I just wanted to die.

"Are you mad because I knew?" His voice cut through the dark; snapping me from my thoughts with the unexpectedness of it.

I wasn't mad about that, I'd known what I was doing; I was angry at myself for getting involved in the first place. I should have kicked him out of the bar as soon as I saw him sitting on the pool table. The Amy of old would have done exactly that. Instead, I had led him up the stairs, played cat and mouse, a half-arsed seductress knowing that everything he was doing was only to stir me up, to get back at me for trying to play games in the beginning.

The only difference was the joke really was on me. I knew Sean was joking, that he was deliberately trying to make me uncomfortable by overdoing the charm and flirting. I had known the whole time and yet I had still bought into it. As if a part of me had believed there might have perhaps been some underlying meaning behind those heated looks.

For a moment I had actually allowed myself to believe that maybe it hadn't been a game, the way he'd looked at me was so … Wow! I really was no better than those stupid girls of his that bowed before him, that were willingly led on by his charms and that smile, a flex of a muscle.

That was Sean.

I had been playing in the big league trying to outplay a player, and I had been well and truly defeated through my own stupidity.

I shook my head. "I'm not mad."

"You're a terrible liar."

"Oh, so I'm a liar now, am I?"

"Well, based on this little game tonight, yeah, you kinda are."

Oh no, he d'int!

"Excuse me? Games? That's rich, coming from you. You're the master of game playing."

His lips twitched. "Actually I like to think of myself more as the Messiah of Games."

I crossed my arms. "Wow, you must be really bored, resorting to playing games with little Amy, the publican's daughter. Stuck here with me when you could be out parking at the Falls or walking some bimbo home for a quickie. Instead, here you are, trapped in my room for God knows how long. This really must be rock bottom for you."

My voice wasn't a whisper anymore I was so angry. It got to the point where I couldn't care less if Adam heard me, or came barging into my room with an entire brigade to see what was going on.

I hated Sean Murphy. I hated his smug, shitty games that treated people like nothing more than objects to admire and use to stroke his ego. I was all but ready to storm over to the door to rip it open and tell him to get the fuck out!

That's right! The *real* swear word, I was *that* pissed.

"What makes you think I don't want to be here?"

Wait.

What?

Sean stalked towards me, backing me into the door. I thudded against it, my mouth gaping in surprise.

"Let's get one thing straight, Amy Henderson. I don't put myself anywhere I don't want to be. And yeah, I knew what you were doing; I didn't need Adam to give me some bullshit spiel about staying away from his precious cousin. Unlike you, when I walked up those stairs, I wasn't playing any game. But I guess that's the big difference between you and me."

Before I realised what he was doing, he reached for the handle. He flung the door open and walked out into the hall, pushing his way out of my room without so much as a backwards glance. I stood in the hall, stunned at what had just happened.

What did he mean he wasn't playing? He had to have been.

I hadn't even given a second thought to Adam until I heard the loud snore over the animated play of music. Adam was passed out cold with the game console still in his hand. I watched the words flash across his screen.

Game over. Game over.

I sighed, walking over to click the power off.

It was game over, all right.

Chapter Thirty-Two

My heart stopped.

My watch read eleven a.m. After a double-take through one squinted eye, I sat bolt upright, leapt out of bed, and ripped the bedroom door open, a feeling of dread spiking through me. There was no way Chris would have let me sleep in this late, not in a million years.

I instinctively looked into Adam's room, half expecting him to still be passed out in his bean bag, but all I found was an empty room. I rushed to check Chris's room but I was greeted with the same empty reception. My last checkpoint was Dad's apartment, but again, nothing. I stood in the middle of the lounge gathering my thoughts when I heard distant shouts and banging. I headed towards the balcony to see what all the noise was, but stopped and thought better of it.

It wasn't until I was mid-shower that it dawned on me. I dropped the toothbrush and clasped my soap-sudded head in dismay.

"Shit! The working bee!!"

I ran around in nothing more than a T-shirt and my undies, dragging a brush through my tangled wet hair, cursing the world and everyone who lived in it. Of all days, why hadn't Chris woken me? Of all days, searching through my dresser to pull out my aqua Mambo mini, I stood on something pointy.

"Ah, faaaaar out." I threw my miniskirt in a fit of rage as I sat on my bed and rubbed at the sole of my foot. It was then that I realised exactly what I had stood on.

The Rubik's Cube.

I picked it up and held it in my palm. In the light of day and after a rather haphazard night's sleep, all I could do was cringe at the way I had behaved last night. I was not some siren, some sexy vixen … *obviously.* What had I been thinking? What had possessed me to think that I could honestly pull that off?

Maybe I *was* still little Amy, the publican's daughter.

I cupped my head in my hands – when had everything become so complicated?

***

After the mad rush of getting dressed, I decided to take a breath and focus on making myself look semi-decent. Blow-drying my hair, putting on natural toned make-up and some Fire and Ice perfume. I wanted to look nice at the working bee, but I sure wasn't going to admit to myself why.

I stood back and gave myself a long, hard look in the full-length mirror. Hmm. The miniskirt was not exactly working bee attire, but I could at least make a grand entrance even if I wasn't entirely sure what greeted me downstairs.

Swinging around the bannister and into the foyer of the restaurant, the very last thing I expected to see was Ellie and Adam standing on drop sheets. They were singing Van Halen's 'Why Can't This Be Love' into their paintbrushes as it blared from a paint-splattered old radio. They laughed at each other as they applied brush strokes of paint on the wall.

"Will you two concentrate?" Tess's voice called out over the music.

I hadn't even noticed her cross-legged on the floor near the skirting boards with an edging brush. She shook her head and went back to her work until her eyes landed on me.

"Amy, hey!"

Ellie and Adam spun around, no doubt spotting the look of confusion on my face as I eyed the stacked cans of paint, drop sheets, rollers on extenders, all waiting to go. Adam cringed and hid behind Ellie, grabbing her by the shoulders like a human shield.

"Get off me, you have paint all over your hands!" Ellie squirmed away.

Adam's brown puppy dog eyes blinked at me. "Do you still love me?"

I eyed the brush in his hand. "You're painting; I will say anything to keep that going."

Adam smiled. "I'll paint the whole hotel, doesn't worry me." He turned to attack the wall again with renewed vigour, taking it as a sign of forgiveness. I would have probably pushed the issue but I was distracted by the paint cans near the bar.

Picking one up, I tilted my head to read the permanent marker scribbled on the lid. My eyes narrowed as I looked from the lid to the wall and back again.

"Portland Stone?" I said, mainly to myself.

"It's a great colour, don't you think?" Tess groaned as she climbed up from the floor and admired the partially painted wall.

Huge ten-litre cans were stacked on a drop sheet. I hadn't planned to repaint the dining room; it wasn't something I had worked into the budget. To me it was just a crazy pipe dream and, apart from my mum, no one knew what colour I liked, bar one other person … Sean.

"Where did all this paint come from?" I asked.

It wasn't a difficult question; well, at least I thought it wasn't, but the looks Ellie and Adam cast each other and the way they were stammering with unease made me ask it again. "Where did the paint come from?"

Adam rubbed the back of his neck; he cleared his throat and stepped forward, as if volunteering for the firing squad or something.

"Uh … It, um, fell off the back of a truck."

Ellie nodded quickly. Tess scrutinised her fingernails and avoided my questioning eyes.

"Off the back of a truck?"

"Yeah, the darnedest thing." Adam shrugged.

Right, so I obviously wasn't going to get anywhere here, but I would get to the bottom of this. I pushed my way through into the main bar where Chris was. He held up his hand to silence me as he spoke into his mobile.

"Yeah, we have some stuff in Uncle Eric's shed, but extra wouldn't hurt. Yeah. Just need some muscle power to tidy up that vine, it's a bloody mess out there ..."

I sighed impatiently, which only gained me a dirty look from Chris.

I wasn't exactly sure why I had to be so silent – there was a thunderous noise blasting out the front of the hotel that had my attention faltering from Chris for a brief moment.

What the hell is that?

I shrugged off the thought, and waved my hand in front of Chris on the phone.

"Yeah, no worries, mate, that would great ... Okay, see you soon." Chris ended the call. "What now?" he asked, looking at his phone, annoyed.

My mouth gaped – what was that supposed to mean? I shook it off.

"Chris, where did the paint come from?"

Without meeting my stare, Chris answered in a monotone, pre-rehearsed, robotic voice. "It fell off the back of a truck."

Oh, okay. So this was the way it was going to be – I sleep in once and everyone had already pre-plotted the day without me. Even though I knew exactly where the paint had come from, I wanted – I *needed* – someone to confirm it for me. It wouldn't have been cheap and there was so much of it.

I really didn't like the thought of any more of Sean's charity, but I also didn't like the opposite prospect – that I'd receive some huge bill in the mail for something I hadn't planned on fixing in the first place. After last night's episode, I wouldn't be surprised if he wanted to rip the beams out from the very balcony he'd fixed.

"Fine, be like that," I said to Chris.

I would continue my investigation elsewhere. I walked to the front door to head out towards the commotion out front. I paused before pushing my way out.

I turned back to Chris who was just pocketing his phone. "Why didn't you wake me?"

Chris shrugged. "You locked up for me two nights running. Seemed only fair."

"Yeah, but today's the working bee. I thought that—"

"We have everything under control. Some of Uncle Eric's mates are coming around to get stuck into the beer garden and there's more people coming to lend a hand by lunch, but don't worry, they have all been sworn to secrecy."

"Good!" I nodded. "Wait, shit! I haven't organised lunch!" I panicked.

"Lunch is at one. Melba and the McGees are prepping in the kitchen – they've picked up the meat and the salads are done. Don't stress, it's fine."

"Oh."

"See what happens when you sleep in?" Chris said with a smirk.

I pushed open the front doors and stepped outside to be greeted by a misty spray in the face and the deafening hum of Toby's pressure washer. Wearing nothing but shorts and a red bandanna tied around just below his eye line, he worked on blasting the dust, dirt and cobwebs from the brickwork and beams. Stan was on standby with his broom, sweeping the excess water from the verandah and scrubbing away any stubborn, lingering cobwebs.

Stan spotted me and smiled, yelling above the pressure washer. "Looks all right, doesn't it?"

I looked from the side Toby had already done to where he was going and the difference was remarkable. With all the dust collected over the years removed it was as if the Onslow had received a new paint job. Under the layer of dust the paintwork had been protected from the elements (at least the dust was good for something). It was an amazing transformation.

I tore my eyes from their handiwork.

"Hey, Stan, the paint inside—"

"IT FELL OFF THE BACK OF A TRUCK."

I flinched and then my shoulders slumped. "Oh, Stan, you too?"

He grimaced. "Sorry."

"You're all right, I think I know."

Toby turned the pressure washer off and, mercifully, silence fell. He pulled down his bandanna and wiped the excess water from his brow. He walked over towards us, playfully spraying the excess water still left in his gun at Stan's feet, making him jump.

"Don't! That shit will take your skin off."

"Relax, it's only a bit of water, isn't that right, Amy?"

Before I could agree or disagree, Toby grabbed me, embracing me in a huge, soppy, saturated bear hug. "Toby, don't!" I pushed him away.

I now sported a wet patch all down my side. "Now look what you've done." I pulled my sopping top and skirt away from my skin.

"Relax, Amy, it's only a bit of water," Stan said.

It seemed *all* the Onslow Boys were smart-arses.

My mouth twisted as I tried my best not to look at their boyish grins.

I shook my head. "Boys!"

Chapter Thirty-Three

Sean wasn't anywhere to be seen and so far my investigative skills had failed me miserably.

Apparently, my sleeping in had given him a chance to word them up not to tell.

As if I wouldn't work it out, anyway. It must have meant that he dropped the paint off this morning and didn't stay. I didn't know how I felt about that – either he legitimately had something else to do or he was avoiding me. I didn't want to ask the boys any questions because, if anything, I told myself I was giving way too much thought to Sean Murphy's whereabouts.

There was something adamantly clear in my mind, though, now more so than ever: I really didn't want to have to owe him anything. I thought back to last night and what could have happened, or what Sean had been about to say before we were interrupted. Guess I would never really know. It's not as if having Sean in my bedroom would have a repeat performance.

After overhearing Chris's earlier phone call about the shed, it triggered a memory.

Soon forgetting my soiled, damp clothes, I walked back inside with a new mission. "Hey, Chris, is Dad's Jeep still in the shed?"

"Yeah, why?"

"Do you know where the keys are? I need to go into town."

"Gee, I don't know. Sleeping in, forgoing hard work – I don't know if I support these lifestyle changes, Amy."

"I'll get Adam to run me through some boot camp drills later," I said with a roll of my eyes. "Do you know where the keys are?"

Without a word, Chris backtracked to a hook over the register that housed a series of keys. He picked out a key chain with a little figurine of Bart Simpson and threw it over the bar to me. I caught the jingling mass with a huge smile.

"Thanks."

"You never got them from me, and you keep it fuelled up."

I was stunned that Chris was even agreeing to let me take the Jeep – I guess it prevented me from borrowing his ute or, heaven forbid, catching a ride with a six-foot-three Onslow Boy. Ha! Fat chance of that.

"All right, I won't be long. Do we need anything?"

"No, I'm right. For Christ's sake, just drive careful."

***

Like a kid on Christmas day, I skipped all the way towards Dad's Brunswick green boat shed that sat about a hundred metres beyond the back of the hotel. Pulling the heavy double doors open to an expansive array of tools, mower, fishing gear, boat, and ta da! Dad's soft-top, army-green Jeep Cherokee.

Running my hand along the bonnet and skimming my way in between the boat and the driver's side door, I unlocked the beast and slid behind the wheel. Nostalgia filled me as I drummed my fingers on the steering wheel with glee.

Dad had taught me to drive in this Jeep, I got my Ls in this car, and I had always had dreams of grandeur of being the first to get my P plates because I was the eldest in my year.

My friend, Tammy, and I had had it all planned: I would get my licence then cruise around town, pick her up and head to the Point with all the cool kids. Of course, my little banishment to the city soon dented that plan quick smart.

The car was stuffy; dust particles danced in the sunlight that filtered through the windscreen. I tipped the visor up and down, familiarising myself with my surroundings. I shuffled through the junk in the console, popped open and rustled through the glove box.

"No way!"

I pulled out a cassette tape and held it up to the light. I squealed in recognition of the familiar cover. I snapped it open and there it was in my sixteen-year-old handwriting: *Roxette*.

I fired up the beast and popped in the tape, turning up the volume as 'Joyride' blared from the speakers.

"Ooooh, yeah!" I put the car into gear and slowly edged my way out of the shed, accelerating around to the front of the hotel. I tooted the horn at the boys and waved like a mad thing.

I turned right on the bitumen road, opting for the long, scenic way into town, past Stan's parents' caravan park and sweeping towards Horseshoe Bend down a leaf-lined trail with beautiful lake views. I cruised along, singing at the top of my lungs, the wind flapping my hair all around the cabin. 'Fading Like A Flower' came on and I thought I would die of happiness. Not wanting my journey to end, at the crossroads I opted to turn onto MacLean's Bridge, the impressive, sweeping bridge that crossed Lake Onslow. I felt exhilarated that I still knew all the words as I sang like a Eurovision contestant, putting so much passion into my performance that I nearly sideswiped the side of the bridge.

Shit! Okay, Amy, settle down.

I placed both hands back on the wheel in a sobering moment, before grinning to myself and chucking a U-turn on the Perry side of the bridge. I sailed back over towards town, directly at the very reason I had decided to go to town in the first place. I had to complete my cunning plan. It was so clever, it bordered on pure genius.

"I'll show you and your Portland-Stone-paint-fell-off-the-back-of-a-truck, Sean Murphy."

I almost felt like chucking my head back and cackling, but that sounded a bit scary even to me so I opted for singing to Roxette's 'Dangerous' instead.

***

The bell above the door let out a magical ding, alerting Jan and Roy to my entrance as I walked into their store. They offered up immediate warm smiles.

"Hi, Jan! Hi, Roy!" I beamed.

"You look really well, honey, been keeping you busy on the hill?"

"You know it." I offered her a double-fingered pow-pow motion and thought, *What is wrong with me*? Music really must soothe the savage beast.

"How can we help you, young Amy?" Roy asked with a smile.

I wanted to grin evilly, but instead, I opted for cool, calm, and matter-of-fact, like I had rehearsed in the car. "Oh, I just need to run an errand."

"Can I help?" Roy said.

"I hope so, I just need to pay some money on Sean's account; he asked me to drop in."

I waited, hoping I wasn't met with confusion, as I had just assumed this would be the place. It was the sole store in town with a hardware section and I guessed that Sean would hold an account here.

"Ah, yes, of course, come through, come through." Roy started towards the back of the store where all the home hardware and DIY essentials were housed.

Bingo!

Until now I hadn't needed to use my account with my 'essentials money' from my parents. Aside from the odd food shopping and cleaning products, I hadn't touched it at all. It was ridiculous, all that had happened to the hotel, all that had been cleaned, repaired and renovated thanks to Sean's generosity… Well, it had to stop.

The money was to be used at my discretion so that's what I was doing. Besides, it was for hotel stuff so I was sure my dad would approve. It's not like I was going to Amcal to blow it all on Revlon products, however tempting it was.

Roy waddled behind the counter. A balding, portly man with bandy legs, Roy lived in his navy blue overalls, changing only his flannelette shirt every day to mix up the look.

He retrieved an A4, navy exercise book from under the counter. Opening it, he licked his thumb and flicked through the pages.

"Now let's see, M for Murphy, Murphy, Murphy, Murphy … Ah, here we go!" He pointed to a page.

By this time, I had pulled out my cheque book and held my breath, bracing myself for the figure. I wasn't completely sure what I could contribute to the cause; it all depended on how massive the damage was.

Roy spun the book around to face me. "That's what's owing. – how much did you want to put on it?"

I sighed with relief. The tally read $465. I had thought it would have been much worse than that, running into four figure sums, at least. This, I could do. I wanted to make a statement, and paying off a portion wasn't as grand a gesture as leaving a clean slate.

As I wrote out the cheque, I envisioned the look on his face when he came in to pay the bill and grinned to myself. Now *that* I would like to see. I had absolutely no remorse filling out a cheque for the $465. I knew between the verandah, the locksmithing, and the paint, all that would have exceeded the $465 mark. I signed off and tore off the slip and handed it to Roy with a smile. It was like a huge weight had been lifted.

I wasn't getting free labour or special treatment, I was paying my own way and it felt good. I would keep my smug knowledge to myself, though. I knew Sean would eventually find out but if he wanted to be Mister Cryptic, fall-off-the-back-of-a-truck, I could be Miss Oops, my-pen-slipped-on-my-cheque-book.

Roy wrote me out a receipt and sealed the deal by placing the cheque in the cash register and slamming it shut. I felt like I could face anything, until I heard my name.

"Amy?"

Chapter Thirty-Four

I could hardly believe what I was seeing.

A lean, Amazonian, modelesque woman stood in front of me in three-quarter-length Lycra pants and a black sports bra that exposed a flat, toned tummy.

She didn't wear a skeric of make-up – she didn't have to; her skin was radiant and flawless without it. The only thing that masked her face were the silken wisps of brown hair that fell from her sleek, perky ponytail, which fell to the middle of her back. But it was those eyes, those big, blue, innocent eyes that I would know anywhere – they were the only thing that hadn't changed.

Once I had stopped gawking like an idiot I managed to voice the only thing that popped into my mind.

"Tammy Maskala?"

"Oh, my God, Amy!" She laughed and folded her arms around me, almost squeezing the life out of me. I wrapped my arms tentatively around her, and yep, she was toned all right.

"I knew it was you; I heard your voice and thought *that* has to be Amy Henderson."

The last time I saw Tammy was a couple of years ago and, um … she'd changed somewhat.

She had morphed from a mousey, knock-kneed schoolgirl into a bronzed, Amazonian beauty queen.

"Wow, so what are you doing with yourself these days?" I asked, trying not to openly stare.

"Oh, you know, I dabble …"

I smiled in good humour – dabble probably meant she worked part-time at the local video shop, or waitressed of a weekend.

"Yeah," she continued, "I'm a personal trainer and studying for my double degree in biomedicine."

My smile faltered. Holy shit, she was a fucking rocket scientist! I wanted the ground to open up and swallow me. Even though it was just Tammy Maskala, the sweetest girl I had ever known, and I knew my twisted stomach hearing of her success was pretty rotten, the shock of seeing her was something that would take some time to sink in.

Oh, please don't ask me what I'm up to. Please don't ask.

"So what have you been up to? I can't believe it's been so long."

Oh, you know, bar room brawling, scrubbing urinals, playing mind games with an older man, and that's just the summer. I am actually a deferred university student-slash-couch potato leeching off my parents still.

"I'm on a break from uni and just came back to manage and oversee the renovations at the hotel." It was kind of the truth. She didn't need to know the details.

Tammy's blue eyes softened. "I heard about your dad."

Just what I wanted. Pity.

"And I saw the flyer around town for the working bee. It's actually funny I ran into you here because I was going to come and volunteer."

"No!" I blurted out a bit too vehemently, causing Tammy to blink in surprise.

"Um, it's just that we're simply inundated with volunteers. It's actually getting a bit ridiculous. Everyone's enthusiasm has been overwhelming so we've had to put a cap on things."

Oh my God, what is wrong with me?

"Oh, okay, well, if you need anything let me know. I cook a mean barbecue."

I was flooded with guilt seeing her sweet, coy smile, the same one I remembered. She had 'changed' but she was still the same.

"Thanks, Tam."

We said our goodbyes, which included an open-ended "we must catch up," like people say when they know they're not going to follow through with it; it's just what you do.

As I left the store, I was gripped by an overwhelming sadness. Sometimes, and of late it was most of the time, I really didn't like the person I had become. At least when I was a teenager I could be excused for being immature, but now I had no excuse. Words played through my mind.

"Unlike you, when I walked up those stairs I wasn't playing any game. But I guess that's the big difference between you and me."

The memory of Sean's words cut me to the quick. I slammed the car door behind me. He was such a hypocrite! He was the biggest game player of them all.

"He assured me you're not his type."

That bothered me more than anything, and the fact that it *did* bother me bothered me a whole lot more. Christ! I banged my head on the steering wheel, once, twice, three times. I sat up to see Tammy had just come out of the shop and seen my little display of self-loathing.

Shit! She smiled weakly and gave a small wave as she put her headphones back on and started to jog across the road, in a long-legged, graceful way. I watched her in my rear-view mirror, still hardly believing how much my old best friend had changed. I turned the ignition and Roxette's 'She's Got The Look' blasting from the speakers, taunting me. I slammed my finger on the eject button.

"Yeah, yeah, yeah, she's got the look," I muttered.

Whatever!

As I drove back to the Onslow, the wind in my hair, my spirits lifted as I thought about the mission I had just accomplished in fixing up Sean's account. I smiled a small, knowing smile. It was the only secret I had been keeping of late that I could truly be happy about. By the time I sped up Coronary Hill and made a wide, sweeping turn into the drive, I had started grinning like a fool. That was, until I nearly drove straight into a truck. I slammed on the brakes, my heart leaping in fright at the unexpected thing in the drive.

"What the—"

The massive tray to the semi was tilted, pouring white pebbles onto the ground. A cloud of dust carried on the air as the load dropped onto the drive.

I shut off the engine and got out, my brows creased in confusion until I saw an unmistakable speck in the distance, leaning casually on a rake. In his bone-coloured work pants and white singlet top, he actually looked like a catalogue model for work gear, but I quickly wiped that from my mind. I slammed the car door and crunched my way across the new stones towards Sean, who was now pushing the massive pile with his rake. He hadn't even seen me; he was too busy signalling to the driver to move forward before whistling and telling him to pull up.

"What's going on?" I yelled over the truck's engine.

Sean turned, sporting an expression of pure innocence. "What?"

I pointed to the mountain of pebbles.

Sean followed my line.

"Oh, right." He nodded as if he had just caught on. "Now this," he pointed, "this really did fall off the back of a truck."

I just shook my head. I had thought I was so clever, paying his account, but all that was now obliterated by a truck full of fine white pebbles that were resurfacing our large driveway. As far as I knew, the driveway had only ever been partly re-stoned by Dad via the odd tandem trailer; it was just too expensive to lay it down by the truck load.

A truck load just like the one before me.

If Sean was angry at me from last night, he said nothing. His mischievous eyes looked down on me in a silent challenge, smirking from the bottle of water he took long, deep swigs from, his eyes firmly set on me. It was the Sean of old, and if he didn't want to bring last night up then I wouldn't either, and I certainly had no plans to, until, of course … I *did*.

"Why aren't I your type?" I blurted out.

Oh my God … shut up!

Sean choked on his water and coughed so hard he banged on the wall of his chest, his eyes watering.

I swallowed deeply, almost wishing that the truck would back up and bury me in a mass of pebbles rather than having to wait for his answer.

"Sorry?" he croaked out.

Oh, shit! Did I seriously have to repeat myself? Maybe he hadn't heard the question over all the noise, but the way he was looking at me now with this uncertain, troubled look in his eyes, I had no doubt that he had.

"Never mind!" I said, my voice a little too high, a little too cheery. "I better go see how they're getting on with the kitchen." I walked a wide berth around Sean – knowing how lightning quick he was with his reflexes. I didn't want him to try to stop me, or demand that I explain what I was talking about.

He didn't.

I walked a straight, determined line towards the Onslow steps.

Don't look back. Don't look back.

I was adamant in that much until I managed a quick glance across the drive as I opened the main door and our eyes locked. His attention was only snapped away when one of the workmen called his name. I took that moment of distraction to dive into the Onslow and hoped that I could hide myself away for the rest of the summer.

If not, at least for the rest of the working bee.

Chapter Thirty-Five

I followed the sound of 'April Sun In Cuba' blaring from a radio out in the beer garden.

The sound was momentarily out-blasted by a power tool and some barked orders.

The sliding glass door was left open, revealing a war-zone-like mess beyond: piles of raked leaves and overgrown hangings of ivy that had been pulled and cut away, revealing slithers of sunlight to pierce through the space. It was an absolute mess, but somehow I managed to see beyond all that. Instead, I saw something else entirely. I saw a mass of people all working together.

A weathered, older man was hand-sawing an overhanging branch, Stan was sanding down the picnic tables, while Ringer followed along after him and applied a fresh lacquer on the exposed wood surface. Adam was wrestling rather unsuccessfully with the blower-vac, while Tess worked at lining up the plastic cups along a little trellis table, ensuring that the horde of workers had a supply of cool beverages. I hadn't entirely lied to Tammy – it seemed we were crowded with volunteer helpers. A gathering of people of varying ages carried rubbish loads and clippings – they were basically gutting the whole space in order to build it up again. I wasn't wholly familiar with many of the faces but at a guess I'd say some were Dad's mates lending a much-needed hand. I swallowed hard, overwhelmed with heartfelt gratitude.

"Beep-beep," sounded the upbeat voice of Tess's dad, Jeff McGee. He ushered me out of the way, carrying a tray of sausages.

"The restaurant's looking good, Amy," he shouted over his shoulder.

Holy crap, the restaurant!

Lured by the music and voices, I had completely bypassed the restaurant. I dived back inside. How could I have missed it? The walls were now coated in a warm, crisp, clean beige. Portland Stone. It had lifted the entire space. I could hardly believe it was already finished.

The sound of money rattling in a tin snapped me from my inspection as Ellie appeared beside me.

"Want to enter the raffle?"

"Raffle?"

Ellie held a tin and a raffle booklet. "Yep! It's part of the fundraiser – first prize wins a meat tray donated by Don the butcher."

I smiled. "Probably not a good idea if I enter. If I win, people might suspect foul play."

Ellie nodded. "Very true. Probably not a good look."

"I tell you what looks good, though …" I turned to give the room my full attention again.

Ellie grinned with pride. "Not bad, huh?"

"You guys did an amazing job."

"Ah, well, as much as I would like to take all of the credit, we did have a little help."

I curved my brow.

"You didn't honestly think the three of us could have done it so quickly on our own? Between Tess's meticulously slow painting and Adam's 'ooh, I love this song' disruptions with *every* song on the radio, we would never have finished." She shrugged. "So Chris called in some reinforcements."

"Hell, yeah, I did," Chris said. I turned around to find him leaning against the open sliding doorway. His face grubby with dirt, his white shirt and jeans covered in grime, he wiped his brows with a gloved hand.

"Welcome back," he said, readjusting his sleeve. A pang of guilt spiked through me as I thought how I had been busy joyriding while everyone else had got their hands dirty. Even strangers were working harder than I was. Truth be known, I hadn't exactly expected anyone to show up to the working bee, but I had obviously underestimated how the locals felt about my dad.

I curtsied. "I am but your humble servant, Christopher."

"Ha! That will be the day." He pushed off from the door frame and headed back towards the beer garden. "How about you help out with the barbecue?" he yelled over his shoulder.

Barbecue? Now that I could do!

***

A long line of dishevelled, grotty workers waited patiently as one by one they claimed their well-earned lunch. Sausages or hamburgers with onions and coleslaw.

"God bless Don the butcher." Tess's mum, Jenny McGee, smiled. "That man is a saint."

"I can't believe he donated all this for the working bee." I looked over the massive pile of meat on the barbecue.

"That's Don for you," added Jeff as he stirred up a pile of cooked onions on the barbecue.

I was on bread and meat duty, having been given the task of asking, "Onions or coleslaw?" Tess was on drink duty, with Coke, Diet Coke, Fanta, or Solo at the ready.

We worked like a long-lined production team, not missing a beat, feeding the hungry masses with a joke and a smile. Yeah, I could work the Henderson charm all right.

Ringer got to the front of the queue and grinned like a fool. "Just coleslaw please,

Amy."

"What, no onions with your burger? Got a big night planned then?" I teased.

"You never know your luck in the big city." He laughed.

"Wise choice, Ringer – onion breath, not hot!" My eyes settled on a group of Dad's friends. "I think there are going to be some really unhappy wives tonight."

Ringer grimaced as he moved on to grab a drink from Tess. I was still laughing when I turned to the next in line.

"What will it…?" I paused, my words falling short as Sean stood before me, with an unnerving gleam in his eyes.

"Be?" he finished off my sentence.

From being someone who was totally killing it on the food station, proving myself to be quite the caterer extraordinaire, I had managed to completely lose my nerve and turn into jelly in one foul swoop. I stammered and clumsily knocked over the sauce bottle, only to nearly fall backwards as my legs hit the back of the esky.

"Whoa, look out!" laughed Jeff.

Smooth, Amy, real smooth.

Acting as if nothing had just happened, I quickly gathered myself, trying not to look at Sean's crooked grin. Instead, I grabbed for a slice of bread and confidently looked at him.

"Sausage or burger?"

Sean watched me unflinchingly. "Burger."

Right, easy. Get it together, Amy.

I grabbed the tongs and a pattie and placed it on the buttered bread. Yep, no problem. So far so good.

"Onions or coleslaw?"

"Coleslaw, thanks, Amy." The way he spoke my name on his lips sounded too intimate for such a public place. It sounded low and promising.

Oh my God, maybe there was a gas leak on the barbecue because I was clearly losing my mind. I worked lightning fast to hand over his hamburger with a serviette, just wanting him to move along the line and be gone.

"Ha! No onions for you either, Murph?" Jeff asked.

Sean grinned. "Well, you never know your luck in a small town." He was speaking to Jeff McGee, but he was looking directly at me. He grabbed for the sauce and applied it liberally to his burger, then placed it back on the table and winked at me. I watched Sean make his way over to join Toby and Stan at one of the finished tables.

"You might want to close your mouth," Tess whispered, elbowing me in the ribs. "There's a few flies hanging around the barbie; you don't want to swallow one."

I snapped my mouth shut, forcing myself not to blush furiously. I couldn't figure Sean out. It seemed that last night's stint hadn't changed his ways and, although he had left my room in a bit of a tizz, he certainly hadn't carried it over to today.

Chapter Thirty-Six

The smell of cooked onions and barbecue smoke stinks!

After everyone had gone home I jumped in the shower. I lathered my hair into a soapy beehive, singing into my Pantene bottle as Eric Carmen's 'Make Me Lose Control' blasted from my little radio. I was squealing up a storm until I heard pounding on the bathroom door.

"Amy, I beg you, stop!" Adam's muffled voice yelled through the door.

"What? Don't you like my singing?" I shouted back.

"Sounds like you're strangling a cat in there."

"Pfft, whatever, I know I'm fabulous!" I snapped my finger like a diva and would have almost sounded convincing … if I hadn't started choking on Pantene bubbles.

Oh God, gross!

I dressed and walked through the hall with my hair twisted into a turbanesque towel piled on top of my head. I smiled a small, secret smile – the strip of hallway between Chris's and Adam's rooms always smelled like overpowering aftershave as they got ready on any given night before they went downstairs. Had for years. It was a fascinating behind-the-scenes case study, and I was the only one privy to it. Would girls ever know the lengths they went to? Sometimes I wondered who was worse at taking forever to get ready, me or the boys. I paused at Adam's open doorway and watched him apply a styling product to his hair.

I wolf whistled as I turned to enter my room. "You'll break all the girls' hearts tonight."

He sighed. "It's the burden I must carry in life."

I sat on the edge of my bed, towel drying my hair, when Adam called out, "Hey, do you have a hair dryer?"

Oh God, it was official – the boys were worse than me.

"Um, yeah."

He stood in my doorway. "Not for my hair – my shirt didn't dry on the line and the collar's still damp."

"Well, wear another one."

"I can't, this shirt's the one; I'm in a navy shirt mood tonight." Rolling my eyes, I grabbed my hair dryer from my lower bedside cupboard.

"Here, but it's a boomerang, all right? It comes straight back."

Adam looked at the hair dryer warily.

"And hurry up before my hair dries."

"Why don't you let your hair dry naturally?"

"Because it goes all wavy and mental," I said. "We inherited the Henderson kink, remember?"

"Ah, yes," Adam said gravely. "The generational curse of the Henderson kink."

"Exactly, so hurry up."

Adam went to leave but paused, as if thinking carefully about what he wanted to say next.

"This is completely out of my forte ..." He shrugged. "But why not try *not* straightening your hair to within an inch of its life?"

"What?"

"Well, I know that's what chicks do, but I don't know, I think it looks too ..."

"Sleek? Shiny? Silky?"

"Severe."

"Oh."

I looked in the mirror, chewing thoughtfully on my lip, watching my long hair beginning to dry into the foreign waves I had always fought against.

I sighed. "Well, I'm definitely going to need some hair product."

Before I could back out of the thought, Adam disappeared and returned with a lime green tub.

"Try this."

I took it from him, eyeing it sceptically. "Let it dry naturally, huh?"

Adam shrugged, like he really wasn't that emotionally invested.

A slow smile spread across my lips as my eyes flicked from the tub of hair product then back to Adam.

"What?" Adam went all broody.

"Thanks, Adam, you're like the sister I never had."

"Shut up!"

"No, really, it's a beautiful thing: you borrow my hair dryer and give me hairstyle advice."

"All right, I'm out of here." He threw the hair dryer on my bed, making a quick exit.

"Aw, come on! Don't be like that. What about your shirt?" I laughed.

"I'll wear another one."

***

Seeing as I was trying something different, I opted for a smoky eye shadow and thought about walking into Adam's room to ask if it made my eyes pop, but then thought better of it. He'd probably kill me if I did that.

I patted my lips with a clear lip gloss and pressed them together, staring at the long waves that cascaded over my shoulders. With a bit of hair product I had aimed for the tousled look and, I had to admit, it didn't look too bad.

I swung myself around the bannister in a whizz of motion and smacked hard into

Chris as he came up the stairs.

"Ah, Jesus, Amy." Chris rubbed at his arm. "Stop swinging on the stairs like a chimp."

My mouth gaped as I rubbed my shoulder. "I'll give you chimp, you chump. Get out of my way!"

Chris continued to rub his own arm and glowered at me, but there was something different in his expression.

"What?" I snapped.

"You look different." He spoke in a way that made me think he didn't wholly approve.

"Is that a good thing or a bad thing?"

"I'll let you know."

Stupid hair. I probably looked ridiculous.

"Max starts tonight," Chris said as he walked past me towards his bedroom.

"Oh, my God, I forgot. How did his interview go today?"

A part of the working bee had been to meet with some potential staff. I had left it to Chris to take care of that while I had cooked the barbecue. The report was obviously promising if he was starting tonight.

"He worked behind the jump at the golf club, has good references, and seems pretty switched on."

"Excellent."

"It doesn't mean we can slack off, though; not until he learns the ropes."

I made a face behind Chris's back – he was always such a killjoy.

I tried to act all casual, even attempting to lean my elbow on the bannister for effect, but I just felt ridiculous. I cleared my throat. "Many in the bar?" I called up to him.

The click of Chris's bedroom light sounded as he came back out, wrestling a clean T-shirt over his head. He finally freed himself of the cocoon and I instinctively reached out to push his messed-up hair back into place.

"What did you say?" he asked, tilting his head away to avoid my fussing.

"Many downstairs?" I tried to keep my voice even as I followed Chris down the hall towards the stairs.

"A few. It's only early."

Always so full of information.

"Oh," I said, a little deflated.

"Stan and Sean just got here, though."

I misstepped and had to grab onto the bannister to prevent myself from ping-ponging my way down the stairs. I thanked God that Chris was in front of me so I could recover from my fumble. It was only seven o'clock – usually no one would traditionally venture out unless it was for dinner and we couldn't even offer that yet. I almost wanted to trek back upstairs and blow-dry my hair pin straight and wipe off my make-up. The last thing I wanted was to look like Olivia Newton-John at the end of *Grease*. Fortunately, I wasn't dressed in Lycra but I was feeling uneasy that maybe I was a bit done up, a bit overdressed just to be working behind the bar. Usually anyone just opted for non-assuming black and here I was in dark, fitted bootleg jeans and an electric blue, fitted V-neck that would no doubt have me marched straight back upstairs to change if my dad was here. The look from Chris was enough. Yeah, it was snug but it wasn't that bad.

Oh God, is it?

Too late. It was time to start my shift.

Chapter Thirty-Seven

There he was.

Sean stood out amongst the crowd as he always did: tall, tanned and chiselled. His dimples were exposed with each heartfelt smile he flashed. I remembered from years ago that his careless hair was always cropped so short you couldn't usually make out its colour. But this summer it was thick and wavy brown, lightened from days in the sun. His eyes focused earnestly and respectfully in conversation, the conversation he was having with …

"Whoa. Is that Tammy Maskala?" Chris appeared next to me.

I glowered across the room to where she stood, tall, lean, and toned. Her halter clung to her curves and her long, sculpted legs were exposed under her black miniskirt. She had her handbag draped casually on one shoulder, her long brown hair swept over the other.

Her laughter rang out across the room at something Sean had said. Oh God, even her laugh was delightful.

"Yeah, that's her," I said, unenthusiastically. Anyone would think she was my lifelong enemy, instead of my high school best friend.

"If you want to go hang with her you can knock off if you want," Chris said. "We're not exactly run off our feet."

Great, the one time I wanted to keep myself busy was the night I could knock off and socialise.

I sighed. "Thanks."

"Gee, don't sound so enthused," Chris said sarcastically.

I grabbed myself a raspberry vodka Cruiser, twisted the lid off, and took a deep swig. I could retire upstairs for the night if I wanted, just disappear, but I knew I couldn't do that. I cursed my inquisitive nature and psyched myself up to go into the poolroom bar. I couldn't exactly sit in the main bar – there was no one else around. It would look pathetic. Funnily enough, that was exactly how I felt.

I needed a plan of attack. I would waltz in and simply ignore them. They were just like any other customers tonight. I would hone in on someone else.

Bic Runga was playing a melodious tune on the jukebox and all of a sudden I wished for some hard rock instead of this romantic mood setter. I searched for familiar faces, making a conscious effort not to look Sean and Tammy's way. Ellie and Adam were playing to the death on the pool table. I spotted Stan at the bar, delving into his pocket and putting his spare change on the counter. I made a beeline for him and plonked myself on the stool next to him.

"Hey, Amy." Stan's smile was always warm and genuine; I felt kind of bad for what I was about to ask.

I looked at him intently.

"Stan," I said.

He sat down next to me, his smile slowly fading.

"What's up?"

"I need you to do me a favour."

Stan nodded. "Sure, Amy, anything."

Bless his heart.

I cleared my throat, trying to summon the words. "Stan, I need you to laugh at everything I say and find me absolutely irresistible."

Stan's brows rose in shock. He shifted on his seat, looking down.

Oh God, is he blushing?

He looked bewildered. "... Um, okay."

I picked up my Cruiser to clink with his beer in unified cheers. "Do I even want to know?" he asked.

"Stan, I don't even think *I* want to know."

"Is this as good a time as any to laugh?"

"Please do," I said.

And with that Stan started to laugh uproariously as if what I said had been delightfully entertaining and charming. I counterbalanced Stan's routine with a hair flick.

It was official. I had hit rock bottom.

For someone as genuine as Stan, he played the part like a pro. In the moments that followed, he subtly edged his chair closer, started buying me drinks, and laughed at what seemed were ridiculous moments to us. Like when I asked him to pass a straw, and he laughed and smiled. But to any onlookers it seemed genuine, especially coming from Stan. It must have looked pretty convincing, because Chris twisted the top off my Cruiser with wary eyes that flicked between Stan and me as if he wasn't wholly comfortable with what he was witnessing. In those moments, Stan lost form – he clammed up, paranoid about Chris thinking he was hitting on me, which would be a definite no-go zone.

"Don't stress about Chris, you know he's broody and threatening on his good days," I assured Stan.

I didn't know what was happening behind me between Sean and Tammy. I didn't want to know. I couldn't even bring myself to look in the direction of the pool table when a triumphant cry rang out as Ellie potted the black.

I would never have glanced around if it weren't for the delicate, gentle tap on my shoulder. I turned with a guise of surprise, even though I had somehow known exactly who it was the moment she had touched me.

"Oh, Tammy, hi!" I said with over-the-top enthusiasm. "I didn't know you were here."

Liar!

"I kept thinking all day about the working bee and I just thought I would come down and have a look. It's amazing, Amy, you've done a brilliant job."

Her voice was smooth, like silk, and her smile was subtle, earnest, and beautiful. Even I was in danger of crushing on her.

Sean appeared behind Tammy, trying to catch my attention. He mouthed and pointed, "Is that her?"

Oh, hadn't all his Christmases come at once? I ignored him and instead smiled at Tammy.

"Thanks, Tammy. I had a lot of help."

Her eyes darted expectantly from me to Stan. "I'm sorry, how rude of me, is this your boyfriend?"

Stan choked on his beer mid-sip. I tapped him on the back as he fought for air. "Oh no, this is Stan. We're just friends."

"Oh, I'm sorry, I just thought that ... Never mind." Tammy blushed crimson, just like she would have when we were younger.

"I just got roped into playing pool." She cringed. "I'm afraid I'm not really good."

Sean was racking up the billiard balls behind her. "Stan the Man, do you and your *date* want to play doubles?"

It was a none-too-subtle jab from Sean and the corner of my mouth twitched.

So he had noticed.

"You're on!" Stan said.

"It's on like Donkey Kong!" Sean called as he chalked his cue.

The way he moved to bend and line up the white billiard ball with such fierce concentration, I half expected him to paint stripes across his cheeks and let out a war cry.

"Should I be scared?" whispered Tammy with a glint of good humour in her eyes.

"Only if you don't pocket a ball," I replied.

Tammy's eyes widened. "Why? What happens then?"

The sound of the white ball smashing into the billiards was always an ear-piercing crack when Sean was behind it. More often than not he pocketed one ball (if not two) on the break. That's why he always wanted to go first. So typical.

I tore my eyes slowly from the pool table to look at Tammy's alarmed, blue-eyed stare.

Oh right, she asked a question. "Pub tradition has it that if you don't pocket a single ball in a game you have to ..." I deliberately broke off, grimacing for effect as I witnessed Tammy turning back into the timid schoolgirl I knew. I didn't want to take such pleasure at slowly torturing her; although the look on her face was priceless.

"Have to what?" she croaked.

"Well, you have to drop your dacks and do a lap around the pool table."

Tammy's mouth gaped in horror.

I shrugged. "Or, in your case, hitch up your skirt, I guess."

"Amy, you're up!" Stan called.

I jumped up from my stool. "Don't worry, you'll pocket a ball, I'm sure."

She didn't.

Thanks to my misspent childhood, it was really a battle between me and Sean, making it a fast game. Every time he finished a shot, he would hand me the cue with a smug, knowing look, his fingers brushing against mine. I thought it was deliberate, but knew better when Tammy awkwardly lined up for another cringe-worthy shot. Sean, being the caring partner he was, guided her through every shot, leaning next to her, pointing out the best solution.

"You see where the light hits the edge of the ball? That's where you have to hit it. You need to slice it on that angle and it will glide into that pocket," Sean said gently.

"Yeah, Tammy, just tap it gently, not too much force," Stan added.

I spun around to glare at him. "Whose side are you on?"

Stan grimaced. "Oops, sorry."

Now Sean was guiding Tammy on how to hold the pool cue correctly, his hands manoeuvring hers in the right places. I turned away, rolling my eyes and sighing impatiently at how long the shot was taking because of it. Even more annoying, something darker spiked in me every time they spoke to each other, or touched, or laughed. It blackened my mood, but if anything, it made me play like a demon. I channelled my annoyance into fierce competitiveness and determination. Every time I pocketed a ball, I lifted my eyes to Sean, who casually leaned against the wall. It was like I only had one opponent to beat, and Stan and Tammy didn't exist. The game was solely between Sean and me.

After all the guidance and touchy-feely in the world, Tammy still missed the shot. No, seriously; she totally missed everything. Her cue slipped in her hands and clipped the white billiard awkwardly, sending it in the opposite direction. We all cringed with apprehension – it was only a matter of time before she tore through the felt tabletop. Sean smiled in good humour, offering her patient words of reassurance, even though I could see his frustration bubbling under the surface.

Tammy blushed and became more and more flustered with each failed attempt, apologising profusely. Sean displayed nothing but the patience of a saint. Which was quite rich, I thought, knowing that if I was on his team playing as badly as Tammy he would have no doubt called me out on it. Both teams' billiards had at last been pocketed except for the final, infamous black ball.

"Come on, Stan! You got this, home and hosed." I called words of encouragement as my partner lined up for a tricky, but doable shot.

Sean taunted from the sidelines. "No chance, Stan, there is no way. It's too hard."

With immense concentration that had him frowning and comically biting on his tongue, Stan ever so gently tapped the white ball with the cue. It glided directly up the felt. It rolled almost in heart-stopping slow motion. It was going to hit the black ball, that was certain, but as the white ball ran out of momentum on its way across the table it tapped into the black and rolled both balls closer and into a direct, match-winning line. We all sighed as one; Stan and I with disappointment and Tammy and Sean with relief.

Before Stan and I could cast each other looks of despair, Sean was on the move, grabbing Stan's cue and chalking it up frantically as he stood in front of Tammy.

"Now, Tam, you got this," he said. "There is no way you can miss this, it's that easy."

Stan threw me a grin and I couldn't help but grin back. Yep! It was Tammy's turn. Although, worry did creep past the edges of my mind. It was an easy shot – surely, surely now was not her time to get it together. After all this, *Tammy* winning the game? Oh God. My grin fell from my face. This was bad; this was really bad.

Tammy nodded at everything Sean whispered to her. Brows narrowed, it seemed her inner warrior had appeared for battle. I half expected Sean to rub Vaseline on her brows, pop in her mouth guard and rub her shoulders before she stepped into the boxing ring.

By now we had gathered quite the crowd of onlookers, both amused by Tammy's dreadful technique and no doubt, entertained by how Sean and I were matching each other shot for shot.

What I hadn't expected were the cheers and whoops of encouragement for when Tammy lined up the cue.

"Come on, Tam, you can do this!"

"Come on, honey, bring it home, all the way."

My eyes darted around at the newly-formed Tammy fan club. She had the whole room cheering for her. How had this happened? When had she turned everything around?

I straightened, fighting to uncrease my forehead and tone down my penetrating glower at my former best friend as she lined up for the shot. Sean leaned next to her, his hand placed lightly on her back as he whispered into her ear some last words of advice. I gripped my Cruiser so hard I feared the bottle might shatter in my hand.

"You okay?" Stan whispered.

I snapped out of my terminator vision and half smiled, before taking a swig.

"Never been better." I took another long, deep swig.

"Tammy! Tammy! Tammy!" the crowd began to cheer.

Oh, for God's sake.

I took another swig, hoping against hope that she would miss. I envisioned after Tammy potted the game-winning ball, the uproarious crowd would engulf her, lifting her onto their shoulders to parade her around in her victory, after she and Sean embraced passionately.

I felt sick.

"All right, all right, everyone, keep it down for a minute," Sean said, motioning everyone into silence.

It was so quiet now, even the jukebox volume had dimmed and all I could hear was the drumming of my heartbeat pounding against my chest.

Miss, miss, miss, miss echoed in my mind as Tammy drew in a deep breath and pulled her elbow back slowly, then tapped the white ball into motion.

Chapter Thirty-Eight

The white ball glided along the felt. It tapped the black, pushing it smoothly and directly into the pocket.

So perfectly and tapped so directly, the white ball followed the black into the pocket, meaning Stan and I were the winners! Perhaps someone should have explained the rules to Tammy who, after her double-pocketed shot, squealed and jumped up and down like a lotto winner.

"Oh, my God! Oh, my God! Oh, my God!" She bounced up and down. "We won! We won!"

The spectators slowly peeled away. Sean pinched the bridge of his nose when the white followed through. He ran his hands through his hair before smiling at Tammy.

"You're a winner all right, Tam, just not tonight."

It slowly registered with her that what had happened was not something to celebrate. The volume to the jukebox was turned up and everyone went back to their usual business.

"We lost?" she said, the look of dismay lining her face.

"Well, look on the bright side, you pocketed a ball so now you don't have to do the table run with your skirt hitched up," I said, genuinely feeling for her.

"Good game, everyone." Stan beamed as he came over to shake my hand and Tammy's.

As Sean unloaded the balls out of the pockets for the next players, I couldn't help but steal a moment to shake his hand. Good sportsmanship and all that.

I sauntered smugly up to him, holding out my hand. "Bad luck, but you're a plucky kid and I like your style. Maybe if you keep practising, who knows?"

Sean grabbed my hand, engulfing it in his. It was as if an electric current exchanged between us. He held my hand, shaking it slowly but firmly. My mouth went dry as he looked down at me in amused silence, telling me I was a little smart-arse. His lips twitched but he didn't let go.

"You're loving this, aren't you?" he asked.

I shrugged. "It's always nice to win."

"I'm not talking about winning." He squeezed my hand before letting go, his fingers sliding across mine in a slow caress that made my tummy tingle.

His eyes never left me as I struggled for something to say, but as quickly as the oddly electric moment had swept over us, it was just as quickly doused with an ice bucket of water.

"You and Stan make a good team," he said in all seriousness.

There was an edge to his words that had me thinking he wasn't only talking about playing pool.

I smiled. "He's a good guy."

Sean nodded and looked away. "That he is. He suits you."

Whoa, okay, this was definitely not about playing pool.

"Oh yeah, I was thinking of even getting him to walk me to my bedroom later," I joked.

Sean's eyes darted back to mine, a deep burning behind them as his brow creased. My smile slowly faded.

I had meant for it to be a lighthearted quip, but it had gone down like a lead balloon.

Tammy came to stand beside me. "Hey, Amy, sorry to be a party pooper but I have a ten-kilometre run in the morning so I'm going to head."

A ten-kilometre run? Of course she does.

"No worries, thanks for stopping by." I struggled to focus on Tammy. Sean had turned into Mr Broody before me.

"Thanks for the game, Sean. Sorry I was such a disappointing partner," she smiled sheepishly.

Sean's mood lifted. "You a disappointment? Not possible," he said, shaking his head, his beautiful eyes making contact with Tammy's, causing her to look down and blush.

"Yeah, well, drive safe!" I threw in, breaking their moment.

Sean finished the last of his beer. "Hey, Tam, you think you could give me a lift home?"

"Oh, yeah, of course, sure."

My head pivoted around between the two of them. "Uh, Sean lives at the old Ellermans' lake house," I said. "It's on the other side of the ranges," I added helpfully, hinting that it wasn't exactly on her way.

"Oh, I don't mind." Tammy waved me off. "I never get tired of seeing that place."

Sean smiled. "You sure it's all right?"

"Absolutely!"

My heart sank as Tammy jangled her keys from her bag and gave me a hug goodbye. I couldn't look at Sean. Instead, I turned to make my way towards the bar, but it couldn't prevent me from hearing the cat-calls and laughter as a few blokes egged Sean out of the door as he followed Tammy.

"Don't do anything I wouldn't do, kids," teased one local.

I guess I knew what type was Sean's: Tammy Maskala.

***

The next day, the hotel shone like a newly polished diamond, inside and out thanks to the raving success of the working bee. Toby and Ringer were in the bar replacing the down lights with new bulbs while Chris reaffixed the blackboards that housed the new lunch and dinner menus. It wasn't a broad selection, but it would be enough to satisfy. Fisherman's basket, steak and chips, Guinness pie and mash, vegetarian lasagne and the crowning glory … chicken parmigiana.

"Well, I don't know about anyone else but I reckon you'll have the usual suspects trial the menu," Toby said as he climbed down from his stepladder.

"It's nine a.m. and you're already thinking about lunch?" Chris threw over his shoulder. "Is this straight?"

"No!" the three of us said.

"What do you mean the usual suspects?" I asked Toby.

"Don't you know? We're all lobbing here for lunch. Sort of a working bee celebration."

I was going to argue that I didn't know; my head was all over the place at the moment so there was every possibility that I had been told but it just hadn't registered.

"Don't stress, Amy, they'll be paying customers," Chris said. He thought he was so clever, reading my mind.

To be honest, it was the last thing I was thinking about. "I wasn't even thinking about that," I defended.

Chris just ignored me as he stood back from the blackboard and took a good look. "Bloody hell, crooked as a dog's hind leg," he mumbled to himself.

Toby and Ringer worked on in awkward silence. Great! They probably thought I was being a tight arse, worried about people not paying their way at lunch. I cursed Chris and his big mouth. But how could I defend my real thoughts, and explain that the reason I was walking around like a space cadet was because all I could think about was Tammy and Sean?

I fought against it, tried not to think about them, but as I had tossed and turned last night, punching my pillow and kicking the sheets off my bed, all I could think about was the two of them. Alone in the night, the car stopping, Sean inviting her into his sprawling, beautiful house on the lake that I was secretly dying to see inside of. He would give her the grand tour and there would be lots of blushing moments and stolen looks. They would bond with getting-to-know-each-other conversations. Aside from her gorgeous exterior, he would soon realise that she was a fitter-than-fit biomedical genius.

Unlike me, Tammy was the complete package. She would cutely confess she'd had a crush on him when she was younger and blah, blah, blah. I'd felt sick just thinking about it, and, more to the point, utterly miserable.

I couldn't even focus on the progress we'd made at the hotel, on the truly amazing effort all our friends had made in dedicating their time and money. I felt awful not feeling more emotionally invested in what was really happening.

I let the boys battle with their finishing touches while I busied myself brewing a coffee from the machine, hissing and whirring some frothy hot milk, the dark coffee oozing slowly into my cup, blacker than deep rich molasses, but not quite as black as my mood.

I hadn't bothered to blow-dry my hair this morning, instead letting it dry of its own accord. I shuffled my bunny slippers across the floorboards, carefully carrying my coffee.

I eased the sliding door open and stepped out to the beer garden – the new and improved beer garden. All that remained of the previous mess was a pile of clippings by the side entrance that Ringer said he was going to dispose of after he had finished up with Toby.

After a long-awaited, much-needed trim, the morning rays of sunlight finally pierced through the ivy canopy. I could even manage to sit on a chair that was now freshly repainted, and the table top also sported a slick new coat. The concrete had been blasted clean by Toby's dad's pressure washer and looked bright and brand new. I sighed as I took a seat, almost laughing to myself that this is exactly what Dad would have done. Well, the old Dad. He would have religiously shuffled out here with his coffee in the morning – all that was missing for me were the paper and a packet of cigarettes.

Sitting out in the beer garden made me feel close to my dad; sitting in his space, imagining him looking around the garden in deep thought like he always did. I would often walk past the sliding glass door and see him staring off into the distance and wonder what he was thinking about. Surely once Dad came home and saw this place looking like new again, once he sat back out here like old times, he would realise that he couldn't let it go. That this was home.

Dread swept over me – what if the new and improved Dad didn't sit in the beer garden? Maybe the new Dad would be running alongside Tammy Maskala for ten kilometres instead. My mood blackened at the thought of it, and, like a bad dream, as if conjuring up some cursed image simply by thinking of it, the sliding door opened and out popped Tammy's head with a brilliantly beaming smile.

"There you are! They said I could find you out here," she said as she stepped through the sliding door.

Oh, fucking perfect!

The last person I wanted to see.

She had short shorts on with a matching hot pink sports bra … *as you do.* Her perky ponytail swished from side-to-side as she approached. She hooked her bag over the chair, placed her water bottle on the table and sat down.

Make yourself at home.

"Been for your run?" I asked unenthusiastically as I sipped on my coffee.

Tammy stretched. "Yeah, this morning; I had some brekkie and showered so I could come over."

And then got back into her skimpy sportswear for a trip to the pub. Awesome.

I stirred my coffee and stared into the cup.

"So did you have a nice night?" I tried to keep my voice even, non-committal, and as soon as the words were out I inwardly grimaced. Why did I care? I didn't want to hear all the details, the last thing I wanted was to be bloody Tammy Maskala's confidante in life again, bosom buddies; it wasn't as if we had anything in common anymore.

Tammy took a swig of her water bottle, shook her head and smiled. "You know, it is so funny how I used to be so terrified of talking to Sean Murphy, remember?" She laughed.

Remember? How could I possibly forget?

"Yep!"

"I don't know why. He is so sweet and funny and easy going," she said dreamily.

Each trait she listed was like a knife in my chest.

"Well, good things come to those who wait," I deadpanned. Okay, I was going to have to try to fake nice a lot more, but I couldn't. With each word Tammy uttered I sank deeper and deeper into depression.

"He's even taking me out on his boat today; we're going waterskiing. I love waterskiing! I may not be able to play pool, but waterskiing … now that I can do."

Wow, that really felt like a punch in the face. Sean had never offered to take me out on his boat. Maybe she really was his type; it was something I would never be able to do. My long-standing phobia of the lake meant it was a definite no-go zone, but here Tammy was about to go full blast into the water sports with him. My heart sank.

"Awesome," I said in my best upbeat voice.

"You should come out. Stan and Ringer are taking their boats out, too, everyone is going." Tammy insisted.

"Oh no." I clicked my fingers. "I have to work the bar today." I thanked God – the thought of being out on the lake made me feel nauseated.

"Oh." Tammy's shoulders slumped. "That's a shame."

"Yeah, a crying shame," I agreed, finishing the last of my coffee.

Tammy's head was tilted to the side as she watched me intently. "Sean's going to meet me here. He shouldn't be too far away, actually."

"That's awesome." Ugh, I really needed to extend my vocabulary.

"He is so sweet." She smiled to herself.

"Yeah, I know, you told me that already." I sighed, turning my now-empty coffee cup with my fingers.

"Have you been to Sean's house? It is *amazing*!" She straightened.

"Yeah, I bet," I nodded, turning my cup on its saucer round and round.

"So let's work this out …" She started to count on her fingers. "… Sean Murphy's funny, sweet, *gorgeous*," she emphasised. "He has a nice car, beautiful house …"

It was like I was being slowly tortured, as if I needed Tammy to reiterate all the wonderful things I knew about Sean. But she had only spoken to him in one night and she had already gathered all this from him.

I knew it all already, though, and more. He was generous, he constantly made smart-arse quips that I supposed would have been funny if they weren't directed at me and he was gorgeous (I wasn't blind to the fact that in any room your attention always turned to Sean). He wouldn't have to say or do anything other than just stand there and exist, and he had that cute dimple that magically appeared with each boyish grin. The way he looked at me, his blue eyes watching and waiting for every infuriated reaction; they would then change into something completely different at the thrill of knowing he got under my skin. I knew all those things about Sean Murphy, I just didn't bundle them with nice house, nice car, nice package. There was so much more to him than that.

"Yeah, he's all those things," I agreed.

Tammy sighed dreamily. "It's hard to fathom that he could be all those things and," she leaned forward, looking directly at me, "be so good in bed."

Chapter Thirty-Nine

My cup flew out of my hand and smashed into a thousand pieces against the concrete.

It was fitting, really, as it was exactly the same thing that had happened to my heart.

Tammy looked expectantly at the mess and back at me in horror. I wondered if it was the same horror I wore on my own face as I felt a raw, searing emotion rise up inside of me.

"Oh, my God, Amy, you *do* like him," she said, astonished.

I rapidly blinked, praying that the tears would not come as I moved quickly to kneel down and pick up the pieces of porcelain. My hands were shaking and fumbling as I tried to grab the shards.

"Oh, my God, I am such a bitch," Tammy cried out. She knelt down beside me, grabbed my hands and forced me to look at her.

"Amy, Amy, look at me! I was joking, I didn't sleep with Sean."

I froze and peered into her earnest eyes that were filled with mortified apologies.

"I'm sorry, I'm such an idiot. I only said it because … well, because I had a feeling but I wasn't sure. I just wanted to see how you reacted."

I pulled away from her. "Were you satisfied with my response, then?" I asked coolly.

Tammy touched my shoulder gently. "Does he know how you feel?"

Oh, fuck off!

I stood still, not wholly confident that I could stop myself from bursting into tears. My heart raced at a million miles an hour.

"Tammy, you've been around for all of five minutes, so thanks, but I really don't need your advice."

Tammy crossed her arms. "You may not want it, but you're going to get it anyway."

I gaped, stunned at Tammy's sternness – this was a hard-arse Tammy.

"It may not be any of my business, but I'm not stupid or blind. I may only have been on the scene for five minutes but that's all I needed to know that you two obviously have something going on. So you can go on sulking into your coffee cups in the beer garden or you can march up to him and tell him how you feel and bloody well just get on with it."

"And what makes you so sure?"

"Because this whole love and hate thing you two have got going on, it ain't fooling anyone."

Tammy and I both flinched when Ellie's head poked through the sliding door.

"Sorry to interrupt, but I just thought I would let you ladies know … The Onslow Boys have arrived." Ellie winked and closed the door.

***

Tammy and I walked back towards the main bar when I paused.

"Hang on a sec, I'll be back in a minute."

"What?" Tammy said.

I pointed to my feet, and her eyes dropped to my fire engine red bunny slippers. She started to laugh.

"Fair enough."

Before I realised what I was doing, I hugged Tammy. I don't know why – maybe because beyond the physical changes she was still the girl I knew, the kind-hearted Tammy Maskala. The relief that swept over me that nothing had happened between her and Sean was overwhelming. She hugged me back.

"I'll meet you in there," she said, and she let me go with a smile.

Running in bunny slippers up a staircase was no easy task, but I managed to ditch the slippers, reline my lips with balm, check the hair and spray some Fire and Ice perfume in record time.

"Sean's downstairs."

I jumped at the unexpected voice. I spun around to see Adam leaning in my doorway munching on an apple.

"What have I told you about sneaking up on people?" I said. "And why are you telling me Sean's downstairs?"

Adam bit a big chunk out of his apple with a grin, before backing out of the door without a word.

"Adam?" I ran after him. I followed him down the stairs, trying to get him to elaborate. Instead, all I got was Adam throwing his apple core over his shoulder for me to catch.

"Ugh, Adam! You are so gross!" I juggled the apple core to the bin in the restaurant bar, grabbing for some hand soap to scrub boy slobber off my hands.

The sound of laughter echoed out from the main bar and caused my heart to slam against my chest as I built up enough courage to make a grand entrance.

I had to act cool and confident, as if nothing was amiss, as though his evening with Tammy hadn't kept me up all hours of the night, graphic images floating through my thoughts. I had to just be normal … whatever that was.

I breezed into the bar sporting my best winning smile, causing everyone to turn and look my way.

Toby, Tess, Stan, Adam, Ellie, Tammy and Ringer all looked at me like something was wrong. I then met Sean's eyes that had the same puzzled expression.

Oh, my God, did I have something on my face?

Tess broke the silence. "Someone's happy."

I scowled. Was the fact that I smiled so utterly shocking to people? Was I such a sad sack in life that the mere thought of being upbeat and perky was so hard to fathom?

"Must be love," Adam said with a wink.

I chose to ignore him entirely.

"I am happy," I shrugged. They didn't need to know that I was almost confined to a blubbering mess beforehand at the thought of Tammy and Sean.

"It must have been that joke I told you in the beer garden?" Tammy laughed.

"Oh, yeah, that was hilarious." I glared at her.

Ringer piped up. "Joke? What joke? Tell me, I love a good joke."

I went to change the subject but was distracted by Sean as he moved towards the bar, placed his empty glass on the counter, and looked directly at me.

"You ready?"

My heart stopped. "For what?"

Tammy jumped off her stool and headed over.

"Oh, Amy, I was just telling Sean that I forgot I had something on this afternoon so I can't go waterskiing. So I said you would be happy to take my place."

I stared blankly at Tammy wondering what the hell she was playing at.

"I spoke to Chris before and he has your shift covered." She sported a wide-eyed 'just go with it' look that actually freaked me out a little bit.

"Amy… waterskiing?" Adam said with a laugh. "Now that I've got to see."

"It's not a spectator sport, idiot!" I snapped.

I met Sean's serious gaze; it was as if the thought of me wanting to go waterskiing was so utterly unbelievable to him, and it was, or maybe all humour had left him because he was disappointed Tammy wasn't coming. All of a sudden, I felt really uncomfortable. Tammy had meant well, but just because she was certain she knew how I felt about Sean, how could she assume it was mutual? Because from the look he was giving me it was clear it wasn't.

"You really want to go?" he asked in all seriousness.

I swallowed, straightening my spine. "Sure."

"We're going out on the lake."

I looked around, uncomfortable with all the questions in front of an audience.

"I know," I said quietly.

Sean studied me for a long moment as if he was gauging whether or not I was telling the truth.

He shrugged. "Let's go then."

Oh shit.

***

Sean chucked me a life jacket that awkwardly engulfed my face. I wrestled it off my head and threw Sean an aggravated glare, but he was too busy whistling and clearing some space on the boat by picking up empty soft drink cans and other bits of rubbish; he was such a boy.

After quickly disposing of the evidence, he dusted his hands on his boardies and looked at me expectantly as I stood on the jetty. I clasped the life jacket across my chest like a shield, warily looking on at the sleek speedboat, bobbing on the water as Sean's heavy frame took up most of the space.

I felt like such an idiot; it was so long ago and although my near drowning was a distant memory, being back, being with Sean, washed all the underlying fear I had of this vast stretch of water right over me.

Sean stepped forward and reached his arm towards me. "Need a hand?"

I breathed deeply, reining in my emotions as an ever-increasing mountain of terror threatened to override me. I swallowed it down like a bitter pill and channelled it into something else. Determination. Not knowing how long this new feeling would last, I used it to propel me towards the boat. In one fluid movement I threw the jacket into Sean's chest with an oomph, and without much thought leapt into the boat and made my way to sit in the passenger seat before my legs gave way. I wanted to puke, I wanted to put my head between my knees in the recovery position, but as Sean sat behind the wheel beside me, I lifted my chin in defiance. I could feel his eyes on me; he was no doubt sporting a cocky grin. When nothing happened, I broke from intently looking out onto the lake like a brave warrior. Instead, my eyes flicked, confused, towards Sean, whose eyes looked wary.

"What?" I asked.

"You sure you want to do this?"

God, this was my chance to say no, to tell him I had better get back to the Onslow, and perhaps leave it for another day, set a fabricated date for some time in the New Year and then flee town. Yep, this was mercifully my chance for a blessed escape – he'd left it wide open for me to chicken out. So when "Yeah, I'm fine" fell from my mouth with the same false bravado that had lifted me into the boat in the first place, my inner monologue screamed.

The part of me that didn't want to strangle myself with the cord of the life jacket wanted to cry as Sean fired up the boat, flipping on his sunglasses and casting me a pearly white smile.

"Well, good, then. Let's go!"

***

"Sean! Stop the boat, STOP THE BOAT!"

It wasn't a car, so he couldn't just slam on the brakes and pull over to the side and let me out, but Sean worked quickly to at least slow us down.

I have to admit, to his credit, it was pretty slow and I knew it would be killing him as he shifted in his seat, looking out onto the lake, the engine purring, but he was stuck driving Miss Daisy. It took us quite a few minutes to reach out onto a clearing and soon enough the stretch of water surrounded us. My outburst had snapped Sean into instant alarm as he worked with lightning speed to stop the boat and move towards me.

"What's wrong? Do you want to go back?"

I violently shook my head, unable to take my eyes from the water. I was frozen in place, hands clasping the chair, turning my knuckles white.

It was five minutes into the journey when I had the plan, the devil on my shoulder telling me what to do. I debated on and on in a whirr of movement until finally the devil in me won and that's when I screamed for Sean to stop the boat.

"Amy?" Sean gently touched the side of my face, snapping me from my daze.

Breaking my eyes from the water, I turned to him, to his intense eyes, his forehead furrowed in concern. He shifted closer beside me, consuming the narrow space.

I looked away. I couldn't allow myself to be comforted by him, by his touch. I stood, pressing for room, making him shift aside.

"Amy, what's wrong?"

I gazed at the shoreline, my eyes transfixed on the Onslow where it rested on the crest of the hill like an emerald jewel with its painted green tin roof. From here it looked normal, no hint of what was once its dark, dank, depressing underbelly.

It taunted me up in the distance, up high on the hill, singing to me, challenging me. The Onslow had almost defeated me, but it had not succeeded. A surge of raw determination rose in me, the thought of it belonging to someone else; I couldn't let that happen. I had to fight, take a stand and suck it up, Princess. I had to face my fears, and in order to do that I had to start from the beginning. Breaking my eyes from the hotel, I stared into the murky water, stepped up, and just as I heard Sean call my name in a blind panic, I took a deep breath and dived into the water.

Chapter Forty

I sank deeper than I thought I would, not that I had given it much thought at all ... obviously.

Memories surrounded me and the all-too-familiar sensations flooded my senses as fast as the water filled my mouth. Before the same blinding panic overcame me, I struggled my way upward, kicking as hard as I could. I burst through the water, gasping for air, disorientated, struggling to keep my head from going back under.

Something grabbed the back of my shirt before moving to sweep around my stomach and started side-stroking me back towards the boat.

"Jesus Christ, Amy! What the hell?" Sean growled in my ear.

I coughed and spluttered, fighting for air. He swung me around and I instinctively latched onto the boat and clawed frantically to anchor myself. Sean's arms latched on too, caging me in protectively, my back pressed against the rapid rise and fall of his chest as I felt his breath flow heavily onto my neck.

"What the hell do you think you were doing?" he asked, dumbfounded. "Didn't get enough the first time you nearly drowned?"

I drew in a long line of glorious air before managing to gain my voice. "I was jumping in at the deep end."

Sean laughed, pressing his forehead into my shoulder. "Bloody hell, you need to come with a warning label."

I couldn't bask in the glory of my daredevil attempt to conquer my fear, I was too busy shaking uncontrollably as the adrenalin wore off and shock set in.

"You're shaking like a leaf; come on, let's get you out of this water."

Sean hitched himself onto the boat with such grace, like he had done it a million times before, no doubt. I still held onto the ledge of the boat with a fierce grip – without the press of Sean's body behind me, securing me in place, I felt incredibly vulnerable. But before I could let it worry me, he grabbed my wrists.

"Come on."

He groaned as he lifted me up and out of the lake, giving me the leverage to hook my knee onto the edge and push up and onto the boat. He did it so easily, as if I had weighed nothing more than a feather instead of a fully clothed woman, wringing wet. I stumbled into a kneeling position and a pool of lake water settled around me. I fought to keep my heart from racing and my entire body from shaking.

Sean shifted towards a metal storage box. Flipping it open he rummaged inside and retrieved a blanket. He spun around, proud as punch, and chucked it at me with a grin. The sun shone behind his massive shoulders, the rays glistening on the droplets of water that ran down his toned body – he looked like some Greek statue. It would have been enough for most girls to kneel before him and worship. Instead, I met his eyes and burst into tears.

Sean's smile fell; I saw that much before I buried my face in my hands and unashamedly, uncontrollably sobbed.

"Hey, hey, hey …" He hurried to me and gently pulled my wrists away from my face. "Oh, Christ, Amy, please don't cry. I have a blanket and a first aid kit but nothing for tears."

Sean's attempt to lighten the mood only caused me to cry more. Before the next series of chest-hitching sobs came, without a word he pulled me into his arms, holding me tight. I was engulfed in them, my head pressed against his chest. I could hear the rapid beating of his heart and I felt instantly warm, even more so when he swept the blanket around me and gently rubbed my back.

"Shhh," he whispered into my temple.

I was slowly calmed by the soothing motion of his whispers and the feel of the hypnotic circle he traced on my shoulder blades. It only took a moment to snap out of my anguish and become acutely aware of the feel of Sean's bare skin under my hands. My arms were wrapped around him, threatening to squeeze the life out of him, but I knew he could take it. It was like embracing a boulder, except instead of cool stone I felt warm flesh. His skin was so soft, my dampened cheek rested right near his heart, goose bumps formed on my flesh for a whole other reason now. My cheeks flamed as I became painfully aware of how good I allowed myself to feel in his arms. The thought completely sobered me from hysteria. I let my arms fall instead, grabbing the blanket and wrapping it around me. I shifted away from his touch. Sean lifted his arms and allowed me to go. He looked at me as if not knowing quite what to make of the crazed, chin-trembling lunatic before him.

After a long silence he moved towards the front of the boat.

"I guess we're not waterskiing today, then," he said with a gentle smile. "If you want I could take you to my lake house?" He didn't look at me when he spoke. Instead, he focused on the fuel gauge with immense concentration

"W-what?" I struggled to my feet, gripping the blanket tighter around me.

"Or I could take you back?"

The blanket entwined in my legs as I hurried forward. "No!" I all but blurted out.

Sean slung his arm on the back of the driver's chair, his eyes trailing over what must have been a somewhat dishevelled state. My eyes bloodshot from my tears, hair damp and dank from murky lake water, the grey of the blanket stained with dark, wet patches as it wrapped around me. Even though his eyes made me want to shift awkwardly under their scrutiny, I held myself there, looking back at him, keeping my spine straight.

Just when I thought Sean's icy gaze could slice into me, a small smile tugged at the corner of his mouth. "You sure?"

I pulled the hem of the fabric upwards so as to manoeuvre my way into the passenger seat next to him.

"How fast does this thing go, anyway?"

Sean's smile widened. "How fast are you willing to go?"

I felt my heart spike in not so much fear, but in a surge of excitement. Okay, there was an ounce of fear involved. I was with Sean, the same oaf that used to fling me around on rollerblades, the very same boy who used to get great delight from hearing my screams of terror. Except that was then. This boy seemed different. When he held me before, there was no joy in seeing me suffer; there was only strength and an unexpected tenderness. I quickly wiped it from my memory.

"Just get going, Grandpa."

"Grandpa?" he said incredulously.

I cringed inwardly for a moment at the potential dangers of taunting the likes of Sean. Teasing him would make him react in a way that would no doubt propel us across the water like a bat out of hell. I swallowed deeply and grasped my blanket tighter.

He turned the boat key to blast it into life, shaking his head with a laugh.

"What?" I said.

He smiled, cleaning his sunnies on his shorts before sliding them on and placing his hand on the throttle.

"You're a bloody lunatic."

Chapter Forty-One

Sean didn't go fast – well, not as fast as I'd expected he would.

Sure, he had picked up the pace, but it wasn't in a water-churning, charge of thrill-seeking, death-defiance speed. He probably thought my little episode was enough of an adventure for both of us in one day.

I still didn't feel wholly comfortable on Sean's boat, surging across the mass of water, the spray of the lake water cooling my face. Diving into the lake with a 'let's conquer my fear head on' tactic wouldn't completely erase my worries, but it had been a start in the right direction … I guess.

Sean steered the boat around a tight bend and then another. It was commonly known as S-Bend Junction and it led into the mouth of another lake system. Yeah, I know, S-Bend; it wasn't very imaginative but like most things in Onslow it was simple and to the point. We travelled out onto the widest stretch of the lake, into open water. My memory pre-empted the boat as it veered right towards the shore and tree line a little farther along the bank where I knew the Ellermans' lake house would be, or rather Sean's lake house now.

I shifted forward in my seat and the blanket fell around my waist as I became distracted by the sight in front of me. I had seen it a hundred times before – the times I'd gone fishing with Dad and my cousins we always passed by the Ellerman lake house. Those fishing trips were always kind of boring for me, talking about footy and tackle, but every time we went past the Ellermans' place, my interest piqued for a moment.

The large, two-storey house was set amidst gum trees. By way of greeting, the first thing to see as boats rumbled past was the large dock as it floated seamlessly over the water's edge. I had seen traces of envy even in my dad's eyes each time we had passed. There was no doubt that it was an impressive space and every local's dream home. Fishing, swimming parties – we had all dreamed what it would be like. Although, being a rather understated man, Mr Ellerman probably never much used the house to its full social-gathering potential. Not like I was sure Sean did.

I didn't even try to hide my goofy smile as we edged closer to the private mooring that led out across from the decked platform. Sean secured the boat to the jetty with practised ease, and I could have appreciated the view as his muscles flexed and body arched, but my attention lay elsewhere, my gaze fixed firmly on the house.

I had never been this close before and I could hardly believe I was actually going inside for a sticky beak.

My mum would be so envious; she had often talked about what the inside might be like and I couldn't wait to tell her what I found. And then, I wondered as to how I might explain that I was at Sean Murphy's house in the middle of the day, on my own, for no good reason. Maybe I'd skip telling her about it at all.

Sean helped me onto the jetty and helped me gain my land legs. I dropped the blanket and took his hand as he steadied me onto the deck.

I squinted up at the house, frowning. Something had changed about it but I couldn't quite put my finger on exactly what. I moved forward, my eyes feasting on the massive structure. Then it clicked and I spun around to face Sean.

"You've changed the windows!"

Sean was crouched near the deck, tying up his boat, his back muscles rippling under his smooth, tan skin. I was momentarily distracted from anything to do with windows before he answered.

"Indeed I have," he said, straightening to his feet. He towered over me. I suddenly felt incredibly small and surprisingly uneasy as I tried not to look at the wall of flesh I was faced with.

Sean smirked, deliberately brushing against me as he passed. I rolled my eyes. The landing wasn't that narrow; I was on to him. God, he was unreal.

I felt like an excited puppy, my six steps equal to Sean's one long stride as I followed him up towards the house. A long trail of steps curved up and around the property leading into the established garden that momentarily shielded us from the open. My skin instantly cooled in the shade of the towering gums and bottlebrushes. Stepping up onto the final landing that led towards the windows, I looked back out over the lake and my breath hitched. It was one thing to look at the lake house from below in the water, but from here, looking out, it was another thing entirely: the long stretch of glimmering water met with the distant backdrop of lush, rolling ranges.

I felt the press of Sean next to me, following my line of vision.

"Not bad, huh?" he asked.

"It's beautiful." I turned to look towards the windows, and noticed on closer inspection that they weren't actually windows. I stepped forward, touched the frames and examined them. My head snapped around to Sean who watched silently on with his arms crossed and a devilish glimmer in his eyes.

"These are doors. You put doors in?"

Sean said nothing. Instead, he bent down to the front doormat, flipped the edge up and retrieved a key. I arched my brow.

"That's not very original," I mused.

"And now you know my secret, so I may just have to kill you."

"Well, can I look at your house first?"

"Is that your final request?" He slotted the key into the lock, a dimple forming in his cheek as he smiled. My heart spiked, but I quickly put it down to the excitement of being here at the lake house, definitely not down to Sean's dimpled smile.

My focus snapped back to the doors. With great delight, Sean peeled back the wall of glass, pushing the doors sideways like a giant concertina, instantly exposing the inside to the out. What once had been aligned with large wooden latch windows had been replaced by large bi-folding doors. It had transformed the dated-looking lake house into a sleek, more modern home. I went to step inside but paused, casting my eyes down at my sodden clothes.

"Oh, um, I'm pretty wet," I said. "I don't want to make a mess." I pulled at my soppy clothing.

"I'm sure the Murray pine floors can take it."

"Holy crap, you have Murray pine flooring?" I charged inside, forgetting the wet footprints I left behind. I entered the massive open space, my eyes trailing upwards to the cathedral ceilings. I turned around in a daze as my bare feet padded on the cool, high gloss floorboards. The light that flooded through the now giant opening of the bi-folding doors shone on the flooring, making it look like glass. An imposing brick fireplace ran from ceiling to floor. I could only imagine how inviting the lake house would be in winter – hell, anytime of the year; it was simply amazing.

Sean stood casually to the side, a hint of amusement in his eyes as he watched me circle around like I was Charlie in Willy Wonka's chocolate factory.

I paused, unable to hide my confusion.

"Where's your furniture?" The living area was massive all right, even more so with the lack of any semblance of someone living there … at all. Aside from several boxes that lay in the corner, there was nothing else. Nothing. The place was empty.

Sean shrugged. "I just had the floors re-polished."

Okay, that made sense.

A faint breeze blew in off the lake. I instinctively wrapped my arms around my body.

"I think we best get you out of those clothes."

"WHAT?" I said a little bit too loudly as I spun around to face Sean, who was wickedly grinning at me, holding up his hands.

"Hey, you need to get your mind out of the gutter; I just meant you're wet. You're going to get sick if you stay in those funky clothes."

Ha! It was summer; they wouldn't take long to dry. Seeing as the word 'funky' was in Sean's vocabulary, I felt rather uneasy and wanted to secretly smell my sleeve.

Oh God, do I smell like funky lake water?

Sean disappeared for a moment and I took a chance to smell my hair and feel my arms. I had smelled better; only faint remnants of the morning's conditioner remained.

Sean came back from the hall that led out into who knew where and flung me a towel much like he had the life jacket, both of which hit me in the face.

"You can use my en suite if you want. The main bathroom is out of action."

"What's this?" I juggled my towel under my arm as I held out another piece of material I hadn't realised had been bundled with it. It was a black T-shirt with yellow piping and the emblem of a tiger on the back with 'Murphy' in block letters sprawled above it; it was an Onslow footy T.

"You can use my washer and dryer if you want. Thought you might want to be comfortable."

I looked at him warily but he said it all so matter-of-factly, no hint of amusement. It was uncomfortable. Anything other than cocky sarcasm and I wasn't quite sure how to handle it.

"Thanks," I managed.

He tilted his head behind me. "Last door at the end of the hall."

I padded along the cool, gloss floors from the bright, open light of the living area to a dark, long hallway. I would have thought that the bedrooms would have been upstairs, which intrigued me even more as to what may be above. But as I continued along, I soon discovered that it wasn't merely a hall towards a bedroom – it was like an entire wing that led off the main house. I made my way to the last door, a big, beautiful wooden door with antique brass handles. Everything in this house was grand. I tentatively opened it, expecting another empty space, so when I was met with a queen-size mattress lying on the floor, right in front of a wall of glass that looked out over the lake, I drew in a long breath. I could only imagine how wonderful it must be to wake up to such a view.

The bed covers, bottle-green sheets and burgundy and green plaid doona, were all askew and unmade. There was an indentation still visible on the pillow where Sean had slept. I wanted to reach out and touch it, but thought better of it. Aside from a lamp that rested on the floor next to the bed, the only other furniture was a rustic chair that sat in the corner piled high with clothes.

I shook my head. *Such a boy!*

I opened the only other door, which I assumed was the en suite.

Wow. Now *this* was grand! It would have been quite the luxurious bathroom suite back in the seventies: gold tap fixtures, an avocado sink and retro-patterned, mission-brown tiles that covered the walls from floor to ceiling. It was an assault on the eyes. But it was large, with a his-and-hers sink that gave me space to unload my cargo. A skylight prevented the dark colours from overpowering the space and provided enough natural light for me to take in my reflection.

I flinched back. *Holy sweet Mary, Mother of God!*

My hair had started to dry into a matted, dreadlocked mess and to say that my attire made me look like I had been dragged through a hedge backwards was a massive understatement. I couldn't peel my clothes off quickly enough and hop into the shower. Scrubbing the grimy lake water off with a cake of Imperial Leather soap, I praised God that Sean had a stock of conditioner.

After running my fingers through the knotted tendrils of my hair and towelling it dry, I stood back to look at my new reflection. I was swamped by Sean's massive T-shirt, which swam on me to the knees. If only my mother could see me now. I wrapped my towel and sodden clothes together and crept back into the living room. Sean was nowhere to be seen. I wanted to find out where the laundry was.

Where is he?

My eyes rested on Sean's back through the opening of the doors. He was standing under a cascade of flowing water from an open shower on the deck. In a hypnotic, circular motion, he ran a cake of soap along his chest and pushed his head forward, letting the water fall across the back of his neck. His eyes were closed. I stood, frozen to the spot – my only movement was my teeth involuntarily digging into my bottom lip. I couldn't take my eyes off him as he moved his shoulder blades from side to side under the water. The shower sprayed a massaging cascade across his broad back, then turned into the stream above his head.

I swallowed deeply. Clasping my bundle tightly I was about to turn and look for the laundry by myself, but then Sean's eyes flicked up and locked onto mine.

Sprung!

Chapter Forty-Two

"Laundry?" I all but screamed out in a high-pitched question.

Sean smiled, the big, broad, tooth-exposing kind.

So embarrassing.

He pointed to the opposite hall.

I all but ran toward the hall, scurrying through multiple doors that led to the wrong room. *Seriously, how big is this freaking house?*

I finally found the laundry room, which was ludicrously large for just washing clothes. It was long and narrow and also dated with sleek, seventies yellow tiles that had been ripped off the wall midway in what I could only guess was the beginning of Sean's handiwork.

I unloaded my clothes into the washer and thanks to an easy-to-find bucket of laundry powder I had my sodden clothes flooded with cold water and churning in no time. I was lost, staring down at the hypnotic winding of the washing machine, when a pair of shorts sailed over my head and landed in the recess.

I dropped the lid and spun around to see Sean standing in the doorway with a white towel wrapped low around his waist. I swallowed deeply, squared my shoulders and acted as if I hadn't been perving on him only moments before. I made a cool, confident line to brush past him and return to the main living area. He made no effort to move so my shoulder skimmed across his bare chest. I made a distinct effort not to look, but could only imagine his cocky grin broadening like the Cheshire cat.

Idiot!

***

My clothes finished their short cycle. I placed them in the dryer and Sean finally gave me the grand tour (after he had mercifully put some clothes on).

Making our way up to the last of the stairs, we reached a massive landing with a big arched window that looked out onto the lake.

"The rooms up here have the best views," Sean said, remaining on the top step as I wandered into the room.

Like a bug to light I walked to the window and pressed my fingers to the cool glass, gazing out over the rippling lake that sparkled, sunrays bouncing off the water.

"I'll say," I said. A foggy mist formed against the glass as I pressed my face against it.

I turned to Sean who still hadn't moved from the staircase.

Is he crazy?

"Why don't you have your room up here?"

It then dawned on me, as it should have when we walked up the staircase: Sean walked with his shoulder pressed against the wall, the fabric of his shirt gliding against the surface. He didn't even step onto the landing, which took me back to the Onslow balcony where he had been paralysed with fear.

"Let me guess. Heights?" I said.

"Let's just say it's not my favourite part of the house." Sean crossed his arms and leaned heavily against the wall.

"Why did you buy a two-storey house, then?" I laughed.

"Because I wanted it," he said in all seriousness.

"Really?" I asked. "And do you always get what you want?" I crossed my arms, mirroring his stance.

Sean's lips curved into that infamous devilish grin. "Always."

"Did you want Tammy to come with you on the boat instead of me?" The words had tumbled out of my mouth before I could stop them, and this time I had nowhere to escape. I was pinned by his unwavering gaze; it was as if he was almost taken back by the question. He shifted uncomfortably, the usual confident, cocky facade melting away. My heart threatened to stop, too mortified to go on as I took his silence as a *yes*.

Instead, he looked back up at me. "We would be skiing at MacLean's by now instead of doing laundry," he said.

I inwardly cringed, breaking from his eyes. "Yeah, sorry about that."

Sean smiled. "It wouldn't be anywhere near as entertaining, though."

His smart-arse confidence had returned.

"Yeah, yeah," I said. "I'm a lunatic; tell me something I don't know." I turned back to the window. I couldn't believe that I was standing in this grand lake house. Furthermore, it didn't seem real that Sean was only in his mid-twenties and the owner of such prime real estate. It was amazing, but I would never tell him that – his head was big enough as it was.

Sean was self-made wealthy; I could respect that. I respected it more than my current situation. Deferred uni procrastinator living with Mummy and Daddy and still, at the age of nineteen, receiving a ludicrously generous allowance. Still sleeping in my childhood bedroom and keeping secrets from my parents so I wouldn't get in trouble.

I was a real catch.

All of a sudden I didn't feel the need to look over every aspect of the house anymore; if anything, looking around the house only made me more depressed. I wasn't jealous of Sean – he deserved to enjoy the fruits of his labour; he worked hard and played hard. But me, I scrubbed down a cool room and I thought the world was against me? I needed to get a grip – if I wanted something to succeed I needed to stop bitching about it and just do it.

"What's going on in that head of yours, Henderson?" Sean asked.

I broke away from looking out at the breathtaking views. Sean was missing out big time with his phobia.

I smiled at Sean, which seemed to make him warier, more guarded.

"I think a break away from the Onslow is just what I needed," I said. "I'm going to go back with a clear head."

"And clean clothes," Sean added.

"A clean slate."

"I think that dip in the Onslow knocked some sense into you."

"Maybe," I said with a smirk.

"That or the lack of oxygen."

"I wasn't under the water for *that* long."

Sean half turned to walk down the stairs. "I didn't mean the lake."

I frowned at him, confused.

"I saw you watching me shower on the deck." His grin was now cheesy, infuriating. "You practically stopped breathing."

"Oh, pa-lease," I scoffed, begging myself not to blush. "I was checking out the outdoor scenery. You were actually in my way, *as usual*."

I overtook him on the stairs and flashed him an annoyed look as I went by.

I was seriously over my stay at Chateau Murphy – clothes dry or not, I was out of here. I had a hotel to save.

"Do you always bite your lip when you admire nature?"

I went to retaliate but thought better of it. *Christ! Had I been biting my lip? Frack it!* Trust him to catch me – now I would never live it down.

"So how long will my clothes take?" I asked as we headed towards the laundry, side by side.

He tugged at my baggy Onslow footy T. "What do you want them for? I think this looks good on you."

"Uh, yeah, I don't think so."

"You think it might raise some eyebrows if I were to drop you off in that?"

"Unless you have a serious death wish I think I'd better hang until my clothes are ready. Besides …" I smiled sweetly, "I support the Perry Panthers, not the Onslow Tigers."

"Ouch! You mean to say you're a Perry Penguin fan?" he teased. "That's just wrong!"

"Oh, and you're not biased or anything, are you, Sean Murphy?"

"I am, one hundred percent biased and you should be, too; you're a born and bred Onslowian. Where's the loyalty?" Sean seemed genuinely horrified about my betrayal of the Onslow Tigers.

I peered in at the laundry to find the dryer still rumbling, spinning the load. I propped myself on the bench to wait it out.

"What do you care? You don't play for them anymore, anyway."

Sean's demeanour iced over – it seemed I'd hit a nerve.

I had a vague memory of overhearing conversations about Sean's sudden end with football.

Before I could stop myself I asked, "Why did you stop playing?"

Sean's expression became uncharacteristically sullen. He thought for a moment, as if searching for the right words. He reached for the hem of his shorts and lifted his knee up onto the counter next to me and pointed to a scar. "My war wound."

Without thinking I reached out and traced my finger along the faint pink scar. "What happened?"

Sean didn't move his leg; he was frozen, watching me trace the line down and then up again slowly over the puckered flesh. He swallowed deeply and opened his mouth to speak but must have changed his mind again. Just as I thought he was about to say something, we were interrupted by the beeping of the dryer. He snapped out of his daze and I drew my hand away.

He walked over to the dryer. "It's over," he said, still serious.

"What, your footy career or the load?" I teased, in an attempt to lighten the mood.

Sean turned his back to me and wrenched open the dryer, gathering up the clean clothes.

"Both," he said and slammed the door shut.

Wow. Note to self: don't mention footy.

Sean handed me the warm pile of clothes and I placed it on the bench. I grabbed my T-shirt first to flick it out before the creases set in.

"Oh. My. God."

"What?" Sean frowned.

I held the T-shirt against my body. It was now only big enough to fit a five-year-old. I quickly grabbed for my shorts and they, too, were a shrunken shadow of their former selves.

"What happened?" Sean laughed.

"What does it look like? They've shrunk!" I cried in dismay, holding up the pieces of fabric in horror.

I had been so impatient, so distracted I hadn't even thought about it. I flicked out the tag to read the words out loud: "Do not tumble dry."

I banged my forehead on the overhead cupboard once, twice, three times.

"So, no MacLean's Beach, then?" Sean said, trying not to smile.

"Definitely not."

"Do you think you could make up an excuse for me and just take me home?" I pouted.

"I didn't have any grand illusions you would actually be out there waterskiing with the masses, Amy."

"I know, I just thought I could make an appearance."

"You still could." Sean smiled, letting his eyes roam over my attire. "You look pretty good to me."

Against my better judgment, I smiled back. "Yeah, I'm sure all the people at the boat ramp are going to think so, too." I cringed at the very thought of trying to make my way from the jetty back to the hotel in Sean's massive, baggy T-shirt.

"Relax, I'll drive you back." Sean moved towards the door.

"Really?"

"Really."

He stopped in the hall, turning back to face me. "What's in it for me, though?"

I paused. "What do you mean?"

"Well, you know all about fair trade and all, and this is a favour, so you kind of owe me one in return." His eyes twinkled deviously.

I swallowed, trying not to lose my cool as I eyeballed him directly. "Well, what do you want?"

His lips twitched into a small, crooked curve. He looked up to the ceiling, deep in thought. "Hmm," he said, "what *do* I want?"

My heart beat faster as he dragged the moment out. He finally ended the torture and exposed his brilliant line of white teeth with a wink.

"I'll let you know."

Chapter Forty-Three

Mercifully only Chris and Max were around when Sean dropped me off. But still, I didn't want them seeing me, either, especially not Chris.

"Just pull in around the back," I said, my eyes darting across the car park.

Sean grinned from ear to ear as he watched me fidget nervously in my seat.

"You don't have to enjoy this so much." I glowered at him.

"What was that? Drop you off out the front?"

"*Don't you dare!*"

It was my only hope that no one was loitering in the beer garden or still finishing up some tasks left over from the working bee. I had devised a clear-cut, meticulous plan for Sean to drop me off by the back entrance so I could cut through the beer garden and scarper through the back entrance and up the back staircase and be fully dressed again with no one the wiser. I prayed the door had been left unlocked. *God, please let it be open.*

Sean turned the ute to the right to sweep around the back and he slowly pulled to a stop under a big towering gum that shielded us from the blistering sun.

He killed the engine but kept his arm casually slung over the wheel, his eyes trailing over my attire with an air of amusement.

I folded my arms and tilted my head, combatting his amusement with a dirty look.

He snickered and shook his head. "It always seems that every time I bring you home you're missing some article of clothing. Shoes. Shorts. Shirt. Seems to be a pattern with you."

"Only around you it is," I said.

"I can't help it if you can't keep your clothes on around me," he teased.

"Oh, ha ha!" I said sarcastically. "So Tammy Maskala went home unscathed, then?"

Sean's eyes narrowed, all humour disappearing from his face. "What's with all the Tammy questions?"

"Nothing; just seemed like you two hit it off last night." I looked back out of the window, suddenly finding the roof line fascinating.

"Well, we played pool," he said.

"Really badly," I threw in.

"Really badly." He nodded. "And then I went home. I had to give a bloke a quote this morning and fix up some roof flashing that moved in that storm we had a few weeks ago … but why am I explaining all this to you?" he said in frustration.

An awkward silence filled the cabin. I could see in my peripheral vision Sean staring at me as I looked down into my lap. Why was I asking these questions? Why did I always shoot him a sarcastic jab about all the girls he would be rendezvousing with, or who he chose to invite into his house? It wasn't exactly like he cared if Stan had walked me to my bedroom or anything – he hadn't asked, so he obviously didn't care.

I breathed in a sigh of relief, grateful that Tammy hadn't talked me into anything as ridiculous as telling Sean how I felt. Not that I knew exactly how I felt. I knew I didn't like Sean looking or speaking to Tammy, and anytime he got close to her I could feel my blood boiling under the surface. Tammy had obviously suspected something in the five minutes she had been on the scene, and Adam made no secret in taunting me any chance he had. Chris and Mum certainly didn't approve of us hanging out.

"Why do you care what I do, Amy?" Sean asked seriously. It was so direct, so unexpected. He wasn't playing games, he was calling my bluff.

My face flamed and I wished the ground would open up so I didn't have to answer him. Maybe I really was that spoilt, immature little girl who used to loiter on the stairs and eavesdrop on everyone's private business. Maybe I was just a busybody by nature and that's why I had to know.

But I knew that was a lie. Above all, I *did* want to know about Sean and what he was doing and who he was with. I held my breath every night hearing the front door of the bar open and secretly hoped he would walk in. In the beginning he had annoyed me, infuriated me to the point where I wanted nothing more than to get away from him. But I never really did. I didn't want to admit it, but I was desperately addicted to Sean Murphy and I didn't know how to process that revelation.

The one thing I would do for myself now to stop from feeling so exposed was to lie through the skin of my teeth.

I met his eyes, unblinking. I replied in all seriousness, "I *don't* care what you do." Of all the lies I had been telling of late, that was the biggest one of all.

I thought he might have said, "Good!" Or at least nodded his head, or sagged in relief at my admission, but his stone-like expression never changed; he didn't even so much as blink as he looked at me.

Instead, he reached out, gathering a fist full of fabric of the black, baggy T, and pulled on it.

"Come here," he said, low and demanding. I sat frozen, my mouth dry as my eyes flicked to his hand and then back up to his face. I swallowed deeply.

My mind was fuzzy, desperate to work but it couldn't. When I made no move, didn't pull away in my moment of confusion, I felt the fabric of my top pull tighter. Sean slid closer, pulling me to him as he leaned forward. Removing his hand from the wheel he cupped the back of my neck and covered my mouth with his. I exhaled a long lingering breath as I melted against his body, the slack of my shirt loosening as I slid closer into him. I grabbed the fabric of his shirt in my fist and drew him closer. His tongue teased ever so gently inside my mouth, giving it to me but not his all; it was as if he was dancing, a promise of things yet to come. He let go of my shirt and slid his hand around my waist along my back, causing a tingly sensation across my skin as I knew I wore nothing more than his silky, baggy footy shirt and my knickers.

It was an insanely erotic thought that I felt so exposed to him and yet so utterly shielded under the dark canopy of the gum tree. A moan escaped my lips as his tongue finally pushed deeper into my mouth. I felt him smile against my lips, pleased with my response. Just as I pushed myself into him, silently pleading for more, he slowly drew away. His eyes burned into mine before they fell to my mouth, watching my shallow breaths escape past my kiss-swollen lips. His own breath laboured and I almost felt that I could die and go to heaven when his tongue ran across his lower lip as if savouring the taste of me.

"Now tell me you don't care," he said, his voice low and raspy.

I straightened in the passenger seat, looking directly into his smug, brilliant blue eyes. "I don't," I said, none too convincingly.

Sean leaned back against his seat, laughter escaping him as he shook his head at me.

"Typical pig-headed, stubborn Henderson," he said.

My mouth gaped. "That will be the last time you insult my family name, Sean Murphy."

"Or what?" He quirked a brow.

I smiled wickedly and leaned forward. "Or I'll bar you from the pub."

He shook his head. "You wouldn't do that."

I mirrored him with the curve of my brow. "Oh, wouldn't I?"

He reached out and slowly ran his thumb over the seam of my lips. "Life would be dull without me."

I fought not to bite my lip at the hypnotic feel of his thumb gently caressing my lips. I had to blink to focus. "No, it wouldn't," I whispered, my chest rising in small, shallow breaths.

Sean looked pleased with himself, working me like I was putty in his hands. "Fair enough. Run back to your tower, little Amy Henderson. I won't bother you tonight."

"Aren't you coming for lunch?" I said all too quickly, disappointment spiking through me.

He shook his head. "I have a job."

"But we're testing out the new menu," I said incredulously.

"It's for a mate. You know what they say," he started up the engine with a boyish grin, "no rest for the wicked."

I truly believed that, because as far as wicked was concerned Sean was the President, Vice President and Treasurer of Wicked, and that was based solely on his lip service. My heart raced at the memory of his tongue in my mouth.

"Well, what about tonight?" I tried to opt for casual, but I could hear myself, how I sounded. I knew I was coming across just like all the other needy girls. Maybe I had been too harsh to judge all the girls that pawed over Sean; maybe they had been kissed by him and needed a hit like it was their drug of choice. I had actually felt pity for them, but more so for myself. What had I become?

"The boys are coming over tonight for a few beers; do you want to come?" My heart spiked at the invitation. I fought not to leap and shout a resounding, 'Hell, yes!'

"I'm working tonight, but if it doesn't get too late I might come out." I shrugged.

"All right." He smirked and put the ute in gear. "You better go before someone sees you and assumes you're an Onslow Tiger supporter."

"Heaven forbid." I laughed and slid out of the ute and slammed the door closed.

Sean shook his head in dismay. "Such a traitor."

I stepped backwards, lost in the moment of watching him back out and turn the wheel. He locked eyes with me and saluted before he pulled around and headed back to the front and down Coronary Hill. I gave a small wave and watched the dust cloud settle and listened to the sound of his engine fade off into the distance. I stood there for the longest time, trying to unravel what exactly had just happened, before I edged my way through the gate into the beer garden. I touched my lips in deep thought, smiling. I had kissed Sean Murphy, or, more to the point, he had kissed me.

He. Kissed. Me. Holy crap!!

I laughed to myself before swinging around the bottom staircase and quickstepping up the stairs, giddy and happy at the unexpectedness of the day's events. I didn't know, however, just how unexpected they would become as I stopped still at the sound of my name.

"Hold it right there, Amy Henderson!"

Chapter Forty-Four

Any feeling of stomach-tingling excitement over what had gone on only a mere moment before was ripped out from under me with such gut-wrenching force, I thought I must have misheard, or maybe I had dreamed it? But as I slowly turned to gaze down at the bottom of the stairs, the reality hit me like a ton of bricks.

"Mum?"

There she stood, her arms crossed and shooting icicles with her cool, blue eyes.

I hesitantly descended the stairs. "What are you doing here?"

Her hard gaze trailed over my attire. Of all the people in the world to catch me like this, my mother had to be *the* worst. I would have sooner run into Chris or the entire Onslow Tigers footy team.

"You're early." I smiled weakly. "By a whole week."

"We thought we would surprise you," Mum said coolly, her perfectly manicured brow arching.

Well, it had worked – *surprise*! As in nearly giving me cardiac arrest surprise. Normally by now my mum would be flinging her arms around me, her gold bangles jingling with every movement as I was suffocated by the hovering cloud of her expensive French perfume. But she hadn't budged, she just stared me down.

My heart pounded; surely she hadn't seen me in the car with Sean? I discreetly flicked my eyes out towards the entrance and breathed a small sigh of relief. You couldn't see beyond the thick canopy of ivy, even from my vantage point on the stairs. I inwardly thanked Dad's mates for not being too heavy-handed with the trimming at the working bee.

"Where's Dad?" I lifted my voice, aiming for light and breezy, hoping that if I didn't play into my mum's mood, or acknowledge my state of dress, it would cease to be an issue. No such luck.

"He's inside, talking to Chris and the apparent new staff member that was put on without our knowledge."

Crap!

He was already in there, talking – there was no chance to corroborate any story with Chris or Adam or *anyone*.

The jig was up.

"Um, look, I better get ready, there's a booking for lunch that I'm a part of."

"As in your friends? Chris mentioned it."

"Um, yeah, it's a kind of a get-together." I wanted to say as a private celebratory drink for all the hard work we'd put in, but I didn't want to say anything until I had spoken to Dad.

"Well, I wouldn't bother, I told Chris to cancel it. Your father and I want to settle in. You can catch up with your friends another time."

"They wouldn't be in anyone's way," I said. "You had no right to—"

"For God's sake, Amy, this is not a holiday camp, and although it seems that you have been treating it as such, it is still a place of business."

My mouth gaped open. She had cancelled my lunch plans so she could preciously kick back in their apartment? An apartment that would be uninhabitable if I hadn't have scrubbed and cleaned and washed and repaired it. The very fact that she had accused me and my friends of leeching off the Onslow made my eyes burn with such anger that I clenched my fists and met her stare dead on.

"Are you kidding me? You don't know anything," I bit out.

Mum's brows rose in surprise before creasing back into a hard line.

"What I do know is you better make yourself decent and change out of *Sean Murphy's* top before your father sees you."

For a moment I thought she was telepathic and then I inwardly cringed at the memory that 'Murphy' was plastered across my back with the number nine, Sean's old footy number. I might as well have had a bright fluoro arrow pointing to me, flashing 'SEAN'.

My mum shook her head. "Honestly, Amy, I am so disappointed in you." And with that. she unfolded her arms and walked away, leaving me on the stairs feeling like I was that sixteen-year-old girl getting banished all over again.

***

There was no way I could perform damage control on my own. Adam was out with everyone at MacLean's still, poor Chris was probably getting drilled by Mum and Dad downstairs, and they were no doubt humiliating me in front of him. I could just imagine it now.

"*I should have known better; she has done nothing but lounge around since she deferred uni.*"

"Sleep all day, party all night; it's time she got her life together."

I squeezed my eyes closed, breathing deeply. There was nothing for it: I had to face the music and if it meant telling them a few home truths, then so be it. I had done all I had to protect Dad. I had fought to save the Onslow – it looked a billion times better than it had when I'd arrived, and business was slowly picking up again.

But if they could only see what they wanted to see, that I was frivolous and irresponsible and off gallivanting with boys rather than working in the pub, well, I couldn't help that. Mum had come in with dagger eyes for her huge disappointment of a daughter; but what I really needed was to talk to Dad, and alone. I didn't hold out much hope as I changed into some cutoff jeans and a singlet top, scooping my hair up into a high ponytail. My concentration faltered as I heard a knock on my bedroom door. At first I half expected Chris's grim face to peek through the crack as he unleashed how much trouble we were in, so when I saw my dad stick his head in the door, I let my arms fall slowly from adjusting my hair as I warily watched him step into my room.

As soon as his grey eyes settled on me, he smiled.

"G'day, Chook."

It was a sentiment and warmth that had me remembering the Dad of old. There was no malice or anger behind his words.

I hadn't realised I had been holding my breath until that point, but as soon as he said my nickname I let all my defences down and quickly closed the distance between us. I threw my arms around him and burst into tears.

"Hey, hey, hey, what's all this?" Dad rubbed my shoulders.

I pulled back, wiping my eyes as I tried to speak, but the words were just a series of nonsensical noises. I felt like a child who had just fallen over and was too wracked with shock and sorrow to explain what had happened.

"Amy, come on, love, sit down." Dad sat on the edge of my bed and motioned for me to sit beside him. I did. He gently rubbed me on the back, his soft, grey eyes pained to see me upset – it made me want to cry even more. I knew how Dad didn't deal with me or Mum crying at all and it was the one thing that gave me the strength to pull myself together before he joined me in sympathy. Dad was hopeless like that.

"What's with all the waterworks? Did you miss your old man that much?" Dad tried for light and jokey, but it did little to raise anything more than a weak smile from me as I brushed away the tendrils of hair that had fallen from my ponytail.

"Dad, I don't even know where to begin," I said with a sniff.

Dad squeezed my hand. "How about at the beginning?"

***

It felt like I had talked forever as my dad sat and patiently listened to everything I unloaded. From the way I had come home to find the place in such a shocking state, to find the Onslow wasn't even open most of the time under Matt's management. I even told him how I had fallen through the balcony and how Sean had been an integral part in helping me. I told him how Chris and Adam had come to the call as had all of my friends and even Dad's friends. Because we all loved the Onslow.

I told him about how we had all pulled together to bring it back to the way it should be, the way it was. I even told him about Melba, knowing she would be mad at me for doing so, but I was tired of secrets. With each confession, it was like a weight had been lifted off my shoulders.

With every piece of information, as it all spilled out, I saw my dad's face become grimmer and grimmer, the colour practically draining from his complexion.

That's when I stopped, remembering how Dad shouldn't be exposed to stress. I bit my lip and fell silent.

My dad was silent too, thoughtful as he rubbed his brow.

He sighed. "Is that all?"

"Isn't that enough?" I asked.

Dad patted my knee. "It's enough, Chook, it sure is enough."

"I'm sorry I didn't tell you," I said, sniffing and wiping my bloodshot eyes.

My dad's eyes met mine. "Don't be sorry, Chook, I'm the one that's sorry. I put too much trust in the wrong people for my own selfish reasons. I was too caught up thinking I was helping my family but all I did in the long run was hurt them."

I squeezed Dad's hand. "I don't blame you, Dad. You're a Henderson, remember? As I've been told a lot lately, we're pig-headed and stubborn. You just have to learn to reach out for help when you need it – there's no loss of pride in that."

Dad looked at me, as if he was seeing me for the very first time. "You've done an incredible job. When your mother said she wanted to come up here I was braced for a lecture on how I had let the place go. But when I pulled up in that drive ..."

"The newly re-stoned drive," I added.

Dad smiled. "The newly re-stoned drive," he corrected, "I thought I was dreaming. I haven't seen this place sparkle since my grandfather owned it. Your mother didn't understand my emotion but as I walked in the front bar and saw the shine on the windows, the gloss of the bar ... it felt like the days of old." He shook his head. "It was magic, Amy."

I smiled, thinking how I would have loved to have seen his reaction.

"Furthermore ..." Dad stood. "I think it's safe to say you saved my marriage. One look at the apartment or the downstairs kitchen would have earned me divorce papers." He laughed.

"Yeah, well, it's not you Mum's angry with," I said.

"Leave it to me, Chook; she just needs to be set straight on a few home truths first. And that's up to me to do. I've been keeping too many secrets and that can't be too good for the old ticker."

"It seems like we are on an even keel when it comes to keeping secrets," I mused.

"Well, how about we agree to an open-book policy from now on, hey?"

"Deal." I smiled. My heart swelled with hope, the way Dad had described the Onslow as magic. Every ounce of blood, sweat and tears I had poured into this place, I couldn't have been more proud of what we had achieved. What *I* had achieved.

"I love you, Dad."

"I love you, too."

Chapter Forty-Five

Mum and Dad had retired to their apartment for the afternoon.

With my lunch plans cancelled it gave me a chance to savour my thoughts on what exactly had unravelled today. Walking through the restaurant, I waved at Melba, who smiled from across the dining room as she set a table with cutlery.

I froze. A new-found dread swept over me. She didn't know.

I casually stepped into the main bar.

"Chris," I whispered.

The cool room door flew open. Chris carried a slab out to the main bar and I flapped my arms about, waving him over dramatically.

He placed the slab on the bar. "What?" He frowned at me as he broke the plastic open.

"Has anyone told Melba that Dad is back?"

Chris froze mid-unpack, his eyes locking with mine.

My shoulders sagged. "Oh, shit!"

Without another word, Chris and I hightailed it towards the restaurant, but just as we were about to enter, Chris grabbed my arm and pulled me back.

We were too late.

The sound of muffled voices filtered through from beyond the divider. Chris stepped past me and peered through the crack of the partition.

"What's going on?" I whispered. After a moment I pushed past Chris to see for myself. There was Dad, standing in front of a very unhappy Melba. He had no doubt come down to grab a drink or something and they had probably given each other the fright of their lives.

Chris and I stood back, grimacing at each other.

"Just as well our lunch was cancelled," I said.

"Better leave them to it," Chris said as we slowly walked back to the main bar.

I wanted to stay and spy on them but I thought better of it.

I hadn't even had a chance to get Chris's version of what had happened when Mum and Dad had first walked through the door. I was suddenly oh, so grateful that I hadn't been working this afternoon … and then my mind switched back to what I had been doing instead. I had been making out with Sean Murphy. I was glad I hadn't been here, for once.

I must thank Tammy big time for her initiative.

The bar door was flung open and a familiar chorus of voices trailed into the main bar. Adam, Ellie, Toby, Tess, Stan and Ringer all piled in, sun-kissed and damp from their morning spent at MacLean's Beach.

"There she is," said Toby.

"Amy, where have you been? I thought you were coming to MacLean's?" Tess asked, her eyes soft with concern.

"Sorry, I got a bit sidetracked."

I could have told them that I had gone to Sean's instead, followed by a heavy make-out session since that's what had had me truly distracted … but I decided to skip that part.

I leaned in, lowering my voice. "Dad's back."

The stunned silence was contagious; it almost made me laugh, especially as Ringer slowly looked up to the ceiling as if expecting the vision of my father to appear from his apartment.

"Holy shit," Adam said. "They're early."

"Did he say anything?" Ellie asked.

"Well, lunch is cancelled."

"Yeah, we got that message," said Stan, holding up his phone.

"Well, I told Dad everything and he was really good about it, but as far as Mum goes … I'm going to leave it for a day or two, let them settle in. At a guess, I think everything seems to be okay." I breathed out.

"Are they still going to put the Onslow on the market?" Toby asked in all seriousness.

I looked expectantly at Chris, who only shrugged in response.

"I haven't touched on that yet, but I am pretty hopeful. Dad was blown away by what we've done so I think it will be okay."

"Well, that's cause for a drink," announced Ringer as he moved towards the bar. All weary, sullen faces soon melted into old, familiar smiles as I rounded the bar to help out Chris and everyone lined up for drinks.

Just as the trash talk began about who had stacked it on the lake and who was the champion waterskiier, Toby's mobile rang.

"Sean! What's up, mate?"

I stiffened. My eyes instantly flew to Toby at the mention of Sean's name.

"Yeah, no, you're right, there was a change of plans; we're not having lunch now."

My concentration faltered as I caught Tess eyeing me as she thoughtfully chewed on the straw of her drink. I quickly busied myself by filling up a pot of beer for Stan.

"So, a slab of VB? Yeah, no worries, fix me up later. Do you want anything else? All right, no dramas. See you tonight." Toby pressed 'End', tucking his mobile back in his pocket.

"Drink orders from our gracious host," Toby said.

"You guys coming?" Ellie asked Chris and I.

"Shouldn't be a late one here – we'll be there." Chris said.

It was the first time Chris had ever spoken for me as an attendee. I was impressed – maybe things were finally changing.

"Don't go thinking you can write yourself off tonight just because your mum and dad are home to hold the fort, though," Chris said to me in all seriousness.

I knew it had been too good to be true. Chris always was the big brother I never had. Or ever wanted.

***

As our friends drank, Chris and I kept an ear out to the conversation in the dining room. We all listened, waited, until we were certain Dad had gone back up to the apartment. As soon as we heard the heavy-footed steps stomp up the stairs, everyone rushed towards the restaurant, elbowing and nudging each other out of the way, fighting for pole position to see what was going on. Chris cut them off at the pass, motioning for everyone to cool it as he pressed his finger to his lips for silence. He then motioned me forward and pushed me through the partition. I stumbled into the restaurant … Real smooth.

Melba had her back to me as she flicked a tablecloth out over a table. The sign that she was still in the building was surely a good one. I tentatively crept towards her, wary, extra nervous, since I had an audience.

I cleared my throat and Melba paused briefly before continuing what she was doing.

"You can tell them all to come in if they want," she said. "Herd of elephants thundering around. Honestly, I could have heard you lot all the way from Perry."

I turned to glare at the partition that slowly peeled open as they stepped sheepishly into the restaurant. Chris came and stood beside me.

I shook my head at him. "Remind me never to do a bank job with you lot."

Chris just shrugged his shoulders.

"Everything okay, Melbs?" I asked.

"Why wouldn't it be?" She moved to the next table and flapped the tablecloth in the air before spreading it evenly across the wood.

"So, you and Dad …"

"He is as pig-headed and self-centred as ever," she bit out.

Oh dear, this is bad.

Her sharp eyes narrowed on me before briefly softening. "And never in my life have I ever seen that man admit he was wrong or say he was sorry."

My shoulders slumped. She was right: he was as stubborn as a mule when it came to admitting defeat; maybe there was something in people saying I was my father's daughter.

"Never in all my life," she said, "but today … he did both." Her eyes had a light sheen to them.

Chris and I looked at each other as if we had both mistaken what Melba had just said.

"I don't know what's happened to that man since he's been gone – detoxing, health scare … maybe seeing this place brought back to life, who knows? But any man who knows when he's wrong and *says* he's wrong, well, that's the kind of man I want to work for."

"Dad apologised?" A smile broadened across my face. "So you're staying?" I tried not to get too overwhelmed by the possibility.

Melba suppressed her own smile as she continued to work. "Try to get rid of me."

We all grinned like fools, relieved that whatever had been exchanged between Dad and Melba was a means to a peaceful resolution. Maybe Dad had changed, and if this was a sample of what the new, improved Dad might be like, then I approved.

In all the confusion, no one had thought to relay to the McGees that our lunch had been cancelled, but in true good-natured spirit they soldiered on anyway and worked instead on surprise feeding Mum and Dad with samples of the new menu. A none-too-subtle work of genius on their part to show my parents how well the kitchen was functioning. Of course, the McGees weren't going to be able to run things forever, but that was where Melba came in. She had spoken of a lady and daughter she'd met through the local Rotary Club who were looking for kitchen work. A shy, single mum of five who had worked as a shearer's cook and in RSL clubs around the state; and her daughter Penny was sixteen and looking for some part-time work around school. Melba had scheduled to give them a trial next weekend, but she said they were keen to be trialled mid-week.

It was all coming together: Max was working out behind the bar, and judging from the polished plates that came down from upstairs, it seemed Mum and Dad approved of the menu.

Mid-afternoon I crept up the stairs towards my room, thinking I would just let Mum and Dad be. Everyone had gone home and I wanted to take a moment for myself in all the chaos that had unfolded in such a short amount of time – nearly drowning, lake house tour, a hot pash with Sean Murphy, Mum and Dad's unexpected arrival and teary confession. I was exhausted. I'd thought this was just going to be a night like any other.

I crept past the apartment and closed my door behind me, leaning against it with a sigh. Now Mum and Dad were home it almost felt like a weight had been lifted, like I could go back to being a young person again and enjoy the summer like I was supposed to have been doing. Sean's Onslow Tigers polo shirt lay crumpled on my bed where I had thrown it earlier as I had rushed to get changed. I picked it up, tracing the embroidered lines of 'Murphy' across the back where it would display bold and proud across his broad shoulders.

A small smile tugged at the corner of my mouth as I lifted the jersey to my face and inhaled the fabric; it was crisp and clean. I was disappointed because it didn't smell like him. Sean's cologne was always intoxicatingly sharp and musky. Not that I had never wanted to admit he smelled so amazing.

There were a lot of things I didn't want to admit about Sean Murphy. About how my heart rate would spike when he walked into a room; how, even though he absolutely infuriated me, I got such a thrill whenever he was near. I didn't want to admit the comfort I took from his presence, and in his arms, at times when it meant nothing more than just that: being my rock. And he always was – without ever asking, he was there. I had let down my barriers, new feelings flooded me, but there was still an overriding emotion that I couldn't shake.

Fear.

Everything was panning out so smoothly, but what if what had happened today with Sean was simply what happens with Sean?

He kisses a girl and then moves on, no strings attached, just a bit of fun. I had seen it time and time again as he had left the pub with a different girl each night, a trail of lovesick, zombie-like girls clawing at his heels, pawing after him.

I didn't want to be one of those girls, deliberately trying to catch his attention, hoping against hope that he would find it in his heart to so much as smile my way or say hello.

Had kissing Sean been a huge mistake? Would it change the relationship we had with one another? He had asked me to go to his place tonight with the others ... but what if it was awkward? I couldn't bear the thought. Through all my denial over the past few weeks, there was one thing that had become clearer than anything else.

I needed Sean Murphy.

I needed him around me like he was an integral part of my body; without him I couldn't function. He kept me sane by driving me insane and it wasn't until I was faced with the thought of that changing that it began to worry me – really worry me. I was afraid of what faced me tonight – I didn't know what his agenda was but I had my own, and it was clear. I loved the way he kissed me and I wanted to do it again.

Chapter Forty-Six

Chris was working Max through the quieter shift into lock-up and he was proving to be a real asset.

He was fast, efficient and ready to try a mid-week shift on his own – it wasn't like any one of us would be far if there was an emergency. Still, I could see the pained uncertainty in Chris as he trained Max to close. He found it difficult to let go of the reins and delicate tasks, the little control freak, unless it was to me. Then, he was more than happy to boss me around, and he took a particular pleasure in telling Adam what to do, too.

At some point, I must have drifted off to sleep, splayed across my bed with Sean's shirt folded into a makeshift pillow. I dreamed about turning up at the lake house for the gathering only for him to completely ignore me. Then, I followed him around like a lost puppy, but every time I spoke to him or tried to get his attention, it was as if he saw straight through me, as though I didn't even exist. It was so real and utterly devastating, as if he had ripped out my heart.

A light tickle across the pad of my foot stirred me from my nightmare. Another stroke and I kicked out against the sensation.

"Wake up! Wake up! Wake up!" sing-songed an upbeat, breezy voice.

I stirred, wondering if the voice was somehow part of my dream. I squinted into the darkness, shifting onto my elbows. A fuzzy silhouette stood before me.

"Tammy?" I croaked.

"Get up! Get up! Get up!" She flicked my light switch on-off-on-off-on in a series of torturous clicks that had me groaning and pulling Sean's shirt over my face to shield me from the offending strobes of light.

"Ugh! Go away," I said, my voice muffled.

The light stopped flicking.

"Umm, what is this?" The polo shirt was ripped from my face, Tammy holding it out before her, inspecting it with a curved brow. She looked down at me, her big, blue eyes bugging out in horror.

She gasped in mock outrage. "What. Did. You. Do?"

I pulled myself up to a sitting position and ignored her question. "What time is it?" I smacked my lips together, my mouth was so dry.

"It's seven-thirty, and don't change the subject," Tammy demanded.

"Seven thirty?" I peeled back the blind to see that the light was dimming as the sun melted into the horizon.

Holy crap, how long have I been out for?

"Amy!" Tammy stood with her hands on her hips.

I yawned and stretched, feeling my bones click and pop. "Yes, Tam?" I blinked at her with an air of butter-wouldn't-melt-in-my-mouth innocence.

She threw Sean's polo in my face. "Explain yourself!"

I peeled it off, trying and yet failing miserably to hide my smirk.

I shrugged. "There's nothing to tell."

"Why is Sean Murphy's shirt in your bedroom?" She crossed her arms. "I'm scandalised."

I rubbed my rumbling stomach as it demanded food. "How about we scoot downstairs, have dinner, and I tell you all about it?"

Tammy grinned. "Deal!"

***

Tammy chewed thoughtfully on a chip. "Wow, you don't muck around."

I straightened. "It's not like I planned it; it just happened."

"Aren't you glad you conquered your fear of the boat?" Tammy beamed.

"Well, I wouldn't say conquered it. It's not like I will be waterskiing anytime soon." I brushed a crumb off my lap. "So what time do we lob up at the party?" I looked at Tammy expectantly when she didn't answer.

"I'm sorry, Amy, I can't go. I have to get up at five and head to the city for a uni thing."

My heart plummeted. I hadn't realised how much I had been relying on Tammy being my wing woman, which was ironic considering how intimidated by and jealous of her I had been. I felt really stupid about it now. Tammy must have read the look of disappointment all over my face.

She tried her best to pacify me. "Tess and Ellie will be there, though."

"No, it's all right," I said. I had never been one to be shy and nervous and have to rock up to a party with the girls, or had an inexplicable need to accompany my friends to the toilets. I had never really understood that. I had gone to hundreds of parties on my own and not once felt intimidated, so why now? Why did I feel so vulnerable that I needed to walk in with someone in tow? I shook off my ridiculous insecurity and smiled, changing the subject to Tammy's city expedition.

After Tammy parted with a lame, "Don't do anything I wouldn't do," I rushed upstairs to beat Adam to the bathroom to get ready. I skipped every second step and spun around the top bannister to dive into the bathroom only to be met with a locked door and the horrific wailings of Adam singing Cliff Richards' 'Wired For Sound.' *Good God!*

I pounded on the door.

"Adam, hurry up!" I yelled.

He sang louder.

"Don't even think about it; I'm next." Chris poked his head out from his room.

My eyes narrowed. "No way! I'm a girl. I need longer to get ready."

"Uh, yeah, but I have muscles to wash," Chris said and he flexed his biceps. "And that doesn't take five minutes."

I rolled my eyes. *Vomit!*

"Who's manning the bar?" I said.

"Max is until I get ready and then I'll show him how to lock up. So, as you see, I need to get ready before you."

I stomped my foot on the ground. "For God's sake, it's only Sean's place. Why are you even bothering?"

"Exactly." He gave me a knowing look.

To be honest, I had never really cared about my appearance. There hadn't been much point to make-up and hair products at an all-girls boarding school. I hadn't even started worrying about that stuff until I'd graduated and come home, so fighting over the bathroom – especially with two boys – was all new to me. Chris was looking right at me as if he was looking straight into my thoughts.

"Just hurry up," I bit out, spinning around to storm into my room. I guessed I could use the time to pick out what to wear –another disturbing ritual I had developed.

Ugh! I was such a girl.

***

It was nine o'clock by the time Chris stepped into the hall with a poof of steam appearing behind him like a magician. He was meticulously rolling up his shirtsleeve when I pushed him out of the way.

"Don't leave without me," I said, slamming the bathroom door.

By ten-fifteen, one of them was banging on the door and I heard whining yells.

"Amy, let's go!" called Adam.

"Everything's locked up; time to move it," Chris added.

I wanted to torture them for longer but I couldn't. I was giddy. I wanted to get to Sean's. I checked my complexion and outfit one last time and collected the essential supplies, lippy and pocket concealer, to pop into my bag before I opened the door and stepped out to the hall. Both Adam and Chris were leaning against the wall looking bored and impatient. Until their eyes landed on me.

Adam raised his brows. "Whoa, cuz!"

I looked down at my attire – was it too much? Oh God, I wanted to change.

"You're wearing a dress?" Chris's brow furrowed in confusion.

I shifted awkwardly under their scrutiny. The vivid green, lacey, summery dress that flowed to above my knees was something my mum had bought me years ago in an attempt to get the tomboy out of me. I had never worn it; instead, it had hung in my cupboard all this time with the price tag still attached. Seeing as I was pushing my comfort zone today, I decided to try it on and, to my surprise, along with my tousled waves that fell over my shoulders, I didn't hate it.

"Do I look all right?" I flattened the fabric out with my palm, self-conscious of how different I felt, and of Adam's and Chris's reactions. "Do you think I should change?" I bit my lower lip.

Chris closed his eyes and rubbed at his temple as if the very thought of me changing was going to give him a migraine. "Amy, if it were up to me, I would want you to change," he said.

My heart sank as my fears were confirmed; I looked ridiculous.

"But seeing as you're not going to I will have to settle with taking a shotgun with me to the party instead."

My eyes flicked up to meet Chris who scratched his jaw with a smile.

"You're such a moron, Chris," Adam said, shaking his head. "He's saying you look beautiful."

"Oh," I said. My heart silently ached at the gesture from my sweet, over-protective cousins.

Chris pushed himself off the wall. "Come on, let's go."

Adam slung his arms around my shoulders as we followed Chris down the hall, spinning his car keys around his fingers as he walked.

"Maybe we should all change," said Adam.

"Oh?" I curved my brow.

"Do you think this party can handle so much Henderson beauty? I mean look at us ... We're gorgeous!"

My laughter echoed as we reached the landing.

"Well, you and I are, anyway," Adam whispered.

Chris paused on the staircase looking back at us incredulously. "I'm standing right here, you know."

Our laughter was interrupted, light flooding the landing as the door to my parents' apartment opened.

Dad walked out in his dressing robe. "You're off, then?" he said.

"Yep," Adam said with a grin. "We're burning moonlight."

Just as we were about to continue our descent, Dad said, "Amy, love, do you think we can have a chat before you go?"

I looked from Dad to Chris and Adam. "Um, sure." I made my way warily up the stairs.

"Do you want us to wait?" Chris asked.

"You blokes head off," Dad said. "This might take a while. I'll drop her off."

Adam and Chris exchanged glances, before they headed down the stairs. I felt a little uneasy until I met my dad's kind, grey eyes.

"You look beautiful, love," he said. "Don't worry; we'll try not to keep you too long."

Mum sat on the couch in her silken nightgown and matching pyjamas, massaging hand cream into her hands. She looked up from her task, her face lighting as I entered the room. "Aw, you look lovely. Where are you off to, then?" Before I could answer, Dad, being Dad (who knew everything), answered for me.

"There's a party at young Sean's tonight," he said, taking a seat in his chair.

Mum's eyes narrowed and her smile fell. "I see." She moved aside on the couch and tapped the space next to her. "Take a seat, honey, we have some things to tell you."

I would usually have plonked on the couch with an air of ease, grabbed the remote control and made myself at home.

But tonight I had other plans.

"Your father has told me a few things and I wanted to say I was sorry for how I acted towards you earlier today. I was just a bit … shocked, that's all."

Mum looked at me pointedly and I knew exactly what she was referring to when she meant 'shocked'.

My mum rubbed my knee. "But now I know what you've been doing, what your friends have done and how you've really stepped up, honey. We are so proud of you."

My nerves melted away at her words, and I smiled at my dad who I loved so much. He had explained things to Mum like he'd said he would. Told her some home truths and probably made her see that the hotel was a thing to be saved, that it meant so much to me and so much to him and that it could shine again. That it could be something to bring us together, not tear us apart.

Mum squeezed my hand. "We have some good news."

I edged forward, keenly buying into Mum's excitement. "With everything you have done, and all the hard work you've put in, we are pretty certain that we can get an even better price at auction!"

Chapter Forty-Seven

My heart stopped and my smile dropped. I looked from Mum's beaming face to Dad, who couldn't even bring himself to look at me.

"What?" I whispered.

"The real estate agent is coming out tomorrow and he is pretty certain that with all of the improvements, we could very well make Onslow real estate history." Mum all but squealed in excitement. "Isn't that great?"

Her enthusiasm was short-lived as she read the horror plastered all over my face.

I shook my head, looking at Dad as if he was a stranger.

My voice broke as I started to speak. "So everything I did, everything that I worked for was for nothing?"

"Not nothing, honey. Mum said. What you did has helped so much. We are so—"

"Proud of me? Yeah, I can tell," I scoffed, staring at my hands that were balled up into angry fists in my lap.

My eyes burned as I looked up at my dad's profile. "So you're going to sell? Just like that?"

"It's not just like that." Mum straightened. "We have thought this through, haven't we, Eric?"

Dad made no move; he just stared away as if looking at me would admit his faults, as though looking me in the eye would seal the fate of the Onslow.

"Answer me this, Mum," I said, turning back to face her. "Is it something you *both* want or something *you* want?"

"I cannot believe you are *still* so surprised about this, I told you ..."

"That's right! You told me, you never asked me. I'm a member of this family too, even though I'm sure you've forgotten that. While you've been off living your second honeymoon, I've been here, working my fingers to the bone to save our home."

I walked across to kneel in front of Dad in his chair, my eyes brimming with tears. "Dad, you said it, you told me what it felt like to see the hotel today, that you hadn't seen it shine this way since your grandfather owned it. You said it was like magic. Are you willing to put a price on that?"

Dad finally turned his head to face me; his sad eyes looked across at me, really *looked* at me. I held my breath waiting for him to speak.

"Amy, sometimes no matter how hard it may be, we have to be smart about things. We have to make decisions with our heads, not with our hearts." He wiped away a tear as it slid down my cheek, and with those words, my heart shattered into a million pieces. I stood, pulling away from him. I glared down at my father, a stranger.

"That's the thing about us Hendersons, Dad," I said. "We think with our hearts. I don't know who you are anymore."

"Amy, that's enough." My mother stood too. "You need to realise that you can't always get what you want in life."

I couldn't believe the hypocrisy coming out of my mother's mouth. "That's rich, coming from you," I said.

Mum's eyes narrowed as her cool, hard, stare seared into me. Her tone was low and threatening as she said, "Get out before I do or say something we will both regret."

"There's nothing you could possibly do right now that could hurt me any more than you already have," I said. I strode towards the door, ripped it open and slammed it behind me with an almighty force. I moved as quickly as I could down the stairs before my tears really fell.

And fall they did.

***

Like a dishevelled Cinderella, I sat on the back staircase in the beer garden with my face in my hands. It was after midnight. I had been sitting in the dark for hours, lost in a deep misery that I couldn't bring myself out of. Without a lift I had no way of getting to the party, not that I felt like it now, anyway. How could I face them? All the people that had gone above and beyond to help me? I felt like I had betrayed them, used them, just to gain a better selling price for the Onslow.

I felt sick. Utterly deflated. Exhausted by the reality that churned around and around in my head. How could they sell? Would they ever really know how good our lives could be now that the hotel was better than ever? Now that Mum and Dad had rekindled their commitment to one another? I was here to help, to do what I could to make things easier. Dad wouldn't have to do it on his own.

Maybe that was the case I needed to plead – I needed to calmly and maturely talk through the positives of why we should keep it, instead of losing my shit and flying off the handle like always. I needed to rationalise and negotiate with them. I dreamed up all these winning scenarios. So why was it I didn't feel the least bit lifted or confident?

I breathed out a shallow, shuddery breath. At the end of the day, I knew Dad would not stand up to Mum, and more than that, I knew once Mum saw the dollar signs, there would be no changing her mind. I felt a deep burning anger against Mum, Dad, but mostly myself. How could I have been so stupid? I should have let the hotel fall down around us all – the stress and pressure I had put on myself and others and oh, God, the working bee, the fundraiser. How was that going to look? We would have to refund all the donations and try to get out of it in some way to save face.

I wrapped my arms around my legs and pressed my forehead against my knees. How was I ever going to face anyone? I almost wanted to be banished all over again. I felt my stomach clench as tears welled in my eyes, my throat, my heart, when I heard a voice pierce through the darkness.

"All dressed up and no place to go?"

My head snapped up, stunned by the unexpectedness of the sound, the familiar sound that made my heart thunder against my chest. I wiped at my eyes, trying to focus my blurry vision through the darkness.

A silhouette stood in the shadows of the beer garden entrance. I slowly unfolded my legs, standing, while bracing myself on the bannister with the fear that my legs would give way.

I hoped I wasn't seeing or hearing things, because right now I needed it to be true more than anything. In that moment I needed to be rescued, to be caught, to be saved from the sorrow that constricted me with every breath. I stepped forward, afraid that if I did the breeze would stir and my shadow would fold into the night. Instead, the darkened figure stepped from the viney shadows into the moonlight, his handsome face lit with an eerie glow that shone on his perfect smile.

It was all I needed. I crossed the distance, relief flooding me as Sean caught me in a flying run. I threw my arms around him, almost knocking the wind out of him, burrowing my face into the warmth of his chest. I held on, never wanting to let go, and within the safety of Sean's arms once again the tears came.

"Hey, hey, what's wrong?" He cupped my face, his eyes serious, worried, as they searched mine.

I shook my head, I didn't want him to see me like this; I couldn't tell him, I couldn't bring myself to reveal how selfish my parents were. It was one thing for *me* to think it but I couldn't bear Sean to.

"Can you take me away from this place?" I whispered.

Sean swept his hand lightly along my dampened cheek. "Of course I can." And without another word, his hand slid down the line of my arm and laced his fingers into mine, a small, sad smile spreading over his lips.

"Come on, let's get you out of here."

And just like Sean, without even knowing the reasons why, he just did. Without a word or a worry, he saved me.

Chapter Forty-Eight

"GET OUT!"

We stood, paused in the doorway of Sean's bedroom, taking in the scene before us. Ringer was lying passed out and face down on Sean's mattress.

"Ringer!" Sean growled, kicking the corpse-like leg that spilled over onto the floor. "Get up!"

I cupped my hand over my mouth and tried to contain my laughter. It didn't help when Ringer stirred from his slumber, slowly lifting his head, sporting a cockatoo-crested hair-do.

"Come on, mate, give us a go," Ringer croaked, half asleep.

"I'll give you a bloody go if you don't get off my bed!"

Ringer groaned, slowly lifting himself onto his elbows and smacking his lips together as if he had an unsavoury taste in his mouth. He squinted up at Sean before comically doing a double-take in my direction. I offered a little wave as I peered from behind Sean's brooding frame.

A wicked smile spread right across Ringer's face as he looked from me to Sean and back again.

"Oh, I see," Ringer said, beaming from ear to ear.

"Ringer," Sean warned.

Ringer held up his hands. "All right, all right. Cool it, Romeo, I'm going."

Ringer dragged himself into a sitting position, still disorientated from sleep. He fumbled a ciggie from his pocket, flicking it into his mouth like a pro. He patted his other pockets, locating a lighter.

Ringer gingerly stood, obviously still drunk from the boys' drinking session. Sean opened the door and stood aside in a none-too-subtle hint to get out.

"You can smoke that outside," Sean said, his face still lined with a dark broodiness. I had to bite my lower lip to stop from smirking.

Ringer shuffled his feet towards the open door and paused before Sean, the very same cheeky grin appearing as he looked at Sean and then me. I turned slightly to mask the blush I no doubt sported across my cheeks.

Ringer tapped Sean on the shoulder. "You're a brave man, Seany, boy. Don't do anything I wouldn't do." He winked and quickly made his way in a zigzag down the hall after Sean pushed him out.

"Crash in the spare room, Ringo! Sleep it off!" Sean called down the hall.

"Aye-aye, Captain!" Ringer saluted before tripping over his own feet and knocking into the wall. "Oh, shit-fuck!"

Sean sighed deeply, shook his head, and shut the door.

I sat on the edge of the bed, still no more than just a mattress on the floor. "I thought you said they'd all gone home," I said, unable to contain my laughter any longer.

Sean smirked. "Yeah, well, I'll do a head count next time."

Without tearing his eyes from me, he clicked the lock on the bedroom door. My smile fell, panic rising in me at the sound; a sound so delicate and innocent, yet it held perhaps the biggest meaning of all. Just me and Sean behind a locked bedroom door. I swallowed deeply.

"So you don't mind if I … you know … stay?" I asked. I tried not to fidget. I didn't want Sean to think I was as nervous as my constantly churning insides made me feel.

He folded his arms and leaned against the door, his eyes searing into me. "Must be pretty bad if you're running away from it."

"I'm not running away," I said defensively, causing Sean's brows to rise.

"Really?" he mused.

My breaths felt laboured; the locked door made me claustrophobic as my mind whirred through a series of explanations. Of course I was running away, what else could there be to it? The more I thought about another possible truth, the more anxiety spiked inside me. Although I absolutely wanted to run away from my parents and all the bullshit, there was an underlying truth that I simply couldn't allow myself to admit. Above it all.

I want to be here.

I wanted to be exactly where I was, locked in this room, alone with Sean, sitting on his bed, gazing up at him as I was now. Taking in the masculine lines of his suntanned body, the slight stubble from his unshaven cheeks, his dishevelled hair that was in need of a haircut.

I stared down at my hands. "Listen, just do whatever you do like I'm not even here," I said. "Don't let me change your ritual; I don't want to be in the way."

"You're not in the way," he said as he moved to open his wardrobe. "I'm going to take a shower, do you want one?"

My eyes snapped up. "No!" I yelled a bit too readily. "Uh, no thanks." I cleared my throat. "I'm fine."

Sean paused in the door of the en suite, his brow curving.

"I didn't mean with me."

"Oh, pfft, I know," I said.

Oh, God help me!

Sean looked as though he wasn't wholly buying it.

Had things changed because of today's kiss? The playfulness in Sean had vanished somehow and everything about our exchange had become so wooden, so unnatural. I missed his smart-arse quips and cockiness. I missed the devilish twinkle in his eyes.

Maybe he was just tired? But here I was alone, all dressed up, lying on his bed, such an easy target and he hadn't even so much as made a single innuendo about my being here. Maybe the kiss had been nothing more than a spur-of-the-moment thing to him. Perhaps Sean would let me have the bed, come out of the shower and say goodnight while he went and slept elsewhere.

Oh my God, is that what he would do?

I would be mortified. But then, I guessed I would know for sure. Whatever had happened between us this afternoon was nothing more than a typical Sean thing to do; it had just been a no-meaning kiss. All of a sudden I didn't want to be there.

My heart sank as I heard the falling of the water and the clanking of the pipes in the wall while Sean showered. I sighed, unstrapped my shoes and set them aside. Whatever happened, whatever Sean did or didn't do, I was grateful to be away from the Onslow. A yawn escaped from me as I stretched my arms above my head; fatigue settling in my weary bones. I was so tired. Tired of it all, but as soon as I heard the water cease and the shower sliding panel open, I had never felt more awake.

"Shit," I whispered.

I dived to the light switch and plunged the bedroom into darkness before running around in a flurry, not sure what my next move should be.

Shit! Shit! Shit!

The basin tap ran and I heard the unmistakable whooshing sound of Sean brushing his teeth. As he tapped his toothbrush on the sink, I dived onto the mattress and ripped the covers back, plunging underneath. My heart drummed so violently I was sure Sean would hear it in the next room.

Pretend you're asleep, pretend you're asleep ...

I tried to slow my breathing; having darted around the room like a headless chicken hadn't helped at all. My mind raced when an alarming thought came to me: I was in Sean's bed, in the dark ... What was I thinking?

Just make yourself at home, Amy! Suggestive much?

This was not good. Before I could do anything about it, I heard the sound of the en suite light switch off and the door screech open. It was so hard to control my breaths. I could only concentrate on breathing in and out, in and out. I had my back facing the en suite door. I could make out the sound of Sean's padded footsteps; it seemed like forever. I waited for the sound of the door unclicking and opening, for him to make his exit down the hall and leave the bed to me in some gentlemanly gesture.

So when I felt the mattress dip next to me, my eyes snapped open. Sean slid underneath the covers and settled gently next to me – his only movement was to align his pillows as he lay down. He exhaled a deep, comfortable sigh of fatigue.

Oh my God, oh my God!

I didn't dare move. I didn't so much as breathe.

Oh crap, my nose was itchy. Why was that always the way? I wiggled my nose like Samantha off *Bewitched*, praying that it would be enough. The bed moved behind me and I froze.

Sean coughed and rolled ... away from me?

I felt his breaths change, become deep and soothing, in and out, in and out. My eyes narrowed. I waited for a long moment before I rolled onto my back with a deliberate, loud sigh.

Nothing.

I coughed and adjusted my pillow, and waited. Still nothing. Now I was getting annoyed. I glared at his bare back, a broad landscape lit by the moonlight that filtered through the window. I pulled the blanket up to my chin, allowing my arm to gently rest along the line of his back, skin to skin.

Oh my God, he was shirtless.

My insides twisted – his skin felt hot pressed next to mine. I was wide awake, staring at the ceiling, more infuriated and frustrated than ever with the sound of his soothing breaths. I sighed aloud once again and kicked one leg out of the bed. I was *so* obviously awake, there could be no doubt.

Sean didn't move and I contemplated punching him in the back of the head, but instead, after what seemed like hours having passed (okay, maybe minutes), I did something far, far worse.

I sat bolt upright in bed. "You have got to be fucking kidding me!"

That got his attention. Sean turned slightly towards me.

"What?" his tired voice croaked in the dark. I leaned across him and gave little thought to how awkward the actual manoeuvre was. He actually got a face full of my boobs as I reached across him for the touch lamp. In a frantic three taps, the bedroom glowed, causing us both to wince against the light.

"Jesus, Amy!"

I tried to keep my voice from shaking, from seeming like some bunny-boiling psycho, but I couldn't help myself.

"Are we honestly going to do this? Lie in the dark and pretend that this is just what happens, that me being in your bed is all casual and non-weird, that we'll both just drift off to sleep?"

Sean rolled onto his back with a groan, rubbing his eyes. "I *did* drift off to sleep."

"It might be normal for you, Sean Murphy, to just kiss a girl midday and then act as if it never happened. Then later, lock her in your bedroom and lay next to her with …" My eyes widened. "Oh my God, have you even got clothes on?"

Sean looked at me wearily. Ripping back the covers, he revealed black silk boxers.

"Satisfied?"

My mouth gaped. Looking at his chiselled six-pack lying in front of me, I quickly averted my eyes from his half-naked body.

"No, let me guess." He pulled himself up onto his elbows. "That's the thing, isn't it? You're not satisfied."

My eyes snapped up to meet his crooked smirk; he was becoming more awake and alert every second.

"Excuse me?"

"What do you want from me, Amy?"

I blinked, taking in the question, searching for an answer. *What was my argument again?*

Sean sat up and leaned his elbows on his knees. His eyes burned into me. "Do you want me to fuck you? Is that what you want?"

I gasped, my mouth dropping open. "How dare you speak to me like that!"

Sean smiled, satisfied, as if I had given him the exact reaction he had been hoping for. "Then go to sleep."

"I will not be told what to do, especially from the likes of you." I glowered at him. I should have slapped him across his smug face a second ago when the moment had called for it.

Sean leaned back against his pillow, folding his hands behind his head, studying me seriously as if I were a bug under a microscope. "What if I told you to come over here?" he asked. "Would you?"

Frustration boiled in me; I dug my nails into my leg to stop myself from screaming.

"Stop playing with me," I bit out.

All humour had disappeared from Sean. His eyes burned into mine. "I told you …" He reached out to the lamp next to the bed and, with a delicate tap, plunged us both into darkness. "I don't play games."

Chapter Forty-Nine

I sat up in the bed, frozen to the spot.

It was as if all thoughts were wiped from my memory. After a long moment, I heard him chuckle.

"Relax, Amy, go to sleep."

Sean turned again, making himself comfy nestling under the blankets. This time, I wasn't angry when I stared at his back. Instead, something else stirred in me – he wasn't playing with me, or using me as an object. Maybe he just didn't see me that way?

But as the darkness consumed me and my shoulders sagged in defeat, the exhaustion of the day hit me again and I let down my guard to all the things I had promised myself that I wouldn't lie about anymore. No more secrets, no more denying how I felt, and that included the infuriating lump right next to me. I just wanted to forget all the things that plagued my thoughts; just for one night I wanted to forget, to feel something other than guilt, and hopelessness, and even though I had no real way of knowing, I knew what I wanted. I could obliterate it all … just for one night.

Sliding down under the blanket, I edged myself up close behind Sean. I slipped my hand slowly under his arm and along his bare stomach. I pressed my lips to his shoulder blade.

"Sean?"

Sean's breathing changed. I felt it as soon as my hand glided over his ripped stomach. Pressing into him, I felt him tense under my touch. I smiled, feeling a certain surge of power in taking him by surprise.

"Amy?" His voice was low and raspy.

I bit my lower lip, thinking that perhaps I should say goodnight and force sleep on myself, welcome the uncomplicated aspect of that and be happy. But that wouldn't make me forget, or feel, so instead I whispered into his shoulder.

"I don't want to play games anymore."

Silence ensued. A long, painful silence. The only measure of Sean I had was his heart thundering against my palm.

What was he thinking? Oh my God, had I made a horrible mistake? Just when I was about to awkwardly peel my arm away and curse myself for even uttering those stupid, stupid words, Sean turned.

In one fluid motion, he forced me to draw my arm back as I was suddenly face to face with his beautiful, serious eyes. I read his wary expression, lit by the rays of moonlight that shone through the window. His throat worked to swallow as he studied me, wagering on whether I was serious or not.

I had no way of voicing it; I didn't know how. Instead, I sat up and hitched myself onto my knees. Slowly, without tearing my eyes from his, I peeled one spaghetti strap from my shoulder and then the other. I slid my dress down and pushed it below my belly button. Sean's eyes watched me intently, his jaw clenched. I shimmied the dress over my hips and around my legs, throwing it across the room. Now I had bared myself to him there was no going back, nothing else to shed; because I then did something so bold, so unexpected, I honestly didn't know I had had it in me.

I straddled him. I had morphed into the femme fatale I had always joked I could never be. Any doubts of his desire were soon erased when I felt the press of him intimately against the sheer scrap of my underwear. His chest rose and fell heavily at the unexpected movement. His eyes burned into me now with a deep need I had never seen before. It excited me.

I grabbed his hands and placed them on me. A gasp escaped from my lips at the feel of his work-roughened hands on my skin. His fingers gripped me as I moved my hips, revelling in the feel of his touch. This was how I wanted to forget, just like this. I felt all the sadness, doubt, and anger evaporate and channel into something else entirely. Above all this, I needed something more. Before another second passed I found it, or, rather, it found me. Sean sat up and claimed my mouth with an all-consuming passion.

I loved the way he kissed me. It was nothing like the kiss from only that afternoon. He kissed me now so deeply, so unapologetically as if each draw from my lips was needed as much as the air he breathed. As though he needed my mouth with such utter desperation or he would simply not survive.

He rolled me onto my back, shifting my legs apart with his knees. His arms pressed on either side of my head, caging me in with his muscled biceps. He smelled like soap and tasted of minty toothpaste, his hair still damp from the shower.

I traced my fingers through his curls, fisting a handful at the nape of his neck that rewarded me with a moan of pleasure that I captured with my lips. As long as Sean was touching me, I was in paradise. I knew what I was doing was bad, that we were crossing a line that would change everything.

I still wanted to do it.

"You're not going to go to sleep, are you?" Sean whispered against my lips.

I smiled, my eyes locking with his. "Do you want me to?"

Sean lowered his wicked mouth and pressed his soft lips against my neck. His hips rocked against me making my breath hitch. "What do you think?"

A thrill spiked in the pit of my stomach. It was hard to think. I tried to grasp onto the edges of my mind. Sean pressed against me again, capturing my gasp with his lips as he kissed me deeply with his hot, delving tongue.

I was lost, completely and utterly lost to him. I closed my eyes and arched against his delicious weight pressing down on me; my fingers digging into his narrow hips as the silk of his boxers rubbed along my thighs. With every blinding sensation, 'trouble' still managed to enter my mind, but all was lost when Sean's wicked hands moved to peel the offending fabric of my underwear away.

His heated eyes locked with mine as he took his time, as if asking a silent question and expecting me to still his hand that now slid slowly up my shin, along my thigh and between my legs. This was trouble all right; being in Sean Murphy's arms, being in his bed was diabolically wrong, catastrophically bad. I was undeniably doomed. Yet still, it was completely and utterly without a question the only place I wanted to be.

Chapter Fifty

The most awkward thing in the world?

People *knowing* you've had sex.

Ringer munched thoughtfully on a piece of toast at the breakfast bar, his amused eyes darting between Sean and me as if he expected details.

"So, you kids sleep all right?" Ringer asked, beaming at us.

Sean threw him a warning look and Ringer winked at him as he sipped on his OJ.

Such a smart-arse.

I pinched my leg under the table, praying I wouldn't turn crimson. I had completely forgotten Ringer was even here. Oh God, how loud had I been? Mortified by the thought, the sooner I got away from Ringer's all-knowing eyes the better.

"Did you want something to eat?" Sean asked. He pushed his chair back and headed for the fridge. He was cool and casual as always, no sign of him blushing or smiling to himself like I was trying not to do.

"Oh, no thanks, I better get back and face the music," I said with a weak smile.

Ringer skulled the last of his juice and belched, long and hard. "I'm headed that way if you want a lift."

"Thanks." Although the thought didn't enthral me, I knew Sean had things to do.

***

A series of impatient honks sounded from Ringer's car. I rolled my eyes at Sean.

"I better go. My chariot is somewhat impatient."

"Sorry to subject you to him," Sean said with a smirk.

A silence settled over us. He swept a tendril of hair from my cheek. His eyes were filled with a million unsaid things.

"Amy, there's something you should know."

My heart pounded against my ribcage. He was going to give me some spiel about last night being a mistake, or that we should just stay friends, I just knew it. I couldn't breathe with the tension that swept between us. Our trance was broken with the sound of another long drawn out series of honks.

"Aaaaaammmmyyyyyyy …" Ringer called.

I blinked out of my daze. "Well, see ya!" I shouted, turning to walk quickly to the car.

***

I felt sick. And it wasn't just the smell of the burrito that Ringer had had to pull up at the corner shop for on the way home. He licked his fingers and struggled, awkwardly shifting gears, all the while trying not to spill his food.

"Seriously, Ringer," I said with a grimace, "you just ate."

He spoke with a mouth full of food. "Urm, erh, growing berh."

"You're disgusting!"

I tried not to think about the "something" Sean had to tell me or about the look of apprehension in his eyes. Whatever he had to say wasn't good and right now all I wanted to think about was the good stuff, like what we had done until the condoms ran out.

I got Ringer to drop me around the back so I could do my walk of shame without the whole family looking on. I was looking for a nice, private exit from his car, until he sounded the horn and started shouting out of the window.

"Come on, drop and give me twenty push-ups!" Ringer yelled.

Adam was out the back entrance doing some warm-ups.

Oh, perfect.

I wanted to slide down in my seat. Adam hadn't seen me yet, but it didn't take long for him to register who was in the passenger seat. His arms slowly dropped from over his head, and a dark look spread across his face.

"Thanks, Ringer," I muttered sarcastically, getting out and slamming the car door.

"Anytime, babe." He saluted before backing out and spinning away with a chorus of still more animated honks.

I inhaled, readying myself to meet Adam's uncertain frown as he took in last night's clothing, my wet hair and make-up free face. I was holding my shoes in my hand so as to tiptoe more effectively up the back staircase.

Adam's eyes darted to me, then towards where Ringer's car had torn away, then back to me again. A look of horror spread across his face as it all clicked into place.

"Oh my God, you totally shagged Ringer?"

I placed my hands on my hip. "Oh, yeah, I totally shagged Ringer," I said. "Jesus, Adam!"

The horror was replaced with confusion. "Where have you been then?"

I sighed. "He dropped me off from Sean's." I wanted to mentally slap myself for the admission, but I had been so focused on Adam's assumption that I had been secretly rendezvousing with Ringer, it just came out.

Adam's brows lifted. "I see." He nodded like that made more sense. "So you're going to tell me you didn't …"

"Shut up!" I snapped, storming past him.

Adam shook his head. "I wouldn't go that way if I were you."

I paused. "Why?"

"Everyone's having a family brunch in the beer garden."

I grimaced. "Everyone?"

"Uncle Eric, Aunty Claire, Chris, Melba, Toby, Tess."

My eyes widened. Oh my God, did they know the Onslow was getting put on the market? Had Mum and Dad announced their plans before I'd had a chance to do damage control? Adam must have read the look on my face.

"They know. Everyone knows. That's what they had to tell you last night, isn't it? That they were still going to sell."

I nodded. Reality came flooding back, punching me in the face. I was trying to think how this had all just spiralled out of control.

"When did Mum and Dad tell you lot?"

Adam sighed. "They didn't."

Confusion must have filled my face as Adam rolled his eyes in frustration, grabbing my arm.

"This way!" He dragged me towards the front. I did my best not to stumble with his quick pace and the sharp pebbles that dug into my bare feet.

"Ow-Ow-Ow … Adam slow dow—" My words broke off as we turned the corner of the hotel to the front and I skidded to a halt. Shrugging off Adam's hold, I moved slowly forward; the stones that dug into my feet were the least of my worries. I crunched along the drive to stand before a giant auction sign with bold letters that proudly stated, 'Opportunity Knocks'. My worst fears were realised.

I felt sick.

Chapter Fifty-One

You know when you have hit rock bottom?

When you sit in a bar getting drunk at three o'clock in the afternoon, talking to old Ray Mooreland, an alcoholic sheep farmer.

3 p.m.: "I mean, what are they even going to do, Ray? Retire? Pfft, what a joke."

3.25 p.m.: "Not once, Ray! Not ONCE did they even ask me. How bloody disrespectful can you be?"

3.40 p.m.: "Oh, and get this, get this, right …? You won't believe this …"

4.01 p.m.: "What I'm trying to say, Ray, is I get it, I do! They want to go and enjoy life, I get that, but, like, what about me? Where do I come into it?"

4.10 p.m.: "I mean, Ray, the thing of it is, and hear me out when I say this … The thing of it is … Umm, what was I saying?"

The bar room front door screeched open and Chris and Sean pushed their way through.

"Oh, thank fuck for that!" Ray jumped up from his stool, grabbed his hat and made for the door. Pausing next to Chris and Sean, he said, "Listen, she's a sweet girl and all, but now you deal with it."

By this time, I had managed somehow to stumble my way over to the jukebox and, tipsy or not, I would always have my favourite song selections memorised: 2981, 4739, and my absolute favourite, 2217. Carly Simon's 'You're So Vain' started up and suddenly I didn't care about anything. I didn't care about my parents or about the uncertain looks I was getting from Chris and Sean. All I cared about was the music as I spun around the pool room singing at the top of my lungs.

Chris turned a horrified expression to Max behind the bar. "What the fuck, Max?"

Max, a lean, baby-faced blond guy, shrugged. "You try saying no to her. I mean she's a paying customer and the boss's daughter, what was I supposed to do?"

Sean rubbed his whiskers, fighting not to smile.

Chris stalked over to me. "Is this how you deal with things? Getting drunk mid-afternoon and flailing around like freakin' Stevie Nicks on crack?"

Sean sidled over towards me and leaned against the jukebox, his eyes alight with amusement. "Looks like you've put some money over the bar, sweetheart."

I shimmied over to the bar, picked up my Tutti Frutti and saluted them with a

"Cheers." I sipped from my glass and smacked my lips together in appreciation.

Earlier, in my rage, I drove down the street and withdrew as much cash as my credit limit allowed me from Mum and Dad's generous allowance. I figured I had earned it, after all, and felt no guilt whatsoever about spending it on cocktails.

"Oh, that's great! That's just great!" Chris glowered at me, his hands on his hips. "Where's Uncle Eric and Aunty Claire?"

I shrugged, peering into my empty glass. "They went out, probably going midlife-crisis shopping, I don't know."

Suddenly I didn't feel so lively anymore. I pressed my forehead to the bar in an attempt to stop the room from spinning.

"I think I'm going to be sick."

"Don't you bloody dare!" Chris called from across the room.

"Mate, we better get her out of here – if the parentals rock up and see her like this …"

Sean didn't need to finish his sentence.

In serious danger of wanting to curl up and fall asleep at the bar, I was saved from sliding off my stool by a set of steely, muscled arms. They picked me up as if I weighed no more than a feather. I squinted through half-lidded, blurry eyes. Staring into a pair of unmistakable blue eyes.

"You're so beautiful," I whispered.

He smirked. "And you're a hot mess."

"Thank you." I smiled, leaning my head against the wall of his broad chest.

Sean laughed. "It wasn't a compliment."

Chris led the way, opening doors as Sean carried me up the staircase.

"I like it when you walk me to my room," I mumbled.

"Shhh," Sean whispered into my temple.

"What did she say?" asked Chris.

"I don't know – something about the moon?" Sean suggested. "She's pretty out of it."

I went to correct him, but my head refused to lift.

"Yeah, well, bring her in. This will fix her up." Chris's voice echoed. *Are we in a tunnel?* We had been travelling up the stairs just a moment before. I longed to feel the feathery softness of my mattress, the warm embrace of my doona that smelled like lavender. Oh, how I wanted to just collapse in a heap and sleep the rest of the summer away.

So when I was set down and leaned up against a cold, tiled wall, I thought maybe I was dreaming.

That's when I heard the water.

It took two Onslow Boys to pin me in the shower recess as they assaulted me with ice cold water that poured from above. I screamed and flailed and wanted to slide down to my knees and just sob bitterly, but Sean held me upright by the back of my shirt.

"I hate you!" I screamed.

Sean laughed. "Come on, now, that's just the drink talking."

"No it's not, I know what I'm saying, don't treat me like a fracking child." I gurgled the last word, coughing, spluttering and finally sobbing as I tried to push Sean away in a limp-wristed motion. I was pathetic.

"A fracking child?" Sean said. "See you're back to your old self again."

I let it all out now, in bone-jarring sobs. I slid to the bottom of the shower and Sean let me go.

Chris shut off the tap and grabbed me a towel.

"Here you go, Chook."

I glared up at him. "And don't think I've forgotten your part in this. I hate you, too."

Chris looked at Sean and shrugged, like 'what's a guy to do?'

He opened his mouth to speak and then paused, cocking his head to the side. His brow creased and he placed his finger to his lips for us to be quiet. I was too busy shivering my arse off.

Chris crept to the door and opened it just a crack, listening intently. He winced and swore under his breath.

"Shit, they're back!" Chris ran his hand through his hair anxiously.

"You stay here and I'll coax them back downstairs. Get her to her room, all right?" He opened the door a crack and slid sideways through it out to the landing.

Sean replaced him at the door, listening, waiting for the voices to fade down the stairs. Knowing Chris, it wouldn't take him long to figure something out. And he did.

"Coast is clear, come on." Sean tried to wrap an arm around me but I slapped him away.

"I don't need your help," I glowered, stumbling rather inelegantly to my feet.

Bloody spinning room.

"Yeah, I can see that," Sean mused.

I pushed past him, zigzagging down the hall like a ball in a pinball machine, leaving a trail of wet footprints on the carpet. I could hear Sean laughing as he followed from behind. God, what an arse.

I spun around so fast Sean nearly collided with me. "You think this is funny? It's just a giant joke to you!"

Sean sighed. "No, I don't."

"Do you even know why I'm upset?" I demanded.

Sean nodded. "Chris came and saw me."

"You should be relieved. At least now you'll get paid." I spun around to stomp into my room.

"Do you think I even care about that?"

"I care!" At least something good could come from the sale: I wouldn't be indebted to Sean anymore.

He sighed and looked up to the ceiling as if praying for God to give him strength.

"You don't get it, do you? You just don't get it." Sean's eyes darkened.

I searched through my drawers for a dry top, ignoring him when he stalked over to me, grabbing me by the arm and forcing me to look into his searing eyes.

"Yeah, it's sad and shitty and all those things. But home is where this is." He pointed to my heart. "That's what makes it a home. Wherever you go, whatever you do, it will be home because you're there. You take the memories with you."

"It's not that simple," I whispered under my breath.

Sean ran his hand through his hair. "I blame your parents."

"Ha! Join the club." I crossed my arms in defiance.

"Not for that." Sean's eyes burned into me.

"For what, then?"

"For spoiling you to within an inch of your life, for turning you into being so damn materialistic you can't focus on the things that really matter."

It was as if Sean had plunged a knife and twisted it into my heart. Anger boiled inside me, or was that vomit? Wait … no, it was anger. And fury threatened to blur my vision.

"You're calling me materialistic? This coming from the man that owns a whopping great lake house, who has a boat and a car. So you could just give it all up tomorrow and that would be all right, would it?"

"Yes," he said coolly.

I scoffed. "I don't believe you."

He was silent for a moment, watching me. "Then you don't know me at all."

"Well, you obviously don't know me, either."

"I know the Amy Henderson who rolled up her sleeves and scrubbed urinals, the Amy Henderson who violently attacked thieving staff members, the Amy Henderson who looks fear in the face and plunges into it anyway. The Amy Henderson who was in my bed last night." He shook his head. "But *this* Amy Henderson in front of me, the one who gets shit-faced in the middle of the day when things don't go her way and throws the mother of all pity parties for herself, you're right. I *don't* know her."

Silence fell between us. A long, tense silence.

"Well, I'm sorry I'm such a huge disappointment to you," I said. "But I won't be sorry for how I feel. I can't just accept it."

Sean reached out and brushed my cheek. "You're going to have to."

I pulled away from his touch; I'd had enough of being lectured. I couldn't believe the one person I'd thought above anyone else I could rely on was now siding with my parents.

"You should go," I said.

I could feel Sean's gaze on me. I silently begged that he wouldn't argue, he'd just move, and was relieved when he slowly walked to the door.

He paused at the threshold. "I'm not asking you not to care, but you just need to realise what's important, what you really want in life."

"And what is it that *you* want out of life?" I scoffed.

Sean smiled. "I'll let you know."

***

To Mum and Dad's credit, they kept me in the loop to the best of their abilities, but it was Chris who gave me all the juicy details.

I sat with Chris and Adam on the outside picnic table, sharing a packet of salt and vinegar chips and downing a double-shot raspberry lemonade. I stole Adam's sunglasses from the top of his head to mute the blinding sunrays that did absolutely nothing for my thumping headache.

"Look at you! Hung like a wet towel," Adam smirked.

All I could manage at that point was to flip him off as I sipped on my lemonade.

"Apparently there's a Sydney buyer really interested – they want to turn it into a bed and breakfast," Chris said, staring sullenly into his Coke.

My heart plummeted. "Already? A bed and breakfast?"

"That's bullshit!" Adam added. "The last thing the Onslow needs is for some crusty upper-class toffs retiring from the city to turn the place into a B & B."

Chris shrugged. "Don't shoot the messenger." He traced the lines of condensation on his pot glass, his troubled stare masking something deeper.

"There's something else going on, isn't there?" I said. "Spill!"

He looked up at me. "Huh?"

"I can read you like a book. Spill it."

Chris sighed. "I wasn't going to say anything because I don't want you reading too much into it."

Adam and I both straightened. This wasn't going to be good.

Chris went to speak but then thought better of it, as if he was thinking about how to put it.

"Chris!"

"All right, all right. Don't get too excited but it looks as though the McGees might put in a bid."

Adam and I looked at each other. My heart spiked with approval.

"Are you serious?"

"Now, see, that's what I mean, Amy, I see that manic, hopeful look in your eyes and I don't want you getting your heart set on it."

"But that is seriously amazing!" I squealed and then instantly regretted it. "Do you think they will?"

Chris ran his hand through his hair. "There are a few interested parties, and as far as I know they're one of the front runners."

"Sa-weeet." Adam smiled.

"But don't go saying anything, all right? I mean it, not even to Tess or Sean or anyone." Chris looked at me pointedly when he mentioned Sean and my mood instantly darkened.

"Where is Sean, anyway?" asked Adam. "I haven't seen him around."

"Pfft, how should I know? I'm not his keeper."

Chapter Fifty-Two

Days went by and there was still no word from Sean.

Chris said he was pretty tied up with work, heading to the city a couple of times through the week. Somehow it did little to appease me. Every time I thought back to our last heated exchange, anytime I wanted to sulk about it, I snapped myself out of it. I didn't want people to think I was the sullen, spoilt brat he'd called me. Even my parents had been surprised by my civilised behaviour, though, to be honest, my worry over Sean's absence overrode my concerns for the hotel.

***

Shuffling into the main bar mid-morning, I paused mid-stride as I spotted a gift box on the bar.

"Ooh, what's that?" I asked Chris, eying it sceptically.

"Sean dropped it off this morning," he said, unenthusiastically. He pushed it towards me. "It's for you. I don't know what's going on with you two, but it's probably not a good idea to worry your mum and dad over your love life right now," he added.

My heart spiked in delight, but I quickly stamped it back down. I was thrilled, but still mad at him. "Ha!" I said. "What love life?"

Chris cocked his brow at the white gift box tied meticulously with a turquoise, silk bow.

"Good point, I'll get rid of it," I said.

I carried the box into the kitchen, hearing a chorus of upbeat chatter. Jenny McGee rolled out pastry beside a production line made up of Melba, Tess and Ellie peeling and chopping vegetables.

"Oooh, what've you got there?" crooned Ellie.

"Just a little something." I frowned, placing the box on the counter.

"From a secret admirer?" asked Jenny.

"Not exactly," I said, picking up a carrot stick and munching on it thoughtfully.

"Well, what does the card say?" Tess pointed at the box.

I frowned. "There is no card."

"Uh, yeah there is." Tess wiped her hands on a tea towel, picked up the box and pulled out a business-card-sized card tucked underneath the turquoise silk.

How could I have missed that?

"Ahhh!" I jumped from my position about to grab it from Tess, when it was quickly plucked from her hands by Ellie.

"Oooh, writing." She smiled.

"Ellie!"

She held her hand up, her brows rising as she read the note. "Oh." Ellie's blue eyes widened in surprise.

"What?" I frowned.

It was enough to have Jenny and Tess clambering to see what was on it. Even Melba peered over their shoulders.

I threw my arms in the air. "I give up."

A look of astonishment lit all of their faces.

"Well, what does it say?"

Tess cleared her throat. "He has such tiny handwriting." She squinted.

"I said I would let you know what I wanted. – Sean."

I glowered at the box.

"Whatever the hell that means, this is huge!" said Ellie.

"Yeah, such a poet," I said sarcastically.

Ellie laughed. "No, Amy, you don't get it. In Sean terms, this is massive."

I looked blankly at their expectant faces.

Tess rolled her eyes. "Sean Murphy doesn't chase girls and he sure as hell doesn't send gifts in pretty little boxes with silky bows."

Ellie nodded. "What's going on between you two, anyway?"

"Trust me, it's a long, uninteresting story."

"Well, let's see how uninteresting," said Jenny, looking pointedly at the box on the counter.

"Yesss! Let's open it." Ellie clapped excitedly.

Tess started unravelling the folds of the bow. "Okay, place your bets, ladies; I call chocolate."

"Earrings," Ellie threw in.

"Perfume," said Jenny.

I leaned forward, allowing myself to get carried away with their excitement.

"And the winner is …" announced Tess. She flipped the box open and her smile slowly fell away. "Oh."

The others almost crushed Tess as they peered into the box, the same looks spreading across their faces as their eyes looked sheepishly up towards me, causing butterflies in the pit of my stomach.

"What? What is it?"

Tess smiled sadly. "It's, umm …"

"Oh, for God's sake, Tess!" I snatched the box out of her hands and peered inside.

My audience nervously watched on, on standby to console me as soon as it registered what was in the box.

So when a goofy grin spread across my face and I started to laugh hysterically, they gave one another puzzled, sidelong looks. They must have thought I had lost the plot.

"Amy, are you all right?" Tess asked cautiously.

I shook my head. Reaching into the box, I held up … a Rubik's Cube. All twisted in a multitude of colours.

"It's not much of a gift, is it, honey?" Jenny said gently.

"Yeah," Ellie added. "The boy clearly doesn't know how to buy for a woman."

I sighed. "It's perfect."

"Really?" frowned Ellie.

It really was, all twisted and messed up.

Just like us.

Chapter Fifty-Three

My parents wanted to keep things normal – as normal as anything could be under the circumstances.

So when Dad announced we were going to have a disco the weekend before the auction, well, I kind of thought he might have been taking the piss.

He wasn't.

I realised as much when I looked at Mum across the dining table and was met with an earnest smile.

"Really?" I frowned.

"Well, weren't you going to plan something for the weekend, anyway?" Dad asked, cutting into his steak.

"Yeah, but that was before." I tried not to cringe.

"How about we give ourselves permission, for one night, to just try to forget all the bad stuff," Dad said.

I traced the line of peas on my plate, recalling the last time I had attempted to make myself forget. I had ended up in Sean Murphy's bed. And though it had been a beautiful beginning … it hadn't ended so well.

I would have thought a disco so close to the auction wasn't a great idea, but my parents were adamant: it was what they wanted. I didn't know if it was a way of masking it as some kind of goodbye party, or they were trying to cheer me up. If that was the case, it kind of had the opposite effect. Come Saturday, the whole place was chaos, getting the beer garden ready for what would be our last Henderson gathering at the Onslow before it was bought by some blow-in from the city and turned into a B & fracking B. It was my deepest hope that the McGees would put in a bid. According to Chris they had gone to their bank manager and crunched some numbers so that was a promising sign.

I forced myself not to think about it, but every time I descended the hotel stairs or perched myself on a bar stool I couldn't help but feel I was counting down to a time when I would never be able to do this again.

***

Before I was even awake, my mobile beeped twice, alerting me to a message.

Thinking it most likely Tammy, I rolled over in my bed to grab it from my bedside to check, when my heart just about stopped.

Sean.

Amidst the insanity of the weeks that had followed from that night, I hadn't seen Sean much. I hadn't seen him much *at all.* He had landed a massive building project in Maitland that had him working away until the weekends. I managed to convince myself that it was just bad timing. I had so much going on at the Onslow and he was working away, so the fact that nothing had progressed from that night was just because of the circumstances.

That's what I tried to tell myself, anyway; I had convinced myself that it had been a bad day. I had been after an escape, just one night. After all, I'd sought him out, pushed him. It had been a one-off, obviously. Sean had made no promises, or declarations of undying love … the thought of which always brought me back to the day after, when he had wanted to tell me something. I had feared him giving me the friendship spiel so much I had legged it quick smart. Looking back now, I wish I had listened, instead of now waiting, hoping to hear from him or see him. Missing him. If I had heard him out at the time, at least now I would know one way or another. My life was in limbo in all aspects. No wonder I couldn't sleep. And the more I didn't hear from him the angrier I was at him. I did miss him, but it didn't mean that I would be falling over him come weekends, or be pathetic and overly grateful whenever he felt like sending a random text. I had some pride.

1 New Message:

Sean: Unravelled the cube???

My brows narrowed. That was it? Three words? I hit reply, smiling evilly to myself.

To: Sean.

I'm sorry do I know you???

It took twenty seconds for my phone to beep again.

1 New Message:

Sean: So that's a no then?

I went to reply but thought better of it. Instead, I put my phone on silent and tossed it back on my side table.

Yep! I was still mad at him.

***

At Saturday night's disco, I watched as my parents faked their way through the night with an award-winning performance of upbeat gaiety. Seriously, they almost had even me convinced life was good.

They talked of exciting new chapters in their lives and how much they were looking forward to it. I thought it best to keep my distance from them and their friends as I was in danger of giving up the jig – one look at me and anyone could have told life wasn't a bed of roses.

I sidestepped along the edge of the dance floor, watching my parents from across the garden, concentrating on the cracks that I expected to see in their cheerful facade. In a moment's pause, my mum turned to Dad and looked at him, *really* looked at him.

Although I would usually cringe and roll my eyes at their moments of wedded bliss, I saw something tender exchange between them. Dad had his arm around the back of Mum's seat and he leaned in to whisper something in her ear. She laughed, like *really* laughed and it was for the first time in, well … forever that I had seen them look so happy. Together. I was never so grateful that they had each other, that they had reconnected. It made me feel like anything we could face we could do together, as a family. I smiled, turning to make my way towards the bar when I slammed into someone.

Sean.

My knee-jerk reaction was to whack him as hard as I could. "Ow! Look where you're going!" I cried.

"Not the face!" Sean held his hands up protectively.

"Relax – punching you in the face would hurt me more than it would you, I'm sure," I said, shaking my hand and wincing. Hitting Sean was like hitting granite.

"No doubt. I am blessed with a ludicrously chiselled jaw line."

"Ludicrously chiselled?" I scoffed.

"Sure, check it out!"

Sean reached for my hand and brought it up to his face. My fingers traced his freshly shaven jaw, something I didn't usually see. I took a good look at him: he was freshly shaven, wearing a short-sleeved dress shirt and navy jeans. He looked ludicrously good.

"You feel it?" he said, a small glimmer of amusement in his eyes.

I felt my traitorous heart pound against my ribcage as my fingers traced a line down his jaw. I snapped out of my trance. We were in a public beer garden. I pulled my hand away and cleared my throat, trying not to look too embarrassed.

"It's not *that* ludicrous," I said quietly.

Sean was still looking at me, I could feel it, but before he could say anything, Tammy let out a loud squeal in the distance.

"Oh my God, I love this song! Amy … Come on!"

She disentangled herself from the crowd and grabbed my hand.

"Come on, let's go!"

She hauled me through the throng of partiers, whether I liked it or not, although it was a welcome save from the possible awkwardness I had under the surface that bubbled up at the very thought of talking to Sean.

It didn't take long to let the music override us – everything else just swept away. I couldn't help but look over, keep track of Sean's movements. It was fine; he had made his way towards a table to sit with the Onslow Boys. Their heads bowed every now and then in conversation, Toby moved to refill glasses; Ringer arrived and slapped their backs and joined the fray. But one thing I was adamantly aware of was Sean's searing gaze as he sipped on his beer, the disco lights flickering across his smug face. Maybe he was just looking at the dance floor, but either way I felt eyes on me.

I was keenly aware of my body, my movements, making every dance move less high school social, more city nightclub, putting more effort into it as Tammy did. I swayed my hips, hands over my head, moving to the music.

Let him watch.

There was always a part of every girl that the same. Although we complained about the boys who chose not to take to the dance floor with us, we all secretly loved the fact that they all stood around the edges and watched. There was something so male, so sexy about the ones who thought themselves too cool to join in.

And then, of course, there were the ones who did join in. They weren't uncool. Well, some were, but there were the boys that took to the dance floor and melted right in with their own quirky, at times lame, dance moves that added to the fun. Right now, it proved to be Ringer and Stan as they sidled up next to Tammy and me, busting a move. We gradually formed a little circle of the four of us, taking turns in the middle for a dance-off. But unlike most dance-offs this was to outdo each other by attempting the daggiest, worst dance moves we could think of. Ringer mimicked a sprinkler move, and then I mocked him by miming starting up a whipper snipper before trimming the hedges. Tammy did the classic *Saturday Night Fever* diagonal point, but Stan took the title with the worst impersonation of the robot I had ever seen. We were all hunched over, laughing so hard I had to hold Tammy upright. Stan broke into a horrifically bad shuffle-step-shuffle moon walk.

Ringer, Tammy, and I bowed to the winner of terrible moves, yelling, "We're not worthy!"

The lights dimmed and the music changed pace. I went to walk off the dance floor to avoid all the loved-up slow dancers and catch my breath, when someone gently grabbed my elbow.

Sean.

Tammy grabbed Stan. "Come on, Stan, buy me a drink, I'm dying here." Tammy pushed him past me, whispering, "Talk to Sean."

The problem being it was the loudest whisper in the southern hemisphere and Sean smirked.

Kill me now!

He grabbed my hand and turned me into a spin. "You heard her – talk to Sean."

The DJ was playing 10CC's 'I'm Not In Love.' While most couples were head to chest, romantically shuffling and swaying to the music, Sean's eyes bore into mine, bristling with an underlying tension.

His lips twitched "Nice dance moves earlier."

"As if we were being serious."

"Sure."

I lifted my chin defiantly. "Well, I have no regrets."

He leaned down; I could feel his lips brush against my ear. "Neither do I."

Sean's voice was low and sexy. We weren't talking about bad dance moves anymore.

I tried not to think too much about how good it felt to be in his arms, or how my heart betrayed my mind with its insistent pounding. I battled so hard against my feelings, but looking up into his familiar blue eyes, all my mid-week convictions that I felt nothing for Sean Murphy came crashing down. I wracked my brain for small talk, half hoping that Sean would strike up a conversation first, but as I looked up at him, unlike me, he seemed completely comfortable, like words weren't necessary.

Sean's hand slid down gently, cupping my lower back, the heat of him pressed against me. The multi-coloured flickers of the disco lights flashed across his handsome face. He smelled so good, my defences came down and I melted into him, just a little.

I closed my eyes, willing myself the strength to walk away; the song was coming to an end. Sean saved me from making that decision.

Letting go of me, he backed away with a long, lingering look, before melting into the sea of bodies and leaving me breathless and alone on the dance floor.

Chapter Fifty-Four

"Amy, have you even been listening to a thing I have said?"

I double-blinked. Tess cast a frown to an amused-looking Toby.

"Sorry, I just have so much going through my mind at the moment." I grimaced.

"The auction?" Toby asked.

Oh yeah, the auction. I'd forgotten about that.

If I were to be honest, it was the first time I had thought of it all night and I felt a little bit guilty over the fact. My eyes trailed over the crowd. I spotted Chris standing with a group, animatedly retelling a story with wild hand gestures that had his audience captivated. Adam and Ellie were burning up the dance floor as 'Video Killed The Radio Star' blared from the speakers. They were so into their own outrageous Kate Bush-esque moves they had pretty much cleared the dance floor.

Tess and Toby followed my line of vision. Toby shook his head. "They're going to end up taking someone's eye out."

"Truly terrifying," Tess agreed.

My attention was swayed by my mother's unmistakable burst of laughter. She sat at a table with all my parents' friends holding their glasses up in a toast. To the naked eye it looked like all the Hendersons were having the time of their lives. The auction seemed like the furthest thing from any of our minds. Sure, it had just popped into mine, but I couldn't help but feel a little miffed. Was I the only one really affected by what was happening? Happening eleven a.m. Monday morning? This really was the last event we would host.

I need a drink!

I zigzagged through the crush of bodies and made my way towards the beer garden bar. Max was flat out attending to the drunken hordes. I wedged myself into a space at the end of the bar, thinking that he would get to me when he was ready.

I felt the press of someone behind me and before I had the chance to move, I heard the unmistakable voice yell out: "Another VB and a raspberry Cruiser, thanks, mate!"

I turned to stare up at Sean.

"It's raspberry you drink, right?"

"Thanks."

Sean squeezed next to me, handing over a twenty and passing me my Cruiser.

"Having fun?" he asked before sipping on his beer.

I shrugged. "I guess."

Sean leaned his back against the bar and his gaze trailed over the sea of people in the beer garden. "Sounds like you need a distraction."

"Well, I have been distracted by Adam and Ellie's alternative dance moves."

Sean's eyes darted off into the distance. He slowly raised his beer to his mouth. "I wasn't talking about that kind of distraction," he smirked, before taking another long sip.

My eyes narrowed in confusion as I looked up to study his profile. Sean didn't break away from whatever he was looking at, so I thought maybe I had misheard him.

He pursed and smacked his lips together, as if savouring the remnants of his beer before turning to face me, holding his beer up mid-sip, mostly to disguise what he was saying to me.

"Leave the back door unlocked tonight," he said before skulling the rest of his beer and placing the empty glass on the bar. He winked down at me before stalking through the crowd and disappearing out of the side exit into the night.

***

Oh my God! Oh my God!

I grabbed a pile of clothes and shoved them in the bottom of my cupboard. Ripping my bra off the handle of my door I shoved it in my bedside drawer. I frantically straightened out my doona cover and studied my reflection in the mirror for the hundredth time.

Did he mean what I think he meant?

Sean had vanished for the rest of the night. My head was so firmly in the clouds I kept getting sympathetic looks from everyone.

"Poor Amy, she is really taking it hard."

"She's just not herself tonight."

If only they knew the truth. My first port of call was to make sure that the back door to the beer garden staircase was in fact unlocked; I twisted and left it ajar. Mercifully, Adam and Chris and everyone were headed up to the Point tonight. But not me. No one questioned my sincerity when I said I had a headache and didn't really feel up to it.

I peered down the long, darkened hall to see that no slither of light shone from underneath my parents' door. I tiptoed back into my room and shut the door.

I took a deep, calming breath. My clock radio read twelve-forty a.m. I started to wonder if maybe Sean had been joking; maybe it had been so long since we had last hung out that I had forgotten how to read his smart-arse innuendoes. I paced my room, a worried line etched in my brow.

I am such an idiot. He was probably sitting on the bonnet of a car at the Point with his arm slung around some floozy, having a good old laugh at me. With each passing minute, anger boiled within me.

He's not coming. He is not coming.

I chewed anxiously on my thumbnail, scowling at the wall, shaking my head. I was such an idiot.

Nearing on two a.m., I resigned myself to the fact that he wasn't coming and felt filled with self-loathing. When would I ever learn? Sean Murphy would never change.

I furiously brushed my hair, cursing the day I ever met Sean Murphy. With each stroke I spat a word of commentary.

"Arrogant!" *Stroke.*

"Egotistical!" *Stroke.*

"Infuriating!" *Stroke, stroke, stroke.*

I threw the brush on my dresser, knocking over the white gift box that sat there. I stared at the tipped box, slowly reaching over to stand it back up, the weight inside plonking against the cardboard. I reached inside and retrieved the Rubik's Cube. I glared at it. Surely I should have taken this as a sign that there was rarely ever a serious moment with Sean; even his 'I'm sorry' gift had to have a smart-arse undertone to it. I thought back to the horrified looks on the girls' faces in the kitchen. They had thought I'd lost the plot when I seemed happy about receiving not chocolates or jewellery, but a Rubik's Cube from Sean.

I re-read the card:

'I said I would let you know what I wanted.'

"A Rubik's Cube? What are you trying to say? Pfft, idiot!"

I sat on my bed, punching and fluffing up my pillows, leaning against my bedhead. I studied the multi-coloured, twisted cube, the colours speckled all over its surface.

He's messed it up good and proper.

I turned it over and over and held it up to the light, when I sat up suddenly. I pulled the lampshade closer and squinted at some small, black markings on some of the squares.

What the ...?

I turned the cube around and around. Seemingly random black lines were marked all over the cube.

I started twisting, seeing if it would become clearer. The markings appeared to only affect the red blocks but until I unravelled the grid I couldn't make out what they meant. My heart raced looking closely at the lines. Were they letters or numbers? Some of them were horizontal, others diagonal, this one a squiggle; what the hell were these lines? After a while, I forgot about the markings and intently worked on unscrambling the mismatched pieces, manipulating it back into its original state. My heart was pounding. Shit! I couldn't get it. I kept over-rotating or making mistakes.

"God damn it!" I threw the cube across the room, running my hand over my brow. I got up and paced, glaring at the cube where it had landed in the corner.

I sighed. "Suck it up, Princess. You can do this."

I bent down to try again and took in a deep breath. My eyes flicked over the cube as my hands started working and twisting in a methodical fashion. I counted the turns in my mind, and eventually the cube began unravelling in my hands. With a final twist I all but laughed in relief. It sat in my hand, completed. Triumphant, I turned the cube in my hand to ensure that all was as it should be, but as I held it up to the light and exposed the red side, my smile fell away.

There, written in Sean's unmistakable penmanship, my fingers traced the permanent marker scrawled across the squares.

'I want you.'

And before the words had even sunk in, I heard the handle to my bedroom door twist.

Chapter Fifty-Five

With barely enough time to close the door behind him, Sean caught the look on my face and stilled.

"Amy, what's wro—" His eyes flicked to the Rubik's Cube.

In one fluid motion, I threw the cube onto my bed and closed the distance between us, violently pushing him against the door before drawing him closer and pressing my mouth against his.

Any moment of surprise Sean may have felt instantly melted into need as his hands fisted in my top and yanked me up against his body. His hands moved to my hair as his hot, silken tongue pushed deeper against my uneven gasps.

'I want you.' It was all I needed to know. Like the multi-coloured, messed-up cube that only he and I could understand the meaning of. The weight behind Sean's words was more than I could ever have hoped for. I didn't need any 'I like you's' or 'I love you's.' Above everything else, the simple fact was that he wanted me.

I broke away from the kiss, hovering so close to his lips, his shallow breaths heating my face.

"I want you, too," I whispered.

Realisation dawned across Sean's face, his eyes brightening as his lush mouth tilted in approval.

"Clever girl!" He laughed softly before pressing his lips to mine again.

Grabbing for the fabric of my shirt, he peeled it upwards and off in one clean swipe, throwing it across my room. My hands grabbed frantically at Sean's belt, flicking and looping it to access the button on his jeans. His hands covered mine to make faster work of it. My impatient, shaking fingers failed me as they moved up to work at the buttons of his shirt. I couldn't do it fast enough. In a maddening sense of urgency I pulled his shirt apart, a shower of buttons littering the floor.

I bit my lip, stifling my smile. "Sorry about that," I said, peeling his shirt back over his broad shoulders.

"Fuck the shirt," Sean muttered against my mouth as he edged me backward onto my bed.

Sean stood before me, breathing hard. He slowly pulled his white singlet over his head, exposing his bare skin in the lamplight. I lay, transfixed by how utterly beautiful he was. An immense, explosive pleasure rippled through me with the knowledge that we were equally desperate for one another. I read it in the heat of his eyes. My own swept over him in a long, lingering caress, as if I was committing every angle, every line to memory. Reluctantly tearing my eyes away, I rolled over to turn the lamp off near my bedside, but Sean grabbed for my ankle and dragged me towards him.

I squealed at the unexpectedness of it as his hands skimmed up my thighs and pulled me closer to him.

"Shhh … You'll wake up your parents."

I sat up on the edge of the bed, his lips finding mine. Sean kneeled beside the bed, forcing my legs around his hips. I gasped as his beautiful, clever hands dug into my thighs and pulled me closer to him.

"Wait a minute, I have to turn the light off." I panted against his mouth.

Sean's hand glided upwards to my hips, sliding underneath my skirt.

"No, I want to see you," he whispered.

I frowned, shaking my head.

Sean's lips pressed against the crinkled line of my forehead, the pressure melting the line away, as his mouth moved to work a maddening trail down my neck.

"Leave it." He spoke his words into my heated skin. Suddenly all my worries about the lamplight were forgotten as Sean hooked his fingers into the elastic of my knickers.

The springs of the bed groaned a loud, infuriating sound as I moved under Sean's wicked touch.

I stilled, digging my nails into Sean's shoulders as he manoeuvred himself on top of me.

I winced. "The bed's too loud."

A glint of amusement lit Sean's eyes as he stood, pulling me to my feet. Reaching past me he pulled the doona off my bed and onto the floor with a shower of pillows. I had to stifle my laugh as Sean grinned down at me, stepping into a slow, lingering kiss. He motioned towards me gently, down to our new makeshift bed. He edged my legs apart and settled his delicious weight on top of me.

"Better?" He cocked his brow.

I smiled, threading my fingers around the tendrils of his hair at the nape of his neck.

"Much better."

He kissed me with a deep, intoxicating caress as he whispered against my mouth once more. "I know what will make it even better." Sean's wicked mouth lowered over my body, kissing a sweet trail of blinding madness as I cradled his head and arched into each knowing stroke.

Sean gently parted my legs wider, running his strong hands down my stomach. Leaving a tingling trail as his heated eyes watched mine, he shifted into place, dipping his head and placing a soft kiss on the inside of my knee. He traced a burning line on my smooth inner thigh.

This was forgetting in a way I had never dreamed was possible, so utterly mind-shattering. I inhaled, feeling fabric peel away, exposing me to Sean so completely. I breathed deeply, bracing myself for what was to come as his head lowered.

Surely he isn't …

He did. I had cursed him for dominating every thought of every waking moment of my day, for making me care way too much about the effect he had over me, the effect he had not just on my mind, but in that very moment on my body, as well. My hands fisted into the doona underneath me, my body no longer my own. I mentally cursed Sean Murphy, gasping in a series of blinding blinks and shallow breaths.

Damn him, I thought, *damn him*!

Never could I have believed that letting down my guard could feel so good and never could I have imagined that in that very moment, lying on my bedroom floor on a makeshift cluster of blankets and pillows, I would unravel so completely.

Chapter Fifty-Six

I would be such a crap poker player.

Since Sean's late-night sneak in and early-morning sneak out, I had only seen him once. One time. He came into the bar later on Sunday afternoon for a few quiet ones with Toby. I tried for cool and casual as I channel-flicked the television in the main bar while the boys talked to Dad about footy. I tried my best at pretending I wasn't affected by Sean's presence. Sean, the boy who I had, only a mere hours before, been having sex with on my bedroom floor.

He was so painfully close I didn't dare meet his knowing eyes. But, of course, me and my cursed, inquisitive nature couldn't help myself. I wiped down the bar next to Dad, glancing up from under my heavy, sleep-deprived eyelids to be rewarded with a flash of Sean's smile, or the sound of his laughter that had my stomach twisting in nervous pleasure. He was wearing a crisp, white T that complemented the tan of his skin.

It was absolute torture being so close to him, yet not interacting, hiding the new bond we now officially shared, but I was so paranoid people would get the 'they just did *it*' vibe, I couldn't talk to him; I couldn't be normal. Which was ridiculous. And I knew it was, but there was no way anyone would suspect that Sean Murphy and Amy Henderson were involved in any way.

Well, apart from Tammy who knew and Adam who had guessed, and Ringer who teased and Mum and Chris who threatened and, holy shit, was there anyone that didn't know? I casually looked at Dad in my peripheral vision and swallowed hard.

I have to get out of here.

I chucked the remote aside and made my way out from behind the bar.

"Where you going, love?" Dad broke from his conversation to look at me with interest, as did Toby and Sean.

Crap! I just wanted to sneak away.

It took all my strength to not automatically flick a glance at Sean; I could feel his eyes burning into me.

"Oh, um … I'm just going to see if Mum needs any help before the auction tomorrow," I stammered.

Dad's brows rose in astonishment. I guess me helping out in any way for the auction *would* be rather unexpected. These past three weeks for them had been the equivalent to living with a time bomb. I had flared up over the littlest of things. I was just tired and completely over my over-analysing thoughts. But it had all come down to this.

One more sleep.

So what had changed? What had mellowed me into the point of not obsessing about the inevitable? What had made me accept that it wasn't the end of the world, that in time I would get over it, made me realise that maybe I had been a bit of a diva about the whole thing, that maybe there was more to life than the Onslow Hotel?

My eyes flicked past Dad, locking briefly with beautiful, blue eyes and then and there I knew what had changed.

It was as if all else failed to be important. Maybe it was how Dad felt when he looked at Mum, the way I had seen him looking at her last night. I thought back to six weeks ago, how even sitting up in his hospital bed on oxygen he had looked so happy because he'd had Mum and me by his side. It wasn't just about gaining a new lease on life; it was about *having* a life.

'You take your memories with you.'

Sean had taught me that.

I smiled at my dad with a casual shrug. "I don't mind."

Dad's shoulders sagged in relief. "Thank God, Chook, she is driving me to drink."

"It's true," added Toby. "I saw him reach for the full cream milk for his cup of tea before."

I looked incredulously at Dad. "Don't you bloody dare!"

***

Monday morning – the day had come. The morning of the auction was so tense you could cut the air with a knife. It seemed the entire town had shown up on the steps of the Onslow to watch how things unfolded. Apparently there were half a dozen serious bidders in contention. I didn't care what the others planned for the place; my heart was solely set on the McGees.

We'd eaten dinner with them the night before, and I could tell Mum and Dad didn't want to put too much pressure on them so they kept things pretty light, but Chris, Adam and me knew they would be the perfect new owners. The time they had put into the restaurant these past few months had been such a big help and a massive success. People flocked back to have meals now and the Onslow had gained quite the reputation as the place to go if you wanted a hot meal and a cold beer.

Like the days of old.

The McGees' biggest opponents were the retired toffs from the city who wanted to turn the Onslow into a B & B. They had come out and inspected several times. I had loitered on the staircase, eavesdropping on their plans of knocking down walls and laying carpet over the hundred-year-old floorboards. It was horrifying. Another potential buyer was Gary Brewster, the insipid local pharmacist. What he wanted with the Onslow was anyone's guess – rumour had it that he wanted to convert it into a home for himself and his high-maintenance wife. It would make for a rather grand mansion on the hillside, I guessed.

But it wasn't meant to be anything like that – the Onslow had served the community for over four generations. It was a place to gather after a hard week's work, to catch up with mates, or to secretly pash your crush in a shadowy alcove. It was supposed to be filled with music and laughter, a meeting point for functions and discos, for lonely widowers to sit at the bar on a graveyard shift and be kept company by the barman. It was a rite of passage for every local eighteen-year-old to come in and have their first drink. It was where the Onslow Boys would meet up and play pool and fill the jukebox with shrapnel.

Gary Brewster couldn't win today, he just couldn't. The thought of the Onslow shutting its doors to the public broke my heart. It hurt more than worrying about moving back to the city to live; it was the end of an era and I could tell my dad knew it, too.

Dad sat in the beer garden with his paper and a green tea. He was turning the pages but I knew his mind was elsewhere. Mum was busy roaming through the hotel, waving freshly baked bread around and setting out flowers for last-minute inspections. I had argued with her that she didn't want it to seem too appealing, that after all we didn't want the McGees to have too much competition. But as with all things, Mum's motto was, "There are no friends in business."

I had discovered Dad in the garden as a result of escaping her flurry of activity.

I pulled out a seat, scraping the legs along the concrete.

My dad's weary eyes snapped up from his paper. "Hey, Chook."

I sighed, rubbing my hands nervously on my thighs. "Not long now."

He smiled a small smile. "No."

I had thought I was in a pretty good place, that I had finally accepted and would be all right, but sitting opposite my dad's sorrowful eyes I felt a lump rise in my throat. Keeping the hotel just for me wasn't enough; they'd had to want it, too. I could see in my dad's grey complexion, the lines etched around his eyes, that he was stressed, anxious and tired.

So tired. In reality, his heart hadn't been here for a long time. He had been oblivious to the hotel as it had fallen down around him. I had just never thought to look beyond the rubble.

"Dad?"

"Yeah, love?"

"It's going to be all right. I know I haven't said that to you, but whatever happens… I just wanted you to know that."

"It hasn't been an easy decision, love, but I just …"

"It's okay." I squeezed his hand. "You don't have to explain."

I didn't really have anything else to add; I mean, what was I meant to say in times like this? Good luck? Here's to the end of life as we know it? Hardly felt right. Instead, I shifted my seat back, got up and wrapped my arms around him for a silent moment before pecking him on the cheek and walking away.

***

The agent had said it would probably be best if we remained inside during the auction, but I couldn't stomach not knowing what was happening outside. Melba was on standby, fetching Mum and Dad cups of tea, while Chris's parents, Aunty Lynda and Uncle Ray, buzzed around anxiously, speculating what *it* would go for. That's right, '*it*', as if the Onslow, our pub, my home, was worth nothing more than money now. That it wasn't a family home that had been handed down for generations, that it wasn't a part of me. The talk of money made my stomach turn and I could feel a familiar anger boil within me.

I have to get out of here.

As I shoved the front door open and joined the bustling crowd outside I was hit with a fresh summer breeze that blew in from the lake. I tried to convince myself that it was the reason my eyes had become so shiny. The car park was packed, filled with unknown cars and faces. My skin crawled at the idea of all these people clambering around me, around my home. I scanned the crowd frantically for a familiar face, any face, but more urgently I searched for Sean. I hadn't seen him since yesterday in the bar with Toby, and through the chaos we hadn't even spoken. But I had never doubted that he would be out here somewhere, that he would have come, knowing what today meant for me.

I momentarily entertained the possibility that he had *not* come. A coldness swept over me at the thought. I really didn't want to have to think about how I would feel about that.

I let out a long, shuddery breath as I tried to rein in my emotions as they battled inside me. I felt a reassuring squeeze to my shoulders and I spun around to see Tammy's warm, comforting face.

"You all right?" She offered me a sad smile.

The only thing that prevented me from losing it was the fact that Toby's parents stood nearby. Matthew Morrison playfully bumped my chin with his fist.

"She's all right!" he said, trying to lighten the mood.

I smiled in good humour, but my legs shook underneath me. I clenched my hands into fists to stop the tremor that would give my nerves, my dread away.

"Have you seen Sean?" I scanned the crowd once more, my eyes darting amongst the nearing crowd as an anxious hum of voices settled over the masses. They looked over their pamphlets and murmured in clusters, speculating about what was to come: how much the hotel would go for, what it would become. Everywhere I looked a new-found dread made my heart rate spike. Mr Brewster, the pharmacist, and his stiff-upper-lipped wife stood to the far right, whispering to one another, their beady eyes trailing hungrily over the exterior of the hotel.

My eyes passed over the crowd before locating a familiar face. Tess smiled and offered a small wave, standing by her parents who were in deep conversation, their faces masked behind their brochures. I allowed myself a moment of peace, of hope, of relief. They were here. It looked like they were really going to bid.

As time marched on towards the hour, I knew that Sean wasn't coming. A numbness filled me, the crowd a mesh of shapes and colour that I refused to look over anymore.

I was snapped out of my trance by an irritatingly chipper voice.

"Oh, turn that frown upside down, Miss Henderson. The sun is shining – it's as if Mother Nature herself has blessed us with this beautiful day."

I blinked at a balding, beanpole of a man in a suit as he wrestled with one of the auction flags on the verandah. He looked more like a creepy funeral director than an auctioneer.

He dusted off his hands and straightened his tie. "Make no mistake, folks, we will sell today." He beamed, as if I should be bowing down to him in gratitude, as if he had just given me the best news of my life. I glared at him unenthusiastically and he soon got the hint.

He coughed. "Right, better get this show on the road." He excused himself.

I felt the press of someone next to me. "What a wanker!"

I turned to find Adam and Ellie by my side. I didn't have to voice the fact that I was happy to see them. Adam and I gave each other a silent exchange just through a look, a look that said 'I know'. Even though he could be so infuriatingly annoying, as he gave my hand a reassuring squeeze I had never been so happy to have him with me.

Max slid in between him and Ellie. "Look out – grey suit, two o'clock," he said in a low voice.

We all turned to where we thought two o'clock was, which, naturally, was all in opposite directions.

"Where?" Ellie whined loudly, stepping on tiptoes.

Max sighed, shaking his head, and pointed. "There."

We looked over to the outskirts of the gathered crowd on the drive to a tall man in an expensive grey suit, who was talking into his mobile phone.

"Sydney buyers," Max added glumly.

My heart sank.

I turned, expecting to see a mirrored image of hopelessness in Adam, but instead I was surprised to see a wry smile. I followed his line of vision, confused at what could evoke such a look at a time like this.

I froze. In the very distance the crowd was parting, and continued to do so in a wave of annoyance as people stepped aside. Making their way towards the Onslow steps, like they had a thousand times before, were Toby, Stan, Ringer and Chris, all led by Sean.

Emotion so raw slammed into me as I watched him lead the Onslow Boys towards the hotel. I fought the urge not to run across the drive and fling my arms around him, so grateful to see him appear out of the crowd. Toby peeled off to stand near Tess and her parents for support, but Sean and the others made a direct line up the steps and closed the distance between us. Stan was talking to Sean but he wasn't paying attention, too busy taking in the crowd on the verandah. His expression was serious and intense until his eyes found me.

I held my breath as our eyes locked on each other. Sean's broody exterior soon melted into a familiar warmth that instantly soothed me. I felt like I could face anything now he was there, that everything would be okay.

There was no time to exchange pleasantries as the auctioneer banged his gavel and called for the crowd's attention, motioning everyone into place as the murmurs fell into silence and people crept forward to attention. I half expected the boys to pause and stop where they were near the steps, but Sean strode towards me.

Paying no attention to the commotion, he walked straight over, never once taking his eyes from me. He winked at me, flashing a devilish smile that caused my heart to skip a beat.

In front of the entire town of Onslow, he stood … by my side.

Chapter Fifty-Seven

Once again I was lost.

The auctioneer started to fire up the crowd with his witty charm and brainwashing spiel.

"Ladies and gentlemen, it's as if Mother Nature herself had blessed us with this fine day," he said with a jovial laugh.

"Ugh! Is he serious?" Ellie groaned.

"I think this bloke needs to think of some new material for his stand-up routine," Adam added under his breath.

There was a collective snicker amongst our group, but it failed to raise any humour in me. I fazed in and out of the auction as it unfolded before me, catching only the edges of what he was calling out.

"Make no mistake, ladies and gentlemen, this is a historical landmark, lovingly developed and maintained over successive years by four generations of the Henderson family."

Each word was like a knife in my heart. I could feel my chest tightening, my eyes welling when something unexpected happened. Fingers laced with mine, palm pressed to palm, a reassuring squeeze that broke my misery spiral as I looked to my side.

Sean.

I studied his profile – he never broke the stern lines of his face as he, like the rest, stoically watched on.

"Here we go," muttered Stan.

"Okay, ladies and gentlemen, let's do what we came here to do and find this grand old lady a history-breaking new owner. Bearing in mind, this property comes with no bar code – you can't scan happiness."

I squeezed Sean's hand so hard I thought I might break it.

"Don't be shy, ladies and gentlemen, raise those hands to the sky, nice and high so I can see them. Where we at? Where will we begin? Today's the day to make your claim on this wonderful lakeside property. Look at those views, ladies and gentlemen, the best in town. Can't you just picture yourself downing a cold one from these balconies? It could be you. Who will start me off? Don't be shy."

This was it. Oh, God, this was it. My heart pounded hard in my chest as I waited for the first bid.

Silence. I allowed myself a foolish moment of hope when no one spoke. Maybe it wouldn't sell. Maybe I could keep it. Maybe I could stay—

A voice called from the crowd. I closed my eyes, my heart plummeting as the faceless voice slammed me back into reality, into a living nightmare.

"Four hundred?" the auctioneer asked, blinking. "It's a cheeky low bid, sir, but nevertheless I'll take it. Where we at? Where we at? Who wants the rope?" he called.

Mr Brewster raised his hand to the sky. "Four fifty!"

The suspense was terrible; it was a blur of faceless calls and clichéd shouts from the auctioneer that had my mind whirring in a blind panic until I heard the unmistakable voice of Jeff McGee.

"Six hundred!" He raised his hand.

My head snapped up to attention. Sean shifted beside me, too, as we both tensed at the new bidder – the McGees.

"I have your six hundred, sir. Where we at, people, where we at?" He turned towards Mr Brewster who glowered at the McGees and sternly nodded, raising his hand.

"Six hundred and fifty," he called.

"Thank you, sir, I like your style," the auctioneer crooned.

Toby squeezed Tess's shoulders. Her colour had drained from her face and her eyes were as wide as saucers as her dad raised his arm again.

Mr McGee: "Six sixty."

Mr Brewster: "Six seventy."

Mr McGee: "Six eighty."

Mr Brewster: "Six ninety!"

An anxious Jeff McGee raised his hand one more time. "Six nine five."

That's when I saw it; the look from Jenny McGee as she squeezed Jeff's arm and they met each other's eyes.

They were at their limit.

No-no-no-no-no.

I bit my lip, my eyes blurring as dread swept over me. I looked at Sean – his jaw pulsed with tension as he watched the auction. I turned to see Chris looking grim as we waited for Mr Brewster to make a decision. He muttered urgently to his wife and an agent who had approached, no doubt encouraging them to push on.

I hadn't realised I was holding my breath until it came out in a long shudder when Mr Brewster raised his hand. "Seven hundred."

The crowd murmured and all eyes were on the McGees.

Jeff looked stone-faced, straight and stoic, like he could take on the world. I would have believed he could if it wasn't for the sad, defeated eyes of Jenny McGee, who looked upon her husband.

It felt like an eternity as another agent approached the McGees, whispering and trying all their best lines to convince them to go just one more.

I was frozen, my heart the only movement as it drummed in my ears. My eyes never wavered from the McGees until … Mr McGee lowered his head and shook it. *No.*

They were out.

I felt my world fall away. I had had my heart set on the McGees buying the Onslow, keeping it in the family, so to speak. With them as owners, nothing would have changed; it would still have been run as a hotel and would have held the same people and memories as before.

But now Mr Brewster nodded in triumph and the auctioneer called for the crowd's attention. I could see the cogs turning in Brewster's head as he pictured his new mansion for himself and his awful wife. I couldn't believe it had come to this. My heart ached.

"Seven hundred and fifty."

What the frack?

Everyone looked around them, dumbfounded as to where the call had come from. Even the auctioneer seemed a bit jilted until he finally located the arm raised high.

On the edge of the crowd, an arm was raised in the air from the grey-suited businessman.

The Sydney buyers.

"No!" My chin trembled.

It was one thing to think of the Brewsters getting their claws into my home, but for the rich city buyers to come in and turn it into a bed and breakfast? To tear down its walls, to strip it of all its history and turn it into something that didn't belong in our community? I couldn't bear it.

I broke away from Sean's hold and pushed through the crowd of stunned onlookers before the tears fell. It was too much; too much to take. I ripped the bar room door open to see my parents, holding each other's hands. They looked just as stunned as I did. I stormed past them towards the restaurant staircase.

My dad reached out to me. "Honey—"

"Don't!" I shrugged him off and ran for the staircase, *my* staircase, for what would be the very last time.

Chapter Fifty-Eight

"The Brewsters didn't get it."

I lifted my head from where it was buried in my knees, my face stained with tears and my cheeks flushed from crying so hard my chest ached. I didn't know why I had come up to the balcony. What had drawn me there? Maybe because it was where it had all begun.

My blurry vision settled on my dad who stood between the open French doors. If I'd had any energy, I probably would have screamed at him. Was he happy? Were Mum and Dad pleased with the money that would now line their pockets as they began their 'new chapter'? Were they happy with the deal they had made with the Devil to make it so?

"Grey suit?" I croaked.

Dad nodded his head, his face expressionless.

I scoffed, shaking my head. "Awesome."

"It was a bit of a battle but you probably heard it from up here," Dad said.

I had been so immersed in self-pity and hopelessness I hadn't paid any attention to the sounds below. My world had crumbled as soon as Jeff McGee had shaken his head *no*. After that, little else had mattered.

"Wow! A bed and breakfast," I said. "How quaint." My words dripped with sarcasm.

My dad's brows narrowed as he picked at the edge of the door frame.

"Is that what you think they'll do?" he asked.

I glowered at him incredulously. "Dad! I was there; loitering on the steps when they brought the architect in. They were going to rip this out and smash that down. They know exactly what they want." I was so furious with him, with how blasé he was being. It was as if the hotel meant nothing to him. Our ancestors would be rolling in their graves.

"Well, why don't we ask him what the new owners have planned?" Dad's head tilted to the apartment.

My mouth gaped open and a new fear spiked through me. I pulled myself to my feet.

"Don't you dare," I whispered. "I don't want to see anyone."

"Even me?"

Sean appeared beside Dad in the doorway. My shoulders slumped in relief. Had Dad not been standing right there I would have run into his arms and cried into him.

"Look, love, I don't want to be rude. It will just take a sec to have a talk with the bloke," Dad said.

Before I could protest, Dad stepped aside and Mr Grey Suit walked through the French doors with a briefcase. He was tall, but not as tall as Sean, and he was polished, sleek. No doubt about it, he was from the city. He had a no-nonsense grace and all-business attitude that had me self-consciously running my fingers through my hair as I silently cursed my dad.

Sean sidestepped and leaned against the door, watching on in stony silence.

Ugh. I didn't want to speak to him – what was there to say? I wished the balcony would just open up and swallow me… again!

"You must be Amy. I'm Duncan Lawler." He reached out to shake my hand.

I unenthusiastically took it.

"Forgive my daughter, Mr Lawler, but as you can appreciate it has been a rather stressful day," my dad said.

"Of course," nodded Duncan.

"Maybe, Mr Lawler, you can alleviate some of my daughter's misconceptions. Are the new owners turning it into a B & B?"

He frowned. "Please, call me Duncan. And, uh, it is my belief that there are no plans to turn it into a B & B."

"See?" nodded Dad.

I remained unmoved. "Forgive me, Duncan, if I don't hold my breath over that."

Duncan smiled. "Is there anything I could do or say to make you think otherwise?"

I smiled sweetly. "Unless you drag the owner up here butt-naked, singing 'Zip-a-Dee-Doo-Dah' while simultaneously cartwheeling…"

Duncan burst out in laughter. "Well, um, I'll put it to them if you like."

I nodded and looked out over Lake Onslow when Duncan turned to Sean.

"What say you, Mr Murphy? Do you know the words to that song?"

My head snapped around. Sean hadn't moved an inch, still leaning against the door with his arms folded. He broke into a slow smile.

"I would be confident with everything but the cartwheel," he said without taking his eyes from me.

I was stunned – no, make that horrified – trying to grasp what was happening.

Sean straightened. "Amy, meet Duncan Lawler, my solicitor."

I shook my head in disbelief. "But, you're the Sydney buyer's solicitor."

Duncan shook his head. No.

I looked at Dad, searching for answers. "The Sydney buyer dropped out, love," he said gently.

I breathed hard: in, out, in, out. I felt dizzy. "Did you know?" I accused Dad, but Sean cut in before he could answer.

"No one knew."

I shook my head in disbelief. "Why didn't you tell me?"

Sensing the tension in the air, Dad moved off the balcony to the French doors.

"Duncan, um, would you care for a drink downstairs?"

Duncan moved quickly. "That would be great." He nodded at me before turning to shake Sean's hand. "We'll have some more paperwork for you to sign before you leave."

Dad walked over to kiss me on the cheek. "Go easy on him, love," he whispered. "He remortgaged his lake house to buy the Onslow."

Dad pulled away before seeing the look of horror in my eyes. He touched my cheek and made his way to follow Duncan, not before pausing in front of Sean.

"No one knew, eh?" Dad curved his brow.

Sean coughed, looking sheepishly at the floor. "Well, no one bar one." Sean's eyes lifted, a smile curving his lips.

"Do I need to guess?" Dad asked.

"If you were me and you could choose to go partners with someone in this place, who would you choose?"

Partners?

Dad broke into a slow smile. "You and Chris are going to do just fine." He held out his hand.

Sean visibly sagged as he took Dad's hand, but before he could register the movement, Dad pulled him into a manly hug, slapping him affectionately on the back, before pulling away with a sniff.

"The real estate guy was right – it's turned out to be a beautiful day." Dad sighed. I knew he was fighting his emotions, yet it wasn't the pang of sorrow and loss but the resounding relief of knowing the Onslow was going to be in safe hands.

I didn't know what to feel.

With the click of the apartment door sounding, I stood stock still, staring blankly at Sean.

He sighed. "I wanted to tell you … I tried to tell you."

"When?"

"The day after you stayed at my house, right before Ringer gave you a lift back."

I didn't have to think hard; I remembered the exact moment he was talking about. Vividly. How could I have been so stupid? I'd panicked and fled before giving him the chance, fearing the worst: the 'we should just be friends' spiel.

"Why didn't you tell me another time? You had plenty of chances."

"I thought about trying again, but come on. Amy, you thought putting up scaffolding was charity; what would you have said about *buying* the Onslow?"

I bit my lip. To be honest, I probably wouldn't have liked it. I didn't know what was wrong with me – any kind, helpful gesture he made I met with bull-headed defiance. Apart from my paying off his account, which, in the scheme of things, meant nothing, I had never been anything other than a burden to him financially. What had I to offer him? I felt sick.

"Sean, I'm so sorry." My voice shook.

Sean's brows creased in confusion.

I shook my head. "I wish I never came home. I'm sorry for the day I ever came crashing into your life."

"I'm not." Sean's eyes burned unflinchingly into mine for so long I had to look away. "Hey," he said gently, "I'm *not*. You are the only girl I have ever met who didn't want something from me. The only one who didn't look at me and see money, a car, a house, my devilish good looks."

That made me laugh.

Sean took in a deep breath and stepped forward.

"And because of that, I wanted to give them to you. I should have told you." He swallowed deeply before taking another hesitant footstep out into the open, onto the balcony.

I pressed my back against the railing, seeing Sean work through his paralysing fear to cross the balcony towards me.

With each step my heart rate spiked.

"You should have told me."

"I wanted to, so many times." He took another deep breath before another step.

"Did you try last night?" I bit out.

Sean paused halfway across the balcony. "Well, in my defence, I was going to until you attacked me." He smirked.

I blushed crimson, looking away from his playful eyes.

Sean took another deep breath before striding across to me and the railing. I reached out my hand – he took it, stepping into me and grabbing a nearby pole before glancing down.

"Holy shit, it's high." He spun away, his breathing heavy.

I moved in front of him, turning him away from the view, my eyes flicking over the beautiful lines of his face. It was now ghost white with fear.

I smiled. "What are you doing?"

He let out a shuddery breath, closing his eyes. "It's called diving in at the deep end," he said, before forcing his eyes open to look down at me.

I shook my head. "I seriously can't pay you back for this."

Sean laughed, as if he had almost forgotten to be terrified. He snaked his arms around my back, drawing me close. "I understand why you're spoilt within an inch of your life."

I frowned, puzzled.

"Who could help but want to give you the world?"

"But your home, Sean. You remortgaged your beautiful home?" I felt hot tears burn my eyes.

"You're my home." Sean stared down at me, his breath laboured for a whole other reason as he slowly closed the distance between our faces, brushing his lips against mine, gently at first, and then more insistently, cleansing me of all the worry and fear as I slid my hands up and along his broad back. He slowly drew away.

I sighed, shaking my head.

Sean's eyes narrowed. "What?"

"It's not enough."

Sean looked down at me incredulously. "I'm standing on the edge of a balcony, kissing you; I spent seven hundred and fifty thousand dollars on your hotel; and it's not enough?"

I shrugged. "I was kind of hoping for naked cartwheeling. The balcony's been reinforced, you know, I think it could take it." I grinned.

Sean shook his head. "There is only one girl in the world I would stand on the edge of a balcony for."

"And do naked cartwheels?"

"That too." He nodded.

I laughed. Hmm. I might have to hold him to that one day. "Wow," I said, "you must really love me." It blurted out before I could stop it. My playful smile faded as the words hung between us.

Sean's eyes ticked over my face in a long study. I thought he wouldn't say anything, that mercifully he mightn't have heard me, but then he broke the silence.

"More than you could ever know."

Epilogue

My feet dangled in the cool, murky lake water as I sat on the deck, chewing thoughtfully on the end of my pen.

My brow creased as I re-read one of the sentences I had written. My concentration was quickly interrupted by the sound of running and the whoosh of a six-foot-three torpedo somersaulting past me and bombing into the lake, spraying me with a shower of water.

"Sean!" I screamed, trying as best as I could to protect my paperwork.

His head broke through the surface and he flicked the excess water from his hair like boys tend to do. He was grinning from ear to ear.

"You're such a bloody child!" I said, glaring.

Sean stroked over to me, his cold, wet hands making me gasp as they latched onto my legs.

"You looked like you could do with a cool down."

"It's not funny, Sean, you've wet all my enrolment forms for uni," I said, blowing on the smudged writing.

I had left it until the last minute to fill in my transfer papers, but it hadn't exactly been in the forefront of my mind lately. Well, not until it had finally become clear to me what I wanted to do with my life. Inspiration comes in all sorts of strange forms and, although nothing had immediately changed with Sean buying the hotel, there were some developments that had been pretty exciting.

I had joked with Sean that he was now my boss and how he was sure to get a real kick out of that fact, but when he had in all seriousness shrugged and said, "I'm going to need an interior decorator," my heart had spiked with approval.

Now that I could do.

Bringing the Onslow into the new century was a passion Sean and I shared. I could help him with ideas and he was a skilled enough contractor to do the big work himself. So when we had joked that I should do this for a living, it had been a total light bulb moment. So here I was, filling in transfer papers from my uni in the city to the Maitland campus, only half an hour away, where I could study interior design. It was perfect.

Sean kissed my knee before lifting himself effortlessly out of the water to sit beside me.

"Sorry," he said earnestly, a small dimple creasing his cheek when he smiled.

I shook my head. "Damn you, Sean Murphy."

Sean's brows rose in surprise.

"You make it so hard for me to stay mad at you."

He broke into a boyish grin, before leaning forward to kiss my neck.

"Good," he whispered into my skin.

I squirmed against the sensation.

Sean leaned back, his eyes sparkling with delight. "It's been an interesting day."

I wasn't the only one who'd had a moment of self-discovery recently. Sean had been approached by the president of the Onslow Tigers to coach the seniors; he'd got to reconnect with his love for the game in a different way. This season I could already see myself sitting in the stands, freezing my butt off, barracking for the Onslow Tigers, and I couldn't wait. I played down my interest with the odd taunt about how the Perry Panthers were going to dominate the season. Sean just shook his head – these days, rendering him speechless was so easy.

"Of course! I forgot. How was the meeting?" I shifted with interest.

"It was just a short catch-up; the real one will happen next week," he said, playing with the frayed edge of the towel I sat on.

My eyes narrowed. "You were gone a long time."

Sean shrugged. He closed his eyes and linked his hands behind his head. "Oh, I just had to run some errands. The funniest thing happened."

"Oh?" I straightened.

"Mmm. I dropped into Roy's hardware to pay an account."

I froze, my eyes widening.

"Did you?" I tried to keep my voice even as I casually turned away from him. I caught Sean peeking at me, one eye open.

"Mmm. Apparently I have a secret admirer."

"Is that right?" I said, looking out onto the lake with the deepest fascination.

"It appears someone has paid out my *entire* account."

"Ha! Imagine that?" I still refused to look down at Sean.

"Yep! All two thousand, eight hundred and eighty dollars of it."

My head spun around so fast I nearly did myself an injury.

"*What*?" I managed to croak out. My heart leaped into my throat as I tried desperately to remember the day I had made a cheque out to Roy at the market-come-hardware store. Had I gotten it wrong? Had Roy gotten it wrong? Nearly three thousand dollars? Oh my God, I wanted to peel away and check my balance.

My panicked thoughts were interrupted by a chuckle. "Seems like you are your father's daughter, after all." Sean leaned up on his elbows.

I blinked, staring down at him, confused.

He smirked. "I saw the signatures, Amy. It seems you and your dad took it upon yourselves to undo my charity work."

Dad? Dad had paid off some of Sean's account, too?

Sean sat up, looking directly into my eyes. "You didn't know about your dad?"

I shook my head, totally dumbfounded, before my eyes snapped up to meet his face. "Go on, say it."

The corners of Sean's mouth tugged upward in amusement. "Bloody pig-headed, stubborn Hendersons." He leaned in, slowly claiming my mouth in an achingly tender caress, before he slowly pulled back.

"And I'm mighty glad to know them."

That One Summer
A Summer Series Novel, Book Three

Published by C.J Duggan
Australia, NSW
www.cjdugganbooks.com

First edition, published December 2013

Edited by Sarah Billington|Billington Media
Copyedited by Anita Saunders
Proofreading by Sascha Craig, Lori Heaford, Frankie Rose
Cover Art by Keary Taylor Indie Designs
Book formatted by White Hot Ebook Formatting
Author Photograph © 2013 C.J Duggan

That One Summer is also available as a paperback at Amazon
Contact the author at cand.duu@gmail.com

That One Summer

Loving Chris Henderson would be wrong. Diabolically disastrous. I mean, what is there about him to love? He's moody, bossy, brooding, a control freak, and that's on a good day … but there was one achingly obvious fact that haunted my every thought, every minute of every day …

He sure could kiss.

As the countdown to the new millennium begins, there is one thing everyone agrees on: no one wants to be in Onslow for New Year's Eve. So that can only mean one thing: road trip!

No longer the mousey, invisible, shy girl from years ago, Tammy Maskala is finally making up for all those lost summers. A new year with new friends, which astoundingly includes the bossy boy behind the bar, Chris Henderson.

She likes her new friends (at least most of them), so why does she secretly feel so out of place?

After chickening out on the trip, a last-minute change of heart sees Tammy racing to the Onslow Hotel, fearing she's missed her chance for a ride. The last thing she expected to meet was a less-than-happy Onslow Boy leaning against his black panel van.

Now the countdown begins to reach the others at Point Shank before the party is over and the new year has begun. Alone in a car with only the infuriating Chris Henderson, Tammy can't help but feel this is a disastrous start to what could have been a great adventure. But when the awkward road trip takes an unexpected turn, Tammy soon discovers that the way her traitorous heart feels about Chris is the biggest disaster of all.

Fogged up windows, moonlight swimming, bad karaoke and unearthed secrets; after this one summer nothing will ever be the same again.

Dedicated to Jenny.
We met under the most extraordinary of circumstances,
that has now grown into the most extraordinary of friendships.

"Always remember to be happy because you never know who's falling in love with your smile."
- Anon

Chapter One

Christmas night, 1999

Honestly! Whose idea was this anyway?

My hands slid along the hallway plaster, my only guide in the pitch blackness. One tentative foot in front of the other, I slowly skimmed along the carpet.

The only thing that pierced the silence was the faint calling from downstairs.

"87-cat-and-dog-88-cat-and-dog ..."

Oh crap!

I shuffled along more urgently, my fingers scrabbling along the wall, hands searching faster. I was nowhere I wanted to be, that was for sure. Not that I knew where I was, exactly. Even in the long, dark hall I knew I was way too exposed.

I was too old for this.

My searching hands dipped into an alcove. Ah-ha! The feel of glossy moulded panels caused my pulse to race. Blindly, I fumbled at the new sensation under my fingertips, my heart skipping a beat when my palm brushed ... a *handle?*

Eureka! A door.

"99-cat-and-dog-100 ... Ready or not, here I come!"

Oh my God! Please open, please open.

Grabbing the handle, I wasn't sure what I feared the most – the door being locked or the sound of the handle twisting.

I braced my hand on the panel. Pushing inward, the door gave way but my relief was short-lived as it let out a painfully loud creak. I paused, frozen with the tension of possibly being discovered. Had I given myself away? I panicked as heavy footsteps sounded on the staircase, closing the distance. My eyes widened.

"One, two, Freddie's coming for you ... Three, four, better lock your door." His voice sing-songed tauntingly up the stairs.

I threw caution to the wind and opened the door quickly, slipped through and shut it gently behind me with a click they probably could have heard in China. I winced at the sound and stood still.

Trying to control my breathing, I abandoned the door behind me, edging into the room; the all-consuming darkness was disorientating. I flailed my arms outward like a deranged zombie and stopped abruptly when my knees hit the edge of a … bed? My fingertips rested on the spongy surface, anchoring myself.

Yep, a bed, that's great. What now?

The footsteps made their way slowly down the hall and my mind raced in a panic-fuelled flurry.

The footsteps stopped outside the door. "Come out, come out, wherever you are!" the voice from the hall called.

My instinct was to dash back to the door, press myself up against it and prevent him from entering and catching me. But before I made the move, something grabbed my elbow, spinning me around. My shocked scream was quickly muffled by a hand that clasped across my mouth, the other hand pulling me close.

"Shhh," a voice breathed, so close that their breath parted my fringe.

With wide eyes and flared nostrils, my laboured breathing was the only thing that wasn't frozen. I tried to fight against the iron-like grip, but it only got me another "Shhh", and an aggravated one, at that. The silhouette in front of me tilted his head, listening to the sounds of the footsteps outside. They were so close, but it wasn't the *sound* that made me fear he was right outside the door. A flash of light danced momentarily under the door crack.

A torch? That was cheating!

I could feel the shudder of a suppressed laugh through his torso as I remained where he'd pinned me, pressed against the silhouette.

"Cheeky bastard," the voice whispered.

A whisper isn't the easiest way to identify a person in the dark. I reached up instinctively and gripped my fingers around his arm, trying to get him to remove his hand from my mouth. Before I could struggle further, he slowly moved his hand, but not before pressing his finger onto my lips as if accentuating the need for silence.

I wasn't an idiot.

The light had moved on from the door, and the footsteps receded down the hall. With the coast clear, I was about to lash out at the dark figure, but before I had the chance, I flinched as a hand unexpectedly clasped mine. I was yanked through the darkness – roughly yanked forward and manoeuvred into a new space. Hangers clanked and I squinted my eyes closed as clothing hit my face. Then the sliding panel of the closet shut behind me.

Behind us, I mean.

"We're in a wardrobe," the voice whispered.

No shit, Sherlock!

The stuffy interior gave a new meaning to blackness. In times like these I instinctively wanted to light a match, if I had one. Not that it was the greatest idea, surrounded by so much cotton in such a confined space. It would really give a whole new meaning to 'Murder in the Dark'.

Murder in the bloody Dark.

The silhouette was no longer a silhouette or a shadow; there was only blackness. I couldn't see a thing. The only knowledge I had of his presence was the heat that pressed against my arm in the confined space.

Unlike the dirty cheat Ringer who had somehow found himself a torch, all the better to hunt us down with in the not-so dark, I didn't have a source of light. On the one and only day that the Onslow Hotel was closed to the public we had all agreed to meet up for some late night Christmas drinks. After a full day spent with an annoying, loud, extended family and a belly full of Christmas food, it was a welcome refuge of sorts to hang out in the quiet bar. Until Amy's bright idea of: "Let's play Murder in the Dark."

My best friend, Amy, grew up here so I would often find myself perched at the Onslow bar after all the drunks had been herded, stumbling out the door. Ever since Amy had come home this summer and we had reconnected our friendship, I had found myself not just with my high school best friend back, but a whole new group of friends that came with her. For the first summer since, wow, I was sixteen, I was hanging with my best friend, and strangely enough 'the Onslow Boys'.

Huh, I was hanging out all right. That was when I realised that I was actually pressed up against an Onslow Boy right now.

But which one?

Alone in the dark with an Onslow Boy. Most girls' prayers would have been answered. The jury was still out for me.

Seeing as the annoyed whisperer had forbidden me to speak (even though it seemed he was obviously allowed to), I reached out and found his shoulder. I patted my way across his collarbone, neck, chin, cheek, lips – soft lips – nose … gently touching the contours of a freshly shaven face. Hmm … nice cheekbones. I momentarily wondered who it was, but as my fingers traced the creases deeply etched above his eyes, I knew instantly.

I smiled, dropping my hand.

"Hello, Chris!

Chapter Two

A blinding light pierced the darkness.

Chris squinted in the harsh light, his broody face lit by the luminous rays from his mobile screen. "How did you know it was me?"

I winced against the foreign light, pushing it away.

"It was easy. No one has a frown quite like you."

As if on cue his frown deepened, the phone highlighting his face like a nightmare. Of all the Onslow Boys to be trapped with it had to be the moody one.

"You know, that light would have been handy about five minutes ago," I said.

"Yeah, well, he would have found us for sure, then," he said, his attention fully focused on his screen as he thumbed through his messages. His serious expression was unchanged.

"Well, hiding in a wardrobe isn't exactly a genius plan."

His eyes flicked up. "Really?" he deadpanned.

I shrugged. "It's the first place I'd look."

Chris lowered his phone, the light still filling the small space. "I suppose you have a better idea, then?"

I straightened, suddenly feeling exposed by the light, and Chris's expectant, cold stare.

"Well … anywhere would be better than here."

With you.

Chris stared at me for an unnervingly long time; I kind of hoped the screen would flick off and plunge us both back into darkness again.

The only movement that had me believing that Chris wasn't cast of stone was the slight tilt to the corner of his mouth. He reached out and slid the door open.

"After you." He motioned with a sweep of his hand.

"Sorry?" My eyes widened.

"You think you have a better place; lead the way then."

Oh crap.

I lifted my chin and slid past him out through the opening while his mobile's screen was still lit and I could see where I was going.

It was short-lived, though. Just as I was about to get my bearings, the light shut off

– or, more to the point, Chris had deliberately pocketed his phone.

Idiot.

I was back to square one, edging my way across the foreign space until my legs hit the edge of the bed. *Again.*

Okay, what now?

Just as my serious lack of a plan was about to be exposed, Chris tapped me on the shoulder.

"Shhh …"

What? I didn't say any… Uh-oh …

Footsteps thudded their way back down the hall. Before I had the chance to so much as panic, Chris pushed me to the carpet. I blindly followed Chris who was frantically sliding under the bed; he pulled me under next to him so fast I was surprised I didn't get a carpet burn.

My heart thundered against my ribcage and a new fear spiked inside me, pumping adrenalin through my body. My breathing was hard and frantic, but that had nothing to do with the footsteps outside.

It was seeming impossible not to breathe right in Chris's face.

Well … this was awkward.

I was so intimately wedged up next to Chris I could feel the press of his lips on my brow. His left arm was trapped under my body, his other hand rested on my shoulder blade. My palms were pressed against his chest; I could feel the erratic beat of his heart slamming violently against my hands.

I swallowed deeply. Now wasn't a good time, but hey, we were under a bloody bed. I was sure my whisper wouldn't be heard outside.

"Chris? Do you think you could move over a bit?" I whispered into his neck.

He breathed out loudly. "I can't."

"Why?"

His fingers touched my lip again, probably necessary, but nevertheless infuriating.

"I WILL FIND YOU. IT'S ONLY A MATTER OF TIME," Ringer shouted, his steps echoing as he jogged down the hall. The torch beam flashed on the floor outside as he passed. Chris's body physically sagged with relief.

"Good ol' Ringer, he isn't the sharpest tool in the shed," Chris chuckled.

I shook my head in disbelief. "Hasn't he found *anyone*? How is that possible? Not even with a torch?"

"I think we'll be safe here for a bit," said Chris.

"Don't be so sure," I mused.

"Why?"

"Under a bed, Chris? I mean, really?"

"Oh for … What is it now?"

"It's the second worst hiding spot you could think of."

Chris shifted, but all it did was draw him closer. "I didn't see you find any place better."

"You didn't exactly give me a chance."

Chris scoffed. I could feel him flex his hand under my collarbone; no doubt my weight on top of his arm was cutting off his circulation. My body lay flush against him, my chest pressed up against his. I could feel every breath, every pulse, every beat of him. I cleared my throat.

"Um … Are you sure you can't move over?" I asked.

"*Yes*."

"Why?"

"Because there's a saxophone case digging into my spine."

"Saxophone case? How can you possibly tell?"

Chris's shoulders shifted in awkward shrug. "We're in my room."

Chapter Three

Oh …

Okay, so I didn't know what to say to that exactly. It wasn't every night of my life that I found myself pressed up intimately against an Onslow Boy, in the dark, in his bedroom, in his bed. Well, okay … under his bed. Still, it did make for interesting conversation.

So what did you get up to on the weekend, Tammy? Oh not much, just front spooning with the local publican of the Onslow Hotel.

Maybe I wouldn't say that. To a lot of people, Amy's dad was still the publican! He'd just recently sold the pub to his daughter's boyfriend, Sean, and her cousin Chris (on paper, they officially took over in the New Year), but still, after decades of Eric Henderson being at the helm, it might take people a fair while to get their head around the change. Yes, I most definitely wouldn't mention that, especially seeing his daughter Amy was my best friend. Gross. That would be disturbing on so many levels.

The building was eerily silent now; there was no sound from outside the room. No sound *at all.* My neck was beginning to ache from the awkward position I was trapped in, pressed up against Chris, holding my head off the ground. Maybe now that Ringer had disappeared into the night to murder the others I could relax. But if I did that, I would be resting my head on Chris, and that would be weird. On the other hand, we couldn't really get much closer than we were now. And this was all his bright idea, anyway.

I tried not to think about it as I let my rigid posture melt against his. My head rested against his shoulder and I found instant relief. I could feel Chris's muscles tighten as I relaxed against him. I could tell he was looking down at me, his scowl probably deepening as I settled in for the night. Oh well … what else was new?

I sighed. "I don't think Ringer is very good at this game."

Chris scoffed. "Ringer couldn't find his way out of a brown paper bag." I felt his body shift, almost as if relaxing too … but not quite.

"So … a saxophone, huh?" I said.

"Yeah. Year Seven band. I wasn't very good." He said it as if it was an embarrassing confession.

Ha! Chris Henderson not good at something? Mr Perfectionist, 'you do it my way or the highway', control freak.

Not likely.

"I find that hard to believe." I yawned, closing my eyes. Mmm, Chris's shoulder was actually quite comfy.

"Hard to believe what?"

My eyes snapped open.

Oh crap, had I actually said that out loud?

"Oh, I just meant that …" I was saved by the creak of the door opening. This time it was my hand that instinctively flew to cover Chris's mouth. Covering his warm, soft lips I was momentarily distracted by the foreign sensation of it, until the torchlight danced around the edges beyond the bed. Chris's hand slowly clasped my wrist, pulling it away from his mouth. Instead of remaining still like I thought he would now that we were under threat, he drew me closer. His hand splayed along my shoulder blades, protectively pushing me into his chest. My face snuggled into the alcove of his neck; I could smell the remnants of his musky cologne and couldn't help but smile. In all of my mum's romance novels a man always smelled like sandalwood and pine. I thought that was just in trashy novels, but as I breathed in, Chris really *did* smell like that; he smelled divine.

Oh God, now was not the time to be thinking of Mills and Boon. I knew why Chris drew me near; my back was at risk of being exposed by the searching torch beam should it skim past. I leaned further into him, away from the edge of the bed. If the saxophone wasn't digging into him before it sure would be now. I bet he was glad he never took up the tuba.

Wait a minute … Why was it so quiet? Where was Ringer's cliché horror movie commentary? I waited for shadows to dance around the dark room, but they didn't. The torchlight had gone. Holy crap, while I'd been too busy thinking about romance novels and tubas … where had Ringer gone?

I lifted my head from Chris's shoulder. He was so still, as if he was wondering the same thing. I wish I knew Morse code; I could have tapped out the question on Chris's chest.

Where was Ring …

"BWAHAHAHAHA …"

A hand latched onto my leg and dragged me out of my hiding spot only far enough until my ankles were exposed. I let out a blood-curdling scream, right in Chris's face.

"Ringer! Let go, you …!"

"Are you ticklish, Maskala?" Ringer asked, threatening to take my shoe off.

I kicked out against him. "Don't you dare!"

He let go of my foot, there was a click and the room flooded with light. I scurried my way from underneath the bed, Ringer standing by the doorframe hunched over in fits of hysteria.

"Oh yeah, laugh it up." I army crawled out from under the bed, struggling to find my footing. "I wouldn't be so smug if I were you, it took you long enough to find us."

Ringer's eyes lit up. "Us?" His smile soon faded as Chris crawled out after me, a look of surprise lining his face as his eyes flicked between the two of us.

"Oh … *I see*." He wiggled his eyebrows.

I burned crimson; I wanted to tell him not to look at us like that, that it wasn't what it looked like, but I was cut off by Chris.

"Of course you bloody see; where did you get the torch, you cheat?" He brushed imaginary dust off his jeans. He didn't seem the least bit embarrassed by Ringer's smug expression.

"Hey, there's nothing in the rule book that says you can't have a visual aid," Ringer defended.

"What rule book?" Chris's younger brother Adam appeared in the doorway, his best friend Ellie standing next to him with her arms wrapped around her body.

"You took bloody long enough." She glowered at Ringer.

Ringer held up his hands in surrender. "Hey, I looked, I really did, but I couldn't find you anywhere."

"Well, next time, try checking the cool room," Ellie said, rubbing vigorously at her bare arms. Maybe there *were* worse places to hide than in a wardrobe or under the bed.

Adam puffed out his chest. "See, I told you it was a good spot to hide."

Ellie rolled her eyes, something she did often around Adam. "You're right, why would he think anyone would be stupid enough to hide in there?" She turned to us, as if seeing us for the first time. "So where were you guys hiding?"

All eyes focused expectantly on me and Chris. I tried to think of something to say that didn't sound so lame as hiding under a bed, but there was no sugar-coating it.

Just as I was about to openly confess our location, Chris beat me to it.

"Oh, Ringer found us in bed together," he said, brushing past me with a parting wink.

My mouth dropped open. "No, he didn't," I insisted, quickly following him out into the hall to avoid their knowing smirks.

"You may be ashamed of our love, Tammy, but sooner or later we must declare it to the world," Chris called over his shoulder as he headed down the hall.

Stunned, I paused in the hallway. "H-he's only joking," I stammered, turning back in time to see him head down the stairs.

Adam's smile broadened. "Of course he is, and that's the most interesting thing of all."

I spun back around to face him. "Why?"

They were all looking at me. Ellie glanced at Adam and then Ringer, a huge grin spreading across her face. "Because Chris doesn't joke … ever."

Ringer elbowed Ellie. "Must be love."

"Oh, shut up!" I scoffed, before marching down the hall and leaving their sniggering behind.

Yep! I was way too old for this.

Chapter Four

Now was my chance.

A chance to escape before Amy appeared from hiding and bullied me, as usual, to stay longer, drink more, and play Cupid with any red-blooded male within a ten-kilometre radius. It was her thing. And Chris was most definitely within a ten-kilometre radius.

I noted, relieved, that the Three Stooges didn't follow; instead, they headed to Adam's room. I tiptoed across the landing, ready to turn onto the staircase.

"Hold it right there, Maskala!"

I paused mid-step; at first I thought I was being paranoid, that maybe I had conjured up Amy's voice in my head. I looked around, confused when I didn't see anybody, worried that I was losing it.

"And where do you think you're off to?"

I was losing it. The voice trailed down from above me, like some heavenly being. My head darted to where I thought it was coming from and, sure enough, I was met with a familiar, beaming smile.

The manhole cover had been shifted to the side and Amy's face peered down at me from beyond.

"Boo!" She grinned. With expert ease, one leg appeared from the opening, then the other. She climbed out, lowering herself by swinging like a monkey, something she had obviously done a hundred times before. She dropped onto her feet with an 'ooph' before straightening and dusting her hands.

"I have never lost a game of Murder in the Dark yet," she said triumphantly.

I shook my head. "A misspent childhood," I said as I picked a cobweb from her hair.

"That's what I said." Sean dropped to the floor after her, making a much louder thud with his six-foot-three frame. He still managed it with the agility of a jungle cat; it would almost have been graceful if it wasn't for the over-obsessive, paranoid brushing off of imaginary creepy crawlies and cobwebs. He shuddered.

"Next time we hide in the cool room," he declared.

Amy rolled her eyes. "That's the worst hiding place you could ever think of."

"You could always hide under a bed," I added.

Amy scoffed. "No one would be stupid enough to hide under a bed; you might as well have a neon arrow pointing to you."

My smile faded as I cleared my throat. "Anyway, I better get going, I have to ..."

"Go for a run in the morning," Amy said in a robotic, bored voice as she looked at me. "I know."

I smiled coyly. Was I really so predictable?

It was my morning ritual to go for a good run; my body craved the outlet, having my muscles burn and my adrenalin soar with the crisp, fresh morning air. Most people thought I was mad, but in a lot of ways it was my sanity; it calmed my overactive imagination. I didn't expect anyone to understand, I sure knew Amy didn't.

"Off you go then, GI Jane, I'll see you at twelve."

My brows lowered in confusion.

Twelve? Twelve?

"You are still coming?" Sean asked.

My eyes glazed over; I bit my lip and tried for the life of me to remember what the hell was happening at twelve.

"Hello?" Amy laughed. "Sleepy Sunday Session at the lake house."

"Oh," I said, "riiiighhhht. Of course ... TWELVE." I nodded.

Amy looked at me side on as if contemplating something, that maybe I had lost my mind for forgetting such a momentous occasion.

Truth be known, I was still getting used to the sudden change in my social life. Since Amy had returned to Onslow from being away all these years, I had suddenly been plunged into a new scene with new acquaintances and situations that I still didn't exactly know how to deal with. It seemed I was part of 'the gang', since I was involved in every drinking session, lunch, dinner, lake excursion, party and ritual Sunday sessions at Sean's lake house. It was nice to be included, to be around people that were funny and friendly.

Then why was it that I felt like I didn't belong? Amy had been my best friend until she was shipped off to boarding school after we'd snuck out together late one night. It sounds a little extreme, but considering what happened that night it really hadn't been.

My parents had been mad too, but they wouldn't have dreamed of sending me away, not that they had the money. Now she was back in Onslow we had picked up our friendship where we'd left it, but now that she had Sean too, I couldn't help but feel like a third wheel sometimes. I knew they tried their best to include me in everything and they liked having me around, but they often drifted off into knowing smiles and glazed, mushy looks that made me want to sidestep away. But who could blame them? It was the honeymoon period and they were crazy about each other. Who was I to rain on their parade?

A flash of light flickered across our faces, momentarily blinding us.

"There you are!" sing-songed Ringer. "Where were you two love birds nesting?"

Amy cut me a dark look, a light shake of her head as if warning me not to say a word.

"We were up in the ceiling," Sean said proudly.

Amy closed her eyes and breathed deeply as if counting silently to stem her anger; all she could manage was a whack to Sean's arm.

"What?" he asked, surprised. "What was that for?"

"Cut it out, you two," Adam said from the stairs in his best mock stern voice, as if imitating his Uncle Eric. Ellie, as usual, was not far behind.

"Hey, guess what?" Adam said, leaning on the stair bannister. "Chris made a joke."

Amy's eyes narrowed in confusion. "Chris doesn't do jokes."

"Chris doesn't so much as smirk, let alone joke," Ellie agreed. "It was the equivalent of unearthing a volcanic ash-ravaged village after centuries of …"

"It's not that rare," said Sean.

"I don't know, it's pretty rare," said Amy.

Sean smirked, rubbing the whiskers on his jaw line, throwing a cheeky grin toward Ringer. "We've seen it before."

Ringer grinned and nodded. "Yep! The one and only time you'll see Chris happy is when he's getting some; am I right or am I right?" He held up his hand to Sean.

Sean just looked at him. "Mate, I'm not high fiving you."

I couldn't help but laugh. I loved the way the Onslow Boys would rough-house and trash-talk each other. I looked at Ellie and Adam expectantly, to exchange our own amused smiles, but when my eyes met inquisitive stares from Ellie, Adam and now Ringer …

Coldness swept over me.

"You don't say?" mused Ellie, staring at me.

Wait, surely they didn't think ...

My eyes widened with horror. Their curious gazes and smirks made heat flood to my cheeks.

"GOODNIGHT!" I said too loudly as I brushed past a confused Amy and Sean and headed down the stairs, quickstepping through the restaurant, dodging a Christmas tree, and into the bar. Chris was propped up on the bar watching TV. I couldn't even look him in the eye as I rushed past, clasping at the front door handle and tugging violently, almost jarring my arms as the door refused to give. I fumbled at the deadbolt, attempting to lift and tug, but it was stuck.

Come on, come on, come on!

I felt the press of Chris next to me as he moved to unbolt the door from the bottom, then the top with expert ease.

"I'll do it, just calm down. You okay?" he asked, the usual serious gaze back in place.

I scoffed, pushing my hair behind my ear. "Next time do me a favour – hide in the bloody ceiling."

Chapter Five

There was one thing that was for certain: no one wanted to be in Onslow for New Year.

"I would sooner die than be here at the stroke of midnight," said Ellie as she smeared a palmful of tanning oil over her shoulder.

"Turn!" called Amy.

Without missing a beat, Ellie, Tess, Amy and I turned from our backs onto our stomachs like synchronised rotisserie chickens, at least according to the boys.

Resting our chins on our forearms, our view changed from the shiny lake stretching toward a long deck that led up to Sean's lake house. The deck was the perfect sunbaking platform; sure, it was hard as a rock, but there was no chance of sand in the belly button so that was a definite plus.

I straightened my towel and repositioned myself as best I could to notice that my view had altered since our last rotation. I lifted my sunnies to spy a figure sitting at the outdoor table near the barbecue. Elbows resting on the tabletop, leaning over an open binder, chewing on the end of his pen, scowling intently at the page, was Chris.

He wore his practically trademark Levi jeans and black T; it didn't scream summer attire, but then nothing about him ever did. His lips moved gently as if talking to himself, shaking his head in frustration as he heavily marked something on his page. Any moment of lighthearted jokester from last night was clearly long gone.

He was, like most times I saw him, sporting the same serious exterior, as if he was always working a shift behind the Onslow bar, not off the clock, hanging with his boys. My gaze shifted toward the lake again where Sean and Toby stood, shirtless, in the distance at the end of the jetty, wrestling with tangled fishing line and arguing over whose fault it was. Ringer and Stan were fishing on the opposite side, casting each other dubious looks as they suffered through the long-standing tradition of Sean and Toby's alpha male dance with one another.

I suppose I should have been relieved; during my warm-up before my run that morning I had suffered more than one moment of dread at the thought of meeting up with everyone at twelve. In fact, like usual, I had psyched myself up into a state, to be prepared for taunts about what Chris and I had gotten 'up to' last night that had caused Chris to crack a smile. I had even gone so far as to take a deep, steadying breath as I walked down the steep incline of Sean's driveway, preparing for the array of questions that would surely follow. Even though there was nothing to tell (like, seriously, *nothing*), it didn't matter. I had always hated confrontation and it seemed like that would never change.

So when I arrived at Sean's place and was met by nothing more than cheerful hellos and earnest smiles, it became perfectly clear: I didn't know these people at all. No wonder I always felt so out of place.

"Tammy." My attention snapped back to the frying corpse beside me. "You're blocking my sun," said Amy.

"Oh, sorry." I moved to lie back down on my stomach, fidgeting to get comfy. Resting my chin on my arms again, I sighed a long, deep, contented sigh, shutting my eyes and letting the heat of the sun's rays warm my skin. My peace was soon disturbed by a none-too-subtle elbow knocking into mine. I peered to my left just in time to catch Amy wink at me with a cheeky grin.

"Oh, I don't know, Ellie, what's wrong with counting down the New Year in the beer garden?" Amy asked in all seriousness.

Ellie's head bobbed up, her white-rimmed sunnies masking the dark, searing stare that no doubt bore into Amy.

"Are you serious?" Ellie hitched herself up onto her elbows. "It's 1999, Amy, we're counting down into *the new* millennium, a new century! As if I'm going to spend another year sitting in the beer garden of the Onslow Hotel … No offence."

Amy shrugged. "None taken."

"Isn't the world supposed to end, anyway?" asked Tess in a sleepy, mumbled voice.

"Exactly!" Ellie straightened. "And I'll be damned if I am going to spend my last moments on this earth at a Blue Light disco singing 'Auld Lang Syne' with my parents."

"It won't be like that," Amy piped up. "Do you honestly think Sean would let it be like that? That I would?"

I knew Ellie had meant 'no offence', she had even said it herself, but I could tell by the incredulous tone in Amy's voice that she was getting a bit shitty that Ellie was depicting the Onslow so negatively.

I mean, if the choice was death over spending time there, then yeah, I could see why one would be pretty insulted by that.

On paper, the weeks leading up to and beyond Christmas looked like they had been pretty turbulent for Amy and her family. They had sold the Onslow Hotel, but in reality it wasn't as if anything much had changed; even though the Onslow sported a new sign on the front verandah boasting 'Under New Management'.

It had been a huge relief for everyone that Sean and Chris had bought the hotel and not one of the city types with bulldozers on standby.

Well, it was a relief for *almost* everyone. I spied Chris rip a page out of his folder and screw it up.

Closing my eyes, I attempted to zone out of Amy and Ellie's bickering, pressing my forehead against my arms, hoping that if I kept out of it I would soon just melt into the deck and avoid the drama. Whatever they chose for New Year's was fine with me.

It had seemed like a perfect plan and I was just starting to doze off in the warm sun when Amy elbowed me again, completely jolting me from my Zen-like state.

"Amy!" I glowered, rubbing my ribcage.

"Did you know about this?" Amy's voice was high and squeaky, which always meant trouble.

"Know about what?" I asked, mystified by her heated question. What had I missed?

Amy tilted her sunnies back and twisted herself to sit and face toward the jetty, glaring over at the boys.

"RIGHT!" she said before launching herself to her bare feet and stomping along the deck toward the long jetty where the Onslow Boys sat fishing.

"Uh-oh …" Ellie sing-songed.

"I thought she knew; I thought everyone knew," Tess added quickly, biting her lip, worry lines etched in her brow.

"Knew what?" I asked, watching Amy close the distance between her and Sean.

What the hell had I missed?

"Amy was under the impression there was going to be some grand New Year extravaganza at the hotel this year," Ellie said.

"And then I just asked if we should wait until the boys got back from their camping trip." Tess grimaced.

"Camping trip?" I asked.

"Yeah, the camping trip Amy obviously had no idea about." Ellie sat up, crossing her legs. "You too, it seems? The New Year's Eve boy bonding expedition they've planned." Ellie shrugged. "Adam mentioned it. They go into the bush, chant and share feelings and stuff."

"Not exactly," a voice said from above.

The three of us swivelled around and found a silhouette towering over us, blocking the sun.

Chris.

"Please don't smash my illusion of what you boys actually get up to," smirked Ellie. "Adam paints quite the vivid picture."

"I bet he does," Chris said, staring off at Amy and the boys in the distance. The three of us followed his gaze to see Sean who, smiling upon Amy's approach, was now not quite so happy.

Amy stood in her lime green bikini, her hands on her hips whenever they weren't furiously flailing around.

Sean held his hands up as if asking a silent question, something that seemed to infuriate her even more.

Their body language said it all.

Toby, Ringer and Stan shifted awkwardly, throwing each other wide-eyed grimaces, no doubt wishing they could be anywhere else in that moment.

"Trouble in paradise?" called an approaching voice. Adam walked through the back bi-fold doors onto the deck, cracking a can of Coke and taking a fizzy sip. He stopped beside Chris. Adam hip and shouldered his brother, causing his drink to fizz over and spill onto the deck.

Chris eyed his younger brother much like he did everyone, as if he was a bug under a microscope that needed to be stepped on. The two Henderson brothers stood side by side, Chris swiping Adam's Coke can out of his hand with a gentle shove to his shoulder before taking his own sip.

"Help yourself," said Adam good-naturedly. "I backwash anyway."

Chris choked mid-sip, working into a coughing fit, rasping insults toward his brother. Adam beamed like he'd just been showered in compliments.

"You're a bloody dickhead," rasped Chris. He worked to pour the remnants of the can out, the brown fizzy stream dribbling and disappearing between the cracks of the decking.

"Watch it, Boss Man, Sean will use you as a mop when he sees that on his deck," laughed Adam.

Chris flicked the excess drops from the can before crushing it in his hand.

"Somehow," Chris said, frowning toward the jetty, "I think Sean has bigger fish to fry."

And that's when we heard the scream.

Chapter Six

There was a loud splash and I couldn't be sure who had hit the water first.

Toby, Ringer and Stan were hunched over in hysterics as Amy and Sean flailed and splashed about in the water. Their bent-at-the-knees, tears-in-the-eyes laughter made me doubt it had been entirely an accident.

Ellie, Tess and I scrambled to our feet and followed Chris and Adam over to the jetty. We didn't know whether to laugh or offer support as one hand then another appeared from beyond the decking, splaying themselves on the surface, anchoring themselves into place.

"I swear to God, Sean Murphy, you're a dead man!" panted Amy as she struggled to hoist herself onto the deck.

Sean clamped his two large hands onto the jetty boards and pulled himself out of the water with ease.

"*You* pushed *me*!" He laughed.

"And you pulled me in!" Amy shouted, as she tried to claw her way onto the platform, rather unsuccessfully. Now on deck, pooling water at his feet, Sean offered her a hand.

"Don't touch me!" Amy slapped his hand away.

"Aw, come on, Amy, I'll take you bloody camping."

"Whaaat?" groaned Chris.

Sean ignored him; instead, he was trying not to appear amused as Amy hooked her heel on the edge of the pier and awkwardly tried to pull herself up with very little success.

"Don't bother," she bit out. "I don't want to go anywhere with you."

Amy always did have a stubborn streak.

"Yes, you do," Sean said. He bent, grabbed her firmly by her arms and ignored her slapping at him as he pulled her up and out of the water as if she weighed nothing. He set her down on her feet, which was all the better for her to glare up at him.

The glare was lost on Sean. His mischievous eyes twinkled as he looked down on Amy. Absolutely no one could doubt he loved her, that he was fully consumed by her, when he looked at her like that. It made my heart unexpectedly pang with jealousy. No one had ever looked at me like that.

"I'll take you camping," he repeated in all seriousness.

The boys sure stopped laughing then.

"Sure we will," added Adam. "You can cook us meals and keep the camp tended to while we do men's business."

That earned Adam a jettyful of murderous stares, none deeper or more intimidating than Chris's.

Just as I was about to tease him on behalf of the sisterhood for being so angered, he spoke.

"They're not coming."

"Excuse me?" Amy's murderous attention turned from Adam to Chris.

"Here we go," sighed Ellie.

"You heard me." Chris unapologetically locked eyes with Amy, as if the subject was somehow non-negotiable.

This was a mistake, a big mistake.

Amy crossed her arms. "I don't believe this. So, what? No girls allowed? Is that what you're saying?"

Adam slapped Chris on the shoulder and said, "It's been nice knowing you, buddy," before he sidestepped away.

Now everybody's attention was fully focused on Chris.

Sean scratched the back of his neck, grimacing. He turned to me. "What you think, Tam? You've been pretty quiet."

I flinched at the question.

Oh God, leave me out of it ...

Now, much to my horror, all eyes shifted to *me*.

So much for avoiding confrontation.

"Oh ... um ..." I fidgeted under their scrutiny. "Well ... I don't know." My eyes locked briefly with Chris's. They were burning into me like laser beams, his folded arms an open scowl of distaste that made me feel like he just wanted me to get on with it. It made me fluster even more. "Well, we could just, um ..."*Oh God, help!* "We could always take a vote?"

Take a vote? Seriously? I inwardly cringed; I needed to just shut up.

Chris scoffed at my answer, plunging his hands into his pockets. He looked over the group.

"What? You can't be serious," he said.

My eyes darted over the others who all looked as if what I had said made perfect sense. *Surely not*. Sean laughed, squeezing my shoulders as he moved behind me.

"Nice one, Tam!" Sean beamed. "We shall take a vote. All those in favour of the ladies coming with us for our New Year's camping extravaganza, raise your hands."

Sean led the way, holding his hand straight up in the air, followed by a rather smug-looking Amy. Tess, Toby and Ellie also raised their hands to the sky, followed by Ringer and Stan. Adam raised his hand, smiling at Chris, clearly taking immense joy in the outcome.

"Those against?" Sean called, causing everyone to plunge their arms down comically fast.

Chris never moved. Not once. In fact, he was so still that if it wasn't for the deep sigh emanating from him, I would have sworn he had turned to stone.

"Well, what do you know – a fucking landslide," Chris bit out.

"Sorry, mate, the people have spoken," Sean said, hooking his arm around Amy and leading her toward the lake house, leaving a trail of water behind them.

"Better make room for our make-up bags, Chrissy babes," crooned Ellie as she walked past Chris, following them to the house.

Toby guided Tess to follow, offering Chris an amused shrug.

"Well, show's over. Come on lads, better check those fishing rods; I fancy smoking a kipper for breakfast." Adam slapped Stan on the back.

"You don't know much about fishing, do you, mate?" quipped Stan.

I smiled, watching the boys make their way back toward the jetty, exchanging trash talk as they went. But then I realised I was now alone with Chris and his angry eyes. He didn't need to say a word for me to know he thought I was solely to blame for ruining his New Year's plans, as if my bright idea had backed him into a corner. Maybe it had? So, in true Tammy Maskala fashion, I did what I liked to do best. I smiled apologetically and brushed past him, refusing to meet his eyes as I made a beeline toward the house for a speedy escape. Even in my hasty departure, call it paranoia, I guess, I couldn't help but feel Chris's eyes burning a hole in the back of my head.

Chapter Seven

Opening the door to my one-bedroom flat, I threw the keys on the little table by the door.

Peeling off the strap of my knapsack, I pinched the bridge of my nose with a sigh, praying that what lurked at the front of my brain was not the beginning of a migraine. I'd been an idiot – too much sun and not enough fluids. A migraine was a reasonable punishment, really.

Even though the sun was now dipping in the sky, taking the edge off the scorching heat, my flat was still painfully warm. I flicked the cooler switch on and it chugged to life. I pulled the curtains closed, shielding my eyes from the blinding, late evening sun. If nothing else, I would have to shower the tanning oil off of me before bed. I had to manage that much before I slunk into a world of pain. I slumped onto the soft couch and shook it from my thoughts.

No, Tammy Maskala! Stop it. It's positive, positive, positive, remember?

Positivity: my new mantra. I'd try to use it before the New Year so at least, by the turn of the new century, looking on the bright side would be second nature.

A niggling piece of me doubted my chances.

I rubbed at my throbbing temples; I could be as positive as I liked, but that wouldn't have any effect on the onslaught of a migraine in its first stages. There was no amount of positive thinking that would keep that at bay. If anything, the less thinking I did the better, which was fine by me – the less I thought about the murderous look Chris Henderson had given me the happier I would be.

I had voiced my unease with Amy.

"Tammy, please," she had said. "Have you ever seen the way he treats *me*?"

I suppose, but I wasn't like Amy. She was so sure of herself; whatever room she walked into she dominated. She could play pool, skull a beer, hell, she could even arm wrestle each of the Onslow Boys. They were her friends, not mine, so when one of them gives me a dirty look, unlike Amy, I'm not about to tell them where to go.

I had to think, though. I had to think of an excuse to get out of this New Year's camping trip. Talks had begun as soon as we entered the lake house that afternoon. It seemed settled, a non-negotiable trip up the coast to the Port Shank Music festival to count down the New Year. That was the plan, a plan that had somehow automatically included me. Chris had sulked his way into the house, perching quietly on a stool at the counter as everyone talked excitedly around him. The two of us seemed like the most unenthused of the group. Maybe I should have bloody voted against it.

Thinking was overrated. My head throbbed with pain.

With a whimper, I dragged my feet across the carpet and up the hall to the bathroom to two crucial things: a cool, clean shower and a medicine cabinet with my painkillers.

Wow. My life rocked.

***

I knew the drill. After my shower I shuffled to bed and darkness, and tried not to move, just let sleep take me over before the pain, before the blinding nausea I hoped I could beat. And it might just have worked. The pounding in my temple was nothing to do with pain; it was owing to the incessant ringing of my phone instead. It jolted me awake, momentarily disorientating me until I recognised the continuous, shrill rings. I scrounged for the only source of light at my fingertips as I pulled my digital clock radio into view.

Whoa!

It was ten o'clock at night; I had been asleep for four hours. I patted my bed for the phone, wondering who would be calling me at this hour. I had my answer the instant I accepted the call. Pounding music bled through the receiver.

"TUESDAY!" Amy shouted.

Half asleep, I waited. I figured she was probably talking to a customer.

"Tammy? Are you there?"

"I'm here." I yawned.

"Oh my God, are you in bed? Already?"

"I had a migraine."

"Riiight," Amy drawled, as if she wasn't entirely buying my story.

"Tuesday," she repeated.

"What about it?"

"That's when we leave. For the New Year's trip."

My heart pounded in my chest. *So soon?*

My mind went blank and I couldn't speak. I was in shock at the urgency, but of course it was urgent. New Year's Eve was Friday; yeah, of course we had to leave sooner rather than later.

"Tammy, you *are* coming." Amy's voice sounded dark.

"Oh well … I …"

"Tammy, if you don't come, I'm going to be really pissed," she said.

"I just think that maybe it's turned into more of a couples' thing."

"A couples' thing?" Amy repeated, as if she could hardly believe what I'd just said.

"Well, you know, you and Sean, Tess and Toby, Stan's bringing his new girlfriend. And, well, Adam and Ellie have each other to hang with, and Chris and Ringer can do their fishing things."

In other words I had gone from the usual third wheel to a spare tyre; I really didn't want to be the awkward tag-along.

"It is sooo not a couples' thing. Remember, this was originally a boy bonding expedition that we happen to be gatecrashing. If anything, it will be more of a chance for us girls to kick back while the men go hunt and gather for us."

"You sound just like Adam." I laughed.

"Ugh, kill me now," Amy said. "So that's it. You're coming and we leave Tuesday. We'll discuss the finer details later, plus something else you might find *very* interesting."

"Now hang on a sec, I didn't say … What would I find interesting?"

"Oh, just a certain something a certain someone said about you."

"What?" I croaked. *What had they been saying about me?*

"I might have overheard a certain Onslow Boy talking about you, that's all."

Onslow Boy?

"What? When? Who?" I stammered.

"See you Tuesday!"

Chapter Eight

Tuesday gave us one day – ONE day.

What the hell do you take camping, anyway? I had no idea; as far as nature was concerned I liked to run through it and around it, not live in it. Sleeping with ants and snakes and God knows what else was *not* my thing.

I had to think of an excuse.

I invited the girls to lunch at the Bake House Café in town to learn more about what exactly was going on for Tuesday. It also gave me a chance to invite Amy half an hour early before Ellie and Tess arrived, to grill her about who had been talking about me and exactly what they had said.

Maybe Chris had been slagging me off to his mates, but by the tone of her smug voice I doubted it was anything like that. I really hoped it wasn't, but then again at least I would have a good excuse for not wanting to go.

I heard the ding of the bell above the café door and expected to see Amy's beaming grin as she scanned the tables, looking for me. I straightened expectantly with an inviting smile, only for it to drop clean off my face when Chris appeared instead.

SHIT.

I slid under the table, my spine making an infuriatingly large fart-like sound against the linoleum seat as I disappeared out of view. What was I doing? Oh God, I hoped he hadn't seen me. How was I going to explain this?

"Ah, young Chris! Good to see you, how's things?" called Norm the baker from out the back.

I grimaced under the tablecloth.

Just go, just hurry up and go.

"Yeah, good thanks, Norm."

Legs walked on the other side of the table, along the line of cabinets as he no doubt looked over the baked goods. I dared not even breathe.

They chatted about their businesses, about the Onslow. Chris seemed in no hurry to order.

My legs ached and my neck cramped, hunched over under the table; apparently it was time to chat. It was odd, hearing Chris talk to Norm. I didn't think I had ever heard Chris string together so many sentences before, and come to think of it, not only was he speaking, but he sounded … normal. Lighthearted, almost.

It was unsettling.

"What are the specials today, Norm?" There was a bang as Chris slapped the counter.

Just grab a bloody pie and go.

"Oh, now hang on a second, young fella, Betty left the list here somewhere."

I sighed, hearing Norm rummage through papers.

He rummaged.

Rummaged.

Rummaged some more.

"Ah, here it is!"

HALLELUJAH!

As Norm rattled off a painstakingly long list of specials, I couldn't help but check my watch every five seconds, ever aware that Amy would be rocking up at any minute and I would be busted. My skin prickled with embarrassment. Why did I think myself so smart as to organise a meeting half an hour before the norm? If I had just said twelve thirty I could have avoided this altogether.

"Sounds good! I'll go for the number seven, thanks, Norm."

Finally!

"Excellent choice! Eat in or take away?"

"Eat in, thanks."

I cringed and closed my eyes. *Nooooooooooo …* This could not be happening.

There was no crawling my way out of this one.

Literally, there wasn't, because I had thought about it, but there was no way I could get out of this without being caught doing so.

The Bake House was a long, gallery-style set-up, booths on one side of the wall and cabinets and service area on the other. Depending on where he chose to sit… If he sat toward the door, his back to my table, I might have stood a chance.

I tried to slow my breathing, to not move even an inch as I listened to the direction of his footsteps. Mercifully they headed in the direction I had hoped they would, away from me and toward the door.

I was going to be okay, I could get out of this with relatively minimal damage to my ego.

"Is this today's paper, Norm?" Chris called out.

"Sure is, help yourself," Norm's voice called from out the back.

I heard the rustling of a newspaper in the distance, followed by footsteps closing in toward my direction.

Oh no-no-no-no …

He was walking this way, all right. His unmistakable Levi denim-clad legs swaggered into view, so painfully close I could reach out and touch them, maybe even trip him. I momentarily entertained the thought before brushing it from my mind.

My heart drummed so fiercely I could swear Norm would have heard it out back. My mouth went dry as I watched every single footstep make its agonising way toward …

He was going to sit at my booth!

This could not be happening, this could not be happening.

Try and explain this, Tammy, when Amy rocks up and you're nestled under Chris's table.

I edged myself as best I could out of touching distance, my eyes widening as the seat dipped under Chris's weight.

His kneecap was barely inches away from my forehead.

This was not okay.

I heard him casually cough as he turned the pages of the newspaper.

"Onslow skate park opening to mark the New Year," he read aloud. "Outdoor cinema a raving success."

Was he serious?

"Locals fight to save historic gum tree ... School wins local funding bid ... Girl trapped under Bake House dining table."

My head snapped up so quickly I headbutted Chris's knee.

"Ahh ..." I clasped my head where it hurt.

Chris slid out of the booth and lifted the skirt of the tablecloth to look at me.

Was he seriously laughing at me?

"Are you okay?"

"I'm fine!" I snapped. Trying to gain some form of composure, I clawed at the seat with one hand, trying to slide out from underneath as I nursed my eye socket.

Chris moved to the side and offered me his hand. I would have slapped him away, but I really did need the help; I had been crouching in such an awkward position my legs were numb and refused to work.

"Easy now, don't hurt yourself."

Ha! Too late for that.

I managed myself into a seated position once again, Chris standing before me. I couldn't bring myself to look at him – for one, I couldn't stand to see his smug smirk and two, I only had one functioning eye.

"Christ, are you okay, Tammy?"

I winced, rubbing my eye. "I think so."

"Don't do that, here let me look." Chris pulled my hand away. "Look at me."

I slowly managed to lift my eyes to him and to my surprise he didn't look smug at all. His brow was furrowed in concern as his fingertips gently pressed around my eye.

He whistled. "Looks like you're going to have one hell of a shiner."

"From your knee? Perfect!" I grimaced.

"Hey, Norm, do you have any ice?" Chris called out.

"Oh no, Chris, don't. I'm fine," I pleaded. But it fell on deaf ears as Chris worked on securing some ice cubes in a cloth Norm organised for him.

"What happened?" Norm asked, the look of alarm spread across his face.

"It's all right, Norm, no one's going to sue you," Chris half laughed as he sat next to me, holding the ice-cold package to my face. Chris continued to pacify Norm. He seemed more shaken than I was. Apparently his wife, Betty, didn't leave him in charge very often and if anything happened on his watch it wouldn't be worth his life.

A broad smile spread across Chris's face. "It's all right; it will be our little secret," he said as he winked at me.

I grabbed the cloth from Chris's grasp, unnerved by his kindness, by the lightness of his mood and the transformation of his smile, a smile that lit his entire face. I must have been staring at him, a deep frown etched across my face as if I were sitting next to a stranger.

In a way, I kind of was.

"Tammy, are you all right?" His smile melted into a grim line, as if unnerved by my catatonic stares.

If anything was going to give me a migraine, an old-fashioned knee to the head would do it.

I cleared my throat, scooting away on my seat. "I'm fine … Thanks."

Taking the hint, Chris climbed out of the booth, watching me with uncertainty.

"You sure?" he said as he sat down opposite me.

"I'll live."

If embarrassment wouldn't kill me first.

Chris opened his mouth to speak when the chime above the front door sounded and Amy entered. Her smile dropped with surprise when she laid eyes on us and her brows furrowed in confusion.

"Jesus, Chris. What. Did. You. Do?"

Chapter Nine

"It was an accident!" I said quickly.

Amy's attention broke slowly away from Chris to me.

"What happened?" she asked.

Oh crap. It was enough that Chris must have worked out that I had hidden under a table to avoid him, but did I really have to say it out loud?

I hadn't been prepared for questions; there was no easy way to explain this, especially with Chris's dark-set eyes burning into me.

I ran into a door? Slipped on a tile? Got kneed in the face by your cousin? The latter, the fact, sounded the least believable and by far the hardest to explain. Still, the truth would set you free, right?

"I uh …"

"She got hit in the head with a salt and pepper shaker," Chris blurted out.

Huh?

"What?" Amy's frown deepened.

"Yeah, well, she asked for me to pass the salt and I … uh … overshot the mark."

"Jesus, Chris!" Amy exclaimed. "What were you thinking? You're not hanging with the Onslow Boys now; Tam's not going to catch it like Sean would, you're such a Neanderthal."

Amy plonked down in the seat next to Chris and punched him in the shoulder. "I hope you said you were sorry."

Chris's brows rose as he looked at me. I could tell he was trying not to smile.

"Of course I said I was sorry; even fetched ice for her face."

"So you bloody should." Amy shook her head and rolled her eyes at me. "Boys!"

I smiled a small smile. I felt kind of bad that she was giving Chris such a hard time. For a split second I had actually believed that I was hit in the face by a salt shaker.

"Let me look," Amy prompted, leaning forward.

"Oh it's nothing, really."

I tried to slap Amy's hands away, but there was no use. Once Amy had something in her head she would not let go.

I heard Amy gasp as she removed the ice-filled tea towel from my eye.

"Whoa, you're going to have a ripper of a black eye."

Awesome.

Norm appeared from the kitchen and set a cup of coffee in front of me. "Here you go, Miss Maskala."

"Oh … I didn't …"

"No, that's all right, it's on the house. If there is anything else you need you just sing out. Just rest up and take it easy."

Oh, now this was getting too much.

"Thanks, Norm." I smiled weakly.

I wanted to slink down in my seat, to hide under the table in mortification, but that was what had got me into trouble in the first place.

Norm returned a minute later, plonking down Chris's number-seven special order in front of him. Amy and I stared at his plate.

Chris straightened in his seat, his eyes aglow with hunger. He readily grabbed his knife and butter sachet when he glanced up and paused. His eyes shifted from me to Amy and back.

"What?"

"Really?" I asked. "Banana bread?"

"What's wrong with that?" Chris asked warily.

"Nothing, I guess, I just assumed a number seven would have been a steak, or a greasy fry-up of bacon and eggs or something." My lips twitched, fighting not to smirk at his dainty serving of toasted banana bread.

"Yeah," Amy said with a laugh. "Man food."

"It's got walnuts in it," Chris defended.

"Whoa. That's hardcore." I grinned.

Chris ignored us and instead opened his sachet in a huff, slapping the butter onto his bread.

Norm came back with a pen and notebook.

"Now, was there anything you wanted, young Amy?" he asked, writing the date on his pad.

"Oh, I don't know." She turned to Chris. "What do you say, Angela Lansbury? Do you want to share a pot of tea with me?"

Chris dropped his knife with a sigh. "Norm, can I have this for takeaway?" He pushed his plate away.

"Aw come on, don't be like that." Amy leaned her head on his shoulder.

Chris nudged her. "Get off me or I'll throw a salt shaker at you, too."

Amy mock gasped. "Hey, Norm, might pay for you to confiscate your salt and pepper shakers just in case they fall into the wrong hands."

"Salt and pepper shakers?" He looked up from his notepad, troubled.

"Yeah, just to lower the injury rate." Amy winked at me.

Norm scratched his head in deep thought. "But we don't have any salt and pepper shakers, only individual sachets."

Oh SHIT!

My eyes widened as big as saucers, flicking to Chris who had closed his eyes in a moment of dread.

The confusion spread from Norm to Amy.

"But you said that …"

The door chime sounded. "Ugh, I'm starving!" said Ellie.

"You're always starving," Tess said, as they pushed their way through the front door.

I braced myself for the onslaught of 'What happened to you?' questions. How were we going to explain it this time?

"Chris," Ellie said, surprised. "What are you doing here? Oooh, banana bread, yum!"

"Here, have it." Chris pushed the plate toward Ellie. "I've lost my appetite."

"It has butter on it already, but no salt," Amy said, her eyes shifting between us knowingly.

Ellie plonked down in the soft leather booth next to me. "Gross. Why would I need salt?"

Amy shrugged. "Stranger things have happened."

Norm coughed. "I'll, uh, leave you all a minute to decide."

Chris shifted uncomfortably in his seat, checking his watch. "I better get back; here, Tess, have my seat."

Amy slid out of the booth, letting Chris out. He stood, grabbed his wallet from his back pocket, thumbed out a twenty and chucked it on the table.

"Keep the change, Norm," he called.

Norm poked his head into the café from the kitchen. "Thanks, mate, see you next time."

Chris shifted his attention back to our table.

"So you ladies are still coming camping, I take it?"

"You betcha," Ellie said through a mouthful of banana bread.

The corner of Chris's mouth curved upwards. "You do realise there are no power points in the base of the gum trees to plug your hairdryers into."

Amy rolled her eyes with annoyance. "Shut up!"

"As if we're that naïve, Chris," scoffed Tess.

As for me, I made an instant mental note.

Don't. Pack. A. Hairdryer.

"Just so you know." He shrugged. "Seeyas."

Our eyes locked briefly before he nodded goodbye and left, the sound of the door chiming and slamming shut.

I looked back at the girls, each one staring at me. I was suddenly aware that I had been left to a pack of wolves. I could almost hear the cogs of speculation turning in Amy's head as she tried to unravel the mystery between me, Chris and the salt shaker in the bakery.

It sounded like some demented version of Cluedo.

I grabbed a menu. "Let's order, shall we?" They were all quiet for a moment, taking my cue to peruse the menus. I started to relax, just a little, thinking that maybe I had escaped the questions altogether.

"Oh my God!" Tess gasped. "Tammy – what happened to your eye?"

Ugh. Kill me now.

Chapter Ten

I had a tendency to hide things, even from the people closest to me in my life, just like I had hidden my slightly puffed-up, bruised eye.

I tried to squeeze out the crusty contents of a thousand-year-old foundation tube I found in the bottom of my bathroom drawer. A testament to how long it had been since I had worn make-up. I wasn't sure mixing it with water had helped much, but I kind of knew that my parents wouldn't even notice and I had never been so thankful for their diverted attention.

"Well, I think it's wonderful!"

Of course she did; my mum thought everything was wonderful. I followed her into the crowded garage, skimming sideways to dodge old light fixtures, fishing rods and bicycle pumps, a pile of retro seventies tiles, a dust-covered cabinet housing bolts and a whipper snipper cord. I accidentally banged into a box of home brew bottles – they tipped sideways but I mercifully caught the box before glass shattered on the floor and I juggled them back into place on top of the old ride-on mower.

My mum had somehow navigated her way through the space with expert ease, like she had done a million times before. I followed the track she had worn in the second-hand carpet on the concrete floor. I sighed, shaking my head as I always did whenever I saw this place. My dad had a garage sale addiction and was always in search of the next treasure. You would often find him sitting on the verandah in his second-hand bottle-green corduroy chair, scouring the *Trading Post*. There was one thing Mum and I both agreed on: the chair was hideous.

"Well, I *don't* think it's wonderful," I said. "I don't want to go on a New Year's couples' retreat."

"Hmm," Mum said as she struggled to unlock the door at the end of the shed. I couldn't help but smile. Mum always kept the end room (her office) locked like Fort Knox, as if anyone would want to steal the treasures that lay within.

The garage filled with light as Mum got the door open and manoeuvred her way into her self-confessed 'woman cave'. It hadn't been without a fight that Dad had agreed to sacrifice prime square footage for Mum's office. It gave him less room for storing his crap.

I followed Mum into her office – or rather workshop, really. Inside housed shelf after shelf of handcrafted, unique pieces of Nina Maskala pottery. It was unique all right – no two ashtrays were the same. And there were lots and *lots* of ashtrays. It seemed that Mum had moved on from such humble ashtray beginnings and since branched out into vases, fruit bowls and …

Oh my God, what was that?

My mum followed my eye line.

"Do you like it?" She beamed, picking up her piece with pride.

I swallowed deeply. Whatever it was, it was hideous. "W-what is it?"

"It's my new thing I'm working on; it's a flower."

That's a flower?

"What do you think?"

Oh, dear Lord. How did I tell my mum that her flower looked like a vagina?

"I'm going to make a whole bouquet of them!"

A bouquet of vaginas.

"I thought I could make up baskets and bouquets and donate them to the local nursing home."

"What does Dad think of them?" I eyed the flower sceptically.

"Oh, I gave up showing him my work ages ago; he would only ever grunt a reply."

"Well, I definitely think you should seek his approval."

"Yes." She tilted her head and admired her handiwork. "They are rather beautiful."

Mum placed the flower back onto the mantel and turned to me, her eyes meeting mine, and for the first time today I felt like I had her full attention.

"Go!" she exclaimed, raising her brows. "Honey, you need to take a break. Make the most of your break from uni and just go have fun with your friends."

It wasn't that simple. Of course, I didn't explain the sole reason for not wanting to go.

Yeah, perhaps I would be a third wheel.

Sure, I didn't fancy being confronted by the endless array of questions from Amy, the ones I knew I couldn't avoid forever.

The last thing I wanted was to go into the embarrassing details. With Chris at the bakery until Ellie and Tess showed up, I'd missed my chance to find out which Onslow Boy had said what about me, so my brilliant plan? I had ended lunch early with the 'I've got a headache' excuse so I wouldn't get grilled by Amy. Yep! I used the old 'I have a headache' excuse, a new low. Mind you, since I was holding an ice pack to my face it was extra believable.

But I couldn't tell my mum any of those reasons.

Aside from my own personal anxieties about going on the trip, any excuse would seem lame; they all sure sounded lame to me.

As if on cue, I was startled by my mobile buzzing and vibrating in my pocket. The screen flashed *Amy*. Biting my lip and staring at the screen, I winced as I was about to do something I had never done before, especially to Amy.

I pushed the mute button, silencing the phone.

It was official, I was a shitty friend. No, even worse.

I was a coward.

My mum's shoulders sagged as she read the look on my face.

"You're really not going, are you?" Mum said with a sigh.

I shook my head, cementing the decision and pocketing my phone again. I would tell Amy tonight, once I had psyched myself up a bit, worked out what to say. So that was it: I was not going. I'd made up my mind. I waited for the onset of relief to flood me, but instead I couldn't help but wonder. If this was what I really wanted then why did I feel so miserable?

Chapter Eleven

Okay, so I didn't expect that.

I hung up the phone, feeling quite mystified with the conversation that had just gone down. I had psyched myself up in order to have the 'I'm not going' speech ready for Amy. I had even thought of multiple comebacks and reasonings in my defence. I had taken in a deep breath, sat down on my bed and prepared myself for what was to come, so when Amy had said, "Okay," I had fallen into surprised silence.

Okay?

And it wasn't even a short, sharp okay, or a 'pfft whatever' okay. It was a chirpy, upbeat 'no worries, maybe next time' okay. I didn't know what to say to that.

"If you change your mind, we leave at lunchtime tomorrow. I better go, I have a million things to do. If I don't see you tomorrow then I'll just see you next year. Next millennium!" Amy laughed before hanging up the phone.

Not only had I not expected that in a million years, I was not prepared for how utterly shit it made me feel. I straightened my spine. Yep, I had made the right decision. It really was no big loss. I wasn't going and Amy was obviously happy and preoccupied by the big trip anyway. It would be a good chance for her to get away and spend some time with Sean; she wouldn't want to spend the trip babysitting me anyway.

It seemed I had seriously over-thought my own importance to the expedition.

Good. What a relief; I was officially off the hook, good news indeed. I eyed the handwritten notes I had made in point form, all the reasons for not going, the list I had apparently not needed anyway. I flipped over the paper, my lips pinching into a smile as I recalled how yesterday, before leaving early from my 'headache', Tess had handed out stapled A4 sheets of an itinerary she had worked on. Apparently she had quizzed Toby on the details and customised it into a schedule that we could all follow. She had even gone so far as to make a list of travel essentials and recommendations. Tess was truly adorable, if not a little neurotic. A rather endearing fact, really, and I could totally relate. Aside from the long-forgotten foundation tube in my bathroom drawer, my little flat was organised on an OCD level of standards. It kind of had to be – my life didn't allow for anything less. Aside from my part-time job as a personal trainer I was studying full-time for my Bachelor in biomedicine. I needed to be organised, especially since I had a new social agenda that meant every spare minute was spent with Amy and the Onslow gang.

Well, *had* been with. Now it seemed I would have a couple of days all to myself, more time to …

Well, to work on scrapbooking my trip to China like I had always wanted to, to re-categorise my CD collection, rework a new fitness track for the new clients that would inevitably start up a fitness regime in the New Year. It was always a busy time for personal trainers, the start of a new year. New Year's weight-loss resolutions ruled. But until then, I could even go down to the Onlsow for a quiet drink if I wanted to, knowing that Chris wouldn't be there to serve and stare daggers at me. Yep! I had so many projects I could take care of – repainting the laundry, cleaning out my wardrobe … Lots to do.

I paused for a moment. New Year's Eve … Oh God, I had visions – visions of me sitting wedged in between my parents on their sofa, watching Mum's favourite movie, *The King and I*, for the millionth time. A coldness swept over me – so many hours to fill over the next few days.

No, Tammy! Positive, positive, positive!

***

I sat bolt upright in bed, clutching at my heart, breathing heavily. I was twisted in my sheets, a light sheen of perspiration across my skin. My eyes blinked at the whirring of the ceiling fan as I gathered my bearings.

Oh, thank God, it was just a dream.

I closed my eyes and breathed in deeply, burrowing my head in my hands. *Just a dream*, I repeated over and over. *Just a dream, just a dream, just a dream.*

I had dreamed that Mum had roped me in to making bouquets of clay vaginas over the holidays. Hundreds and hundreds of them – they filled Mum's woman cave to the ceiling, vaginas towering over, threatening to topple and bury me forever. Actually it wasn't a dream; it was a nightmare, and potentially my fate for the next week if I didn't escape Onslow.

It was ten a.m., a massive sleep-in by my standards. No doubt I was mentally exhausted from the day before, if not suffering a mild concussion from being kneed in the face. After having fallen asleep reading Tess's itinerary over and over, I had awoken with a new attitude. Scrapbooking and painting the laundryroom was not a positive way to enter the new millennium.

Peeling the sheets back, I dived out of bed and grabbed my phone on the way to the bathroom. I rang Amy's mobile but it went straight to message bank.

"Hey, Amy, it's me. I changed my mind. I'm coming; I'm definitely coming, so wait for me, okay? See you soon."

I ended the call, smiling at my new-found feeling of excitement. This was going to be great – a road trip! A better chance to hang out with fun people and escape Onslow. What had I been so afraid of? Ellie was right – the thought of staying in Onslow was horrific; I would sooner be a third wheel.

If nothing else, the journey would prove to be a spectacular one. The boys had planned to take the route up the Queen's Highway, through the ranges and along the remote coast. Apparently it was one of the most picturesque highways in Australia, or so it said on the itinerary.

Shoving clothes and my make-up bag into my green Esprit beach bag, I was grateful now that it was a lunchtime start; I was going to need every spare minute and still I felt like I wasn't ready.

I ticked off the list methodically:

- ✓ Sunscreen
- ✓ Lip balm
- ✓ Leave in conditioner

I laughed, wondering if the Onslow Boys' list read the same.

- ✓ Any personal medication needed

Oh crap! My migraine tablets, way to go, Tess! Pedantic people were often picked on, but you could never accuse them of being unprepared. Highly organised people would always have the last laugh. I circled the sentence as a reminder to grab them before ticking off other key items.

My pen hovered on the sheet.

Sleeping bag? Bugger!

Chapter Twelve

My mum was officially a saint.

After a mini-freakout and blind panic over all the things I didn't have from the list, I had rung Mum, jabbering away like a lunatic as I watched the clock count down before my eyes. I had tried Amy again but she was obviously busy sorting out her own list. I left another frantic message.

"Wait for me, I am coming!"

Mum, sensing the urgency, arrived in record time. She carried two armfuls of goods from the Land Rover as I shut and locked the door behind me.

"Leave them, Mum, there's no time! I'm going to be late."

Mum let the contents of her arms spill back onto the back seat. "I guess that means you need a lift?" Mum curved her brow in good humour.

I pecked Mum on the cheek. "Would you?"

Mum shook her head. "Hop in."

The wheels screeched as we turned the corner crazy fast. It wasn't because of the time limitations – Mum always drove like that. You always knew when Mum was nearly home; you could hear her turning up our street and roaring into the driveway.

Dad always shook his head. "She is going to go straight through that bloody garage one day," he'd say.

It was our own personal joke.

Accompanying Mum's horrendous driving was Mum's horrendous music. Barry Manilow blared out of the speakers. Any time we stopped at the traffic lights, I would slink down in my seat and pray no one noticed me, although Mum did draw attention our way, slapping the steering wheel and singing at the top of her lungs:

"*At the Copa, Copacabana*

Music and passion were always the fashion

At the Copa ... they fell in love!"

Ugh, seriously, take me away from this place.

The light took a painfully long time to turn green, but when it did Mum slammed her foot onto the accelerator as she bore through town like Steve McQueen on the streets of San Francisco. She flew up Coronary Hill and made a large sweep into the drive. I instinctively turned down the music.

"Thanks, Mum. You're a lifesaver." I hopped out of the car, working to open the back door to retrieve my things. I had never been so happy for Dad's garage sale obsession – everything I needed to complete my list had been found in the garage.

"Did you want to have a look and check if what I grabbed is all right?" Mum called from her seat.

I slammed the passenger door, shouldering my cargo and dragging the big duffle bag from Mum along the stone drive.

"No, it's okay; it will be fine. Thanks heaps."

Mum smiled. "I knew you would change your mind, I read it all over your face yesterday."

What? Surely not. Yesterday I had been displaying my most resilient 'I am so not going' look. And I'd meant it, too.

"Don't look so puzzled, Tam, I can read you like a book. Go have fun with your friends and stop stressing for once."

"I don't stress." I lifted my chin.

Mum shook her head, as if not believing a single word. Not that I could blame her, I didn't believe them myself.

Mum started up the engine. "Behave yourself, especially with those Onslow Boys in tow." Mum winked.

"Mum!" I looked around in horror.

"I mean it, Tammy – condoms were the one thing I couldn't find in the garage."

"Oh my God! I'm going!" I blanched, juggling my baggage and wanting to get far away from my mother's awkward jokes. Not that they were entirely jokes.

"I'll see you next year," she called, before pulling into gear and circling out of the drive, Barry Manilow's 'Mandy' following her down the hill.

I waved, watching the dust settle in the drive. Could she be any more mortifying? Luckily no one had come outside to witness it.

I continued to drag the duffle bag Mum had packed with travelling essentials toward the hotel verandah. Bloody hell, what had she packed, a freaking toaster and kettle? This thing weighed a ton. All of a sudden I wished I could take a moment to examine the contents of the bag; with Mum in control, God only knows what else she'd thrown in there. Her openness and honesty seriously creeped me out sometimes. You would never catch Amy's mum talking like that. Not in a million years. And as if conjuring her into existence, I heard Claire Henderson's voice.

"Hello, Tamara." She always called me that. "I hope you had a nice Christmas."

Claire Henderson sat comfortably in a white Adirondack chair on the verandah of the Onslow Hotel, wearing white capri pants and halter, her thick, ash blonde hair in a high ponytail, her eyes shaded by Chanel sunglasses, her perfectly manicured hand holding an iced tumbler with clear liquid. No doubt her infamous lunchtime G and T.

"Hello, Mrs Henderson," I groaned. Backing up toward the hotel, pulling my bag up the steps …

Thump-thump-thump.

Clearly out of breath by the time I got to the verandah, it was of no surprise that Claire Henderson hadn't budged from her shady recline; Claire Henderson didn't do 'help'.

She lifted her sunnies to spy my bags as I let them fall by my feet.

"And what have you got there?" she asked.

I fought to catch my breath, placing my hands on my hips. "Camping gear," I managed to breathe out, stretching my aching back.

Claire's confused blue eyes snapped up. "Camping gear?" she asked.

"For the road trip," I said.

If Claire Henderson didn't have a face full of Botox, she would have probably been frowning at me right then, but seeing as she was unable to do that, I had to take the blank stare instead. Maybe Amy hadn't told her about it. It *had* happened kind of quickly, I suppose.

"The New Year's road trip," I repeated.

"Oh, honey, I don't know how to tell you this." Claire Henderson sat up straight.

"Tell me what?" I asked.

"Sweetie, they've already gone."

Chapter Thirteen

This morning?

"But I'm sure the itinerary said twelve ..." I fumbled the papers out of my pocket, my eyes ticking side to side until I found it clear as day: 'Meet at the Onslow at twelve.'

"See?" I all but shoved the paper into Claire's face.

"Yes, well, apparently the boys wanted an earlier start; I would have thought Amy might have mentioned it."

"Well, I wasn't going to go, but then I left her a message this morning letting her know I was coming."

"And she never got back to you?"

I shook my head, folding up the itinerary and tucking it back into my pocket.

Claire sighed. "She was running around like a headless chicken this morning, squawking orders at everyone. The new time threw everyone off, maybe she forgot to check her messages?" Claire said soothingly.

"Yeah, maybe," I said, although we both knew when it came to Amy and her new beloved Nokia phone, she was rarely parted from it and checking it every five minutes. There was no way she would have not received my several messages.

A pit formed in my stomach. Maybe Amy hadn't wanted me to go? Maybe she was punishing me; after all, I was the one that had ignored her phone calls. She might have been mad at me for not telling her what really happened at the Bake House. I would have left me behind too.

I looked over my pile of camping gear.

Well, this was awkward.

"Oh, leave that there, Tamara. Come inside and I'll get you a drink."

I sidestepped away from my gear, not really wanting a drink. Instead, I just wanted to call up Mum and get her to take me away from here. I could lock myself away, scrapbook and paint my laundry like I had originally planned. I swallowed down the tears that threatened to bubble to the service. My best friend didn't want me around.

I followed Claire as she pushed against the main door. Eric Henderson was perched at the bar, talking to Max, one of the barmen, who was restocking the fridge.

Both sets of eyes turned expectantly toward Claire and me, confusion dawning across Eric's face the same way it had with Claire.

"Don't ask," Claire said; maybe I looked more upset than I realised.

Eric held up both hands as if silently stating, 'I'm not saying a word.'

"Max, can you please get Tamara a drink – anything she wants, our shout." Claire squeezed me reassuringly on the shoulder before motioning me to sit at the bar. Even though they weren't the owners anymore, not much had changed; they were still living in their apartment upstairs until they found a place to buy. Sean had made it perfectly clear that there was no rush. They spent most of their time living in their town house in the city anyway, except for occasions like now when they agreed to hold the fort for what would be Sean and Chris's last chance to get away before they officially took over. My heart sank; they would be well and truly winding their way through the picturesque scenery of the Perry Ranges by now, all laughing and joking, full of excitement. I didn't want a drink; I just wanted to call for a ride home.

"Can you excuse me for a minute? I just have to make a call." I smiled weakly, sliding off the stool and making my way outside, pulling my mobile out of my pocket. Looking at the blank screen was a painful reminder that there were no messages from Amy, not a one.

I phoned my parents number, hoping that Mum had made it back in time to pick up. I mentally calculated her speed and the distance – yep, Barry Manilow would have sung her home well and truly by now. On the fourth ring, Mum's voice answered.

"What did you forget?" she asked.

"Can you come pick me up, please?"

"Pick you up? Why?"

Hot tears burned under my lids; I didn't want to have to tell her. I felt like a complete idiot standing here next to my things on my own. No doubt Claire was relaying to Eric and Max what had happened; it was just so embarrassing. The sooner I could get away from here, the better.

"They left without me." I bit my lip, trying not to get emotional.

So when Mum laughed hysterically down the phone, it snapped me momentarily out of my misery and into confused anger.

"You think that's funny?" I scoffed.

"Oh, honey, I think it's hilarious."

Wow! I knew my parents often lacked a sensitivity chip, but this was downright mean. What a way to kick a person when they were down.

Mum contained herself as best she could before speaking. "I suppose it's time to come clean," she said. "Promise you won't get mad?"

"What are you talking about?" I exclaimed.

"Well, call me a traitor, but I may or may not have called Amy after you left last night."

"What?"

"Okay, so I did. I gave her the heads up that you were going to call her to tell her you weren't coming."

"WHAT?"

"Oh, Tam, I saw it all over your face; I knew you didn't mean it. I just wanted to tell Amy not to be too harsh on you, that you would most likely change your mind by morning. I know my daughter, honey."

My mouth gaped in horror, at the utter betrayal by my own mother, by my own friend. It all made sense now; Amy was so light and easy-going on the phone at my news, I should have known.

"And I was right, you did change your mind," Mum said.

"So what?!" I scowled at the phone, furious. "What difference does it make? They've still gone. You could have given Amy all the heads up you like; I left her enough messages but she still left without me. Your little theory is seriously flawed, Mother."

"Yes, I know they left this morning," Mum said.

I threw my arms up in despair. "Yeah, well, seems like everyone is in the know except me."

"Relax, Tammy, Amy didn't want me to stress you out by the early departure, she didn't want you to change your mind again, which, knowing you, you probably would have."

I scoffed. She was probably right but I would NEVER admit that.

"Yeah, well, that's brilliant because you may not have realised this, Mother, but I am actually stranded here with no ride now," I ranted. "So can you please come and pick me up?"

She sighed. "Tammy, you have a ride."

"Oh, do I? Really?" I asked sarcastically, staring out at the near-empty car park. "How interesting. And who, supposedly, am I riding off into the sunset with, huh?"

"That would be me," a voice said from behind.

Chapter Fourteen

I squealed, spinning around so fast, startled by the unexpected voice.

Chris?

"What are you doing here?" I clutched a hand to my heart.

"You ready?" he asked unenthusiastically, eyeing my pile of goods before frowning back at me. "We're only going for a few days, you know. You've packed enough for an Amazonian jungle expedition."

"I … I like to be prepared," I stammered. And this, well, this I was definitely not prepared for.

Chris sighed. "I'll get the car." He made his way toward the steps before pausing. My heart still pounded fiercely when he turned to look back up at me, a small twitch curving his lips. "You might want to finish your phone call."

Oh shit, the phone!

"H-hello, Mum, are you there?"

"As I was saying … You have a ride and by the sounds of it you just found that out for yourself."

"Chris Henderson," I whispered into the phone.

"Apparently he wasn't leaving till later anyway, so it worked out all right. Besides, Amy said it would give you two a chance to sort out your stories, whatever that means?"

I knew exactly what it meant. It was Amy's way of punishing me, of punishing Chris. I had read it all over his glowering expression. For someone who didn't want girls on the trip in the first place, being stuck in a car the whole trip with me would be his worst nightmare.

Well, join the club.

"I'm not going," I said.

"Tammy, don't be like that," Mum chastised.

"Like what? This is like unravelling a Miss Marple murder mystery, there are so many twists and turns."

"Just go catch up with your friends and relax."

"I am so over this." I shook my head, tears of frustration threatening to spill over.

"Tammy, you are going to have to learn to just relax. Your friends are expecting you and I think it was nice of Chris to agree to take you."

The thought of the awkward hours stranded in a car with him made me want to leave my things behind and hide. Under a bed. Though that would be the first place he would look.

The sound of a thundering V8 engine neared and suddenly all thoughts of escape seemed hopeless.

"I better go, my ride is here," I said, my words dripping with sarcasm. "Say hi to Amy for me next time you chat to her,"

"Try to remember to have fun, love. Remember your mantra: positive, positive, positive."

"Goodbye, *Mother*." I ended the phone call.

Pfft ... Positive, positive, positive.

I would have to desperately dig deep to find any trace of positive energy in me, and just as I thought I might grasp onto some small fibre of it, my eyes landed on my ride.

What. The. Hell.

***

"So what do you think?" Chris stood with his elbow leaning casually on the open door of his jet black panel van. He looked up at me expectantly. "Pretty sweet ride, huh?"

"If you're a serial killer," I said, cautiously descending the steps.

Chris's head snapped around with surprise, his eyes almost as dark as the van itself. He slammed the car door and folded his arms, glowering at me as I approached.

"I'll have you know, Toby and I have spent the better part of six months fixing this old girl up."

I wrinkled my nose. "Really?"

"It's got a 308 and a four barrel carby."

"Why, it could be grease lightning," I smirked.

I didn't think a death stare could vary in so many ways, but Chris had mastered a variety of pissed-off stares like no other. The one he was now casting me was a whole new level of anger.

Oops.

I cleared my throat and looked away, suddenly super aware that the last thing I should do was alienate my ride, but then the thought did occur to me: did I want to be trapped in a car with Chris Henderson for three days? Three long, insufferable days – could I subject myself to any more death stares, sneers, scoffs and deep sighs? Maybe I would be doing myself a favour if I gave him good reason to leave me behind. Before I fully acclimated to the idea, my attention was snapped back to the present and the duffle bag that landed at my feet.

I frowned toward the verandah where Chris had moved and was readying himself to turf my other bag down.

"Hey! Watch it," I snapped. "You might break something." It was a possibility, though I didn't know exactly what. Maybe Mum had slipped in a crockery set? Who could honestly guess?

"Let me guess," Chris said with a smirk as he slung my beach bag over his shoulder and trotted down the steps. “Hairdryer?” He threw a cocky smile and grazed my shoulder as he passed, heading for the van. My eyes burned into his back as he opened the double doors to chuck in my bag. He turned to me expectantly, his hand out for me to pass him the duffle. I snatched it up, trying not to let the strain of its weight show as I lugged it over and carefully placed it into the back. I attempted to, anyway. With a rather inelegant lack of grace, I hitched it up onto my knee, trying to be all cool and casual, as if I was totally in control …

I so wasn’t.

Chris plucked it from me as if the bag weighed nothing and turfed it into the back.

“Careful!”

“Relax, it landed on the mattress.”

Mattress?

I peered into the back. Sure enough, a mattress lined the whole floor up to the front bucket seats. The windows were blacked out and the inside walls were lined with black carpet. Oh, ick. All it needed was some leopard-print cushions and a disco ball.

It would seem that black was a common theme throughout Chris’s van, and the colour matched his mood.

Chris slammed the back shut. Viewing time was over.

I half expected him to say, “Let’s get this show on the road,” or “We’re burning daylight,” but instead I got a rather lacklustre, “Get in.”

Yep! Three long days.

Chapter Fifteen

Claire and Eric waved us goodbye in a pearly white-smiled send-off.

Claire looked utterly relieved that Chris was giving me a lift. He'd saved the day.

"See! All's well that ends well." She smiled as she hugged me goodbye.

Disappointment must have been etched in every crease of my face when I thought I had been left behind; I wondered what expression Claire and Eric read in my face now? I could only imagine my attempt at a good-humoured smile was coming across as nothing more than a pained grimace at best.

I opened Chris's car door and slid into the passenger seat, the leather sticking to my skin in the heat. I dipped my sun visor to shield my eyes from the bright sun glare. The sun's rays reflected off the newly polished dashboard that still smelled like Armor All spray. It was sickly sweet and smelt brand new.

Chris slid behind the steering wheel beside me, flicked down his visor and a pair of sunnies fell into his lap. He scooped them up and quickly put them on. That was a bonus, I thought. I wouldn't be able to see his guaranteed eye-rolls and those death stares. The engine roared to life as Chris fired up the black beast and my senses were assaulted with the growl of the engine and Bruce Springsteen mid-chorus, singing 'Brilliant Disguise' through the speakers.

Normal people would apologise and turn down the volume. Normal people would say something, anything at all, before shifting the steering column into gear. But not Chris. Instead, he placed his arm on the back of my headrest as he craned backward, reversing out, before shifting gear and pulling us away from the Onslow drive.

Most people would offer a cheery double honk to Claire and Eric as they waved from the verandah, but not Chris. He lifted one finger from the wheel in a half-hearted wave as we sped away.

It was so like him; everything was understated. I guess I was amazed that he had managed to string together a handful of sentences at all in order to communicate anything. We sat in silence. I couldn't believe I was going to spend three whole days cooped up in this car with him. It was going to be the longest three days of my life.

Surprisingly, after a little while he did start talking. It was about his car, but it could have been worse. And he did seem rather animated about it. I tucked that knowledge away for emergency conversation material in the hours of awkward silences that were sure to come.

I was actually relieved that Bruce Springsteen filled what would have been an otherwise unbearable silence. I peered at him out of the corner of my eye. He'd propped his arm on the ledge of the open window and his black hair fluttered in the breeze. He was usually so staunch and straight, unmoving, but now he seemed … well … kind of relaxed.

He turned his head every now and then to view the passing lake scenery; he tapped on the steering wheel and whistled lightly to the chorus of a song; he pulled at his safety belt as he straightened in his seat a bit. Was this an insight into a whole other, chilled-out side to Chris, I wondered?

He slouched down and seemed to melt into the leather of his seat a bit. It was the first time I had seen his shoulders relax, as if the more distance we put between us and the Onslow the more comfortable and clear-headed he became.

Interesting.

Chris leaned forward to lower the music, but it was too late now; there was a ringing in my ears.

He had nice hands, tanned by the sun, tidy fingernails; he could totally be a hand model with hands like those. If you were going to notice Chris and like him, his hands would probably be the first thing that would draw you to him, seeing as his face was always an intimidating scowl. It wasn't the first time I had noticed his hands – there had been countless times he had served me a drink at the bar, or handed me change and I had noticed how nice they were. The second thing I noticed about Chris (if I was noticing things) was his shoulders. They were so square, so symmetrical; he looked like he was a swimmer. He had great posture, even when he stood behind the bar between customers, with his arms folded – his stance was straight, proud, expectant. Yep! Your eyes would trail from those hands to those shoulders and usually be met with a piercing flick of the deep brown eyes that would cause you to quickly look away, or caused *me* to, anyway.

He had been pretty intimidating in the beginning, but as time wore on I just found him downright rude, no matter how lovely his hands and shoulders may be.

"What are you staring at?" Chris's voice pulled me out of my thoughts.

Oh crap! Was I staring?

I snapped my head away to look out of the window. "Nothing."

"They're not that white, are they?" he said.

My attention moved from the window to Chris again with a confused frown.

"Sorry?"

His head tilted downward as he shifted his leg a little to expose … a kneecap.

I smiled. "You're wearing shorts?"

"You don't have to sound so surprised." He lowered his leg.

"I don't think I've seen you in shorts before." My eyes trailed over his tan cargos; it seemed that in line with nice hands and shoulders, Chris had nice legs. *Okay, best not to stare*, I thought. But then something grabbed my attention.

"You have impressively tanned legs for someone who lives in Levi's," I mused. "You don't sun-bake in a pair of budgie smugglers on the weekends, do you?" That would just be too much.

Chris burst out laughing, so loud and abruptly it caused me to flinch at the unexpectedness of it. Laughter from Chris was as rare as seeing him in shorts.

"Budgie smugglers?" he asked.

"Yeah, you know, Speedos, Y-fronts,"

"I know what they are, Tammy, and the answer is *no*, no I don't do that." He grinned, concentrating on the road.

I took a moment to study Chris, not out of the corner of my eye this time but to unapologetically study him. I wanted to fully absorb the rarity of his smile, of his good humour, because let's face it, it would probably be the first and last time I saw it.

I curved my brow. "So exceptionally tanned legs but no weekends spent in budgie smugglers, eh? Curiouser and curiouser," I smirked.

Chris coughed. His face flexed back into those familiar stern lines as he straightened in his seat. "Tamara?"

I cocked my head. "Yes, Christopher?"

His lips twitched as he fought not to smile. "Stop staring at me."

And as quickly as the moment had come it was gone again. He controlled his smile and settled back into his regular serious, no-nonsense Chris.

"I can't help it," I said, reluctantly shifting my gaze back out to the road. "It's so very fascinating."

"What, my legs?" He shifted, as if checking them out.

I didn't answer; I relaxed in my seat, resting my head on the seatbelt strap.

Nope, it wasn't his legs that were fascinating. It was his smile.

Chapter Sixteen

It had been a rather animated start.

One I'd hoped would be a bit of an ice-breaker, but it did little to fully thaw his icy exterior. An hour and a half into the journey we were cruising through the winding terrain of the Perry Ranges in stone-cold silence – well, aside from Bruce Springsteen on repeat who now felt like a close and personal friend of mine. He was the buffer that saved me from feeling *completely* uncomfortable. If I had been travelling with any other Onslow Boy, there would have been free-flowing conversation, constant chatter and incessant flirting, not that I revelled in such things. Flirting to me was so very alien I didn't quite know how to do it. And with the Onslow Boys there was always a shameful amount of flirting.

Maybe this was the best outcome. I didn't wholly feel a part of the Onslow gang; I struggled at witticisms or keeping up with the banter of in-jokes and shared memories I knew nothing about. I was usually just a bystander, smiling in good humour or laughing politely at things I didn't really understand. Amy was so comfortable and boisterous with these guys, nothing worried or fazed her. Mum's words echoed through my consciousness. 'Just try to relax, Tammy.'

I scoffed at the thought. *Relax?* I didn't know the meaning of the word – my mind was a constant churning of worry. The only peace I really afforded myself was when I went for my runs and worked on my fitness circuits. Any other time my mind would race at a million miles an hour, never at peace. It hadn't taken my doctor long to pinpoint that my migraines were brought on by stress, that with a combination of full-time study and my fitness job I was running myself thin. He advised me that something had to give. Pretty amusing, really – it didn't matter how physically healthy and fit my body had become, my mind was still as frazzled as ever. Maybe a few days of sitting in contemplative silence with Chris would do me good, keep me occupied in a different sense. A welcome distraction from reality, from working out, studying. Just me (and Chris) and the road to a new year – hell, a new century. This might actually be good for me. I squared my shoulders.

Positive, positive, positive.

"So why did you hide from me at the Bake House?" Chris asked.

Oh crap!

I didn't know where to look. Especially now, as Chris flicked his sunnies up onto his head and glanced at me expectantly. The canopy of towering gum trees flickered shadows across his face as the afternoon sun battled to pierce through the dense bushland lining the road.

"Oh, I was just joking around." I gave a quick laugh, wiping a crease from my lap.

"You were avoiding me," he pressed, his tone serious.

"I wasn't avoiding you," I said, squirming under his scrutiny. A bubble of unease surfaced in my chest, but then a thought popped into my head. I looked pointedly at him. "Why would I do that?"

Ha! Ball's back in your court. Maybe it would make him have a think as to why anyone might want to avoid him; he wasn't exactly a ray of sunshine and considering the last time we interacted he had given me such a penetrating death stare ... Have a think about *that,* Mr Henderson.

I watched his reaction – there was no evidence of him even taking in the question, as if he wasn't even giving what I had said a second thought.

He shrugged. "You tell me," he said matter-of-factly, as if he wasn't even particularly invested in the answer.

Unease turned into anger. Was he so blind to himself? Did he have no real sense of why I would perhaps want to go to such lengths to avoid him? His nonchalant attitude made me feel like a bit of a weirdo, as if I just did random weird things all the time. I expected him to shrug, roll his eyes and say, "Chicks."

I narrowed my eyes at him. Maybe it was time I did him a favour. "I hid because, frankly, at that moment you were the last person on Earth that I wanted to see."

Chris's brows rose. "Really?" he said, a mixture of amusement and intrigue lining his face.

I crossed my arms. "Just because your friends put up with you doesn't mean I have to. If the choice is to be subjected to your pissy-pants attitude or hide under a table, well I clearly choose the latter."

"Pissy-pants attitude?" He glowered.

I leaned closer. "Believe me, that's sugar-coating it." I looked back out of the window, conversation over.

A long silence settled between us. An immense sense of satisfaction swelled in my chest, a feeling of pride, I guess, from staring down the beast and telling him what for. Maybe honesty really was the best policy.

I snuck a glance at him, scowling at the road ahead. Then again, considering we weren't anywhere near our destination, this was going to be one hell of a road trip.

Nevertheless, I still felt empowered, until, of course, my attention was caught by the chuckle coming from beside me. That smile was back. Chris rubbed his jaw line in humoured wonder as he glanced at me.

"Not bad for someone who doesn't like confrontation," he mused.

My brows narrowed. I had never told him that, I had never admitted that to anyone; it was my own Achilles heel and something I would never voice out loud. I shifted uneasily.

"And what makes you think I can't handle confrontation?" I lifted my chin in defiance. "I can handle it just fine."

Chris tilted his head incredulously. "Tam … you hid under a table."

Oh, right.

I didn't know what was more infuriating – the fact that he was so obviously right or that he had called me Tam. It sounded so foreign on his tongue, so strangely intimate. Usually any of the boys would playfully call me Tammy, Tamara or Tim-Tam. Sean and Amy would occasionally call me Tam, but no one else and *especially* not Chris.

It was unsettling.

I closed my eyes and rubbed at my temples, a dull ache slowly surfacing in its old, familiar way. I rubbed the back of my neck. I needed to relax – the last thing I needed was a migraine. My best form of avoidance of Chris was to stare out of the window, but the constant whirring and flashing of scenery going by was a sure-fire way to induce an instant migraine. My eyes needed to focus on nothing; I just needed to be still and silent. Luckily, Bruce had remained turned down and was really only acting as croony background music. I swallowed deeply, trying not to fear the worst.

I shifted in my seat, making myself more comfortable.

"What's going on?" Chris said. "Will you stop fidgeting?"

At this point I really couldn't care what Chris thought. Fine, I would sit still for a while and hope that maybe I was being paranoid, that perhaps I had just been worked up from the chaos of the morning and the pent-up frustration. Maybe I was dehydrated. If I sat still with my eyes closed, maybe I could rein this thing back in.

"You okay?" Chris's voice pierced the darkness.

"Hmm," I said. "Fine."

I breathed in deeply, wishing I had paid more attention to the meditation techniques I was taught when I was a teenager. For now I would try for stillness, for silence. That could work – just breathe, relax. Shut off my thoughts and let go.

I concentrated on my breathing and not the thunder of the engine. I could feel my shoulders sagging and my body melting into the leather bucket seat as I calmed my mind and my body into believing everything would be okay. And just as I was about to breathe a sigh of relief, my eyes blinked open.

I sat up straight in a panic. "STOP THE CAR!"

Chapter Seventeen

Oh no-no-no-no-no ...

As soon as Chris had jolted the car to a violent stop on the gravelly side of the road, I unbuckled myself and almost kneed him in the face as I scurried over the back of the seat like an uncoordinated spider.

Hmmmph. I landed fair on my back; bless the mattress for breaking my awkward dismount.

"What the hell, Tam? What happened? What are you doing?" Chris asked as he swivelled in his seat to watch me. I crawled over the mattress to my Esprit bag, unzipped it and dumped the contents out onto the mattress.

No-no-no-no-no ...

I scrambled through my belongings, fearing the worst. Surely I couldn't be so stupid? I stilled. Leaning back on my heels I delved into the pocket of my shorts and retrieved Tess's list. I unravelled it and sure enough there it was, boldly circled, the only thing not ticked off the list.

Any personal medication needed.

My heart sank. In all the chaos of searching for bloody sleeping bags and other essentials I had organised through Mum, I had completely forgotten to pack the most important thing of all: my migraine medication. My heart pumped and a light sheen of perspiration made the nape of my neck sticky, or was that just the onset of sickness? Oh God, I was in trouble.

A blinding streak of light assaulted me. I shielded my eyes against the offending rays. Chris stood before me, holding open the back door to the panel van.

"What did you forget?" He sighed. Ha! Now he just sounded like my mother.

I held up my hands, slapping them on my thighs in defeat; I shook my head. Hot tears welled in my eyes as my traitorous chin began to tremble.

I tried to scoop up my belongings in between horrid sniffling sounds that came involuntarily out of me, as now did the water works, gushing tears from my eyes.

Just *perfect!*

A hand snaked gently around my wrist.

A perfect hand.

"What's the matter?" Chris's voice was soft. "What can I do to help?"

I looked up at his face. The hard lines had melted into something that looked like … concern? I pulled my hand away.

"I just forgot something really important," I said, trying to keep it together.

Chris's brows rose in alarm. "Oh … right." He straightened and the gentle hand let go of my wrist. Shoving his hands in his back pockets, he attempted to look casual, but he looked anything but. "Well, we might be able to find a petrol station or something up the road to find what you need."

I shoved my belongings back into my bag, pausing only to meet Chris's eyes in confusion.

"What I need?"

He cleared his throat. "Um, yeah … You know."

I raised my brows in silent question.

He sighed in agitation. "Where you can get … girl stuff," he whispered the last words, as if someone might overhear him on the side of a highway in the middle of nowhere.

It took a moment for the penny to drop and I broke into a weak smile. "Ooooh, I see." I nodded. "Chris, I don't need a tampon." I had great joy in watching him squirm at the sound of that word.

"Oh, right. Okay. Well … good." He moved, refusing to look at me as he slammed the door on my smirk, coating me in soothing darkness again. At least his moment of unease had momentarily snapped me out of my despair.

I placed my bag aside, took a deep breath and climbed back over the seat again. Chris waited until I had settled in before he opened the driver's door and slid in beside me. He gripped the steering wheel and looked ahead as silence settled over us; this time there was no Bruce to mask it.

I sighed, pushing my fingers back through my hair, gathering the tendrils at the base of my neck. "I forgot my pain medication."

The infamous crease pinched between Chris's eyes and I knew what he was thinking: 'Is that all?'

"Oh, right," he said as he clicked his seatbelt into place. "Well, we can always pick up some Panadol at the next servo."

I shook my head. "I wish that would work. I get really bad migraines, like *really* bad. My vision goes and I get nauseous and the pain …" I broke off. I didn't want the tears to come again. That would just make it worse.

"How often do you get them?" Chris asked.

"Usually about once a fortnight, lately more frequently," I said.

"Do you know what causes it?"

Stress.

I shrugged. "Just prone to them; I guess I'm just lucky like that."

"Are you getting one now?" His eyes studied me like I was a bug under a microscope.

I bit my lip. "I really hope not." My voice shook. Truth be known, I had become so reliant on having my painkillers at hand come an attack, and I was at least able to shut myself away in the comfort and darkness of my own home and manage myself through the pain. But not like this, stuck in a van in the middle of bushland with a moody, silent boy who probably thought I was just being a drama queen.

Chris's knuckles brushed against my arm, snapping me out of my thoughts. "Here," he said, holding out his sunglasses. "Put these on."

My gaze lifted from the sunglasses to his face as the corner of his mouth pinched into a smile.

I grabbed them from him, my fingers brushing his. "Thanks," I said.

Chris cleared his throat as he placed his hand on the steering wheel and he started up the engine again. "Well, let's get this show on the road."

I tried not to laugh and slid on his sunnies.

Normal suited Chris.

***

We had been travelling for an hour, maybe two? I couldn't be sure. All I knew was a storm was brewing and as black clouds rolled in, so did the familiar migraine pain. There was no denying it now, this was definitely a migraine.

Tears burned my eyes – what once had been worry of potentially being far away from home without my medication had now become a bone-jarring reality. I'd never thought that such a beautiful, picturesque trip through the wide open spaces and leafy ranges could feel so claustrophobic.

As the panel van hummed forward through sweeping turns and bends, it only reinforced how completely out of my comfort zone I was. I could almost feel the colour drain from my face as my skin became clammy and spots danced across my vision, forcing me to keep my eyes shut tight behind the sunglasses. I guess I turned out to be the perfect travel partner for Chris – there was no small talk from me, I was all about silence. I left him alone and he left me alone. I just wanted to crawl into a hole and block out the whirring of the engine, the motion of the car sweeping around bends, which only heightened my nausea. I tried desperately not to think about vomiting or passing out, but the more I thought the more miserable I became.

At some point I must have drifted off, awakened only by a feathery touch to my cheek.

"Tam?"

The car was still, the world was silent, save for the odd bird call in the distance. I stirred gently, not wanting to move in case I was thrust into the pain that spiralled its way through my head in excruciating pulses with every movement.

I felt a palm cup my forehead, then my cheek.

"You're burning up."

That was the last I heard before feeling my passenger door fly open and a voice near my face spoke gently.

"Tam, we've stopped at a rest area. There are toilets here if you want to freshen up."

My bladder agreed that that was an excellent idea, the only thing that could possibly have made me move.

"That a girl. Come on, I'll help you." A hand clasped onto my arm, strength for me to lean on, to help me stand. I eased myself out of the car and clutched at my temples.

Squinting through blurred vision, I could see a hexagon-shaped concrete block in the distance that housed the public toilets back off the road amid the bushland. It was like a beacon to me as I broke from Chris's hold and headed slowly over.

"You all right?" he asked, following closely behind. It was kind of reassuring to think that if I stumbled he would break my fall. I waved him off, managing nothing more than caveman-like grunts as I shuffled toward the toilet block. The last thing I needed was for Chris Henderson to help me to the toilet. I stumbled forward, determined to force myself through the door, out of his sight. Then I could crumble.

"Whoa!" Hands grabbed my shoulders and steered me to the left. "Not that one."

Oh, right, maybe I did need his help.

Thankfully, the toilet block was cool and dark inside. I managed to do what I needed without passing out and waking up in a compromising position. It's amazing how determined you can be even on the edge of delirium. Mind you, I didn't get a chance to fall into mindlessness with Chris calling out every minute, asking if I was okay. I didn't know which of us was more frightened of me hitting the women's toilet floor, him or me?

I splashed cool water onto my face and the back of my neck and squinted at my cloudy reflection in the rest room mirror. I didn't need a whole lot of light to know I was as white as a ghost, my eyes bloodshot, my hair in disarray.

I was an absolute train wreck, but right now, I couldn't care less. I had to get out of there, the churning of my nausea made only worse by the dank surroundings of the toilet block. I edged my way outside and spotted Chris pacing then jerk to a halt when he saw me.

Chapter Eighteen

Was I dreaming?

There was no noise, no thumping V8 engine, no Bruce. Nothing but silence – beautiful, underrated silence. Something cool pressed against my forehead; a soft sensation smoothed over my head. The movement was hypnotic, back and forth, sweeping and dividing the tendrils of my hair. I snuggled deeper into the dream. My cheek felt warm, in stark contrast to the cool feeling on my forehead. This was a strange dream, one that I didn't want to wake from. I felt safe, rested; no pain reached me here. I wanted to stay forever. The stroking motion through my hair stopped.

No, don't stop. I squirmed. Something touched my shoulder blade, a delicate squeeze.

"Tammy?"

No, no, I wasn't ready.

"Tam?"

There was that name again.

The cold compress swept away from my brow and ran a delicious cool trail along my cheek and around to the nape of my neck, causing my eyelids to flutter open.

"Tammy, you better drink something, you need to keep your fluids up." The squeeze to my shoulder turned into a series of gentle taps.

I squinted and blinked, trying to focus on a light glow in the distance. I groaned and rubbed my face before stretching one arm up to the heavens, expecting my bones to crack and pop. I savoured the sweet, sated feeling of unravelling from sleep, but most of all basking in my blissful new reality: no pain. It was over. As I stretched, the back of my hand whacked against something.

"Jesus, Tammy, watch it!" A strong hand grabbed my wrist. "You nearly took out my eye."

I lifted my head a little and looked around me. My head was resting on a thigh? I sat bolt upright and my head slammed against something hard.

"Faaaaar … Tammy!" I swivelled around, clutching the back of my head to see Chris gripping his jaw, his face contorted in badly disguised surprise and pain.

"Bloody hell, you just got rid of one migraine." Chris winced as he worked his jaw to check it wasn't broken.

I bit my lip. "I'm sorry, you just startled me."

Startled was an understatement. I took in the darkened surrounds lit only by some crude camping glow wand or something wedged in the corner. My knees dipped into the spongy mattress. We were in the back of the panel van. My eyes settled on Chris who sat with his elbows resting on his knees, looking pissed off as he continued to rub his jaw. This was definitely not a dream.

"W-what time is it?" I asked, looking past him through the windscreen. It was completely dark.

"After eight."

"EIGHT?"

"You were out cold." Chris shrugged. "Must have needed it."

Wow, eight. I was out cold, all right. The last thing I remembered was coming out of the toilet block, and then nothing. Nothing until I felt the coldness on my forehead. I spotted a face washer near Chris's foot. I smiled. I thought I had been dreaming, but with that and the smooth, rhythmic feeling of fingers running soothingly through my hair, it seemed I definitely hadn't been. And the warmth against my cheek was Chris's thigh? I swallowed deeply. I could feel my face flame and was thankful for the dim lighting. My eyes slowly lifted to look at Chris.

"Thanks," I said.

Chris's brows lifted in surprise. "Wow. This is not the normal reaction when girls wake up in the back of a panel van."

I cocked my brow. "Oh? Been many, have there?"

Chris stretched out his arms, folding them behind his head as a boyish grin lined his face. "Hundreds."

"Lots of damsels in distress?"

"I'm actually thinking of painting a red cross on the side of the van."

"Sounds lucrative; you should charge by the hour," I said, throwing the wash cloth up at him. He caught it with impressive reflexes.

I took a moment to study this playful side of Chris, taking in the lines of his face, the jagged folds of his hair that were ruffled in a casual messy, cool way. He wasn't beautiful like Toby, cute like Stan or oozing charisma and raw sex like Sean did. He was something else entirely. As much as I hated to admit it, he was the epitome of handsome – silver-screen good looks, smouldering, broody, he was an utter enigma.

But who was the real Chris?

I secretly wondered which other girls he may have had here in the back of his panel van in the past. I tried to pinpoint any of the girls that strutted around the Onslow like a conveyer belt of sex, ripe for the picking. I hadn't really been into the pub scene until getting back in touch with Amy recently, but still, even I could recognise the whispers and doe-eyed looks girls gave him as they held out their hands to Chris at the bar for their change. It was somewhat amusing – Chris didn't even give them the time of day, but that didn't stop them from trying. Maybe that was a part of the attraction?

I couldn't exactly guess who may have caught his attention, I couldn't even imagine who he may have invited into the van, or up the stairs to his bedroom, or into the beer gar …

I stilled.

"You all right?" Chris shifted with unease.

My eyes snapped up to lock with his. I quickly looked away again, my mind racing at a hundred miles an hour. My cheeks burned as my memory flashed back to a time – the only time – I had seen Chris with a girl, something I had completely forgotten until now.

"Yeah. Nothing. I'm fine."

***

It wasn't an unusual state of affairs for Amy and me to sneak out. To us, our parents were utter killjoys when it came to anything beyond ten p.m., which basically left an entire social scene out of reach, locked beyond our front doors, unexplored. At fifteen, it was an injustice of gargantuan proportions. More so for Amy whose older cousins, Chris and Adam, taunted her nightly by coming and going as they pleased. They were a little older, sure, but the big difference was that they were boys. Such double standards.

On one warm summer night, Amy and I had planned to pull off the ultimate deception and sneak out for Todd Macki's eighteenth. Word on the grapevine was that it was going to be epic. Pretty much every teen in town was going to gatecrash; we simply had to go. The plan was for me to sneak out and ride across town to the Onslow, hiding my bike behind a bush in the beer garden. Amy would 'accidentally' leave the fairy lights on in the beer garden and I would tiptoe through, having not broken a leg in the dark. The dim lights were a much-welcome sight as I fumbled my way up the back staircase to the top landing near the back door of the second storey. The plan was that I would wait there until precisely five past twelve at which time I would tap our secret knock on the back door panel to signal that I had arrived and the coast was clear.

I prided myself in being a masterful creature of the night that could slide along the edges of blackness with the elegance of a jungle cat. In reality, I was just smart enough to remove my jangly bracelets and wear my sensible (quiet) Converse sneakers to trek to our meeting point.

Wrapping my arms around my legs, I settled in to wait on the landing and glanced at my watch: eleven forty-five, early as usual.

I sighed. *Always better to be early*, I thought, as my gaze traced the star-lined sky, my lips tilting into a devilish grin. My parents would be livid if they knew my whereabouts right now.

Impatient and bored, I had felt bold, brimming with confidence and self-assurance.

Maybe Amy was (by some miracle) running early. There was no point in us both waiting around, twiddling our thumbs for the next twenty minutes when we could be at the party of the decade. I sat up and my fist hovered over the back door, ready to make contact when laughter floated up from below.

My eyes had widened, heart had pounded and I'd dived onto the platform. My palms connected with the wooden landing and I'd squeezed my eyes shut, praying no one could see me. The laughter dipped into conspiratorial whispers as footsteps continued down below. I opened my eyes, listening intently to the movements. A gap in the decked landing let in a faint slither of a subtle glow from the fairy lights beneath. I squinted, fixing my eye slowly to the gap, searching out the people whose voices lingered in the shadows under the stairs.

Even through the tiny crack it didn't take me long to find them. Broad, square shoulders were bathed in the subtle glow of the lights in the small space under the stairs. I had gasped and pressed my face into the slatted wood as the shadows moved beneath. A small hand slid along his shoulder, gripping the fabric with such force I thought it might tear. He pressed her back against the post, her fair skin illuminated white in the light as she gasped at the unexpectedness of it. She affixed her hungry stare on him as he lowered his mouth to hers. My eyes widened as the heated scene played out before me. I couldn't turn away. I had never felt more scandalous than at that moment in my life. At fifteen I had never seen or experienced anything like it. Excitement twisted in my stomach seeing her gasp as he trailed his mouth down her neck. I bit my lip as I watched his fingers slide slowly, wickedly against the girl's collarbone, only to hook the strap of her top and peel it slowly downward, revealing a small, milky white breast. An unexpected feeling shot through me at the sight of his thumb teasing the pebble-like bud as he kissed her once more, and my, *how* he kissed her. I felt the pang of jealousy – never had I ever been so wanted, so desired. I imagined for a moment that I was that girl in the dark, that I was the one who was pressed up against the beam, as he slowly lowered his head to trail kisses along my exposed skin. The girl arched her back, her neck twisted in exquisite madness, her fingers folded through the dark tendrils of his hair. Her breath had hitched as his tongue slid teasingly along her nipple.

"Chris!" she gasped, the word carrying its way up the stairs.

I flinched backward and kicked a pot plant off the landing. I covered my face to stop from screaming as I heard the plant shatter below. Before I could worry that it might have landed on anyone, the back light to the beer garden flooded the space. I scrambled backward, out of sight. It seemed I wasn't the only one concerned with being discovered – hearing the muffled giggles beneath me as they scurried out of the space. I leaned forward and peeked over the ledge just enough to see Chris running out of the side exit of the beer garden, leading the girl by the hand as they fought to catch their breath from laughing. He looked back at her with a boyish grin, as if he would follow her to the ends of the Earth, as he pulled her through the gate and into the darkness beyond.

I sat back, plastered against the bricks of the hotel, my breath laboured, my cheeks aflame from all I had seen.

I could only hope that I would remain undiscovered. The back light switched off again and I had shaken my head, trying to clear the fog. I eyed my watch in the gloom: one minute past twelve. I had exactly four minutes to gather myself and try to forget what I had just witnessed.

Chapter Nineteen

I had never told a soul about that night.

In fact, I had forgotten all about it. How was that possible? I must have felt so intensely wicked and mortified about my secret spying that I had blocked it out of my mind altogether, until now, as I thought back to Chris's fingers stroking my hair, entirely innocent, simply to comfort a sleeping girl.

Heat still flooded my cheeks at all the confused emotions fifteen-year-old Tammy had felt on that night. It also cemented the knowledge that Chris may have been distant, moody and mysterious, but he sure knew how to treat a girl.

I had no doubt that he had had his fair share, under the beer garden steps, in his room, in this van. I couldn't bring myself to look at him, suddenly annoyed at the feelings that twisted in my stomach, at the thought of him having girls in there, anywhere. It was the same feeling I'd got that night, a sharp unexpected jolt of jealousy. It was pathetic. Stupid.

Jealous over Chris Henderson? I don't think so.

"Are you okay? You look kind of flushed." Chris's voice snapped me from my lurid thoughts.

"I'm fine!" I said too quickly. "Migraine's gone, I'm good to go." I crawled toward the front seat.

"Where are you going?" Chris asked.

I paused mid-climb, looking back at him expectantly. "Oh, um, I'm okay to keep going."

Chris twirled the face washer casually around his finger. "I thought we might set up camp here for the night; we're nowhere near any fine eatery or civilisation, but the toilet block is here, which is something I guess."

My heart pounded as I lowered my leg and slid down to sit on the mattress beside him. "But the itinerary said we would stop in Calhoon first night; isn't that where the others would be expecting us?"

Chris shrugged. "We've lost too much time with the late start and the unplanned stopover." He eyed me expectantly. "Besides, we're in pretty thick roo country and I don't fancy busting up my windscreen by ploughing into one."

No. I didn't want that either.

"Best make camp here."

My heart sank; I had grand visions of catching up with the others, setting up tents and swags together, even perhaps us girls persuading the boys to stay in a hotel, although I didn't much like our chances. At best it would be an established camping ground with hot showers – the height of luxury. Instead, no thanks to me, we were hours and hours behind the others, stuck in the middle of nowhere in the back of a panel van.

"You hungry?" Chris grabbed a shopping bag and rustled around inside it. "It's not exactly Michelin Star cooking, but Melba rustled me up a batch of salad rolls and a pack of Anzac biscuits. Aw sa-weet!" he cried. "The old girl has chucked in some frozen Primas, God love her." Chris pulled out the drinks, beaming like he was a kid at Christmas. He chucked one over to me that I juggled into catching.

I eyed the juice box sceptically, a grin pinching at the corner of my mouth. Amy had often complained that Chris was Melba's favourite. This might just work out in my favour. I couldn't help but speculate that Melba hadn't packed lunch for Adam or Amy. *Interesting*, I thought.

Amy being the only girl and Adam being the charismatic charmer, it surprised me that Chris was the favourite.

"Thanks," I said, watching Chris set aside his precious goods. He lined them up straight like soldiers and set the bag aside.

"It probably wouldn't hurt for you to take it easy, anyway," he said. "We can get your medication when we hit Calhoon tomorrow." He passed me a salad roll.

"It's a nice idea," I said, "but there is one small problem."

"What's that?" Chris asked through a mouthful of roll.

"They're prescription meds." I sighed.

He swallowed. "Bugger."

"Yep." I picked at my soggy bread roll.

"Drink!" Chris's voice sounded firm. "You need to keep your fluids up," he insisted.

"Forever the barman," I mused.

"Keeping people hydrated is my profession," he said, breaking the plastic straw of his Prima and shoving it into the fruit box. I couldn't help but smile at him; Chris, the serious, no-nonsense publican, sipping from a Prima like a boy in a schoolyard. He looked so unguarded, so innocent, and then my mind flashed back to his taunting mouth in the beer garden that night. Looks were deceiving. He wasn't as much of a puzzle as people believed. He was just understated – unlike the other Onslow Boys he was private and didn't wear his emotions on his sleeve. No; instead, he lurked in shadows and drove black panel vans with the windows blacked out. What was that saying? It's the quiet ones you have to worry about? Great! And I was stuck with him tonight.

Not feeling hungry, I wrapped the remainder of my roll back up and placed it aside. "I might freshen up a bit before I call it a night," I said. "Do you need help to set anything up?"

The gurgling sounds of the straw sucking up the last remnants of juice answered me, before Chris crushed the packet with satisfaction. "Nope! It's okay, I'll set up camp."

Relieved, I grabbed my toiletries before he changed his mind and roped me into setting up some complicated camping apparatus.

I struggled with the latch of the back door, jiggling and twisting, even going so far as to put my shoulder into it, which got me nowhere, either.

I struggled with the stupid thing until I felt the press of Chris lean against my shoulder and place his hand over mine.

"Not like that." His words breathed out near my cheek. "Like this." He twisted and lifted the handle with ease, freeing the lock and pushing it open, mercifully giving me room to move from the heat of his torso.

"Thanks," I said too quickly, as I gathered my things and moved toward the toilet block. Fumbling my goods, flustered, I dropped bits and pieces along the way.

Please don't be watching. Please don't be watching ...

I managed to steal a glance back toward the car before going into the Ladies' toilets. My eyes briefly locked with his amused ones as Chris sat casually on the edge of the van, a crooked grin curving his lips.

Bugger.

Chapter Twenty

I took my time cleansing, scrubbing, toning and moisturising.

It was as close to a shower as I was going to get. I changed into my nightwear and pulled my hair up into a high ponytail and out of my face. Even though I had slept a good portion of the day away, I was bone tired, and suddenly grateful that Chris had made the call to stop for the evening even if we were a good six hours behind schedule. Driving on into the night and reaching Calhoon at four in the morning wouldn't put us in good stead for the next day's leg – driving tired was not only dangerous for Chris, but getting overtired was another migraine trigger for me. No, I needed a good night's rest. So I took my time, allowing Chris to set up tent and get changed himself while I busied myself brushing my teeth.

I didn't know exactly what warranted camping attire, but Tess's list recommended flannelette PJs as the coastal roads can be chilly of a night, even in summer. I knew we weren't that far into the journey, or maybe it was the fluoro lighting in the toilet block that flickered with a disco of bugs buzzing above my head, but the night was still stifling, the air thick and warm. As I stood in my white and navy striped PJs, the only nightwear I had packed, I stretched out the collar and fanned myself. I'd probably be grateful for it as the air cooled and I settled in the tent for the night, but not yet I wasn't. I packed all my gear back into my toiletry bag. Chris had had enough time to set up. I zipped up my toiletry bag and made my way outside.

I paused. A frown etched my brow as I neared the van, following the dull light and soft music that filtered out of the open back door. I spotted Chris perched on the end of the mattress, his foot hitched up on the tow bar. He was relaxed, whistling along to the tune.

He straightened and sat up when he saw me approaching.

"Feel better?" he asked.

I kept walking, peering around the other side of the van, bewildered. I did a full circle around it, checking in all directions.

"Where's the tent?"

Chris pushed his hands in his pockets, a perplexed line creasing his brow. "What tent?"

My pulse spiked in anxiety. "The sleeping tent?" I envisioned a large, multi-winged tent that could house a family of five, with even a shady verandah part to sit in outside on deckchairs. Like the one on the front of camping shop catalogues, that kind of tent.

"Oh." Chris cocked an amused brow and scratched the back of his neck. "Ya see, the thing is …" He tapped on the mattress beneath him. "I don't do tents."

I squared my shoulders, a grave look on my face. "That's not camping," I said coolly.

Chris smiled, reaching in to grab his bag. "You'll thank me in the morning." He winked, shouldered his backpack and headed for the toilet block.

***

Okay, no sweat. We would just sleep in the back of the van. The very confined, claustrophobic van.

It appeared that in my absence Chris had been busy – he had placed all the baggage aside (well, most of it was mine; he was a light traveller, so it would seem) and set the mattress up with fresh black sheets and a navy plaid doona. To top it off there were two lumpy pillows that looked like they had seen better days. The bed was made army-style immaculate, crisp and taut; you could really bounce a coin off it. I was impressed, but not surprised. If Chris did something it was always with military precision. I knew Chris's goofball of a younger brother was in the army but maybe they had gotten it wrong? Maybe Adam and his lighthearted wit and people skills needed to be behind the bar and Chris needed to be shipped off to the South Pacific or wherever they go to these days?

I stood with my hands on my hips eyeing our sleeping quarters, the very *cosy* quarters that Chris had no doubt planned on sleeping in alone until I had crashed the party. No worries, we were both adults here, no problem. I had my sleeping bag. I grabbed for it, unclasping the pull string and dumping out the – whoa! Hot pink roll. Okay. I could work with this. In one flick, I uncurled the sleeping bag and pulled it apart, revealing a …

"Oh my God," I said aloud. I looked on in horror at the giant caricature of Punky Brewster with two thumbs up. Dad and his bloody impulse purchases at garage sales. Sure, this would have been handy, and no doubt I would have loved it … when I was five! Knowing Dad, it had probably been buried in the garage for the past fifteen years. A very delayed discovery indeed.

I am not sleeping in this. I could only imagine how amusing the Onslow Boys would find it. I quickly gathered it back up, rolling it and shoving it back into its cover, cursing and punching it in with all my might.

Why doesn't anything go back in the way it comes out?

I heard Chris's footsteps crunching on the gravel as he approached the car, rounding the back of the van with a towel slung over his shoulder.

I eyed his damp hair with interest. "Did you have a bath in the sink?"

"Just a freshen-up." He brushed past me and chucked his bag in the back.

Wow, he smelt good, like he was ready for a night on the town. He had even changed his T-shirt with a new black one. I fought not to smile as I envisioned his wardrobe in his room filled with nothing but identical black T-shirts all hanging in a line.

I guessed I should really know that; I mean, I had been in his closet only a few days ago. Not that I had paid much attention … to the clothes.

"Aren't you hot?" Chris's voice snapped me from my thoughts.

"Excuse me?"

"What's with the flannies?" Chris's eyes looked me over with guarded amusement. There was nothing I hated more than the up-and-down look; the kind you got when walking into the Onslow on a Friday night. Except this was not a look of appreciation. He was looking at me like I was an idiot.

Damn Tess's list.

"I thought it might get cool on the coastal road." I adjusted my top.

"Well, we've got a ways to go before we find out, so if I were you I'd get changed; there's no A/C in this hotel." Chris leaned in, grabbing a pillow and shoving it under his arm.

I opened my mouth to say that I didn't have anything else to wear, when I paused and watched him make his way to the front passenger door. He hopped in the front of the car with his pillow.

"W-what are you doing?" I asked, climbing into the van and crawling toward the front. I rested my elbows on the back of the bucket seat where Chris was making himself at home, punching his pillow and shuffling himself into a recline.

"What's it look like? We've a big day tomorrow – early start." He lay with one arm behind his head, his body partially skew-whiff. He looked really uncomfortable.

"You can't sleep there!" I insisted. "You have hardly any room."

"It's all good; I've crashed on worse couches." He sighed, closing his eyes.

I stared down at him for a long moment. I didn't know whether to be flattered by the gentlemanly gesture or annoyed that he found the mere thought of sleeping next to me so offensive.

"You're being ridiculous," I said. "There's plenty of room for both of us on the mattress."

Kind of.

"We can even sleep top to toe if you want?" I suggested.

Chris laughed. "At the risk of kneeing you in the head again, I think not. Go to sleep, Tam."

I took a moment's pause as if waiting for him to speak again, but it was obvious that the topic was closed. Fine, I thought, let him suffer from leg cramps and a bad night's sleep; it was his problem, not mine.

I pulled the back doors shut and fixed myself on top of the doona.

What was his problem, anyway? He didn't have to act like he might catch something off me. Heaven forbid he'd get girl germs.

I nestled onto the mattress, trying not to focus on the fact that he was lying just near my head, divided only by a seat.

"Goodnight, Chris," I said.

A deep sigh emanated from the darkness.

"Goodnight." The sound of his body shifting on the leather seat screeched as he tried to manoeuvre into a more comfortable position. I bit my lip; he must have been so uncomfortable.

I shook the thought from my mind. I couldn't let myself worry about Chris and his comfort, because I had my own to worry about.

Stupid flannelette pyjamas!

Chapter Twenty-One

It was still dark when we hit the road.

I didn't exactly know if it's just what you do when you're on a camping trip (get an early start) or if he was just trying to make up for lost ground. My guess was that Chris had had the worst night's sleep possible and was awake, anyway. I tried not to take so much pleasure in it, so refrained from bursting out into an 'I told you so' dance. Plus, it was too early for that stuff.

We had a six-hour drive to Calhoon ahead of us. The idea of it made me want to cry. It also meant that the others would no doubt have moved on to the next point by the time we reached it.

All I wanted was a shower – a long, hot shower.

"I don't suppose Melba packed breakfast by any chance?" I looked at Chris behind the wheel. He was sporting some serious bed hair.

"No," was his clipped response.

Geez, sorry I asked.

Having forgone my morning run, my foot bounced up and down in the footwell. I tapped out a beat on my knees. I felt completely restless. Considering we were in the middle of nowhere, running in remote wilderness probably wasn't a good idea. I guess, if anything, if anyone *had* stumbled across us, we were the dodgy-looking ones in our black serial-killer van. I smiled to myself – I wondered how many a poor passer-by last night had avoided the rest stop, having seen our dodgy car parked there. I sure would have kept going.

"So, if it's not Grease Lightning, what do you call it, then?" I asked.

"It doesn't have a name." He looked at me like it was the most ridiculous question he'd ever heard.

"Every car has a name," I said. "Black Betty? The Beast? She needs a name."

"She?"

"Of course, all cars are girls," I said. "So, really? No name?"

"Well …" Chris paused, as if changing his mind about what he'd been going to say.

"'Well, what?" I straightened in my seat, intrigued.

"The boys have a name for it." He fought not to smile.

Uh-oh.

"What?"

Chris glanced out of the window, a smile broadening across his face. "You don't want to know."

Oh, now I did!

I went to press further but he promptly changed the subject.

"There's a petrol station and cafe about fifty kilometres from here, we can stop there for some breakfast."

Food? God, yes!

I wanted to clap my hands together and squeal at the thought. Though a lot of girls had phobias of eating in front of boys, I was not one of them; I loved my food. I was a constant source of hatred and envy owing to my fast metabolism, but truth be known, I worked my butt off – quite literally. Fitness was everything to me; though sometimes my diet did lack the certain balance that you'd think a personal trainer should have. A New Year's resolution, for sure. Like the rest of the world, I planned to eat healthier. I kind of felt like a hypocrite being a personal trainer some days, telling mums and businessmen what to do when I didn't necessarily do it myself. I needed to be hypnotised or something. No Monte Carlo biscuits in between meals!

"I don't know what kind of selection they have," Chris added. "Probably just your typical potato cake and Chico Roll from the bain-marie." He almost looked apologetic.

I wanted to laugh – people always assumed that I was a muesli and yoghurt girl based on my athletic nature. Ha! Perhaps I could get away with it after all. Live a lie until I was caught scoffing down a chocolate Chokito for afternoon snacks. Let Chris think I was healthy on the inside, I thought.

I switched my mobile on. I had kept it turned off in an effort to save its battery.

"Don't bother, there's no reception up here," Chris said.

"Well, I guess I can't be completely mad at Amy, then," I said, mainly to myself.

"Why would you be mad at Amy?" Chris asked. It seemed like he was genuinely interested.

I sighed. "My mum and Amy conspired against me in a way to get me on this trip."

"You weren't going to go?" he asked, surprised.

"I seriously didn't think I was, but apparently – and this is the most infuriating part – my mum can read me like a book. It's pretty frustrating when someone knows what you're going to do before you even make the decision to do it."

Chris frowned. "I don't get it; how did they conspire against you?"

"I told my mum I wasn't going and it took me all afternoon to pluck up the courage to tell Amy. And when I did call her she was suspiciously okay about me not going."

"Well, that doesn't sound like Amy at all," Chris agreed.

"I know! It should have been a massive red flag. Apparently my mum had rung her to tell her I was coming and to expect a phone call."

He laughed. "Ah-ha!"

"Yeah, the plot thickens. Amy didn't want Mum to tell me about the departure time being brought forward in case I really did freak out and didn't want to go. So how did you get roped into it, anyway?"

"I wasn't going to leave until today, do a nonstop drive to Point Shank, have the alleged time of my life and then head back. But when Amy came and begged me to go early because I had to bring you, well, the plan changed somewhat."

I cringed, embarrassed. "Sorry."

Chris shrugged. "I was coming anyway."

"So what tactic did she use against you?" I asked. "Guilt? Blackmail? Torture?"

Chris smiled. "I shall never reveal my weaknesses."

"Did she promise you banana bread?" I teased.

Chris burst out laughing. "That's it. You know my weakness."

"Hmm," I said with a sly smile. "Handy to know."

A silence fell between us, but it wasn't awkward; it was light, easy, comfortable.

"Thanks for bringing me, Chris. I mean, for waiting, or leaving early. Or whatever you call it, thanks." I looked at his profile until he glanced my way, his brown eyes meeting mine for a moment before returning to the road.

"It's nothing." He shrugged.

I smiled and looked back out of the window.

It wasn't nothing.

***

I hummed a happy tune as I forked another helping of pancake into my mouth, swinging my fork from side to side as if I was conducting an orchestra. I was in heaven – blueberry pancake heaven. I looked up to see Chris perusing his newspaper in silent study.

"What are you looking at?" I asked with a mouthful of batter.

He shook his head as he lifted his paper with a shuffle. "Nothing."

To think I used to be intimidated by those eyes. Now I had managed to spend some time around them I must be getting used to the varying degrees of his stares. There was the 'I'm so bored right now' deadpan, or the 'I wish you would just shut up right now' stare-down, and there was the 'Kill me now' look that was usually followed by a sigh of frustration. I munched thoughtfully on my breakfast, amusing myself no end with profiling Chris. Of course, there were other looks too. Like the humour that flooded his eyes when he laughed – not that that happened often. Or the look of concern that had been etched on his face when he watched me make my way to the toilets yesterday when I was unwell. Those moments made me uncomfortable; they were glimpses of something so foreign I didn't know how to react to them. Bitter, moody and silent Chris I could handle, but anything else had me stumped. Luckily they were fleeting moments.

A double beep sounded from somewhere, making me jump.

"And hello reception!" Chris announced as he delved into his pocket and grabbed his phone, flicking through the screen.

"There's service here?" I grabbed for my own.

"Yep!"

I turned it on, waiting for any magical ding. And sure enough, one-two-three-four chimes went off.

"Someone's popular," Chris said without taking his eyes from his message.

The first was a missed call alert from my mum, probably wondering if I was okay or if she was forgiven. The first text message said as much.

Gello sweety, hop youtt hsving fun, ring me when u can. Lobve mum.

Yep, that was Mum all right. At least she got a couple of words right.

There was one missed call from, hello-hello: Amy Henderson. Followed by a message.

I am so-so sorry, please don't be mad. I was totally freaked out that we had to leave early and when your mum called I was worried that she was wrong that you wouldn't change your mind and come. Aunty Claire said you guys had left and I am SO HAPPY, yay for Chris!! Even though I totally had to blackmail him. Can't wait to see you. Travel safe and see you soon!!! Xxx

My shoulders slumped. How could I possibly stay mad at her, or Mum for that matter? As I re-read the message, one thing bothered me.

I totally had to blackmail him. I knew I had joked about it, but something kind of bothered me that she'd had to resort to such extreme measures to force him to take me, and what could she possibly have over him, anyway?

"Any news?" Chris's voice snapped my attention away from my screen.

"Oh, just from Mum and Amy. You?"

"They've left Calhoon, but have decided to stop over for the night and camp at Evoka Springs. It's only a few hours past Calhoon. They said they would wait for us to catch up."

My eyes brightened. "They're going to wait?"

"Yep!" Chris finished texting back and hit send. "We should get there about three this arvo if we have a good run."

"Oh, we will. No migraines here!" I saluted.

"All right, well, we'll get some food and drinks for the road and keep going then." He paused, looking down at my plate. "After you've finished your pancakes, of course."

I grinned like a Cheshire cat. "Of course!" I picked up my fork and continued to eat and hum with much enthusiasm. When a day started with pancakes it was destined to be a good one.

Chapter Twenty- Two

I prided myself in being a pretty patient person, really.

But this was ridiculous.

So much for having a good run and getting to our destination by three. I glowered across the road to where Chris paced in front of the Black Cat Cafe (that, incidentally, *did* serve the best pancakes ever). I sighed, flicked off my shoes and placed my bare feet on the dash as I watched him laugh and pick at the peeling paint of a fence post as he talked animatedly.

It was his third call that ranged from serious and business-like to upbeat, chatty laughter. I wondered who he could be chatting to – or, more importantly, who was putting that smile on his face. He did know about the Black Cat Cafe and the landscape of this trip pretty well. Maybe he had made the voyage a few times before with the boys. Or maybe he had a mistress at every port or petrol station. Maybe he was hooking up a booty call for when we got to Calhoon – a widowed cougar with fire-engine red lipstick and manufactured curls.

If we ever *did* get to Calhoon.

I eyed the flashing charge button on my mobile and figured I had some time to kill. I dialled Amy's number and she answered on the second ring.

"Tammmyyyyyy!" she squealed down the phone, so loud I had to hold it away from my ear.

"I've changed my mind, I'm not coming," I said dryly.

"You better bloody be!" she shouted.

"Relax," I said. "It's just a joke. Wouldn't miss it for the world."

"We're leaving Calhoon about lunchtime, but we'll wait at Evoka Springs for you guys."

"EVOKA SPRINGS, BABY!" someone shouted in the receiver.

"Piss off, Ringer," Amy snapped

"Someone's excited." I laughed.

"You wait until you get up here; it's so beautiful, you are going to bow down before me and thank me for getting Chris to bring you."

"Yes, about that …" I glanced out of the passenger door. Chris was still on the phone. "How did that come about?"

"Well, *as usual*, he was being his normal whinging, whiny self. 'I'm coming, I'm not coming, I'm going, I'm staying'. Actually, kind of sounds like you."

"Shut up!"

"Anyway, after he had a moan about leaving early I told him to quit his shit, he could come later if he absolutely had to, and that it actually worked out pretty well because you would be rocking up at twelve."

"I'm sure he was thrilled about that," I mused.

"Oh no, don't tell me he's being a dick?" Amy asked.

"No, no, he's all right. I just wondered what on earth could *make* Chris Henderson do anything."

"Oh, it was easy. Blackmail."

I laughed out loud. "Ah, yes." My stomach churned. What was I anxious about? "Must have been something pretty good," I said, trying for a lighthearted 'I don't really care that much' tone.

"Well, yeah, *hello*," Amy said, like it was the most obvious thing in the world, and that I should automatically know what she was referring to.

I, of course, had no idea and my silence must have told her as much.

"Oh. My. God. That's right, at the Bake House; I didn't get a chance to tell you, did I? You left early."

My mind searched back to that day and I suddenly remembered the whole reason why I had planned to meet Amy early. It was to quiz her about her cryptic message about what a certain Onslow Boy had said about me. My heart pounded against my ribcage and my mouth went dry.

"So? So what about it?" I said quickly, my eyes widening as I spotted Chris looking both ways before crossing the road toward the car.

"I can't believe I forgot to tell you."

"Told me what?" I all but shouted as Chris walked in front of our car.

"That I overheard—"

Beep-beep.

My phone went flat.

"Noooooooo!" I screamed at the blank screen in frustration. Chris paused at the driver's door before leaning in the open window and looking cautiously at my phone, then me.

"Something wrong?"

I threw my dead phone on the dash in a huff, running my fingers through my hair. *Nope, nothing I can't find out ... in six hours!* Six long, painful hours. Hours of speculation.

Wait a minute.

I sat up. "Can I use your phone?"

"Sorry." Chris slid behind the wheel and slammed the door. "Mine's as flat as a tack."

Of course it bloody was, Mr Have-a-chat.

Of all the times for him to actually find his voice and want to have a nice long chinwag, it had to be now?

He revved the engine and I sat, broodily staring off into space. What had Amy overheard? Who had been talking and could she have used it against Chris as blackmail? Was he the one talking about me? Was it good? Bad? Or was someone confiding in him? And why did any of it matter so much?

Chris ejected his Bruce Springsteen tape and reached for the glovebox. "Here, pick a tape. You can program the next leg of the journey."

Chris nodded his head toward the stash. I took my feet off the dash and tentatively grabbed for a couple of cassettes. I read the cover of the first one and grinned from ear to ear.

"No way!"

Chris eyed me with interest.

I couldn't get the tape out of the cover quick enough.

I slotted it into the player; I turned the volume up. 'Rhiannon' flowed out of the speakers.

Chris smiled. "Nice choice."

"Are you serious? I love Fleetwood Mac."

"They're one of my all-time favourites," he agreed.

The next several hours seemed kind of manageable – maybe music really did soothe the savage beast?

***

We rolled into Calhoon after lunch, a pretty little town with elm tree-lined streets and old Victorian charm. A nice little tourist attraction not too far away from the coast and Evoka Springs. The engine rumbled as we turned down the main street, with Fleetwood Mac's 'Tusk' blaring from the sound system, echoing conspicuously down the quiet street.

"Just going to make a quick stop," Chris said. I jumped, startled by his voice. It had been a couple of hours since he'd last talked, in typical Chris style. He pulled into a car space and nodded toward the shops. "There's a shop there if you want to grab a cold drink or anything. Back in a minute." Before I could respond, Chris had dashed across the road and walked down the street. I yawned. It was somewhat unnerving that I was getting used to all his little Chris-isms.

I stepped out of the car, stretching my arms to the sky, groaning as I heard my bones click and pop from sitting down for so long. I stepped up onto the kerb to stretch my legs for a bit. I didn't want to wander too far from the car, as Mr Genius had taken the car keys with him and, nice town or not, the last thing I wanted was for the van to be hijacked.

Not that anyone would want it.

Still, my Punky Brewster sleeping bag was in there and to lose that really *would* be a tragedy.

I perused the window display of the local real estate agent, daydreaming over all the in-ground pools and water views that were selling for a fortune. How lucky people were that could afford a place like that, I thought. I wondered if they knew it.

Tourists probably stopped off in Onslow and looked at our real estate and thought the same thing. How lucky we were to live in Onslow. And here we were fleeing from it, cringing at the very thought of being stuck there for New Year's Eve. I wondered if anyone from Calhoon had fled and headed for Onslow to count in the New Year. I grabbed a fresh bottle of water from the shop next door and headed back to the car. I sat in the passenger seat with the door open, sunning my legs, and eyed my watch with annoyance.

Come on, Chris!

I was itching to get to Evoka Springs, to hang out with the others, catch up with the girls, grill Amy over the thing she hadn't gotten a chance to tell me.

I drummed my fingers impatiently on the dash, watching the slow tick of the dashboard clock. Ten minutes had gone by. I let out a frustrated sigh. My legs were getting hot, getting that tingling that starts to happen when you're on the verge of burning. I lifted my feet into the footwell and slammed the car door.

I closed my eyes and took in a deep breath. "*Men*," I sighed.

"What about them?"

I yelped, jumping at the unexpected voice and at Chris's head poking in the open window of the passenger door.

"Jesus, Chris!" I slapped his shoulder and clutched at my heart. "You scared me to death; don't do that."

He chuckled as he made his way back to the driver's side.

"Sorry about that," he said as he got back into the car. "Here, consider this a peace offering." He threw a yellow package in my lap.

"What's this?" I eyed it sceptically, as if half expecting it to explode in my lap.

Chris put his seatbelt on. "Open it and see."

I looked from the package to him and back again with guarded uncertainty. I tried to tear away the sticky tape that held the parcel shut. Chris watched on with silent amusement.

I peered into the bag and stilled. My eyes widened as I looked back at Chris. He was now openly grinning.

"Are you kidding me?" I exclaimed. "When …? How …?" I stammered inelegantly as I dumped the contents of the bag onto my lap.

My migraine medication spilled out.

"I called your mum this morning and asked if she could get the Onslow chemist to fax a copy of your painkiller prescription through to Calhoon so you could get it filled."

I stared at the bottle in awe. "That's what you were doing this morning? All those phone calls?"

"It took a few. Your mum, the Calhoon chemist for their fax number, the Onslow chemist to give them the details … They were all pretty helpful. Seems like it's pretty important stuff you got there."

My eyes watered with relief at having my pills with me. But most of all, my heart swelled with gratitude. He'd been so thoughtful. I lifted my gaze to meet his, unapologetically, tears and all.

"This is amazing … Thank you," I whispered, my voice threatening to break.

I thought Chris might have been embarrassed by my girly display of emotion, that he would have shrugged it off the way he usually did, or maybe just done what he did best and stayed silent. Instead, he looked right back at me. His gaze ticked across my face in silent study, before a crooked line pinched in the corner of his mouth.

"Most girls get sentimental about flowers," he teased.

I sniffed, wiping my eyes, and gave a small laugh. "Not this girl. Food and meds keep me happy."

"Well, you're easy to please, then."

I could feel his eyes still on me as I placed the bottle back into the bag.

"Get me to a phone charger and I'm all yours," I joked.

Chris's good humour was replaced with awkward surprise.

Oh God, what did I just say? I wanted the ground to open up. *Why couldn't I just learn to seriously shut up!*

Chris cleared his throat and adjusted his side mirror.

"Well, in that case …" He started up the car and threw me a cheeky grin. "Let's get you charged, then."

Chapter Twenty-Three

"Taaaaammyyyy!"

I was all but knocked over by a fierce, bone-crushing bear hug as Amy collided into me at a run.

"You made it!" she squealed, dragging me around in circles as though we were playing Ring a Ring o' Roses.

Sean stood next to Chris, watching.

"How come you never act like that when we reunite?" Chris asked Sean in blank-faced seriousness.

Sean slapped Chris on his shoulder. "Don't worry, mate, I assure you there's a song in my heart."

Amy dragged me down a sloping dirt track. "Come check out our camping spot, it's wicked."

I couldn't help but laugh and throw the boys a worried look as she led me away, linking her arm with mine.

"Boy, am I glad you guys are here," she said.

"Miss me that much, did you?" I joked.

But Amy's serious expression never faltered. "Let's just say I'm hoping some fresh company melts the ice, so to speak."

Before I could ask what that meant exactly, I heard distant cries.

"Tammy!" Ellie shouted from her deckchair, alerting Tess and Adam to our approach.

Adam stared pointedly at his naked wrist. "You're late!"

"Better late than never." Tess beamed as she hugged me. "Good trip?"

"*Yeah, right*," Adam scoffed. "The poor girl was subjected to Chris for two days, can't you see how incredibly fragile she is?"

"Well, best take a seat, Oh Fragile One." Ellie hopped up, offering me her seat.

I obliged. "Where is everyone?" I looked around the convoy of vehicles parked on an angle like a wind break. Gear and tents were all set up.

"Toby, Ringer, Stan and Belinda have gone down to the river to go fishing," Ellie said unenthusiastically.

"Belinda?" I asked. *Who was Belinda?* "Is that Stan's new girlfriend?"

"Sure is, isn't she, Ellie?" Adam grinned and nudged Ellie with his foot.

Ellie grimaced. "She hates me!"

"What? Why?"

"Probably because I'm his ex," she said. "But even if I wasn't – trust me, she and I are like water and oil. We do not mix."

"That's brilliant, Ellie; it perplexes me why you even needed to copy my science homework when you have such insightful knowledge about liquid components," Adam teased.

She glowered. "I'll turn your nose into a liquid component if you're not careful."

Adam cat-called, holding his hands up in surrender. "Easy, now."

I leaned toward Amy to whisper, "Is this the ice that needs thawing?"

Amy cringed. "I wish."

I followed her eye line toward Tess. She sat on the nearby log; her eyes may have been watching her two best friends, but she looked a million miles away.

I threw a questioning look to Amy.

She sighed. "I'll tell you later."

***

After the initial hysteria of our arrival, I managed to take in the beauty of the bushland surroundings. I sat in one of the camping chairs, enjoying the cool breeze. It was so quiet. Soothing. It was hard to believe that we were on our way to the coast when we were so thickly enclosed by trees.

Adam said that once we broke out of the ranges in the next leg, it would literally be like turning a corner and bam, the ocean would be right there in front of us. I couldn't wait. Time spent *not* jammed into a car, another bend, yet another hour. Although I relished being out in the open at the campsite, I couldn't help but find myself glancing up the track to the panel van where Chris and Sean stood, peering under the bonnet. Catching up on men's business, no doubt. A familiar voice called from behind, shattering my focus.

"NO WAY! He brought the SHAGGIN' WAGON!" Ringer called.

I spun around. "The what?"

A shirtless Ringer strode up the track with a fishing rod slung over his shoulder. Behind him trailed Stan, Toby and a petite girl with a pixie haircut.

Ringer passed me, admiring the van. "The Shaggin' Wagon; that's what it's called," he laughed.

"THAT'S what you call it?" I asked Ringer in horror, standing up from my chair.

Ringer shrugged, dumping his fishing gear in the back of Sean's ute. "The mattress is a bit of a red flag, don't you think?"

"Shut up, Ringer," warned Chris as he approached from the track. He gave Ringer a shove as he joined our group.

Ringer shoved him right back. "How many miles has she clocked up now, you old stud?"

The macho rough-housing escalated, scuffing up dust as Ringer trapped Chris in a headlock.

Ellie sighed. "Yep, the gang is back together."

Ignoring the caveman display (and seriously wanting to forget the only reason the van could possibly have that name), I turned back to the group.

"You must be Belinda?" I smiled, reaching out to offer a hand to the unfamiliar girl.

"Hey." She smiled coyly and took my hand. "Tammy, right?"

"That's me," I said.

Belinda's eyes sparkled with a warmth that made me instantly like her. She was such a delicate thing, she only came up to Stan's shoulder, with jet black cropped hair and alabaster skin that would no doubt burn easily in the sun. She was pretty much the exact opposite to Ellie's blonde, bouncy self.

"We were just about to give Tammy a tour of the campsite," beamed Ellie.

Belinda's sparkling, friendly eyes dimmed as they flicked toward Ellie, as if the sun had gone behind a cloud. "Oh, okay, cool." She nodded.

Yep, Ellie might have well been right about Belinda's lack of love for her, but in true Ellie style she just met Belinda's tension with a pearly white smile, as if she hadn't noticed anything out of the ordinary.

Tess linked her arm through mine. "Welcome to paradise." She led me away from the settling dust and dirty looks.

Toby took the lead toward the camp ground. "That's Tess's and my home." He pointed to an army green, two-man tent.

"Yeah, they're just the plebs outside the city walls," added Adam.

Passing another dome-like tent, Toby continued. "Bell and Stan's humble abode." He grazed his hand along the side of the red canvas.

"And mission control, here is Adam, Ellie and Ringer's chateau." We came to a multi-roomed tent with an awning and fold-out table and chairs, with long life milk, stacked baked beans and a box with Cruskits and Vegemite, amongst other things, spread out on the table.

"I am so glad you're here," Ellie said. "You can bunk in with us."

"Yeah, this is where all the hot, single people stay." Ringer propped his elbow on Adam's shoulder and raised his eyebrows in a 'hubba-hubba' motion.

Stan shook his head. "Ignore him."

"Yeah, we do," added Belinda with a cheeky grin.

I scanned the grounds where they had made themselves at home – everything was spick and span and in such well-aligned order. My body seemed to relax somewhat. The neat campsite really spoke to the OCD in me. I wondered if the boys were usually so well organised, or whether it was something to do with Tess's organisational skills that had influenced the group.

I turned to Amy. "Where are you and Sean camping?"

Amy folded her arms. "We've been voted off the island."

I blinked at her, confused. "Sorry?"

"Honeymoon section is that-a-way." Adam pointed to the woods.

"Fine by us." Sean threw Amy a knowing smirk that caused her to blush and look away.

"Ugh, seriously, you two, quit it," Ringer said, wrinkling his nose in distaste.

"Ah, someday, Ringer." Sean slung his arm around Ringer's shoulders and looked up whimsically to the sky. "Someday, you too will be shunned from the group over the love of a woman."

Ringer shucked Sean's arm off. "I would sooner … drive the Shaggin' Wagon." Ringer sneered as if the very idea was so unsavoury.

Chris's eyes darkened. "I'll pretend you didn't just say that, young Ringo."

"Uh-oh, mate, anything but the car." Adam's eyes darted from Ringer to Chris and back in mock horror.

"Mate, it's a bucket of rust; you're kidding yourself," Ringer argued.

"You seem to forget that I found him that bucket of rust," Toby said.

"You know what I mean – you're dreaming if you think you're going to pick up any chick in that car." Ringer laughed.

"He picked up me."

All heads snapped toward me.

I shrugged, playing it cool. "I think the van is hot."

Literally. I nearly died of heat exhaustion last night.

Toby broke into a slow grin as he took in Ringer's troubled expression.

"Really?" Ringer asked.

"Oh yeah," I said taking a step forward. "The shiny black paint … The spongy … soft …mattress … The purr of the engine vibrating through your body." I stood right next to him, whispering in his ear. "So. Hot."

I was so close I could hear Ringer swallow deeply. His Adam's apple bobbled up and down and he cleared his throat as he stepped back a little, away from me, not knowing where to look or what to say.

Ha. I couldn't help but giggle as I turned to catch the bemused faces of the group.

"Wow," breathed Adam. "There is something so insanely hot about a woman defending a car."

Everyone burst out into startled laughter. All except Chris, who just looked at me with those intense brown eyes and a crooked grin on his face.

Ringer puffed out his chest. "So, uh, Chris … do you think I could borrow your car next weekend?"

Chris paused. "Let me think about it."

"Really?" Ringer's brows rose in surprise.

"No," Chris said short and sharp, unfolding his arms and leaving the group. He brushed past me sideways, his hand gently squeezing mine as if to say 'thanks'. It happened so quickly I thought I might have imagined it. All the same, it made my stomach twist in excitement at the unexpectedness of it.

"Aw, come on, Chris, you know I was only kidding." Ringer followed him, his thongs crunching down the track as he pleaded his case.

Toby watched on as the two walked across the camp clearing. "The only way Ringer is going to get near that car is if Chris runs him over in it."

Stan laughed as he slung his arm around Bell and started toward the makeshift kitchen.

"Well, the night is young," said Stan.

Chapter Twenty-Four

"*What is that*?" I asked, though I knew the answer.

I was no expert on camping paraphernalia, that was for certain, but my heart skipped a beat when I spotted something unmistakably familiar in the campsite.

Adam followed my eye line. "It's a solar shower," he said, as if it was the most obvious thing in the world.

The canvas bag was hanging from a tree not too far away from the camping kitchen, on full display; there was no privacy screen, just a bag dangling from a makeshift rope, the showerhead dripping onto the muddy earth where people had used it before. Right now it seemed like the most beautiful thing I had ever seen.

"Do you want one?" Amy asked. "It's not very warm, but it does the job."

My eyes lit up. "I would do anything for a shower."

Sean's brows rose. "Anything? Did you hear that, Chris? She'll do anything." A wicked smile plastered across his face as he waited for Chris's reaction.

The reaction never came. Chris ignored him and disappeared inside the large canvas tent.

It was my cue to leave, avoiding Sean's gleaming eyes. I didn't have time to take the bait. I was on a mission.

***

The walk back down the track to the campsite seemed a lot longer in thongs and a bright, floral bikini. I slung my towel over my shoulder and pulled my ponytail loose, the second most amazing feeling in the world. The first would no doubt be the shower I was headed for.

I was almost giddy with excitement – having spent last night in my flannelette PJs in the back of the van had felt like the equivalent to wrapping myself in cling wrap and sleeping in a sauna.

I couldn't wait for this.

"Don't take too long," Ellie called from her camping chair. "We're heading into town."

My heart sank a little. "We are?" The last thing I really wanted to do was get back into the car.

Amy took my towel and hung it on a tree branch. “Yep, us girls thought we would do some shopping,” Amy chirped as she handed me a bar of soap. “Plus,” she said under her breath, “we wanted to get Tess away for a while.” My eyes instinctively moved to Tess who was intently reading a book in the shade.

Was something going on with Tess? No doubt Amy would tell me when she could. I thought that this was the whole idea of the road trip, to get away for a while, but apparently some of us needed to get away from the getaway.

“Come on, tell the truth,” said Adam. “Now say why you’re really going into town.”

Amy cut Adam a dark look that did little to intimidate him.

Ellie straightened. “Well, you needn’t think I’m going out in my cut-offs and singlet top.”

“Going out?” I questioned.

“Uh, yeah, apparently there’s a great little pub in Evoka,” said Amy. “We thought we might head down there tonight.”

“Bloody hell, is that why you’re going to town? To buy an outfit?” Sean laughed.

“*No*.” Amy glowered. “We just thought we’d get some supplies, seeing as we were in such a rush to leave, thanks to you boys wanting to leave so bloody early.”

“The early worm gets the fish,” Sean said.

Amy scoffed. “I haven’t even seen your fishing rod in the water yet.”

Sean wrapped his arms around Amy and nuzzled her neck. “That’s because I’ve had better things to do.”

There was a collective groan. “Get a room, you two,” said Adam.

I wrestled with the showerhead. “How does this thing …” and before I could finish my sentence a stream of cold water hit me in the face. I spluttered and gasped at the unexpected icy cold that ran down my skin.

“Oh-my-gosh, oh-my-gosh,” I breathed out as I vigorously rubbed soap over my shoulders and stomach, thinking that maybe the friction would warm my skin, or just to get washed as quickly as possible. I whimpered through the motion.

I wiped the water out of my eyes, only sensing that someone was standing near at the exact moment that they reached over my head and twisted the nozzle. The freezing water blasted hard and fast all over me and I gasped in shock again.

I heard a chuckle. “Warm enough?”

I blinked through the droplets of water to see Chris standing next to me. That had me gasping for a completely new reason.

He was wearing nothing more than a pair of footy shorts. I took in the ripped lines of his biceps, and his impressive broad shoulders that narrowed in toward his waist. I took in his tanned, smooth skin that shone in the afternoon sun.

Chris usually worked inside, or stood glowering by the sidelines on any one of our gatherings. I had never seen him so *exposed* before, and boy was he exposed.

Dribbles of water ran down his arms as they worked, adjusting the stream some more. The clear rivulets splayed down his chest and rolled down his toned, taut stomach. I wanted to reach out and follow their line with my finger.

Wait, what? I snapped my thoughts away from following the descending crystal beads.

A cold shower right now was actually exactly what I needed.

"Hang on a sec," Chris said as he trotted back to the camp kitchen, disappearing behind the canvas flap. He returned with a full water jug.

"Here's something I prepared earlier," he smirked. "Tilt your head back."

Without hesitation I did as I was told. He trickled a deliciously warm stream of water over my head, washing the suds from my drenched tendrils of hair.

I closed my eyes, forcing myself not to groan with pleasure at such a welcome sensation as he slowly, almost teasingly, dribbled the stream over me. All too quickly it was over and the cool stream from the showerhead overtook any feeling of warmth Chris had thoughtfully afforded.

I smiled brightly at him. "Thanks."

I almost felt the same heated warmth from Chris's coffee-coloured eyes as he stared down at me. It was the first time I had held his stare, and it didn't hold anything other than kindness.

My stomach fluttered with butterflies.

"Do … do you want me to leave it running?" I stammered.

Chris broke into a smile, the tooth-exposing kind, as heeyed the showerhead. "Sure."

I nodded like a zombie, passing him the rose-scented cake of soap, his fingers brushing mine.

"Thanks."

"That's okay," I said. I reached for my towel in a daze and stepped aside as Chris moved forward to take my place.

Shivering I wrapped the towel around me before looking up and pausing. Everyone was sitting and standing around the campsite, watching with such deep-set, if not amused, interest.

Geez. All they needed were some 3-D glasses and a bucket of popcorn.

I blushed crimson; in those mere moments under the water I had completely forgotten we had an audience, that our exchanges were not just limited to us and us alone anymore, that we were part of a group – a smug, staring group.

I wrapped the towel tightly around my body, pushing the soaked tendrils of hair over my shoulder. Amy came over with an extra towel for my hair, her brow curved with interest. I braced myself for the insinuating comments that might come as she handed me the towel.

She folded her arms and looked at me as I rubbed my hair vigorously.

"Wow," she whispered. "If this is how you two behave in public, I don't want to even know …"

"I'm going to get dressed!" I piped up before marching up the track toward the panel van, my thongs squelching with every step as I dared not make eye contact with anyone.

As far as showers went, that was definitely the most mortifying one I had ever had.

***

"Come on, let's go! Let's go!" Amy called as she wound down the window.

With my hair still wet, I jogged toward Sean's Toyota twin cab ute where Amy sat behind the wheel. I opened up the passenger door and climbed inside. Ellie, Tess and Belinda sat in the back, all buckled up for the expedition.

"I can't believe Sean is letting you take his car," said Ellie. "It must be love."

Amy was too busy adjusting her seat to reply. "Bloody legs like a spider," she muttered under her breath. She pulled her seat forward so she could touch the pedals.

"Who has legs like a spider?" A set of tanned elbows rested on the open driver's window, startling us all.

"Bloody hell, Sean!" Amy slapped at him.

Sean flashed his pearly whites. "What time will you be back?"

"Never you mind," called Ellie. "This is women's business."

Sean grimaced. "You're going to talk about feelings and crap, aren't you?"

Amy smirked. "Most definitely."

"Well, in that case," he said, pecking her on the forehead, "take your time."

Amy rolled up the window before starting the car.

"Dare you to drop a big wheelie," I joked.

"No way!" she said. "It wouldn't be worth my life." Instead, she settled for a polite double toot, waved goodbye, and pulled out onto the road.

Chapter Twenty- Five

So we didn't exactly launch *immediately* into talking about our feelings.

But by the glimpses I caught in the back seat through the rear-view mirror, maybe we needed to.

Ellie looked bored, Tess looked sad and Belinda looked like she would rather be anywhere else.

I cleared my throat. "So! What's our first port of call?" I said in my best upbeat voice.

"I don't think there's a lot to choose from in Evoka, but it's the closest thing we have at our disposal," grimaced Amy.

"I know what is in Evoka," sighed Tess. "Hippy shops with wind chimes, stress balls and crocheted beanies."

"How do you know?" asked Belinda.

"My mum dragged me to the Mother's Day market here one year. Not a lot to choose from." Tess shrugged as if she didn't particularly care, though.

"If the only dress shop in town is limited to tie-dyed products I will be so annoyed," said Ellie.

"Surely it won't matter. I doubt the Evoka pub is black tie," I said reassuringly.

Ellie examined the end of her blonde ponytail for split ends. "It's only the second day and I am already bored out of my mind."

"Well, don't you dare say that in front of the boys." Amy flicked a warning look in the rear-view. "The last thing I need is Chris saying, 'I told you so.'"

I wanted to defend Chris's honour, I don't know why, to say that I didn't think he would say that, but then I thought better of it.

It was twenty minutes down a winding dirt road before we hit the smooth bitumen that led into town. The first sign of civilisation was passing a shack set back off the road among thick bushland.

Amy started laughing hysterically.

"What's so funny?" I asked, glancing at the others. They looked just as perplexed by the outburst as I felt.

Amy fought to contain herself. "Did you see that place back there?"

"What about it?" asked Belinda.

"That's the pub." Amy slapped the steering wheel.

"Whaaaat?" groaned Ellie.

"Definitely not black tie," added Tess.

I glanced back, seeing nothing but a line of bitumen as we sped forward. "Did the sign really say 'Villa Co-Co'?"

"Better grab ourselves some tie-dye, ladies," Amy continued to laugh.

Ellie shook her head. "I would sooner die."

***

Evoka was a blink-and-you'll-miss-it kind of town; it housed a small local supermarket, post office, pub, butcher and a one-stop tourist shop with said hippy incense and scented oils, woven baskets and postcards. After seeing the 'Villa Co-Co' pub, we reached an unspoken agreement that finding an outfit for a night out seemed less important than it had before. Instead, we opted for some peaceful roaming around the tree-lined streets. Regardless of its humble setting, Evoka was a beautiful place and the last stop before the towns that dotted the coast along the way toward Point Shank.

We pushed our way through the front door to the tourist shop, assaulted immediately by the powerful fumes from the incense that burned on the counter. The shop was cluttered with an array of interesting artefacts, from bejewelled elephant statues to wind chimes and dream catchers; you had to really look amongst the collection in order to take it all in.

I sidestepped between two tables piled high with tea towels and gem stones, and took extra care as I manoeuvred my way through the small space. I spotted a cardboard sign on the counter that stated in permanent black texta: 'You break. You buy.' I tucked in my elbows. I really didn't want to be stuck with buying a dragon sculpture holding a crystal ball or something equally hideous. And a broken one, at that. My gaze skimmed along the cluttered shelves as I edged my way toward the back of the store.

I was open to the idea of finding a souvenir for my parents, perhaps, and paused at a stand that housed guardian angel pendants. I tilted my head to read the scripture on the little cards and froze.

The hair on the back of my neck rose at the low growling from behind me. A deep, guttural growl that taunted me, practically dared me to move. My eyes widened as I caught the reflection in one of the outlandish gold-plated mirrors on the wall of the most massive dog peering at me through the beaded curtain from out back. I locked eyes with the beast and realised I had made a big mistake. It flinched back and barked an ear-piercing bark.

I screamed.

The others raced around the corner and paused, seeing me pressed up against the wall on tippy toes.

"Aww, look at the puppy," Ellie crooned.

"Puppy?" I squealed. "It's a bloody monster."

"It's a Saint Bernard." Amy waved me off like I was being overdramatic. As she edged closer to the bead curtain she held her hand out tentatively for the beast to sniff it.

"Hello, beautiful, what's your name?" she cooed.

The giant stepped forward and sniffed the air, before flinching back and barking incessantly.

"Aww, it's okay, we won't hurt you," Amy said over the noise.

"WINSTON! NO!" a woman cried. She parted the beaded curtain and pulled on the dog's collar, edging him into the back room. "Go on, you know you're not allowed in here." She groaned as she pushed the resisting eighty-odd-kilo beast away.

The woman closed the door behind her, muffling the outraged barks from behind. Breathless, she smoothed over her frizzy, salt and pepper hair as she smiled at us with coffee-stained teeth.

"Can I help you?" she asked brightly. Aside from us disturbing Winston, she seemed utterly delighted to see us.

"Um, we were just looking, thanks. Sorry to frighten your dog," I said.

"Oh, not at all." Her bangles jingled as she waved off my sentence as if it were nothing. "He likes to think he's a guard dog, but he's nothing but a giant teddy bear. Are you ladies passing through?"

"We're camping near here; we thought we would just pop into town to do some shopping." I smiled.

"We were kind of looking for a clothing store," Belinda added. Ellie cut her a dark look as if to be quiet, which Belinda ignored. "We were wanting to go out tonight, but we didn't really pack anything suitable."

"Going out?" the lady asked. "In Evoka?"

I wanted Belinda to shut up, too. Somehow handing out all our personal information didn't sit right with me; it was the kind of scene you would see in a horror movie. You know, where there's a group of campers that stop off at a gas station and tell the innocent-enough shop man exactly what they were doing and where they were going, only to be picked off one by one in the dead of night by a masked, chainsaw-wielding psychopath. I glanced around to see any sort of apparel in the shop.

"Villa Co-Co, is it?" asked Tess. "That's the pub, right?"

The lady's eyes suddenly lit. "Of course! Villa Co-Co … What fun!"

"Really?" I asked sceptically.

"Oh yes, Peter and Jan have just come back from Bali and they throw one hell of a party." She walked around from behind the counter, her long velvet skirt swooshing along the floorboards. "Follow me, ladies," she sing-songed as she walked toward the back of the shop.

We all looked at each other, uncertain exactly what to do, when Ellie shrugged and made the first move after her.

In a tentative line, we manoeuvred our way to the back of the shop, where the lady unravelled a plastic sheet off a clothes rack and wheeled it out from the corner.

"If you're going out, you're going to have to look the part," she said.

Amy smirked as she folded her arms. "It's not black tie, by any chance?"

The lady looked puzzled at the question. "Yes, you're not from around here, are you?"

"No. No we are not," I agreed.

***

After being pointed in the direction of a changing room, we took turns in flicking through the clothes of the woman's hidden stash, giggling over the eclectic array of fashion.

"Oh my God, is she for real?" whispered Amy as she held up a bat-winged '80s power suit.

"I think it's hilarious," added Belinda as she pressed an electric blue Lycra dress against herself.

"Hey, can I have a look at that?" asked Ellie as she took it from Belinda. "You know, if you took the shoulder pads out of this, it wouldn't be so bad …" she mused.

Amy disappeared into the changing room, which was really just a curtained corner. "Villa Co-Co won't know what hit it," she called.

"You're not seriously contemplating wearing any of this?" I whispered to the curtain.

"Why not?" laughed Tess as she tried on a 1920s-style hat. "It would be worth it just to see the looks on the boys' faces."

Amy poked her head out from the curtain. "YES! We should totally pick something for tonight."

Bangles and tinkering china approached. "Ladies, I have made you some Devonshire tea. We have a lovely courtyard in the back. You can talk over your outfit decisions."

"Um, I think I love Evoka," Ellie said, draping her dress over her shoulder and following the lady out of the back French door.

"Ta-da!" Amy flung back the curtain, sporting a leopard-print miniskirt and a black lace spaghetti strap top. She actually looked really good, and my heart sank a little as I eyed what was left on the rack.

"I love it!" beamed Tess.

"I can't wait to see Sean's face," Amy said as she adjusted the straps.

"Wow, we are really doing this, aren't we?" I asked.

"Yep. It's all or nothing," said Belinda.

Taking on board their expectant looks, I sighed and went back searching through the rack. It was all well and good to rock up at the local pub tonight having made some questionable fashion choices, but something deeper niggled inside my mind. It was more than being the centre of attention, or looking like a fool in front of the girls; I didn't care about that. But I didn't want to look a fool in front of the boys.

In front of Chris.

Chapter Twenty-Six

Belinda was kind enough to wait for me as I used the changing room.

Although, in reality, I really didn't need or want her to. I would have been perfectly happy if she had just gone out to the courtyard with the others while I stayed behind the curtain and stared miserably at my reflection.

"I don't know about this," I said, biting my lip.

"Come on, show me," Belinda called.

"I just don't think …"

"Tammy, now."

I sighed deeply. "Okay."

I peeled the curtain back and stepped out from the alcove, facing another full-length mirror next to where Belinda sat on a stool.

I turned, trying to look at myself from all angles, only to be stilled by Belinda's wolf whistle.

"That is hot!" she said.

"I look like a belly dancer." I pulled down my midriff top that exposed my belly. The long, flowing white skirt pulled around my legs with a shimmering gold embossed pattern etched across the layers. The white was a stark contrast against my tanned skin.

"A *hot* belly dancer," Belinda added.

I knew she was just being nice; I didn't really know her so what else was she supposed to say? You look like a dog?

"Ringer said you had a bangin' body." Belinda folded her arms.

"What?" I turned, wide-eyed.

She shrugged. "I asked him what you looked like, and he was very accurate in his description. Come to think of it, very *detailed*." She tilted her head in deep thought.

I turned back toward the mirror. I wondered if that was the conversation Amy had overheard? I still had to clear up what she had blackmailed Chris with. If that was it, I felt a little disappointed and I didn't want to admit the reason why. Somehow I had convinced myself that maybe Chris had said something about me. I shook the idea from my mind – who had I been kidding? He would have been the last person to say anything at all, let alone about me.

I sighed. "I am sure Villa Co-Co is the party capital of Evoka, but I think I'll pass."

Stepping back into the change room, I was suddenly overwhelmed by a deep-seated misery. Sometimes I wished I could just let go, just stress less and enjoy myself like the others, but I was always plagued with doubt, with worry. Afraid of not fitting in, which was ironic as I sabotaged every chance of fitting in by constantly stepping aside from everyone.

Belinda was still waiting for me as I stepped back out and placed my outfit back onto the rack. She offered me a small smile. "That's okay, I won't dress up either. It was a silly idea."

"Belinda, you don't have to …"

"No, it's okay," she said as she slid off her stool. "I'm not a sheep; I don't follow others just because they're doing it."

Maybe she was just trying to make me feel better?

Somehow, I didn't think so. It turned out, I kind of liked Belinda. I liked her quiet strength and understated presence.

"Come on, I may very well need your back-up while I break it to the others," I said, making our way toward the courtyard.

"I wouldn't be too worried – how many fights break out over Devonshire tea? None, I'm guessing; it's just not civilised."

"I hope you're right," I said with a laugh.

***

I was relieved the others bought their outfits anyway, even though they decided that maybe Evoka wasn't exactly the right place to try them out. They vowed that they would wear them out somewhere, though.

"It's a shame, really," said Amy, heaving her bags along as we walked toward the car. "That's actually the first time I've seen Tess laugh in a while; I think the silly fashion parade was a good distraction for her."

I glanced back at the others trailing several metres behind us; I felt a pang of guilt surge within me. "Now I feel bad that we're not dressing up."

"Huh? Oh, no, don't be silly, it's going to take more than stepping out in fancy dress to cheer up Tess long term," Amy said.

"What's going on? Is Tess okay?" I pressed, taking the moment to find out once and for all the mystery behind Tess's sad eyes.

"I hope so, I hope this trip gets better for her than it started, but I think she is at a bit of a loss as to what to do, and none of us really know what to say to her."

Do about what? What didn't I know? I remained silent, hoping Amy would continue.

"It's Toby," she said. "He's been really distant of late, we've all noticed it. And the first night we camped they must have had a humdinger of a fight in the car because they weren't even speaking to each other when they arrived and I could tell Tess had been crying."

"Well, all couples fight," I said. *Yeah, like I was some expert.*

"Not Tess and Toby. Not like this. I would have shrugged it off as well, but I can see it too. Like how he sat by the fire most of the night, just staring into the flames. He's so distant, so not himself."

"Does Sean know anything?" I asked.

Amy sighed. "He says he's going to have a talk to him, pull him aside and see what's going on."

I nodded. "Maybe some time alone together will be good for them; you know, Toby and Tess."

We approached the car. Amy slung her bags in the back of the ute, glancing at the others' approach. "I hope so," she said, "because I really don't like where this is headed."

"Where's that?" I asked quickly.

"The one other time I saw Toby distant and agitated like this."

"When was that?"

"The last time he broke up with his girlfriend."

***

"Those little shits!" cried Ellie.

We slowed down as we made our way past the Villa Co-Co hotel, only to see Ringer's car parked out the front.

"I can't believe they went without us! I bet they've been there all afternoon." Ellie glowered out of her window.

"Should we go in?" I asked, wondering if Amy would slow down and do a U-turn. Instead, her brows narrowed and she pumped the accelerator.

"Pfft. Let them have their macho boy bonding."

Amy stared at the road with an evil grin.

I cocked my brow and glanced into the back for support. "Amy, you scare me when you look like this."

"Let's just say, we have a full tank of fuel, and I happen to know there is late night shopping in Calhoon."

Ellie gasped. "You're not seriously thinking of trekking back to Calhoon?"

"Well, ladies, if we're going to make a fashionably late entrance, we might as well do it in style."

I bit my lip, a thrill spiking in my stomach as I turned to see the same manic look in the others' eyes. Amy glanced in her rear-view mirror, no doubt seeing the elated smile across Tess's face.

Amy turned to me. "What do you think?"

Without hesitation, this time I decided for once to be a sheep. This time I'd follow the crowd, and I'd jump in with both feet.

"Let's do it!"

Chapter Twenty-Seven

It was dark by the time we returned to the campsite.

We sort of expected to find a note with 'gone pubbing' left for our convenience, but instead we found Stan reclining in his fishing chair with a stubby, staring into space. His entire face lit up when he saw us approach.

"Hey," he said, standing up quickly. "What took you so long?"

"Just a side-trip shopping adventure," said Ellie as she held up her bags with glee. She turned to Tess. "Come on, we'll get ready in the big tent."

Tess cringed. "I have never gotten ready in a tent before."

"That makes both of us," Ellie said. She held the canvas partition back for Tess.

I turned to smile at Bell and Stan, but they were too busy reacquainting themselves with one another with doe-eyed looks.

And that's my cue to exit.

I took my bags to the van, my second home these days. Amy headed toward the woods. "Meet back at the car in fifteen!" she called back.

Ellie's head poked out through the canvas. "Fifteen minutes? Are you serious?"

"Fifteen minutes," Amy repeated.

Oh-crap-oh-crap-oh-crap.

I ran as best I could up the slanted dirt track toward the van. The others may have never gotten ready in a tent before, but *I* had never gotten ready in the back of a *panel van* before.

This was going to be interesting.

I made my way around the back, juggling my baggage to reach for the back handle, praying that Chris hadn't locked the car. As the magical click sounded and I pulled the door open I was flooded with relief. I threw my shopping bags in the back and hopped inside, ensuring to leave the door slightly ajar so the interior light stayed on. Light was a necessity when applying mascara. Unlike the gypsy skirt in Evoka, in a cute little shop in Calhoon I had managed to find a fitted, white summer dress with vintage lace embroidery. It was so delicate, so light and feminine and cost an absolute fortune from one of those indie clothes designers. Still, I had fallen in love with it and felt like I wanted to walk into the Villa Co-Co and see Chris from across the bar, and I wanted for once to stride into a space with absolute confidence, offer a coy smile perhaps as I locked eyes with him. I had run through all the scenarios as I'd looked over my outfit in the changing room. And then, of course, I had snapped out of my daydream.

Why was I so intent on making a good impression on Chris?

I didn't know where my head was at lately, and it didn't help that I had seen a different side to Chris the last couple of days: a caring side, a lighthearted side. But why wouldn't he be? He's on holidays and we were all relaxed (well, aside from Toby and Tess – that was a worry). I was sure it wouldn't take long for Chris to seep back into his old, grumblebum ways, especially around his friends.

And then I had another scenario go through my mind: me entering the Villa Co-Co and being completely ignored by him while he drank with the boys. It was a possibility – just because we were forced to travel together and he had done a few nice things didn't mean he thought of me any differently.

I blinked a couple of times, snapping out of my thoughts. I had to hurry up; I had done nothing more than lay out my dress and accessories as I sat back on my heels, obsessing about stupid 'what if?' scenarios.

I had too much to do in too little time, and too little space, so it would seem. I balanced awkwardly on the spongy mattress as I undressed and slipped on my new under things. I had really gone all out, going so far as to buy some new perfume, which I sprayed liberally over my half-dressed body. I smiled to myself as I sprayed it on the mattress as well. Won't that have the next girl Chris brings back here guessing. I stilled, a familiar pang of jealousy twisted in my stomach.

I didn't want there to be another girl.

Right! Enough of that, time to get a wriggle on – quite literally, as the best way to get this thing on was to step into my new dress. Leaving the lip glossing and moisturising till the very last minute, my hair and face could happen on the way to the pub. I tried my best to stay upright but the spongy floor underfoot was making it somewhat of a challenge. I swayed from side to side like a drunken sailor, trying to manage one foot through the opening of the dress. I bent over so as not to hit my head on the ceiling and braced one hand against the van wall to steady myself. I tentatively stepped in the dress, and started to shimmy the dress up with my free arm. I was on the home stretch as I managed to pull the tight-fitting dress over my hips. I released the wall to use both hands.

Almost done.

And with those famous last words, the back door to the van flung open and I was blinded by a harsh light.

I screamed and covered my bra as I fell over, squeezing my eyes shut, as if by some kind of miracle it would make me disappear.

"Don't look at me! Don't look at me!" I yelled. Worrying less that it could be an axe-wielding maniac breaking into the van than simply someone seeing me in my underwear.

"It's a little late for that," said an unmistakable voice.

My eyes snapped open to find Chris casually leaning in the open doorway of the panel van, torch in hand.

"Don't you knock?" I yelled, trying for angry and less mortified as my arms wrapped around my white lace bra.

"I was actually more worried that the interior light was left on – a flat battery in the morning would not be ideal," he said in all seriousness, as if seeing me half naked in front of him was the least of his worries.

That idea actually made me *more* uncomfortable. He didn't even look me over with any type of male appreciation. Sure, I had wanted to make a good impression, but this certainly wasn't how I had planned to go about it.

"What are you doing back here anyway?" I asked, annoyed as I turned my back on him to finish hitching my dress up over my shoulders.

"Just seeing what was taking so long, but then we had to remind ourselves that it was probably taking you all four hours to put your make-up on."

"Ha! Well that's … where … you're … wrong," I said, struggling to reach around behind me to the back of my dress to zip it up.

Oh crap!

Chris sighed. "Come here."

I turned, wide-eyed. "W-what?"

"Come here," he repeated, trying to stop his lips from twitching as he turned the torch off and set it aside.

I swallowed deeply and tentatively stepped forward. He held out his hand, to help me out of the van. I took it, almost feeling an electric current pulse from his skin as it touched mine. Goosebumps formed on my flesh that had little to do with the warm summer night, or the fact that the back of my dress was open, exposing me in a new way. He helped me down from the van, guiding me to the ground. He was bathed in a rich yellow glow from the interior light. For the first time I actually took in the fresh, clean lines of his navy polo shirt, and his dark Levi's were back. His jagged, jet black hair was dry from his shower earlier and my mouth involuntarily pinched into a smile as I realised he was freshly shaven.

"You sure it didn't take *you* four hours to get ready?" I mused.

A familiar pinch formed between his brows as he circled his finger in the air. "Turn around."

I did as he asked, still clasping my hands to my front to hold my dress in place. He pulled the fabric together and gently manoeuvred the zip upward. He paused only to gather my hair and slide it over my shoulder so he could pull the zip all the way up. I managed to glance back at him, taking in the dramatic lines etched on his face in concentration. He had edged the zip all the way up and my new dress tightened over my body the way it should.

"Thanks," I said, and went to move, but his hand stopped me.

"Hang on a sec, there's a button thingy here."

I could feel him fumbling with the fabric at the nape of my neck, struggling to slot through the button. I could feel his breath on the back of my neck, more so when a deep sigh of frustration blew out as he struggled to master the button loop.

"Having trouble?"

"It won't defeat me," he said through gritted teeth.

I smirked, holding my hair to the side and stretching my neck out so he could work on the infuriating, delicate button.

After a long moment and a few curses under his breath he said, "There! You're good to go."

"Thanks," I sighed, adjusting my dress. I spun around. "What do you think?" I mentally slapped myself as soon as the words fell out. Chris was not my BFF or one of the girls, what did I expect him to say?

So when he said, "Nice," it shouldn't really have felt like he was knifing me in the heart.

Nice ... Nice? A cup of tea was nice.

"Wow, thanks, you really know how to make a girl feel special," I said coolly, reaching for my clutch, concentrating on packing the things I needed for a night out on the town. Lipstick, compact, money, ID. I shoved each piece in my bag with irritated force.

I turned expectantly to him and was startled by the fact that he had moved next to the panel van door. I grabbed the other, pulling to shut it, but he stopped me. He caught the door and my eyes met his.

"What did you want me say?" He stared down at me with a quizzical narrowing of his brows.

Beautiful, stunning, gorgeous, let's forget about the others.

I blinked, trying to compose myself. It was just a simple question.

I let go of the door, leaving him to shut them. "I don't want you to say anything," I said lowly, turning to make my way down the track to meet the others.

Chapter Twenty-Eight

I was met by a rather sheepish-looking Bell and Stan.

I paused. "Bell, you're not dressed?"

Belinda smiled coyly, taking in her cut-off jean shorts and T-shirt. "Oh yeah, um, if it's all the same I think we might just stay here." She looked at Stan beside her.

"Oh, a romantic night in, then?" I teased.

Stan sighed. "Not exactly."

Before he could explain, we heard, "HEADS!" A football hurtled through the darkness, and we quickly ducked.

Ringer jogged into view, laughing. "Sorry," he said, before he scooped the ball up near Stan.

Ringer pushed in between Bell and Stan, slinking his arms around their shoulders. "We're going to have so much fun. Anyone up for charades?"

I cringed, thinking that the dodgy-looking Villa Co-Co sounded far more appealing. "Where's Amy?" I asked, looking for Sean's car.

"Oh, um, she said she would meet you there." Belinda winced.

"What?" My head snapped around.

"She said you could catch a lift back with Chris."

Oh did she now?

"You're going to need two cars to bring back the drunken hordes anyway," Stan added.

I heard Chris's footsteps from behind. "You ready?" he asked unenthusiastically as he stood beside me.

Wait until I catch up with my traitorous friends.

"Lead the way." I smiled sweetly.

Chris turned to Ringer who was busy handballing the footy to himself. "You sure you're not coming?"

"And suffer through Sean and Toby having a deep and meaningful?" He shuddered. "I think not."

My interest piqued. Maybe Sean was actually taking the opportunity to have a heart to heart with Toby; maybe it would help and Tess and he would be all right. I really hoped so.

I did as best as I could to keep up with Chris's long, determined strides.

"We're in Ringer's car," he called over his shoulder as he made his way toward the large, canary yellow Ford.

I expected many things from Chris, but one of them wasn't opening the door for me. It stopped me in my tracks.

His elbow rested on the door frame, his brows rising expectantly. "Something wrong?"

"Uh … no, not all," I said, quickly moving to slide into my seat. The door closed after me as Chris sauntered around the front of the car toward the driver's side.

Ha! Who said chivalry was dead?

I worked to quickly apply some gloss onto my lips in the dark, patting the strawberry flavour on my bottom lip and pressing them together. In the mad rush I had had little chance to do anything else. I self-consciously ran my fingers through my hair before Chris opened the door and slid in next to me. Beyond the strawberry scented lip gloss, Chris's sharp, musky aftershave filled the cabin.

Aftershave on a fishing trip? Interesting.

"So Villa Co-Co, huh? Sounds like a very happening kind of place," I mused.

Chris started the car, flashing a grin.

"I'll let you be the judge of that."

***

Villa Co-Co was a single-storey weatherboard hotel with a large verandah out the front. It sat back in the leafy confines of a blue gravelled drive that led off the main road. Blue, red and yellow party lights flashed along the entire length of the verandah roof. The only tropical clue bearing support to its name were the fish fern and bird's nest palms housed in multi-coloured pot plants dotted around the entrance.

I closed the passenger door. "I don't think we're in Kansas anymore, Toto."

What struck me was the distance we had to park away; the makeshift car park on the abandoned dirt lot beside the hotel was absolutely packed with cars. One car was being pressed up against by a couple with wandering hands and thrusting tongues as we walked past. I quickened my steps to catch up to Chris.

"There weren't that many cars here before." I clasped my arms around myself, warily eyeing the figures that loomed near the entrance of the hotel.

"Must be the full moon that drives people out," Chris said, looking up at the large illuminated disc in the sky.

I gulped, looking at the eerie face smirking down at me from above. "Yeah, brings out all the crazies, you mean."

Chris stopped and I ran into his back with a yelp. There was a devilish glint in his eyes as he smiled, slow and wicked. "You have no idea."

Before I could question him, he laced his fingers with mine in a firm grip and led the way inside.

Chris pushed his way through the front door and music assaulted my senses. I winced at the sound and the smell of cigarettes. It was as if all the oxygen had been sucked out of the room, and for that matter the lighting too. It was so dark inside it seemed like we were in a nightclub, minus the sticky drink-stained carpet. Rose Tattoo's 'Bad Boy For Love' screamed from the speakers. I involuntarily stepped closer to Chris, squeezing his hand tight, just to make sure he didn't let go. This was one crowd I really didn't want to get lost in. Unlike the subtle warm lighting that lit the open, airy Onslow Hotel, this place was small, dark and loud, and crammed with bodies ranging from the soiled work clothes of the toothless local timber cutter to the rowdy local in a grass-stained cricketing outfit shouting for shots at the bar. A group of girls chewed speculatively on their cocktail straws as they looked Chris up and down. Their eyes dimmed as they landed on me. And that wasn't even what dominated the entire bar space – lining the bar was a sea of leather-clad, tattooed, hairy bikers. All we needed was a drunken sailor and a go-go dancer and it would truly complete the picture. Chris smiled down at me as if he were revelling in my unease.

"Want a drink?" he shouted, smiling wickedly as he dragged me nearer the bar.

"No! No." I dug in my heels. "I mean shouldn't we find the others first?"

Safety in numbers, right?

I could only imagine what the others were thinking of this place; they were probably in a corner somewhere, looking on with the same wide-eyed horror that I was. The sooner I located them, the sooner we could all link arms and make an escape back to the cars and the campsite.

No wonder Ringer had returned – that should have been a red flag right there.

My gaze swooped around the dark, crowded space, hoping that one of the flashing party lights would flash onto a familiar face. And it did.

"Oh. My. God."

Chris followed my eye line to fix on what had me so stunned.

"Is that Ellie?" I asked. "She's dancing in a cage."

"Are you honestly surprised?" laughed Chris as he started to lead me through the crowd, drinks forgotten.

"Uh, you mean am I surprised at Ellie or the fact that there is a human-sized cage in the bar?"

Go-go dancer – check.

"Fair point," he said. He manoeuvred us through the crowd with expert ease and guided me toward a booth near the back of the pub. It sat next to a stage that had band equipment set up on it. The name scrawled across the drum kit read 'Spank the Monkey'. I could only hope that it was their night off.

Sean, Toby and Adam sat at the table completely unaware of our approach until Chris slammed his hand on the table, causing their heads to comically spin around and their hands to grab for their beers.

"Look what I found," Chris announced, tilting his head toward me. "She was chatting up some bikers at the bar; thought I better intervene." He guided me toward a seat.

"How about you go dance in a cage somewhere?" I smiled sweetly as I sat down.

"Oh no you don't," Adam piped up. "Ellie has five more minutes."

"So there's a time limit, is there?" I asked.

"There is when there's a bet on," Adam grinned.

"A bet?" Chris asked. He sat next to me so I shifted a little on the bench seat. There wasn't much room; I felt him pressed right next to me, his body heat elevating my own.

I was somewhat distracted when Toby spoke.

"Adam bet Ellie she wouldn't have the guts to dance in the cage for ten minutes."

I couldn't help but laugh. "It's Ellie, of course she's going to take the bet."

"Exactly." Adam beamed. "Best bet I ever lost."

We all tilted our heads toward the cage where Ellie was imprisoned.

"With a friend like you ..." I shook my head, trying not to find it so funny.

Adam finished the last of his beer. "I better go and see how she's doing; do you think she would find it funny if I tried to slip a fiver in the cage?"

"I think you might get kicked in the face," I said with a laugh.

"Now that I would pay to see," said Sean.

Adam flipped us the bird, picked up his empty beer glass and disappeared into the crowd.

I wondered where the other girls were but I didn't need to wonder for too long. An ear-piercing scream was so shrill it could be heard over even the loudest of music.

"Tammy!" Amy screeched as she dragged Tess through the masses, pushing people out of the way to reach our table. "You made it!"

"No thanks to you," I glowered.

"Oh, don't be like that." She waved off my words.

"You know you are going to give me serious abandonment issues if you keep leaving me behind," I said.

"Not to worry, Chris will always be there to give you a lift," Amy said with an obnoxious wink-wink. Oh my God, she was such a dork, I half expected her wink to come with a nudge-nudge. And the fact that she had done it in front of everyone, I could feel myself blanch. I had thought that her leaving me behind to ride with Chris was some form of punishment. It appeared not. She raised her brows in a 'hubba-hubba' kind of way and looked between me and Chris. Oh my God! Was she seriously trying to play Cupid? My insides twisted.

"How much have you had to drink?" Sean mused suspiciously.

"Not much." Amy shrugged, swaying on her feet.

Tess held up six fingers behind Amy's back. Not that that told us much: six shots or six pints? Whatever it added up to, it was six of something too many.

"You always were a two-pot screamer," said Chris.

Amy's eyes cut Chris an acidic look. "At least I know how to have fun," she snapped.

"Tammy, come dance, this place has the BEST music," she said, leaning over Chris and grabbing my hand. Amy's tunnel vision as she strode away, regardless of who or what was between her and the dance floor, made my moving past Chris jerky and awkward. I tried not to decapitate him as Amy pulled at my arm.

"Sorry," I whispered as I almost fell on top of him when trying to get to my feet. Tess took my other hand.

"Just go with it." She laughed as we were dragged through the crowd to what I guessed was a dance floor.

Go with it? I thought. *As if I had any other choice*.

Chapter Twenty- Nine

I didn't know how Ellie managed to dance ten minutes in a cage, but she did.

Ten minutes on the dance floor and I was looking for an exit. It wasn't that I was unfit; I mean, I ran marathons for fun. But this was a different kind of marathon. No fresh air, no natural light, and no fluids for hydration. My enthusiasm was fading fast.

I bumped into a couple dry-humping next to me who were certainly getting rehydrated with each other's fluids. I cringed and danced away. By now Ellie was free from her cage and getting swung around the dance floor by Adam with their famous version of dancing. Kind of like … If Kate Bush and Mick Jagger had a love child, it would dance like Adam and Ellie.

I was doing my best nonchalant sidestep away, when one of my favourite songs started. I turned to point at Amy, who was already pointing at me, and we squealed with excitement at each other as the Eurythmics' 'When Tomorrow Comes' blared from the speakers.

I was filled with renewed energy all of a sudden and transported to my youth as Amy and I started to dance and sing all the lyrics to a song we knew off by heart. It didn't matter that we were in a dive of a hotel, surrounded by seedy strangers – at that moment it was just Amy and me on the dance floor. It was as though we were at a school social or at the blue light disco at the back of the Onslow, bullying the DJ to play our favourite songs.

It was just us, two best friends having a good time, until I felt the slide of a hand along my lower back. I spun around in surprise and collided with a chest; I looked up and my eyes locked with Chris's.

"Do you want a drink?" he asked, leaning toward my ear, his breath tickling my skin.

Momentarily dazed, I nodded yes. His hand left my waist and he peeled off toward the bar. My heart pounded – having realised it was Chris vying for my attention, even after the jolt of excitement had shot through me, as quickly as it had come the disappointment soon followed as he left.

What had I expected, for him to take my hand and lead me onto the dance floor like Patrick Swayze? Chris didn't do dancing; he did staring sullenly from the side, or trash-talking about guy stuff with the guys. I was an idiot to think anything else.

"What was that about?" yelled Amy, dancing in front of me.

I shrugged. "Nothing."

"That look on your face doesn't say nothing," Amy said. "What did he say?"

"He just asked if I wanted a drink."

"Ugh! Forever the barman." Amy rolled her eyes.

I couldn't help but think she was right; it was always as if he was on duty, as if he couldn't just relax and be himself, whoever that was. I thought I had seen glimpses of it in the car, but that's all it was, a taunting flash of someone else that never stayed around.

"What's going on?" Tess intervened, trying to catch her breath as she took a moment from tearing up the dance floor.

"Oh, Chris is getting Tammy a drink," Amy said.

"Nice of him to ask me, I'm dying here," Tess said, fanning herself.

"Where's Toby?" I asked. It was an innocent enough question, but when the light dimmed in her expression I regretted it immediately.

"He went back to the campsite," Tess said.

"Oh." It's all I could manage; this was definitely not normal Tess and Toby behaviour. Any talk Sean must have had with him – if he had – obviously hadn't helped.

I felt kind of stupid about the pang of disappointment I had over being asked if I wanted a drink. Seriously. If that was my biggest issue …

An ice-cold sensation pressed against my back and I gasped and jumped away, spinning around to see a devilish gleam in Chris's eyes.

"Here you go," he said, passing me a raspberry Vodka Cruiser.

I took it from him. "Thanks … I guess."

He just grinned and walked back to the table where Sean sat.

"Ugh! Seriously, when are you two just going to get it on already?" said Amy.

A flushed Ellie leaned her elbow on Tess's shoulder and wiped sweat from her brow.

"Sorry?" I asked, trying not to choke on my drink.

"Why don't the two of you just do it already?" she repeated.

I laughed nervously, hoping it didn't sound forced. "How much have you had to drink tonight?" I asked.

Ellie straightened. "I'm as sober as a judge."

"A cage-dancing judge," I mused, sipping on my Cruiser, hoping that the subject would be changed, and fast.

"What are we talking about?" Adam appeared next to Ellie, passing her a beer.

"NOTHING!" I said a bit too quickly, casting the others a dark, warning stare.

They ignored it.

"Be warned, Adam, you might not have the stomach for this," said Amy.

"The stomach for what?" asked Adam, his eyes widened in expectant excitement as if what we were discussing could possibly be gory or disturbing.

I had to get out of there; I needed air and plenty of it. I had to break away from their knowing looks. The *last* thing I wanted was for them to confide in Adam, Chris's brother. I knew he was kind of one of the girls, being Tess's and Ellie's best friend and all, but still. At the end of the day, he was Chris's younger brother. I could only imagine that this kind of knowledge would be used as hours and hours of torture against Chris.

"I'll be right back, I just have to get some air," I announced quickly, before dodging my way through the crowd. I hit the front door, pushed it open and ran out to grab the wooden rail. I took a deep breath; the clean air was glorious – it was as if I could get drunk on the stuff. Instead, I eyed my bottle of vodka, still in my hand. I stared at it for a long moment; well, if I was going to be drunk it might as well be on the real stuff. I tipped the bottle back and sculled the bottle until my eyes watered.

"Whoa, easy there," Adam's voice spoke from behind me.

I lowered the bottle again, catching my breath and coughing.

"You know, drinking alone is pretty sad," he said, leaning against the railing.

"I don't think you could ever be alone at Villa Co-Co," I said.

"Ah, yes, I dare say each and every one of us will take a little piece of Villa Co-Co away with us." Adam dreamily looked off into the distance.

"Hopefully not alcohol poisoning," I added.

"Yeah, well, that's Amy's department, maybe Ellie's, and if the night pans out right it's sure as hell going to be Tess's problem."

"How is Tess?" I asked and immediately thought I probably shouldn't have.

Adam sipped thoughtfully on his stubby, the same darkness casting over him as it had Tess. "She doesn't say too much to me, probably because she knows that I'll lose my shit. But put it this way – by the end of this trip, Toby and I will be having words and I won't be pussyfooting around like Sean does."

Adam spoke each word as if it was a dark promise; it chilled me to the bone. "What's he done, anyway? What is wrong with Toby?" I asked. "Seems like no one knows. Maybe that should be the question that's being asked."

Adam shrugged. "That's the problem, no one knows, I don't even think Toby knows or if he does he's not saying, but my loyalty is to Tess not him, and if he doesn't man up and talk to her soon then I'm not going to just stand by and watch him hurt her."

I grimaced. "I know it's hard, but try to think about what Tess wants, what she needs in a friend right now."

Adam sighed. "I knew you'd be all logical and reassuring and shit."

I smiled. "Sorry about that."

"Ah, that's all right." He straightened. "Do you want me to give you some reassurance?"

"Um, okay …"

Adam leaned closer to me. "I won't tell anyone."

Chapter Thirty

I looked at Adam, thoroughly bewildered.

My mind raced with questions, but I didn't get to ask even one of them as the door behind us opened and music flooded onto the verandah.

"Oi, your women are looking for you." Chris stood in the open doorway, glowering at his younger brother.

"Ha! Only because they're too tight to buy their own drinks." Adam grinned. He peeled himself off the railing and made his way to the open door. "I was going to take Tammy back to the campsite; she has a bit of a headache ..."

I did? What was he on about?

Adam continued. "Do you think ...?"

"I'll take her," Chris snapped, never taking his broody expression off me.

I couldn't take my dumbfounded eyes off Adam.

Headache?

"Thanks, bro!" Adam tapped Chris on the shoulder, stepping back through the door. He winked at me and mimed that his lips were locked and he had thrown away the key.

My breath hitched; is that what he had meant? That he wouldn't say something to Chris? What? That I liked him? I guess I should have been relieved, but the last thing I needed (aside from Amy playing matchmaker) was for Adam to none too subtly try to hook me up with his brother.

His broody, fuming, scary-looking brother who stood in front of me.

He stalked over to me, took the bottle from my hand and threw it in the nearby bin. "Let's go."

"But I haven't ..."

"Now!" he growled over his shoulder as if the point was completely non-negotiable.

Geez, what did I do?

I hurried after him, stumbling in my footwear, the stupid over-strappy, blister-inducing heels that Ellie had convinced me to buy.

"Chris." I stopped to take off one shoe, then the other. "Wait."

Either he hadn't heard or he just chose to ignore me as he stalked off into the car park.

Ugh. What a bloody child.

I thought maybe removing my shoes would help me move faster, but as I winced and hopped on the sharp gravel it kind of had the opposite effect.

"Ooh-ah-ooh-ah—ah." I limped my way across the never-ending stretch, my anger building with each painful step.

Just. You. Wait. Chris Henderson.

Chris had reached the car long before me. He had flung the passenger door open and was glowering at me, waiting for my arrival.

There was the Chris I knew.

"Get in." He pointed.

Pain being the least of my worries now, I stormed the final couple of metres and threw one shoe in the car then the other. I slammed the car door shut and pushed Chris against it.

"Don't you dare speak to me like that!" I yelled. "I'm not one of your lackeys, you can't boss me around like that, and what's with the freakin' attitude?"

"Have you taken one of your tablets?" he snapped.

"What?"

"I'm guessing you're one of two kinds of stupid," Chris said.

What the hell?

"One, you haven't taken your medication to stop your migraine or two, you have *and* you've been drinking. Either way it makes me want to throttle you."

My mouth gaped open. I was completely taken aback by every offensive rant that came from his mouth, before I thought about it.

"Chris!"

"You're right, I can't tell you what to do, but have enough sense to realise that your actions affect other people."

"Are you going to let me explain?"

"You know, Tammy, I'm not always going to be around to give you a ride and if you think ..."

"For fuck's sake, CHRIS, I DONT HAVE A FUCKING HEADACHE!" My scream echoed through the car park so loud I wouldn't have been surprised if the music had stopped and the entire population of Villa Co-Co had heard.

Chris's brows rose in confusion. "Then, why did you say—"

"*I* didn't say. I never said. *Adam* was the one who told you I had a headache, *Adam* was the one that suggested you take me home, *Adam* was—"

"But why would he do that?" Chris asked, confusion etching his brows.

"My God!" I tugged at my hair in frustration then put my hands on my hips. "I'm guessing *you're* one of two kinds of stupid. One, you're blind or two, ignorant. Or both. Either way it makes me want to throttle *you*."

Chris's mouth pinched at the corner. "What's with the freakin' attitude?" he said.

Touché.

I sighed. "Why do you think they left for the camping trip early and blackmailed *you* to stay back and drive me? Why did they leave for Villa Co-Co without me and have *you* take me? Why suggest I have a headache so *you* can whisk me away into the night?"

Chris crossed his arms over his chest, his expression unmoving and unreadable as he waited for me to spell it out.

He was really going to make me do it.

I buried my face in my hands.

God give me strength.

I looked him dead in the eye. Best to get it out of the way – now that Adam knew, there would be no peace, anyway. "Because they're playing matchmaker." I waved my hand, motioning between us. "With you and me."

I braced myself for Chris to laugh, or openly grimace, or maybe blush, but he did none of those things. I waited. I tilted my chin up a little; I wasn't going to cave with embarrassment. I was going to stand my ground.

The only thing that thawed my resolve was when Chris broke into a brilliant white smile.

"What?"

Chris leaned against the car, his smile growing wider and wider as his devilish eyes watched my troubled expression.

"What's so funny?"

Chris hooked his hands behind his head, looking like the cat that got the cream. I couldn't help but break into a smile myself; this unexpected reaction was contagious.

"What are you thinking?" I said.

Chris looked me dead in the eye. "Let's give them what they want."

Chapter Thirty-One

My smile evaporated from my face in shock.

"W-what?" I swallowed.

"They are so obviously bored with their own petty existences."

"Yeah," I said. "I guess?"

Chris pushed off the car, moving to stand before me, the same devilish twinkle in his eye. "Well, let's give them something to talk about." He inched closer to me.

"What are you suggesting?"

"You might have to call on your academy award-winning acting skills."

"Go on."

"Here's an idea," he said. "We pretend that we're having a summer fling, but we don't admit anything. We act kind of cuddly but flat-out deny anything's going on. What do you think? They'll drive each other wild speculating. It will kill them. Plus, it'll stop them from playing Cupid if they think it's already happened."

My grin matched Chris's. "Sounds pretty devious."

"No more than they are."

True.

"So you in?" He held his hand out to me. I looked at it for a long moment before giving it a firm, business-like shake.

"I'm in." I paused, thinking. "So how do we start this masterful plan of deception?"

"First we'll have to plant the seed," Chris said as he opened the car door for me.

"Oh? And what's that going to be?" I asked with interest.

"The person with the biggest mouth."

***

When we arrived back at the campsite we found Ringer throwing Maltesers in the air and trying to catch them with his mouth. Having witnessed one roll from his lips onto the ground only to be picked up and placed back into the packet, we both respectfully declined his offer when he passed it our way.

"You guys weren't gone long," Ringer said with a mouth full of chocolate.

"No, I had a headache," I said, trying not to look at Chris.

"Yeah, well, Villa Co-Co isn't the place to nurse a headache," said Ringer.

"Where's Romeo and Juliet?" asked Chris as he propped himself on a nearby esky.

"You know young lovers." Ringer grinned, nodding toward their tent.

"What's Toby's excuse, then?" The words fell out of my mouth before I could stop them.

Both boys looked at me, unable to answer, because, unlike everyone else, Toby was a complete enigma.

"Anyway, I'm going to turn in for the night. Better rest this head of mine. Night, boys."

"Night, Tammy," said Ringer.

"Night," Chris said, trying not to smile.

I tentatively walked toward the path, my strappy heels dangling from my hand. I winced with every sharp stick or piece of bark that dug into my feet. It must have looked like I was doing the walk of shame, the infamous ungodly-hour stumblings of a girl with messed-up hair and raccoon eyes. I smiled to myself, lost in my thoughts before a new thought entered my mind.

I was heading toward the van.

I stilled. Was I sleeping in the van tonight? I mean, that's where all my stuff was, but would that be weird? Sleeping in Chris's van and not the tent. I bit my lip and looked back down the track. I couldn't go back, that would be awkward. My mind raced at a million miles an hour, conflicted by what to do.

"Night, Tammy." I jumped, startled when a voice pierced the darkness.

I muffled my cry with my hands.

A rich chuckle emanated from the dark like a nightmare, until a light flicked on.

"Sorry, I didn't mean to scare you," Toby said, trying not to laugh as he stood from his camping chair.

I clutched at my heart. "Jesus, Toby, you nearly copped a shoe in the face."

I had walked straight past Toby and Tess's tent and hadn't even realised. The treetop canopy above us cast deep shadows eerily all over the camping ground; not even the light of the full moon could penetrate in some places. Toby's torch shone at my feet.

"Why aren't you wearing them?"

I held up my heels. "Hiking boots they are not."

Toby nodded. "I don't know much about women's shoes, but I'm guessing you're right."

"The blisters on my feet think so too."

An awkward silence fell between us, and just as I was about to say goodnight and continue my awkward, painful trek up the track toward the van, Toby spoke.

"Hang on a sec," he said. He shucked off his shoes and handed them out to me. "They're about ten sizes too big, but I assure you I haven't any foot diseases; they will be definitely more comfortable than those."

I stared at Toby's sneakers, taken aback by the kindness. Of late I had heard nothing but the whispered speculation about Toby and Tess and how Toby was being a jerk. I hadn't thought much of it, and, to be honest, I didn't really know him. I hadn't talked to Toby much outside of the group setting.

He shook the shoes. "Go on, take them."

I so badly wanted to ask him what was wrong between him and Tess, why he was shutting down. I wanted him to tell me that everything would be all right, that they would be all right because, let's face it, we all believed if Toby and Tess couldn't work it out, no one could. I took his Converse shoes.

"Thanks," I said, taking them and placing them on the ground and slipping my feet inside. They were comically huge but compared to the sticks and sharp gravel they were like walking on clouds.

Toby smiled, looking at my feet. "There you go," he said.

It was the first real smile I had seen from Toby in a long while. Although I was so desperate to ask, I didn't dare. He wasn't really my friend anyway, and he had probably gotten enough grilling from his real mates asking him what the matter was.

If they didn't know, he sure wasn't going to tell me.

But then all of a sudden he did.

"Do you ever feel like you have so much to say, but you just don't know how to say it?" he asked out of the blue.

I stilled, almost forgetting to breathe as I took in his words. Toby was talking, and he was talking to me. I didn't move, afraid I'd spook him.

I kept it simple. "I feel like that all the time."

His eyes flicked up to meet mine, as if he was trying to gauge if I was serious. Toby sighed and pushed his hands deep into his pockets. "Every time I go to speak, or try to confess …"

I inwardly cringed. Confess wasn't a good word; it implied that he had done something wrong. My heart thundered in my chest.

"Sometimes," I said, "you just need to say it, no matter how it sounds. Some things are better out in the open. Better said than left unsaid."

God that sounded confusing; did that even make any sense?

Toby nodded like he completely understood.

"You'll know when the time's right to talk about it. Whatever it is you need to talk about." I tried to sound soothing, but I was worried I wasn't being any help at all.

"Yeah, I will," Toby said, lost in his own musings. And then just like that he snapped out of his deep thoughts. "Well, be careful walking in those shoes – they might be more comfortable but they might not be much easier."

"Oh yeah," I said, blinking, refocusing. "Thanks, though, you're a lifesaver."

"Night, Tammy."

"Night."

I turned to shuffle my way up the slanted gravel track. My mum had always taught me never to judge anyone unless you walked a mile in their shoes; I just had never expected to be walking in Toby Morrison's, literally.

***

I punched my pillow for the millionth time, trying to get comfortable. It was impossible, considering it was partly the crappy pillow's fault, but mostly it was because I was lying in the dark, on the mattress, still in my dress.

In the back of the van, I had struggled and fallen, nearly dislocated my shoulder trying to undo the back of my dress. If I'd had access to a pair of scissors I would have had no qualms about shredding the bloody thing into a million pieces.

Frustrated, I had crumpled to the mattress, giving up, trying to think of the silken fabric as soft against my skin instead of the reality of its scratchy lace edgings. I would never have had this problem if I had bought the bloody hippy dress from Evoka.

Where the bloody hell was Chris?

Probably planting the seed like he had planned, sitting with Ringer at the campsite, although me crashing in the van tonight was no doubt going to be a topic of conversation.

A wicked smile lit my face. I could always call out from the van. "OH, CHRIS! I NEED YOU TO TAKE MY CLOTHES OFF!"

I giggled to myself; I was so funny. Wouldn't they just love that? It would not be the most subtle of planted seeds. I thought it was probably better to just try to sleep instead before I did do something stupid. Little did I know that as far as doing stupid things was concerned, Chris was going to take the whole freakin' cake!

Chapter Thirty-Two

I hadn't even realised I had fallen asleep until two things happened:

The door to the van opened and I was hit in the face with a piece of plastic.

"Sorry," Chris laughed.

I hitched myself up onto my elbows and winced against the van's bright interior light. "What was that?" I croaked, looking around me for the flying missile.

"Trust me, you don't want to know."

Well, NOW I did!

I sat up, stretching my arms to the roof as I continued to look around the mattress.

Chris climbed into the van, leaving the door ajar, and rummaged through his bag.

"Uh, you know how we were going to plant the seed, subtly?" he said.

I lifted the bedding, still searching for the mystery missile. "Hmm," I managed, blinking to wake myself up.

He cringed. "Well, I might not have been quite subtle enough."

"What are you talking abo—" I froze, my eyes fixing to the very *thing* that had hit me in the face. I scooped it up and turned it in my hand, as if studying a wondrous object. My eyes flicked up in horror to see Chris almost bracing himself for me to lose my shit.

"Are you serious? A condom?"

Chris ran his hand through his hair. "I know, I know."

"THIS is NOT subtle," I said.

"Well, I didn't ask for it," Chris defended.

"So what? You just stumbled onto this on your trek home?" I asked in wonder, trying not to think how I had come about wearing another person's shoes.

"Honest to God, I didn't even get the chance to plant the seed with Ringer, we were too busy talking about other stuff and I thought, well, maybe the fact you were sleeping in my van might be subtle enough anyway, and just as I was calling it a night he stopped me, went into his wallet and chucked *that* at me. And then I chucked it at you."

Chris was rattling on in a blind panic, as if what he was saying was so far-fetched I might not believe him and was about to call him on it.

It was curious to see the usually cool, calm, collected Chris fumble over his words.

I started laughing and threw myself back on the mattress. A wry, relieved smile broke across his face.

"I'm glad you think it's funny," he said, throwing the blanket over my head, muffling my laughter.

I peeled off the cover, hitched myself up onto my elbows and watched as Chris stood outside the open end of the van and brushed his teeth.

"What did you say when he gave it to you?"

"Whert curld I serh?" he asked with a mouth full of foam before he shoved the brush back into his mouth.

"You should have reminded him I had a headache."

Chris choked on some toothpaste as he fought not to laugh.

I buried my head in my hands. "Oh my God, Chris. We're living a lie."

I lifted my head only to face a wall of exposed abs as Chris stood outside the van, peeling his top off. I quickly looked away, nuzzling down in my bedding and turned onto my side. A moment after Chris had rinsed his mouth out, the back of the van dipped under his weight as he once again rummaged around in his bag. I heard him as he shucked off his shoes and undid the belt and zip of his pants before shutting the back door and plunging us both into darkness.

All of a sudden, the van felt claustrophobic, far too small for the both of us. I held my breath, bracing myself until Chris climbed over the seat and made himself comfortable in the front.

But he didn't. Instead, he lay down next to me. My eyes widened. He puffed up his pillow and shimmied himself into a little spot, his arm pressing against me as he made himself comfortable.

"You got enough room?" he asked.

"Yep, plenty," I lied.

Chris was so close I could feel the heat from his skin; I could hear every intake of breath he made.

I lay frozen in an awkward twisted position, afraid to move. It was like being trapped under the bed playing Murder in the Dark all over again, except this time I didn't have to fear Ringer – well, not until the morning and this time it would be for a whole other reason.

Oh my God, Ringer thinks we're having sex! Which means by morning everyone will think we've done it and they'll all be looking at us with 'they have just totally *had sex' eyes.*

I sighed.

"What's wrong?" Chris asked.

"Oh nothing, this bloody thing itches," I said, which wasn't a total untruth. I clawed at my dress.

Chris hitched himself onto his side. "Are you still wearing your dress?" he asked, laughing.

"Pfft, no!"

Chris reached out, carefully sliding his hand up my arm to my shoulder, feeling the delicate lace of the material. "Yeah, you are. Why?"

I lifted my chin. "Because it's actually quite comfy."

"When it's not itching?" he repeated.

"Yeah, well aside from that."

"You can't get it off," Chris spoke in such a way that I could completely imagine him grinning, thinking it so hilarious that I couldn't get out of my own clothes. "Did you even try?"

"Of course I tried," I snapped.

"Whoa, okay, I see it's a touchy subject," he said as he pulled himself up to a sitting position. For a moment I thought he was actually offended and was making a move toward the front seat.

"W-where are you going?" I sat bolt upright.

Chris paused. "Nowhere. Turn around." His voice was low.

"Chris, it's fine, I was nearly asleep. I can just …"

"Does everything have to be a bloody debate with you?"

My mouth gaped. "No."

"Then turn around."

This time I did as he asked.

No biggie. He's done this before; it's the same as before. Except the zipper is going down instead of up, and he's half dressed, and in the dark, in the back of the Shaggin' Wagon with a condom floating around somewhere. Yep! No big deal whatsoever.

Chris gently swept my hair to the side, his fingertips lightly grazing along the back of my neck. It was just as he had done earlier in the evening, but somehow the dark heightened my senses; I could feel his breath on the back of my neck; I could hear him swallow deeply as his fingers gently worked on the buttoned clasp at the top. Just like he had struggled before to do it up, he was having trouble undoing it. He shifted closer; I could feel his leg press into my tail bone. I could hear my own laboured breath that seemed so painfully loud, but it was nothing compared to the thunderous beating of my heart that was practically deafening to my ears.

I bit my lip – a part of me wanted him to hurry up, but an even bigger part of me wanted him to take his time.

"Got it." His words were low and close to my ear.

He then, with an agonisingly slow and steady hand, peeled the zipper downward. It was as if he was unravelling me. I pressed my lips together, closing my eyes, as I briefly imagined that this wasn't just about a clumsy girl wanting to get out of an itchy dress, but it was because he wanted to undo my dress. Because it was Chris and me, in the back of his van. Because I was a girl he had seen from across the room, a girl he had walked with and guided through the dark, a girl he didn't have to pretend he was sleeping with to play a joke on his friends.

I almost gasped at the maddening sensation of Chris's thumb as it accidently grazed my bare back. I leaned back a little, hoping that more would come of it, but as quickly as it had been there it was gone, until I felt the press of his lips resting on my shoulder.

It was utterly distracting until his beautiful hands slid over my bare shoulders, pushing the fabric of my dress so that it fell forward. I grabbed the material, lightly brushing my fingers against his as I pulled the material down toward my waist. Chris's breathing quickened and he watched me, motionless for a long moment, almost as if he was contemplating what to do next.

I turned my head, my cheek so near his; even in the dark I could sense his lips were close. If he didn't know where to go from here, *I* sure did. Just as I was about to make the next step, an easy one, by closing the distance between us, he took the next bold move.

"Goodnight!"

He shifted back, lay down and rolled over, facing away from me.

I stared at his back in stunned silence, half naked and bitterly disappointed.

Chapter Thirty-Three

After that, sleep did not naturally follow.

Instead, I lay there in my bra and undies, staring up at the ceiling, wondering what it was exactly he had found so repulsive about me. I had worked myself into such an over-exhausted state of worthlessness and frustration. The worst thing was I knew Chris wasn't asleep either; you could always tell by a person's breathing if they were asleep or not. Sleep was full of deep, relaxed breaths, and there was nothing relaxed about Chris. He lay with his back to me, probably wondering how he would possibly face me in the morning. Well, I would make it easy for him, I thought.

As soon as the first slither of sunlight even threatened to lighten the sky, as quietly as I could I rummaged through my bag to find my running gear: my Lycra three-quarter pants, sports bra, my ankle socks and runners. With my water bottle, I wrapped it all up, deciding I could get dressed outside the van; it wasn't like anyone would be up at this hour, anyway.

I slowly unclicked the door and slid out. I glanced back at Chris's apparently sleeping body. A pulse of anger shot through me as I remembered how humiliated I had felt last night. I wished I had just slept in the bloody tent. I slid out the back of the van and gently closed the door before quickly getting dressed and jogging along the walking track.

I had thought that running might clear my head; that it would be a welcome return to feel my muscles cry and my lungs burn as I pushed myself to stride longer, run faster. I would run until either I vomited or could push through it, but as I collapsed against a tree, sweat dribbling down my back, my cheeks flushed with heat, there was nothing clear about my mind at all.

I was still haunted by his touch. Had I imagined his laboured breath? The way he had gently caressed my skin? I could almost still feel the burn of his lips on my shoulder.

I trudged back up the path. Up ahead I could see the gang hovering around the makeshift kitchen, heating up baked beans on the campfire as the billy boiled.

My face flamed with embarrassment. Ringer had probably blabbed about the condom he had so thoughtfully gifted Chris and me. I slowed my pace as I headed back toward the campsite. *Let Chris face them first.*

***

I saw him before he saw me.

Standing shirtless by the makeshift kitchen, spooning a mouthful of Nutri-Grain, he was listening intently to Sean who sat on a folded out camping chair holding a captive audience. So captive, a dribble of milk slid down Chris's chin, which he wiped away with the back of his hand.

God, how could such a thing be so sexy? I needed to have an ice-cold solar shower.

I was grateful for Sean holding the spotlight; it made my approach from the track of less interest than I had anticipated. I received only distracted glances and half-hearted waves from the enthralled group that surrounded Sean. The only person who didn't seem so enthralled was Chris, whose deep brown gaze locked with mine briefly before I quickly looked away, sliding into the spare space next to Bell.

"What's going on?" I whispered.

Bell grinned, munching thoughtfully on a toast finger. "Sean was just retelling a gripping tale of love and loss," she said with a giggle.

"But mostly loss," added Stan quietly out of the side of his mouth. He and Bell exchanged looks and caught a case of the giggles.

Sean's eyes darkened. "It's not funny."

"No, it's not," added Chris as he sat beside Adam on the opposite side of the table. "It's bloody hilarious."

"Okay, what have I missed?" I looked around the snickering group.

Toby stretched his arms toward the sky before linking them behind his head, a mischievous glint in his eyes. "Sean thought he'd try to get all chummy with the owners of Villa Co-Co."

"I would call it more like flirting." Amy crossed her arms, a smirk curving her mouth.

"True. There was some shameless flirting going on," Toby agreed.

"Get stuffed, she was old enough to be my mother," piped up Sean.

"Which makes it all the more disturbing," mused Amy.

"Anyway, I don't know if you saw Jan? The Madame of Villa Co-Co?" Toby asked me.

I tried to cast my memory back; I hadn't really been there that long. I did remember a short, dumpy, overtanned lady with spikey, peroxide hair swanning around the place in a kaftan and fake acrylic claws. For the briefest of moments I had entertained the notion that she looked like a human-sized pineapple. Could she be …

"Oh my God, the Pineapple?"

They all burst into the loudest, most hysterical laughter, none laughing louder than Adam who banged the table with his hand and grabbed his stomach.

"That's her." Toby pointed at Sean. "The Pineapple!"

The only person not laughing was Sean. He sat rubbing the stubble of his chin with a wry smile. "All right, all right, get on with it, Tobias, you're enjoying this way too much."

Toby tried to regain his composure as he wiped his eyes. Tess sat next to him, catching her own breath as she waited with glee for him to continue. They both seemed normal and relaxed. I hoped this was a good sign.

Toby cleared his throat. "Anyway, the Pineapple."

Ringer snorted.

"Shhh." Ellie elbowed him.

"So, I'm not sure how it happened exactly but the Pineapple honed in on the great almighty Sean; she must know a businessman when she sees one, who knows? They were talking about business and hotels and all the stuff that would make you want to take a cyanide pill, it was so utterly boring." Toby groaned.

"Except for you, Chris, you would have loved it," Amy pointed out.

"Sounds riveting," Chris deadpanned.

"Anyway, as the night wore on, I think her top got lower so the cleavage got bigger and bigger."

"There was a lot of cleavage," grimaced Tess.

"And with each shift of her low-cut top, her hand would motion the barman for another jug of beer."

"So the Pineapple had big jugs?" I asked Sean, trying not to laugh.

He shook his head. "Massive."

"There were jugs everywhere," Toby exclaimed, holding his hands up with dramatic flair. "Anytime Sean finished another jug, she would be like, 'Let me get this one, let me get this one.'"

"Where were you, Amy?" I asked.

"Rolling my eyes next to him."

"We learned about how she and her husband have just returned from Bali because they import furniture, and how they want to open up a restaurant over there, all really fascinating stuff, and we thought, you know, these people are quite switched on really. But we sort of really didn't realise how switched on and business savvy they were until it was closing time," said Toby.

By now my elbows were on the table; I had fully leaned forward, just like the others had been before.

"What happened at closing time?" I bit my lip.

"The Pineapple disappeared and a waitress slipped Sean a folded piece of paper with a smile."

Before I could ask if the Pineapple's phone number was on it, Sean sighed. "A hundred and seventy-eight bucks."

"What?"

"Mate, you ruined my punchline!" Toby slapped the table, annoyed.

I must have looked confused until Chris spoke. "The Pineapple was running a bar tab the whole time."

I tilted my head in sympathy, but Amy continued to shake her head.

"Some savvy businessman you are," she scoffed.

I patted Sean on the shoulder. "Never mind, you weren't to know she was a rotten pineapple," I said, trying not to laugh.

I stood to make my way for some brekky, making a conscious effort to not make eye contact with Chris. If there was one thing I could sympathise with Sean about, it was that you couldn't always judge a book by its cover. That I knew for sure.

Chapter Thirty-Four

"I wouldn't bother with that if I were you."

Ringer's voice snapped me from my daydream as I stood beside the solar shower with my cup of tea, mentally psyching myself up to have a shower and then get changed.

I turned to where he was busy packing up chairs.

"I have to," I said.

There were just no two ways about it; I had to wash off the sweat from my run, I had to feel human if I was going to sit in the van with Chris again for hours and hours. Something I was *not* looking forward to.

"Just do what the rest of us are gonna do." Ringer groaned as he lifted a twenty-litre esky onto the back of the ute's tray.

I looked expectantly at him.

He rolled his eyes. "Tammy, where are we?"

I looked around.

Um, nowhere?

"We're at Evoka Springs." He said it as if it were the most obvious thing in the world.

"Yeah, so?"

"So do you know why people stop here?"

"Gemstone elephant statues?" I said, taking a sip of my tea.

"Evoka SPRINGS, baby!" Ringer pointed behind me. "See down that track, where Sean and Amy's love nest is?"

"Hmm."

"Well, about three hundred metres beyond that is a giant watering hole."

"Heated springs?" My eyes lit up. "Why didn't you guys tell me yesterday?" I shuddered at the memory of the icy water.

"Uh, not heated exactly – actually, it's just like a big river – but the water is warm as."

Oh, okay, so that sounded better than an ice-cold shower. And I didn't fancy my chances of Chris offering to pour warm water on me again. If anything, Chris seemed more likely to pour ice-cold water on heated situations.

I tipped the dregs out of my cup. "Are you going down?" I asked.

"We all are! Better get your swimmers on." He shrugged. "Or not, doesn't worry me." Ringer winked and flashed a cheeky grin.

***

I jogged up the path, feeling all the expected excitement of not wanting to get left behind as I rushed to change into my swimmers. The last thing I hoped to see was Chris coming down the track in the opposite direction, dressed in nothing but his black footy shorts with a towel slung over his shoulder.

God, he looked good.

I snapped my thoughts from such perviness. Besides, I was still mad at him from last night, wasn't I? Oh no, was I starting to turn into an Amy clone? Holding a grudge and being dramatic? I really didn't want to be like that; besides, what was his crime, not finding me irresistible?

No, I didn't want to be that girl. So, in the true spirit of *positive, positive, positive*, I met Chris's guarded eyes with a bright smile.

"Going for a tub?" I called, making my way toward him.

Don't look at his shoulders; don't linger on his pecs; eyes up front and centre!

He held up a cake of soap with a smirk.

"I hope that is environmentally friendly?"

His face seemed to relax a little; the guard came down. "Absolutely," he said with a grin. "The fish are going to smell like roses."

He had the most beautiful smile. How had I missed it before? Maybe because it was so rare, but when he smiled in front of me it was utterly transforming; Chris was like the sun appearing from behind the clouds.

I wanted to get to know him, the real him. I didn't want to dismiss him in petty anger because he didn't make a move last night; I wanted to find out what pushed his buttons, what made him tick. I had seriously contemplated getting a lift with Adam and Ellie or Stan and Belinda rather than spend another day with Chris in the van, but I never entertained the thought for long. I had grown quite fond of the van.

Of Chris.

"So, has Ringer mentioned anything to you?"

My eyes blinked at his question. Oh God, that's right, last night's gift from Ringer.

"Oh, um, no, actually. I was kind of expecting the worst. You?"

Chris shook his head. "Not yet. Give it time, he'll strike when we least expect it."

"It's like Murder in the Dark all over again."

"So what's our plan of attack today, then?" Chris asked, toeing a circle in the dirt.

"As in?"

"Operation Summer Fling?" He looked at me, a glint of amusement twinkling in his eyes.

My heart skipped a beat. Was he serious? After the way last night had ended I had thought maybe it was just a joke, but did he still want to go through with it?

"You mean, plant more seeds?" I asked, afraid to hope.

He shrugged, squinting up at the sky. "Keep 'em guessing, I reckon."

My stomach twisted in excitement. "Okay, I'm really not an expert at this or anything."

"Would you like me to lead the way?" Chris asked, sporting a cheeky grin.

I blushed. "You might have to; you seem to be naturally more devious than I am."

His brows rose in surprise. "Oh, really?"

"Well, hiding in cupboards, under beds, making secretive calls to local chemists ..."

Chris nodded as I spoke. "I am pretty sneaky."

"*So* sneaky," I agreed. "So the problem is, how will I know how to react to you when I have to?"

All humour faded from Chris's eyes as he looked into mine. There was nothing but smooth calmness in his expression, no aggressive lines etched above his brow. He looked so much younger than usual. I wanted to look away but I couldn't; his gaze pinned me into place. A slow, crooked smile pinched the corner of his mouth.

"Oh, trust me, you'll know," he said, and just as I thought he had robbed me of all breath, he slid past me on the walking track and continued on his way toward the campsite.

***

The stillness of the tranquil surrounds were disturbed by the Tarzan-like hollers injected into the air every time one of the boys launched themselves at a run at the long rope from the embankment. They flew through the air and plunged into the water of the Evoka Springs.

It was Chris's turn to take the rope. His biceps pulled into taut, moulded curves that stretched just as impressively as his back muscles when he reached and pulled for the rope. Wearing Chris's sunnies, my eyes secretly gazed at the line along his ribcage as he inhaled a deep breath before launching himself into the air. My breath hitched when he flung into a backward somersault, plunging feet first into the murky water. I straightened from my recline, lifting the sunnies from my eyes and holding my breath until his head poked up out of the water with that famous hair flick boys do. As soon as he broke the surface everyone cheered. They had good reason to; it had been impressive. I just melted back on my towel in relief, placing Chris's oversized man sunnies back on.

As tradition had it, Bell, Tess, Ellie, Amy and I were all lying, sun-baking on our towels, watching the alpha males trying to outdo each other with testosterone-fuelled antics. After we had gone for a dip, washing our bodies and hair with flowery-scented soap, we lounged on our towels, refreshed and sunkissed.

While the others chatted about the things they missed, like hairdryers and running hot water, I lay silently, propped up on my elbows, watching Chris's body slowly appear out of the water. It was as if a movie was playing out in slow motion before my eyes – he ran his hands back through his hair as the excess water dribbled down his tanned skin. We hadn't said two words to each other since we had all congregated by the river over an hour ago, so although I knew he planned on planting a seed of intrigue, I guess he hadn't meant he would necessarily do it anytime soon. Heck, if at all. But as he made his way up onto the bank his eyes locked onto me, he winked, and strode toward me.

Oh-crap-oh-crap-oh-crap ...

I shifted myself into a seated position, not knowing what that wink meant until he came over. Chris stood above me, shaking the excess water off his hair, causing me to flinch and scream.

"Chris, doooon't!"

He collapsed onto my towel beside me, laughing.

"You're an idiot," Amy glowered, wiping off wayward droplets from her shoulders.

He ignored her; even turning his back on me so he could watch as Adam took the rope.

So what, that was it? Was that his idea of planting the seed? Seriously? Share my towel? Prop himself here after some tomfoolery and get dry?

That was something any of the Onslow Boys would do on a regular basis. I didn't know if the wink had meant he was going to try something to arouse suspicion or not, but my lips twitched in silent amusement. Two could play at this game.

I shifted onto my knees. "You look tense, Chris," I said, placing my hands on his shoulders to balance myself. I could feel the flex of his muscle twitch under my unexpected touch.

To his credit (apart from that), he didn't bat an eyelid. "Yeah, I must have slept funny," he replied, kinking his head from side to side.

I scooted closer, kneading at the base of his neck. Chris stretched his head forward, involuntarily groaning as I pressed my thumbs into the muscle.

"There?" I asked.

"Mmm-hmm," was his only response as he brought his head forward, shutting his eyes.

I didn't dare look to my left where Amy was no doubt watching with distaste, and I didn't want to bring my eyes forward to possibly lock eyes with a smug Onslow Boy.

I knew that if I made any kind of connection I would be brought undone; I wasn't a very good liar.

I worked my thumbs into Chris's taut back muscles that were so incredibly tight and knotted. And then I thought about how tense he was all the time, in his job, in his life. Why *wouldn't* he be all knotted up like a pretzel?

Being a bit of a fitness freak, I was not unaccustomed to sports massages – if anything, it was one of my addictions in life, so I was pretty well versed in using an array of techniques to get the blood flow into tissue. I bit my lip, concentrating on the vast landscape of Chris's back. His skin was so soft, so flawless under my touch. I was mesmerised by every hypnotic circle I pushed into his flesh. Chris's eyes were still shut and only the odd sound of pleasure escaped him.

"I'm not hurting you, am I?" I whispered in his ear.

"No, it's good, don't stop," he mumbled sleepily.

A twist of pleasure knotted in my stomach as I gently raked my fingertips down his spine, causing him to shiver.

I smiled. "Chris Henderson, are you ticklish?"

"Don't even try it."

"How very interesting …" I raked my fingers tauntingly upward.

"Tammy," he warned.

My little public display would certainly have everyone speculating by now. I slowly ran my fingers toward his ribcage.

But I was stopped by a blood-chilling scream from the water.

Chapter Thirty-Five

My stomach plummeted to the ground.

Chris moved like lightning – he was up and off my towel before I'd even blinked. He powered his legs along the ground as he entered the water, the river turning into a mesh of churned foam as Chris, Sean, Stan, Toby and Adam converged toward Ringer. I hadn't even noticed him swing into the lake.

I stood, my hands bracing my cheeks as everything played out like a horror movie. Chris and Sean dragged Ringer out of the murky water. It was turning pink around them.

That's when I saw the blood.

"Get a towel!" Sean yelled as we all moved out of their way.

"What happened?" cried a tearful Ellie.

Ringer's jaw was clenched as he manoeuvred himself onto a nearby log before Adam skidded along the sand with a clean towel ready for his foot, which was flowing with blood.

"Jesus, mate." Adam cringed as the blood stained the towel immediately.

"I stepped on a bloody bottle neck or something," Ringer hissed through gritted teeth.

Chris crouched beside Ringer, popping a bottle of water with his teeth. "Sorry, mate, this might sting but I've got to clean the wound, make sure there's nothing in it."

Ringer nodded. He was white as a ghost and looked a bit woozy, propped up only by Sean's steely grip on his shoulders.

I didn't like the look in Chris's eyes; they read that what he was about to do was going to hurt him more than it would hurt Ringer. I doubted entirely if that was true, but he poured water over the wound anyway. Ringer tensed and Ellie grabbed his hand.

"It's going to be all right, Ringo," she comforted him, looking wide-eyed at the emerging wound as Chris's water cleared the sand away and revealed just how bad the cut was.

It was deep.

Adam looked away. "Tess, can't you do something? You're a doctor."

Tess's eyes widened in alarm. "I'm a pharmacist," she emphasised. "It's a bit different."

"Well, what about you, Ellie? You're a nurse," Adam said in a panic.

"A *dental* nurse." She shook her head. "Ask Tammy, she's the biomedical genius." She pointed at me.

I was about as qualified in such things as anyone else, but before Adam accosted Toby's mechanical skills, I pointed out the obvious.

"It's going to need stitches. We need to wrap it in something clean and apply pressure, a T-shirt will do. We have to stop the bleeding until we get back to camp to the first aid kit."

"We'll have to go to emergency in Calhoon and get it seen to," Stan said.

"Well, we'll pack up the site and wait for you to get back. Whether we have to stay another night or go back, we will," added Sean.

"Hello, I'm right here, you know."

We all looked at Ringer.

"Sorry, mate." Sean grinned.

"Come on, get me to the bloody hospital."

The four hundred metres back to the campsite seemed to take an eternity, probably more so for Sean who carried Ringer on his back. We wasted little time in applying a bandage and propping him up across the back seat of Stan's car.

"We'll wait for you here," Toby said through the open window.

"Don't you bloody dare," Ringer called from the back seat.

"Mate, we're not leaving without you," Toby glowered.

"If you don't go, you won't make it to Point Shank in time for New Year's and I'm already ruining these guys' lives." Ringer nodded toward Stan and Bell and winced.

"Hey, we volunteered," Bell said sternly to him.

Sean rested his arms on the windowsill fixing his earnest gaze on Ringer. "Stop being a tool, Ringo. We're not leaving without you."

Ringer's eyes were full of pain, but utter sincerity. "Go," he said.

"Get fucked! We're staying," said Sean.

"We'll call you from the hospital," said Stan as Bell climbed into the passenger seat beside him.

"We'll be here."

Stan shook his head. "At least hit the coast today, settle in Portland, if anywhere. We'll see what then." Stan fired up the engine.

We all stepped away from the car as Stan backed out and reversed around. An immense sadness filled the atmosphere as Ringer pressed his hand against the window then waved goodbye. We all smiled and waved him along, calling out well wishes and that we'd see him soon. And just as the car disappeared through the bush scrub, the frantic rush of panic from moments before and the shock of what had happened fell upon us in stony silence.

I stared off into the distance, feeling numb and worried for Ringer. Even though I knew he would be okay, taking Ringer, Stan and Bell from the group changed everything. Just as I was about to let the reality wash over me, I felt a hand pull at my elbow. It tugged me around and before my glassy eyes could register what was happening, Chris had pulled me into a fierce embrace. His arms enveloped me in such warmth, such strength that I melted against his bare skin. My cheek burned against his chest as I wrapped my arms tightly around him. His hand smoothed over my hair just like it had that time when my consciousness had danced between wake and sleep in the van that night.

It could have been his way of stirring speculation amongst the others, but something in his embrace told me it wasn't about that; it wasn't about making a show for anyone else, it was that part of Chris, the kind, seldom-exposed Chris that had come out to comfort me, to support me yet again. I never wanted any other Chris to steal him away again. But just as easily as the emotion had come, it slid away into a stony grave as he peeled his arms from me.

"I better help pack up," he said, clearing his throat.

"Sure," I said, hoping I wasn't blushing. "I'll start packing the van."

Chris paused, his dark brown eyes studying me for a long moment. "Do you still want to travel in the van?" he asked.

Would it be weird that I did? Or was the deal for Chris to drop me off with the others so I could catch a ride with Amy and Sean the rest of the way? Was he finally able to offload me and get rid of the annoying girl he'd had to pick up because his cousin had blackmailed him? I suddenly felt really stupid, shifting awkwardly under his gaze.

"Um, is that okay?"

Chris's expression never faltered as he shrugged. "If you want."

I did want.

But wow. He didn't have to act so enthusiastic about it. He was so hard to read. Although I don't know what I had expected – for him to crumble to his knees and beg me to go with him? No, I didn't expect that, but, hey, I hadn't expected the hug either.

I nodded. "All right, I'll start packing the van, then."

Yep! No biggie, travelling alone with Chris. That's what I told myself over and over again as I headed toward the van. Then why was it my heart wanted to leap out of my chest?

***

It didn't take me long to get everything secured and packed in the back of the van. I shut the door with a sigh, thinking to make myself more useful with the bigger pack-up of the campsite.

I peeled the tent flap back to help Amy pack up the last of the food.

I smiled, handing over the half-used carton of long life milk when something triggered in me. A long-forgotten conversation stemming back to my flat mobile phone.

Blackmail.

"Oh my God," I laughed.

"What?" Amy stilled.

"It's been such a crazy couple of days, I can't believe we still haven't finished our conversation from days ago."

Amy's brows narrowed and she looked at me like she had no idea what I was talking about.

I looked around to ensure we were alone in the tent; I kind of felt a bit stupid bringing it up again. Still, we were going to be separated for probably another whole day of travel and I really did want to find out what was so juicy that she could blackmail Chris about. Maybe I could use it to my advantage.

"What you used to blackmail Chris with, you never got a chance to tell me."

Amazement spread across her face. "I can't believe we haven't finished that conversation – what has become of us?"

"I know," I laughed.

"I'm sorry, my head's been all over the place lately. Just when I thought this trip would be about relaxing I've been nothing but stressed."

"Everything's all right, though? With you and Sean?"

"Oh God, yes, amazing, good. No, I just meant the whole Toby–Tess saga, Bell not liking Ellie, no hot showers and now Ringer. Don't say anything to Sean, though, I'm acting like I love every minute of this hellish trip."

I couldn't help but feel that somehow I had gotten the better end of the deal; following on later with Chris, it had kind of kept us away from all the group's drama.

Amy gathered up a box. "Help me with these boxes to the car and we'll finish this conversation once and for all."

Chapter Thirty-Six

Why did I feel so nervous?

As if carrying boxes of breakfast goods to the car was the equivalent to walking Death Row? Maybe I didn't actually want to know the answer anymore. What if what Amy had to say would make me think differently about Chris, about the Chris I had come to know these last couple of days? I felt sick.

Amy slid the box along the back tray. I handed her my box and she did the same. She turned to me with a speculative look in her eyes.

"What is going on between you and Chris, anyway?"

Oh no! I didn't want to have *this* conversation. Amy had that juicy 'tell me more' look in her eye, but the truthful answer was incredibly dull. Besides, that would defeat the purpose of our devious faux flirtations. Chris's faux flirtations, anyway.

"No way, I'm not stalling this conversation again," I said, pointing the finger at her.

She shrugged. "Fair enough, but I'm guessing you already know it."

"Know what?" I screamed to the sky. This conversation was so hyped up in my head it was destined to be anticlimactic.

"Well, I was lingering in the bar one late night lock-in… I pretty much just left the boys to their own devices and was cleaning up in the main bar when a certain conversation emerged that piqued my interest."

I curved my brow. "About?"

"You!" Amy smiled broadly.

My heart thundered so fast in my chest I thought it might explode.

"So naturally I pretend I'm not listening and start stocking the fridge," Amy says with pride.

I am frozen on her every word: frozen solid, afraid to move in case she stops talking or we are interrupted.

"So I heard your name and who should be singing your praises but none other than *Ringer*." Amy accentuated his name with excitement.

My shoulders slumped. I had kind of expected it all along. Ringer speaking highly of me wasn't exactly a secret, he openly flirted with me any chance he got, but he flirted with everyone. It was his calling card, more so now that Sean was shacked up with Amy.

Amy continued. "So he's talking about how fit you are and how banging your body is and he can't believe you're single and all that, and then the conversation changed and they were talking about some random that he hooked up with the weekend before, and I swear those boys are the worst gossips I've ever met."

Yep. Definitely anticlimactic. I tried not to seem overly disappointed as I smiled politely.

"Anyway, I don't remember what piqued my interest again – maybe it was because they were paying Chris out about something, I always like to see that – but I think they were questioning his bachelor status and running off a list of names of people he rated. They were throwing names at him left, right and centre. Sharnie Maynard, Ellie Parker, Julie Hooper, Laura Pegg – he was just shaking his head, not answering – you know, giving his best Chris Henderson stony death stare – but then something interesting happened."

"What happened?"

"Sean mentioned your name and his face completely changed."

I started breathing quickly, my chest rising and falling rapidly. I refused to take my eyes from Amy, I didn't dare ask what she meant but I didn't need to as she leaned in closer to me.

"It was like a light switch went on. Sean said 'Tammy Maskala' and his eyes lit up; it was all they needed to give him absolute hell about you for the rest of the night. It was like they had discovered this massive secret about him."

"What did he do?" I breathed out.

Amy laughed. "After he went bright red? He tried to kick them all out, threatened to cut off the beer supply and bar them for life. But you know what?"

I shook my head.

"He never denied it. Not once." Amy beamed smugly.

"So that's what you blackmailed him about?" I whispered.

"I said if he didn't pick you up and give you a lift I would tell you everything I overheard that night about him having the hots for you."

I blanched. "You didn't!"

Amy puffed out her chest. "I did."

Amy then moved on to how utterly amazed she was at how shocked I seemed considering the way we had been acting with each other. The shower, us sneaking off early last night, the shoulder massage … There was no mention of the condom, thank God. Amy revelled in it all. But I was still digesting what between us had been real and what was fiction.

"It's so obvious you two are into each other, and I would usually be all about the details, but Chris is my cousin so it's kind of gross." Amy grimaced as if she were torn between wanting to know and never, ever wanting to know.

"Well, I'll spare you, because, in all honesty, nothing has happened."

"Sure-sure," Amy said as she sauntered back toward the tent.

"It's true," I called after her.

Amy shook her head. "You are the worst liar." She laughed and disappeared through the canvas flap.

I stood in the middle of the clearing, confounded by my new-found knowledge.

Chris *actually* liked me. It wasn't all a prank. Then why hadn't he made a move on me last night? I'd sure given him the opportunity. He hadn't even looked me over in the way a male appreciates a woman with my lacey white dress last night; in fact, I think his word was 'nice', not exactly high praise. He was happy to pretend to be into me for the boys' benefit, but if he really did like me, why was he holding back?

Oh crap, I don't know.

All I knew was, I was afraid to hope, but desperate to know. Amy's story was interesting, but having spent the last two days with Chris it had done nothing but conflict my emotions. With every flash of tenderness from him there was an equal display of broodiness.

I sighed. I wondered what the next leg of the road trip would bring. If there was one thing that was for sure, I was going to push some Chris Henderson buttons and in order to do that I might just have to play my own little game.

Chapter Thirty-Seven

Knowledge is power, right?

Then why was it that I didn't feel the least bit powerful? Amy's words played over and over in my mind, and as I analytically turned every one of them over in my head, by the time I had readied myself to get into the van, I had all but convinced myself that Amy must have gotten it wrong.

Seriously, it was just a look. Big deal, so his 'look' changed.

Hardly an admission of undying love. So what if he hadn't denied the taunts? Chris wasn't the sort of person to bow down to pressure – well, unless he was blackmailed by a pesky younger cousin.

A line pinched between my brows, a mirror image to Chris's as I approached him from the track. I doubted his troubled look was a product of overzealous obsessing about feelings, though. No. Instead, his troubled eyes flicked up to me.

"Are these yours?" he asked, holding a pair of size ten men's navy Converse shoes. His gaze shifted from them to my petite size six feet and back to these mysterious objects. He turned them over in his hands, inspecting them as if they were a newly discovered ancient relic.

Oh crap! Toby's shoes.

"Ah, no. Actually I better return them."

I reached for the shoes but Chris lifted them out of my reach.

He cocked his brow. "Bring men's shoes home often, do you?"

I sighed. "Yes, I am quite the kleptomaniac with a foot fetish. You better guard your Italian leather loafers with your life," I quipped.

A spark of amusement glinted in his eyes, but the frown remained. "I don't own Italian leather loafers."

"Really?" I questioned. "You don't rock them out with white knee-high socks?"

The corner of Chris's mouth pinched. "No, but I'll look into it."

I reached for them again but he was faster than me, lifting them even higher. If I had been his younger brother I imagined his next move would have been to place his hand on my forehead and, pushing me back, laugh as I wildly swung arms. Luckily, he didn't go that far.

"Hmm, interesting," he said mainly to himself as he held one shoe up to the sun, inspecting it.

I placed my hands on my hips. "You can talk. I may have confiscated a pair of shoes on my travels, but let's not forget what you brought back last night, Christopher Condom!"

Just as my words spilled out, proudly thinking myself quite the word player, the sound of a branch snapped from behind me. My eyes widened; I could almost feel a cold shiver run down my spine as I turned and had my worst fears confirmed.

Adam stood at the edge of the track, arms crossed casually across his chest, grinning from ear to ear as if enjoying the show.

"Sorry to interrupt," he said. The bright, devilish white flash of teeth was almost blinding as he looked from Chris to me.

Did I really just call him Christopher Condom?

I wanted to die.

Of all the people to overhear *that* particular conversation, it had to be his little brother Adam. I could almost see the speculative cogs turning in his head as he filed Christopher Condom into the 'remember for all eternity and use against Chris' file.

I didn't have to look at Chris to know he would be scowling. I didn't want to know if it was directed at me or Adam.

"What do you want?" Chris bit out.

Plunging his hands into his pockets. "Hey, I'm just the messenger; Sean said it's time to go."

Taking advantage of the moment of distraction, I grabbed the shoes out of Chris's hands.

"I best return these, then," I said. I looked straight ahead, not daring to meet either pair of their eyes as I moved past Adam and made my way down the track.

Mortified!

***

Seeing only the indented bark chips and scuffed-up dirt as any remnants of Toby and Tess's campsite, I made my way toward Toby's lone blue Ford ute, thinking if neither was around I could just slip the shoes in the back of the tray. I was about to veer off the track and cut through the scrub to make my way to the clearing where his car was parked under a towering gum. Skimming my way through the branches, working to push myself through the thicket, I stopped when I heard raised voices beyond the scrubby barrier.

Not wanting to do an Adam and stumble into a private conversation, my eyes darted around for a quick, silent escape.

But as the heated conversation escalated, the last thing I wanted was to be discovered, so I had little choice but to crouch behind a bush and ride out the storm.

My heart pounded; I tried to keep still, slow my breaths and not think about the uncomfortable position I had settled myself into. I was soon snapped out of my worry for comfort when I heard what sounded like Toby's voice.

He was yelling. Pleading with someone. Oh no, had I stumbled across him and Tess fighting? I had thought everything looked okay at breakfast. At least, they were sitting next to one another. And Toby had seemed in good spirits – everyone was.

But clearly not now.

I clenched the shoes to my chest like a life vessel, saddened by the conversation I couldn't quite make out. I was glad. I didn't *want* to hear it.

Then, of course, as if the Gods were conspiring against me, the voices grew louder. They shifted closer to me, so close I could make out the outlines of bodies through the bushes as I crouched lower so as not to be discovered. I held my breath.

A slender, blonde figure stormed away, pausing only when Toby snared her elbow.

"Ellie, wait!"

Ellie?

Ellie spun around, her eyes glassy and wild. "You have to tell her!"

Toby's hand dropped from her; he seemed broken, exhausted. "I can't."

"It's driving her crazy, the way you're acting. She's not stupid, she knows something is going on."

Toby's eyes were downcast. He slowly shook his head as he mulled over Ellie's words. "It would ruin everything," he said.

Ellie wiped away a stray tear.

"Hey, come on." Toby stepped closer and rubbed her shoulder. "You're supposed to be happy, not sad."

She sniffed and smiled weakly. "I am. I am happy. I just can't wait for it to be over."

My stomach churned. Whatever was going on, it didn't sound good.

Toby sighed, pulling her into a hug. "Not much longer."

What. The. Fuck?

I couldn't witness any more.

I had been holding my breath for so long I was in serious trouble of passing out. I felt nauseated, bewildered, horrified, angry.

I mean, seriously. What the fuck?

I edged away from them, scrambled to my feet and stormed in the opposite direction. I was so mad at what I had heard I didn't care if they heard me. Let them bloody hear me. I burst through bushes, crunching a determined line back up the track, my heart pounding, my mind racing, anger bubbling under the surface of my skin before the last defeated emotion slammed into me and my stomach plummeted. I stopped, bent over, hands on my knees as I caught my breath.

Poor Tess. Poor, sweet Tess.

I squeezed my eyes shut, hoping against hope that what I had witnessed was just a dream, that I would wake up any minute, or maybe even that I'd simply misinterpreted what they'd been saying. Maybe I was on the wrong track entirely.

But as I opened my eyes, blinking and focusing on the pair of shoes I still held in my hand, grasped so tightly my knuckles were white, I didn't think I was. Anger gave way to sadness. I knew I probably shouldn't have jumped to conclusions – hell, only moments before Adam had walked into my own conversation and probably come to his own inaccurate conclusions.

I tried to soothe myself that maybe what I had overheard hadn't been wildly inappropriate, that Toby's distance couldn't be so disturbing. If this was a glimpse of the new century to come then I wanted no part of it.

Not. For.

I threw one of Toby's shoes.

A. Single.

Then I threw the other one.

Minute.

They both ricocheted off the same gum tree and disappeared in the thick scrub. It afforded me a moment of satisfaction, but it didn't last for long. I continued my heavy-footed stride up the track. So determined was I to leave the memory behind me I didn't even see Adam until my shoulder bumped into his as he walked in the opposite direction.

Startled and shunted out of my troubled thoughts, I snapped, "Watch out."

Adam steadied me with his hand. "Sorry," he half laughed. "Whoa, woman on a mission. Don't worry, we won't leave without you."

I scoffed. "Since when has that ever been a problem?" My words dripped with sarcasm.

Adam tilted his head as he studied me. In moments when Adam was serious (which weren't very often), you could really see the resemblance between him and Chris; the familiarity of his focus almost caused me to melt from my defensive stance.

"Are you all right?" he asked, genuinely concerned.

I wanted to blurt out what I had just seen and heard; I wanted to scream it from the treetops so Adam could tell me not to be ridiculous and that I was overreacting. I wanted desperately to be pacified, assured that everything was going to be okay.

Instead, I said, "I'm fine." I broke my gaze from his sexy, Chris-like eyes.

As I moved past him he caught my arm. "Hey, Tammy. Don't let my brother upset you. I know he can be a dick sometimes but you know what he's like." He shrugged.

What was he talking about?

I tugged my arm free as something primal peaked inside me. I had been in a hell of a mood this afternoon but something in Adam's words that had been meant to comfort rubbed me the wrong way.

This was so not about Chris. But if it had been … I shook my head. "You don't know him at all. None of you do, you only see what you want to see. You think just because people seem good and pure on the outside that it means they're good people? Sometimes people need to stop with the wisecracks and smart-arse innuendos and have a proper look at the person inside, because as it stands, if I had to choose between being stranded with any of you lot or Chris, believe me, I would rather be stranded with him, a hundred percent."

And just as I was about to lift my chin and stride away like a bad-arse, someone cleared their throat from behind me.

Chapter Thirty-Eight

Not again.

Adam nervously rubbed the back of his neck and openly cringed. I didn't need to guess too hard who was behind me.

Chris displayed a perfect poker face, as if he hadn't just overheard my mad rant about him.

"Ready to go?" he asked.

I nodded, staring at the dirt as I turned coyly back to Adam.

"Bye," I said quietly, like a chastised child.

I was so embarrassed. Adam's mouth had gaped several times during my impressive spiel. I had thought he was trying to butt in, to defend himself and the group from my rage, but thinking about it now, he was probably trying to warn me of the captive audience behind me, the audience I now brushed past on my way toward the van.

This had not been an ideal start to the day. I mean, seriously, it's not like we were all hanging out in a maze, accidentally turning a blind corner and happening upon heated *private* conversations. We were camping, for goodness sake. Even if Chris had overheard my character appraisal of him, I couldn't have been gladder to get into his black panel van and get some distance from everyone else for a while.

Maybe Ringer, Stan and Bell were the lucky ones, away from all the drama, the drama that was no doubt going to get a whole lot worse.

Mercifully, Chris didn't mention a thing. He simply slid in behind the wheel and fidgeted himself into comfort, inspected the side mirror, selected a cassette and adjusted the volume. He oversaw every action meticulously, like a pilot ticking off his protocols in the cockpit of his aeroplane. I had become accustomed to his little ritualistic tics over these last few days – the familiarity comforted me, and Lord knows I needed to be comforted. Chris pulled into gear and edged us away from what had been our temporary home and I let the sweet sound of Bruce crooning out of the speaker soothe me away from my troubled thoughts.

We pulled behind a line of cars at the mouth of the track that led out of the grounds and spilled off onto the main road. Sean's suntanned arm rested on the open window of his twin cab at the front of the queue, Amy by his side with her legs on the dash.

"Next stop, Portland," he shouted out of his window, saluting his brow and turning onto the main road.

Adam followed next in Ringer's bright canary yellow Ford, Ellie readjusting her ponytail in the rear-view without a care in the world. They edged out, followed by Toby's blue ute idling directly before us. My eyes burned into the back of them, my mouth agape as I saw Toby flash a smile at Tess, saying something that made her laugh. So light, so normal as if the only person carrying the weight of impending doom was me.

The burden was heavy, lodged in my chest. I swallowed it down as I slid Chris's sunglasses over my eyes.

Soon it was our turn and we pulled onto the main road and fell into place behind the conga line of cars winding their way toward the coast, a step closer to Point Shank.

***

I can't exactly say I was uncharacteristically quiet; I wasn't a chatterbox to begin with, nor a social butterfly. That was probably the one thing Chris appreciated about me, how I was perfectly content with silence, so he didn't mind me being his plus one. But there is silence and there is *silence*, and my silence this time was electric and generated a swirl of tension between us.

A part of me wanted to tell Chris what I had heard between Toby and Ellie. These were his friends, he had a right to know. Maybe he'd tell me what to do. Did I do anything? Did I confront Toby? Tell Tess? Accost Ellie? Or did I mind my own business and stay out of it entirely? My leg jiggled up and down as I mulled it over. It was a nervous habit – it always bounced like that when I was anxious – and apparently it was very annoying, or so Chris said as he reached over and clamped his hand on my knee.

My whole body stilled. The feel of Chris's hand on my bare leg burned my skin and wiped my memory clean of all my thoughts and troubles. Anytime we came into contact, no matter how big or small, my body reacted in the most disturbing of ways.

"Stop it," he said, moving his hand away and leaving a warm impression on my skin. I almost wanted to start moving my leg just so he would reach over and touch me again. I crossed my arms and bit down on my thumbnail, concentrating fiercely on not jiggling my leg.

"He'll be all right, you know." Chris's words broke me away from my thoughts, my eyes shielding their confusion behind his sunnies.

When I didn't answer he continued, "Ringer – he'll only need a few stitches. Trust me, I've seen him banged up worse over the years."

Oh God. Ringer. I'd forgotten all about him.

I inwardly cringed, feeling even worse. *Poor Ringer, poor Tess. Who else could I pity?*

"You weren't even thinking about Ringer, were you?" Chris asked, glancing at me and back at the road.

I chewed on my lip. "No," I admitted, hating how guilty I sounded when I said it.

Chris sighed. "You're not worrying about my bonehead brother, are you? I threatened him with grievous bodily harm if he goes stirring."

My mouth involuntarily curved upward. I could totally imagine Chris had done exactly that.

"Although, thinking about it," he continued, "probably a bit harsh considering."

"Considering what?" I asked.

"Well, we are kind of provoking them to talk about us, so we can't exactly get mad if they do."

"True. Still, you don't want to be known as 'Christopher Condom' to your mates, do you? You know how a nickname can stick."

Chris laughed. "I'm guilty of handing out a few myself."

"Oh? Like what?"

Chris winced. "You know Alan Pasternack?"

My smile fell from my face. "You didn't."

"I did."

I didn't know whether to openly gasp or be impressed. Alan Pasternack was a year below Chris at school and had been famously known for being the paper delivery boy whose mates bet him one hundred dollars to cut his hair into a mullet. He never saw the hundred dollars and the mullet stuck around a bit too long. But more famously than that, Alan got a nickname: Pastel-Knacker. It was both cringeworthy and highly amusing and all of a sudden I saw the Onslow Boy in Chris, in the devious, boyish grin he flashed.

It was kind of hot.

I controlled my urge to smile and looked out of the window as I said, "Kids can be so cruel."

"Well, I imagine there isn't much word play on a name like Tamara Maskala."

I thought back to a less happy time. "I think the worst I got in school was Tamara Mascara."

"Not the most imaginative lot," Chris mused. A service station loomed on the horizon and Chris flicked the indicator on. "Better top up," he said, veering off the main road toward the mustard and off-white service station.

"Mmm," I responded, my mind miles away, this time not haunted by the present but by the past.

Chris pulled into the servo, unclipped his belt and slid out.

"Did you want anything?"

I shook my head.

Minutes passed, but it could have been hours for all I knew as I stared off into nowhere, shucking off my shoes and hugging my legs so as not to jig them while lost in my thoughts.

A burst of warm air flooded through the front seat as Chris opened his door and slid back inside, juggling an armful of drinks and chips: two of everything.

He rustled through his goods. "Chewy?" He held out a Juicy Fruit packet. I smiled, held out my hand and he flicked two white parcels onto my palm.

"Thanks," I said, popping both into my mouth. I chewed my gum and watched Chris's profile as he took a long swig on a bottle of creamy soda. I was thankful that he didn't press me for my thoughts, demand to know what was wrong. He wasn't that guy.

It seemed I was more guarded than I realised, although I should have known, seeing as how I kept my guard up even with Amy, my best friend. It wasn't normal to keep things bottled up, was it? Keeping things to yourself, keeping secrets? Look at Toby and the colossal mistake he was making by not speaking up. Not that I had such a burden of my own, still not thinking Chris would really care to know. I decided against my better judgement to voice my thoughts.

I grabbed my knees tighter and parked my gum in my cheek so I could talk without chewing. "When I was in Year Seven, I remember all the boys compiled a list."

Chris lowered his drink, looking at me as if surprised his quiet companion was suddenly speaking. Or surprised I was out of the blue talking about when I was in Year Seven. Or both.

He shifted in his seat, facing me to listen.

"It was a list of the perfect dream girl; if they could take traits from each girl in our group, what would it be? So they chose Melinda Smart's legs, Fiona Martin's face, Amy Henderson's body, Carla McKay's hair ... something of each girl in our group. They even chose hands, eyes, personality."

"Sounds like Frankenstein's bride," mused Chris.

I laughed. "Yeah, pretty much."

"So what part were you sacrificing?" Chris asked, screwing the lid back on his drink and placing it aside.

I stared at my knees. "They didn't want anything from me." I shrugged. "Not even my brain."

I said it so matter-of-factly I didn't expect for Chris's good humour to slide away, for his eyes to narrow. I wasn't looking for pity; it was just what had been on my mind.

The mind is funny how it can flow like a stream; wash from one subject to the next. Tammy Mascara wasn't even all that bad; it certainly wasn't my worst memory. Being the frizzy-haired, shy girl in school hadn't been easy. I hadn't fit in then and I didn't now, but that was okay. Even though many of my personal traits remained the same, I was happy to say I wasn't that shy girl anymore. I had worked hard to ensure that.

Chris opened and closed his hand on the steering wheel, focusing on the motion, deep in thought.

"Yeah, boys do things like that," he said quietly. "In fact, I probably would have done the same thing if I'd been there."

What was he saying? That he wouldn't have picked any part of me as his dream girl, either? Something panged inside me, a raw emotion that bubbled to the surface and pooled into a toxic slick.

It was an honest admission. I just hadn't expected my heart to sink so much.

"Mine would have been a bit different, though," he said, his brow furrowing, concentrating on the flex of his hands as they clasped the steering wheel. Clench and relax, clench and relax. Perhaps this was his leg jiggling equivalent. I was considering reaching out to stop it in a moment; I smiled a small, secret smile at the thought.

His hands slid over the wheel, his beautiful hands.

"Oh, and what would have made yours so different?" I half laughed, hoping it didn't sound too forced.

His hand stilled. Gripping the top of the wheel, he sat straight back in his seat.

"Because if I'd had to choose perfect, I would have just chosen you."

He had said it so clearly. Matter-of-fact. So certain, and now his eyes were on me, deep and burning as if a fist had wrapped around my heart and squeezed it to a stop.

I swallowed deeply, looking at him, waiting for him to break into laughter, to say 'just kidding' and start the car up and be back on our way.

But he didn't.

"I would choose your legs even when they're jigging and driving me to distraction. I'd choose your face because it creases into something so amazing when you find something funny (which, incidentally, isn't often enough for my liking).

"I'd choose the way your cheeks go red whenever you're embarrassed, just like they are now.

"I'd choose the fact that you're smart, kind and funny and you don't even know it." His eyes ticked over my face in a long, silent study. "It's a pretty big list, but yeah. I'd choose everything about you."

My chin trembled like I was a small child.

"Well, you obviously don't remember the frizzy-haired girl from school, because I assure you if you did—"

"I remember," he said, cutting me off. "I remember the knock-kneed, shy girl who used to drink raspberry lemonade in the restaurant and openly swoon at Sean Murphy every time he came into your vicinity."

I cringed. Yep, he remembered me.

Chris smiled. "You're not as invisible as you think."

Chapter Thirty-Nine

There was nothing like the blast of a car horn to pour ice water over a moment.

Sean pulled in behind us, honking his horn in a series of annoying rhythms.

"Way to go, lead foot!" he shouted out of the window.

The whole way from Evoka Springs, Chris had overtaken every car until he'd had an open road in front of him. It had earned him some jeering, lewd hand gestures and aggravated toots along the way from Sean, Adam and Toby, but Chris had just coolly saluted and flattened the accelerator pedal to the floor.

As I checked my flushed cheeks in the rear-view mirror, a yellow car appeared in the reflection as Ellie and Adam pulled in next. Seeing them brought me back to reality. They pulled into a parking bay. Toby and Tess wouldn't be far away.

"It's not my fault you drive like an old woman," Chris called back.

As he went to open the car door I grabbed his arm.

"Do we have to go with the others?" I said.

Chris's gaze dropped to where my hand rested. I quickly drew it away, my mind whirring over how best to explain my outburst.

From the look on his face, Chris was wondering the same thing.

Please don't ask me why. I didn't want to face Toby and Ellie. I honestly didn't know what I'd say to them if I did.

He silently appraised me as if I were some puzzle that had to be solved. I braced myself for the questions to begin, so when he did nothing more than open his car door and slide out of the seat, I didn't know how to feel about that. Had I angered him by wanting to ditch his friends? I guessed that was essentially what I was asking.

"An old woman? On behalf of old women everywhere, I resent that," Sean said incredulously as he ambled over to Chris.

"You try lugging all this gear weighing me down – the ute's half full of Amy's beauty products."

"I heard that," called Amy from Sean's ute.

Chris leaned his elbows on the open door of the van. "You going to wait at Portland for the verdict on Ringer?"

"Yeah, I'll call Stan when we get there," said Sean.

Chris nodded sombrely. "Okay. We might push on past Portland, catch up with you at Point Shank." He said it so casually, like it was no big deal, but Sean's eyes immediately darted toward me, then back to Chris.

He flashed a less-than-subtle cheesy grin. "I see," Sean mused.

"What's going on?" Adam sidled up with a bucket of hot chips and a Coke under his arm.

"We're getting ditched," said Sean.

"Get stuffed." Chris half laughed before slinking back into the driver's seat, shutting his door. "I won't be sorry to leave your ugly mugs behind," he quipped, starting up the car. Sean leaned his arms on the open window.

"How do you put up with him, Tammy?" Sean asked.

I eyed Chris. "Oh, you know, he kind of grows on you."

"Yeah, like a fungus," added Adam.

Chris gave him the finger while revving the engine, as if the purring growls were some kind of threat.

"All right then, you know where we plan to meet up?" Sean changed the subject.

"I know the place," said Chris.

"Remember?" Sean held a finger up to his lips miming, 'Not a word.''

What was that all about?

Chris nodded, as if whatever this secret was would be taken to the grave.

I thought I was the only one burdened with a secret, but the boys didn't look burdened – they looked smug. And there was nothing more frustrating than a smug Onslow Boy.

There was no use even asking – they no doubt had some stupid boy code that wasn't going to be broken.

"You're right to go?" Chris asked.

"Yes!" I straightened.

Let's get the bloody hell out of here before Toby arrives.

Chris's brows rose, taken aback by my enthusiasm.

"All right then." He pulled into gear. "See you fellas at Point Shank."

"Keep the home fire burning for us till we get there," Sean said with a wink.

Chris sounded his horn and sped off, leaving the others as nothing more than small dotted figures in our rear-view mirror. I knew what would be happening; they would all be gathering around asking Sean what that was all about. There would be some sarcastic comments made and speculation would run high.

Amy might have even been a bit pissed off that I hadn't spoken to her before leaving. It had all happened so fast I hadn't eve had a chance to think about it.

When the question had tumbled out of my mouth, the last thing I had honestly expected was for Chris to agree and leave the others behind. At best, we had one more night together on the road before we reached Point Shank.

My stomach churned and I didn't know if it was relief or dread that filled me at the thought of reaching our destination so soon. The others may assume it was some secret lovers' tryst, but, in truth, I just couldn't face the group. Couldn't stomach seeing the unhappiness in Tess's eyes. I had to tell her what I'd heard, I knew I did. It was the most confrontational thing I would force myself to do and I felt sick to my stomach just thinking about it. Something needed to be done, I just didn't know if I would do it before or after the New Year. I had exactly one more night to figure it out.

***

I expected Chris to ask why I had wanted to leave the others behind. But he didn't. His stony silence was a welcome refuge; maybe he had simply wanted some peace and quiet too.

But there was this thing wedged between us now, this unspoken elephant in the room. I couldn't believe the others had interrupted us at that exact moment between us, leaving so much unsaid. He had mentioned things that made my stomach twist, but now as I glanced at his profile I saw nothing but the Chris of old, the shut-down, intimidating businessman, though I was well over being intimidated by him. If anything, he was just damn frustrating; his mood transformed within seconds and I just never knew what I was going to get.

I placed the sunnies on top of my head, and turned to look at him – really look at him. "Why are you always so serious?" I asked.

Chris scowled as if on cue, something I found more amusing these days. "What do you mean?" he asked. He rolled one shoulder, guarded. Annoyed.

I watched him intently. "You're not like the other guys."

Chris breathed out a laugh. "Well, I'll take that as a compliment."

I didn't answer.

Chris's humour dissolved. "I have my own brain and I use it. I'm not a sheep. I don't just follow anyone."

"Yeah, but sometimes it's about just joining in and having a laugh," I said.

"So in other words you want me to be a stereotypical Onslow Boy?"

Did I? Did I want him to be a larrikin? Flirty and bubbly, loud and occasionally obnoxious?

That wasn't Chris.

Chris stared intently at the road. "To be honest, I really don't care what people think. If a group of girls made a list of the perfect Onslow Boy, do you really think they would want any part of me?" he said with a smirk. "Ninety percent of the time I'm the only sober person, the buzz kill, the responsible one coaxing girls down from tabletops, breaking up fights, cleaning up vomit, calling last drinks, being designated driver."

"Why's it always you, though?"

"Someone's got to do it. If they're going to be idiots, I just want to make sure they're being safe idiots."

And just like that I saw the real Chris. Responsible, hardworking, always looking out for others, and not giving a damn what it took.

I realised I didn't have to try so hard to work out what made Chris tick – it boiled down to 'what you see is what you get'.

My heart swelled; I was overcome with attraction for the boy by my side. He didn't think himself an Onslow Boy? Oh, he was an Onslow Boy, all right. He was the glue that held the ship together. The group would not function without him, and most alarmingly of all, I knew I couldn't function without him, and it both thrilled and scared me to death.

I decided I would tell Chris about Toby, seek his advice; *but not yet.*

For now I had something else that needed to be said. "Don't you dare change for anyone, Chris Henderson."

You're perfect.

Just as I had thought, Chris didn't take compliments well. He shifted in his seat and glanced uncomfortably out of the window.

He laughed nervously. "Does this mean I make the list?"

"Yeah, you're okay, I guess," I teased, trying not to think of his perfect hands, kissable lips, and shoulders that I wanted to dig my nails into.

I swallowed. Yeah, best not to think about it.

He curved his brow at me. "Just okay?"

"Well, all right then, how about NICE." Ha! There's a word for you.

Chris's smile faltered a little. I could just see his brain ticking through memories and landing on having called my evening attire 'nice' just last night.

Now he understood how gutting it was.

"You know that nice for me means 'absolutely beautiful', right?" he asked.

What?

I crossed my arms. "No, I didn't know that."

Chris smiled. "Well, now you do."

Chapter Forty

We wound our way through the last of the bushy canopy.

As we grew nearer to Portland, the real sign of change was the ochre-coloured rock formations that intermittently sliced their way through the green landscape. Mercifully, it was on Chris's side of the car in which the scenery plunged into a sheer drop with only a flimsy white railing in front of it that didn't look like it could prevent a tricycle from plummeting over the edge, let alone a souped-up panel van. I would personally have preferred a six-foot-high lead fence.

My skin felt sticky against the leather seat and I didn't know if it was owing entirely to the warm afternoon sun beating down on us through the windshield, or the fear of death that made my stomach reel every blind corner we took.

I thought better of it than to make conversation with Chris as he drove; I wanted his full attention on the road. I had even turned down the music a little so he could give the drive his full concentration. Beside me and my white-knuckled terror, Chris seemed really relaxed, elbow propped up on the windowsill, the warm breeze riffling through his black hair. Every so often he casually admired the beauty of the countryside, not in the least bit affected by the drop directly beside him.

I wanted to scream, "Eyes on the bloody road!" but as quickly as he looked away from the road he looked right back again.

The only words Chris had spoken during our commute through the hills were, "Not long now."

I didn't know entirely what that meant. Not long now until we arrived somewhere? Not long now and we would plummet to our deaths?

Considering he had announced that it wasn't long over an hour ago, I was very underwhelmed thus far.

But just as I thought I couldn't stand rocketing around the windy, steep hillsides any longer and would put my head into the recovery position between my knees, he said, "Tammy, look!"

Suddenly all my anguish seeped away, replaced by a bright, beaming smile. As out of nowhere we had turned a corner and bam! The ocean was right there. It was like a magic trick, as if Mother Nature had tucked away this little piece of heaven in the corner of the world, as though she had wanted to surprise us or reward us for surviving the road of death.

I'd take it. The long stretch of blue-green water surged into a delicious foamy mass against the rocks below. Now I found myself not afraid, but instead leaning over toward Chris to peer down the rocky incline.

Even though we grew up with Lake Onslow on our doorstep and were constantly in danger of being waterlogged most of our lives, there was always this mystique and wonder about the ocean. It always managed to take my breath away, especially when it appeared from nowhere.

"We're about twenty-five kilometres from Portland, so we're making good time."

"Are we stopping in Portland?" I asked, confused.

Chris dipped his sun visor against the blinding sun. "No, we'll push on through."

***

I felt pangs of regret as we drove in one side and out the other of the huge coastal town of Portland. It stretched along a vast promenade opposite a white sandy beach that was swarming with bikini-clad and shirtless tourists. People were everywhere: strolling, shopping or dining in the endless line of quirky cafes that dotted along the promenade.

Our jet black panel van roared as we made our way down the main street; it seemed so out of place in this bright, sparkling coastal town.

I could only imagine the others setting up camp here for the night, walking these streets after the evening sun had kissed the horizon. I kind of envied them. It was a far cry from the nothing that was Evoka, that was for sure. I wondered if it was too late to change our mind, to stay here and soak up the bustling atmosphere. But as we rolled farther on, down a strip of man-placed palm trees, we drove by the 'You are now leaving Portland' sign and my shoulders involuntarily sagged.

I felt like when I was a kid and my parents had just driven passed a McDonald's without stopping for a Happy Meal – the disappointment was palpable.

"Don't worry," Chris laughed, as if amused by my childlike wistfulness. "I know a better place than Portland."

I straightened with interest. "Really?"

"If you're keen, it's about five hours from here but if we crash there tonight, Point Shank is only three hours beyond that."

My heart plummeted.

Another five hours' driving today?

"Okay," I said, trying not to sound too miserable.

"It's pretty busy in town, but there's a place just up the road that serves the best fish and chips in the southern hemisphere. You want to stop?"

Poor Chris, it was like he was trying to placate my disappointment by littering the journey with little treasures so as to make it more bearable.

He had been so good. Without even questioning why, adding to all the other ways he had looked out for me, he had agreed to break away from the others. He had helped me when I'd had the migraine, he had hunted down my prescription and medication, he'd helped me into my dress, *helped me out of it ...*

I slammed the lid closed on that memory, of the embarrassing way I had tilted my head to the side, begging for him to make a move, and he had. In the opposite direction.

Yeah, best not to think about that. The remnants of that night still burned with shame, even after Amy had told me of her discovery of just how much he liked me; even after he had given me quite possibly the best compliment of my life earlier on today.

Because if I'd had to choose perfect, I would have just chosen you.

My heart may have threatened to break through the wall of my chest at the time, but now I just felt … nothing. Because I knew it wasn't for real. If I had learned nothing else these last few days, it was that Chris wasn't really in charge of his own emotions. He was a fever one minute and Antarctica the next. He seemed to struggle on any level of personal connection; the only thing he seemed to do was Band-Aid a feeling, say things that would make me feel better, like now.

Chris eased the car toward a car park. I looked at the restaurant we were pulling into …

"Does that say 'The Love Shack'?"

Chris cut off the engine and we looked up at a one-storey weatherboard cafe with bi-fold doors that opened onto a small deck with a huge red sign flashing 'The Love Shack' at us in neon.

The lobster on the sign was bending his claw into a thumbs up.

I raised my brows at Chris.

"Hey, I said they had great fish and chips, not that they would feature in *House & Garden* magazine."

"Uh, no. That would require taste," I half laughed.

"Well, I assure you the taste is there, it's just all in the food and trust me – that's all that matters."

He opened his door.

I slid out from my side, not taking my eyes from the hideous, flashing sign. If someone had told me that I was going to enter The Love Shack with Chris Henderson, I would have laughed – laughed like I was right now.

"Cut it out," warned Chris, trying to act like it wasn't funny.

I imitated the thumbs-up lobster and laughed even more.

Chris just shook his head and walked on without me.

Chapter Forty-One

Oh crap! Chris was looking at me.

He was looking at me with a smug 'I told you so' glint in his eyes as he licked the excess dribble of lemon off his salty fingers.

He sat across from me with the stretch of blue ocean at his back; it seemed so inappropriate that I was glowering at such a beautiful boy in such a beautiful place. It took all of my willpower not to glance at his lips as he pressed them together, savouring the tangy flavour.

I was still chewing thoughtfully on the most amazing piece of flake I had ever tasted in my life. I had known it would be the second I'd placed the lightly battered white flesh on my tongue.

Damn it!

"So?" Chris asked, a devilish curve teasing the corner of his mouth.

I snagged a chip out of my basket with a casual shrug. "It's all right," I lied.

Chris laughed at me and pressed his back against his cane chair. He stretched his arms into the air and linked them behind his head as his bright, toothy smile spread across his face.

"Just all right, huh?"

Attempting not to smile was impossible, I was such a terrible liar. I scrunched up my face and avoided those deep, knowing eyes. "Yeah, if you like that whole insanely delicious flavour thing, it's all right, I guess."

"Ha! I knew it." Chris slammed his hand on the tabletop, the vibration causing the salt shaker to tip on its side.

We both reached for it and grabbed it at the same time. Chris's hand rested on mine. My eyes flicked up to his face, which was now no longer lined with the lighthearted humour from a moment before. I went to move my hand away but his fingers were clasped over mine. He gave them a light squeeze.

He spoke lowly. "Careful, you know how dangerous these can be."

It took me a moment to remember. The last time we had sat alone opposite each other was when I had hidden from him under the table at the Bake House.

Not my proudest moment. Heat flooded my cheeks at the mortifying memory of that day. It also didn't help that I was more than a little aware of Chris's scorching hot skin resting on mine. I moved to sit the salt shaker upright. Chris slid his hand away, his gaze still pinning me to my seat. I brushed the excess salt off the table, trying to act casual. I could feel Chris's eyes watching my every movement.

Stop staring. Change the subject.

I cleared my throat, dusting the salty granules from my hands. "So where are we stopping tonight?"

Chris's eyes lit up as he tipped back on his chair. "Oh, just a little place I know," he said with a wolfish grin.

I cast him a dubious look. "How incredibly cryptic of you."

"It's hard to explain; you'll see in five hours' time." He dunked his chip in a blob of tomato sauce.

Five. Long. Hours.

***

Upon dusk, we veered off the main road down a side track. Finally.

My temple had been pressed against the window for the last few kilometres and I straightened up and looked around. The headlight highlighted a wooden sign with words I didn't catch as we sped by. The sudden turn made my heart leap with excitement. We had been driving in one long, straight line for hours having left the beauty and the wonder of the coast disappointingly behind. No longer dancing along its edges, we had headed inland only to be faced with flat, uninspiring country that made me wish we were winding through the hills again … almost.

I didn't know how Chris was doing it, hours upon hours of endless driving. I noticed him stretch his neck, or roll his shoulders in fatigue sometimes. I had even offered to take over for a bit, but that had just earned me a wry smile and a polite decline.

Probably some kind of territorial thing. Whatever; fine by me. I had dozed fitfully along the way, trying anything to kill some time. Of course, it didn't help that the only real reprieve from the heat had been our open windows. I didn't know if Chris wanted to conserve petrol or prevent his car from overheating or what other reason there was for not using the air con.

The last of the sun was melting down for the day, cooling the air and bringing with it a reprieve from its scorching rays, which was something, at least. The others were no doubt long settled in near the beach around Portland somewhere, setting up camp, catching up with one another, looking after Ringer.

My mind flashed back to this morning to Toby and Ellie. I pinched the bridge of my nose – I didn't want to think about them right now. This morning seemed like a lifetime ago and I kind of wanted to keep it that way. I moved to massage my temples and let out a weary sigh.

"We're nearly there," said Chris.

I stretched in my seat, wondering where 'there' was. I envisioned a glorious big bathroom with heated showers, maybe a hut with a king-sized bed. Instead, Chris veered off into an open, sandy clearing and slowed the van to a complete stop. He turned off the engine and drummed his steering wheel in excitement.

“We’re here.” He grinned, flinging his door open and sliding out.

I glanced around, examining where *here* was exactly. And just as I had suspected, *here* looked like nowhere. No toilet block, no showers, no public barbecue or picnic tables. Nothing.

Chris had said he would take me somewhere better than Portland. Having remembered the thriving cafes, glistening sand and stretching ocean, I grabbed at the open window and stared tentatively into the fading light.

Absolutely nothing.

Chris stood near my door, stretching his arms toward the stars with an almighty groan. His T-shirt lifted and exposed a flash of ripped muscle. All of a sudden I didn’t feel so dismal about our situation. Still, I would have liked some answers. I unclicked the passenger door and pushed it open. My legs felt like jelly, my circulation obviously cut off from below my waist.

“Where are we?” I winced.

“Shh …” Chris held up his hand. “Do you hear that?”

I stilled, listening intently. What was I listening for?

“I don’t hear anything,” I whispered.

“Listen,” he snapped.

I was in no mood to play Murder in the Dark, I Spy or Listen to the freakin Noise. I just wanted to have a shower, a long, hot sho—

I froze. I *did* hear something: a low, unmistakable rumble. I wondered how I could possibly not have heard it to begin with. My eyes widened as my gaze locked onto Chris. He smiled wide and bright.

“Change into your swimmers,” he said, doubling back toward the car.

I didn’t question, I just moved, quickly rustling through my gear and ducking on the opposite side of the van from where Chris was also changing. I had gone from fatigue to heart-pounding excitement. Adrenalin pumped through my veins as I tried to guess at what lurked beyond the fading light.

I secured my bikini string on my hip as I walked around the van and collided with Chris, his head entrapped inside his T-shirt as he tried to pull it over his head.

“Watch it,” his muffled voice said.

I tried not to laugh; it was a position I had been trapped in many times in a women’s changing room.

I stepped forward, gathered the fabric and pulled upward. “Hold still,” I laughed.

I didn’t actually do much, as Chris managed to yank it off his head, his hair all ruffled and standing on end, which caused me to laugh even more.

“Don’t laugh, I could have died.” He scowled.

I shook my head. “Honestly, how old are you?”

He didn’t answer, he just looked at me, his eyes darting at my attire, and then quickly back to my face. It was so fleeting, but there was no mistaking the meaning in his eyes.

It was the look I had hoped for last night in my new dress. Instead, I found it here, standing before him in my turquoise bikini. I concentrated on keeping my own gaze nice and high, away from his black footy shorts and the wall of bare taut, tanned skin just begging me to look. I would not give him the satisfaction.

"That sound better be a running shower," I said.

Chris chucked his T-shirt inside the open window of the van. "Even better." He tilted his head and started toward some bushes along the perimeter.

I called after him, "So, what, I'm supposed to just follow after you, am I?"

Chris shrugged. "Or you could stay here, by yourself."

I glanced around. Hmm, alone, scantily clad in the quickly fading light … I had seen enough horror movies where Jamie Lee Curtis screamed her way through some trying times. Yeah, not gonna happen.

"Chris, wait up."

Chapter Forty-Two

A fence? We were climbing over a fence.

Or, rather, what once was a fence and was now just a low lying wire string that had seen better days. Still, the barrier was a universal statement for keeping people out and away from something forbidden, something private, or in this case, something breathtaking.

My feet sank into the sandy embankment as I cautiously followed Chris down the steep dune. As I stepped carefully toward the horizon, I watched as the sunlight bled into the expansive, deep blue sea, but our obvious main focus was what Chris was striding for.

Closer than the sunlight glistening off the ocean was a man-made ocean pool, a barrier built up with concrete and sandstone, creating a calm expanse of water that contrasted with the rhythmic crests and swells beyond it as the ocean pummelled its edges.

The wind and sea spray tickled at our skin in the darkness, lit only by a line of towering, wrought iron street lamps. Just two were lit; all the others were dark. Damaged, smashed by bored delinquents, no doubt.

But they weren't here now. The beach was deserted.

"Are we allowed to be here?" I asked, struggling to find purchase in the sand.

"Which answer would you be happy with?" asked Chris.

"Uh, the law-abiding one."

"Then, yes, absolutely we're allowed to be here."

A sense of foreboding chilled my blood as Chris led me up the grassy track. The grass was long and wild, only partly trampled down, which suggested it wasn't well used.

"Is this safe?" I asked, hating the shaky sound to my voice. My bare arms were speckled with goosebumps and I tried to rub them away. I wasn't cold in the balmy December breeze, but nervous with the worry that what we were doing was wrong, that what we were about to do was forbidden.

Chris turned his amused focus on me as he walked backward through the grass. "So many questions!" he said with a laugh, before spinning around to concentrate on his steps.

I wanted to ask how he knew about this place, but clamped my mouth closed, thinking better of it.

No more questions. Stop being a wimp and just go with it.

I swallowed down any reservations I had and decided to enjoy my surrounds. We were no longer cooped up in the car, we were alone, just the two of us without the others and their drama, and tomorrow we would finally reach Point Shank. The others may have been settling in at Portland, even going out for tea and the clubs maybe, but Chris was right; he had taken me somewhere better than that. He had brought me to a secluded slice of paradise, even though we were probably trespassing. I quickened my pace to walk beside him, our arms brushing with every unsteady step we formed in the sand.

"Just answer me this, then."

"Mmm?"

"There isn't going to be any police tape or chalked outline of a body up here, is there? That's not the reason no one's here?"

Chris laughed. "I hope not – that would be a serious buzz killer."

And the icing on top of a long day, I thought.

My stomach twisted with excitement as we reached the railing that linked the way down toward roughened concrete steps, part of the sweeping barricade that surrounded the pool. On top, the whole perimeter of the concrete fortress was divided with steel poles with a single chain linking them together – not much of a barrier between the seeming protection of the man-made water hole and the entire ocean beyond.

Unlike me, Chris didn't seem nervous at all. As he walked along the wide edge of the pool he seemed comfortable, right at home. For some unknown reason I followed him exactly, stepping in his footsteps as if we were walking in a minefield. Why on earth wasn't this place swarming with tourists? The air was still thick and warm and the full moon rose in the sky, adding to the minimal, eerie light the two lonely lamps cast over half the pool. No amount of lighting or lack thereof would make it less uninviting, though. Unlike the ocean, it was free of seaweed and creatures of the deep … or was it? What if a shark had catapulted on a wave over the ledge? Or an octopus had wanted a sea change (so to speak)? I'd watched the Discovery channel; I had seen it happen.

I chewed on my lip thoughtfully, ready to plant myself on a concrete step and sit this adventure out.

Chris sighed. "The tide cuts off the main access from the beach, see?" He pointed toward a rocky, harsh landscape. "That's why no one's here. Plus there's a bigger pool over in Breckon Beach. That one's patrolled and popular with late night swimmers. This place would have been the go back in the '80s maybe; now it's mainly used by athletes who want to do laps without having to worry about hairy-backed men in Speedos and screaming kids."

"But we're here; I mean, we made the effort to come here, so why don't others?"

Chris ran his fingers along the chain-linked pole with a casual shrug. "Maybe they do. Maybe late night lovers come skinny dipping here at midnight … Who knows?" He stepped toward me, his hand skimming over the chain.

"You mean there might be an Onslow Boys equivalent on their way here right now? The Breckon Beach Boys?" I said, looking back to where we had walked from.

"Christ, I hope not," Chris laughed. "I'm kind of enjoying the serenity."

Yeah, the serenity littered with my thousand paranoia-infused questions. Lighten the hell up, Tammy!

I turned back around and flinched. Chris was standing close, really close, leaning on the railing with amusement.

"Guess we better not muck around then." Even in the night-time shadows I could tell that amusement lined his face; I could tell simply by the way the words had fallen off his tongue. They were tauntingly suggestive. If he thought it was funny to make me squirm under his penetrating stare, well, I wouldn't give him the satisfaction.

I lifted my chin. "Keep dreaming, Henderson. I'm not skinny dipping," I said proudly. "I don't care how secluded this place is."

The light of the moon illuminated the brilliant flash of Chris's toothy smile. "More's the pity," he said. "To be honest, I'll be amazed if you even get in." He walked right up to the edge of the pool.

"Why wouldn't I?" I said quickly.

Chris stretched his arms to the sky. "You just don't strike me as a girl who gets out of her comfort zone much."

Comfort zone?

My entire summer had been spent out of my comfort zone. This whole trip had been massively out of my comfort zone. But I had done it. Against all my better instincts, here I was. I had even been prepared to potentially do something last night with Chris that was completely out of character. I had wanted him to kiss me – everything in my body language had screamed as much at him. He would have to have been blind not to have understood that much last night, but he had known. Of course he had. Why else would he have spun around so fast other than to avoid me?

I felt not so much the burning of humiliation rising in me, but more the burning of anger.

He didn't know anything about me. So what if I didn't want to go skinny dipping? Just because I had some safety-related questions over the creepy, poorly lit, abandoned pool, I was a girl who never pushed the boundaries? That never went against the grain?

Fuck you, Chris Henderson.

My brows narrowed and all of a sudden I hoped that I was illuminated well enough that he'd see just how angry his statement had made me.

I pushed past Chris, my feet slapping angrily against the cool, wet concrete as I glanced out toward the massive pool.

"You don't have to, you know," Chris said, looking uncomfortable. "I just thought that it was kind of a cool place to bring you after a long trip."

Oh, now he was trying to be nice and supportive?

Underneath the glow of the pool light, I stood close enough to count all the different shades of brown in his eyes, eyes that ticked across my face as if trying to solve the mysteries of the universe through me. Then they lit up, as if at that very moment he had realised what my determined, serious gaze meant.

"Tammy, wait …"

It was too late. In an act of defiance, as he reached out toward me, without a second thought I dived into the water.

Chapter Forty-Three

I had been so proud, so confident.

Until I hit the water.

Not only was the pool filled with salty ocean water, I wasn't entirely convinced that the water hadn't made a direct line from an Antarctic iceberg itself. The ice-cold water sliced against my skin.

I broke through the surface, gasping with the shock of it. The freezing assault on my body that had not long ago been clammy and warm from the trek through the dunes now stung in bitter pain. But my next gasp had nothing to do with the paralysing sensation of the water.

I was met with a far bigger problem.

Oh my God! Where was my bikini top?

My feet found purchase on the bottom of the pool, allowing me the balance to be able to cover my breasts with one arm while clawing frantically through the impossibly dark water with the other. At least, I hoped it was impossibly dark.

Shit, shit, shit, shit, shit ...

"Looking for something?"

My eyes locked onto him, still standing on the pool ledge, the perfect viewpoint. My brows narrowed. Chris held up a scrap of material. Corded, turquoise strings with two triangles that dangled from his hand, dancing in the summer breeze.

This couldn't be happening.

"I feel like I'm living in a *Carry On* movie," Chris joked before clearing his throat and forcing himself to be serious. "Look, I was just trying to stop you from diving in, but, um, I kind of only stopped part of you." He swung the bikini top around his finger, averting his eyes from me.

I had never been so glad of dodgy lighting.

Chris braced himself for some kind of homicidal rant about my top, but, truth be told, as my body slowly acclimated to the freezing water, it felt good floating, my weight suspended and soothed from the stiffness, aches and pains of the day's travel. As the water cradled me, carried me, it swept all my cares away with it.

"What are you standing there for?" I called. "You look like a coat hanger, get in already."

Chris's eyebrows lifted in surprise.

"What's wrong? Cold water out of your comfort zone?" I jabbed.

Chris took a deep, chest-expanding breath. I couldn't tell if it was to psych himself up or if he was praying for patience.

"Well, here," he held up my top. "You want me to chuck you this?"

Maybe it was the calming sway of the water that lapped at my skin, or the protection of shadows, the feeling of the open air and summer breeze that rippled across the water's surface. Maybe plunging into the murky depths of the unknown had made me reborn?

I didn't know, but what I did know was that I felt free, and I liked it. I liked it a lot.

"Keep it!" I yelled, working quickly to edge my bikini bottoms down. I slid them from my legs and scrunched them into a ball. "Here," I called, and I threw them toward Chris. He caught them in shock and held them up, his brow curving.

I just smiled and removed my arm from my chest, unaware if he could even see me. But I didn't care. I kicked myself away from the ledge, deeper into the shadows.

Chris had moved closer to the lamp light; for a moment I thought he was walking away, again reaching the edge and backing off, backing away from me.

Panic spiked inside me. What had I done? Maybe I'd misread it; maybe he didn't want to get into the water with me, after all. Had what I had done in a bold, wild moment repelled him so much that he didn't want to swim at all now?

In the depths of the shadows I watched him warily, watching intently as he made his way toward the railing and worked on tying the strings of my bikini together and looping my bottoms onto the steel pole as if for safekeeping. Under the light, I caught the bemused smile and the slight shake of his head that I'm sure I wasn't meant to see. He moved toward the edge of the pool and his eyes landed on me. I hunched my shoulders under the water. Even under the protective cover of darkness Chris's eyes locked onto mine easily enough. So easily, and so readily, his smouldering, dark eyes burned directly into my soul.

I didn't feel protected by the shadows anymore – if anything, I felt like I was under a giant spotlight.

All my bold confidence gushed out of me, poured into a locked box I couldn't begin to unlock again. I felt nervous. I was so exposed.

Chris's mouth broke into a wolfish grin. "So much for not skinny dipping," he said, popping the top button of his black footy shorts.

My breath hitched as he unzipped the fly, causing the shorts to loosen a little. I quickly looked away. I was completely out of my depth.

Chris didn't dive; instead I heard the padded steps of his feet followed by an almighty splash. Water sprayed over my head and back.

His head broke the surface, gasping in a breath of horror.

"Holy shit, it's fucking freezing!" He flailed around much like I had as the shockwaves ripped through him.

I laughed, completely unsympathetic to his suffering.

"It's beautiful," I said with a sigh.

"Please tell me it gets better?" he asked, his voice filled with tremors.

"It does," I said. "Put your shoulders under. It's worse if you don't."

Chris lowered his broad, bare shoulders and my stomach twisted with regret at having given him such advice. Still, his beautiful face was visible, looking at me like he was going to say something but hadn't made up his mind whether to release the words.

I wanted to hear them. "What?" I asked.

Chris shook his head, fighting against the smile that tried to break through his lips. "Nothing."

"You were going to say something."

"Was I?" he asked with interest.

"Yeah, I could tell. What were you going to say?"

Chris dipped his head under the water for a second and smoothed his hair back off his face; he looked like he was modelling for Dolce & Gabbana, he was so breathtaking by moonlight. Although we were in a large, almost Olympic-sized pool, and we were metres apart, I couldn't help but be acutely aware of how completely naked we were in it. My heart raced with nerves as Chris swam toward me and latched onto the concrete edge in the shadows.

I swallowed, trying not to seem uncomfortable by his sudden nearness, by the fact that he was so close I could feel his breath near my shoulder.

Alarmingly, it wasn't embarrassment, or wanting to edge away that made me feel uncomfortable. I wasn't either of those things. It was a whole other sensation that spiked in the pit of my stomach that made me breathe quickly and have trouble keeping my thoughts focused and gazing above the waterline.

It was the same way I had felt last night when Chris had helped me undress in the dark van.

I inwardly scoffed. *Yeah, and that turned out so well. Christ, Tammy, get a grip of your hormones, you sex-starved maniac.*

Starved? Yeah, that was kind of an understatement; it had been a while, a long while actually. And now there was a naked Onslow Boy next to me. No wonder I felt a little unsettled! Okay, *really* unsettled.

I tried to keep cool, to look calm and casual, just like he appeared to be. Obviously my naked presence didn't have the same effect on him. That knowledge would help me stop from doing anything foolish like I had last night.

"So? You were going to say?" I tried to keep the conversation flowing, distract myself from his nearness. His *nakedness*.

Serves me right – I got into this, now I had to suffer the consequences.

Chris stood up on the pool floor, exposing his broad shoulders as the water lapped below his ribcage. I remained hovering with my shoulders under the water; I didn't have the luxury of standing.

Chris rubbed his jaw line, laughing.

"What?"

"I wasn't going to say it," he said.

"Say what? What were you thinking?" I pressed.

Chris lowered his shoulders in the water again, never moving his gaze from me as the humour in his eyes disappeared.

"I was thinking, alone in the dark with a naked, beautiful girl. This is soooo much better than Portland." He grinned.

A shiver ran down my spine and I knew it had nothing to do with the chill of the water. My heart slammed against the wall of my chest and my stomach twisted with the sheer thrill of Chris's confession.

Beautiful girl. Did he really think I was beautiful?

He was grinning like a fool, so maybe he was just joking.

"Are you sorry you left the others?" I asked, then inwardly slapped myself. Why had I just asked that? Some things I really didn't want to know the answer to, and I had the feeling that was one of them.

Chris's brows knitted together in deep thought, but he still didn't break eye contact, studying me. There was no smile, no cheeky glint of humour. It had all melted away, replaced by the stony exterior of the Chris of old. I literally braced my bare back against the concrete wall, the rough edges digging into my skin.

"Seriously, you want to know?" he asked.

After a second, I nodded involuntarily. I didn't want to know. I didn't want him to say, 'We should have stayed in Portland,' or 'I wish the others were here right now, it would be so much more fun,' or 'Are you kidding? Of course I wish we were with the others - being stuck here with you is a nightmare.'

I was snapped out of my thoughts as Chris glided through the water, and edged closer to me and my naked body. He stopped so close I dared not even move. If I did, I would brush against his bare skin and might not be able to fake the fact that it wouldn't mean anything to me.

"You really want to know?" His voice was husky and serious.

I swallowed, wishing I could just slink away into the depth of the dark water and disappear.

Escape.

But then he said, "Tammy, there is no place else I would rather be than right here, right now, with you."

Before I could take in the weight of his words, Chris edged closer, slow but deliberate.

Placing his hands on either side of me, caging me in against the pool wall, his body that sheltered me from the breeze that rolled in off the ocean was now replaced by his breath, warm and welcome on my skin. He was so close, but not touching.

I wondered if maybe it was a test: a test of wills, of who would break first. I desperately wanted to reach out to him, to bring my shaking hands up and slide them over his shoulders, to press skin to skin, drawing him near and crushing against him, like the stirrings of waves slamming against the rocks.

Chris was like a rock, a boulder hovering over me, barricading me in, his heated eyes ticking tauntingly over mine. If this was a test of wills, I forced every weakness in me to stand firm, defiant. I had made the first move last night and been rejected.

Not again.

Don't move, Tammy, don't look at his eyes – focus. Ignore the curve of his bow-shaped mouth. Christ, it looked so kissable. Try not to think about that, try not to think about the flex of his muscles so near your face, try not to think about ... oh God.

I swallowed as his leg brushed against mine, the sensation too raw, so unexpected I forced myself not to reach out and pull him toward me. As if reading the moment of weakness on my face, Chris smirked.

Cocky bastard.

He could torture me if he must, but I would not fold. No way, no how, not again. As I was about to run through the same chant in my head, over and over again to cement my stance, I suddenly didn't need to.

Chris folded first.

Chapter Forty-Four

I had expected him to pull away.

It had never occurred to me that he would close the distance between us. I had been so distracted, busy battling my own desires, controlling my urges, that I didn't notice until it was happening.

The heated look of need in his eyes made my heart stop. His gaze dipped to my lips.

I wasn't a girl being led into the dark Onslow Hotel beer garden. No, this was better. Much, much better.

I closed my eyes, waiting for him to tell me this was a mistake, waiting for him to stop. Instead, his fingers skimmed along the dip of my spine causing me to suck in a breath. My eyes flung open, locking with Chris's wicked gaze just before his mouth descended slowly onto mine. His kiss was achingly tender, brushing against my lips, capturing the breath he drew out of me, then a gasp as his body pressed against mine. My back grazed against the rough, concrete wall but the pain slicing into my skin was the furthest thing from my racing thoughts as I felt Chris's desire push against my stomach. I lifted my hands to slide over his slick shoulders just like I had fantasised. I opened my mouth to him, his hot tongue teasing mine like I had hoped it would. What had begun as a slow, soft exploration turned into frantic, deep, burning need as Chris kissed me hard. Tasting the salt from the ocean on his lush mouth, it was as if all our reservations were swept away. My arms circled around his neck, drawing him closer, pressing skin against skin with no apology. There was no room for pleasantries, just deep-seeded desire as Chris fisted my hair, tilting my head for better access to my mouth.

He broke away from his drugging kisses, his lips hovering close. "Is this what you want?" Chris breathed into my mouth.

He grabbed my leg and hooked it around his waist. I gasped as he pressed against me.

This was what I wanted, *he* was what I wanted – of this I was certain, even if just for one night.

I wanted Chris in every way.

I bit my lip, answering his question by skimming my hand along his shoulder, down his chest, over his stomach and dipping below the water.

Even in the shadows I could see his face transform – his eyes fluttered closed and he breathed out a long, shuddery breath across my neck. He wrapped his hand around mine, guiding me up and down below the water.

This was madness. Our intensity for one another, the way our mouths found each other as if we fitted together so perfectly there was no question what was going to happen.

"Tammy, look at me," Chris said, his voice raspy.

I lifted my eyes, almost shy, despite the way my hand slid across the most intimate part of him. He swallowed hard, stilling my movements.

"Are you sure?"

My lids were heavy and my body shivered against every sensation, against the slide of Chris's palm over my belly as he brushed the backs of his fingers over my breast.

"Yes," I breathed.

"Because if you want, I'll stop," he whispered, cupping my breast and kissing my neck.

Like hell I wanted him to stop.

I hooked my other leg around his waist, leaving nothing to his imagination. He claimed my mouth, kissing me so fiercely and rocking his hips against me. I thought I had died and gone to heaven.

This was really happening; it didn't get any closer than this. Chris drew back a little and positioned himself to glide his way inside me. He was teasing, gentle, soothing me for what was to come before he pushed, and just before he did, panic twisted in my stomach.

"Chris, wait," I said.

He froze. "What's wrong?"

I bit my lip, feeling awful for stopping right before, but better than after.

"Do you, um, do you have ... protection?" I asked, my voice small. I inwardly cringed, hoping it wasn't a mood killer. My gaze lifted, expecting to see his face crease with disappointment.

Instead he backed away a little, which was almost worse. His brows lifted and his eyes, once cloudy and deep with need, blinked as if clearing the fog.

"Shit, Tam, I'm sorry, I didn't even think."

This was what I had been afraid of, the sudden burst of reality slamming home. I braced myself for more apologies, for mutterings that what we had done was a mistake and it wouldn't happen again.

I cursed myself for stopping him, but some things were just non-negotiable.

No part of him was touching me now. I wrapped my arms around myself, my body aching as the heights of the pleasure and heaven I had felt a mere moment before were ripped from me.

"Hey, Tam." His hand touched my cheek, forcing me to look at him. "It's all right, we just got carried away is all, but we stopped in time."

I closed my eyes, feeling the hot moisture pool behind my lids.

"Yeah, stopped before you did something you would live to regret," I said, pushing away from the wall and moving to pass him.

"Whoa, wait a sec." His hand snaked around my wrist and he pulled me back. "This isn't over, not for me," he said seriously.

I stared up at him, my mind whirring in maddening circles, fearing to hope.

"What are you saying?" I whispered.

He pulled me closer, circling his arms around my waist. "What I'm saying is I want to go to the ends of the Earth with you."

He swept a wet tendril of hair away from my brow, cupping my face, before lowering his mouth against mine so tenderly I melted against him.

"And, furthermore, if we're going to do this, we have to do it right. In every way." His thumb brushed tenderly across the seam of my kiss-swollen lips.

My heart swelled; I was falling for what could be the most amazing person I had ever met. It was almost impossible to comprehend that I was once so intimidated by him, hiding under tables and dreading the hours spent by his side on this trip. I knew this tender side to him was not always front and present, that it was often overshadowed by the equally brooding, bossy, moody part of him. But I couldn't help but be completely and utterly in awe of all that was Chris. To me, he was bloody near-on perfect.

Chapter Forty-Five

I had never felt more alive.

Chris turned around as I stepped out of the water and grabbed for my bikini. I slipped into it lightning fast. I glanced anxiously toward Chris's back as he looked out over the ocean. My lips tilted up at the endearing gesture, considering the heat and passion of only moments before.

Securing the knot at the nape of my neck, I scooped up Chris's shorts.

"All done. Here!"

He turned in time to catch them.

"Lucky they didn't get swept away," I said.

"Well, that would have been awkward," he said, pulling them on under the waterline. "I don't see any fig leaves I could have used in their place."

"Oh, I don't know," I said, looking out at the dunes. "We could have gotten creative. Worst-case scenario we could have made you a nice mankini out of my bikini top." I laughed.

Chris grimaced, lifting himself out of the water. "I think I would have opted for a moonlight nudie run, for both our sakes."

I combed my fingers through the knotted tendrils of my hair. I may have been refreshed from the swim, but as the salty seawater dried on my skin it certainly didn't leave me feeling clean.

As if reading my very thoughts, Chris grabbed my hand. "Ready for that shower?"

My eyes narrowed; he was just teasing me, and a shower was an impossibly cruel taunt.

"You should never joke about such things," I said, looking at him sceptically.

"I wouldn't dare," he smirked and led me up the concrete steps. We reached the very top and stopped.

"See?" he said, tilting his head forward.

There it was – an outdoor beach shower. "Does it work?" I asked, trying not to dance on the balls of my feet.

"There's only one way to find out." Before his last words had left his mouth the race was on.

Not only did it work – and sure, it was cold, but I couldn't have cared less – but it was clean, fresh water that flowed over my salty body and I had Chris by my side, playfully nuzzling my neck and skimming my ribcage in tortuous, ticklish circles.

No one had ever made my heart pound so hard just by the look in their eye before. My body flooded with heat even after an ice-cold shower.

The second thing I wanted perhaps more than a clean shower was to get back to the van and fast.

***

Even walking back up the sandy dunes to the track seemed more manageable when Chris was holding my hand. I had to fight the urge to stop him in his tracks and kiss him like crazy, but he strode a long, determined path back to the van – so determined I struggled to keep up. As we made our way through the clearing, my heart rate spiked as I saw the panel van in the distance. We closed in and I instinctively moved to the back doors but Chris stopped me. Instead, he pulled me toward him and lifted me onto the bonnet of the car.

I squealed at the unexpectedness of it. The engine still felt warm underneath me as Chris pushed his body between my legs, cupping his hand behind my neck and drawing a deep, passionate kiss from me. My insides were on fire and adrenalin coursed through me at the thought that he was going to do me on the bonnet of his car.

Oh, how my life had changed.

His hands rested on either side of my hips, and he leaned forward and stole another kiss.

"Wait here," he said against my lips, before he drew away and walked to the back of the van. I pressed my fingers to my lips, and, still tasting the remnants of his salty kisses, I smiled. I hoped that he was searching for something in particular. So when he returned holding a … towel? I couldn't help but feel bitterly disappointed.

He threw it toward me, catching it before it engulfed my face.

"Thanks," I said, smiling weakly as I started to towel dry my hair. "What's that?" I eyed the folded square of black fabric in his hand.

"Oh, I thought you might want to do away with the flanny PJs tonight. I have a clean T-shirt." He handed it over to me. "It will swim on you, but it will be more comfortable."

This time my smile was genuine as my fingers traced the soft black material in my lap. Here I was, like a sex-crazed nympho thinking about nothing but wanting him to grab a condom, and his first thought was getting me into comfortable clothes, not pulling me out of them. Chris had even changed into a dry pair of board shorts.

I blanched at my wicked thoughts.

I towel dried the end of my hair in a daze, my bones weary from a long day as I pushed my wanton desires aside.

"Here." He laughed, taking the towel from me, and, draping it over my head, rubbed vigorously, to the point that I complained.

If he thought this was sexy …

"Ow-ow-ow!"

He pulled the towel away, breaking into a fit of laughter as he looked over my tousled hair, rubbed into the consistency of straw.

"Shut up," I said, glowering at him as I ran my fingers through the untamed mass.

Chris smiled so brilliantly I couldn't be mad for long. He grabbed for the T-shirt, flicked it out, and bunched it up to the neckline.

"Arms up," he announced.

I rolled my eyes. "You're actually enjoying this, aren't you?"

"Well, I don't fancy my chances of explaining to everyone how you managed to get pneumonia in the middle of summer," he mused.

I lifted my arms straight up, allowing him to drape the over-sized T-shirt over my head, yanking it free with a forceful pull as I poked my arms through the sleeves.

Under the T-shirt, Chris's hands skimmed around my back as he pulled the strings to my bikini free. A thrill shot through me. I may have been covered by the T-shirt, but it didn't make what he was doing any less exciting. He moved up to the nape of my neck and gently tugged the cord with expert ease. The bikini fell away as he pulled the material free.

I watched as his Adam's apple bobbed in his throat, his hands skimming along the edges of my breasts and down my ribcage to the bikini strings at my hips. My breath caught in my throat. He stilled for a moment, carefully watching my face for my reaction, before he slowly started to slide my bikini bottoms off me. I leaned back on my hands, lifting my bottom so he could free them and slide them down my legs.

I had never felt sexier, perched up on the bonnet of a black car in nothing but an oversized black T-shirt, with Chris's hungry eyes on me.

I knew what was to come; I sensed it in the intense way we looked at one another, in the way our chests heaved, the way my body arched toward Chris at the slightest touch. Blame it on the summer holidays, the full moon or the moonlight swim. I didn't know exactly what was to blame but all I knew was my blood burned with need for him.

Regardless that in the light of day it could be a colossal mistake. I didn't care; all I cared about was the next instant he touched me or kissed me. I slid slowly off the bonnet.

He had made the most important first move tonight, so now it was my turn to make the last. I grabbed his hands and laced them with my fingers, pulling him toward the van. Stepping past the passenger door he stopped me dead in my tracks and my heart sank.

"Tam, hang on a sec." Chris let go of my hands and pulled open the passenger door. "Don't want to cover the mattress with sand," he said, tilting his head with a cheeky grin.

My eyes fell to our bare feet caked in wet sand. Relief flooded every part of my being as I dived into the front bucket seat and slid across.

Chris followed me in and closed the door.

Chapter Forty-Six

We were, once again, just two people in the front seat of a car.

Well, a little bit different than any way we might have occupied the front seat before.

I straddled Chris's lap, his fists gripping the material of the T-shirt at my hips. Our hot, delving kisses stole the ability to breathe from us both as we frantically clawed at one another. I ran a trail of kisses teasingly down his jaw line and neck to his collarbone. He groaned with approval and grabbed the backs of my knees, pulling me closer to him still. I gasped at the friction. Chris kissed me so passionately, murmuring words between his draw of breath as he tauntingly skimmed his hands under my T-shirt.

"Let's get in the back," he breathed into my mouth.

"What about the sand?"

"Fuck the fucking sand," he said, motioning for me to lift off him. We frantically manoeuvred our way over the back seat and crashed clumsily onto the soft mattress in a heap.

We couldn't help but laugh at ourselves; we had finally made it here, to the darkened, secluded van. I took the moment to mention the main issue.

"So, um, do you still have Ringer's … you know?" I asked, feeling heat flood my already flushed face.

Chris sat up. "Shit, yeah, hang on a sec …" He stilled. "FUCK!"

I flinched. "What?" My eyes widened and I sat up.

Chris ran his hands through his hair in despair.

"How could I be so freaking stupid?" He threw himself back on the mattress.

"Chris? What the hell?" I shifted onto my knees, alarm rising in me more every second that passed.

He sighed deeply, hitching himself onto his elbows. "I put it in a really safe place," he deadpanned.

"H-how safe?" I asked, fearing to know the answer.

"I tucked it in one of the shoes you brought back last night."

My eyes widened, horror overriding my worry.

Toby's shoes? The shoes I had thrown against a tree in a fit of rage?

"Why would you do that?" I asked.

"Well, I didn't want it swimming around the back of the van, I wanted to hide it, so I just shoved it in there when I was packing up the van."

"You know, wallets are also handy places to stow such things," I said.

"Yeah. Well, I didn't think of that at the time, obviously."

I cupped my face with my hands before something dawned on me. "Wait a minute, you watched me take those shoes from you, knowing I was going to return them to their rightful owner, knowing full well that ..."

"I swear, it completely slipped my mind. There is no way I would have let you. I just ... I don't know. Got distracted." He sighed, before the lines in his face transformed into pain. "Whose shoes were they, anyway?"

"Toby's," I said.

Chris scoffed. "Well, he's going to get a nice surprise next time he tries them on."

Um, yeah. About that ...

I chewed on my thumbnail. I looked at Chris eating himself up over a foolish mistake. I could have kept it to myself, but thought better of it.

"He's going to get a bigger surprise than you think," I said, cringing at what I was going to say.

Chris's brows lowered. "What do you mean?"

"Well, they didn't exactly make it back to Toby," I confessed.

Chris lifted one brow. "Oh?"

"Before you get too excited, they're not here," I said quickly.

A bemused tilt formed in the corner of Chris's lips. "Where are they, then?"

I squirmed under his gaze. "They may or may not be up a tree, back in Evoka."

Chris blinked, as if he wasn't fully comprehending.

"Why are they up a tree?"

To tell Chris why meant explaining why I'd been so pissed at him and I really didn't want to have to revisit this morning's fight. Not tonight. I just wanted to forget; in these glorious moments in Chris's arms, I wanted all the worries and the weight of the world to melt away.

"A prank gone wrong, you might say."

"That's an understatement." Chris sighed, throwing himself back onto the mattress.

I lay down next to him and placed my head on his chest. "Is now when you tell me not to stress because you have one in your wallet, anyway?" I asked, hoping against hope.

Chris scoffed. "Well, to be honest, it was originally going to be an all-mates' fishing adventure; I didn't see the need to stock up."

I felt both disappointed and relieved. I lifted myself onto my side, staring down at him.

"What, no woman in every port?" I teased.

"What?" Chris asked, confusion etched on his face.

"Nothing," I said, settling down, resting my head back on Chris's bare chest. His heart pounded hard and fast against my temple; it was soothing, as was the familiar feeling of Chris folding his fingers through my hair.

I still didn't know whether to laugh or scream – against all the odds of trying to forget the disaster of this morning's run-in with Toby and Ellie, my actions had only led to completely backfire tonight.

Was this the universe's way of punishing me for being a coward and wanting to leave the trouble behind me, to avoid confrontation for as long as I could? Maybe it served me right – my fence-sitting ways in the past hadn't exactly gotten me far. If anything, the moment I stepped out of my comfort zone, look what happened: I was lying in Chris Henderson's arms, and I had never felt more alive.

I wanted to hold onto that, and I wanted to release the burden I carried with me. Maybe by talking to Chris about it he might be able to help. He had known Toby all his life, after all.

I lifted my head off his chest. "Chris?" I whispered, touching his shoulder.

I was met with silence and the sudden realisation that he was no longer stroking my hair. Instead, he lay there, sound asleep. His chest rose and fell slowly, his beautiful bow-shaped lips relaxed and no lines etched his brows in worry or stress. He looked so peaceful.

My heart ached for him – he had had no sleep last night after our awkward exchange. He had then had a long day's worth of driving, only to end it with a moonlight skinny dip with me.

I smiled at the memory of every kiss, every touch. I didn't want to wake him, especially not to tell him about Toby. I would let him get a good night's sleep, rest up for the last leg of the journey tomorrow. If anything, I had to fight the selfish urge to wake him up to assure me that no matter what, in the light of day there would be no weirdness or regret between us.

I had seen it so many times before – late night Saturday rendezvous usually led to awkward avoidance the next day. The one thing in our favour was that there had been no alcohol involved, but still Chris wasn't the most predictable creature I had ever met. I tilted my head, looking down at the sleeping, gorgeous Onslow Boy. His features twisted into a familiar frown in his sleep. I didn't know what was racing through his mind to cause such a worrisome look, but I did what I had often thought of doing before brushing the insane moment away.

I leaned over him and gently kissed his forehead. I felt the puckered worry lines melt under my lips and I smiled, lifting myself slowly to admire my handiwork.

Chris shifted slightly and I froze, hoping he wouldn't wake. He pressed his lips together and a fleeting frown creased and disappeared as he sighed.

I moved now. Edging my way carefully to lie beside him.

"Tam?" his voice croaked.

"Yes?" I whispered.

"You got to put the pool cues back."

I bit my lip to stifle my giggles. Dreaming of work. No wonder he scowled in his sleep.

"Okay, I will," I assured him, lying down in the space beside him.

"Tam?" Chris called out.

I sighed. "Yes, Chris?"

"I love you." He turned onto his side leaving me stunned, silent and staring at his back.

Chapter Forty-Seven

You can never read too much into a dream.

How could I possibly? It was just a dream; he had no control over it, he had been dreaming of pool cues only seconds before, for Christ's sake. And if I believed that dreams had any weight to them, considering my reoccurring dream in which my teeth fell out, I was in serious trouble.

The night had left me frustrated, confused and in a bed full of sand for no reason. Sure I was clean and comfortable without my flannelette PJs, but the only problem now was that my thoughts plagued me, making sleep fitful.

I awoke with the sun streaming across my face, an unexpected intrusion considering the panel van's windows were blacked out. Shifting onto my side and shielding my eyes, I peeked through one squinted eye to spot a blurry silhouette standing at the open doors of the panel van.

"Morning," Chris beamed.

I sat up, stretching and groaning. I brushed my matted locks of hair to the side and cringed at its Brillo pad-like consistency. Suddenly I became very aware of my appearance.

Chris stood in the doorway, a warm, friendly smile spread across his lips as he leaned casually against the open door. He was dressed in navy shorts and white T with an open checked shirt over the top. He looked like he belonged in a David Jones catalogue, and here I was looking like a bag lady.

"Morning," I croaked.

"You hungry?"

I rubbed my stomach; it was hollow and begging for substance. "Famished," I said.

"Get dressed and we will hit the road." Chris stepped back in the sunlight and stretched his arms to the sky.

He seemed awfully chipper. It was a welcome sight to wake up to. I'd had a fitful sleep plagued with dreams of waking up with a note next to me, telling me he had hitchhiked back to Onslow – Happy New Year. So when I had woken to Chris's beautiful smile instead, butterflies fluttered happily in my stomach. Or maybe it was hunger? No, it was definitely butterflies, and it was nice.

By the time I got dressed into some cut-off denim shorts and a lime green singlet top, I had opted to throw my hair up into a messy bun style. Using my drink bottle I washed my face and brushed my teeth, staring off into the distance, admiring the sandy, scrubby surrounds and how different everything looked in the light of day.

What did look different, as in a hundred times better, was Chris Henderson. He whistled animatedly to the radio as he leaned over a map he had spread across the bonnet, the very bonnet he had slid my bikini bottoms off me on last night.

I blanched at the memory as my eyes wandered over the curve of pronounced muscle that flexed whenever Chris shifted, the same muscles I had explored only hours before with my hands and mouth. I shook my head, blinking away last night before I choked on my toothpaste. Now that would not be a good look.

I rinsed my mouth out, quickly spraying a zigzag line of Impulse body spray over me and dabbing on some strawberry Lip Smacker. I casually made my way around the front of the van, with a casual, no-big-deal attitude.

So we nearly had sex last night. That's what happens: people hook up and get on with it, people dream, people declare their love and then they wake up and start their day like normal. No big deal at all. Nope, nothing to write home about here; just a normal summer fling.

I stood by the side of the bonnet and leaned my elbows casually on its surface, hoping I didn't look too try-hard.

Chris's serious eyes flicked up to me with brief acknowledgement and then back to the map.

Hmm.

"I'm trying to see if there's a shorter route to Point Shank."

My heart pounded, worry licking at the edges of my overactive imagination.

"That keen to get rid of me, huh?" I teased, regretting the words as soon as they had fallen from my mouth, even more so when Chris's less-than-amused eyes flicked up to meet mine for a second before going straight back to the map.

He ignored me. "If we go this way it's about three hours." He traced his finger along a red line. "But if we go this way, we should be able to shave off about half an hour."

I nodded, looking at the map. It could have been a map of Berlin for all I knew. If I never reached Point Shank it really wouldn't have worried me; I would have forgone the seaside city famed for its New Year's Eve festival of bands and fireworks. I would sooner have stayed here, if we'd had the proper supplies like food, hair conditioner and condoms. This place would be paradise. But I knew we wouldn't stay.

I shrugged. "Which way is closest to food?"

That caused Chris's lips to tug into a crooked line. "This way." He pointed at the map.

I frowned. "The long way?"

Chris nodded.

Ha. What do you know, I was paying attention, I thought to myself proudly.

Chris folded up the map. "The long way it is."

"Oh, um, is that okay? I mean, we can go any way, it doesn't really matter. I can wait, I'm not that hungry. Seriously, go the shortcut if you want." I was babbling, I knew I was; it was a clear sign of my anxiety. It was like an out-of-body experience in that I could see myself and hear myself but I couldn't make myself stop.

Chris stared at me, amusement lining his face. He stepped forward and the subtle motion made me shut up instantly. Or it could have been the finger he placed on my lips.

My eyes narrowed but not because he had silenced me. I quite liked him touching my lips – it caused a familiar heat to flourish – but my eyes darted from his face up to his hair. I grabbed his wrist, drawing his hand away.

"Your hair's wet."

Chris ran his hand through his messy, damp hair. "Went for a morning dip. I didn't want to wake you."

Something inside me panged, annoyed at him for not waking me to freshen up with him before the last leg of the journey. The result had him looking like sex and sunshine, and I looked like sludge and death. So he had slept like a baby and had a morning dip. No wonder he was in such a jolly mood.

I crossed my arms, hoping I didn't appear as resentful as I felt; I didn't want to do an Amy and sulk for the rest of the trip.

"You talk in your sleep, you know." The words fell out of my big mouth.

Seriously, Tammy. Shut. Up.

Chris's brows rose in surprise. "Yeah? What did I say?"

I love you – I love you – I love ...

I shrugged. "Just mumbling, mostly."

"Must have had something on my mind." He half laughed, moving around the car to put the map back into the glovebox. "You know what they say about dreams?"

I moved to the passenger door and opened it, listening with interest.

"No, what?" I asked.

"They say if you dream it, it won't come true."

I forced a smile on my face, trying to be pacified by Chris's words. I mean, great – so my teeth wouldn't fall out, but his words also hit a nerve in me.

Was this his way of covering himself? Maybe he remembered his dream last night and was just whacking a disclaimer on it, unsure of which part I had witnessed.

Either way, it wasn't the way I had wanted to leave our little paradise. There had really only been awkwardness on my end of things. Chris was so relaxed, with not even any acknowledgement over last night's heat between us; it was like it had never happened.

I didn't know how I felt about that. I had been dreading so much any potential 'talk' I might be faced with in the light of day, but now there was no recognition whatsoever, as though I had imagined the whole thing.

It made me feel a bit shitty. I know that's what happens with some boys – they hook up with a girl and then go about life again. I wasn't going to be a *Fatal Attraction*, bunny-boiling 'do you want to be my boyfriend?' psycho, but I had at least thought that the exchange between us last night had been real. Intense. I knew how he had made me feel and I knew he'd felt something too.

Or at least I thought I'd known.

Suddenly I was really relieved that we didn't have a condom, because if this was how I felt about him after just fooling around then I would have been a thousand times worse if we had slept together. It was a painful realisation. Things were different in the light of day, all right.

All I had to do was put on a brave face for the next three hours.

Crap!

"Why don't we take the short way?" I said.

Chris paused before sliding into the car. "Didn't you want something to eat?"

I looked out of the passenger window, trying to keep my emotions in check. "It's okay; I'm not that hungry anymore."

Chapter Forty-Eight

The short way was both a blessing and a curse.

Although I had claimed to have lost my appetite, try telling my ravenous stomach that. I felt nauseated and was quiet throughout the trip. I didn't entirely know if it was because I was just hungry or because my insides were churning with anxiety and bitter disappointment. Considering I had dreaded our arrival at Point Shank only yesterday, now we couldn't get there soon enough even if it did mean having to face Toby and Ellie. I cared little now. I was over game players and the deception. Arriving at Point Shank meant that I would at least get a distraction and alternative company. As soon as possible I planned to give Chris some space and move into the 'singles' tent; I didn't want to be a needy nympho following him around.

Chris never asked why I was so quiet, which was more natural than anything. If there was one thing we had fallen into over the last three days it was the ability to have comfortable silences; it was one of the things I had liked most about us. Except now the silence hung in the air so thick you could carve it – for me, anyway. I was sure Chris was none the wiser over my whirring thoughts of inadequacy that only served to make me more miserable.

Over an hour into the journey we had managed to grab some takeaway food and kept going toward Point Shank. Chris seemed anxious to keep up a quick pace and when we were a mere twenty minutes from Point Shank, Chris suddenly became fidgety and unsettled. He shifted in his seat, drummed the steering wheel and adjusted his side mirror several times. I had almost been tempted to tell him to settle down, but then the scenery changed and once again we were on the outskirts of civilisation, whirring past a mixture of shops, cafes and people. Finally we approached a sign that cemented where we were: 'Point Shank NYE Beach Bash' was scrawled across a giant banner, high above the main street. There was an air of excitement, a mass of people converging on a densely populated city to see in the New Year. We'd made it.

Having arrived early on New Year's Eve itself, it was a relief knowing that at least we would have time to unwind and settle in before the madness of tonight's festivities began.

Now for the first time I actually wished the others were here too. We had arrived early, so what would we do? Locate our campsite and sit in the van all day until the others caught up? My mind wickedly flashed to a way we could kill time, but I quickly stomped that out.

Yeah, that was not going to happen.

Considering we had spent a few nights in the solitude of quiet, bushy surrounds or coastal beach culs-de-sac, now we had hit Point Shank everything seemed … loud. And visually over-stimulating. There were shouts, 'woot's and screams from merry crowds of people lining the streets, enjoying their official last day of the twentieth century. We drove past a packed caravan park where tents were dotted side by side with barely a spare patch of grass in between. There were caravans, trailers, utes, boats and four-wheel drives cluttering every inch of the road; it took us every second of our free time to manoeuvre our way through the town.

My fantasies of Chris pulling off the main road and winding through side streets to take me to some undiscovered, secret location overlooking the ocean seemed less and less likely. My heart sank.

Maybe coming here was a bad idea?

I thought Chris would say as much, seeing as he was the one actually navigating through the chaos, but he didn't seem in the least bit fazed. If anything, he was excited. I then had visions of the boys wandering off tonight, partying into the New Year. What if Chris met some girl? What if he brought her back to the campsite – what then? Sleep toe to toe with Ellie?

I really had to shut my mind down.

"So, is the camping ground nearby?" I asked, hoping that the hill we were driving up was closing in on our destination. If nothing else, there would be facilities for a hot shower and a toilet that wasn't a bush. I was desperate for a real shower.

"Not exactly," Chris grimaced.

I straightened in my seat. "Oh?" I pressed, preparing myself for the bad news.

Only four more hours past Point Shank and we're there.

"We're not exactly 'in' a camping ground," said Chris.

"Sounds ominous."

"Oh, it is." Chris flashed me a bright, pearly smile that caused my traitorous heart to jump.

My hands became clammy – the possibility of no showers, no toilets, no privacy ran through my mind in a long line of hideous scenarios. This was originally an all-boys trip and roughing it to them was no big deal. And then my mind flashed back to the last conversation Chris had had with Sean before leaving the petrol station.

"All right, then, you know where we plan to meet up?" Sean had said.

"I know the place," Chris had replied.

"Remember?" Sean had then held a finger up to his lips and mimed 'not a word'.

Oh God. What kind of hellhole had they planned to take us to? Was this some form of punishment because we gatecrashed their road trip? Was it some kind of prank Sean wanted to play on Amy that we all had to suffer through? If I had dreaded arriving at Point Shank before, now I wanted to turn around and go back home without stopping.

"Okay, I'm scared," I admitted.

Chris laughed. "Oh relax, it's not that bad. It's just going to take some … adjusting to."

Oh God, it must *be bad.*

***

I gazed out toward a grassy embankment, divided by pavement then the sandy beach. By now I was all beached out; I was no longer bewitched by the beauty of it. If anything, I was filled with so much dread and anxiety, the blue water and golden sand just whizzed by in a blur. To think I could have painted my laundry by now and be helping Mum sell her clay vaginas at the market instead.

I had never thought that would be a more appealing option than road tripping with my friends.

My thoughts were jolted back to the present as Chris pulled off the road onto the side.

I sat patiently. He probably wanted to get something out of the back. I kept looking out of the window.

"What's wrong?" His voice snapped me away from the view.

"What?"

"You're disappointed?" he asked.

My eyes met his; was he asking about last night, or Point Shank? The last thing I wanted to do was be the whingy tag-along.

I swallowed, shaking my head. "No," I lied.

"Well, we're not far, so we can settle in and wait for the others," Chris sighed, tilting his head from side to side.

"Sounds like a plan." I tried to sound upbeat but I knew I was not pulling it off.

"God, my neck is killing me. I might get a massage," he said.

Was he asking me for a massage? Is that what he was hinting at?

"Where do you suppose I could pay for one?"

No, he wasn't asking me for one.

"I don't like your chances of finding anywhere on New Year's Eve," I said.

"Maybe, but I think any place with complimentary fluffy white robes and room service should be able to offer something. I don't know, someplace ... well ... like that." Chris pointed over the road. There was a massive, sprawling, sandstone-coloured resort, lined with palm trees and a giant waterfall feature illuminated with coloured lighting that read 'Point Shank Beach Resort'.

"You can't just walk in off the street and ask for a massage." I frowned.

"Why not?" Chris asked in all seriousness.

"Because you can't."

"Well, it's worth a try; we have some hours to kill. Don't you want a massage?" He pulled the van back out onto the road, indicating a turn into the expansive driveway.

"Not at the risk of getting laughed out of the reception."

"Don't be dramatic."

It was the equivalent to a slap in the face, and my blood boiled at his ignorance.

"The fact that you're a part owner of a hotel mean it's absolutely mind boggling that you don't get how wrong you are," I argued.

Chris defiantly steered into the driveway, the thrumming sounds of the V8 engine echoing as we drove under the resort's sweeping awning.

We so didn't belong here. I wanted to shrink into my seat.

"You are so embarrassing." I smiled politely at the doorman who tried not to look over our car with judgemental eyes.

Chris killed the engine. "How about this: if you're right and they turn me away, I'll give you a massage. But if they say 'Of course, Mr Henderson, welcome to Point Shank Beach Resort, please follow me to your masseur,' then you have to give me a massage on top of my massage." He held out his hand.

He thought he was so clever.

I straightened in my seat. "I am going to so look forward to that massage." I took his hand and yanked it with all my strength.

"Deal."

We both exited the car, offering each other knowing smirks. For someone who ran a business he really didn't have a clue. The doorman opened the door for us.

"Good afternoon," he smiled brightly.

Chris stopped next to him. "Tell me something…" His eyes lowered to the man's name badge. "Graham, do you offer massages here?"

Graham nodded animatedly. "Oh yes, sir, we have a very luxurious day spa."

Chris flashed me a bright white smile. "Excellent."

I rolled my eyes and followed Chris through the door that Graham held open for us.

The first thing that hit me was the chill of the powerful air conditioning, followed by the high, cathedral-style ceilings with luxurious chandeliers that cast a bright glow across the reception's polished surfaces and the reflective gloss of the marble tiles.

Chris and I stood in the middle of the massive reception area: me in my denim shorts, singlet and bird's nest-like hair; Chris in his white T and cargos. We definitely didn't belong here, although you wouldn't have thought it by all the warm smiles every passing member of staff gave us.

We were called up to the main desk, something I was both dreading and looking forward to.

"Welcome to Point Shank Beach Resort, how can I help?" An immaculately kept woman, hair slicked back in a shiny bun, with bright red lipstick, bright sparkling eyes and a figure to die for flashed a winning smile. She made me feel like a gutter rat as I self-consciously tucked a stray hair into place.

"I was just wondering, we have just arrived in Point Shank and we're looking for a place we could get a massage. We have been on the road for three days and had some time to kill and thought we might try our luck." Chris had spoken every word with a sexy grin across his face as he looked Wonder Woman directly in the eyes and pleaded his sad case.

I sighed, amazed at how easily he could turn on the charm when he wanted. More importantly, I braced myself for the answer. The answer that I knew would come, and it did.

I saw it the second her head tilted and her high-wattage smile dimmed a little. "Oh, I'm sorry, sir, but the facilities are reserved for guests only."

Yes!

I grinned so broadly I almost wanted to break out into a dance, chanting, "I told you so, I told you so."

Chris's smile evaporated. He shifted uneasily as he glanced at my big, toothy grin with annoyance. Wonder Woman's eyes passed from Chris to me, probably thinking we were a pair of weirdos, but her professionalism never faltered, not once.

He cleared his throat. "I see."

"Is there anything else I can help you with today, sir? Maybe help yourself to some brochures on the local establishments."

"No, that's okay. Actually, um, there is something else you can help me with."

Chris pulled out his wallet from his back pocket, taking out a white square piece of paper and unfolding it.

Ugh, he was probably asking for directions to our site. I yawned, folding my arms, and admired the decadent display of flowers sitting on the marbled desk.

Chris slid the paper over. "We have a booking for a party of nine, under Sean Murphy."

WHAT?

I spun around so quickly I almost knocked over the massive flower arrangement.

"What did you just say?" I breathed.

Chris smiled, reached out, and swept a loose tendril of hair out of the way of my wild, shocked eyes.

"Welcome to Point Shank."

Chapter Forty-Nine

We followed the porter down a long, carpeted corridor.

I half expected a camera crew to appear from behind a pot plant, announcing I was on candid camera. My eyes skimmed every angle of the luxury digs.

"Are you okay?" asked Chris as he walked by my side.

My mouth gaped as I tried to summon the words; I had been stunned into silence since Chris had booked us in. After his massage ruse I feared I would never believe another word he said.

"What are we doing here?" I laughed, my insides twisting with giddiness every step we took down the hall.

"We thought that seeing as you girls would be roughing it to get here the least we could do would be to end the trip with a bit of luxury. It was Sean's idea."

"Do the others know?"

"The boys do. We wanted it to be a surprise; I think it's been the most difficult secret to keep in the history of mankind."

Chris looked at the room key card he held in his hand. "Here's your room."

I danced on the balls of my feet as Chris tipped the porter to leave the luggage. Chris couldn't open the door quickly enough. He slid the key card into the slot and the magical green light flashed in unison with Chris's smile.

"You ready?"

"Open-open-open!" I clapped.

There is always that moment of wonder when you enter a spectacular room, and after three nights sleeping in the back of a panel van, the apartment I stepped into was as luxurious to me as the Taj Mahal. Glossy white tiles, sleek, modern and massive. I ran from room to room turning on lights, inspecting cupboards and announcing every discovery.

"There's a spa! This one's got an en suite …Whoa, check out the kitchen!"

There were three bedrooms, two bathrooms, a huge open living space, a dining room and a sliding wall of glass that led out onto a balcony overlooking the ocean.

I pressed myself against the glass. "Oh my God, Chris!"

I turned to see him watching me with a glimmer of amusement as he set our bags down. "You approve?"

Did I approve? I had expected the pits of fiery hell, not a clean, crisp paradise.

"I *so* approve," I said, running over to him and throwing my arms around his neck.

I looked up into Chris's eyes. "It's a fantastic surprise."

Chris sobered as he studied the lines of my face; his eyes flicked to my mouth for such a brief second that I almost missed it. He still held me, his hand resting on my lower back. I so wanted to kiss him. My eyes strayed to his mouth, not caring if he caught the unmistakable moment of distraction. He had a beautiful mouth that did wicked things, and although last night had probably meant nothing more than just a bit of fun, I really wanted to do it again.

"I think you're forgetting one thing," he said, causing my eyes to snap back up to his.

"What's that?" I asked.

Chris leaned forward, his lips brushed against my ear and I felt my skin tingle.

"Running. Hot. Water."

***

Reclining in the huge, blistering hot corner spa with my hair completely caked in so much conditioner it was pure white, I channel flicked through my TV.

Yeah. There was totally a TV in the bathroom. I had changed it onto the music channel where Cindy Lauper was crooning 'Girls Just Wanna Have Fun'.

Yeah, they did!

I bit a chunk out of the strawberry that was wedged on the side of my champagne glass, like any classy chick would, and mused how very Julia Roberts this all was, à la *Pretty Woman.* Minus the whole being a paid escort thing, of course.

I had emerged from the bathroom wrapped in large white towels, one around me and one around my head.

"Chris?" I called down the hall. He'd said he would be back in five, that he was going to check out the others' apartments, but I had definitely been in the bathroom for longer than that and expected him to be in the lounge where the TV had been left blaring.

"Hello?" I looked around the apartment.

There was a notepad and pen left on the kitchen bench.

I spun it around, reading Chris's neat handwriting.

Check the main bedroom.

I read it over three times, every time my heart rate elevating and the same insecure girl clawing her way to the surface, turning me into a puddle of nerves. I took in a deep breath and made my way up the hall to the master bedroom, clasping my towel around me tightly before remembering the turban-esque wrap on top of my hair.

Shit! Not a good look.

I unwrapped it from my head and scurried back to the bathroom, throwing it onto the floor. I quickly wiped the foggy mirror and checked my complexion. I ran my brush through my hair before bending over and flicking it back and forth two to three times for that natural, tousled look.

"Okay," I sighed, looking at my reflection and giving myself a pep talk. "Let's go."

The walk down the hall was so incredibly long. The downlights lit the tiles that were cool underfoot. Of course, the main bedroom door was last. I stopped at the door and took a deep breath before I grabbed the gold handle, twisting and pushing it open.

I paused in the doorway, firstly confused until I switched the light on, illuminating the room and causing me to burst out into laughter. I cupped my hand over my mouth, trying to muffle the sound of hysterics as I edged closer to the bed, hardly believing what was laid out on the bed.

No, it wasn't Chris like I had hoped; instead lay a plush, fluffy white robe, the kind Chris had spoken about. I bit my lip, and shook my head. He was turning out to be quite the practical joker.

***

By the time Chris had returned, I was on the rather generous balcony in my fluffy robe, enjoying the ocean views. I heard him enter and smiled to myself, keeping my focus on the waves.

"Nice robe," he said as he settled in the seat beside me.

"What, this old thing?" I tugged at the neatly tied bow.

"Feel better?"

"Almost human."

"Well, enjoy the serenity while you can; the others are on their way. I just spoke to Sean on the phone."

I shifted upright in my seat. "How's Ringer?"

Chris smirked. "According to the staff at outpatients, he is a complete pain in the arse, so, yeah, sounds normal to me. He got eight stitches."

"Are they still coming?"

"Yeah, they're on their way, too, but they won't get here till later tonight."

"Well, we will have to make a big fuss over him when he arrives."

"Yeah, he'll hate every minute of that," Chris said with a laugh. "I hope you bagsed the best room?"

"Indeed I have: master bedroom with en suite." I beamed.

Chris grimaced. "Ellie won't like that."

And with that, all good humour evaporated. "Who's staying in this apartment?"

Chris watched me with interest. "You, Ellie, Toby and Tess, I think. Sean and Amy are sharing with Bel and Stan, and I'm shacked up with Ringer and Adam. Why?"

I'd had no idea that paradise could turn into hell in the span of two seconds, but it just had. Me, Ellie, Toby and Tess all sharing the same apartment? Now that's what you called a Love Shack.

Chris touched my knee. "Tam? What's wrong?"

I looked at him, his eyes narrowed in concern. How could I tell him? How could I complain when all the boys had done their adorable best to surprise us all? How could I be so ungrateful as to complain about my roomies? But how could I also expect myself to cohabitate with them, knowing what I knew?

I couldn't do it; I couldn't live with the very people I was aiming to confront, whose lives I was potentially going to destroy. I couldn't. Not even for just one night.

"Can I stay with you?" I blurted out. "Or can you stay here? Or I don't, I just want, or rather … stay, please?" I was pathetic, a rambling idiot and I half expected Chris's expression to reflect as such, but it didn't. Instead, his dark, broody stare narrowed in a steely gaze.

"Who do you want moved?" he asked, his words dripping with icy intent.

I broke from his gaze. "Ellie," I said lowly, looking down at my hands, almost ashamed I was asking without telling him why.

After a long, drawn-out moment, he said, "Okay."

Without another word or, like always, never even wanting to know the reason why, Chris got up from his chair and left me on the balcony, his footsteps disappearing down the hall before finally I heard the sound of the apartment door.

What must he think of me?

Chapter Fifty

I couldn't even bear to be wearing my robe anymore.

I felt like an utter coward, an ungrateful coward. I wanted to go and pound on Chris's door and blab everything. Tell him exactly why I had wanted to leave without the others, why I couldn't stand to be anywhere near Ellie, but that, above all, the one constant in this whole trip was the complete, unexpected joy of the past three days with him. The person I had nearly made love to last night; the one I still wanted to. And I didn't want to give him up.

I paced the up and down the hall, plagued by the actual problem of not knowing where the boys' apartment was. Of all the times to have the sudden compulsion to confess everything, it had to be the rare moment that Chris wasn't around.

I figured I could find out where he was at reception, so grabbed my key card. I marched for the front door and slammed right into Chris with a yelp. He grabbed my elbows to steady me and I clutched at my chest in surprise.

"I didn't hear you come in," I breathed out, my heart throbbing in my chest.

"You were kind of preoccupied," he said, throwing his key card on the bench.

"Chris, I have to tell you something." I wrung my hands anxiously together.

His gaze burned into me so intently I almost forgot what I was meant to be saying.

He shook his head slightly. "Don't."

I was the one now staring intently at him. "Don't what?"

"Don't tell me," he said.

"Well, you don't know what I have to tell you."

"Is it about you?" he asked.

"Well, no, not really."

"Is it about me?"

"No."

"Then I don't want to know."

Wow.

So much for the pep talk and making myself feel better. I had anticipated pouring my heart and soul out to him, and he would reassure me that no matter what, everything would be okay. There may have been some embracing and heavy pashing in my daydream, too.

But, instead, he had said, "I don't want to know."

I felt a bit gobsmacked, and, to be honest, a bit pissed off.

"Wow, thanks, great pep talk," I said, coolly brushing past him before stopping just before the hallway.

I turned back around to face him. "Do you trust Toby?"

Chris's gaze was so piercing, so intimidating I almost wished I had never asked.

"With my life."

He didn't even think about his answer. It was an honest one. Was the bro code blind to all things? I wasn't sure and I wouldn't find out – not from Chris, anyway.

Soon the others would be here and our time alone would come to an end as we were engulfed by the loud, excited reunion.

I would go back to being on the outer – more so than ever now, as I felt so uncomfortable and awkward around Ellie and Tess. Although things hadn't automatically been awkward from first thing this morning, things would be heading in that direction, and I didn't know how to claw my way back.

***

There was no better way of killing time than drawing the blinds and falling into the welcoming abyss of sleep, nestled on top of a queen-sized bed. The utter bliss of allowing my tense muscles to melt into the soft mattress was exactly what I needed. What I didn't need, however, was to be jolted awake by a loud scream and slammed into by a large flying weight that bounced up and down on the bed beside me.

"OH MY GOD, TAMMY!!!!"

Bounce-bounce-bounce.

Amy?

The light switch flicked on-off-on-off-on before another body sailed through the air and slammed onto the mattress, singing horribly out of tune.

Off the Florida Keys

There's a place called Kokomo

That's where you want to go

To get away from it all ...

Sean.

"Get off!" I pushed them away but it was like pushing at two boulders.

Amy dropped on her side, laughing like a maniac; Sean still lay across my legs, pinning me to the mattress.

"Not bad, huh?" He smiled.

I shook my head. "You're a crafty devil, Sean Murphy."

"Indeed," he said, getting up off the bed. "My job here is done – you're awake." He dusted his hands and disappeared out of the door.

Amy lay next to me on her side, resting her head casually on her hand as she watched him go.

"God, I love that man," she said dreamily. "I have never felt more loved and so blessed than I do having him in my life."

It was a surprisingly candid and heartfelt admission from Amy – so touching to hear her say that.

I would have smiled had I not taken it upon myself at that very moment to burst into tears.

Amy sat up like she had received an electric shock. "Hey, hey – Tammy, what's wrong?" She pulled my hands away from my face.

I shook my head, trying to shrug her insistent hands away. I felt so stupid.

Amy scrambled off the bed and quickly shut the door, before moving to sit by my side.

"Hun, what's wrong?" she asked, brushing the hair away from my face as I hugged my pillow.

I didn't know how to answer that.

Nothing? Everything?

I really didn't know myself, which only made me even more miserable as the sobs hitched at the bottom of my throat.

Amy's chin wobbled. "Tammy, don't cry, please don't, it's going to be all right," she said soothingly, rubbing my back.

There was a knock on the door before it opened a crack and Toby stuck his head in. It only took him a second to realise that it really wasn't a good time.

"Oh, sorry, I didn't mean to ..." he stammered. "I just wanted to ask Tammy for my shoes." He grimaced, as if he really hated to ask.

It was the final nail in the coffin of my pity party as I wailed into my pillow, my shoulders convulsing. I'd completely lost it.

"I'll, um ... I'll come back later." Toby closed the door quickly.

Amy rubbed my back more urgently now, as she shushed me and spoke gentle, soothing words like a best friend should. She also gave up asking questions; instead, she did the one thing I needed. She moved quietly to turn off the light and gently crawled into the bed, shuffling into the space behind my back, sliding her arm around me securely.

"It's going to be okay," she whispered. "I'm here now."

***

The next time I awoke was less of a rude awakening. I woke naturally and rubbed at my sore, swollen eyes before rolling onto my back, expecting to find Amy there. But she was gone. She had probably waited for her psychotic friend to cry herself to sleep, and crept out of the room wishing she had left me behind in Onslow.

I dragged myself out of bed, never having been more thankful for having my own en suite bathroom. I looked at my puffy, bloodshot eyes in the reflection and saw a stranger. I saw a girl so full of misery and self-pity it made my stomach turn. This was what Amy had found. She had no doubt been just as surprised as I had been when Sean pulled into the drive; she had no doubt, in true Amy style, raced up to my apartment to jump around and celebrate with me to share the excitement. Instead, she had found a crumpled mess, crying in her plush suite, offering no more explanation than cryptic sobs.

That wasn't fair. She must have been so worried.

Tonight was the night. It really was; it was the last night of 1999 before the clock ticked over to a new millennium. It would probably be the last time any of us would go on a trip like this together, and after I confronted the people I needed to, it would probably be the last time we were even in the same room together. Things would never be the same again. I just had to work out when to do it.

I either ruined their lives this year, or next year. Neither option was fantastic.

As I washed my face and stared at my sullen reflection in the mirror, I made up my mind.

One more night.

One more night of living the lie, one more night in which we were together, all friends, under the belief that life was grand and weren't we lucky. Yes, one more night to kiss it all goodbye. It was rather poetic really; as we would count down to a new beginning, a new millennium, everyone would be none the wiser that it was all about to end.

Maybe Chris could have been prepared if he hadn't drawn the ignorance-is-bliss card, the one that had made me so furious it probably explained my tears more than anything else.

I had put too much hope in Chris, hope that I could share the burden of Toby and Ellie's secret, that Chris would be there when I needed him most.

But he wasn't.

Before any of this I had been an intelligent, driven person who didn't define herself by anyone else, but during this trip I had become a lovesick mess, dependent on the whims of a sullen, stubborn man. That intelligent, independent woman was still in me, I knew she was, but the person I saw now was more like the insecure, frizzy-haired, invisible girl from long ago.

I don't think so.

I squared my shoulders, delved into my make-up bag and applied some bronzer, lip balm and a touch of mascara – not even waterproof mascara. Now I really *couldn't* shed any more tears.

I ran a brush through my long, light golden brown hair and swept it over one shoulder.

That was better. I felt better by simply looking less pitiful. I hoped that I looked less like I had in the foetal position in a blubbering mess and more like a diva ready to count down to the year 2000. Okay, so I would never be a diva, but at the very least my mind's position for the night was to party like it was 1999.

Chapter Fifty-One

I made my way into the living room and conversation immediately came to a halt.

Awkward.

Ellie, Amy and Tess were all lounging around on the couches with champagne flutes in hand. The boys were nowhere to be seen.

"Hey, Tim-Tam." Ellie jumped up, bouncing her way over to me, embracing me with a hug. I stiffened against her hug. This pretending everything was fine for the night was going to be really hard.

"Hey." I smiled, hoping it seemed real.

"Can you believe this place?" She beamed.

"What I can't believe is that Adam kept a secret," Tess said, moving past Ellie and hugging me.

"Are you okay?" She squeezed me tight.

"Yeah, fine."

Okay, this was going to be really, really *hard.*

"True," laughed Ellie as she topped up her champagne glass. "He is a shocker for keeping secrets."

Unlike you.

"Where are the boys?" I asked as Amy passed me a glass of champagne.

"Probably bonding in the bar," said Tess, "but I think we will allow that." She winked.

"Hells yeah, they can do whatever they like," Ellie said. "They've earned enough brownie points for the next millennium. Cheers, ladies, here's to this year and the next." Ellie held up her flute.

"Cheers!"

We all clinked our glasses together, followed by me sculling mine and holding my flute out for more, much to the amazement of the others.

"Go, Tammy!" laughed Tess.

Yep, everyone was buying it. Good. I sculled my next glass and glanced at Amy mid-gulp; she looked less than happy about my party-girl attitude.

After downing the last of the champagne from my glass, I clinked it down on the kitchen bench with a gasp of satisfaction.

"Let's order room service!"

***

Come seven o'clock and four empty plates of chocolate mud cake, we decided to think about tonight's wardrobe.

"Oh my God, I almost forgot," said Tess as she jumped out of her chair and ran down the hall.

I looked around at the others. They shrugged and shook their heads, obviously none the wiser, either. I heard the rustling of a plastic bag long before Tess reappeared with something behind her back.

"Bell gave this to me before she left Evoka, just in case she didn't make it here." Tess smiled at me. "Close your eyes."

"Um, okay …" I said, obeying.

"Hold out your hands."

I did as she asked, waiting anxiously as she gently placed a plastic bag onto my waiting hands. They dipped slightly under the delicate weight.

"Okay. Open them." Tess clapped.

I opened my eyes to find, yep, a white plastic bag. I peered inside.

"You have got to be kidding me."

"What? What is it?" Amy sidled up next to me.

I shook my head. "It's official, I am completely in love with Bell," I said laughing, as I turfed the bag upside down and a bundle of fabric spilled onto the floor.

The dress from Evoka Springs.

"Oooh, pretty. What is that?" Tess asked.

"I tried this on at the hippy shop in Evoka. I really liked it but I put it back on the rack," I said, rubbing the soft, layered fabric between my fingers.

Ellie's eyes lit up. "That is so what you're wearing tonight."

I stood and held the long skirt to my hips, musing about how I didn't buy it because I didn't want to stand out. I was afraid about what others might think, but so much had changed in two short days and now I wanted to wear it more than ever.

"I feel a fashion parade coming on," announced Amy.

"Quick! Before the boys get back," said Tess.

"Crap! Wait for me – I'll have to grab my stuff from my room," said Amy as she dodged past a coffee table.

"Me too." Ellie followed her out of the room.

Tess stopped mid-step into her room, confusion lining her face. "Ellie, where are you crashing tonight?"

"Ugh! I've been checked into the honeymoon suite with Sean, Amy, Stan and Bell. As if that's not going to be awkward," said Ellie, rolling her eyes.

"Hey, we're not that bad," Amy said, glowering, by the front door.

"As long as you don't keep me awake with your kissy-kissy noises all night," Ellie said as she followed her out of the door. It swung shut with a heavy bang behind them.

So it seemed Chris had made arrangements for Ellie to be placed in their apartment before they had arrived. It had been the last conversation we had had. I cringed at how pathetic I had been, how needy, how pitiful I was when I had asked him to stay. But I didn't see him coming to sleep in the now spare room. As far as I knew he was still sharing an apartment with Adam and Ringer tonight. I was grateful that he had organised it, yet it was still a rather anticlimactic ending to what had been a trip full of surprises.

Since the boys were catching up in the bar, us girls swanned about getting ready. It wasn't a completely awful situation, aside from being stuck between Tess and Ellie and not knowing where to look.

"The honeymoon suite? Poor Ellie." Tess pouted as we went to the main bathroom with our arms full of make-up and hair product.

Yeah, poor Ellie, I thought. If only Tess knew.

It didn't take Amy and Ellie long before they were knocking on the door to be let back in. I opened the door and they walked in with clothes draped over their shoulders and make-up bags in hand, arguing over the gripping subject of whether to wear their hair up or down.

"Well, I'm going for down," declared Ellie as she padded her way to share the bathroom with Tess. I watched her and wondered how she could even sleep at night, how she could be so casual about betraying her best friend and lying to her face.

"You okay?" Amy touched my hand, breaking me from my death stare.

"Oh, yeah, fine." I tried for an airy shrug-off, but Amy was not buying it for a second.

"Well, you weren't quite fine an hour ago."

"I think I was just overtired," I said, avoiding eye contact.

"Oh, well, if that's all it was I kind of feel bad about abusing Chris now."

My eyes snapped up to meet hers. "What?"

"Well, what was I meant to do? You weren't talking and there was only one person who could have made you so upset and that was my idiot cousin. So I may or may not have ripped him a new one."

"You know, when you say I may or may not have, it usually means you did."

"Well, yeah, I totally did." She grimaced.

"Ammmyyyy," I groaned and thumped the back of my head against the hall wall. "He would have had no idea what you were talking about."

"I don't know about that. When I told him how upset you were, he seemed really concerned; it took all my strength to stop him from marching to your room and kicking the door down to see if you were all right."

I inwardly cringed. *Why? Why did she have to tell him about my meltdown? He probably thought I was some oversensitive clingy girl, flipping through bridal magazines and picking out names for our children.*

"Yeah, well, I don't see him breaking down the door to check on me now," I said, my heart sinking a little.

"After the tongue-lashing I gave him, don't be surprised if he gives you some space tonight."

"Ta-DA!" Ellie jumped into the room wearing her tight, electric blue '80s dress with shoulder pads that would make Joan Collins envious. Ellie sashayed her best runway walk down the hall.

"What do you think?" she asked as she cocked her hip, did the three-second pouty stare off into the make-believe crowd before turning and criss-crossing her legs as she swayed her hips back down the hall.

"I thought you were going to take the shoulder pads out," said Amy.

Ellie peered at her shoulder. "They are ludicrously huge, aren't they? But I don't know, they are kind of growing on me."

"Well, be prepared for Adam to give you shit about them for the entire night, then," Amy warned.

"What else is new?" Ellie said, rolling her eyes.

A knock sounded on the door and Ellie froze mid-stride, her eyes bugging out. "Wait, don't let them in," she squealed and ran to hide in the bathroom as best she could in her skin-tight dress.

A part of me wanted to follow her and hide in the bathroom too, my heart slamming violently against the wall of my chest. I knew Amy had meant well but she had turned an already awkward situation with Chris into ... Well ... I guessed I would find out.

As Amy headed for the door, I straightened and lifted my chin.

Remember, Tammy: positive!

Amy squinted through the spy hole before she looked at me with surprise.

"It's Chris and Toby."

Holy shit!

"Wait-wait-wait, don't open the door," I whispered to Amy as I quick-stepped down the hall.

"Where are you going?" laughed Amy.

"I'm getting ready. No! I'm asleep. No! I'm in the shower ... No-no, I'm, I'm ..."

Amy wound her hands in a circle as if to say spit it out. A fist pounded on the door again, making me jump.

"Just go." Amy ushered me away. "I'll say you're on the phone, or trapped under a vending machine or something."

I was going to argue but Amy was already opening the door. I dived into my room and slammed the door behind me, pressing my back against it, trying to still my breath.

Who was avoiding who now?

Chapter Fifty-Two

I was a prisoner.

Sitting on the edge of my bed with my hands neatly clasped in my lap, I heard voices and laughter in the living room. Ellie, Amy and Tess were being sociable; I was the only weirdo who refused to come out and say hello.

I should have gone out and said hello; I was being rude and weird. Regardless of what Amy had said I should have just gone out and pretended everything was okay.

I stood and wiped my clammy hands on my skirt, took in a deep breath. I rested my hand on the gold door handle.

Everything was clearly not okay.

The room would be filled with Toby, Tess, Ellie and Chris, and Amy would burn her speculative gaze into my temple.

And what if Toby was here to pick up his shoes? Just as I was about to back away from the door, the voices in the other room became louder, making their way up toward the hall again. I dared not move (okay, I moved enough to press my ear up against the door).

This is what I had resorted to.

"Well, come down when you're ready, we'll just be in the bar," I heard Chris say.

"Of course you will," scoffed Amy.

Silence.

"She still on the phone?" asked Chris.

"Uh, yeah, must be," Amy said.

Silence.

"Okay! Well, see ya down there," Amy's voice went up a few stress-induced octaves; I had visions of her pushing them out of the door, which was probably what must have happened because when I heard the click of the door shutting my shoulders sagged with relief.

I blew out a long breath and ripped the door open.

"Thank God! I thought they would never lea—"

I froze in the doorway, my eyes locking with Chris's as he leaned on the opposite wall, arms folded across his chest.

Busted.

He cocked his brow with interest. "You were saying?"

My mouth gaped and I looked to Amy for an explanation. She stared at the floor, walls, the ceiling – anywhere but at me.

"I'm so sorry," she mouthed.

Betrayal was a bitter pill to swallow. Still, I didn't have to wonder too hard to guess how it had come about. Chris would have tilted his head for Toby to go out of the door then looked at Amy and pressed his finger against his lips as he motioned for her to shut the door. Then he leaned against the wall opposite my door. I didn't even give him time to settle in and get comfy as it had taken me all of 1.5 seconds to come bursting out.

My brows knitted together as I stared, not at Amy, but locked my eyes firmly on Chris whose own burning gaze darkened as the defiant staring competition began.

Amy shuffled awkwardly next to Chris. "Um, I'll give you two a minute."

I could feel her wanting to grab my attention, for me to give her a nod of forgiveness, but I couldn't break eye contact from Chris; I didn't even so much as bat an eyelid.

"All righty, then," she breathed as she slowly backed away. "I'll just leave you two to it, then."

So he was here and he was pissed off. I could tell that Chris Henderson, a man of few words, was itching to say something. It was as if I could hear the cogs of speculation turning inside his head.

Well, let him speculate. He could stew about it and wonder why I was avoiding him as long as he wanted; it was probably the very question that was dancing on the tip of his tongue.

Just as I was about to speak, Chris pushed himself off the wall and strode over to me.

He grabbed my upper arm and pulled me through the doorway of the bedroom and kicked the door shut behind us. I was barely able to gather my thoughts as Chris pressed me against the back of the door and claimed my mouth in a hot, mind-bending kiss. His lips were demanding, firm, slow, coaxing mine to open for him. I was unable to move, enticingly ensnared by him as his scorching kiss robbed me of all thought, all breath.

He broke away, breathing hard as he stared down at me and gently swept a lock of hair off my brow.

His mouth curved in triumph. "Snap out of it, Maskala." His voice was raw, disjointed, but it was still filled with cockiness as he reached for the door handle. I stumbled aside, my legs like jelly. I touched my lips, staring after him as he made his way to the front door and left without a backward glance.

What the hell was that?

***

Amy's eyes narrowed with worry as soon as they had locked onto me when I entered the kitchen.

She stopped mid-pour of juice into her glass. "Are you mad?" she asked.

Was I mad?

I had just had the most intensely hot pash of my life, a mind-blowing moment that had ended way too soon. My mind was still in a fog, my thoughts fragmented into a million different hazy pieces. Mad? I was *so* not mad.

I pulled out a kitchen stool on the opposite side of the breakfast bar, trying to keep myself from smiling dreamily.

"Tammy Maskala, you have to spill. Now."

My eyes blinked in Amy's direction. "Sorry?"

Amy's lips quivered. "What is going on with you these days? I'm your best friend and I feel like I don't know about anything in your life anymore."

I wanted to deny it, to tell Amy she was exaggerating, but I knew she was right. Of course she was – I had been more guarded than ever these last couple of days and I couldn't explain to her why.

If Amy was truly my best friend, I would tell her the things that plagued my thoughts. The complexities in my so-called love life, the burden of Toby and Ellie's secret – I would, I *should* tell her about it all. But I didn't want to; I wanted to keep it locked away and not talk about the things that worried me.

Then why had I wanted to tell Chris? Ha! That had worked out so well.

"I'm sorry, I just don't know where my head's at lately," I lied.

Amy reached out and touched my hand. "Well, tell me where it's at and I might be able to help."

I laughed. "I wouldn't even know where to begin."

Amy walked around the breakfast bar and propped herself on the stool beside me. "How about we start with Chris?"

She leaned on the counter, holding her chin in her hand as if settling in for the long haul.

So I did it – I unpacked all my emotions and all my frustrations and, to my surprise, something I had never voiced before, not even to myself.

"I like Chris," I said. "I really, really like Chris."

Amy rolled her eyes. "Tell me something I don't know."

That was a surprise. To me, voicing that very thing was an admission of epic proportions. I had kind of expected more shock, more excitement, maybe. But it *was* Amy I was talking to.

I decided to disclose only the things that affected me directly, and tried to ignore the echoed laughter from the spare bathroom as Tess helped Ellie to straighten her hair. I really tried to ignore it.

"So, what are you going to do about loving Chris Henderson?" Amy grinned as she sipped on her drink, a mischievous glint in her eye.

I sighed and shook my head.

Loving Chris Henderson would be wrong. I mean, what was there about him to love? He was moody, bossy, a control freak, and that was on a good day. But there was one achingly obvious fact that haunted my every thought, every minute of every day …

The man sure could kiss.

Chapter Fifty-Three

Apparently I had to cut the shit and take control.

"I'm serious, Tammy, tonight's the night. You have to seize the moment, tell Chris how you feel and just lay it all on the line. He likes you back, I know he does."

From the moment I had finally confessed I liked Chris, Amy had nearly drowned me in these speeches. I think she was quite liking being able to do the 'best friend' advice thing.

"Ow! Amy, watch it." I tilted my head to the side, wincing as she jabbed a bobby pin into my skull.

"Sorry. Anyway, seriously. Men are not complicated." She reached for another pin from her make-up bag.

"We *are* talking about Chris," I said. "I think he invented complicated."

"There!" Amy stood back and admired her handiwork. "What do you think?"

I looked at my reflection, smiling at the unfamiliarity of my long hair cascading down my shoulders in tousled waves. She had pinned back the longer wisps of my fringe and dotted my hair with pins that shone with diamantes. I tilted my head from side to side, looking at it from every angle.

"I love it!"

Amy beamed. "You're going to look so hot!"

"All right, who's next?" asked Ellie as she walked into the bathroom. She slammed her giant make-up case down on the counter.

"Do Tammy. I have to go make sure my outfit doesn't smell like mothballs." Amy skipped out of the bathroom.

"Oh, it's okay," I said, "you don't have to do my make-up." I started to get up from the edge of the bath.

"Don't be silly," Ellie said, pushing me back down, "it's what I do. Now, first we're going to cleanse and tone."

I bit my lip, feeling increasingly uncomfortable whenever I was around Ellie. I gritted my teeth as she worked with expert hands to clean and swab my face.

"You have the most beautiful skin. Must be all the water you drink."

Every sentence was said more to herself than to me, because I didn't respond.

At the end, when she was gently applying the finishing glossy layer to my lips, she said, "Pout, like this." She pulled her lips inward as an example of what she wanted me to do. "That's it." She gently slid the wand over my lips, before stepping back and tilting her head with a brilliant smile. "My finest work yet. Of course, it helps when I'm working with someone as gorgeous as you." She winked.

I wanted to hate Ellie, to openly scoff and scowl at all her words and flinch against every touch, but it was impossible. No matter what higher moral ground I chose to stomp on, one thing was clear: I couldn't hate her, and it utterly killed me.

"Take a look," she said with pride, motioning me toward the mirror.

I stood, expecting to see hooker-red lipstick and overly blushed cheekbones. Instead, to my utmost surprise, the make-up Ellie had used was all bronzes and natural tones. I leaned in closer to inspect the flawless job of glossy golden shades that highlighted my eyes and brought out the contours of my face. I looked amazing.

Damn her, she even did fantastic make-up.

Ellie squeezed my shoulders. "Chris's jaw is going to hit the floor when he sees you tonight." She beamed.

My eyes locked with hers in the reflection, narrowing in confusion.

She shrugged. "Oh please, everyone knows."

I turned to face her. "Everyone knows what?"

"Well, there is obviously something going on between you two. I think it's great." She smiled brightly.

Under normal circumstances I probably would have giggled and confided in her about what had happened these last few days. But, try as I might, even though I enjoyed her company, was entertained by her careless charm and, yes, her ability to apply flawless make-up, resentment still churned in the pit of my stomach and although I had promised myself just *one more night* of carefree, normality and fun, I couldn't stop myself from what I was about to do.

"I'm on to you, you know," I said coolly, causing Ellie's big blue eyes to lock onto mine, the sparkle fading.

"What?" she breathed out, as if the mere weight of my words had knocked the wind out of her.

"Just do me a favour, okay? Just stop acting like everything is okay, because it's insulting."

Ellie gaped; she stammered trying to find some words, but whatever it was she wanted to say, I didn't want to hear it.

"Thanks for the make-up," I said emotionlessly. I walked out of the bathroom, my hands balling into fists at my sides, trying to disguise the tremor. It was a step forward. A step toward the confrontation that had to happen, that would change everything. I felt sick.

What had I done?

***

Well, one thing was for sure, I didn't have to worry about feeling awkward around Ellie anymore, because she avoided me like the plague. She had come out of the bathroom all flushed, walked a direct line to the spare room and closed the door.

"Hurry up, Ellie, we're heading down soon," called Amy before fixing her gaze onto me.

"Bloody hell, Tammy, get dressed already!" She motioned me back into the bedroom.

"Okay, okay, I'm going." I walked up the long hall, trying to cut off my mind.

Stay out of it, Tammy, you already said too much, too soon. Just enjoy the night and forget. Forget about it all. Stress less!

Ha! Stress less. My mum's advice worked through my mind like a constant drill into my brain. I shut the bedroom door and checked my phone on the charger. Several missed calls and messages appeared on my screen. I smiled as I dialled the number for home.

It rang out. I closed my eyes, hot tears burning under my lids.

Crap! Don't cry, Tammy. Don't. Cry. Not now. You can't afford to screw up your make-up.

I hadn't realised how much I was actually relying on hearing my mum's voice. I had sent her a text to say that we had arrived safely, but I was yet to talk to her. I really wanted to before the New Year began. The line clicked over to the answering machine and I listened to my mum ramble on with a five-minute spiel about what to do in the event that she or Dad weren't available. I had begged her for years to change it.

"Hey, Mum, just wanted to give you a call and wish you and Dad Happy New Year. I miss you heaps and I'm having a really good time." I tried to sound convincing, but wasn't sure I had pulled it off. "Anyway, I'll see you when I get home. Try not to party too hard, okay? Love you heaps, bye."

I sighed and pressed the phone to my forehead; I really needed my mum's upbeat words to soothe me, to tell me to 'stress less'. If my apparent mantra was to be positive, hers was not to stress. And in order to do the latter I had to be the former.

I slapped my hand defiantly on my thighs.

"Let's do this," I said aloud to myself. Standing and walking a proud, determined line to the wardrobe, I laid my outfit out on the bed.

No matter what happened tonight, or was going to happen tomorrow, I was going to make the most of what was left of 1999.

Like Amy had said, I was going to cut the shit and take control.

I was going to let Chris know how I felt.

Chapter Fifty-Four

It could have been the dress.

Or it could have been the champagne? Heck, it could very well have been the decision to shut off that crucial part of my brain that plagued me with worry. Whatever it was, I had never felt sexier and more bad ass than I did right now.

I had even decided to act natural around Ellie, leading the way for her to do so as well. It was almost as if we hadn't even had the conversation in the bathroom. But of course, we had, so although we faked it pretty well, I knew tonight we wouldn't be dragging each other onto the dance floor in the name of girl power.

As the four of us stood in the elevator, we each fidgeted with our foreign attire in the reflection of the elevator mirrors.

"Seriously, Tammy, Chris is going to freak out when he sees you," laughed Amy.

My normal response would have been to repel any such notion, but as the glasses of champagne I'd sculled in the suite made the edges of my mind blur, I admired my shimmery white and gold skirt that fell low on my hips and the midriff top that hugged into a V falling short of my belly button. My skin was a deep brown, in stark contrast to the white of the fabric, and my hair pooled into a cascade of soft, loose curls to the middle of my back. I felt beautiful and exotic and for me that meant more than what anyone else might think. For the first time, I actually embraced the thought of dressing up, of socialising. Maybe the New Year would continue for this new Tammy. As long as the alcohol wasn't the sole cause for my new-found confidence, that is, because that could be a problem.

The elevator came to an abrupt, stomach-plunging halt on the ground floor, and when the doors slid open we quickly moved from the claustrophobic space.

The four of us certainly were a motley crew. Ellie, with her electric blue,'80s figure-hugging dress (minus the shoulder pads), had opted to wear her long blonde hair sleek and glossy. To be honest, she needed little else to make a statement; my automatic reaction had been to tell her how great she looked, but I thought against it.

Tess looked beautiful in a powder blue baby doll dress; it looked like it was specially made for her and was by far the least outlandish of all our attires. Amy might have thought my outfit was show-stopping, but Tess would always be the one to turn heads, even if she was dressed in a paper bag.

Amy pulled off black and animal print like no other, and although she had fully intended it to be a bit of a laugh, she looked hot all the same.

"Sex on legs, coming through," I announced as Amy rocked a seriously lethal pair of black stilettos.

"Shut up, Maskala." She looked back at me with a smirk.

We'd aimed to stick out from the crowd, but compared to a lot of others moving around the hotel, we looked disturbingly normal.

I watched as we passed a group of guys wearing coconut shell bras and grass skirts.

We walked out of the reception area and wove our way through the curved garden path, flickering with shadows from tiki torches along its sides. We heard the distant screams and splashes of late night swimmers who still lounged and hung out by the pool bar.

"Where are we going?" Tess asked as we followed Amy further and further into the depths of the resort and its immaculately kept garden.

"The bar's down near the second pool," Amy called back, as she stepped carefully along the stone path. I, myself, gloried in the atmosphere of the summer's evening. It was definitely a lot cooler along the coast than it was at home. I ran my hands along the tops of the foliage that ran along the edges of the path; I didn't have to worry about heels with my beaded, casual sandals and I felt free and fabulous in my sexy attire. I certainly could never have worn this to the Onslow. But none of that mattered here. We passed another group of guys on the path, all wearing sombreros and Hawaiian shirts. They stood to the side and let us pass, bowing graciously.

"Ladies."

We smiled politely and ignored the wolf whistles and invitations to party with them, and followed the distant music that flowed out from the bar.

Soon we saw the glow of the bar up ahead. Double doors led into a darkened building, with only the pulsing lights of a music station lighting the space in neon flashes. It was no darker than Villa Co-Co had been, but the Point Shank Beach Resort bar was clean, open, airy and far more tropical than a couple of potted palms. If anything, this place should have been called Villa Co-Co, but instead the neon sign by the entrance door read 'Hibiscus Nightclub'.

A very handsome staff member waited by the door with a tray of complimentary cocktails and a glow-in-the-dark wristband each (probably tagging us so we didn't double dip on free cocktails, but nevertheless all given with an inviting smile).

Tess was the last to take a cocktail from his tray – it matched the electric blue of Ellie's dress.

Tess sipped it, looking around in wide-eyed wonder. "This is what heaven must be like." She grinned.

I had thought finding the boys was going to be as easy as walking into a bar – there they'd be, propped up against it – but it seems that there were a few more bodies to look through than anticipated. Apparently, the entire guest list at the resort had converged at the bar for pre-celebration cocktails. We carefully pushed our way through the crowd, ensuring as best we could that we didn't spill our drinks – the last thing I needed was a blue streak down my front.

"Do you see them?" shouted Ellie above the music.

I shook my head. "Amy, are you sure this is the right bar?"

"This is the only one here," she said. "That I know of." She shrugged while involuntarily swaying to the beat of the music.

"So much for a grand entrance," laughed Tess.

"Well, let them find us," I said and in that moment it was like a light bulb lit above all of our heads.

"Yeah, let them come to us," agreed Amy, finishing the last of her cocktail.

I followed suit, cringing against the pure alcohol at the bottom of my glass before I slammed it down triumphantly on a nearby table. I pointed to the dance floor.

"Ladies, floor, dance, now," I declared.

Unlike what dominated the jukebox at the Onslow with the usual 'Smells Like Teen Spirit' or the odd Cold Chisel number, we gloriously revelled in the catchy little number of 'Rock the Boat' by Hues Corporation.

We were so lost in the glorious throes of the music, all trying to outdance each other with shimmies and other questionable dance moves, we had completely forgotten about the boys. But then out of nowhere a hand scooped around Amy's waist and whizzed her around in a screaming flurry.

Sean.

How we didn't see him coming, I will never know. His six-foot-three frame stood out above the crowd even more than usual as he was dressed in a sleek, single-breasted black suit with a white shirt and thin black tie. I know I joked before about sex on legs, but, seriously, Sean was raw, and dangerously handsome tonight. Amy seemed to agree; I could see it in the way her eyes lit up, despite how she laid into him with a slap to the upper arm.

"Don't do that, I'm full of blue stuff," she cringed, rubbing her stomach and sticking out her blue tongue at him. "I'm pretty sure we just drank lighter fuel."

Sean ignored her protests, and instead pulled her to him and captured her mouth in a searing kiss that even made my own heart rate spike. I tore my eyes away from them and darted around, seeing if I could spot any of the other Onslow Boys in the crowd, my heart pounding so loudly I was sure everyone would hear it above the music.

Amy drew away from Sean, her eyes smoky and dreamy as she looked up at him. "Hi," she said, smiling coyly.

"Hi." He grinned down at her.

I pushed Sean in the arm. "Where did you come from?"

And more importantly, where were the others?

Sean looked at me as if noticing me for the first time. "Whoa, Tammy?" He looked me over as if he was seeing a stranger.

A pang of insecurity rushed passed my alcohol-induced buzz and clawed its way to the surface.

I was all but ready to sidestep away and change my attire when Amy leaned into Sean, grinning widely. "Do you think a certain someone will approve?" she asked him.

Sean broke out into a knowing grin. "Oh, I think a certain someone is going to fall off his stool."

"Excellent!" said Amy. "That is exactly the reaction we were going for."

She winked at me. I really didn't want to talk about this with Sean, even if it did have cryptic undertones. His attention casually flicked from me to the others, his eyes narrowing at all our revealing outfits.

"I think I'm going to need a shotgun tonight," he mused.

"We can take care of ourselves, Murph. Where are the others?" asked Tess.

Sean smiled. "Bar. It's this way." He pointed to a corridor leading off the main club room. He offered Amy the crook of his arm before leading her off the dance floor. "Come on, ladies, stick with me and I'll make you stars."

***

One more of those blue things. That's what I needed, a pure hit of top-shelf alcohol to still my nerves. I had excused myself from the group, but hadn't exactly announced that I was grabbing a drink from the bar across the room. They would have wondered why I didn't grab a drink at the bar that we were headed to, where the rest of the Onslow Boys were.

Where Chris was.

Oh God.

I took a deep gulp of the cocktail that the bartender slid my way and squeezed my eyes shut with a shudder at the sour aftertaste.

Okay, down this and face the music. Make the entrance you wanted.

Considering the last exchange Chris and I had had, I really should have felt more at ease. I remembered the way he had stalked toward me, pulled me into the room and pushed me against the door. Heat rushed inside me just thinking about it, or was it the alcohol? No, it was definitely Chris.

I downed the last of my hundred percent alcoholic cocktail and made a determined line towards the corridor Sean and the girls had disappeared down. It was a long, subtly lit corridor.

Crap, I thought, *maybe I should have gone with them*, as the remnants of the last cocktail took effect. I steadied myself against the wall, hoping by doing so it would stop the room from spinning. I needed to focus.

As I fixed my eyes on the brighter glow of the bar at the end of the stuffy, dark hall, my gaze zeroed in on my target: oblivious to my watching him, Chris appeared out of the end room and darted down an adjacent walkway.

He was dressed like Sean, in a dark dress suit that even with the briefest glimpse had my stomach twisting and caused my breath to catch in my throat. I didn't need any grand entrance, or any longing looks across a crowded room; all I needed was him. My foggy mind cleared with intent as I moved down the hall quickly, my skirt swooshing around my legs. I dodged the sea of bodies and turned down the same side walkway Chris had.

There he was, leaning casually near the end of the hall, his back turned to me as he thumbed through his mobile phone.

I smiled to myself as I closed the distance between us. He had taken great pleasure in taking me by surprise today, robbing me of all my thoughts, all my breath, all my momentary anger and frustration. Now it was time to return the favour, and what's more, I wanted to do it now, before nerves and doubt rose within me and convinced me that 'Tammy Maskala did not wear provocative dresses, Tammy Maskala didn't swirl cocktails, Tammy Maskala didn't attack unsuspecting men in darkened hallways.'

Because, despite the niggling voice of doubt, tonight I wholeheartedly embraced all those things.

I shut down that voice inside my head and strode toward Chris. I pushed him against the wall with such force that he dropped his phone, but I didn't care. My mouth claimed his with such a deep-seeded need that I grabbed the lapels of his jacket and drew him closer toward me. At first his entire body was rigid in shock as I slammed him against the wall, but his hands eventually lowered to rest on my back as he gave in to my mouth, kissing me in return and moaning his approval as my tongue slipped into his mouth, tasting the remnants of beer and the tang of toothpaste. His fingers dug into my bare lower back; it caused me to gasp his name on his lips.

"Chris."

I felt him freeze, his hand stilling on my back, almost as if he was afraid that if he touched me I would break.

He swallowed deeply. "Well, this is awkward."

Chapter Fifty-Five

"Tammy, it's me ... Adam."

I flinched away so quickly, backed away so fast I slammed into the opposite wall. My hands clasped my mouth and my eyes widened with horror.

Oh my God, oh my God, oh my God.

My eyes focused on what was most certainly and definitely not Chris. *Adam* stood across from me, his hands held up as if begging for a truce.

"Tammy, it's all right, it's just a mistake." He tried to smile in good humour.

All I could manage was to shake my head repeatedly. How could I have not known? How could I have attacked the wrong person? The wrong *brother!*

I cupped my flaming cheeks as all words failed me. This was why you don't dress like a ho, this was why you don't drink like a ho, and most certainly why you don't act like a ho.

I moaned in embarrassed despair and slid down the wall.

Ho-ho-ho!

Hot tears of shame pooled behind my lids and I buried my face in my hands. I couldn't even bring myself to look at Adam.

"Hey, hey, hey. Tam, it's all right." Adam knelt before me. "Come on, look at me." He tried to prise my hands away from my face but I didn't make it easy for him. He eventually won out.

"Tammy, come on. This is getting insulting. I'm not that bad a kisser," Adam joked, which only made my tears fall.

He rubbed my upper arms. "Hey, come on, I know you like Chris; this didn't even happen, it's forgotten already."

I forced myself to look up at him. "I am so, *so* sorry, Adam, I thought that ... that ..."

"I know. It's all right," he said, wiping my tears away. "As far as mistakes go, this was right up there with some of the best of my lifetime."

I scoffed, shaking my head.

"I'm serious," he smirked. "At least in my top five."

"I am so embarrassed. And just so you know, I don't do things like this. I don't dress like a gypsy, scull cocktails, and attack random men in corridors. I just want to make that clear."

"Well, thanks for clearing that up; I really was thinking all those things." His mouth pinched upward in the corner.

"And these bloody corridors are really badly lit," I added.

"Really bad," Adam agreed.

"I mean, it's like an OH&S issue."

"I'm writing a letter to management first thing in the morning," Adam teased.

He did actually help me feel better.

He sat beside me, leaned against the wall and let out a sigh.

"You know what happens in the '90s stays in the '90s," Adam said, looking at his watch. "And as it goes we only have an hour and twenty-five minutes of guilt to live with before the stroke of midnight washes all our sins away."

"Really?"

"Truly."

Adam climbed back to his feet and held out his hand to pull me up. I looked at his hand and then up to him.

"So you're not mad at me?" I asked.

Adam burst out laughing. "Um, *no*. It would take more than being attacked by a beautiful girl's face to tick me off. I am most certainly not mad at you." He grinned down at me.

I slid my hand into his and he pulled me to my feet.

"Well, of all the people to have accidentally kissed, I'm relieved it was you." I cringed with embarrassment.

"Think of it as an early New Year's Eve kiss." He bumped my chin with his fist. "Because I totally kiss girls like that at the stroke of midnight."

I smiled. "Do you think you could do me a favour?"

Adam's brows rose in surprise. "Sure."

"Do you think you could escort me to this bloody bar before I disgrace myself any further?"

Adam's mouth pulled into a crooked smile. "As long as you promise to keep your hands to yourself."

I laughed. "I can only try."

***

By now, I wanted to blend into the wall, to slink into the crowd and hover around the group, unnoticed and unannounced.

No such luck.

Adam pointed across the room to a fully occupied table, where everyone sat, present and accounted for, including Ringer, Stan and Bell.

Amy was the first to see us and she waved animatedly. Everyone turned to look.

"Shit, I'll be right back," said Adam.

My panicked eyes darted to his. "Where are you going?"

He leaned towards me, whispering near my temple. "I have your make-up on my jacket."

I looked at his suit jacket and, sure enough, a light sheen of unmistakable glittery dust was smudged there from our heated embrace.

"Oh God." I swallowed.

"Yeah, I'll take care of it," he said. "Be right back. See you at the table." And just like that, Adam disappeared through the crowd toward the men's room. I wrung my hands anxiously, drew in a deep breath and walked across the room toward the table of our friends. Of course, I didn't think myself so special that I would be the centre of attention as I crossed the floor, but I was very aware of a particular pair of eyes that watched my approach. Chris leaned his elbows casually on the tabletop, talking and listening to Ringer, but his eyes flicked towards me, studying every step I took until I came and stood right next to the table.

"Here she is!" announced Sean. "We thought we had lost you."

Ringer turned in his seat and his eyes widened. "Holy shit, Maskala. What the fuck are you wearing?"

Stan whacked him across the back of the head but it did little to snap him out of his wide-eyed gawk.

"I see they didn't stitch your mouth up," I mused.

"Ha! We should be so lucky," said Sean.

Bell leapt up from her chair. "Here, sit here, Tammy, I'll grab an extra chair." Her smile was not lost on me as Bell quickly vacated her seat next to Chris.

Subtle.

Bell skimmed past and whispered in my ear, "You look hot!"

"Thanks to you, I do." I hugged her.

"Thought you might like it." She winked, moving to steal a chair from another table.

I sat in Bell's vacant seat next to Chris, who made no move from his casual lean on the table as his eyes fixed intently on me, much like they had when he had kissed me.

"What took you so long?" he asked.

I could have looked away, let the pangs of regret for my colossal mistake moments before flood my face with crimson, but instead I was drawn so deeply into the depths of his warm brown eyes. I stared back at him, without apology; it was like we were the only two people in existence and I leaned my elbows onto the table in mirror image of him.

"I was looking for you," I said, so only he could hear.

I felt the press of his knee against mine and it made my heart pound faster. Such a simple touch.

"Well, you found me." He smiled.

"I did," I said, pressing my leg back against his, feeling the heat of him burn through the silky fabric of my skirt.

He broke away from my eyes, fighting not to smile as he glanced at the tabletop and back up at me with a shake of his head.

"What?" I asked with a confused frown.

He leaned in closer, and whispered in my ear. "You have no idea what you do to me." He drew away, his eyes locking with mine.

"W-what do I do?" I breathed out, mesmerised by the varying colours of brown framed by his inky lashes.

He bit his lip, pushing himself back in his seat.

"Remind me to tell you later," he said, a glimmer of amusement in his eyes. "Don't forget."

I shook my head. "Don't worry, I won't."

Chapter Fifty-Six

"So tell me again ..."

"Why have we travelled all this way to sit around a table and look at one another?" asked Ringer.

"Well, you see, we have this friend and he can't walk long distances, or be on uneven ground or basically throw himself into the full-fledged party scene," said Chris.

"What, this old thing?" Ringer pointed to his elevated, bandaged foot with his walking crutch. "It's just a scratch," he scoffed.

"Oh puh-lease, we've had to listen to you bitching for the last two days," said Bell.

"Yeah, 'I'm too hot, I'm too cold, I'm thirsty, I'm hungry, my foot's ouchy,'" mocked Stan.

Ringer grinned with an evil glint in his eyes. "Well, it sounds bad when you say it all together."

"It *was* bad," said Bell.

"So this is it, is it? I'm stuck in here for this monumental moment in history because I'm an invalid? Great – it'll be remembered as that time when Ringer completely ruined our New Year's Eve. I might as well have gone home," sulked Ringer.

"Mate, you know New Year's Eve is the most overrated night of the year, right? It's been a good trip. It doesn't matter where we are or what we do tonight as long as we're in good company," said Sean.

"That's beautiful, Sean, you should really put that on a bumper sticker." Adam arrived at the table, his jacket a little damp, and pulled up a chair. "So we're all frocked up and nowhere to go," he said.

"Don't you start," warned Chris.

"We do look like the Blues Brothers," added Toby as he adjusted his tie.

"Well, I think you look beautiful," Amy said, slinging her arm over Toby's shoulder. "I love seeing my boys suited up, it doesn't happen often enough."

"Maybe we should turn the Onslow into black tie?" mused Chris. "Just for Amy."

"That'll be the day," laughed Sean.

"I'm just saying, there is a massive music festival happening down the road, on the beach, that every man and his dog is at, spending everything in their wallets and having the time of their lives, and you're all here babysitting me," Ringer piped up.

"Ringer, we're not leaving you so just forget it," said Ellie.

"Well, don't think for a second that I wouldn't ditch you lot if the stitch was on another foot," Ringer said, folding his arms across his chest.

"I know you wouldn't, so just drop it, tough man," said Ellie.

Ringer sighed, admitting defeat. "You're all insufferable."

Chris leaned over to me. "Did you want a drink?"

"Uh, no. I think I'll wait, I've had quite an array already."

Chris pulled back and lifted his brow. "I thought I tasted champagne today." His mouth curved.

I blushed at the memory as Chris smugly lifted his stubby to his mouth and sipped.

"There is one line I draw in the sand, though," said Ringer.

Everyone sighed, wishing that Ringer would just accept that we weren't leaving him.

"And what's that?" asked Toby with little enthusiasm.

Ringer shifted awkwardly to stand, gathering his crutch under his arms. "We may be prisoners of my ill-fortuned circumstance …" he said, looking over the entire table. Ringer grabbed his glass and lifted it upwards. "But by God, there will be dancing."

***

We abandoned our table and, in the spirit of Ringer, rallied down the same ill-fated corridor I had been in not long ago.

"Keep your eyes on the time, guys; we'll meet back at reception at ten to," Sean said, grabbing Amy's hand.

I wished Chris would reach for my hand, would guide me down the hall and wrap his arms around me. Instead, we walked side by side next to Stan and Bell.

"What's at ten to?" asked Stan.

Chris shrugged. "Who knows? Some scheme, knowing Sean."

"Well, I must say, I am a fan of his scheming ways. Did you nearly have a heart attack when you pulled up at this place, Tammy?" asked Bell.

My gaze flicked to Chris, who watched me expectantly, as if he really wanted to know the answer too.

"Indeed I did." My mouth twitched.

Stan and Bell led the way down the corridor, dodging bodies loitering in the hall. I kept my gaze forward, trying not to be swept away by less-than-savoury memories of what I had done with Adam.

Chris leaned in towards me.

"Don't think I've forgotten that you owe me a massage."

I blinked, my mind snapping from my daydreams. "Sorry?"

Chris smiled. "You lost the bet, remember?"

I gaped at him. "No, I didn't; you tricked me."

Chris rubbed the back of his neck. "A bet's a bet."

"You're unbelievable," I scoffed.

"Why, thank you," he laughed.

"It's not a compliment."

Chris smiled at my curt response as we entered the main room of the club. He guided me to the side of the dance floor, out of the way of the flow of traffic.

"I guess I kind of tricked you today when you thought I'd left the apartment." He looked down on me.

"You did," I said, hypnotised by the disco lights dancing across his face.

"Are you sorry I did?"

"No."

"Are you sorry I kissed you?"

I shook my head. "No." I reached out and traced my fingers down the strip of his thin black tie. He looked so beautiful in his suit. I had never seen him suited up before; he was born to wear it. He stepped closer to me as if encouraging me to touch him.

A smile tugged at the edges of my mouth as my eyes lifted to his. "You look really nice tonight," I said.

Chris broke into a brilliant white smile, his teeth glowing in the disco lighting.

He looked away and I followed his gaze to the others on the dance floor, to the familiar scene of Sean spinning Amy around like a rag doll and Adam and Ellie tearing up the floor in the most disturbing uncoordinated way.

"Dance with me?"

Chris hadn't looked away from our friends. I watched his profile, thinking I had imagined what he had just said. I had to have. In all the times I had been to the Onslow, I knew one thing for sure. *Chris Henderson most certainly did not dance.*

He broke his eyes away from the revellers and looked at me expectantly. "Well?"

"Are you serious?" I asked.

"I'd never joke about such a thing." He grabbed my hand and led me onto the dance floor.

Chapter Fifty-Seven

Oh, to hell with it, you only live once.

"One beer and one of those horrendously toxic blue cocktails!" I shouted above the pounding of the music.

I felt a body squeeze in next to me. "Make that two beers, and two cocktails, please." Tess waved a fifty at the bartender.

"Having fun?" She leaned into me so I could hear her.

I nodded. "I am. I can't believe I nearly didn't come."

"What? And miss out on hanging with us? Surely not." She elbowed me playfully.

"It feels so weird, I feel like I've hardly spoken to you these past few days."

"Yeah, well, I haven't exactly been the best company lately. I feel actually really bad, I feel like we've dragged the group down," admitted Tess.

"Come on, now you're starting to sound like Ringer," I said.

Tess smiled, but it didn't quite reach her eyes. The most natural thing would be for a friend to ask how things were between her and Toby, to be supportive. But I had been avoiding them ever since Evoka, or otherwise too wrapped up in Chris to fully notice what was happening between them. I looked into Tess's sad eyes. I was such a bad friend.

"Are you okay?" I asked as the barman slid the drinks in front of us. "Put your money away, I got this," I said, handing over a fifty dollar note.

"Thanks," Tess said, reaching for her cocktail like it was a lifeline.

"If it wasn't bad enough that Toby has been running hot and cold this entire trip, now I have to try to deal with Ellie."

I choked mid-sip of my cocktail, working myself into a violent coughing fit.

Oh God.

"Ellie? What about Ellie?" I rasped.

"You haven't noticed? She's not herself tonight, is she? I think she had been crying before but she won't tell me anything."

Oh God, please put two and two together, I thought, *if not now then soon.* I knew I was being selfish, but if she worked it out herself then I wouldn't have to get in the middle of it.

I was by far the worst friend ever – sitting on vital information for Tess, just so I could enjoy myself. I should have come out with it the second I had left the bushes in

Evoka; instead of marching in the opposite direction I should have ploughed through those bushes and confronted Toby and Ellie there and then. How different the trip would have been. We probably would have all turned around and gone back to Onslow straight away.

"Do you think you could speak to Ellie? Try to find out why she's upset?" asked Tess.

If anything, the thought of finding it hard to dislike Ellie wasn't a problem anymore; in fact, looking into Tess's troubled eyes made it all the easier.

"Sure," I lied.

"Thanks, Tammy, you're the best."

If only she knew the truth.

***

"It's not ten to yet, why are we heading back?" called out Adam, trailing behind the group as we headed back up the garden path to the reception lobby.

"Because, as a whole, our time-keeping skills leave a lot to be desired," said Sean.

"Still doesn't explain why we're meeting at reception, anyway," said Stan.

Sean sighed. "Oh ye of little faith, trust me; I have something worked out."

"Amy?" Stan asked.

"Hey, don't look at me, I haven't a clue what Captain Cryptic is up to," she laughed.

Sean, as usual, loved every minute of our confusion.

I leaned into Chris. "Do you know?"

He curved his brow at me. "He's my business partner, he's under contract to tell me everything."

"So do you?" I pressed.

Chris shrugged. "I haven't a bloody clue."

The main foyer was deserted (as would be expected in the lead-up to the most hyped-up occasion of this century). I kind of felt sorry for the lone staff member that had drawn the short straw and had to work tonight of all nights.

Sean walked over to the desk, leaned against it and talked in hushed tones to the cheery fellow behind it. The man nodded at everything Sean said, checked the computer, and nodded some more.

"What on earth is he up to?" Bell said as we all looked on, wondering the same thing.

Sean walked back over to the group, his brows drawn in a no-nonsense, serious frown.

"Right, you have ten minutes to use the little girls' and little boys' rooms, or whatever you need before we meet back here."

"Do I have time to go grab my camera?" asked Tess.

"As long as it doesn't take any longer than ten minutes," Sean said. "Shall we all sync our watches?"

"Oh, for God's sake, Sean. Back here in ten, everyone." Amy rolled her eyes and dragged him to the elevator.

Everyone moved quickly, all in opposite directions – some slid to the elevators to go up to their rooms; others headed for the reception toilets. I thought myself particularly crafty as I headed for the poolside Ladies' room, knowing I would be able to be in and out more quickly. By now, the pool was long abandoned and all the sun-lounge mattresses had been hooked over the backs of the chairs to dry out for the night.

I hurried into the Ladies' room I was almost blinded by the bright fluorescent lighting that reflected off the gold tap fittings and black and gold marbled countertops.

As I finished my business, I made sure I didn't commit the ultimate disaster: I checked for toilet paper stuck on my shoe, or, worse, my skirt tucked into my undies. I unlatched the cubicle and froze in surprise.

Ellie stood by the basin, nervously wringing her hands together. "Hi, Tammy. Can we talk?"

I made a direct line to the sink, pumped the hand-soap dispenser and turned the elaborate gold tap.

"What could you possibly say in seven minutes that I would want to hear?" I said coldly, deliberately avoiding her eyes.

"Do you think Tess will be mad?" Ellie's voice was sad, almost inaudible.

I slammed the tap off. "Oh my God, Ellie! You think?" I yelled, my voice echoing off the tiles.

Tears welled in Ellie's eyes. "You can't help who you love," she said, her chin trembling.

"The thing is, Ellie, sometimes there has to be a line drawn, and you know what that line is for? So you don't fucking cross it." I was so angry, so absolutely enraged that I had been put in this position, to be sought out by her and just before we all had to meet back.

Ellie was crying and my face flushed crimson.

I breathed deeply. "Do you love him?" I asked, not knowing entirely why I did.

Ellie's big blue eyes lifted to mine in surprise. "I think I've always loved him," she said.

"Does he … Does he love you?"

Ellie thought for a moment. "I don't know. As a friend, yes, but I don't know about … more."

"I hope it's worth risking everything for," I said. "Risking your friendship with Tess, your friendship with everyone for." I moved toward the door.

Ellie reached out to stop me.

"Please don't say anything, I don't want anyone to know," she said, her eyes pleading.

The hairs on the back of my neck rose and my blood chilled in a way that almost scared me as I pulled away from Ellie's grasp.

"I have been tortured long enough by your secret; if you don't tell Tess about you and Toby, then I will. Don't think for a second I won't."

I pushed past her, ripping the door open and storming into the night. I was so angry, angry to the point that hot tears burned in my eyes.

Perfect.

"Tammy, wait!" Ellie's panicked call followed me, causing me to walk faster. I had

had enough of talking. I didn't know what Sean had planned, but I didn't really care. I just wanted this year to end and, like Adam said, have all the sins of the '90s washed away forever. Ha! We should be so lucky, because little did everyone know that it was only the beginning, the beginning of a bigger nightmare that would tear us all apart, and the worst of all?

It was up to me to do it.

Chapter Fifty-Eight

I stormed back to reception.

My sole intent was to make it to the elevator without being spotted, only to be stopped dead in my tracks as a hand snaked around my arm, making me yelp.

Chris.

"Where do you think you're going? We've only got five minutes … What's wrong?" Chris's brows narrowed.

Before I could answer, Ellie ran into the reception and skidded to a halt upon seeing me and Chris. Her eyes were all bloodshot and her mascara had smudged a path down her cheeks.

The three of us stared at one another, frozen and silent. To speak was to confess, and now was not the time. No time was the time. I was about to ask Chris to take me away from this place, to just get in his van and drive until it was the New Year and all the hype, all the expectation was over with. I knew he would, too. I knew that, without question, he would take me away and that was what I loved about him most.

Sean broke the silence, his cheerful upbeat voice echoing through the large space as he re-entered the room with Amy in tow.

"Look out!" Sean paused and looked at each of us, one at a time. The scene before him must have been comical. Chris separating two tear-stained, dishevelled chicks.

Sean's eyes narrowed on Chris. "What the hell have you done?"

"Me? I haven't done anything," Chris said incredulously.

"Well, you have thirty seconds to sort it out." Sean jangled a set of keys in his hand.

The elevator door dinged and slid open.

"Finally!" Sean walked away, leaving only Amy's uncertain gaze fixed on us.

"Um, can this wait?" she asked.

"No!"

"Yes!"

Ellie and I spoke at exactly the same time.

I turned to Chris, my rock, my saviour, my …

"You heard the man – sort it out."

My traitor!

Chris brushed a strand of hair behind my ear as he leant down to brush his lips against my temple. "Sort it out," he whispered.

Pulling away, he winked before abandoning me to join the others near the elevators.

I slowly turned to meet Ellie, her hands fisted at her side. Her angry eyes flicked briefly from me to the others. She grabbed my hand and dragged me into the alcove of the nearby Internet kiosk, away from prying eyes.

"Who were you talking about just now?" she asked, her eyes wild, her voice demanding.

I couldn't believe this girl. "Oh, please, who do you think I'm talking about?"

Ellie looked at me incredulously. "Well, Adam, of course, who else could you possibly …"

The penny dropped as she slowly gained her composure; I saw it in her eyes – her big, blue, horrified eyes.

"You thought I was talking about Toby?" she gasped.

Oh God, this was awkward.

"How could you even think that I could do that? Tess is my best friend. Toby is like a brother to me!"

I wanted to crawl into a hole.

"Ellie …"

"Like you said, there are lines you don't cross. To think that you even thought for a second that that was one I would have …"

"Ellie …"

"Oh my God, who have you told? Does anyone else think that?" Ellie cupped her cheeks in horror.

"No! No one," I said, shaking my head. "I haven't told anyone, I swear."

"But why did *you* think that? Did I do something? Say something?" I could see Ellie's mind racing at a hundred kilometres an hour.

I had nowhere to look but at Ellie; I owed it to her not to look away. What could I say? By what they were saying, by how they were acting, I naturally thought they were having an affair?

Oh God, even repeating it inside my head, it sounded really, really lame. And worse – not only had I gotten it wrong, but I had gotten it so very, *very* wrong.

I had ruined the trip for myself, almost ruined it for everyone, based on nothing but a misunderstanding. And now, hurt and tears were in Ellie's eyes, whose crime had been nothing more than having feelings for her best friend. Was it midnight yet? I wanted the Y2K bug to make the planet burst into a ball of fire or whatever was predicted already and end us all.

It was the only thing that could save me from the shame that made my insides hurt.

I stepped forward and grabbed Ellie's shoulders.

"You did nothing wrong, it's just me and my stupid over-analytical imagination." I let go of her shoulders and grabbed her hands. "Ellie, I am so, so sorry. Please forget everything I've said. I guess I was just trying too hard to figure out what was happening between Toby and Tess and you know what?"

"What?" Ellie sniffed.

"It's none of my bloody business; it's none of *any* of our business. Yeah, it's human nature to worry about them, but it's out of my hands. It's something that they have to sort out on their own. I'm just sorry I didn't realise that before. Then I wouldn't have gotten into this mess."

"I guess it was only natural to assume Ellie 'the whore' was the reason," she scoffed sadly.

My shoulders sagged. "Ellie, you are not a whore, you are a good friend – a great friend. If you weren't you wouldn't care about liking Adam and how it might affect your friendship with Tess." Ellie's eyes flicked up to mine, as if something I had said resonated with her.

"Why would Tess be mad if you liked Adam, anyway?" I asked.

Ellie opened her mouth to speak but then thought better of it. I guess I couldn't blame her for feeling guarded around me. When she actually did speak, her words surprised me somewhat.

"Me, Tess and Adam have been friends all our lives. Best friends. Our bond is something that can't be explained and it's so incredibly precious to me I don't know if it's worth risking."

"Well," I said thoughtfully, "I know I'm the last person on the planet that you should probably take advice from right now, but someone showed me that sometimes if you step out of your comfort zone you can experience some pretty amazing things."

"That someone sounds like a very wise person," Ellie mused.

"He is."

Ellie sighed. "Truth is, I don't know the answer right now, and it's not a decision I'll make lightly."

"Well, that's smart too. Even if you don't know now, in time you will and if there is something else that I've learned, it's that best friends are there to listen to you. Don't shut Tess out."

Silence fell between us.

"Ellie, I'm really sorry." I swallowed hard.

She smiled. "You know, you actually scared the hell out of me. You were *so* mad."

I cringed.

"Tammy, I know you don't always feel a part of things with us, but for what it's worth, whether you like it or not you're one of us. You just proved it."

Tears blurred my vision. "I wish I'd proved it in some other way."

"You have; you proved it in the way you care about Tess and Toby, about wanting to do the right thing, by the way you love Chris."

My eyes snapped up to see Ellie's knowing smile.

She nudged me with her hip. "We all know," she said. "How about we just find comfort in the truth and move on?"

It was like music to my ears. Before I could tell her that I wholeheartedly agreed, footsteps sounded up the passage and screeched to an abrupt halt.

Adam.

His brows rose in surprise as he parted his suit jacket and plunged his hands into both pockets of his slacks.

"Sean says if you're not there for countdown he is going to haunt you for the next millennium."

"We're coming," said Ellie. "Just had some gossip to catch up on." Ellie looked at me, her mouth tilting into a crooked line.

Adam's eyes shifted to me uncomfortably and I knew he had just gotten the completely wrong idea. Why the heck would I tell Ellie about my mistaken kiss?

"We were just speculating what Sean was up to, is all," I said. "Any clues?"

"None, but if you hurry up I think we're about to find out."

Chapter Fifty-Nine

"All right, we're all here?" called Sean.

"Yes," we all groaned, completely over the build-up to the big mystery surprise.

Sean pressed the button for the elevator and the doors instantly glided open.

He checked his watch. "This is it, people, the final countdown."

We all piled in, cramming ourselves into the small box like sardines.

Tess earned herself a whack to her temple by one of Ringer's crutches as he hopped inelegantly into the confined space. Amy screamed with pain as Sean accidently stood on her foot, and I was wedged up against Chris's chest. Admittedly, it wouldn't have been the worst place to be if Toby hadn't elbowed me in the spine.

"Shit, sorry, Tam."

I managed to smile through the pain, and thought, *Well, at least I could look Toby in the eye now.*

I felt Chris's hand splay over my bare back, rubbing soothing circles along my skin. Considering he was laughing and joking with Stan next to him, seemingly oblivious to his hand's actions, I wondered if it was as natural for him to touch me as it seemed.

"Where to from here?" Stan asked, his hand hovering over the floor panel.

Sean broke into a brilliant smile.

"The only way is up, Stanley."

Amidst the chatter and the stomach-plummeting jolt that catapulted us upward, I felt the gentle brush of Chris's lips against my brow, a stolen moment between us in the crowded space. I clasped the lapels of his jacket and breathed him in.

With eleven of us trapped in a confined space, you would think that the elevator door couldn't have opened soon enough, but as we piled out of the crammed, mirrored prison, the reality of breaking away from Chris was not a welcome thought … until we stepped out to the foyer. Our mouths gaped open, an unusual silence sweeping over us.

"Oh no, you d'int!" screamed Ringer like a diva.

Before us was a wall of glass, and beyond that wall was a glittering, candlelit terrace with rooftop pool. A long table lined with ice and champagne was the first thing to greet us as we all merged forward, Sean opening the door with pride.

"Best seats in Point Shank," he said.

Chris slapped Sean on the shoulder. "You did good, mate, you did good."

"Why get sand in our shoes when we can hear and see all from up here?" Sean swept his arm out like an emperor addressing his subjects.

"I wonder what the poor people are doing tonight?" joked Adam. He busied himself plunging a strawberry into his mouth from one of the fruit platters.

The breeze whooshed through the folds of my skirt, my hair flailing around as I walked along the terrace, past the pool, to look out over the balcony. The very strip that we had driven along earlier that day was now in darkness, highlighted only by an orange glow of high-powered street lights. Distant screams and laughter carried on the wind, the music from the festival clear and crisp to our ears. For long moments none of us said a word, we just listened and flashed cheesy, happy grins at one another. All those people below didn't have a clue how good we had it up here.

I spun around and clutched my hair at the nape of my neck to prevent it from blowing in my eyes and robbing my vision.

"Sean, I am officially the president of your fan club," I said.

"I'll be the vice president," added Ellie.

Sean pulled up a seat at the far end of the balcony, nursing a Crown Lager and casually crossing his long legs at his ankles.

"I would prefer to call you my groupies," he said, flashing a boyish grin before taking a deep swig.

What made this whole feat even more impressive was Sean's fear of heights. Noting his position, wedged up near the entrance, away from the edge – obviously nothing much had changed.

It only made this decadent surprise even more selfless.

"I think I'm actually glad Ringer injured himself," said Stan, looking down at all the insect-sized people on the footpath.

"Yeah, come to think of it, I don't fancy stumbling drunk along the beach, stepping in vomit and waking up with sand in my bum crack," said Adam.

Chris eyed his brother with interest. "I don't know what you get up to on the beach, but—"

"You know what I mean," snapped Adam.

Chris's brows rose. "Do I?"

Adam ignored him. "This is heaps better."

"What time is it?" I interrupted.

"Time to get moving …" said Stan.

"See!" said Sean. "That's why I wanted to get here early; otherwise we would have missed the bloody countdown."

Amy chucked a wedge of pineapple in her mouth, wincing at the sour aftertaste as she casually slid into Sean's lap. He welcomed her without a moment of hesitation, circling his arms around her.

"How long do we have this place for?" she asked, straightening Sean's tie.

"As long as we want. It's not exactly a space they hire out but I can be very persuasive." Sean pressed his forehead against Amy's, a devilish tic in the corner of his mouth making her blush.

The only person who didn't seem overly impressed or interested in our surprise five-star venue was Toby.

He leaned on the balcony railing, looking out onto the stretch of black ocean across the street.

His sombre mood didn't go unnoticed. Tess tore her eyes away from his back and locked with my gaze. She looked so defeated, so tired, to the point that there were no more tears to shed. She just shook her head and turned away, finding salvation in a fresh glass of champagne. Although I had been more than relieved that Ellie had nothing to do with the wedge growing between Toby and Tess, it still did little to stop my heart from aching for them. I felt the press of Chris next to me as he leaned against the railing beside me.

"You and Ellie all good?" he asked, mid-sip of his stubby, as if trying to disguise his words.

I nodded. "All good."

"I don't have to switch her back to your apartment now, do I?"

"No, I think she is pretty settled in the honeymoon suite," I said.

We looked across at Amy and Sean, making out like two teenagers at a Blue Light disco. I felt a moment of sympathy for Ellie and the company she was keeping. It was a stark contrast between Amy and Sean to the likes of Toby and Tess, and for a moment I found it hard to believe that out of the couples, Chris and I were the least complicated.

Not that we were a couple or anything. Actually, I didn't exactly know what we were. Friends with benefits? We weren't exactly friends and benefits would imply more than second base …

Even on the brink of a new century I realised that I knew just as little now about him as I had at the beginning of the trip.

I studied his stormy profile, marvelling at the strong, chiselled lines of his insanely kissable lips and the faint workings of a permanent wrinkle on his brow from too much frowning.

As if sensing me staring, Chris tilted his head toward me and drew his beer away from his mouth.

He didn't smile, or say a word, he just looked into my eyes and it was in that moment I knew something had changed. Before the trip I would have turned away, quickly broken from his darkened, intimidating eyes. But now, I stared straight back, lost in the depths of them, never wanting to turn away. I wanted to live there.

That was the difference.

However wonderful it was, poolside, on top of a resort about to be showered in a cascade of colours from the New Year fireworks, there was only one thing I wanted, and my eyes spoke as much as they flicked to Chris's mouth: a silent invitation, a whispered promise. I met his eyes once more. I may not have spoken, but he understood every word. Chris turned to me, shielding me from the frantic winds that made my skin form into gooseflesh.

He stared thoughtfully at me for a moment.

"Come here," he said softly, darkly, a promise of something greater to come.

It made me afraid of what might happen if I didn't. I breathed in deeply, feeling an invisible pull between us as I drew nearer. Chris slid his hand along my belly, skimming around to dance along my spine. This was it, this was what I wanted; this was what I had been waiting for. Just as I saw Chris swallow in anticipation, the moment was shattered.

Tess screamed.

Chapter Sixty

All it took was one moment.

Time slowed as people down in the club and on the distant shore started counting down to the new century, new beginning.

They danced, cheered, laughed – surrounded themselves with the warm, glittering night as they rang in the New Year with hopes and dreams for the future. That's what we had all wanted; whether secretly or publicly, we hoped for our lives to change in some way from this night on.

But we'd never thought it would change like this.

Tess's eyes were wide, fixed ahead of her. She stood frozen, cupping her mouth, small whimpers escaping unheard on the breeze. The wind carried the joyful cries of "Happy New Year!" on invisible wings, but up here on the balcony we were silent.

A dull ache sliced my abdomen and my breath caught in my throat. I only remembered to breathe when I felt Chris's fingers lace with mine so tightly I felt he may break me.

An explosion of colour filled the night sky; popping and spiralling in rampant surges, the fireworks cast a magical backdrop against our open-air retreat.

Tess's soft whimpers washed over us; I wanted to go to her, to console her in some way, but I didn't need to. Her gaze dropped to the tiled floor, her watery eyes shiny with hot tears as she shook her head, barely believing the promise before her that would change her life forever:

Toby bending on one knee.

He curled his fingers around Tess's trembling hand, his warm brown eyes fixed on her intently.

"I know you've seen nothing but the worst of me since we left Onslow. But you know me. You know more than anyone that I am never one to love for the sake of being in love, but I love because of you. You make the ordinary man in me feel extraordinary and I want to go on loving and discovering with you for the rest of my days."

Toby delved a shaky hand into the inner pocket of his jacket. He turned the black box and opened it toward Tess, a nervous lilt to the curve of his mouth.

"Please say yes."

In that moment I couldn't feel anything but the squeeze of Chris's hand as I held my breath, watching, waiting.

Tess moved to kneel in front of Toby, wrapping her arms around his neck, the sheen of tears overflowing to trail a path down her face. She looked at him, really looked at him and swept her hand along his jaw line, her thumb grazing his lips.

She shook her head. "As if there could be any other answer."

***

At 12:01 a.m. on the first of January, year 2000, on top of a resort terrace in the coastal town of Point Shank, a group of friends converged on two people: a screaming, crying heap.

We broke the mould that night. We didn't scream "Happy New Year" or vomit up our drinks and get sand in our butt cracks; no, we did so much more.

Us girls cried and pawed at Tess's diamond engagement ring that by far out-blinged every firework in the sky. The boys engulfed Toby with macho congratulatory hugs and ruffles of hair, but none quite as touching as when Sean and Toby embraced, thumping one another in bone-jarring thuds on the back. Toby drew away and nodded his silent thanks. It made me suspect that Sean was the only one who had known Toby's intentions throughout the trip. Thinking about it, he'd probably masterminded the private rooftop terrace space for the perfect backdrop and romantic beginning for his best mate's proposal, let alone everyone else's enjoyment.

I took a moment to break away from the pack and walked over to Sean.

Standing on the very tips of my toes, I kissed him on the cheek. "You are an amazing man, Sean Murphy." I smiled.

Sean's brows rose in surprise. "Now, Tam, I know you have always been desperately in love with me, but you're just going to have to learn to control your urges."

I rolled my eyes. "You're unbelievable."

"What? Did you honestly think I would turn over a new leaf in the year 2000?"

I shook my head. "Don't you dare go changing, Sean Murphy – not one bit."

Sean broke into a wicked grin. "Happy New Year, Tam," he said, bending down to kiss my forehead, before ruffling my hair and walking away.

Well, maybe some things he could *change.*

I wiped the tendrils of hair out of my eyes and spotted Ellie watching Toby and Tess completely lost in each other.

Ellie wiped away what little eye make-up she had left. Her nose was red and her eyes bloodshot from the tears of joy that poured as she witnessed her best friend's proposal.

I stood beside her. "You knew, didn't you?" I mused.

Ellie sniffed and nodded. "Since Evoka. It nearly killed me keeping it under wraps."

I fought the urge to laugh. I had been so wrong, so wrong about everything. I remembered how Ellie had threatened Toby, told him that his weird behaviour was stressing Tess out, how emotional she was because of it.

It was all so clear now. I had thought it to be something so sinister, but it was nothing more than Ellie being a true friend, pacifying a stressed-out fiancé-to-be.

Poor Toby.

I brushed past the bodies flanking the now beaming happy couple. I worked my way in a direct line through to Toby and threw my arms around him. He stiffened in surprise before his arms rested around me.

"I am so sorry about your shoes."

Toby laughed. "Uh-oh, that sounds ominous."

I broke away, fighting the urge to let the tears flow; emotion I hoped would pass for happiness for them instead of the raging guilt that bubbled up within me.

How could I explain that they were up a tree in Evoka? With a condom inside?

"You see …" I started.

"They're gone, aren't they?" Toby said. "It's all right, they weren't my favourite pair," he said.

Mercifully I was saved from admitting it by Adam's grand announcement.

"HAPPY NEW YEAR!" he screamed. He ran, fully clothed, and cannonballed into the pool, splashing water over all of us.

"Adam! Don't be a bloody dickhead!" screamed Amy, shucking the excess water from her arms before she recognised the devious glint in Chris's and Sean's eyes.

"Don't. You. Dare," she warned.

"Whatever do you mean?" said Chris as he innocently set his beer on the table.

"I think she's accusing us of something," said Sean as he began to inch around in the opposite direction.

Amy backed away. "I mean it, you two. Your lives will not be worth living." Amy broke into a run.

But she, of all people, should have known: you can't outrun an Onslow Boy, let alone two … Something I found out the hard way a minute later.

***

I gathered up the saturated layers of my skirt, waited for a moment of distraction and crept slowly through the open glass doors of the terrace, dripping a trail of evidence to the elevators. I pressed frantically on the down button, urging it on with silent prayers.

Come on, come on, come on …

The red digital readout ticked agonisingly slowly up toward the rooftop terrace. Even though I was alone, I hugged my arms around myself, masking the mortifying transparency of my top that evidently wasn't meant to be swum in.

I looked over my drenched state with great annoyance, hoping that the new dress wasn't ruined. It had been fun, though. Aside from Ringer, we had all gone in, clothes and all, a line of dripping wet Onslow Boys in their suits; it looked like we were shooting a music video for a new boy band.

It was actually very hot. Not so hot when Bell pulled me aside and pointed out my little wardrobe malfunction that would have given the video an R rating, however.

As if I had conjured her up with my mind, I heard Bell's voice.

"Hey, wait for us," she whispered, dragging Stan behind her.

I inwardly cringed. I had planned for a crafty exit, but the more of us that left at once would definitely arouse suspicion in the others.

'Shhh," Bell pressed her fingers to her lips. "We're on a mission."

"Oh?" I whispered.

Stan held up a room card with a smile.

Oh God, I hope they weren't referring to a sexual mission.

"Sean organised so Tess and Toby can have a room of their own," beamed Bell. "Kind of like a pre-Honeymoon Suite, I suppose."

Stan nodded. "We have to sneak in to grab their gear and relocate them."

The elevator door dinged and opened. The three of us dived inside, leaving behind three puddles on the tiles as evidence.

We thought ourselves quite the escape artistes as the doors drew slowly closed. We thought we had made a stealthy getaway until we heard footsteps closing in, followed by the screeching of sliding footwear on the tiled floor and an arm that plunged through the nearly-but-not-quite-closed elevator doors. Flinching backward as the doors opened again, a figure squeezed through the opening.

Chris.

Chapter Sixty-One

I made a last sweep around the bathroom before returning back into the hall.

Chris stood in the doorway to keep the door wedged open while Stan and Bell lugged all of Tess and Toby's gear out of the spare room.

"I think that's everything," I said, standing at the front door with Chris.

"Cool," whispered Stan, although I'm not sure why he whispered; we were three floors below the others.

"Now we're going to go and put a trail of rose petals in their new room," said Bell.

"And they have no idea?" asked Chris.

"They haven't a clue," beamed Bell. "We just casually walk back up and hand them the new card and point them that way."

"Yeah, well, remember, you never saw me," said Chris.

'Or me!" I added quickly.

"See who? I don't see anyone, do you, Bell?"

"Not a soul," she said, her knowing eyes shifting between the two of us. "Well, goodnight."

"Night," Chris and I said at the exact same time, not without seeing the subtle wink that Stan threw Chris.

We watched them bundle the luggage into the elevator on their mission. I thought maybe I would feel the sag of relief hit me once the doors had closed and the elevator whirred into life. But I didn't. Instead, I felt the weighty stare of Chris's eyes burning into my profile. I turned, my arms still wrapped around me.

Chris leaned casually against the doorjamb, leaving a damp mark on the wallpaper. His hair was all shaggy and dishevelled and oh-so sexy.

"Are you cold?" he asked, his eyes roaming in speculation over my self-embracing arms.

"No," I said quickly.

Chris nodded, as if accepting my answer without too much thought. He pushed off from the doorjamb, uncrossed his arms and plunged his hands into his pockets.

"Okay, well, goodnight," he said, starting for the hall.

Seriously? Goodnight?

No "Happy New Year", no New Year kiss … Nothing? I didn't get a chance to let the disappointment override me.

I was too busy being fucking pissed off. I knew he hadn't promised me anything, that there was no admission of undying love. But seriously? The knee touching, the hand holding, the slow dancing, the moment we were going to kiss on the terrace? Was I just a boredom killer to him? Was I just a way to pass the time?

No, I wasn't upset; no tears were going to fall from these eyes. I was far too busy glaring incredulously at his back. Chris sauntered a few steps up the hall before he paused and turned back around. I altered my gaze – I didn't want to give him the satisfaction of thinking I cared one way or another if he stayed or walked off the edge of a balcony.

His eyes met mine, a line of amusement curving the corner of his mouth.

"You know, this is the part where you stop me, and ask me to stay."

My mouth gaped, my hands falling to my sides. "And why on earth would I do that?"

Chris shrugged, a casual, one-shouldered shrug like he always did. "Oh, I don't know," he said as he slowly stalked his way back in my direction, trailing his hand along the hall wall. "That's a hell of a big apartment for just one person."

Chris's words suddenly dawned on me. No Ellie, no Toby and no Tess … Just me.

I lifted my chin. "Well, I asked you to stay before."

Chris's brows lowered in confusion. "What? When you asked me to move Ellie?"

I nodded.

Chris was right in front of me now, so close I could feel the warmth of his breath on my face.

"It wouldn't have worked," he said, his voice low.

"Why?"

"Because if I'm going to stay," he said, trailing his finger lightly over my collarbone. "I can't promise that I can keep you quiet." His eyes lifted to mine: dark, smouldering and full of promise. Heat flooded my cheeks as his words hung heavy between us.

My chest heaved as I fought to control my breath, the breath he robbed from me by one look, one touch, one hotter-than-hell insinuation. His eyes dipped lower, roaming over my translucent dress, the wet white clothing I had all but forgotten to shield. What's more, with the way Chris looked at me, the way his eyes burned for me … I really didn't want to. Let him look, let him see, because, as far as I was concerned, tonight I belonged to him.

Chapter Sixty-Two

The apartment door slammed.

A second later, Chris's back thudded against it so fiercely I swear I heard the air escape from his lungs.

Payback, I thought, as I claimed his mouth, working to frantically peel the wet black suit jacket off his shoulders. There was nothing nice or sensual about the way we kissed, the way we clawed at one another's clothing. I worked on pulling and stretching his tie apart as his fingers dug into my hips, skimming over the sheer fabric of what he murmured into my mouth as an "infuriating skirt". I smiled against his lips, revelling in his torture.

Chris edged me backward until I thudded against the opposite door.

"If you tell me you don't have a condom, I swear …" I breathed, before kissing him deeply. He broke the kiss. "If I didn't I would drive straight to Evoka and climb a fucking tree if I had to."

My heart leapt: the way he kissed me so passionately, the way his breath caught when I ran my mouth down his jaw line.

My fingers clawed a slow, taunting trail up over his muscular stomach. He flinched away.

I giggled. "You *are* ticklish."

Chris grabbed me by the wrists and pinned them above my head.

"Best get you out of these wet clothes, Miss Maskala." He nuzzled the words into my neck, causing me to squirm at my own sensitive skin.

He let go of my hands so he could reach for the handle that led into the bathroom. Edging into the space, he flicked the light on, exposing us and snapping me completely out of my sexy mood.

I clasped my arms around my top again.

"What's wrong?" Chris asked.

"What?" I said nervously. "Nothing, I …"

Chris paused. "You have no idea how beautiful you are, do you?"

I tilted my head incredulously. Even I could take a guess that under the harsh bathroom lighting with chlorine-filled hair I looked like a drowned rat. Unlike Chris with his crazy-cool, casual, messed hair and white dress shirt and black slacks that fitted him to perfection.

He moved toward me.

I drew my arms tighter around myself.

He leaned past me and turned the shower on. My eyes widened in surprise and he smiled.

"This will be our third shower together," he mused.

It was an interesting thought; I hadn't even showered once with my ex-boyfriend, and in the space of four days I'd had three showers with Chris?

A hazy steam slowly rose, misting the air. He never took his eyes from me as he undid his cufflinks, first one sleeve, then the other. How could something so simple be so damn sexy?

He then worked down in a slow, confident line, undoing his shirt buttons, until I stopped him.

His face was stony; he probably suspected I had changed my mind. Instead, I took over. One by one, I popped the buttons free with trembling fingers, before finally peeling the fabric apart and pushing it back over his shoulders. It was like unwrapping a present: a beautiful, tanned, flawless present – the one I had been waiting so long for and now had the chance to play with. I smiled at my analogy. My hands lowered to work Chris's belt buckle, but this time his hands stopped me. Instead, his fingers gathered at the base of my midriff top and he slowly peeled it upwards, exposing me so completely to his heat-filled eyes. He pulled it up and over my head and let it fall to the floor. I shut my eyes as his hands trailed a maddening path over my stomach, upwards to cup my breasts as he stole a heated kiss. He slowly led my hands down to his belt buckle again.

He broke away from my mouth. Nuzzling and pressing his lips to my temple, he whispered, "It's going to be so good."

I never doubted it for a second, and all of a sudden I also found my skirt infuriating and it simply had to go as soon as I edged his own infuriating pants down. I only got as far as unzipping his slacks before Chris had his own ideas of bunching and gathering my skirt far enough to slide up my thighs, lifting the barrier between us. He edged me towards the vanity and, without hesitation, propped me on top of it, sweeping off a line of toiletry products that clattered to the tiled floor. A thrill shot through me just like it had when he had lifted me onto the bonnet of the car, and just like he had that night, Chris worked on hooking my knickers around his fingers and edging them over my thighs and down my legs with expert ease.

"You're very good at that," I mused.

"I'm good at lots of things," he said, curving his fingers around the backs of my knees and pulling me closer to him. His words whispered against my mouth as his hand made a slow burning trail along my skin, sliding over my inner thigh and dipping between my legs. Chris was there to catch my gasp as he kissed me and showed me how good he was, how utterly mind-bendingly good he was and how wickedly wonderful and clever his hands were as he pushed me to the edge of madness. My cry rang out and echoed against the tiled room, the steam dampening our skin as I tried my best to keep from falling off the vanity in my boneless, sated state. It took a hot, chaste kiss to bring me back around as I met the smug glint in his eyes.

"Ready to wash your sins away?"

***

My body ached.

Don't get me wrong, it ached in the most delicious way. Lying entwined in 1000 count thread sheets on a queen-sized, feather-top mattress. Having sinned, as Chris called it, in every spot in the hotel room possible, we went to the imaginative lengths that a giant apartment to ourselves could offer. It was the perfect ending to a perfect New Year's Eve.

Ellie wasn't a home wrecker.

Toby loved Tess beyond imagination.

Sean had successfully pulled off a New Year's Eve bash that would go down in the history books. And Chris: well, Chris took me to places and pushed me beyond anything I could ever imagine possible.

I stretched, wincing against my aching body, but absolutely sated in other ways where my muscles were so relaxed I felt like I had woken from a hundred-year sleep. I thought about rolling over, thinking I would find an empty space, maybe a note saying 'Thanks'. Maybe I would hear a million excuses and be given the whole, 'Uh, yeah, I'm not looking for a girlfriend right now' speech. Or worse, palpable awkwardness followed by 'It was a mistake and must never happen again.'

Who'd ever have thought that rolling over could be so terrifying?

As I slowly, tentatively rolled over, blinking against the sunlight, something took me by surprise.

Chris was sitting up in bed, reading a newspaper. I lay on my stomach, looking up at him, transfixed by the familiar crease between his brows as he concentrated. So deep was his concentration that I doubted he even realised I was awake.

And then he cleared his throat.

"Man injured in Point Shank prank … Music Festival reaches record numbers … Coastal earthquake as woman endures multiple orgasms?"

"Oh, stop it!" I sat bolt upright, pulling the paper out of his hands, my cheeks flaming.

"That's not what you said last night." Chris smiled, broad and cheeky as he folded his hands behind his head.

All I could manage was an incredulous shake of my head. "You're unbelievable."

Chris winked. "You know it."

I scoffed and reached out to whack him across the arm, but he was too fast. He grabbed my wrist and then the other. I squirmed and squealed as he wrestled me to the mattress, overpowering me with his strength. The hard lines of his heated bare skin pressed up against me.

My breath quickened as Chris stared down at me, his own chest rising and falling heavily.

Relief flooded me as I looked into his eyes; they were the same eyes, looking at me the same way they always had. Chris was not a mystery anymore.

"You forgot to remind me."

Chris's words snapped me from my daydream.

"Last night when you were at the table, you asked me 'What?', and I said I would tell you later."

I vaguely remembered. "Well, I'm reminding you now."

Chris loosened his grip, his body visibly melting against mine.

"But, if it's to tell me you thought I looked nice …" I warned.

Chris laughed. "No, nice wasn't the word that popped into my mind."

"Good." I nodded.

All humour disappeared from Chris's face as his eyes ticked over mine.

"When you walked into the room I was terrified."

Terrified? Um, okay ... Bring back nice.

"I was terrified because seeing you across the room cemented everything I was afraid to admit. I connected the moment I started falling for you and when you came and sat beside me I knew. I remembered. I loved you from the moment I pulled you into my wardrobe, even more so when I accidentally kneed you in the face at the Bake House, and I was well and truly gone by the time you mocked my black panel van." He smiled.

I felt the pressure inside my chest, my heart wanting to leap out to give all of myself to him. My eyes fixed on Chris as he gently traced a line with his finger along my bottom lip.

"So if you don't mind, I want to take you home." He slid his hand under the sheet across my stomach. "There'll be a few stops along the way …" His fingers dug into my hip, before sliding upwards.

I arched against him. "What did you have in mind?" I breathed.

"I want to finish what we started in the ocean, eat seafood at The Love Shack, run a tab in Sean's name at Villa Co-Co."

I burst out laughing. "Sounds divine."

"And then last, but not least …" Chris smiled wickedly. "We'd better find Toby's shoes."

Epilogue

I found one shoe.

And there was no condom inside it. Aside from the very important, yet unsuccessful, task of Converse recovery, we took our time travelling back to Onslow, winding our way through the terrain we had already explored. It seemed to take less time to return; admittedly, we did find better ways to occupy ourselves. We had kept a pretty tight line travelling with the others home, except for our secret place with the ocean pool – that was our place – and as planned we left a day early from Point Shank to experience it in the way it was intended.

It wasn't until I was on my lone shoe hunt camped up at Evoka Springs for the night that it actually occurred to me that I hadn't suffered from a migraine since way before Calhoon on day one. I walked down the track, swinging the single navy Converse around, smiling at the realisation. I can't say that I was miraculously cured, but I certainly felt different; I hadn't even had the need to remind myself to be positive.

I just was.

After disposing of the evidence of Toby's shoe in the back of the van, I wound my way back down toward the main campsite. Bell, Amy and the boys had gone fishing for a few hours so I decided to join Ellie, Tess, Ringer and Adam sitting in shade at the folded-out camping table.

"I can't believe we are going back to Villa Co-Co," Ellie said, wrinkling her nose in disdain as she feasted on a bag of Burger Rings.

"Oh, come on," said Ringer, stealing a ring from her packet. "You saw the sign, it's Ladies' Night." Ringer raised his brows as if we should have been ecstatic.

Ellie turned, narrowing her gaze. "Now tell the truth, Adam, tell us the real reason you want to go there."

Adam straightened in his seat. "I don't know what you are talking about." He reached for a Burger Ring but Ellie slapped his hand away.

"Oh, nothing about a certain something it said on the sign under 'Ladies' Night'?" said Tess.

Adam picked an invisible hair off his shoulder. "Still no idea. You girls are crazy."

"What's this?" I asked sitting down next to him.

Ellie rolled her eyes. "It's karaoke night at Villa Co-Co."

"Wow!" I laughed.

Adam stretched his arms to the sky. "Wow indeed, ladies, wow indeed. Hope you're prepared, that's all I'm saying." He stood up with a cheeky wink and the three of us staring after him.

"Ladies' Night means cheap booze, right?" asked Ringer.

Tess sighed. "Yep!"

"Well, thank God for that."

"Trust me," said Ellie, "if Adam's singing karaoke we're going to need it."

***

We watched with a mixture of horror and respect as a short, pierced man with a stringy goatee and cowboy hat belted out a well-tuned, passionate version of Bon Jovi's 'Dead or Alive'.

Stan leaned across the table and tapped Adam on the shoulder. "Mate, I think they take their karaoke pretty seriously in Evoka."

"As do I, Stan, old boy. As. Do. I." Adam's eyes scanned the room, assessing the competition.

Chris shifted uncomfortably in his seat, dreading the night more than anyone. Adam and Amy often tried to twist Chris's arm to host a karaoke night at the Onslow, to which his consistent response was always a resounding, "I would sooner poke myself in the eye with a sharp stick."

So it didn't seem likely.

Tess nudged Ellie. "Remember when you and Adam entered the talent show in Year Seven?"

Ellie cut Tess a dark look, but it was too late; Adam swivelled around in his seat.

"The year was 1991," he began. "The competition was fierce …"

Ellie cringed and slipped down in her seat, obviously wishing the ground would open up.

"We practised every night after school; Onslow High didn't know what hit them." Adam's eyes looked far away as if remembering a fine moment in history.

"What did you sing?" asked Sean with interest.

"Adam …" Ellie warned. "Don't."

I could tell Adam danced on the edge, you could see it in his eyes as he looked at Ellie, battling between loyalty to her and his utter desperation to tell a good story.

He shrugged. "I'm afraid I cannot say."

By now, everyone had edged forward on their seats, leaning elbows on the tabletop, waiting to hear what had been so mortifying about a Year Seven talent show. We all sagged in disappointment.

Ellie sighed and mouthed "Thank you" to Adam. He took his beer in hand and gave her a casual wink mid-sip.

Our attention focused back onto the stage as the residential Madame of Villa Co-Co stood front and centre. She wore a lime green kaftan with matching acrylic nails and blue eye shadow. It really brought out the bleached yellow in her cropped spike hairdo. The

Pineapple was in fine form tonight.

"Now, ladies and gentlemen, we have a very welcome guest that has travelled all the way from Onslow to be here with us tonight. Please put your hands together and welcome to the stage …" She looked at her card. "Aaron Henderson!"

It didn't take much for us to break into hysterics. The boys clapped and cat-called, "Go, Aaron!"

As Adam got up from his chair, he confidently strode towards the stage and took the mic.

"Ah, yeah, it's Adam." He smiled coyly toward our table. Bell near on deafened me by putting her fingers in her mouth and whistling.

I never could do that.

Adam cleared his throat. "All right, um, there's been a bit of a change of plans. I'm feeling a bit nostalgic tonight so I thought I might take a trip down memory lane."

"Hello?" said Sean, leaning forward in his chair.

"But I'm going to need your help, because ya see, I can't do it on my own, and there is only one person in this room that can complete this duet …"

"Oh God!" Ellie stared towards the stage, her eyes wide with horror.

"And that person is Ellie Parker." Adam pointed, directing the spotlight to her.

"Ellie! Ellie! Ellie!" Adam chanted into the microphone, encouraging the entire room to join the chorus, none louder than our own table. Toby placed his beer down before grabbing Ellie's hand and pulling her out of her seat toward the stage.

"Traitors! The lot of you." She glowered back at us. It only led us into further hysterics, watching her take each furious step up to the stage where Adam waited, grinning from ear to ear as he handed her a microphone.

"I hate you so hard right now," she said to him.

Adam's smile just got bigger.

"They fight like a bloody married couple," said Ringer.

"They'll get married one day – no one else would put up with them," joked Chris.

"Don't be awful," said Tess.

"All right, now you have to cut us some slack," Adam said. "It's been a while."

It was a pretty high-tech set-up as far as outback pub karaoke went. There was a screen at the foot of the stage for the singers and one mounted on the wall for the crowd to sing along if they so desired.

The music started up just in time for the song title to flash across the screen:

'Islands in the Stream', Kenny Rogers and Dolly Parton.

"No way!" laughed Sean.

"Ugh, I remember it now – hours and hours they practised in his bedroom." Chris grimaced.

"I love it!" I clapped in excitement.

"Better save your enthusiasm until it's over," said Ringer.

Confidently, Adam took the lead with Kenny's lyrics, and he was good – *really* good. We were all stunned into silence. Then Ellie kicked in with Dolly's part and we were all smiling and eyeing each other with surprise. They were kind of … excellent?

"I am beginning to wonder if my little brother really joined the army or if he's been touring the professional karaoke circuits." Chris looked on with a mixture of horror and pride.

By the chorus you could hardly believe that Ellie had protested in the first place. Eye contact, a bit of heart clutching, it was a well-rounded performance that had us all up on our feet singing along, cheering for Ellie and Aaron. He would never live that down.

As the duet faded to a close and the screen went black, the crowd went wild. Adam took Ellie's hand and they bowed. It was an unlikely end to our road trip, a trip that was originally supposed to be girl-free and full of fish, camping, talking sport and drinking beer. Instead, it had ended up so much more and I hoped everyone had enjoyed it as much as I had. I looked over at Chris, marvelling in his laughter, the way he was so completely relaxed and happy. He banged the side of his stubby with the edge of his car key.

"All right, on that rather disturbingly impressive note, I propose a toast." He centred his beer in the middle of the table and everyone followed suit in a multitude of clinks.

"To the new millennium," he said.

"To the new millennium!"

With no takers on stage for karaoke, music started up and we all cheered and headed to the dance floor as Meat Loaf's 'Paradise by the Dashboard Lights' played.

Not one of us opted out of busting a move; even Ringer twisted as best he could on crutches. Who would have guessed that in a dank, dodgy little bar we could find so much entertainment? It wasn't a place you'd want to be involved in an after-hours lock-in or anything, but come closing time, knowing this was our last night away from home, we sang and fist-pumped the air until our voices were hoarse. We belted out the final request of 'Just Like Jesse James' like it was our own personal theme song. I don't know if it was the beer, the music, the atmosphere or – hell, it might have been Villa Co-Co magic – but what happened next was a serious game changer. In the middle of the dance floor, Chris turned me into a spin and pulled me into him like he had done a dozen times before, except this time he held me there. His eyes fixed on mine so intently my smile slowly fell from my face. And for the first time Chris leaned forward and in front of his mates – *our mates* – he kissed me, *really* kissed me. Cupping my face, Chris kissed me with no mind of who saw or what whistles and cheers and taunts came from around us (and there were plenty of those). Chris Henderson kissed a girl for all to see and my heart swelled with absolute tenderness and joy, because that girl was me.

Can't wait to read more about the
Onslow Boys?
Be sure to catch the exciting Onslow Boy Novella's in
C.J Duggan's Summer Series…

Stan

I had plans, big plans, but all that changed the night Bel Evans darkened my doorstep.

Stan Remington is the go-to man. What he doesn't know about Onslow means one of two things: it doesn't exist or it hasn't happened yet.

And when it comes to Onslow, for Stan, being an only child means a guilt-riddled sense of duty to help out at his parents' caravan park every summer of his life: same old town, same old story.

Until Belinda Evans.

The wild and insipid doctor's daughter who spends summer holidays with her family at Remington's Caravan Park, but she's not Stan's problem; that is, until she sabotages his planned weekend escape. Now Stan finds himself not only caretaking the caravan park on his own, but responsible for Bel as well.

Just the two of them.

Under the one roof.

For one long, long weekend.

In a world built by mundane routine and small-town boredom, this summer promises to be anything but boring.

Available Now!

Max

Max Henry thought he'd left the dusty flats of Ballan behind, but when the past slams into his present, suddenly there is no escaping – even if he wanted to.

Melanie Sheehan didn't set out to be a liar, but her last lie landed her in big trouble. Now Mel must suffer a harsh consequence – she's not allowed out of her father's sight.

No friends, no parties, no life.

Since impeccably good behaviour is now all she's about, her dad, renowned Ballan local 'Bluey' Sheehan, is about to finally cut Mel some slack. The catch? While he heads out of town on business, she has to stay at the Onslow Hotel, and he's entrusting Max Henry, the eldest son of Bluey's best mate, to look out for her.

He just doesn't know it yet.

Max, the new head barman at the Onslow Hotel, is the one boy Mel has been crushing on since forever. At a time when Mel plans to go on the straight and narrow, she is about to tell the biggest lie of all. Will Max be able to handle the fiery farm girl or should he be considered the last boy in Onslow to trust?

Pre-Order Now!

Ringer

They say it's the quiet ones you have to worry about, and she was quiet,
very quiet – when she wasn't busy despising me with a burning passion.

Ringo 'Ringer' James has a no-strings-attached policy.

Love them, leave them, and remain the eternal bachelor.

After a summer in which every one of his mates has succumbed to settling down, or so it seemed, Ringer is on the lookout for a quick exit. Having had enough of the stomach-turning love fest witnessed over the past three months, Ringer jumps at the opportunity to help out his mate, Max, by heading to Max's dad's property for a working holiday.

It's just what he's looking for. A remote, dusty homestead in Ballan, with only hard work, a cold beer and a comfy bed to worry about – no women.

Until Miranda Henry.

The privately educated daughter of his boss has returned home from overseas and things are about to get very complicated, very fast. As summer draws to its end, Ringer is about to learn that sometimes attraction defies all logic, and that there really is such a thing as 'enemies with benefits'.

Available Now!

Forever Summer (Novel)
'Adam & Ellie's Story'
By C.J Duggan.

2015

You see there's this boy.

He makes me smile, forces me to listen, serenades me out of tune and keeps me sane, all the while driving me insane. He's really talented like that. But for the first time in since, well, forever, things are about to change. The question is, how much am I willing to lose in order to potentially have it all?

Pre-Order Now!

Coming April 28th 2015
Paradise City
By C.J. Duggan

There's bound to be trouble in Paradise...

When her parents decide a change will be good for her, seventeen-year-old Lexie Atkinson never expected they'd send her all the way to Paradise City. Coming from a predictable life of home schooling on a rural Australian property, she's sure that Paradise will be amazing. But when she's thrust into a public school without a friendly face in sight, and forced to share a room with her insipid, hateful cousin Amanda, Lexie's not so sure.

Hanging out with the self-proclaimed beach bums of the city, sneaking out, late night parties and parking with boys are all things Lexie's never experienced, but all that's about to change. It's new, terrifying … and exciting. But when she meets Luke Ballantine, *exciting* doesn't even come close to describing her new life. Trouble with a capital T, Luke is impulsive, charming and answers to no one. The resident bad-boy leader of the group, he's sexier than any boy Lexie has ever known.

Amidst the stolen moments of knowing looks and heated touches, Lexie can't help but wonder if Luke is going to be good for her… or very, *very* bad?

Pre-Order Now!

Acknowledgements

Writing is a very solitary endeavor, but it is the people by my side that make it so utterly rewarding.

Much love to my amazing husband Mick, for continuously reminding me to eat, drink and sleep. For being the beautiful part of my reality and supporting me in all I do, I know it's not easy but I wouldn't want to share it with anyone else.

I am blessed with such a talented hard working team, these ladies always go above and beyond for me. A special thanks to: Sascha Craig, Sarah Billington, Anita Saunders, Marion Archer and Keary Taylor.

Many thanks to my formatters Karen Phillips, Emily Mah Tippetts.

Always grateful for the love and support of my friends and family, especially Mum, Kevin, Dad, Daniel and Leanne.

My fellow Authors for their inspiration, support and friendship: Frankie Rose, Jessica Roscoe, Lilliana Anderson, Keary Taylor. I adore you ladies and would be truly lost without our daily chats.

To my fierce 'Team Duggan' warriors, for your unwavering support and enthusiasm. For always spreading the word and fighting the good fight to help put the Summer Series out there for the masses. I feel incredibly privileged to have each and every one of you on my team and in my life, thank-you.

To all the bloggers, reviewers, readers who have enjoyed and shared the Summer Series. For taking something away from the story, for loving and embracing the characters. In a world that is often dark enough, it has been an absolute pleasure injecting it with a bit of sunshine.

About the Author

C.J Duggan is an Internationally Number One Best Selling Author who lives with her husband in a rural border town of New South Wales, Australia. When she isn't writing books about swoony boys and 90's pop culture you will find her renovating her hundred-year-old Victorian homestead or annoying her local travel agent for a quote to escape the chaos.

For more on C.J and 'The Summer Series', visit
www.cjdugganbooks.com

Made in the USA
Coppell, TX
13 March 2022